Mario Puzo

THE LAST DON

THE DARK ARENA

CRESSET EDITIONS

This edition published in 1998 by Cresset Editions,
an imprint of Random House UK Ltd,
20 Vauxhall Bridge Road, London SW1V 2SA

The Last Don first published in 1996 by Heinemann
The Dark Arena first published in 1973 by Heinemann

Printed and bound in Australia by
Griffin Press Pty Ltd, Netley, South Australia

ISBN 0 0918 6682 0

THE LAST DON

For

Virginia Altman
Domenick Cleri

PROLOGUE

Quogue
1965

ON PALM SUNDAY, one year after the Great War against the Santadio, Don Domenico Clericuzio celebrated the christening of two infants of his own blood and made the most important decision of his life. He invited the greatest Family chiefs in America, as well as Alfred Gronevelt, the owner of the Xanadu Hotel in Vegas, and David Redfellow, who had built up a vast drug empire in the United States. All his partners to some degree.

Now the most powerful Mafia Family head in America, Don Clericuzio planned to relinquish that power, on the surface. It was time to play a different hand; obvious power was too dangerous. But the relinquishing of power was dangerous in itself. He had to do it with the most skillful benignity and with personal goodwill. And he had to do it on his own base.

The Clericuzio estate in Quogue comprised twenty acres surrounded by a ten-foot-high redbrick wall armed by barbed wire and electronic sensors. It held, besides the mansion, the homes for his three sons as well as twenty small homes for trusted Family retainers.

Before the arrival of the guests, the Don and his sons sat around the white wrought-iron table in the trellised garden at the back of the mansion. The oldest, Giorgio, was tall, with a small, fierce mustache and the lanky frame of an English gentleman, which he adorned with tailored clothes. He was twenty-seven, saturnine, with savage wit and closed face. The Don informed Giorgio that he, Giorgio, would be applying to the Wharton School of Business. There he would learn all the intricacies of stealing money while staying within the law.

Giorgio did not question his father; this was a royal edict, not an invitation to discussion. He nodded obedience.

The Don addressed his nephew, Joseph "Pippi" De Lena, next. The Don loved Pippi as much as he did his sons, for in addition to blood—Pippi being his dead sister's son—Pippi was the great general who had conquered the savage Santadio.

"You will go and live permanently in Vegas," he said. "You will look after our interest in the Xanadu Hotel. Now that our Family is retiring from operations, there will not be much work here to do. However you will remain the Family Hammer."

He saw Pippi was not happy, that he must give reasons. "Your wife, Nalene, cannot live in the atmosphere of the Family, she cannot live in the Bronx Enclave. She is too different. She cannot be accepted by them. You must build your life away from us." Which was all true, but the Don had another reason. Pippi was the great hero general of the Clericuzio Family, and if he continued to be "Mayor" of the Bronx Enclave, he would be too powerful for the sons of the Don when the Don no longer lived.

"You will be my *Bruglione* in the West," he told Pippi. "You will become rich. But there is important work to do."

He handed Pippi the deed to a house in Las Vegas. The Don then turned to his youngest son, Vincent, a man of twenty-five. He was the shortest of the children, but built like a stone door. He was spare in speech, and he had a soft heart. He had learned all the classic peasant Italian dishes at his mother's knee, and it was he who had wept so bitterly at his mother's dying young.

The Don smiled at him. "I am about to decide your destiny," he said, "and set you on your true path. You will open the finest restaurant in New York. Spare no expense. I want you to show the French what real food is all about." Pippi and the other sons laughed, even Vincent smiled. The Don smiled at him. "You will go to the best cooking school in Europe for a year."

Vincent, though pleased, growled, "What can they teach me?"

The Don gave him a stern look. "Your pastries could be better," he said. "But the main purpose is to learn the finances of running such an enterprise. Who knows, someday you may own a chain of restaurants. Giorgio will give you the money."

The Don turned finally to Petie. Petie was the second and the most cheerful of his sons. He was affable, at twenty-six no more than a boy, but the Don knew he was a throwback to the Sicilian Clericuzio.

"Petie," the Don said, "Now that Pippi is in the West, you will be Mayor of the Bronx Enclave. You will supply all the soldiers for the Family. But also, I have bought you a construction company business, a large one. You will repair the skyscrapers of New York, you will build state police barracks, you will pave the city streets. That business is assured but I expect you to make it a great company. Your soldiers can have legitimate employment and you will make a great deal of money. First you will serve an apprenticeship under the man who now owns it. But remember, your primary duty is to supply and command soldiers of the Family." He turned to Giorgio.

"Giorgio," the Don said, "You will be my successor. You and Vinnie will no longer take part in that necessary part of the Family which invites danger, except when it is absolutely necessary. We must look ahead. Your children, my children, and little Dante and Croccifixio must never grow up in this world. We are rich, we no longer have to risk our lives to earn our daily bread. Our Family will now serve only as financial advisors to all the other Families. We will serve as their political support, mediate their quarrels. But to do this we must have cards to play. We must have an army. And we must protect everyone's money, for which they will let us wet our beaks."

He paused. "Twenty, thirty years from now, we will all disappear into the lawful world and enjoy our wealth without fear. Those two infants we are baptizing today will never have to commit our sins and take our risks."

"Then why keep the Bronx Enclave?" Giorgio asked.

"We hope someday to be saints," the Don said, "But not martyrs."

An hour later Don Clericuzio stood on the balcony of his mansion and watched the festivities below.

The huge lawn, carpeted with picnic tables crowned with winglike green umbrellas, was filled with the two hundred guests, many of them soldiers from the Bronx Enclave. Christenings were usually joyful affairs, but this one was subdued.

The victory over the Santadio had cost the Clericuzio dearly. The Don had lost his most dearly beloved son, Silvio. His daughter Rose Marie had lost her husband.

Now he watched the crowds of people mulling around the several long tables filled with crystal urns of deep red wine, bright white tureens of soups, pastas of every kind, platters laden with a variety of sliced meats and cheese, and crispy fresh breads of all sizes and shapes. He allowed himself to be soothed by the soft music of the small band playing in the background.

Directly in the center of the circle of picnic tables, the Don saw the two baby carriages with their blue blankets. How brave the two babies were, they had not flinched when struck with Holy Water. Beside them were the two mothers, Rose Marie and Nalene De Lena, Pippi's wife. He could see the babies' faces, so unmarked by life, Dante Clericuzio and Croccifixio De Lena. He was responsible for ensuring that these two children would never have to suffer to earn a living. If he succeeded, they would enter the regular society of the world. It was curious, he thought, that there was no man in the crowd paying homage to the infants.

He saw Vincent, usually dour with a face like granite, feeding some small children from the hot dog cart he had built for the feast. It resembled the New York street hot dog carts, except that it was bigger, it had a brighter umbrella, and Vincent gave out better food. He wore a clean white apron, and he made his hot dogs with sauerkraut and mustard, with red onions and hot sauce. Each small child had to give him a kiss on the cheek for a hot dog. Vincent was the most tenderhearted of his sons, despite his rough exterior.

On the boccie court, he saw Petie, playing with Pippi De Lena, Virginio Ballazzo, and Alfred Gronevelt. Petie was a practical joker, which the Don disapproved of; it always seemed a dangerous business to him. Even now Petie was disrupting the game with his tricks as one of the boccie balls flew into pieces after the first hit.

Virginio Ballazzo was the Don's underboss, an executive officer in the Clericuzio Family. He was a high-spirited man and was pretending to chase Petie, who was pretending to run. This struck the Don as ironic. He knew his son Petie was a natural-born assassin, and that the playful Ballazzo had a certain reputation in his own right.

But neither of them was a match for Pippi.

The Don could see the women in the crowd glancing at Pippi. Except for the two mothers, Rose Marie and Nalene. He was such a fine-looking man. As tall as the Don himself, a rugged strong body, a brutally handsome face. Many of the men were observing him also, some of them his soldiers from the Bronx Enclave. Observing his air of command, the litheness of his body in action, knowing his legend, *The Hammer,* the best of the "Qualified Men."

David Redfellow, young, rosy-cheeked, the most powerful drug dealer in America, was pinching the cheeks of the two infants in their carriages. Finally, Alfred Gronevelt, still clad in his jacket and tie, was obviously ill at ease at playing a strange game. Gronevelt was the same age as the Don himself, near sixty.

Today Don Clericuzio would change all their lives, he hoped for the better.

Giorgio came to the balcony to summon him to the first meeting of the day. The ten Mafia chiefs were assembling in the den of the house for the meeting. Giorgio had already briefed them as to Don Clericuzio's proposal. The christening was an excellent cover for the meeting, but they had no real social ties with the Clericuzio and wanted to be on their way as soon as possible.

The den of the Clericuzio was a windowless room with heavy furniture and a wet bar. All ten men looked somber as they sat around the large dark marble conference table. They each in turn greeted Don Clericuzio and then waited expectantly to hear what he had to say.

Don Clericuzio summoned his sons, Vincent and Petie, his executive officer, Ballazzo, and Pippi De Lena to join the meeting. When they arrived, Giorgio, cold and sardonic, made a brief introductory remark.

Don Clericuzio surveyed the faces of the men before him, the most powerful men in the illegal society that functioned to supply the solutions to the true needs of the people.

"My son Giorgio has briefed you on how everything will work," he said. "My proposal is this. I retire from all my interests with the exception of gambling. My New York activities I give to my old friend Virginio Ballazzo. He will form his own Family and be independent of the Clericuzio. In the rest of the country I yield all of my interests in the unions, transportation, alcohol, tobacco, and drugs to your Families. All my access to the law will be available. What I ask in return is that you let me handle your earnings. They will be safely held and available to you. You will not have to worry about the Government tracking down the money. For it I ask only a five percent commission."

This was a dream deal for the ten men. They were thankful that the Clericuzio were retreating when the Family could just as well have gone forward to control or destroy their empires.

Vincent walked around the table and poured each of them some wine. The men held their glasses up and toasted the Don's retirement.

After the Mafia dons made their ceremonious farewells, David Redfellow was escorted into the den by Petie. He sat in the leather armchair opposite the Don, and Vincent served him a glass of wine. Redfellow stood out from the other men not only because of his long hair but because he wore a diamond earring and a denim jacket with his clean, pressed jeans. He had Scandinavian blood. He was blond with clear blue eyes and always had a cheerful expression and a casual wit.

The Don owed a great debt of gratitude to David Redfellow. It was he who proved that lawful authorities could be bribed on drugs.

"David," Don Clericuzio said, "You are retiring from the drug business. I have something better for you."

Redfellow did not object. "Why now?" he asked the Don.

"Number one," the Don said, "the government is devoting too much time and trouble to the business. You would have to live with anxiety the rest of your life. More importantly, it has become too dangerous. My son Petie and his soldiers have served as your bodyguards. I can no longer permit that. The Colombians are too wild, too foolhardy, too violent. Let them have the drug business. You will retire to Europe. I will arrange for your protection there. You can keep yourself busy by buying a bank in Italy and you will live in Rome. We will do a lot of business there."

"Great," Redfellow said. "I don't speak Italian and I know nothing of banking."

"You will learn both," Don Clericuzio said. "And you will live a happy life in Rome. Or you can stay here if you wish, but then you will no longer have my support, Petie will no longer guard your life. Choose as you like."

"Who will take over my business?" Redfellow asked. "Do I get a buyout?"

"The Colombians will take over your business," the Don said. "That cannot be prevented, that is the tide of history. But the government will make their life misery. Now, yes or no?"

Redfellow thought it over and then laughed. "Tell me how to get started."

"Giorgio will take you to Rome and introduce you to my people there," the Don said. "And through the years he will advise you."

The Don embraced him. "Thank you for listening to my advice. We will still be partners in Europe and believe me, it will be a good life for you."

When David Redfellow left, the Don sent Giorgio to summon Alfred Gronevelt to the den. As the owner of the Xanadu Hotel in Vegas, Gronevelt had been under the protection of the now defunct Santadio Family.

"Mr. Gronevelt," the Don said. "You will continue to run the Hotel under my protection. You need have no fear for yourself or your property. You will keep your fifty-one percent of the Hotel. I will own the forty-nine percent formerly owned by the Santadio and be represented by the same legal identity. Are you agreeable?"

Gronevelt was a man of great dignity and great physical presence, despite his age. He said carefully, "If I stay, I must run the Hotel with the same authority. Otherwise I will sell you my percentage."

"Sell a gold mine?" the Don said incredulously. "No, no. Don't fear me. I'm a businessman above all. If the Santadio had been more temperate, all those terrible things would never have happened. Now they no longer exist. But you and I are reasonable men. My delegates get the Santadio points. And Joseph De Lena, Pippi, gets all the consideration due him. He will be my *Bruglione* in the West at a salary of one hundred thousand a year paid by your hotel in any manner you see fit. And if you have trouble of any kind with anyone, you go to him. And in your business, you always have trouble."

Gronevelt, a tall, spare man, seemed calm enough. "Why do you favor me? You have other and more profitable options."

Don Domenico said gravely, "Because you are a genius in what you do. Everyone in Las Vegas says so. And to prove my esteem I give you something in return."

Gronevelt smiled at this. "You've given me quite enough. My hotel. What else can be as important?"

The Don beamed at him benevolently, for though he was always a serious man, he delighted in surprising people with his power. "You can name the next appointment to the Nevada Gaming Commission," the Don said. "There is a vacancy."

Gronevelt for one of the few times in his life was surprised, and also impressed. Most of all he was elated, as he saw a future for his hotel that he had not even dreamed of. "If you can do that," Gronevelt said, "we will all be very rich in the coming years."

"It is done," the Don said. "Now you can go out and enjoy yourself."

Gronevelt said, "I'll be getting back to Vegas. I don't think it's wise to let everyone know I'm a guest here."

The Don nodded. "Petie, have someone drive Mr. Gronevelt to New York."

Now, besides the Don, only his sons, Pippi De Lena, and Virginio Ballazzo were left in the room. They looked slightly stunned. Only Giorgio had been his confidant. The others had not known the Don's plans.

Ballazzo was young for a *Bruglione,* only a few years older than Pippi. He had control over unions, garment center transportation, and some drugs. Don Domenico informed him that from now on he was to operate independently of the Clericuzio. He had only to pay a tribute of 10 percent. Otherwise, he had complete control over his operations.

Virginio Ballazzo was overcome by this largesse. He was usually an ebullient man who expressed his thanks or complaints with brio, but now he was too overcome with gratitude to do anything but embrace the Don.

"Of that ten percent, five will be reserved by me for your old age or misfortune," the Don told Ballazzo. "Now forgive me, but people change, they have faulty memories, gratitude for past generosities fades. Let me remind you to be accurate in your accountings." He paused for a moment. "After all, I am not the tax people, I cannot charge you those terrible interests and penalties."

Ballazzo understood. With Don Domenico, punishment was always swift and sure. There was not even a warning. And the punishment was always death. After all, how else could one deal with an enemy?

Don Clericuzio dismissed Ballazzo, but when the Don escorted Pippi to the door, he paused for a moment, then pulled Pippi close to him and whispered in his ear, "Remember, you and I have a secret. You must keep it a secret forever. I never gave you the order."

On the lawn outside the mansion, Rose Marie Clericuzio waited to speak to Pippi De Lena. She was a very young and very pretty widow, but black did not suit her. Mourning for her husband and brother suppressed the natural vivacity so necessary to her particular kind of looks. Her large brown eyes were too dark, her olive skin too sallow. Only her newly baptized blue-ribboned son, Dante, resting in her arms, gave her a splash of color. All through this day she had maintained a curious distance from her father, Don Clericuzio, and her three brothers, Giorgio, Vincent, and Petie. But now she was waiting to confront Pippi De Lena.

They were cousins, Pippi ten years older, and when she was a teenager, she had been madly in love with him. But Pippi was always paternal, always off-putting. Though a man famous for his weakness of the flesh, he had been too prudent to indulge that weakness with the daughter of his Don.

"Hello Pippi," she said. "Congratulations."

Pippi smiled with a charm that made his brutal looks attractive. He bent down to kiss the infant's forehead, noticing with surprise that the hair, which still held the faint smell of incense from the church, was thick for a child so young.

"Dante Clericuzio, a beautiful name," he said.

It was not so innocent a compliment. Rose Marie had taken back her maiden name for herself and her fatherless child. The Don had convinced her to do this with an impeccable logic, but still she felt a certain guilt.

Out of this guilt, Rose Marie said, "How did you convince your Protestant wife to have a Catholic ceremony and such a religious name?"

Pippi smiled at her. "My wife loves me and wants to please me."

And it was true, Rose Marie thought. Pippi's wife loved him because she did not know him. Not as she herself had known him and once loved him. "You named your son Croccifixio," Rose Marie said. "You could have pleased her at least with an American name."

"I named him after your grandfather, to please your father," Pippi said.

"As we all must," Rose Marie said. But her bitterness was masked by her smile, her bones structured in such a way that a smile appeared naturally on her face and gave her an air of sweetness that took the sting out of anything she said. She paused now, faltering. "Thank you for saving my life."

Pippi stared at her blankly for a moment, surprised, slightly apprehensive. Then he said softly, "You were never in any danger," and he put his arm around her shoulder. "Believe me," he said. "Don't think about these things. Forget everything. We have happy lives ahead of us. Just forget the past."

Rose Marie dipped her head to kiss her infant but really to hide her face from Pippi. "I understand everything," she said, knowing that he would repeat the conversation to her father and her brothers. "I have made peace with it." She wanted her family to know that she loved them still and that she was content her infant had been received into the Family, sanctified now by Holy Water, and saved from everlasting Hell.

At that moment Virginio Ballazzo gathered Rose Marie and Pippi up and swept them to the center of the lawn. Don Domenico Clericuzio emerged from the mansion, followed by his three sons.

Men in formal dress, women in gowns, infants in satin, the Clericuzio Family formed a half circle for the photographer. The crowd of guests clapped and shouted congratulations, and the moment was frozen: the moment of peace, of victory, and of love.

Later the picture was enlarged and framed and hung in the Don's study room, next to the last portrait of his son Silvio, killed in the war against the Santadio.

The Don watched the rest of the party festivities from the balcony of his bedroom.

Rose Marie wheeled her baby carriage past the bowlers, and Pippi's wife, Nalene, slim, tall, and elegant, came along the lawn carrying her infant, Croccifixio, in her arms. She put the child in the same carriage with Dante, and the two women gazed down lovingly.

The Don felt a surge of joy that these two infants would grow up sheltered and safe and would never know the price that had been paid for their happy destiny.

Then the Don saw Petie slip a baby bottle of milk into the carriage and everyone laughed as the two babies fought for it. Rose Marie raised her son Dante from the carriage, and the Don remembered her as she was just a few short years before. The Don sighed. There is nothing so beautiful as a woman in love, nor so heartbreaking as when she is made a widow, he thought with regret.

Rose Marie was the child he had most loved, she had been so radiant, so full of cheer. But Rose Marie had changed. The loss of her brother and her husband was too great. Yet, in the Don's experience, true lovers would always love again and widows grew tired of black weeds. And now she had an infant to cherish.

The Don looked back on his life and marveled it had come to such glorious fruition. Certainly he had made monstrous decisions to achieve power and wealth, but he felt little regret. And it all had been necessary and proved correct. Let other men groan over their sins,

Don Clericuzio accepted them and placed his faith in the God he knew would forgive him.

Now Pippi was playing boccie with three soldiers from the Bronx Enclave, men older than him, who had solid business shops in the Enclave, but who were in awe of Pippi. Pippi with his usual high spirits and skill was still the center of attention. He was a legend, he had played boccie against the Santadio.

Pippi was exuberant, shouting with joy when his ball jostled the opposing ball away from the target bowl. What a man Pippi was, the Don thought. A faithful soldier, a warm companion. Strong and quick, cunning and withholding.

His dear friend Virginio Ballazzo had appeared on the boccie court, the only man who could rival Pippi's skill. Ballazzo gave a great flourish as he let his ball go, and there was a loud cheer as he made the successful hit. He raised his hand to the balcony in triumph, and the Don clapped. He felt a sense of pride that such men flowered and prospered under his rule, as had all the people who had gathered together on this Palm Sunday in Quogue. And that his foresight would protect them in the difficult years to come.

What the Don could not foresee were the seeds of evil in as yet unformed human minds.

BOOK I

Hollywood
Las Vegas
1990

CHAPTER 1

BOZ SKANNET'S RED CAP of hair was sprayed by the lemon-colored sunlight of California spring. His taut, muscular body throbbed to enter a great battle. His whole being was elated that his deed would be seen by more than a billion people all over the world.

In the elastic waistband of Skannet's tennis slacks was a small pistol, concealed by the zippered jacket pulled down to his crotch. That white jacket blazed with vertical red lightning bolts. A blue-dotted scarlet bandana bound his hair.

In his right hand he held a huge, silvery Evian bottle. Boz Skannet presented himself perfectly to the showbiz world he was about to enter.

That world was a huge crowd in front of the Dorothy Chandler Pavilion in Los Angeles, a crowd awaiting the arrival of movie stars to the Academy Awards ceremony. Specially erected grandstands held the spectators, the street itself was filled with TV cameras and reporters who would send iconic images all over the world. Tonight people would see their great movie stars in the flesh, shed of their manufactured mythic skins, subject to real-life losing and winning.

Uniformed security guards with shiny brown batons tucked neatly in holsters formed a perimeter to keep the spectators in check.

Boz Skannet didn't worry about them. He was bigger, faster, and tougher than those men, and he had the element of surprise. He was wary of the TV reporters and cameramen who fearlessly staked out territory to intercept the celebrities. But they would be more eager to record than prevent.

A white limousine pulled up to the entrance of the Pavilion, and Skannet saw Athena Aquitane, "the most beautiful woman in the world," according to various magazines. As she emerged, the crowd pressed against the barriers shouting her name. Cameras surrounded her and charged her beauty to the far corners of the earth. She waved.

Skannet vaulted over the grandstand fence. He zigzagged through the traffic barriers, saw the brown shirts of the security guards start to converge, the pattern familiar. They didn't have the right angle. He slipped past them as easily as he had the tacklers on the football field years before. And he arrived at exactly the right second. There was Athena talking into the microphone, head tilted to show her best side to the cameras. Three men were standing beside her. Skannet made sure that the camera had him, and then he threw the liquid from the bottle into Athena Aquitane's face.

He shouted, "Here's some acid, you bitch." Then he looked directly into the camera, his face composed, serious, and dignified. "She deserved it," he said. He was covered by a wave of brown-shirted men with their batons at the ready. He knelt on the ground.

At the last moment Athena Aquitane had seen his face. She heard his shout and turned her head so that the liquid struck her cheek and ear.

A billion TV people saw it all. The lovely face of Athena, the silvery liquid on her cheek, the shock and the horror, the recognition when she saw her attacker; a look of true fear that for a second destroyed all her imperious beauty.

The one billion people around the world watched as the police dragged Skannet off. He looked like a movie star himself as he raised his shackled hands in a victory salute, only to collapse as an enraged police officer, finding the gun in his waistband, gave him a short, terrible blow to the kidney.

Athena Aquitane, still reeling from shock, automatically brushed the liquid from her cheek. She felt no burning. The liquid drops on her hand began to dissolve. People were crashing all around her, to protect her, to carry her away.

She pulled loose and said to them calmly, "It's only water." She licked the drops off her hand to be sure. Then she tried to smile. "Typical of my husband," she said.

Athena, showing the great courage that helped make her a legend, walked quickly into the Pavilion of the Academy Awards. When she won the Oscar for best actress, the audience rose and clapped for what seemed like forever.

In the chilled penthouse suite of the Xanadu Casino Hotel of Las Vegas, the eighty-five-year-old owner lay dying. But on this spring day, he thought he could hear, from sixteen floors below, an ivory ball clacking through red and black slots of roulette wheels, the distant surf of crapshooters hoarsely imploring tumbling dice, the whirring of thousands of slot machines devouring silver coins.

Alfred Gronevelt was as happy as any man could be while dying. He had spent nearly ninety years as a hustler, dilettante pimp, gambler, accessory to murder, political fixer, and finally as the strict but kindly lord of the Xanadu Casino Hotel. For fear of betrayal, he had never fully loved any human being, but he had been kind to many. He felt no regrets. Now, he looked forward to the tiny little treats left in his life. Like his afternoon journey through the Casino.

Croccifixio "Cross" De Lena, his right-hand man for the last five years, came into the bedroom and said, "Ready Alfred?" And Gronevelt smiled at him and nodded.

Cross picked him up and put him in the wheelchair, the nurse tucked the old man in blankets, the male attendant took his post to wheel. The nurse handed Cross a pillbox and opened the door of the penthouse. She would remain behind. Gronevelt could not abide her on these afternoon jaunts.

The wheelchair rolled easily over the false green turf of the penthouse garden and entered the special express elevator that descended the sixteen floors to the Casino.

Gronevelt sat straight in his chair, looking right and left. This was his pleasure, to see men and women who battled against him with the odds forever on his side. The wheelchair made a leisurely tour through the blackjack and roulette area, the baccarat pit, the jungle of crap tables. The gamblers barely noticed the old man in the wheelchair, his alert eyes, the bemused smile on his skeletal face.

Wheelchair gamblers were common in Vegas. They thought fate owed them some debt of luck for their misfortune.

Finally the chair rolled into the coffee shop/dining room. The attendant deposited him at their reserved booth and then retired to another table to await their signal to leave.

Gronevelt could see through the glass wall to the huge swimming pool, the water burning a hot blue in the Nevada sun, young women with small children studding its surface like colored toys. He felt a tiny rush of pleasure that all this was his creation.

"Alfred, eat a little something," Cross De Lena said.

Gronevelt smiled at him. He loved the way Cross looked, the man was so handsome in a way that appealed to both men and women, and he was one of the few people that Gronevelt had almost trusted during his lifetime.

"I love this business," Gronevelt said. "Cross, you'll inherit my points in the Hotel and I know you'll have to deal with our partners in New York. But never leave Xanadu."

Cross patted the old man's hand, all gristle beneath the skin. "I won't," he said.

Gronevelt felt the glass wall baking the sunlight into his blood. "Cross," he said, "I've taught you everything. We've done some hard things, really hard to do. Never look back. You know percentages work in different ways. Do as many good deeds as you can. That pays off too. I'm not talking about falling in love or indulging in hatred. Those are very bad percentage moves."

They sipped coffee together. Gronevelt ate only a flaky strudel pastry. Cross had orange juice with his coffee.

"One thing," Gronevelt said, "Don't ever give a Villa to anyone who doesn't make a million drop. Never forget that. The Villas are legendary. They are very important."

Cross patted Gronevelt's hand, let his hand rest on the old man's. His affection was genuine. In some ways he loved Gronevelt more than his father.

"Don't worry," Cross said. "The Villas are sacred. Anything else?"

Gronevelt's eyes were opaque, cataracts dimming their old fire. "Be careful," he said, "Always be very careful."

"I will," Cross said. And then, to distract the old man from his coming death, he said, "When are you going to tell me about the great Santadio War? You worked with them then. Nobody ever talks about it."

Gronevelt gave an old man's sigh, barely a whisper, almost emotionless. "I know time's getting short," he said. "But I can't talk to you yet. Ask your father."

"I've asked Pippi," Cross said, "But he won't talk."

"What's past is past," Gronevelt said. "Never go back. Not for excuses. Not for justification, not for happiness. You are what you are, the world is what it is."

Back in the penthouse suite, the nurse gave Gronevelt his afternoon bath and took his vital signs. She frowned and Gronevelt said, "It's only the percentages."

That night he slept fitfully, and as dawn broke he told the nurse to help him to the balcony. She settled him in the huge chair and wrapped him in blankets. Then she sat beside him and took his hand to check his pulse. When she tried to take her hand back, Gronevelt continued to hold it. She permitted it and they both watched the sun rise above the desert.

The sun was a red ball that turned the air from blue-black to dark orange. Gronevelt could see the tennis courts, the golf course, the swimming pool, the seven Villas gleaming like Versailles and all flying the Xanadu Hotel flag: forest green field with white doves. And beyond, the desert of endless sand.

I created all this, Gronevelt thought. I built pleasure domes in a wasteland. And I made myself a happy life. Out of nothing. I tried to be as good a man as possible in this world. Should I be judged? His mind wandered back to his childhood, he and his chums, fourteen-year-old philosophers, discussing God and moral values as boys did then.

"If you could have a million dollars by pushing a button and killing a million Chinamen," his chum said triumphantly, as if posing some great, impossible moral riddle, "would you do it?" And after a long discussion they all agreed they would not. Except Gronevelt.

And now he thought, he had been right. Not because of his successful life but because that great riddle could not even be posed anymore. It was no longer a dilemma. You could pose it only one way.

"Would you push the button to kill ten million Chinamen"—why Chinamen?—"for a thousand dollars?" That was now the question.

The world was turning crimson with light, and Gronevelt squeezed his nurse's hand to keep his balance. He could look directly into the sun, his cataracts a shield. He drowsily thought of certain women he had known and loved and certain actions he had taken. And of men he had to defeat pitilessly, and the mercies he had shown. He thought of Cross as a son and pitied him and all of the Santadio and the Clericuzio. And he was happy he was leaving it all behind. After all, was it better to live a happy life or a moral life? And did you have to be a Chinaman to decide?

That last confusion destroyed his mind utterly. The nurse, holding his hand, felt it grow cold, the muscles tense. She leaned over and checked his vital signs. There was no doubt he was no more.

Cross De Lena, heir and successor, arranged the state funeral of Gronevelt. All the luminaries of Las Vegas, all the top gamblers, all of Gronevelt's women friends, all the staff of the Hotel, had to be invited and notified. For Alfred Gronevelt had been the acknowledged genius of gambling in Las Vegas.

He had spurred and contributed funds to build the churches of all denominations, for as he often said, "People who believe in religion and gamble deserve some reward for their faith." He had forbidden the building of slums, he had built first-rate hospitals and top-notch schools. Always, he claimed, as a matter of self-interest. He despised Atlantic City, where under the guidance of the state they pocketed all the money and did nothing for the social infrastructure.

Gronevelt had led the way in convincing the public that gambling was not a sordid vice but a middle-class source of entertainment, as normal as golf or baseball. He had made gambling a respectable industry in America. All of Las Vegas wanted to honor him.

Cross put aside his own personal emotions. He felt a deep sense of loss; there had been a genuine bond of affection between them throughout his whole life. And now Cross owned fifty-one percent of the Hotel Xanadu. Worth at least $500 million.

He knew his life must change. Being so much more powerful and rich, there would have to be more danger. His relationship with Don Clericuzio and his Family would become more delicate, in that he was now their partner in an enormous enterprise.

The first call Cross made was to Quogue, where he spoke to Giorgio, who gave him certain instructions. Giorgio told him that none of the Family would attend the funeral except Pippi. Also, Dante would be on the next flight out to complete the mission already discussed, but he was not to attend the funeral. The fact that Cross now owned half the Hotel was not mentioned.

There was a message from his sister, Claudia, but when he called, he got her answering service. There was another message from Ernest Vail. He liked Vail and was carrying fifty grand of his markers, but Vail would have to wait until after the funeral.

There was also a message from his father, Pippi, who was a lifelong friend of Gronevelt. And whose advice he needed on how to conduct his future life. How would his father react to his new status, his new wealth? That would be as ticklish a problem as dealing with the Clericuzio, who would have to adjust to the fact that their *Bruglione* in the West was so powerful and wealthy in his own right.

That the Don himself would be fair, Cross had no doubt; that his own father would support him was almost a given. But the Don's children, Giorgio, Vincent, and Petie, how would they react, and the grandson, Dante? He and Dante had been enemies since they were baptized together in the Don's private chapel. It was a running joke in the Family.

And now Dante would be arriving in Vegas to do the "job" on Big Tim the Rustler. That bothered Cross because he had a perverse fondness for Big Tim. But his fate had been decided by the Don himself, and Cross worried about how Dante would do the job.

The funeral for Alfred Gronevelt was the grandest ever seen in Las Vegas, a tribute to genius. His body lay in state in the Protestant church his money had built, which combined the grandness of

European cathedrals with brown slanting walls from Native American culture. And with famed Vegas practicality, a huge parking lot, decorated with Native American motifs rather than European religious.

The choir that sang the praises of the Lord and recommended Gronevelt to Heaven was from the university where he had endowed three chairs in the humanities.

Hundreds of mourners who had graduated from college because of scholarships Gronevelt had funded looked truly grieved. Some of the crowd were high rollers who had lost fortunes to the Hotel and seemed mildly cheered that at last they had triumphed over Gronevelt. Women, on their own, some middle-aged, wept silently. There were representatives from the Jewish synagogues and Catholic churches he had helped to build.

It would have been against everything Gronevelt believed in to shut down his casino, but there were those managers and croupiers who were not on the day shift. Even some recipients of the Villas made their appearance and were accorded special respect by Cross and Pippi.

The governor of the state of Nevada, Walter Wavven, attended the funeral, escorted by the mayor. The Strip itself was cordoned off so that the long procession of silver hearses, black limos, and mourners on foot could follow the body to the cemetery and Alfred Gronevelt could pass through, for the last time, the world he had created.

That night the citizen visitors of Vegas gave Gronevelt the final tribute he would have most loved. They gambled with a frenzy that set a new record for the "Drop," except of course for New Year's Eve. They buried their money with his body to show their respect.

At the end of that day, Cross De Lena prepared to begin his new life.

That night, sitting alone in her beach house in the Malibu Colony, Athena Aquitane tried to decide what to do. The breeze from the ocean coming through the open doors made her shiver as she sat on the couch thinking.

It is hard to imagine a world-famous movie star as she was when she was a child. Hard to imagine her going through the process of becoming a woman. A movie star's charisma is so powerful that it seems as if their adult images as heroes, as beauties, had sprung full grown out of the head of Zeus. They never had a history of bed-wetting, never had acne, never had an ugly face to grow out of, never had the shrinking shyness and nerdiness of adolescence, never masturbated, never begged for love, never were at the mercy of fate. It was very hard, now, for Athena even to remember such a person.

Athena thought that she had been born as one of the luckiest people on earth. Everything came to her naturally. She had a wonderful father and mother, who recognized her gifts and nurtured them. They adored her physical beauty but did everything in their power to educate her mind. Her father tutored her in sports, her mother in literature and the arts. She could never remember a time in her childhood that she had been unhappy. Until she was seventeen years old.

She fell in love with Boz Skannet, who was four years older, a regional football star at his college. His family owned the biggest bank in Houston. Boz was almost as handsome as Athena was beautiful, plus he was funny, he was charming, he adored her. Their two perfect bodies came together like magnets, nerve endings high voltage, flesh all silk and milk. They entered a special heaven and to ensure that this would last forever, they married.

Within a few short months Athena became pregnant, yet with her usual bodily perfection, she gained very little weight; she never felt sick and enjoyed the idea of having a baby. So she continued going to college, studying drama, and playing golf and tennis. Boz could overpower her in tennis, but she beat him easily in golf.

Boz went to work in his father's bank. Once she had the baby, a little girl that she'd named Bethany, Athena continued going to school, since Boz had enough money to hire a nanny and a maid. Marriage made Athena even more hungry for knowledge. She read voraciously, especially plays. She was delighted by Pirandello, dismayed by Strindberg; she wept over Tennessee Williams. She grew more vibrant, her intelligence framed her physical beauty by giving it dignity that beauty sometimes does not have. It was not surprising that many men, young and old, fell in love with her. Boz Skannet's friends envied him having such a wife. Athena prided herself in her perfection, until in later years she found that this very perfection irritated many people, including friends and lovers.

Boz joked that it was like a Rolls that he had to park in the street every night. He was intelligent enough to know that his wife was destined for greater things, to know that she was extraordinary. And he could see very clearly that he was fated to lose her, as he had lost his own dreams. There had been no war to prove his courage, though he knew himself to be fearless. He knew he had charm and good looks but no particular talent. He was not interested in amassing a huge fortune.

He was jealous of Athena's gifts, her certainty of her place in her world.

So Boz Skannet went forward to meet his fate. He drank to excess, he seduced his colleague's wives, and at his father's bank, he initiated shady transactions. He became proud of his cunning, as any man does of a newly acquired skill, and used it to hide his growing hatred of his wife. For was it not heroic to hate one so beautiful and perfect as Athena?

Boz's health was extraordinary despite debauch. He clung to it. He worked out in the gym, took boxing lessons. He loved the physicality of the ring, where he could smash his fist into a human face; the cunning of switching from jab to hook; the stoicism of receiving punishment. He loved hunting, the killing of game. He loved the seduction of naïve women, the schematism of romance.

Then with his newfound cunning he thought of a way out. He and Athena would have more children. Four, five, six. That would bring them together again. That would stop her from leaping up and away from him. But by that time Athena could see this for what it was and said no. She said more. "If you want children, have them with the other women you're screwing."

It was the first time that she had spoken coarsely to him. He was not surprised that she knew of his unfaithfulness, he had not attempted to hide it. In fact, that was his cunning. Then it would be he who had driven her away, not she who had left.

Athena observed what was happening to Boz, but she was too young and too intent on her own life to give it the necessary attention. It was only when Boz turned cruel that Athena, at twenty years of age, found the steel in her character, an impatience with stupidity.

Boz started playing those clever games of men who hate women. And it seemed to Athena that he was actually going insane.

He always picked up their dry cleaning on his way home from work, because as he often said, "Honey, your time is more valuable than mine. You have all your special classes in music and drama besides your degree work." He thought she would not detect his spiteful reproach because of the offhand tone of his voice.

One day Boz came home carrying an armload of her dresses while she was taking a bath. He looked down at her, all gold hair and white skin, rounded breasts and buttocks decorated with foamy soap. His voice thick, he said, "How would you like it if I threw this shit right into the tub with you?" But instead, he hung the clothes in the closet, helped her out of the water, and rubbed her dry with rosy pink towels. Then he made love to her. A few weeks later the scene was repeated. But this time he threw the clothes in the water.

One night he threatened to break all the dishes at dinner but did not. A week later, he smashed everything in the kitchen. He always apologized after these instances. Always tried to make love afterward. But now Athena refused him and they slept in separate bedrooms.

Another night at dinner Boz held up his fist and said, "Your face is too perfect. Maybe if I broke your nose, it would have more character, like Marlon Brando."

She ran into the kitchen, and he followed her. She was terribly frightened and picked up a knife. Boz laughed and said, "That's the one thing you can't do." And he was right. He easily took the knife away from her. "I was only kidding," he said. "You're only fault is you have no sense of humor."

Athena, at twenty, could have turned to her parents for help, but she did not, nor did she confide in friends. Instead she carefully thought things out, she trusted her intelligence. She saw that she would never finish college, the situation was too dangerous. She knew the authorities could not protect her. She considered briefly a campaign to make Boz truly love her again so that he would be the old Boz, but now she had such a physical aversion to him that she couldn't stand even the thought of him touching her, and she knew that she would never be able to give a convincing performance of love, though that option appealed to her dramatic sense.

What Boz did that finally forced her hand and made her certain she had to leave didn't have to do with her, it concerned Bethany.

He often tossed their one-year-old daughter into the air playfully and then pretended he was not going to catch her, only doing so with a last-minute lunge. But once he let the infant bounce, accidentally it seemed, on the sofa. And then finally one day he quite deliberately let the little girl fall to the floor. Athena gasped with horror and rushed to pick the baby up, to hold her, to comfort her. She stayed awake all night sitting beside the crib of the infant to be certain she was all right. Bethany had a fearful lump on her head. Boz tearfully apologized and promised he would no longer tease in such a fashion. But Athena had come to a decision.

The next day she cleared out her checking account and her savings account. She made intricate travel arrangements so that her movements could not be followed. Two days later, when Boz came home from work, she and the baby had disappeared.

Six months later Athena surfaced in Los Angeles, without a baby, and started her career. She easily got a mid-level agent and worked in small theater groups. She starred in a play at the Mark Taper Forum that led to small parts in small movies, and then was cast in a supporting role in an A movie. In her next picture she became a Bankable Star, and Boz Skannet reentered her life.

She bought him off for the next three years, but she wasn't surprised by what he did at the Academy. An old trick. This time just a little joke . . . but the next time, that bottle would be full of acid.

"There's a big flap at the Studio," Molly Flanders told Claudia De Lena that morning. "A problem with Athena Aquitane. Because of the attack at the Academy Awards, they're worried she won't go back to work on her picture. And Bantz wants you at the Studio. They want you to talk to Athena."

Claudia had come to Molly's office with Ernest Vail. "I'll call her as soon as we finish here," Claudia said. "She can't be serious."

Molly Flanders was an entertainment lawyer, and in a town of fearsome people she was the most feared litigator in the motion picture business. She absolutely loved fighting in the courtroom, and she nearly always won because she was a great actress and had a superb grasp of the law.

Before getting into entertainment law, she had been the premier defense attorney in the state of California. She had saved twenty murderers from the gas chamber. The worst any of these clients had to suffer was a few years for different degrees of manslaughter. But then her nerves had given way and she had switched to entertainment law. She often said it was less bloody and it had greater and more witty villains.

Now she represented A-picture directors, Bankable Stars, top-notch screenwriters. And on the morning after the Academy Awards, one of her favorite clients, Claudia De Lena, was in her office. With her was her screenwriting partner of the moment, a once famous novelist, Ernest Vail.

Claudia De Lena was an old friend, and though one of the least important of Flanders's clients, the most intimate. So when Claudia asked her to take on Vail, she agreed. Now she regretted it. Vail had come with a problem that even she couldn't solve. Also, he was a man she could feel no affection for, though she usually learned to like even her murder clients. Which made her feel a little guilty about giving him bad news.

"Ernest," she said, "I went over all the contracts, all the legal papers. And there is no point in your continuing to sue LoddStone Studios. The only way you can get the rights back is to croak before your copyright expires. Which means sometime in the next five years."

A decade before, Ernest Vail had been the most famous novelist in America, praised by critics, read by a vast public. One novel had a franchise character LoddStone had exploited. They bought the rights, made the picture, and achieved an enormous success. Two sequels also made a fortune in profit. The Studio had on its drawing board four more sequels. Unfortunately for Vail his first contract had given all the rights to the characters and title to the Studio, on all planets in the universe, in all forms of entertainment, discovered and undiscovered. The standard contract for novelists who had not yet amassed clout in movies.

Ernest Vail was a man who always had a grim, sour expression on his face. For which he had good reason. The critics still acclaimed his books, but the public no longer read them. Also, despite his talent, he had made a mess of his life. During the last twenty years his wife had left, taking their three children with her. On the one book that had become a successful movie, he had made a one-time score, but the Studio would make hundreds of millions over the years.

"Explain that to me," Vail said.

"The contracts are foolproof," Molly said. "The Studio owns your characters. There's only one loophole. Copyright law states that when you die all rights to your works revert to your heirs."

For the first time Vail smiled. "Redemption," he said.

Claudia asked, "What kind of money are we talking about?"

"On a fair deal," Molly said, "five percent of gross. Figure they get five more pictures out of it and they are not disasters, total rentals, a billion worldwide, so we're talking around thirty or forty million." She paused for a moment and smiled sardonically. "If you were dead, I could get your heirs a much better deal. We'd really have a gun to their heads."

Vail said, "Call the people at LoddStone. I want a meeting. I'll convince them that if they don't cut me in, I'll kill myself."

"They won't believe you," Molly said.

"Then I'll do it," Vail said.

"Talk sense," Claudia said amiably. "Ernest, you're only fifty-six years old. That's too young to die for money. For principle, for the good of your country, for love, sure. But not for money."

"I have to provide for my wife and kids," Vail said.

"Your ex-wife," Molly said. "And for Christ's sake, you've been married twice since."

"I'm talking about my real wife," Vail said. "The one who had my kids."

Molly understood why everybody in Hollywood disliked him. She said, "The Studio won't give you what you want. They know you won't kill yourself, and they won't be bluffed by a writer. If you were a Bankable Star, maybe. An A director, maybe. But never a writer. You're just shit in this business. Sorry, Claudia."

Claudia said, "Ernest knows that and I know that. If everybody in this town wasn't scared to death of a blank piece of paper, they'd get rid of us entirely. But can't you do something?"

Molly sighed and put in a call to Eli Marrion. She had enough clout to get through to Bobby Bantz, the president of LoddStone.

Claudia and Vail had a drink together afterward in the Polo Lounge. Vail said reflectively, "Big woman, Molly. Big women are easier to seduce. And they're much nicer in bed than small women. Ever notice?"

Not for the first time Claudia wondered why she was so fond of Vail. Not many people were. But she had loved Vail's novels, still did. "You're full of shit," she said.

Vail said, "I meant big women are sweeter. They bring you breakfast in bed, they do little things for you. Feminine things."

Claudia shrugged.

Vail said, "Big women are good-hearted. One brought me home from a party one night and really didn't know what to do with me. She looked around the bedroom exactly like my mother used to look around her kitchen when there was nothing in the house to eat and she was figuring out how to throw a meal together. She was wondering, how the hell we were going to have a good time with the materials at hand."

They sipped their drinks. As always, Claudia warmed to him when he was so disarming. "You know how Molly and I became friends?" Claudia said. "She was defending some guy who had murdered his girlfriend and she needed some good dialogue for him to use in the courtroom. I wrote the scene just as if it were a movie, and her client got manslaughter. I think I wrote the dialogue and the plotline for three other cases before we stopped."

"I hate Hollywood," Vail said.

"You just hate Hollywood because LoddStone Studios screwed you on your book," Claudia said.

"Not just that," Vail said. "I'm like one of those old civilizations like the Aztecs, the Chinese empires, the Native American Indians, who were destroyed by a people with more sophisticated technology. I'm a real writer, I write novels to appeal to the mind. That kind of writing is a very backward technology. It can't stand up against movies. Movies have cameras, they have sets, they have music and they have these great faces. How can a writer conjure that up with just words? And movies have narrowed the field of battle. They don't have to conquer the brain, only the heart."

"Fuck you, I'm not a writer," Claudia said. "A screenwriter is not a writer? You just say that because you're not good at it."

Vail patted her on the shoulder. "I'm not putting you down," he said. "I'm not even putting down film as an art. I'm just defining."

"It's a lucky thing I love your books," Claudia said. "It's no wonder nobody out here likes you."

Vail smiled amiably. "No, no," he said. "They don't dislike me. They just have contempt for me. But when my estate gets the rights to my characters back on my death, they'll have respect."

"You're not serious," Claudia said.

"I think I am," Vail said. "It's a very tempting prospect. Suicide. Is it politically incorrect these days?"

"Oh shit," Claudia said. She wrapped her arm around Vail's neck. "The fight is just beginning," she said. "I'm sure they'll listen when I ask for your points. Okay?"

Vail smiled at her. "No hurry," he said. "It will take me at least six months just to figure out how to do myself in. I hate violence."

Claudia realized suddenly that Vail was serious. She was surprised at the panic she felt at the thought of his death. It was not that she loved him, though they had been lovers briefly. It was not even that she was fond of him. It was the thought that the beautiful books he had written were to him less powerful than money. That his art could be defeated by such a contemptible foe as money. Out of that panic she said, "If worse comes to worst, we'll go to Vegas and see my brother, Cross. He likes you. He'll do something."

Vail laughed. "He doesn't like me that much."

Claudia said, "He has a good heart. I know my brother."

"No, you don't," Vail said.

Athena had come home from the Dorothy Chandler Pavilion the night of the Academy Awards without celebrating and had gone right to bed. She tossed and turned for hours, but she couldn't sleep. Every muscle in her body felt taut. I won't let him do this again, she thought. Not again. I won't live in terror again.

She made herself a cup of tea and tried to drink it, but when she saw the small tremor in her hand, she became impatient, walked outside, and stood on the balcony looking into the dark night sky. She stood for hours, but her heart still raced in terror.

She dressed. In white shorts and tennis shoes. And as the red sun began to show itself over the horizon, she ran. She ran faster and faster along the beach, trying to stay on the hard wet sand, trying to follow the coastline as the cold water washed over her feet. She had to clear her head. She couldn't let Boz beat her. She had worked too hard and too long. And he would kill her, she never doubted that. But first he would play with her, torment her, finally he would disfigure her, he would make her ugly, thinking it would make her his again. She felt her own fury beating in her throat, and then the cool wind spraying ocean water in her face. No, no!

She thought about the Studio, they'd be frantic, they'd threaten her. But it was money, not her, they were concerned about. She thought about her friend Claudia, how this could have been her big break, and she felt sad. She thought about all the others, but she knew she couldn't afford the luxury of compassion. Boz was crazy, and people who weren't crazy would try to reason with him. He was smart enough to make them think they could win, but she knew better. She couldn't take the chance. She couldn't allow herself to take that chance. . . .

By the time she reached the large black boulders that meant the north beach ended, she was completely out of breath. She sat, trying to slow her heart down. She looked up when she heard the caw of seagulls as they swept down and seemed to glide along the water. Her eyes filled, but she pulled herself back with determination. She swallowed past the lump in her throat. And for the first time in a long time she wished her parents weren't so far away. Some part of her felt like a small child and wished desperately to run home to safety, to someone who could put their arms around her and just make everything better. She smiled at herself then, a crooked, wry smile, remembering when she really believed that was possible. Now, she was so loved by everyone, so admired, so adored . . . and so what? She felt more empty than she thought any human was capable of feeling, more lonely. Sometimes when she found herself passing an ordinary woman with her husband and children, a woman living an ordinary life, she felt such longing. Stop! she told herself. Think. It's up to you. Come up with a plan and carry it through. It's not only your life that depends on you. . . .

It was midmorning before she walked back home. And she walked with her head held high and her eyes staring straight ahead: She knew what she had to do.

Boz Skannet was kept in custody overnight. His lawyer organized a press conference when he was released. Skannet told reporters that he was married to Athena Aquitane, though he had not seen her for ten years, and that what he had done was just a practical joke. The liquid was only water. He predicted that Athena would not press charges, intimating he possessed a terrible secret about her. In this he proved correct. No charges were filed.

That day Athena Aquitane informed LoddStone Studios, the studio making one of the most costly pictures in movie history, that she would not return to work on that film. Because of the attack made on her, she feared for her life.

Without her, the film, a historical epic called *Messalina,* could not be completed. The fifty million dollars invested would be a total loss. It also meant that because of this no major studio would ever dare cast Athena Aquitane in a movie again.

LoddStone Studios released a statement that their star had suffered extreme exhaustion but that in a month she would be recovered enough to resume shooting.

CHAPTER 2

LODDSTONE STUDIOS WAS the most powerful movie-making entity in Hollywood, but Athena Aquitane's refusal to go back to work was a costly treachery. It was rare that mere "Talent" could deal such a damaging blow, but *Messalina* was the Studio "Locomotive" for the Christmas season, the big picture that would power all the Studio's releases through the long, hard winter.

It happened that the next Sunday was the date of the annual Festival of Brotherhood charity party, held at the Beverly Hills estate of Eli Marrion, major shareholder and chairman of LoddStone Studios.

Far back in the canyons above Beverly Hills, Eli Marrion's huge mansion was a showplace of twenty rooms, but the oddity of it was that it had only one bedchamber. Eli Marrion never liked anyone sleeping in his house. There were guest bungalows, of course, along with two tennis courts and a large swimming pool. Six of the rooms were devoted to his large collection of paintings.

Five hundred of the most eminent people in Hollywood were invited to this charity festival with an admission fee of one thousand dollars per person. There were bars and buffet tents and dancing tents spread over the grounds, and there was a band. But the house itself was off-limits. Toilet facilities were provided by portable units in gaily decorated, wittily designed tents.

The mansion, the guest bungalows, the tennis courts, and the swimming pool were roped off and barred by security men. None of the guests were offended by this, Eli Marrion was too lofty a personage for offense to be taken.

But as guests frolicked on the lawns, gossiping and dancing for an obligatory three hours, Marrion was in the huge conference room of the mansion with a group of people most concerned with the completion of the film *Messalina.*

Eli Marrion dominated this gathering. His body was eighty years old but so cleverly disguised you took it for no more than sixty. His gray hair was perfectly cut and tinted to silver, his dark suit broadened his shoulders, added flesh to his bones, insulated his pipe-thin shanks. Mahogany shoes anchored him to earth. A white shirt was vertically cut with a rose-colored tie that pinked his grayish pallor. But his rule over LoddStone Studios was absolute only when he wanted it to be. There were times when it was more prudent to let mere mortals exercise their free will.

Athena Aquitane's refusal to complete a film in progress was a problem serious enough to command even Marrion's attention. *Messalina,* a hundred-million-dollar production, the studio Locomotive, with video, TV, cable and foreign rights presold to cover the cost, was a golden treasure that was about to sink like an old Spanish galleon, never to be retrieved.

And there was Athena herself. At the age of thirty, a great star, already signed to do another blockbuster for LoddStone. A true Talent, of which there was nothing more valuable. Marrion adored Talent.

But Talent was like dynamite, it could be dangerous and you had to control it. You did that with love, with cajolery in its most abject form, you showered it with worldly goods. You became a father, a mother, a brother, a sister, even a lover. No sacrifice was too great. But there came a time when you could not be weak, when indeed you must be merciless.

So now in this room with Marrion were the people to enforce his will. Bobby Bantz, Skippy Deere, Melo Stuart, and Dita Tommey.

Eli Marrion, facing them in this familiar conference room, twenty million dollars worth of paintings, tables, chairs, and rugs, the crystal goblets and jugs totaling at least a half million more, could feel his bones crumbling within. Each day he was astonished how difficult it was to present himself to the world as the all-powerful figure he was presumed to be.

Mornings were no longer refreshing, it was fatiguing to shave, to knot his tie, to button the buttons on his shirt. More dangerous was the mental weakness. This took the form of pity for people less powerful than himself. Now he was using Bobby Bantz more, giving him more power. After all, the man was thirty years younger and was his closest friend, loyal to him for so long.

Bantz was president and chief executive officer of the Studio. For over thirty years, Bantz had been Marrion's hatchet man, and through the years they had become very close, like father and son, as it is said. They suited each other. After the age of seventy, Marrion had become too tenderhearted to do the things that absolutely had to be done.

It was Bantz who took over from movie directors after their artistic cut and made their films acceptable to audiences. It was Bantz who disputed percentages of directors, stars, and writers and made them either go to court to collect or settle for somewhat less. It was Bantz who negotiated very tough contracts with Talent. Especially writers.

Bantz refused to give even the standard lip service to writers. It was true you needed a script to start, but Bantz believed that you lived and died by casting. Star power. Directors were important because they could steal you blind. Producers, no slouches when it came to thievery, were necessary for the manic energy that started a movie.

But writers? All they had to do was make that initial tracing on blank white paper. You hired another dozen to work it over. Then the producer shaped the plot. The director invented Business (sometimes a whole new picture), and then the stars came up with inspired bits of dialogue. Then there was the Creative Staff of the Studio who, in long, carefully thought out memos, gave writers insights, plot ideas, and wish lists. Bantz had seen many a million-dollar script from a big-shot screenwriter paid a million dollars, only to find when the picture was finished it contained not a single plot incident or word of dialogue of the writer's. Sure, Eli had a soft spot for writers, but that was because they were so easy to screw on their contracts.

Marrion and Bantz had traveled the world together selling movies to film festivals and market centers, to London and Paris and Cannes, to Tokyo and Singapore. They had decided the fate of young artists. They had ruled an empire together, as Emperor and chief vassal.

Eli Marrion and Bobby Bantz agreed that Talent, those who wrote, acted in, and directed movies, were the most ungrateful people in the world. Oh, those hopeful pure artists could be so engaging, so grateful for their chance, so accommodating when they were fighting their way up, but how they could change after achieving fame. Honey-making bees turned into angry hornets. It was only natural that Marrion and Bantz kept a staff of twenty lawyers to throw a net over them.

Why were they always so much trouble? So unhappy? There was no doubt about it, people who pursued money rather than art had longer careers, got more pleasure in life, were much better and more socially valuable people than those artists who tried to show the divine spark in human beings. Too bad you couldn't make a movie about that. That money was more healing than art and love. But the public would never buy it.

Bobby Bantz had gathered them all up from the festival going on outside the mansion. The only Talent there was the director of *Messalina,* a woman named Dita Tommey, in the "A" class and known as the best with female stars, which in Hollywood today meant not homosexual but feminist. The fact that she was also a lesbian was irrelevant to all these men in the conference room. Dita Tommey brought in her pictures under budget, her pictures made money, and her liaisons with females caused far less trouble on a picture than a male director screwing his actresses did. Lesbian lovers of the famous were docile.

Eli Marrion sat at the head of the conference table and let Bantz lead the discussion.

Bantz said, "Dita, tell us exactly how we stand on the picture and what your thoughts are on solving the situation. Hell, I don't even understand the problem."

Tommey was short and very compact and always spoke to the point. She said, "Athena is scared to death. She is not coming back to work unless you geniuses come up with something that can erase that fear. If she doesn't come back, you guys are out fifty million bucks. The picture cannot be finished without her." She paused for a moment. "I've shot around her in the past week, so I've saved you money there."

"This fucking picture," Bantz said. "I never wanted to make it."

This provoked other men in the room; the producer, Skippy Deere, said, "Fuck you, Bobby," and Melo Stuart, Athena Aquitane's agent, said, "Bullshit."

In truth, *Messalina* had been enthusiastically supported by everyone. It had received one of the easiest "green lights" in history.

Messalina told the story of the Roman Empire under the Emperor Claudius from a feminist point of view. History, written by males, painted the Empress Messalina as a corrupt and murderous harlot, who one night took on the whole population of Rome in sexual debauch. But in the movie creating her life almost two thousand years later, she was revealed as a tragic heroine, an Antigone, another Medea. A woman who, using the only weapons available to her, tried to change a world in which men were so dominant that they treated the female sex, half the human race, as if they were slaves.

It was a great concept—rampant sex acts in full color and a highly relevant and popular theme—but it needed a perfect package to make the whole thing credible. First Claudia De Lena wrote a script that was witty and had a strong story line. Dita Tommey as director was a pragmatic and politically correct choice. She had a dry intelligence and was a proven director. Athena Aquitane was perfect as *Messalina* and had completely dominated the picture so far. She had the beauty of face and body, and the genius of her acting made everything plausible. More important, she was one of the three female Bankable Stars in the world. Claudia, with her own offbeat genius, had even given her a scene in which Messalina, seduced by the growing Christian legends, saved martyrs from the sure death of the amphitheater. When Tommey read the scene she said to Claudia, "Hey, there's a limit."

Claudia grinned at her and said, "Not in the movies."

Skippy Deere said, "We have to shut down the picture until we get Athena back to work. That will cost a hundred fifty grand a day. The situation is this. We've spent fifty million. We're halfway through, we can't write Athena out and we can't double her. So if she doesn't come back, we scrap the picture."

"We can't scrap it," Bantz said. "Insurance doesn't cover a star refusing to work. Drop her out of a plane, then insurance pays. Melo, it's your job to get her back. You're responsible."

Melo Stuart said, "I'm her agent but I can only have so much influence on a woman like her. Let me tell you this. She is genuinely frightened. This is not one of your temperamental things. She's scared, but she's an intelligent woman, so she must have a reason. This is a very dangerous, a very delicate, situation."

Bantz said, "If she torpedoes a hundred-million-dollar movie, she can never work again, did you tell her that?"

"She knows," Stuart said.

Bantz asked, "Who's the best person to talk sense into her? Skippy, you tried and failed. Melo, you did. Dita, I know you did your best. I even tried."

Tommey said to Bantz, "You don't count, Bobby. She detests you."

Bantz said sharply, "Sure, some people don't like my style but they listen to me."

Tommey said kindly, "Bobby, none of the Talent likes you, but Athena doesn't like you personally."

"I gave her the role that made her a star," Bantz said.

Melo Stuart said calmly, "She was born a star. You were lucky to get her."

Bantz said, "Dita, you're her friend. It's your job to get her back to work."

"Athena is not my friend," Tommey said. "She is a colleague who respects me because after I tried to make her, I desisted gracefully when I failed. Not like you, Bobby. You kept trying for years."

Bantz said amiably, "Dita, who the hell is she not to fuck us? Eli, you have to lay down the law."

All attention was fixed on the old man, who seemed bored. Eli Marrion was so thin that one male star had joked he should wear an eraser on his skull, but this was more malicious than apt. Marrion had a comparatively huge head and the broad gorilla face of a much heavier man, a broad nose, thick mouth, yet his face was curiously benign, somewhat gentle, some even said handsome. But his eyes gave him away, they were cold gray and radiated intelligence and an absolute concentration that daunted most people. It was perhaps for this reason that he insisted that everyone call him by his first name.

Marrion spoke in an emotionless voice. "If Athena won't listen to you people, she won't listen to me. My position of authority won't impress her. Which makes it all the more puzzling that she is so frightened over such a senseless attack by such a foolish man. Can't we buy our way out of this?"

"We will try," Bantz said. "But it makes no difference to Athena. She doesn't trust him."

Skippy Deere, the producer, said, "And we tried muscle. I got some friends in the police department to lean on him, but he's tough. His family has money and political connections and he's crazy in the bargain."

Stuart said, "Exactly how much does the Studio lose if it closes down the picture? I'll do my best to let you recoup on future packages."

There was a problem about letting Melo Stuart know the extent of the damages; as Athena's agent, it would give him too much leverage. Marrion did not answer but nodded to Bobby Bantz.

Bantz was reluctant, but spoke. "Actual money spent, fifty million. Okay, we can eat fifty million. But we have to give back the foreign sales money, the video money, and there's no Locomotive for Christmas. That can cost us another . . ." He paused, not willing to give that figure, "and then if we add the profits that we lose . . . shit, two hundred million dollars. You'd have to give us a break on a lot of packages, Melo."

Stuart smiled, thinking he would have to jack up his price for Athena. "But actually, in real cash put out, you only lose fifty," he said.

When Marrion spoke his voice had lost its gentleness. "Melo," he said, "How much will it cost us to get your client back to work?" They knew what had happened. Marrion had decided to act as if this was just a scam.

Stuart read the message. How much are you going to stick us up for on this little scheme? This was an attack on his integrity but he had no intention of getting on his high horse. Not with Marrion. If it had been Bantz, he would have been wrathfully indignant.

Stuart was a very powerful man in the movie world. He didn't have to kiss even Marrion's ass. He controlled a stable of five A directors, not strictly Bankable but very powerful indeed; two male Bankable Stars; and one female Bankable Star, Athena. Which meant he had three people who could assure a green light for any movie. But still it was not wise to anger Marrion. Stuart had become powerful by avoiding such dangers. Certainly this was a great situation for a stickup but not really. This was a rare time when straightforwardness could pay off.

Melo Stuart's greatest asset was his sincerity, he truly believed in what he sold, and he had believed in Athena's talent even ten years before, when she was an unknown. He believed in her now. But what if he could change her mind and bring her back before the cameras? Surely that was worth something, surely that option should not be closed off.

"This is not about money," Stuart said with passion. He felt a rapture for his own sincerity. "You could offer Athena an extra million and she would not go back. You must solve the problem of this so-called long-absent husband."

There was an ominous silence. Everybody paid attention. A sum of money had been mentioned. Was it an opening wedge?

Skippy Deere said, "She won't take money."

Dita Tommey shrugged. She didn't believe Stuart for a moment. But it wouldn't be her money. Bantz simply glared at Stuart, who coolly kept looking at Marrion.

Marrion analyzed Stuart's remark correctly. Athena would not come back for money. Talent was never so cunning. He decided to wrap up the meeting.

He said, "Melo, explain very carefully to your client, if she does not come back in one month's time the Studio abandons the picture and takes the loss. Then we sue her for everything she owns. She must know she can't work again for a major American studio afterwards." He smiled around the table. "What the hell, it's only fifty million."

They all knew he was serious, that he had lost his patience. Dita Tommey panicked, the picture meant more to her than anyone. It was her baby. If it succeeded she would be among those directors who would be Bankable. Her OK could get a green light. Out of her panic, she said, "Get Claudia De Lena to talk to her. She's one of Athena's closest friends."

Bobby Bantz said contemptuously, "I don't know what's worse, a star fucking somebody below the line or being friends with a writer."

At this Marrion again lost his patience. "Bobby, don't bring irrelevancies into a business discussion. Have Claudia talk to her. But let's wrap this thing up one way or another. We have other pictures to make."

But the next day a check for five million dollars arrived at Lodd-Stone Studios. It was from Athena Aquitane. She had returned the advance money she had been paid to do *Messalina*.

Now it was in the hands of the lawyers.

In just fifteen years Andrew Pollard had built the Pacific Ocean Security Company into the most prestigious protection organization on the West Coast. Starting in a suite of hotel rooms, he now owned a four-story building in Santa Monica with over fifty permanent HQ staff, five hundred investigators and guards under freelance contracts, plus a floating reserve group who worked for him a good part of the year.

Pacific Ocean Security provided services for the very rich and very famous. It protected the homes of movie magnates with armed personnel and electronic devices. It provided bodyguards for stars and producers. It supplied uniformed men to control the crowds at great media events such as the Academy Awards. It did investigative work in delicate matters such as providing counterintelligence to ward off would-be blackmailers.

Andrew Pollard became successful because he was a stickler for details. He planted ARMED RESPONSE signs on the grounds of his rich clients' houses that flashed in the night with an explosion of red light, plus he had patrols in the neighborhoods of the walled-in mansions. Careful in picking his personnel, he paid high enough wages so that they worried about being fired. He could afford to be generous. His clients were the richest people in the country and paid accordingly. He was also clever enough to work closely with the Los Angeles Police Department, top and bottom. He was a business friend of Jim Losey, the legendary detective, who was a hero to the rank and file. But most important, he had the backing of the Clericuzio Family.

Fifteen years before, while still a young police officer, still a little careless, he had been entrapped by the Internal Affairs Unit of the New York City Police Department. It was small graft, almost impossible to avoid. But he had stood fast and refused to inform on his superiors who were involved. The Clericuzio Family underlings observed this and set in motion a series of judicial moves so that Andrew Pollard was given a deal: Resign from the New York Police Department and escape punishment.

Pollard migrated to Los Angeles with his wife and child, and the Family gave him the money to set up his Pacific Ocean Security Company. Then the Family sent out word that Pollard's clients were not to be molested, their houses could not be burglarized, their persons were not to be mugged, their jewelry was not to be stolen and if stolen in error must be returned. It was for this reason that the flaming ARMED RESPONSE signs also flashed the name of the protection agency.

Andrew Pollard's success was almost magical, the mansions under his protection were never touched. His bodyguards were as nearly well trained as FBI men, so the company was never sued for inside jobs, sexual harassment of their employers, or child molesting, all of which happened in the world of security. There were a few cases of attempted blackmail, and there were some guards who sold intimate secrets to the scandal sheets, but that was unavoidable. All in all, Pollard ran a clean, efficient operation.

His company had computer access to confidential information about people in all walks of life. And it was only natural that when the Clericuzio Family needed data, it would be supplied. Pollard earned a good living and he was grateful to the Family. Plus the fact that every once in a while there was a job he could not ask his guards to do, and he would then make application to the western *Bruglione* for some help in the way of strong-arm.

There were slyer predators for whom Los Angeles and Hollywood were like some Edenesque jungle, teeming with victims. There were the movie executives lured into blackmailers' honey traps, the closeted movie stars, sadomasochistic directors, pedophile producers, all frightened their secrets would get out. Pollard was noted for dealing with these cases with finesse and discretion. He could negotiate the lowest possible payment and ensure that there would be no second dip.

Bobby Bantz summoned Andrew Pollard to his office the day after the Academy Awards. "I want all the info you can get on this Boz Skannet character," he told Pollard. "I want all the background on Athena Aquitane. For a major star, we know very little about her. I also want you to make a deal with Skannet. We need Athena for another three to six months on the picture, so structure a deal with Skannet so that he goes far away. Offer him twenty grand a month but you can go as high as a hundred."

Pollard said quietly, "And after he can do what he wants?"

"Then it's a job for the authorities," Bantz said. "You have to be very careful, Andrew. This guy has a powerful family. The movie industry cannot be accused of any off-color tactics, it might ruin the picture and hurt the Studio. So just make the deal. Plus we are using your firm for her personal security."

"And if he doesn't go for the deal?" Pollard asked.

"Then you have to guard her day and night," Bantz said. "Until the picture is done."

"I could lean on him just a little," Pollard said. "In a legal way of course. I'm not suggesting anything."

"He's too well connected," Bantz said. "The police authorities are leery of him. Even Jim Losey, who's such a good buddy of Skippy

Deere, won't use any muscle. Aside from public relations, the Studio could be sued for enormous amounts of money. I'm not saying you should treat him like a delicate flower but . . ."

Pollard got the message. A little rough stuff to scare the guy but pay him what he wanted. "I'll need contracts," he said.

Bantz took an envelope from his desk drawer. "He signs three copies and there's a check in there for fifty thousand dollars as a down payment. The figures in the contract are open, you can fill it in when you make the deal."

As he went out Bantz said after him, "Your people didn't help at the Academy Awards. They were sleeping on their fucking feet."

Pollard did not take offense. This was vintage Bantz.

"Those were just crowd-control guards," he said. "Don't worry, I'll put my top crew around Miss Aquitane."

In twenty-four hours Pacific Ocean Security computers had everything on Boz Skannet. He was thirty-four years old, a graduate of Texas A&M, where he had been Conference All-Star running back and then gone on to one season of professional football. His father owned a bank in Houston, but more important, his uncle ran the Republican political machine in Texas and was a close personal friend of the president. Mixed into all of this was a lot of money.

Boz Skannet was a piece of work in and of himself. As a vice president in his father's bank, he had narrowly escaped indictment in an oil lease scam. He had been arrested for assault six times. In one case he had beaten two police officers so severely they had to be hospitalized. Skannet was never prosecuted because he paid damages to the officers. There was a sexual harassment charge settled out of court. Before all this he had been married at twenty-one to Athena and had become the father of a baby girl the next year. The child was named Bethany. At age twenty, his wife disappeared with their daughter.

All this gave Andrew Pollard a picture. This was a bad guy. A guy who carried a grudge against his wife for ten years, a guy who fought armed police officers and was tough enough to send them to the hospital. The chances of scaring such a guy were nil. Pay him the money, get the contract signed, and stay the hell out of it.

Pollard called Jim Losey, who was handling the Skannet case for the Los Angeles PD. Pollard was in awe of Losey, who was the cop he would have liked to become. They had a working relationship. Losey received a handsome gift every Christmas from Pacific Ocean Security. Now Pollard wanted the police dope, wanted to know everything Losey had on the case.

"Jim," Pollard said, "Can you send me an info sheet on Boz Skannet? I need his address in L.A. and I'd like to know more about him."

"Sure," Losey said. "But the charges against him have been dropped. What are you in this for?"

"Protection job," Pollard said. "How dangerous is this guy?"

"He's fucking crazy," Losey said. "Tell your bodyguard team that if he gets close they should start shooting."

"You'd arrest me," Pollard said, laughing. "It's against the law."

"Yeah," Losey said, "I'd have to. What a fucking joke."

Boz Skannet was staying in a modest hotel on Ocean Avenue in Santa Monica, which worried Andrew Pollard because it was only a fifteen-minute drive to Athena's house in Malibu Colony. He ordered a four-man team to guard Athena's house and put a two-man team into Skannet's hotel. Then he arranged to meet with Skannet that afternoon.

Pollard took three of his biggest and toughest men with him. With a guy like Skannet you never knew what might happen.

Skannet let them into his hotel suite. He was affable, greeted them with a smile, but did not offer any refreshment. Curiously enough, he was wearing a tie, shirt, and jacket, perhaps to show that after all he was still a banker. Pollard introduced himself and his three bodyguards, all three showing their Pacific Ocean Security IDs. Skannet grinned at them and said, "You guys are sure big. I'll bet a hundred bucks I can kick the shit out of any one of you in a fair fight."

The three bodyguards, well-trained men, gave him small acknowledging smiles, but Pollard deliberately took offense. A calculated umbrage. "We're here to do business, Mr. Skannet," he said. "Not to endure threats. LoddStone Studios is prepared to pay you fifty thousand down right now and twenty thousand a month for eight months. All you have to do is leave Los Angeles." Pollard took the contracts and the big green-and-white check out of his briefcase.

Skannet studied them. "Very simple contract," he said. "I don't even need a lawyer. But it's also very simple money. I was thinking a hundred grand in front and fifty thousand a month."

"Too much," Pollard said. "We have a judge's restraining order against you. You get within a block of Athena and you go to jail. We have security around Athena twenty-four hours a day. And I've set up surveillance teams to keep track of your movements. So for you this is found money."

"I should have come to California sooner," Skannet said. "The streets are paved with gold. Why pay me anything?"

"The studio wants to reassure Miss Aquitane," Pollard said.

"She really is that big a star," Skannet said musingly. "Well, she was always special. And to think I used to fuck her five times a day." He grinned at the three men. "And brainy in the bargain."

Pollard looked at the man with curiosity. The guy was handsome as the rugged Marlboro man in the cigarette ads, except that his skin was red with sun and booze and his body build was bulkier. He had that charming drawl of the South, which was both humorous and dangerous. A lot of women fell in love with such men. In New York there had been some cops with the same kind of looks, and they had scored like bandits. You sent them out on murder cases and in a week they were consoling the widows. Jim Losey was a cop like that, come to think of it. Pollard had never been so lucky.

"Let's just talk business," Pollard said. He wanted Skannet to sign the contract and take the check in front of the witnesses, then maybe later if they had to, the Studio could make a case for extortion.

Skannet sat down at the table. "Have you got a pen?" he asked.

Pollard took his pen out of the briefcase and filled out the figures of twenty thousand a month. Skannet noted him doing so and said cheerfully, "So, I could have gotten more." Then he signed the three copies. "When do I have to leave L.A.?"

"This very night," Pollard said. "I'll take you to your plane."

"No thanks," Skannet said. "I think I'll drive to Las Vegas and gamble with this check."

"I'll be watching," Pollard said. Now was the time he felt he should show some muscle. "Let me warn you, if you show up in Los Angeles again, I'll have you arrested for extortion."

Skannet's red face brimmed with glee. "I'd love that," he said. "I'll be as famous as Athena."

That night the surveillance team reported that Boz Skannet had left but only to move into the Beverly Hills Hotel, and that he had deposited the fifty-thousand-dollar check in an account he had at the Bank of America. This indicated a number of things to Pollard. That Skannet had influence, because he had gotten into the Beverly Hills Hotel, and that he didn't give a shit about the deal he had made. Pollard reported this to Bobby Bantz and asked for instructions. Bantz told him to keep his mouth shut. The contract had been shown to Athena to reassure her and persuade her to go back to work. He did not tell Pollard she had laughed in their faces.

"You can stop the check," Pollard said.

"No," Bantz said, "he cashes it and we got him in court on fraud, extortion, whatever. I just don't want Athena to know he's still in town."

"I'll double the security on her," Pollard said. "But if he's crazy, if he really wants to harm her, that won't help."

"He's a bluffer," Bantz said. "He didn't do it the first time, why would he do anything now?"

"I'll tell you why," Pollard said. "We burglarized his room. Guess what we found? A container of real acid."

"Oh shit," Bantz said. "Can you tell the cops? Jim Losey maybe."

Pollard said, "Having acid is not a crime. Burglary is. Skannet can put me in jail."

"You never told me anything," Bantz said. "We never had this conversation. And forget what you know."

"Sure Mr. Bantz," Pollard said. "I won't even bill you for the information."

"Thanks a lot," Bantz said sarcastically. "Keep in touch."

. . .

Claudia was briefed by Skippy Deere. And instructed as was proper to their roles as producer and writer on a picture.

"You have to absolutely kiss Athena's ass," Deere said. "You have to grovel, you have to cry, you have to have a nervous breakdown. You have to remind her of everything you've ever done for her as an intimate and true friend and as a fellow professional. You must get Athena back on the picture."

Claudia was used to Skippy. "Why me?" she said coolly. "You're the producer, Dita is the director, Bantz is president of LoddStone. You guys go kiss her ass. You've had more practice than me."

"Because it was your project all the way," Deere said. "You wrote the original screenplay on spec, you got me and you got Athena. If the project fails, your name will always be associated with that failure."

When Deere left and she was alone in her office, Claudia knew Deere was right. In her desperation she thought of her brother, Cross. He was the only one who could help her, help make the problem of Boz disappear. She hated the thought of trading on her friendship with Athena, and knew Athena might refuse her but Cross never would. He never had.

She put in a call to the Xanadu Hotel in Vegas, but she was told that Cross would be in Quogue and would not be back until the next day. This brought back all the childhood memories she always tried to forget. She would never call her brother in Quogue. She never would voluntarily have anything to do with the Clericuzio again. She never wanted to remember her childhood again, never to think of her father or any of the Clericuzio.

BOOK II

The Clericuzio and Pippi De Lena

CHAPTER 3

THE CLERICUZIO FAMILY legend of ferocity had been established more than a hundred years ago in Sicily. There the Clericuzio had waged a twenty-year war with a rival family over the ownership of a piece of forest. The patriarch of the opposing clan, Don Pietro Forlenza, was on his deathbed, having survived eighty-five years of strife only to suffer a stroke, which his doctor predicted would end his life within a week. A member of the Clericuzio penetrated the sick man's bedchamber and stabbed him to death, shouting that the old man did not deserve a peaceful death.

Don Domenico Clericuzio often told this old story of murder to show how foolish were the old-fashioned ways, to point out that ferocity without selection was mere braggadocio. Ferocity was too precious a weapon to waste, it must always have an important purpose.

And indeed he had the proof, for it was ferocity that led the Clericuzio Family in Sicily to destruction. When Mussolini and his Fascists came to absolute power in Italy, they understood that the Mafia had to be destroyed. They did it by suspending due process of law and by using irresistible armed force. The Mafia was broken at the cost of thousands of innocent people going to jail or exile with them.

Only the Clericuzio clan had the courage to oppose Fascist decrees with force. They murdered the local Fascist prefect, they attacked Fascist garrisons. Most infuriating of all, when Mussolini gave a speech in Palermo they stole his prized bowler hat and umbrella imported from England. It was this peasant humor and contempt, which made a laughingstock of Mussolini in Sicily, that finally led to their ruin. There was a massive concentration of armed forces in their province. Five hundred members of the Clericuzio clan were killed outright. Another five hundred were exiled to the arid islands in the Mediterranean that served as penal colonies. Only the very heart of the Clericuzio survived, and the family shipped young Domenico Clericuzio to America. Where, proving that blood will tell, Don Domenico built his own empire, with far more cunning and foresight than his ancestors had shown in Sicily. But he always remembered that a lawless state was the great enemy. And so he loved America.

Early on he had been told the famous maxim of American justice, that it was better that a hundred guilty men go free than that one innocent man be punished. Struck almost dumb by the beauty of the concept, he became an ardent patriot. America was his country. He would never leave America.

Inspired by this, Don Domenico built the Clericuzio empire in America more solidly than the clan had in Sicily. He ensured his friendship to all political and judicial institutions with great gifts of cash. He did not rely on one or two streams of income but diversified in the finest tradition of American business enterprise. There was the construction industry, the garbage disposal industry, the different modes of transportation. But the great river of cash came from gambling, which was his love, in contrast to the income from drugs which, though most profitable, he distrusted. So in later years it was only in gambling that he allowed the Clericuzio Family to be involved operationally. The rest wetted the Clericuzio beak with a tithe of 5 percent.

After twenty-five years the Don's plan and the dream was coming true. Gambling was now respectable and, more important, increasingly legal. There were the ever-burgeoning state lotteries, those swindles perpetrated by the government on its citizens. The prizes stretched over twenty years, which, in effect, amounted to the state never paying the money at all, just the interest on the money withheld. And then that was taxed in the bargain. What a joke. Don Domenico knew the details, because his Family owned one of the management companies that ran the lottery for several states at a very good fee.

But the Don was banking on the day when gambling on sports would become legal in all the United States as it was now legal only in Nevada. He knew this from the tithe he collected on illegal gambling. Profits on the Super Bowl football game alone, if gambling became legal, would come to a billion dollars, in just one day. The World Series with its seven games would yield equal profit. College football, hockey, basketball, all rich streams. Then there would be intricate, tantalizing lotteries on sports events, legal gold mines. The Don knew he would not live to see that glorious day, but what a world it would be for his children. The Clericuzio would be the equal of the Renaissance princes. They would become the patrons of art, advisors and leaders of government, respectable in history books. A trailing cloak of gold would brush out its origins. All his descendants, his followers, his true friends, would be secure forever. Certainly the Don had the vision of a civilized society, the world, as this great tree shedding the fruit that must feed and shelter humanity. But in the roots of this great tree would be the immortal python of the Clericuzio, sucking nourishment from a source that could never fail.

If the Clericuzio Family was the Holy Church for the many Mafia empires scattered over the United States, then the head of the Family, Don Domenico Clericuzio, was the Pope, admired not only for his intelligence but for his strength.

Don Clericuzio was also revered for the strict moral code he enforced in his Family. Every man, woman, and child was completely responsible for his actions, no matter the stress, the remorse, or the hard circumstances. Actions defined a man; words were a fart in the wind. He disdained all social sciences, all psychology. He was a devout Catholic: payment for sins in this world, forgiveness in the next. Every debt had to be paid, and he was strict in his judgment in this world.

As in his loyalty. The creatures of his blood first; his God second (did he not have his own chapel in the house?); and third, his obligation to all the subjects in the domain of the Clericuzio Family.

As for the society, the government—patriot though he was—never entered the equation. Don Clericuzio had been born in Sicily, where society and the government were the enemy. His concept of free will was very clear. You could will yourself as a slave to earn your daily bread without dignity or hope, or you earned your bread as a man who commanded respect. Your Family was your society, your God was your punisher, and your followers protected you. To those on earth you owed a duty: that they would have bread to put in their mouths, respect from the world, and a shield from the punishment of other men.

The Don had not built his empire so that his children and his grandchildren would someday recede into a mass of helpless humanity. He built and kept building power so that the Family name and fortune would survive as long as the Church itself. What greater purpose could a man have in this world than to earn his daily bread, then in the next world to present himself to a forgiving deity? As for his fellow man and their faulty structures of society, they could all swim to the bottom of the ocean.

Don Domenico led his Family to the very heights of power. He did so with a Borgia-like cruelty and a Machiavellian subtleness, plus solid American business know-how. But above all with a patriarchal love for his followers. Virtue was rewarded. Injuries avenged. A livelihood guaranteed.

Finally, as the Don had planned, the Clericuzio reached such a height that it no longer took part in the usual operations of criminal activity except in the most dire circumstance. The other Mafia Families served chiefly as executive Barons, or *Brugliones,* who when in trouble went to the Clericuzio hat in hand. In Italian the words *"Bruglione"* and "baron" rhyme, however in the Italian dialect *"Bruglione"* means someone who fumbles the smallest tasks. It was Don Domenico's wit, sparked by the Barons' constant pleas for help, that changed the word "baron" to *Bruglione.* The Clericuzio made peace between them, sprang them from jail, hid their illegal gains in Europe, arranged foolproof ways for them to smuggle their drugs into America, used its influence with judges and different government regulators, both federal and state. Help with municipalities was usually not required. If a local *Bruglione* could not influence the city he lived in, he was not worth his salt.

The economic genius of Don Clericuzio's oldest son, Giorgio, cemented the Family power. Like some divine laundress he washed the great spouts of black money that a modern civilization spews from its guts. It was Giorgio who always tried to moderate his father's ferocity. Above all, Giorgio strove to keep the Clericuzio Family out of the glare of public notice. So the Family existed, even to the authorities, like some sort of UFO. There were random sightings, rumors, tales of horror and benignity. There were mentions in FBI and police department files, but there were no newspaper stories, not even in those publications that gloried in depicting the exploits of various other Mafia Families who, through carelessness and ego, came to misfortune.

Not that the Clericuzio Family was a toothless tiger. Giorgio's two younger brothers, Vincent and Petie, though not as clever as Giorgio, had almost the Don's ferocity. And they had a pool of enforcers who lived in an enclave of the Bronx that had always been Italian. This enclave of forty square blocks could have been used in a film of Old Italy. There were no bearded Hasidic Jews, blacks, Asians, or bohemian elements in the population, nor did any of these own a business establishment there. There was not one Chinese restaurant. The Clericuzio owned or controlled all real estate in the area. Of course some of the Italian families' progeny sprouted long hair and were guitar-playing rebels, but these teenagers were shipped to relatives in California. Every year, new, carefully screened immigrants from Sicily arrived to repopulate. The Bronx Enclave, surrounded by areas with the highest crime rate in the world, was singularly free of evildoing.

Pippi De Lena had risen from Mayor of the Bronx Enclave to *Bruglione* of the Las Vegas area for the Clericuzio Family. But he remained directly under the rule of the Clericuzio, who still needed his special talent.

Pippi was the very essence of what was called *Qualificato,* that is, a Qualified Man. He had started early, making his "bones" at the age of seventeen, and what had made the deed even more impressive was he had done so with the garrote. For in America, young men in their callow pride disdained the rope. Also, he was very strong physically, of good height and with intimidating bulk. He was, of course, expert with firearms and explosives. All this aside, he was a charming man because of his zest for life; he had a geniality that put men at ease, and women appreciated his gallantry, which was half rustic Sicilian and half movie American. Though he took his work very seriously, he believed that life was to be enjoyed.

He did have his little weaknesses. He drank heartily, he gambled always, he was excessively fond of women. He was not as merciless as could be wished by the Don, perhaps because Pippi enjoyed too much the social company of other people. But all these weaknesses somehow made him more potent as a weapon. He was a man who used his vices to drain poison out of his body rather than to saturate it.

It helped his career, of course, that he was the nephew of the Don. He was of the blood, and that was important when Pippi broke the family tradition.

No man can live his life without making mistakes. Pippi De Lena, at the age of twenty-eight, married for love, and to compound that error he chose as a wife a completely inappropriate woman for a Qualified Man.

Her name was Nalene Jessup, and she danced in the show at the Las Vegas Xanadu Hotel. Pippi always proudly pointed out that she was not a showgirl who presented herself in the front line with her tits and ass showing, she was a *dancer.* Nalene was also an intellectual, by Vegas standards. She was bookish, took an interest in politics, and since her roots were in the particularly WASP culture of Sacramento, California, had old-fashioned values.

They were complete opposites. Pippi had no intellectual interests, he rarely read, listened to music, or attended movies or theater. Pippi had the face of a bull, Nalene the face of a flower. Pippi was extroverted, full of charm, yet he exuded danger. Nalene was so gentle in nature that not one of her fellow showgirls and dancers had ever been able to pick a fight with her, as they often did with each other to pass the time.

The only thing Pippi and Nalene had in common was dancing. For Pippi De Lena, the feared Clericuzio Hammer, was a veritable idiot savant when he stepped onto the ballroom floor. This was the poetry he could not read, the medieval gallantry of Holy Knights, the tenderness, the exquisite refinement of sex, the only time he reached out to something he could not understand.

For Nalene Jessup, it was a glimpse into his innermost soul. When they danced together for hours before making love, it made their sex ethereal, a true communication between kindred souls. He talked to her when they danced, alone in her apartment, or on the dance floors of the Vegas hotels.

He was a good storyteller with good stories to tell. He expressed his adoration of her in a flattering and witty way. He had an overwhelming masculine presence, which he laid at her feet as a slave, and he listened. He was proud and interested when she talked of books, the theater, the duties of democracy to lift up the downtrodden, the rights of blacks, the liberation of South Africa, the duty to feed the unfortunate poor of the Third World. Pippi was thrilled by these sentiments. They were exotic to him.

It helped that they suited each other sexually, that their opposites attracted each other. It was helpful to their love that Pippi saw the true Nalene but that Nalene did not see the real Pippi. What she saw was a man who adored her, who showered gifts upon her, who listened to her dreams.

They married a week after they met. Nalene was only eighteen, she knew no better. Pippi was twenty-eight and truly in love. He, too, was brought up with old-fashioned values, certainly from different poles, and they both wanted a family. Nalene was already an orphan, and Pippi was reluctant to include the Clericuzio in his newfound rapture. Also, he knew they would not approve. Better to face them with the deed and work things out gradually. They were wed in a Vegas chapel.

But here was another lapse in judgment. Don Clericuzio approved that Pippi married. As he often said, "A man's primary duty in life is to earn his own living," but to what purpose if he did not have a wife and children? The Don took umbrage that he had not been consulted, that the wedding had not been celebrated as part of the Clericuzio Family. After all, Pippi had Clericuzio blood.

The Don peevishly commented, "They can dance to the bottom of the ocean together," but nevertheless he sent lavish wedding presents. A huge Buick, the ownership of a collection agency that yielded the princely income for that time of one hundred thousand dollars a year; a promotion. Pippi De Lena would continue to serve the Clericuzio Family as one of its closely affiliated *Brugliones* in the West, but he was banished from the Bronx Enclave, for how could this alien wife live in harmony with the faithful. She was as foreign to them as the Muslims, the blacks, the Hasidim, and the Asians who were banned. So in essence, though Pippi remained the Clericuzio Hammer, though he was a local Baron, he lost some influence in the palace in Quogue.

The best man at the little civil ceremony of marriage was Alfred Gronevelt, owner of the Xanadu Hotel. He gave a small dinner party afterward, where bride and groom danced the night away. In the years following, Gronevelt and Pippi De Lena developed a close and loyal friendship.

The marriage lasted long enough to produce two children: a son and a daughter. The eldest, christened Croccifixio but always called Cross, at age ten was the physical image of his mother, with a graceful body and an almost effeminately handsome face. Yet he had the physical strength and superb coordination of his father. The younger, Claudia, at the age of nine, was the image of her father, blunt features only saved from ugliness by the freshness and innocence of childhood, yet without her father's gifts. But she had her mother's love of books, music, and theater, and her mother's gentleness of spirit. It was only natural that Cross and Pippi were close to each other, and that Claudia was closer to her mother, Nalene.

In the eleven years before the De Lena family broke apart, things went very well. Pippi established himself in Vegas as the *Bruglione,* the Collector for the Xanadu Hotel, and he still served as Hammer to the Clericuzio. He became rich, he lived a good life, though by the

Don's edict not an ostentatious one. He drank, he gambled, he danced with his wife, he played with his children and tried to prepare them for their entry into adulthood.

Pippi had learned in his own dangerous life to look far ahead. It was one of the reasons for his success. Early on he saw past Cross as a child to Cross as a man. He wanted that future man to be his ally. Or perhaps he wanted at least one human being close he could fully trust.

And so he trained Cross, taught him all the tricks of gambling, took him to dinner with Gronevelt so that he could hear stories of all the different ways a casino could be scammed. Gronevelt always opened up by saying, "Every night, millions of men lie awake figuring out how to cheat my casino."

Pippi took Cross hunting, taught him how to skin and gut animals, made him know the smell of blood, see his hands red with it. He made Cross take boxing lessons so that he could feel pain, taught him the use and care of guns but drew the line at teaching him the garrote; that was after all an indulgence of his own and not really useful in these modern days. Plus there could be no way of explaining such a rope to the boy's mother.

The Clericuzio Family owned a huge hunting lodge in the mountains of Nevada, and Pippi used it for his family's vacations. He took the children hunting while Nalene studied her books in the warmth of the lodge. On the hunt Cross easily shot wolves and deer and even some mountain lions and bears, which revealed that Cross was capable, that he had a good aptitude for guns, was always careful with them, always calm in danger, never flinched when he reached into the bloody guts, the slimy intestines. Dissecting limbs and heads, dressing the kill, he was never squeamish.

Claudia displayed no such virtues. She flinched at the sound of a gun and threw up while skinning a deer. After a few trips she refused to leave the lodge and spent time with her mother reading or walking along a nearby brook. Claudia refused even to fish, she could not bear to put the hard steel hook into the soft center of a worm.

Pippi concentrated on his son. He briefed the boy on basic behavior. Never show anger at a slight, tell nothing of yourself. Earn respect from everyone by deeds, not words. Respect the members of your blood family. Gambling was recreation, not a way to earn a living. Love your father, your mother, your sister, but beware of loving any other woman than your wife. And a wife was a woman who bore your children. And once that happened to you, your life was forfeit to give them their daily bread.

Cross was such a good pupil that his father doted on him. And he loved that Cross looked so much like Nalene, that he had her grace, that he was a replica of her without the intellectual gifts that were now destroying the marriage.

Pippi had never believed in the Don's dream that all of the younger children would disappear into legitimate society; he did not even believe it to be the best course of action. He acknowledged the old man's genius, but this was the romantic side of the great Don. After all, fathers wanted their sons to work with them, to be like them; blood was blood, that never changed.

And in this Pippi proved himself to be right. Despite all of Don Clericuzio's planning, even his own grandson, Dante, proved to be resistant to the grand design. Dante had grown to be a throwback to the Sicilian blood, thirsting for power, strongwilled. He never feared breaking the laws of society and of God.

When Cross was seven and Claudia six, Cross, aggressive by nature, fell into the habit of punching Claudia in the stomach, even in front of their father. Claudia cried for help. Pippi, as the parent, could resolve the problem in different ways. He could order Cross to stop, and if Cross did not, he could pick him up by the scruff of the neck and dangle him in midair, which he often did. Or he could order Claudia to fight back. Or he could cuff Cross against the wall, which he had done once or twice. But one time, perhaps because he had just had dinner and was feeling lazy, or more likely because Nalene always argued when he used force on the children, he lit up his cigar calmly and said to Cross, "Every time you hit your sister, I give her a dollar." As Cross continued punching his sister, Pippi rained dollar bills on the gleeful Claudia. Cross finally stopped in frustration.

Pippi swamped his wife with gifts, but they were gifts a master gives to his slave. They were bribes to disguise her servitude. Expensive gifts: diamond rings, fur coats, trips to Europe. He bought her a vacation house in Sacramento because she hated Vegas. When he gave her a Bentley, he wore a chauffeur's uniform to deliver it to her. Just before the end of their marriage, he gave her an antique ring certified as part of the Borgia collection. The only thing he restricted was her use of credit cards, she had to pay them out of her household allowance. Pippi never used them.

He was liberal in other ways. Nalene had complete physical freedom, Pippi was not a jealous Italian husband. Though he would not travel abroad except on business, he allowed Nalene to go to Europe with her women friends, because she so desperately wanted to see the museums in London, the ballet in Paris, the opera in Italy.

There were times that Nalene wondered about his lack of jealousy, but over the years she came to realize that no man in their circle would dare pay court to her.

On this marriage Don Clericuzio had commented sarcastically, "Do they think they can dance all their lives?"

The answer proved to be no. Nalene was not a good enough dancer to rise to the top, her legs paradoxically too long. She was of too serious a temperament to be a party girl. All this had made her settle for marriage. And she was happy for the first four years. She took care of the children, she attended classes at the University of Nevada and read voraciously.

But Pippi no longer was interested in the state of the environment, had no concern about the problems of whining blacks who couldn't even learn to steal without getting caught, and as far as the Native Americans, whoever they were, they could drown them at the bottom of the ocean. Discussions of books or music were completely beyond his horizon. And Nalene's demand that he never strike their children left him bewildered. Young children were animals; how could you make them behave in a civilized way without flinging them against a wall? He was always careful never to hurt them.

So in the fourth year of their marriage, Pippi took on mistresses. One in Las Vegas, one in Los Angeles, and one in New York. Nalene retaliated by getting her teaching degree.

They tried hard. They loved their children and made their lives pleasant. Nalene spent long hours with them reading and singing and dancing. The marriage was held together by Pippi's good humor. His vitality and animal exuberance somehow smoothed over the troubles of man and wife. The two children loved their mother and looked up to their father: the mother because she was so sweet and gentle, beautiful and full of natural affection; the father because he was strong.

Both parents were excellent teachers. From their mother, the children learned the social graces, good manners, dancing, how to dress, grooming. Their father taught the ways of the world, how to protect themselves from physical harm, how to gamble and train their bodies in athletics. They never resented their father for being physically rough with them, mainly because he did so only as discipline, never got angry when he did so, and then never held a grudge.

Cross was fearless but could bend. Claudia did not have her brother's physical courage but had a certain stubbornness. It helped that there was never any lack of money.

As the years went on, Nalene observed certain things. At first very small. When Pippi taught the children how to play cards—poker, blackjack, gin—he would stack the deck and clean them out of their allowance money, then at the end he would give them a glorious streak of luck so that they could fall asleep flushed with victory. What was curious was that Claudia as a child loved gambling far more than Cross. Later Pippi would demonstrate how he had cheated them. Nalene was angry, she felt he was playing with their lives as he played with hers. Pippi explained it was part of their education. She said it was not education but corruption. He said he wanted to prepare them for the reality of life, she wanted to prepare them for the beauty of life.

Pippi always had too much cash in his wallet, as suspicious a circumstance in the eyes of a wife as in the eyes of the tax collector. It was true that Pippi owned a thriving business, the Collection Agency, but they lived on too rich a scale for such a small operation.

When the family took vacations in the East and moved in the social circles of the Clericuzio Family, Nalene could not miss the respect with which Pippi was treated. She observed how careful men were with him, the deference, the long meetings the men held in private.

There were other little things. Pippi had to travel on business at least once a month. She never knew any of the details of his travel, and he never talked about his trips. He was legally licensed to carry a firearm, which was logical for a man whose business it was to collect large sums of money. He was very careful. Nalene and the children never had access to the weapon, he kept the bullets locked in separate cases.

As the years went by, Pippi took more trips, Nalene spent more time in her home with the children. Pippi and Nalene grew more apart sexually, and since Pippi was more tender and understanding in lust, they grew further and further apart.

It is impossible for a man to hide his true nature over a period of years from someone close to him. Nalene saw that Pippi was a man completely devoted to his own appetites, that he was violent in nature though never violent to her. That he was secretive, though he pretended openness. That though he was amiable, he was dangerous.

He had small personal follies that sometimes were endearing. For instance, other people had to enjoy what he enjoyed. Once they had taken a couple to dinner to an Italian restaurant. The couple did not particularly care for Italian food and ate sparingly. When Pippi observed this he could not finish his meal.

Sometimes he talked about his work at the Collection Agency. Nearly all the major hotels in Vegas were his clients, he collected delinquent gambling markers from customers who refused to pay up. He insisted to Nalene that force was never used, only a special kind of persuasion. It was a matter of honor that people pay their debts, everybody was responsible for their actions, and it offended him that men of substance did not always meet their obligations. Doctors, lawyers, heads of corporations, accepted the complimentary services of the hotel and then reneged on their side of the bargain. But they were easy to collect from. You went to their offices and made a loud fuss so that their clients and colleagues could hear. You made a scene, never a threat, called them deadbeats, degenerate gamblers who neglected their professions to wallow in vice.

Small business men were tougher, nickel-and-dime guys who tried to settle for a penny on a dollar. Then there were the clever ones who wrote checks that bounced and then claimed there had been a mistake. A favorite trick. They gave you a check for ten thousand when they only had eight thousand in their account. But Pippi had access to bank information, so he would merely deposit the extra two thousand to the man's account and then draw out the whole ten thousand. Pippi would laugh delightedly when he explained such coups to Nalene.

But the most important part of his job, Pippi explained to Nalene, was convincing a gambler not only to pay his debt but to keep gambling. Even a busted gambler had value. He worked. He earned money. So you simply had to postpone his debt, urge him to gamble in your casino without credit, and pay off his debt whenever he won.

One night Pippi told Nalene a story he thought enormously funny. That day he had been working in his Collection Agency office, which was in a small shopping mall near the Xanadu Hotel, when he heard gunfire in the street outside. He ran out just in time to see two masked armed men escaping from a neighboring jewelry shop. Without thinking Pippi drew his gun and fired at the men. They jumped into a waiting car and escaped. A few minutes later the police arrived, and after interrogating everyone, they arrested Pippi. Certainly they knew his gun was licensed, but by firing it he had committed a crime of "reckless endangerment." Alfred Gronevelt had gone down to the police station to bail him out.

"Why the hell did I do that?" Pippi asked. "Alfred said it was just the hunter in me. But I'll never understand. Me, shooting at robbers? Me, protecting society? And then they lock me up. They lock *me* up."

But these little revelations into his character were to some extent a clever ruse on Pippi's part, so that Nalene could glimpse part of his character without penetrating to the true secret. What made her finally decide on divorce was Pippi De Lena's arrest for murder. . . .

Danny Fuberta owned a New York travel agency that he had bought with his earnings as a loan shark under the protection of the now extinct Santadio Family. But he earned most of his livelihood as a Vegas junket master.

A junket master signed an exclusive contract with a Vegas hotel to transport vacationing gamblers into their clutches. Danny Fuberta chartered a 747 jet every month and recruited approximately two hundred customers to fly on it to the Xanadu Hotel. For a flat rate of a thousand dollars, the customer got a free round-trip flight from New York to Vegas, free booze and food in the air, free hotel rooms, free food and drink in the hotel. Fuberta always had a long waiting list for these junkets, and he picked his customers carefully. They had to be people with well-paying jobs, though not necessarily legal ones, and they had to gamble in the casino at least four hours every day. And, of course, where possible they had to establish credit at the Cashier's cage in the Hotel Xanadu.

One of Fuberta's greatest assets was his friendship with scam artists, bank robbers, drug dealers, cigarette smugglers, garment center hustlers, and other lowlifes who made handsome livings in the cesspools of New York. These men were prime customers. After all, they lived lives of great stress, they needed a relaxing vacation. They earned huge sums of black money, in cash, and they loved to gamble.

For every junket plane filled with two hundred customers that Danny Fuberta delivered to the Xanadu, he received a flat fee of twenty thousand dollars. Sometimes he received a bonus when the Xanadu customers lost heavily. All this in addition to the initial package charge provided him with a handsome monthly income. Unfortunately, Fuberta also had a weakness for gambling. And there came a time when his bills outpaced his income.

A resourceful man, Fuberta soon thought of a way to make himself solvent again. One of his duties as junket master was to certify the casino credit to be advanced to the junket customer.

Fuberta recruited a band of extremely competent armed robbers. With them Fuberta hatched a plan to steal $800,000 from the Xanadu Hotel.

Fuberta supplied the four men with false credentials identifying them as garment center owners with huge credit ratings, the particulars culled from his agency files. On the basis of these credentials, he certified them for the two-hundred-grand credit limit. Then he put them on the junket.

"Oh, they all had a picnic," Gronevelt said later.

During the two-day stay, Fuberta and his gang ran up huge room service bills, treated the beautiful chorus girls to dinner, signed for presents at the gift shop, but that was the least of it. They drew black chips from the casino, signed their markers.

They split into two teams. One team bet against the dice, the other team bet with the dice. In that way all they could lose was the percentage or break out even. So they drew a million dollars' worth of chips from the casino signing markers, which Fuberta later turned into cash. They looked like they were gambling furiously but were really treading water. In all this they created a great flurry of action. They fancied themselves actors, they implored the dice, they scowled when they lost, cheered when they won. At the end of the day they gave their chips to Fuberta to cash and signed markers to draw fresh chips from the cage. When the comedy ended two days later, the syndicate was $800,000 richer, they had been happy consumers of another twenty thousand in goodies, but they had a million dollars in markers in the cage.

Danny Fuberta, as the mastermind, got four hundred grand, and the four armed robbers were well satisfied with their share, especially when Fuberta promised them another shot. What could be better, a long weekend in the grand hotel, free food and booze, beautiful girls. And a hundred grand to boot. It was certainly better than robbing a bank where you risked your life.

Gronevelt uncovered the scam the very next day. The daily reports showed the markers high even for Fuberta's junket. The Drop at the table, the record of money kept after the night's play, was a figure too low for the amount of money wagered. Gronevelt called for the videotape from the "Eye in the Sky" surveillance camera. He didn't have to watch more than ten minutes before he understood the whole operation and know that the million dollars of markers was so much cigarette paper, the identities false.

His reaction was one of impatience. He had suffered countless scams over the years, but this one was so stupid. And he liked Danny Fuberta; the man had earned many dollars for the Xanadu. He knew what Fuberta would claim: that he, too, had been deceived by the false IDs, that he, too, was an innocent victim.

Gronevelt was annoyed by the incompetence of his Casino personnel. The Stick at the crap table should have caught on, and certainly the Box man should have picked up the cross-betting. It was not that clever a trick. But people went soft with good times, and Vegas was no exception. He thought regretfully that he would have to fire the Stick and the Box man, at least send them back to spinning a roulette wheel. But one thing he could not duck. He would have to turn the whole matter of Danny Fuberta over to the Clericuzio.

First he summoned Pippi De Lena to the hotel and showed him the documents and the film of the Eye in the Sky. Pippi knew Fuberta but not the other four men, so Gronevelt had snapshots made from isolated video stills and gave them to Pippi.

Pippi shook his head. "How the hell did Danny think he could get away with this? I thought he was a smart hustler."

"He's a gambler," Gronevelt said. "They believe their cards are always winning cards." He paused for a moment. "Danny will convince you he's not in on this. But remember, he had to certify that they were good for the money. He'll say he did it on the basis of their ID. A junket master has to certify that they are who they are. He had to know."

Pippi smiled and patted him on the back. "Don't worry, he won't convince me." They both laughed. It didn't matter if Danny Fuberta was guilty. He was responsible for his mistakes.

Pippi flew to New York the next day. To present the case to the Clericuzio Family in Quogue.

After passing through the guarded gates, he drove up the long paved road that cut through a long plateau of grass, its wall armed with barbed wire and electronics. There was a guard at the door of the mansion. And this was in a time of peace.

Giorgio greeted him, and he was led through the mansion into the garden at the rear. In the garden were tomato and cucumber plants, lettuce, and even melons, all framed by large-leafed fig trees. The Don had no use for flowers.

The Family was seated at the round wooden table eating an early lunch. There was the Don, glowing with health despite his near seventy years, visibly drinking in the fig-perfumed air of his garden. He was feeding his ten-year-old grandson, Dante, who was handsome but imperious for a boy the same age as Cross. Pippi always had the urge to give him a smack. The Don was putty in the hands of his grandson; he wiped his mouth, crooned endearments. Vincent and Petie looked sour. The meeting could not start until the kid finished eating and was led away by his mother, Rose Marie. Don Domenico beamed at him as the boy walked away. Then he turned to Pippi.

"Ah, my *Martèllo,*" he said. "What do you think of Fuberta, that rascal? We gave him a living and he grows greedy at our expense."

Giorgio said placatingly, "If he repays, he could still be a moneymaker for us." The only valid plea for mercy.

"It's not a small sum of money," the Don said. "We must have it back. Pippi, what do you think?"

Pippi shrugged. "I can try. But these are people who don't save for a rainy day."

Vincent, who hated small talk, said, "Let's see the photos." Pippi produced the pictures and Vincent and Petie studied the four armed robbers. Then Vincent said, "Me and Petie know them."

"Good," Pippi said. "Then you can straighten out those four guys. What do you want me to do with Fuberta?"

The Don said, "They have shown contempt for us. Who do they think we are? Some helpless fools who have to go to the police? Vincent, Petie, you help Pippi. I want the money back and these *mascalzoni* punished." They understood. Pippi was to be in charge. The sentence on the five men was death.

The Don left them for his walk in the garden.

Giorgio sighed. "The old man is too tough for the times we live in. This is more risk than the whole thing is worth."

"Not if Vinnie and Pete handle the four hoods," Pippi said. "That OK with you, Vince?"

Vincent said, "Giorgio, you'll have to talk to the old man. Those four won't have the money. We have to make a deal. They go out and earn and pay us back and they're home free. If we bury them, no money."

Vincent was a realistic enforcer who never let the lust for blood overcome more practical solutions.

"OK, I can sell Pop that," Giorgio said. "They were just helpers. But he won't let Fuberta off."

"The junket masters have to get the message," Pippi said.

"Cousin Pippi," Giorgio said smiling, "what bonus do you expect on this?"

Pippi hated when Giorgio called him cousin. Vincent and Petie called him cousin out of affection, but Giorgio only did so when in negotiation.

"For Fuberta it's my duty," Pippi said. "You gave me the Collection Agency and I get wages from the Xanadu. But getting the money back is hard so I should get a percentage. Just as Vince and Petie if they get some from the hoods."

"That's fair," Giorgio said. "But this is not like collecting markers. You can't expect fifty percent."

"No, no," Pippi said, "just let me wet my beak."

They all laughed at the old Sicilian idiom. Petie said, "Giorgio, don't be cheap. You don't want to chisel me and Vincent." Petie now ran the Bronx Enclave, chief of the Enforcers, and he was always promoting the idea that the button men should get more money. He would split his share with his men.

"You guys are greedy," Giorgio said with a smile. "But I'll recommend twenty percent to the old man." Pippi knew that meant it would be fifteen or ten. It was an old story with Giorgio.

"How about we pool it?" Vince said to Pippi. Meaning the three of them would share whatever money was recovered no matter from whom. It was meant as a friendly gesture. There was a far better chance of recovering money from people who were to live than people who were to die. Vincent understood Pippi's value.

"Sure, Vince," Pippi said. "I'd appreciate that."

He saw Dante walking hand and hand with the Don far off at the edge of the garden. He heard Giorgio say, "Isn't it amazing how Dante and my father get along? My father was never that friendly to me. They whisper to each other all the time. Well, the old man is so smart, the kid will learn."

Pippi saw that the boy had his face turned up to the Don. The two looked as if they shared a terrible secret that would give them dominion over Heaven and Earth. Later Pippi would believe that this vision put on him the evil eye, and triggered his misfortune.

Pippi De Lena had gained his reputation over the years by his careful planning. He was not just some rampaging gorilla but a skilled technician. As such he relied on psychological strategy to help in the physical execution of a job. With Danny Fuberta there were three problems. First of all he had to get the money back. Second, he had to coordinate carefully with Vincent and Petie Clericuzio. (That part was easy. Vincent and Petie were extremely efficient in their work. In two days they tracked down the hoods, forced a confession, and arranged for compensation.) Then third, he had to kill Danny Fuberta.

It was easy for Pippi to run into Fuberta accidentally, to turn on his charm and insist the man be his guest for lunch at a Chinese restaurant on the East Side. Fuberta knew Pippi was a collector for the Xanadu, they had necessarily done business over the years, but Pippi seemed so delighted to run into him in New York that Fuberta could not refuse.

Pippi played it in a very low key. He waited until they had ordered and then he said, "Gronevelt told me about the scam. You know you have a responsibility for those guys being certified for credit."

Fuberta swore his innocence, and Pippi gave him a big grin and slapped him on the shoulder in a comradely way. "Come on Danny," he said, "Gronevelt has the tapes, and your four buddies already fessed up. You're in big trouble but I can square things if you give back the money. Maybe I can even keep you in the junket business."

To back up his statement, he took out the four photos of the hoods. "These are your boys," he said, "and right now they are spilling out their guts. Laying all the shit on you. They told us about the split. So if you come up with your four hundred grand, you're clear."

Fuberta said, "Sure, I know these boys, but they're tough guys, they wouldn't talk."

"It's the Clericuzio who are asking," Pippi said.

"Oh shit," Danny said. "I didn't know they had the Hotel."

"Now you know," Pippi said. "If they don't get the money back, you're in big trouble."

"I should just walk out of here," Fuberta said.

"No, no," Pippi said. "Stick around, the Peking duck is great. Look, this can be straightened out, it's no big deal. Everybody tries to scam once in awhile, right? Just get the money back."

"I don't have a dime," Fuberta said.

For the first time Pippi showed some irritation. "You have to show a little respect," Pippi said. "Give a hundred thousand back and we'll take your marker for the other three hundred."

Fuberta thought it over as he munched a fried dumpling. "I can give you fifty," he said.

"That's good, that's very good," Pippi said. "You can pay off the rest by not taking your fee for running junkets to the Hotel. Is that fair?"

"I guess," Fuberta said.

"Don't worry any more, enjoy the food," Pippi said. He rolled some duck into a pancake, anointed it with black sweet sauce, and handed it to Fuberta. "This is terrific, Danny," he said. "Eat. Then we do business."

They ate chocolate ice cream for dessert and made arrangements for Pippi to pick up the fifty grand at Fuberta's travel agency after working hours. Pippi grabbed the lunch check, paying cash. "Danny," he said, "you notice how chocolate ice cream in a Chinese restaurant has so much cocoa? The best. You know what I think? The first Chinese restaurant in America got the recipe wrong and the ones that came after just copied that first wrong recipe. Great. Great chocolate ice cream."

But Danny Fuberta had not hustled for the forty-eight years of his life without being able to read the signs. After leaving Pippi he dived underground, sending a message that he was traveling to collect the money he owed the Xanadu Hotel. Pippi was not surprised. Fuberta was only using tactics common in such cases. He had disappeared so that he could negotiate in safety. Which meant he had no money and there would be no bonus unless Vincent and Petie collected on their end.

Pippi drew some men from the Bronx Enclave to scour the city. The word was put out that Danny Fuberta was wanted by the Clericuzio. A week went by, and Pippi became more and more irritated. He should have known that Fuberta would only be alerted by the demand for repayment. That Fuberta had figured out that fifty grand would not be enough, if he even had fifty grand.

After another week, Pippi became impatient, so that when the break came he moved more daringly than was prudent.

Danny Fuberta surfaced in a small restaurant on the Upper West Side. The owner, a Clericuzio soldier, made a quick call. Pippi arrived just as Fuberta was leaving the restaurant and, to Pippi's surprise, drew a gun. Fuberta was a hustler, had no experience in strong-arm. So when he fired, the shot was wide. Pippi put five bullets in him.

There were a few unfortunate things about this scene. One, there were eyewitnesses. Two, a patrol car arrived before Pippi could make his getaway. Three, Pippi had made no preparation for a shooting, he had meant to talk Fuberta into a secure location. Four, though a case could be made for self-defense, some witnesses said that Pippi shot first. It came down to the old truism that you were more in danger with the law when you were innocent than when you were guilty. Also, Pippi had a silencer on his gun, in preparation for his final friendly chat with Fuberta.

It helped matters that Pippi reacted perfectly to the disastrous arrival of the patrol car. He did not try to shoot his way out but followed the guidelines. The Clericuzio had a strict injunction: Never fire at an officer of the law. Pippi did not. He dropped his gun to the pavement, then kicked it away. He submitted peacefully to arrest and denied completely any connection with the dead man lying just a few feet away.

Such contingencies were foreseen and planned against. After all, no matter how much care was taken, there was always the malignancy of fate. Pippi now seemed to be drowning in a typhoon of ill fortune, but he knew he had only to let himself relax, that he could count on the Clericuzio Family to tow him to shore.

First there were the high-priced defense lawyers who would get him out on bail. Then there were the judges and prosecutors who could be persuaded to become stalwart in the defense of fair play, the witnesses whose memory could be made to fail, the staunchly independent American jurors who if given the slightest encouragement would refuse to convict in order to foil authority. A soldier of the Clericuzio Family did not have to shoot his way out of trouble like some mad dog.

But for the first time in his long service to the Family, Pippi De Lena had to stand trial in a court of law. And the usual legal strategy was that his wife and children must attend the trial. The jurors must know that on their decision rested the happiness of this innocent family. Twelve men and women tried and true had to harden their hearts. "Reasonable doubt" was a godsend to a juror wrung by pity.

During the trial, the police officers testified they had not seen Pippi with the gun or kicking it. Three of the eyewitnesses could not identify the defendant, the other two were so adamant in their identification of Pippi that they alienated jury and judge. The Clericuzio soldier who owned the restaurant testified that he had followed Danny Fuberta out of the restaurant because the man had not paid his check, that he had witnessed the shooting, and that the shooter definitely was not Pippi De Lena, the defendant.

Pippi had worn gloves at the time of the shooting, which was why there were no prints on the gun. Medical evidence was given for the defense that Pippi De Lena suffered from intermittent skin rashes, mysterious and incurable, and that the wearing of gloves had been recommended.

As maximum insurance a juror had been bribed. After all, Pippi was a high executive in the Family. But this final precaution had not been needed. Pippi was acquitted and deemed forever innocent in the eyes of the law.

But not by his wife, Nalene De Lena. Six months after the trial, Nalene told Pippi they must divorce.

There is a cost for those who live on a high level of tension. Physical parts of the body wear down. Excessive eating and drinking tax the liver and heart. Sleep is criminally evasive, the mind does not respond to beauty and will not invest in trust. Pippi and Nalene both suffered from this. She could not bear him in her bed, and he could not enjoy a partner who did not share his enjoyment. She could not hide the horror of knowing he was a murderer. He felt an enormous amount of relief that he did not any longer have to hide his true self from her.

"OK, we'll divorce," Pippi said to Nalene. "But I'm not losing my kids."

"I know who you are now," Nalene said. "I won't see you again and I will not have my children living with you."

This surprised Pippi. Nalene had never been forceful or outspoken. And it surprised him that she dared to speak to him, Pippi De Lena, in such a fashion. But women were always reckless. He then considered his own position. He was not equipped to bring up children. Cross was eleven and Claudia was ten, and he recognized the fact that, despite his closeness with Cross, both children loved their mother more than they did him.

He wanted to be fair to his wife. After all, he had received from her what he wanted, a family, children, a bedrock to his life, which every man needed. Who knew what he would have become if it had not been for her?

"Let's reason this out," he said. "Let's split without any bad feelings." He turned on the charm. "What the hell, we've had a good twelve years. We've had some happy times. And we have two wonderful kids, thanks to you." He paused, surprised again by her stern face. "Come on Nalene, I've been a good father, my kids like me. And I'll help you in whatever you want to do. Naturally you can keep the house here in Vegas. And I can get you one of the shops in the Xanadu. Dresses, jewelry, antiques. You'll earn your two hundred grand a year. And we can sort of share the kids."

Nalene said, "I hate Las Vegas. I always did. I have my teaching degree and a job in Sacramento. I've already enrolled the children in school up there."

It was at that moment that Pippi, with a sense of astonishment, realized that she was an opponent, she was dangerous. It was a concept completely foreign to him. Women, in his frame of reference, were never dangerous. Not a wife, not a mistress, not an aunt, not the wife of a friend, not even the daughter of the Don, Rose Marie. Pippi had always lived in a world where women could not be an enemy. Suddenly he felt that rage, that flow of energy, that he could feel toward men.

Out of that he said, "I'm not going to Sacramento to see my kids." He always became angry when someone rejected his charm, refused his friendship. Anyone who refused to be reasonable with Pippi De Lena was courting disaster. Once he decided on confrontation, Pippi took it to the limit. Also, he was astonished that his wife had already made plans.

"You said you know who I am," Pippi said. "So be very careful. You can move to Sacramento, you can move to the bottom of the ocean for all I care. But you take only one of my children with you. The other stays with me."

Nalene looked at him coolly. "The court will decide that," she said. "I think you should get a lawyer to talk to my lawyer." She almost laughed in his face when she saw his astonishment.

"You have a lawyer?" Pippi said. "You're taking me to the law?" Then he began to laugh. His laughter seemed to carry him away. He was almost hysterical.

It was strange to see a man who for twelve years had been a supplicating lover, a beggar for her flesh, her protection from the cruelties of the world, turn into a dangerous and threatening beast. At that moment she finally understood why other men had treated him with such respect, why they feared him. Now his ugly charm had none of that geniality that was so disarming. Oddly, she was not so much frightened as she was hurt that his love for her could so easily vanish. After all, for twelve years they had cradled each other's flesh, laughed together, danced together, and nurtured their children together, and now his gratitude for the gifts she had given him counted for nothing.

Pippi said to her coldly, "I don't care what you decide. I don't care what a judge decides. Be reasonable and I'll be reasonable. Be tough and you won't have anything."

For the first time she was terrified of all the things she loved; his powerful body, his large, heavy-boned hands, the irregular, blunt features she had always thought manly, that other people called ugly. All through their marriage, he had been more courtier than husband, had never raised his voice to her, had never even made a mild joke at her expense, had never scolded when she ran up bills. And it was true he had been a good father, only rough with the kids when they did not show respect for their mother.

She felt faint, but Pippi's face became more distinct, as though framed in some shadow. Extra flesh padded his cheeks, the very slight cleft in his chin seemed to be filled in with a tiny dot of black putty. His thick eyebrows had spears of white in them, but the hair on his massive skull was black, each strand as thick as horsehair. His eyes, usually so merry, were now a merciless flat tan.

"I thought you loved me," Nalene said. "How can you frighten me so?" She began to weep.

This disarmed Pippi. "Listen to me," he said. "Don't listen to your lawyer. You go to court, let's say I lose all the way down the line. You're still not going to get both kids. Nalene, don't make me be tough, I don't want to be. I understand you don't want to live with me anymore. I always thought I was so lucky to have you as long as I did. I want you to be happy. You'll get far more from me than you'll get from any court judge. But I'm getting old, I don't want to live without a family."

For one of the few times in her life Nalene could not resist malice. "You have the Clericuzio," she said.

"So I have," Pippi said. "You should remember that. But the important thing is, I don't want to be alone in my old age."

"Millions of men are," Nalene said. "And women too."

"Because they're helpless," Pippi said. "Strangers decide their lives. Other people veto their existence. I don't let anyone do that."

Nalene said scornfully, "You veto them?"

"That's right," Pippi said. He smiled down at her. "That's exactly right."

"You can visit them all you want," Nalene said. "But they both have to live with me."

At that he turned his back and said quietly, "Do what you want."

Nalene said, "Wait." Pippi turned to her. She saw on his face something so terrible in its soulless ferocity that she murmured, "If one of them wants to go with you, then OK."

Pippi suddenly became exuberant, as if the problem were resolved. "That's great," he said. "Your kid can visit me in Vegas and my kid can visit you in Sacramento. That's perfect. Let's settle it tonight."

Nalene made a last effort. "Forty is not old," she said. "You can start another family."

Pippi shook his head. "Never," he said. "You're the only woman who ever had the Indian sign on me. I married late and I know I'll never marry again. You're lucky I'm smart enough to know I can't keep you, and I'm smart enough to know I can't start over again."

"That's true," Nalene said. "You can't make me love you again."

"But I could kill you," Pippi said. He was smiling at her. As if it were a joke.

She looked into his eyes and believed him. She realized this was the source of his power, that when he made a threat people believed him. She summoned her last reserve of courage.

"Remember," she said, "if they both want to stay with me, you have to let them go."

"They love their father," Pippi said. "One of them will stay here with their old man."

That evening after dinner, the house iced with air conditioning, the desert heat outside too strong, the situation was explained to Cross, eleven years old, and Claudia, ten. Neither seemed surprised. Cross, as handsome as his mother was beautiful, already had the inner steeliness of his father, and his wariness. He was also completely without fear. He spoke up instantly. "I'm staying with Mom," he said.

Claudia was frightened by the choice. With a small child's cunning, she said, "I'm staying with Cross."

Pippi was surprised. Cross was closer to him than to Nalene. Cross was the one who came hunting with him, Cross liked to play cards with him, to golf and box. Cross had no interest in his mother's obsession with books and music. It was Cross who came down to the Collection Agency to keep him company when he had to catch up on paperwork on Saturday. In fact he had been sure that Cross would be the one he would get to keep. It was Cross he was hoping for.

He was tickled by Claudia's cunning answer. The kid was smart. But Claudia looked too much like himself, he didn't want to look at an ugly mug so much like his every day. And it was logical that Claudia go with her mother. Claudia loved the same things Nalene did. What the hell would he do with Claudia?

Pippi studied his two children. He was proud of them. They knew their mother was the weaker of the two parents, and they were sticking up for her. And he noticed that Nalene, with her theatrical instinct, had prepared cleverly for the occasion. She was dressed severely in black trousers and a black pullover, her golden hair was bound severely with a thin black headband, her face framed into a narrow, heartbreaking white oval. He was conscious of his own brutal appearance as it must appear to small children.

He turned on his charm. "All I'm asking is for one of you to keep me company," he said. "You can see each other as much as you want. Right Nalene? You kids don't want me living here in Vegas all alone."

The two children looked at him sternly. He turned to Nalene. "You have to help," he said. "You have to choose." And then he thought angrily, Why do I give a shit?

Nalene said, "You promised that if they both wanted to go with me, they could."

"Let's talk this out," Pippi said. His feelings were not hurt—he knew his children loved him, but they loved their mother more. He found that natural. It did not mean they had made the right choice.

Nalene said scornfully, "There's nothing to talk about. You promised."

Pippi did not know how terrible he looked to the other three. Did not know how cold his eyes became. He thought he had controlled his voice when he spoke, he thought he spoke reasonably.

"You've got to make a choice. I promise that if it doesn't work out, you can have your own way. But I have to have a chance."

Nalene shook her head. “You’re ridiculous,” she said. “We’ll go to court.”

At that moment Pippi made up his mind what he had to do. “It doesn’t matter. You can have your way. But think about this. Think about our life together. Think about who you are and who I am. I beg of you to be reasonable. To think about all our futures. Cross is like me, Claudia is like you. Cross would be better off with me, Claudia would be better off with you. That’s the way it is.” He paused for a moment. “Isn’t it enough for you to know they both love you better than me? That they would miss you more than they would me?” The last phrase hung in the air. He did not want the children to understand what he was saying.

But Nalene understood. Out of terror, she reached out and pulled Claudia close to her. At that moment Claudia looked at her brother beseechingly and said, “Cross . . .”

Cross had an impassive beauty of face. His body moved gracefully. Suddenly he was standing beside his father. “I’ll go with you, Dad,” he said. And Pippi took his hand gratefully.

Nalene was weeping now. “Cross, you’ll visit me often, as much as you want. You’ll have a special bedroom in Sacramento. Nobody else will use it.” It was, finally, a betrayal.

Pippi almost bounded into the air with exuberance. It was such a weight lifted from his soul that he would not have to do what he had for one instant decided to do. “We have to celebrate,” he said. “Even when we divorce, we’ll be two happy families instead of one happy family. And live happily forever after.” The others stared at him stony faced. “Well, what the hell, we’ll try,” he said.

Claudia never visited her brother and father in Vegas after the first two years. Cross went every year to Sacramento to visit Nalene and Claudia, but by his fifteenth year the visits dwindled to the Christmas holidays.

The two different parents were two different poles in life. Claudia and her mother became more and more alike. Claudia loved school; she loved books, the theater, films; she reveled in her mother’s love. And Nalene found in Claudia her father’s high spiritedness, his charm. She loved her plainness, which had none of the brutality of her father. They were happy together.

Claudia finished college and went to live in Los Angeles to try her hand in the film business. Nalene was sorry to see her go, but she had built up a satisfactory life with friends in Sacramento and had become an assistant principal at one of the public high schools.

Cross and Pippi had also become a happy family, but in a far different way. Pippi weighed the facts. Cross was an exceptional athlete in high school but an indifferent student. He had no interest in college. And although he had extraordinarily good looks, he was not excessively interested in women.

Cross enjoyed life with his father. Indeed, no matter how ugly the decision that had been made, it seemed to have turned out to be the right one. Indeed two happy families, but not together. Pippi proved to be as good a parent to Cross as Nalene was to Claudia, that is, he made Cross in his image.

Cross loved the workings of the Xanadu Hotel, the manipulation of customers, the fight against scam artists. And Cross did have a normal appetite for the showgirls; after all, Pippi must not judge his son by himself. Pippi decided that Cross would have to join the Family. Pippi believed the Don's oft-repeated words, "The most important thing in life is to earn your bread."

Pippi took Cross in as a partner in the Collection Agency. He brought him to the Xanadu Hotel for dinner with Gronevelt and maneuvered so that Gronevelt would take an interest in his son's welfare. He made Cross one of the foursome in his golf games with high-rolling gamblers at the Xanadu, always pairing Cross against himself. Cross, at the age of seventeen, had that particular virtue of the golf hustler, he played much better on a particular hole where the bets were high. Cross and his partner usually won. Pippi accepted these defeats with good grace; though they cost him money, they earned his son an enormous amount of goodwill.

He took Cross to New York for the social occasions of the Clericuzio Family: all holidays—particularly the Fourth of July, which the Clericuzio Family celebrated with great patriotic fervor; all the Clericuzio weddings, and funerals. After all, Cross was their first cousin, he had the blood of Don Clericuzio running in his veins.

When Pippi made his once-a-week foray at the tables of the Xanadu to win his eight-thousand-dollar weekly retainer with his special dealer, Cross sat watching. Pippi instructed him in the percentages of all forms of gambling. He taught him the management of the gambling bankroll, never to play when he felt unwell, never to play for more than two hours a day, never to play more than three days a week, never to bet heavily when he was on a losing streak, and always to ride a winning streak with a cautious intensity.

It did not seem unnatural to Pippi that a father should let his son see the ugliness of the real world. As the junior partner in the Collection Agency, it was very necessary for Cross to have such knowledge. For the collections were sometimes not as benign as Pippi had described to Nalene.

On a few of the more difficult collections, Cross showed no signs of abhorrence. He was yet too young and too pretty to inspire fear, but his body looked strong enough to enforce any orders Pippi might give.

Finally Pippi, to test his son, sent him out on a particularly tough case, where only persuasion, not force, could be used. The sending of Cross was in itself a signal that the collection would not be pressed, a sign of goodwill to the debtor. The debtor, a very small Mafia *Bruglione* in the northern corner of California, owed a hundred grand to the Xanadu. It was not a big enough matter to involve the Clericuzio name, things had to be handled on a lower level, the velvet glove rather than the iron fist.

Cross caught the Mafia Baron at a bad time. The man, Falco, listened to the reasoned approach made by Cross, then took out a gun and held it to the young man's throat. "Another word out of you and I'll shoot out your fucking tonsils," Falco said.

Cross, to his own surprise, felt no fear. "Settle for fifty grand," he said, "You wouldn't want to kill me for a lousy fifty grand? My father wouldn't like it."

"Who's your father?" Falco asked, his gun still steady.

Cross said, "Pippi De Lena, and he's going to shoot me anyway for settling for fifty grand."

Falco laughed and put his gun away. "OK, tell them I'll pay the next time I come to Vegas."

Cross said, "Just call me when you come in. I'll give you your usual comp RFB."

Falco had recognized Pippi's name, but there had also been something in Cross's face that had stopped him. The lack of fear, the coolness of his response, the little joke. All of this smacked of someone whose friends would avenge him. But the incident persuaded Cross to carry a weapon and a bodyguard on his future collections.

Pippi celebrated his courage with a vacation for both of them at the Xanadu. Gronevelt gave them two good suites and a purse of black chips for Cross.

At this time Gronevelt was eighty years old, white-haired, but his tall body was vigorous and still supple. He also had a pedagogical streak. He delighted in instructing Cross. When he handed him the purse of black chips, he said, "You can't win so I'll get these back. Now listen to me, you have one chance. My hotel has other diversions. A great golf course, gamblers from Japan come here to play on it. We have gourmet restaurants and wonderful girlie shows in our theater with the greatest stars from film and music. We have tennis courts and swimming pools. We have a special tour plane that can fly you over the Grand Canyon. All free. So there's no excuse that the five grand you have in that purse should be lost. Don't gamble."

On that three-day vacation, Cross followed Gronevelt's advice. Every morning he golfed with Gronevelt, his father, and a high roller staying at the Hotel. The betting was always substantial but never outrageous. Gronevelt noted with approval that Cross was at his best when the stakes were highest. "Nerves of steel, nerves of steel," Gronevelt said admiringly to Pippi.

But what Gronevelt approved of most was the kid's good judgment, his intelligence, his knowing the proper thing to do without being told. On the last morning, the high roller playing with them was in a sullen mood and with good reason. A skillful and ardent gambler, tremendously wealthy from a lucrative string of porn houses, he had lost nearly $500,000 the night before. It was not so much the money itself that bothered him as the fact that he had lost control in the middle of a streak of bad luck and had tried to press himself out of it; the mistake of a callow gambler.

That morning when Gronevelt proposed the moderate stake of fifty dollars a hole, he sneered and said, "Alfred, with what you took off me last night, you could afford a grand a hole."

Gronevelt was offended by this. His early-morning golf was a social occasion; linking it to the business of the Hotel was bad manners. But with his usual courtesy he said, "Of course. I'll even give you Pippi as your partner. I'll play with Cross."

They played. The porn house magnate shot well. So did Pippi. So did Gronevelt. Only Cross failed. He played the worst game of golf the others had ever seen. He hooked his drives, he dived into the bunkers, his ball sailed into the little pond (built on the Nevada desert at enormous expense), his nerve broke completely when he putted. The porn-house magnate, five thousand dollars richer, his ego restored, insisted on them sharing breakfast.

Cross said, "Sorry I let you down, Mr. Gronevelt."

Gronevelt looked at him gravely and said, "Someday, with your father's permission, you'll have to come work for me."

Cross, over the years, had observed closely the relationship between his father and Gronevelt. They were good friends, had dinner together once a week, and Pippi always deferred to Gronevelt in a very obvious way, which he did not do even with the Clericuzio. Gronevelt in his turn didn't seem to fear Pippi yet gave him every courtesy of the Xanadu, except a Villa. Plus Cross had caught on to Pippi's winning eight thousand dollars every week at the Hotel. Cross then made the connection. The Clericuzio and Alfred Gronevelt were partners in the Xanadu Hotel.

And Cross was aware that Gronevelt had some special interest in him, showed him extra consideration. As witness the gift of black chips on this vacation. And there had been many other kindnesses. Cross had total comp at the Xanadu for himself and his friends. When Cross graduated from high school, Gronevelt's present had been a convertible. From the time he was seventeen, Gronevelt had introduced him to the showgirls of the Hotel with obvious affection, to give him some weight. And Cross, over the years, came to know that Gronevelt himself, old as he was, often had women to his penthouse suite for dinner, and from the gossip of the girls, Gronevelt was a catch. He never had a serious love affair, but he was so extraordinarily generous with his gifts that the women were in awe of him. Any woman who stayed in his favor for a month became rich.

Once in one of their teacher and pupil talks, as Gronevelt instructed him in the lore of running a great casino hotel like the Xanadu, Cross dared to ask him about women in the context of employee relations.

Gronevelt smiled at him. "I leave the women in the shows to the entertainment director. The other women I treat exactly as if they were men. But if you're asking advice about your love life, I must tell you this. An intelligent, reasonable man in most cases has nothing to fear from women. You must beware of two things. Number one and most dangerous: the damsel in distress. Two: a woman who has more ambition than you do. Now don't think I'm heartless, I can make the same case for women, but that's not to our purpose. I was lucky, I loved the Xanadu more than anything else in the world. But I must tell you I regret not having any children."

"You seem to live the perfect life," Cross said.

"You think so?" Gronevelt said. "Well, I pay the price."

At the mansion in Quogue, a great fuss was made over Cross by the females of the Clericuzio Family. At the age of twenty he was in the full flower of youthful maleness—handsome, graceful, strong, and for his age, surprisingly courtly. The Family made jokes, not entirely free from Sicilian peasant malice, that thank God he looked like his mother and not his father.

On Easter Sunday, while more than a hundred relatives were celebrating Christ's resurrection, the final piece of the puzzle about his father was made clear to Cross by his cousin Dante.

In the vast walled garden of the Family mansion, Cross saw a beautiful young girl holding court with a group of young men. He watched his father go over to the buffet table for a platter of grilled sausage and make a friendly remark to the girl's group. He saw the girl visibly shrinking away from Pippi. Women usually liked his father; his ugliness, his good humor and high spirits disarmed them.

Dante had also observed this. "Beautiful girl," he said, smiling. "Let's go over and say hello."

He made the introductions. "Lila," he said, "this is our cousin Cross."

Lila was their age but not yet fully developed as a woman; she had the slightly imperfect beauty of adolescence. Her hair was the color of honey, her skin glowed as if refreshed from some inner stream, but her mouth was too vulnerable, as if not fully formed. She wore a white angora sweater that turned her skin to gold. Cross fell in love with her for that moment.

But when he tried to speak to her, Lila ignored him and walked to the sanctuary of matrons at another table.

Cross said a little sheepishly to Dante, "I guess she doesn't like my looks." Dante smiled at him wickedly.

Dante had turned into a curious young man with enormous vitality and a sharp, cunning face. He had the coarse black hair of the Clericuzio, which he kept confined underneath a curious Renaissance-style cap. He was very short, no more than five feet and a few inches, but he had an enormous confidence, perhaps because he was the favorite of the old Don. He carried with him always the air of malice. Now he said to Cross, "Her last name is Anacosta."

Cross remembered the name. A year before the Anacosta Family had suffered a tragedy. The head of the family and his oldest son had been shot to death in a Miami hotel room. But Dante was looking at Cross, waiting for some sort of answer. Cross made his face impassive. "So?" he said.

Dante said, "You work for your father, right?"

"Sure," Cross said.

"And you try to date Lila?" Dante said. "You're sick." He laughed.

Cross knew this was danger of some kind. He remained silent. Dante went on, "Don't you know what your father does?"

"He collects money," Cross said.

Dante shook his head. "You have to know. Your Dad takes people out for the Family. He's their number one Hammer."

It seemed to Cross that all the mysteries of his life were blown away on a sorcerer's wind. Everything was very clear. His mother's disgust of his father, the respect shown Pippi by his friends and the Clericuzio Family, his father's mysterious disappearances for weeks at a time, the weapon he always carried, sly little jokes he had not understood. He remembered his father's trial for murder, dismissed from his childhood memories in some curious way the night his father had taken his hand. Then, a sudden warmth for his father, a feeling that he must protect him in some way now that he was so naked.

But over all this Cross felt a terrible anger that Dante had dared to tell him this truth.

He said to Dante, "No, I don't know that. And you don't know that. Nobody knows that." He almost said, And you can go fuck yourself you little creep, but instead he smiled at Dante and said, "Where the hell did you get that fuckin' hat?"

Virginio Ballazzo was organizing the children's Easter egg hunt with the panache of a born clown. He gathered the children around him, beautiful flowers in Easter garb, their tiny faces like petals, skin like eggshells, hats beribboned with pink, and their faces rosy with excitement. Ballazo gave each of them a straw basket and a fond kiss and then shouted to them, "Go!" The children scattered.

Virginio Ballazzo himself was a treat to look at, his suits made in London, his shoes in Italy, shirts in France, his hair cut by a Michelangelo of Manhattan. Life had been good to Virginio and had blessed him with a daughter almost as beautiful as the children.

Lucille, called Ceil, was eighteen years old and on this day served as her father's assistant. As she handed out baskets, the men on the lawn whistled to themselves over her beauty. She was in shorts and an open white blouse. Her skin was dark with an undertone of rich cream. Her black hair was twisted around her head like a crown, and so she stood a youthful queen created by superb health, youth, and the genuine happiness that high spirits can give.

Now out of the corner of her eye she could see Cross and Dante quarreling, and she saw that for a moment Cross had suffered a crushing blow, his mouth crumpling.

She had one basket left on her arm, and she walked over to where Dante and Cross were standing. "Which one of you wants to hunt for eggs?" she asked, her smile flashing with good humor. She held out the basket.

The two of them looked at her with dazed admiration. The late-morning light turned her skin to gold, her eyes danced in delight. The white blouse swelled invitingly and yet so virginally, her round thighs milky white.

At that moment, one of the little girls began to scream. They all looked toward her. The child had found a huge egg, as big as a bowling ball and painted with vivid reds and blues. The child had been struggling to put it in her basket, her beautiful white straw hat askew, her face wide-eyed with astonishment and resolution. But the egg broke and a small bird flew out, which is what made the child scream.

Petie ran across the lawn and scooped up the young child to comfort her. It was one of his practical jokes, and the crowd laughed.

The little girl carefully straightened her hat, then shouted in a treble voice, "You tricked me," and slapped Petie in the face. The crowd roared with laughter as she ran away from Petie, who was still pleading for forgiveness. He caught her up in his arms and gave her a jeweled Easter Egg dangling from a gold chain. The little girl took it and gave him a kiss.

Ceil took Cross by the hand and led him to the tennis court, which was a hundred yards from the mansion. They sat in the three-walled tennis hut, its exposed side away from the festivities, so they could have privacy.

Dante watched them go with a sense of humiliation. He was very conscious that Cross was more attractive, and he felt snubbed. Yet he felt proud to have such a handsome cousin. To his surprise he found himself holding the basket, so he shrugged and joined the Easter egg hunt.

Hidden in the tennis shack, Ceil took Cross's face in her hands and kissed him on the lips. They were tender, brushing kisses. But when he put his hands under her blouse, she pushed him away. She had a brilliant smile on her face. "I wanted to kiss you since I was ten years old," she said. "And today was such a perfect day."

Cross was aroused by her kisses but only said, "Why?"

"Because you're so beautiful and so perfect," Ceil said. "Nothing is wrong on a day like today." She slipped her hand into his. "Don't we have wonderful families?" she said. Then abruptly she asked, "Why did you stay with your father?"

"It was just the way it worked out," Cross said.

"And did you just have a fight with Dante?" Ceil asked. "He's such a creep."

"Dante is OK," Cross said. "We were just kidding around. He's just a practical joker like my Uncle Petie."

"Dante is too rough," Ceil said, then kissed Cross again. She held his hands tight. "My father is making so much money, he's buying a house in Kentucky and a 1920 Rolls-Royce. He has three antique cars now and he's going to buy horses in Kentucky. Why don't you come over tomorrow and see the cars? You always loved my mother's cooking."

"I have to go back to Vegas tomorrow," Cross said. "I work in the Xanadu now."

Ceil gave his hand a tug. "I hate Vegas," she said. "I think it's a disgusting city."

"I think it's great," Cross said, smiling. "Why do you hate it if you've never been there?"

"Because people throw away hard-earned money," Ceil said with youthful indignation. "Thank God my father doesn't gamble. And all those sleazy showgirls."

Cross laughed. "I wouldn't know," he said. "I just run the golf course. I've never seen the inside of the casino."

She knew he was making fun of her, but she said, "If I invite you to visit me at college when I go away, will you come?"

"Sure," Cross said. In this game he was far more experienced than she was. And he felt a tenderness about her innocence, her holding of his hands, her ignorance of her father and the Family's true purpose. He understood that she was just staking out a tentative claim, the lovely weather, the explosion of celebration in her body of womanhood, and he was touched by the sweet, unsexy kisses.

"We better go back to the party," he said, and they strolled hand in hand to the picnic area. Her father, Virginio, was the first to notice them and rubbed one finger against another and said, "Shame, shame," gleefully. Then he embraced them both. It was a day Cross always remembered for its innocence, the young children chastely clad in white to announce the resurrection, and because he finally understood who his father was.

When Pippi and Cross went back to Vegas, things were different between them. Pippi obviously knew that the secret was out, and he paid Cross some attentions of extra affection. Cross was surprised that his feeling toward his father had not changed, that he still loved him. He could not imagine a life without his father, without the Clericuzio Family, without Gronevelt and the Xanadu Hotel. This was the life he had to lead, and he was not unhappy to lead it. But there began to build up in him an impatience. Another step had to be taken.

BOOK III

Claudia De Lena
Athena Aquitane

CHAPTER 4

CLAUDIA DE LENA drove from her apartment on the Pacific Palisades toward Athena's Malibu house and pondered what she would say to persuade Athena to come back to work on *Messalina.*

It was as important to her as it was to the Studio. *Messalina* was her first truly original script; her other work had been adaptations of novels, rewrites or doctoring of other scripts, or collaborations.

Also, she was a coproducer of *Messalina,* which gave her a power she had never previously enjoyed. Plus an adjusted gross of the profits. She would see some really big money. And she could then take the next step, to producer-writer. She was perhaps the only person west of the Mississippi who did not want to direct; that required a cruelty in human relationships that she could not tolerate.

Claudia's relationship with Athena was a true intimacy, not the professional friendship of fellow workers in the movie industry. Athena would know how much the picture meant to her career. Athena was intelligent. What really puzzled Claudia was Athena's fear of Boz Skannet. Athena had never been afraid of anything or anyone.

Well, one thing she would accomplish. She would find out exactly why Athena was so fearful, and then she could help. And certainly, she had to save Athena from ruining her own career. After all, who knew more about the intricacies and traps of the movie business than she did?

Claudia De Lena dreamed of a life as a writer in New York. She was not discouraged when, at the age of twenty-one, her first novel was turned down by twenty publishers. Instead, she decided to move to Los Angeles and try her hand at movie scripts.

Because she was witty and vivacious and talented, she soon made many friends in Los Angeles. She enrolled in a movie-script writing course at UCLA and met a young man whose father was a famous plastic surgeon. She and the young man became lovers, and he was bewitched by her body and intelligence. He revised her status from comradely bed partner to "serious relationship." He brought her home to his family for dinner. His father, the plastic surgeon, was enchanted by her. After dinner the surgeon put his hands around her face.

"It's unfair that a girl like you is not as pretty as you should be," he said. "Don't take offense, it's a perfectly natural misfortune. And it's my business. I can fix it if you let me."

Claudia was not offended, but she was indignant. "Why the hell should I be pretty? What good does that do me?" she said with a smile. "I'm pretty enough for your son."

"All the good in the world," the surgeon said. "And when I get through with you, you'll be too good for my son. You are a sweet and intelligent girl, but looks are power. Do you really want to spend the rest of your life standing around while men flock to good-looking women who have not one tenth of your intelligence? And you have to sit around like a dummy because your nose is too thick and you have a chin like a Mafia hood." As he said this he patted her cheek and said gently, "It won't take much doing. You have beautiful eyes and a beautiful mouth. And your figure is good enough for a movie star."

Claudia flinched away from him. She knew she resembled her father; the Mafia hood remark had touched a nerve.

"It doesn't matter," she said. "I can't pay your fee."

"Another thing," the surgeon said. "I know the movie business. I have prolonged the careers of stars male and female. Now when the day comes for you to pitch a movie at a studio, your looks will play an important part. That may seem unfair to you, I know you're talented. But that's the movie world. Just think of it as a professional move, not some male-female thing. Though of course it is." He saw that she still hesitated. "I'll do it without a fee," he said. "I'll do it for you and for my son. Even though I fear that once you're as pretty as I think you will be, he will lose a girlfriend."

Claudia had always known she was not pretty, now the memory of her father preferring Cross came back to her. If she had been pretty, would her destiny have been changed? For the first time she took a good look at the surgeon. He was a handsome man, his eyes were gentle as if he understood everything she was feeling. She laughed. "Okay," she said. "Turn me into Cinderella."

The surgeon didn't have to do that much. He thinned her nose, rounded her chin, and scaled her skin. When Claudia reentered the world, she was a handsome, proud-looking woman with a perfect nose, a commanding presence, perhaps not quite pretty but somehow even more attractive.

The professional results were magical. Claudia, despite her youth, obtained a personal interview with Melo Stuart, who became her agent. He got her minor rewrites on scripts and invited her to parties where she met producers, directors, and stars. They were enchanted by her. In the next five years, despite her youth, she was ranked as a Class A writer on A films. In her personal life the effect was equally magical. The surgeon had been right. His son could not meet the competition. Claudia had a string of sexual conquests—some really submissions—that would have made a film star proud.

Claudia loved the movie business. She loved working with other writers, she loved arguing with producers, cajoling directors: the first with how to save money doing the script a certain way, the other with how a script could be done on the highest artistic level. She was in awe of actresses and actors, how they were attuned to her words, making them sound better and more touching. She loved the magic of the set, which most people found boring, she enjoyed the camaraderie of the crew and had no compunction about screwing "below the line." She was thrilled with the whole process of opening a movie and watching its success or failure. She believed in movies as a great art form, and when called in to do a rewrite, she fancied herself a healer and did not look to make changes solely to get screen credit. At the age of twenty-five she had an enormous reputation and friendships with many stars, the closest one being with Athena Aquitane.

What was more of a surprise to her was her ebullient sexuality. Going to bed with a man she liked was as natural to her as any act of friendship. She never did it for advantage, she was too talented; she sometimes joked that stars slept with her to get her next script.

Her first adventure had been with the surgeon himself, who proved to be much more charming and adept than his son. Perhaps enchanted by his own handiwork, he offered to set her up in an apartment with a weekly allowance, not only for the sex but for the enjoyment of her company. Claudia refused good-humoredly and said, "I thought there was no fee."

"You've already paid the fee," he said. "But I hope we can see each other now and then."

"Of course," Claudia said.

What she found extraordinary in herself was that she could make love to so many different kinds of men, of varying ages, types, and looks. And enjoy all of it. She was like an aspiring gourmet, who explored all sorts of strange delicacies. She played mentor with budding actors and screenwriters, but that was not the role she liked. She wanted to learn. And she found older men far more interesting.

On a memorable day, she had a one-night stand with the great Eli Marrion himself. She enjoyed it, but it was not truly successful.

They met at a LoddStone Studio party, and Marrion was intrigued with her because she was not afraid of him and made some penetrating and disparaging remarks on the Studio's latest blockbuster production. Also, Marrion had heard her repel Bobby Bantz's amorous advances with a witty remark that left no ill feelings.

Eli Marrion had given up sex the last few years. It was more work than fun, since he was nearly impotent. When he invited Claudia to come with him to the Beverly Hills bungalow owned by LoddStone, he assumed that she accepted because of his power. He had no idea that it was her sexual curiosity. What would it be like to go to bed with so powerful a man who was so old? That would not have been enough, but in addition she found Marrion attractive despite his age. His gorilla-like face could actually turn handsome when he smiled, which he did when he told her that everyone called him Eli, including his grandchildren. His intelligence and his natural charm intrigued her because she had heard about his ruthlessness. It would be interesting.

In the bedroom of the downstairs apartment of the Beverly Hills Hotel bungalow, she observed with amusement that he was shy. Claudia rejected any coyness, she helped him undress, and while he folded his clothes over a stuffed chair, she got herself naked, gave him a hug, and followed him beneath the bedcovers. Marrion tried to joke, "When King Solomon was dying, they sent virgins to his bed to keep him warm."

"Well, then, I'm not going to help you much," Claudia said. She kissed him and fondled him. His lips were pleasantly warm. His skin had a dryness and waxiness that was not distasteful. She had been surprised by his tinyness when he shed his clothing and shoes, and she considered for a moment what a three-thousand-dollar suit could do for a man in power. But his smallness with the huge head was also endearing. She was not at all put off. After ten minutes of fondling and kissing (the great Marrion kissed with the innocence of a child), they both realized that he was now fully impotent. Marrion thought, This is the last time I will ever be in bed with a woman. He sighed and relaxed as she cradled him in her arms.

"Okay, Eli," Claudia said. "Now I'll tell you in detail why your movie is lousy from a money standpoint and an artistic one." Still gently fondling him, she delivered a penetrating analysis of the script, the director, and the actors. "It's not that it's just a bad movie," Claudia said. "It's an unwatchable movie. Because it has no story sense and so all you have is some fucking director giving you a slide show of what he thinks is a story. And the actors just go through the motions because they know it's bullshit."

Marrion listened to her with a benign smile. He felt very comfortable. He realized that an essential part of his life was over, finished by an approaching death. That he would never again make love to a woman, or even try, was not humiliating. He knew Claudia would not talk about this night, and if she did, what would it matter? He still retained his worldly power. He could still change the destinies of thousands, as long as he remained alive. And now he was interested in her analysis of the film.

"You don't understand," he said. "I can bring a picture into existence but I can't execute the picture. You're quite right, I will never hire that director again. The Talent doesn't lose money, I do. But Talent has to take the blame. My question is, Will a movie make money? If it becomes a work of art, that's just a happy accident."

As they spoke, Marrion got out of bed and began to dress. Claudia hated it when men put on their clothes, they were so much more difficult to talk to. Marrion, to her, was infinitely more lovable naked, strange as that seemed; his spindly legs, his meager body, his huge head, all made her feel an affectionate pity. Oddly enough, his penis, flaccid, was bigger than that of most men in a similar state. She made a mental note to ask her surgeon about that. Did a penis grow larger as it grew more useless?

Now she saw how fatiguing it was for Marrion to button his shirt and put in his cuff links. She jumped out of bed to help him.

Marrion studied her nakedness. Her body was better than many of the stars he had gone to bed with, but he felt no mental flicker and the cells of his body did not react to her beauty. And he did not really feel regret or sadness.

Claudia helped put on his trousers, button his shirt, put in the cuff links. She straightened his maroon tie and brushed back his gray hair with her fingers. He slipped on his suit jacket and there he stood, all his visible power restored. She kissed him and said, "I had a good time."

Marrion was studying her as though she were some sort of opponent. Then he smiled his famous smile that erased the ugliness of his features. He accepted the fact that she was truly innocent, that she had a good heart, and he believed that it was because of her youth. It was just too bad that the world she lived in would change her.

"Well, at least I can feed you," Marrion said. He picked up the phone to call room service.

Claudia was hungry. She polished off a soup, duck with vegetables, and then a huge bowl of strawberry ice cream. Marrion ate very little but did his share in polishing off the bottle of wine. They talked about movies and books, and Claudia learned to her astonishment that Marrion was a far better reader than she was.

"I would have loved to be a writer," Marrion said. "I love writing, books give me so much pleasure. But you know I've rarely met a writer I could like personally, even when I adore their books. Ernest Vail for instance. He writes beautiful books but he's such a pain in the ass in real life. How can that be?"

"Because writers are not their books," Claudia said. "Their books are the distillation of the very best that is in them. They're like a ton of rocks that you have to crush to get a little diamond, if that's what you do to get a diamond."

"You know Ernest Vail?" Marrion asked. Claudia appreciated that he said this without a trace of salaciousness. He must have known about her love affair with Vail. "Now, I love his writing but I can't stand him personally. And he has a grudge against the Studio that is insane."

Claudia patted his hand, a familiarity that was permissible since she had seen him naked. "All the Talent has a grudge against the Studio," she said. "It's not personal. And besides, you're not exactly a sweetheart in business relationships. I may be the only writer in town who really likes you." They both laughed.

Before they parted, Marrion said to Claudia, "Any time you have a problem, please call." It was a message that he would not wish to pursue their personal relationship.

Claudia understood. "I'll never take advantage of that offer," she said. "And if you have trouble with a script, you can call me. Free advice but you have to pay my deal price if I have to write." Telling him that professionally he would need her more than she would need him. Which of course was not true but told him that she had her own faith in her talent. They parted friends.

On the Pacific Coast Highway, traffic was slow. Claudia looked to her left to see the sparkling ocean and marveled at how few people were on the beach. How different from Long Island, where she had visited when she was younger. Above her head she could see the hang gliders sailing just over the power lines and onto the beach. On her right side she saw a crowd around a sound truck and huge cameras. Somebody was shooting a movie. How she loved the Pacific Coast Highway. And how Ernest Vail had hated it. He said driving on that highway was like catching a ferry to Hell. . . .

Claudia De Lena first met Vail when she was hired to work on the movie script of his bestselling novel. She had always loved his books, his sentences were so graceful, they flowed into each other like musical notes. He understood life and the tragedies of character. He had a novelty of invention that always delighted her as fairy stories had enchanted her in her childhood. So she had been thrilled to meet him. But the reality of Ernest Vail was another thing entirely.

Vail was then in his early fifties. His physical presence had none of the grace of his prose. He was short and heavy and had a bald spot that he didn't bother to hide. He may have understood and loved the characters in his books, but he was totally ignorant of the niceties of everyday life. This was perhaps one of his charms, his childlike innocence. It was only when she got to know him better that Claudia discovered that beneath this innocence was an offbeat intelligence that could be enjoyed. He could be witty as a child is unconsciously witty, and he had a child's fragile egotism.

Ernest Vail seemed to be the happiest man in the world at that breakfast at the Polo Lounge. His novels had earned him a solid critical reputation and good but unimportant money. Then this latest book had broken through and become an enormous bestseller and was now being made into a movie by LoddStone Studios. Vail had written the script, and now Bobby Bantz and Skippy Deere were telling him how wonderful it was. And to Claudia's astonishment, Vail was swallowing their praise like some starlet headed for the casting couch. What the hell did Vail think Claudia was doing at this meeting? What dismayed her was that this was the same Bantz and Deere who had the day before told her that the script was a "piece of shit." Not being cruel or even pejorative. A Piece of Shit was simply something that didn't quite work.

Claudia was not put off by Vail's homeliness, after all she herself had been homely until she blossomed into handsomeness under the surgeon's knife. She was even somewhat charmed by his credulity and his enthusiasm.

Bantz said, "Ernest, we're bringing in Claudia to help you. She's a great technician, the best in the business, and she'll make it a real movie. I smell a big hit. And remember—you have ten percent of the net."

Claudia could see Vail swallow the hook. The poor bastard didn't even know that 10 percent of the net was 10 percent of nothing.

Vail seemed to be genuinely grateful for help. He said, "Sure, I can learn from her. Writing scripts is a lot more fun than writing books but it's new to me."

Skippy Deere said reassuringly, "Ernest, you have a natural flair. You can get a lot of work out here. And you can get rich on this picture, especially if it's a hit and especially if it wins the Academy."

Claudia studied the men. Two pricks and a dope, not an unusual trio in Hollywood. But then she had not been any smarter. Hadn't Skippy Deere screwed her, literally and figuratively? Yet she couldn't help admiring Skippy. He seemed so absolutely sincere.

Claudia knew the project was already in serious trouble and that the incomparable Benny Sly was working behind her and that Sly was turning Vail's intellectual hero into a franchise by writing him into a James Bond–Sherlock Holmes–Casanova. There would be nothing left of Vail's book but the bare bones.

It was out of this pity that Claudia agreed to have dinner with Vail that night to plan how they would work on the screenplay together. One of the tricks in collaboration was to stave off any romantic involvement, and she did this by presenting herself as unattractively as possible in work sessions. Romance was always distracting to her when writing.

To her astonishment the two months they spent working led to an enduring friendship. When they were both fired from the project on the same day, they went to Vegas together. Claudia had always loved gambling, and Vail had the same vice. In Vegas she introduced him to her brother Cross and was surprised that the two men hit it off. There was absolutely no basis for their friendship that she could see.

Ernest was an intellectual who had no interest in sports or golf. Cross hadn't read a book for years. She asked Ernest about this.

"He's a listener and I'm a talker," he said. Which struck Claudia as being not a real explanation.

She asked Cross; though he was her brother, he was the greater mystery. Cross pondered the question. Finally he said, "You don't have to keep an eye on him, he doesn't want anything." And as soon as Cross said it, she knew it was true. To her it was an astonishing revelation. Ernest Vail, to his misfortune, was a man who had no hidden agendas.

Her affair with Ernest Vail was different. Though he was a world-renowned novelist, he had no power in Hollywood. Also, he had no social gifts; indeed, he inspired antagonism. His articles in magazines addressed sensitive national issues and were always politically incorrect, but ironically this angered both sides. He jeered at the American democratic process; writing about feminism, he declared that women would always be subjugated by men until they became physically equal, and advised feminists to set up paramilitary training groups. On racial problems, he wrote an essay on language in which he insisted the blacks should call themselves "coloreds" because "black" was used in so many pejorative ways—black thoughts, black as hell, black countenance—and that the word always had a negative connotation except when used in the phrase "simple black dress."

But then he enraged both sides when he maintained that all Mediterranean races be designated as "colored." Including Italians, Spaniards, Greeks, et cetera.

When he wrote about class, he claimed that people with a great deal of money had to be cruel and defensive, and that the poor ought to become criminals since they had to fight laws written by the rich to protect their money. He wrote that all welfare was simply a necessary bribe to keep the poor from starting a revolution. About religion, he wrote that it should be prescribed like medication.

Unfortunately nobody could ever figure out whether he was joking or serious. None of these eccentricities ever appeared in his novels, so a reading of his works gave no insights.

But when Claudia worked with him on the screenplay of his bestselling novel, they established a close relationship. He was a devoted pupil, he gave her all the deference, and she on her part appreciated his somewhat sour jokes, his seriousness about social conditions. She was struck by his carelessness about money in practice and his concern about money in the abstract; his pure dumbness about how the world worked in terms of power, especially Hollywood. They got along so well that she asked him to read her novel. She was flattered when he came to the studio the next day with notes on his reading.

The novel had finally been published on the strength of her success as a screenwriter and the arm twisting of her agent, Melo Stuart. It had received a few reviews of faint praise and some derisive ones merely because she was a screenwriter. But Claudia still loved her book. It did not sell, nor did anyone purchase the movie rights. But it was in print. She inscribed one to Vail: "To America's greatest living novelist." It didn't help.

"You're a very lucky girl," Vail said. "You're not a novelist, you're a screenwriter. You will never be a novelist." Then without malice or derision he spent the next thirty minutes trying to strip her novel bare and showing her that it was a piece of nonsense, that it had no structure, no depth, no resonance in characterization, and that even her dialogue, her strong point, was terrible, witty without point. It was a brutal assassination but carried out with such logic that Claudia had to recognize its truth.

He ended up with what he thought was a kindness. "It's a very good book for an eighteen-year-old woman," Vail said. "All the faults I've mentioned can be repaired by experience, simply by getting older. But there's one thing you can never repair. You have no language."

At this Claudia, though crushed, took offense. Some of the reviewers had praised the lyrical quality of the writing. "You're wrong on that," she said. "I tried to write perfect sentences. And the thing I admire most in your books is the poetry of your language."

For the first time Vail smiled. "Thank you," he said. "I wasn't trying to be poetic. My language sprang out of the emotion of the characters. Your language, your poetry in this book is imposed. It's completely false."

Claudia burst into tears. "Who the fuck are *you*?" she said. "How can you say something so terribly destructive. How can you be so fucking positive?"

Vail seemed amused. "Hey, you can write publishable books and starve to death. But why, when you're a genius screenwriter? As for my being so positive, this is the only thing I know, but I know it absolutely. Or I'm wrong."

Claudia said, "You're not wrong but you are a sadistic prick."

Vail eyed her warily. "You're gifted," he said. "You have a great ear for movie dialogue, you're expert in story line. You really understand movies. Why would you want to be a blacksmith instead of an automobile mechanic? You are a movie person, you are not a novelist."

Claudia looked at him with wide-eyed wonder. "You don't even know how insulting you are."

"Sure I do," Vail said. "But it's for your own good."

"I can't believe you're the same person who wrote your books," she said venomously. "Nobody could believe you wrote them."

At this Vail broke into a delighted cackle. "That's true," he said. "Isn't that wonderful?"

All through the next week he was formal with her while they worked on the script. He assumed their friendship was over. Finally Claudia said to him, "Ernest, don't be so stiff. I forgive you. I even believe you're right. But why did you have to be so brutal? I even thought you were making one of those male power moves. You know, humiliate me then push me into bed. But I know you're too dumb for that. For Christ's sake, give a little sugar with your medicine."

Vail shrugged. "I have only one thing going for me," he said. "If I'm not honest about those things then I'm nothing. Also, I was brutal because I'm really very fond of you. You don't know how rare you are."

Claudia said smilingly, "Because of my talent, my wit, or my beauty?"

Vail waved his hand dismissively. "No, no," he said. "Because you are blessed, a very happy person. No tragedy will ever bring you down. That is very rare."

Claudia thought about it. "You know," she said, "there's something vaguely insulting about that. Does that mean I'm basically stupid?" She paused for a moment. "It's considered more sensitive to be melancholy."

"Right," Vail said. "I'm melancholy and so I'm more sensitive than you?" They both laughed and then she was hugging him.

"Thank you for being honest," she said.

"Don't get too cocky," Vail said. "Like my mother always said, 'Life is like a box of hand grenades, you never know what will blow you to kingdom come.' "

Claudia was laughing when she said, "Christ, do you always have to sound the note of doom? You'll never be a movie writer and that line shows it."

"But it's more truthful," Vail said.

Before they finished their collaboration on the script, Claudia dragged him into bed. She was fond enough of him that she wanted to see him with his clothes off so they could really talk, really exchange confidences.

As a lover Vail was far more enthusiastic than he was expert. He was also more grateful than most men. Best of all, he loved to talk after sex, his nakedness did not inhibit his lecturing, his intemperate judgments. And Claudia loved his nakedness. With his clothes off he seemed to have a monkey's agility and impetuousness, and he was very hairy: a matted chest, patches of furry hair on his back. Also, he was as greedy as a monkey, clutching her naked body as if she were a fruit hanging from a tree. His appetite amused Claudia. She relished the inherent comedy of sex. And she loved that he was famous all over the world, that she had seen him on TV and thought him a little pompous on literature, the grievous moral state of the world, so dignified clutching the pipe he rarely smoked and looking very professorial in his tweed jacket with sewn-leather elbow patches. But he was far more amusing in bed than on TV; he did not have an actor's projection.

There was never any talk of true love, of a "relationship." Claudia had no need for it and Vail had only a literary sense of the term. They both accepted that he was thirty years the elder and, aside from that, no bargain really except for his fame. They had nothing in common except literature, perhaps the worst basis for establishing a marriage, they agreed.

But she loved arguing with him about movies. Vail insisted that moving pictures were not art, that they were a regression to the primitive paintings found in lost caves. That film had no language, and since the progression of the human species depended on language, it was merely a regressive, minor art.

Claudia said, "So painting is not an art, Bach and Beethoven are not art, Michelangelo is not art. You're talking bullshit." And then she realized he was teasing her, that he enjoyed provoking her, though prudently only after sex.

By the time they were both fired from the script, they were really close friends. And before Vail went back to New York, he gave Claudia a tiny, lopsided ring with four different colored jewels. It didn't look expensive but it was a valuable antique that he spent a lot of time looking for. She always wore it thereafter. It became in her mind a lucky talisman.

But when he left, their sexual relationship was over. When and if he ever returned to L.A. she would be in the middle of another affair. And he recognized that their sex had been more friendship than passion.

Her farewell gift to him was a thorough education in the ways of Hollywood. She explained to him that their script was being rewritten by the great Benny Sly, the legendary rewriter of scripts, who had even been mentioned for a special Academy Award for rewrites. And that Benny Sly specialized in turning uncommercial stories into one-hundred-million-dollar blockbusters. Undoubtedly he would turn Vail's book into a movie that Vail would hate but that would surely make a lot of money.

Vail shrugged. "That's okay," he said. "I have ten percent of the net profits. I'll be rich."

Claudia looked at him with exasperation. "Net?" she cried out. "Do you buy Confederate money too? You'll never see a penny no matter how much the movie makes. LoddStone has a genius for making money disappear. Listen, I had net on five pictures that made a ton of money and I never saw a penny. You won't either."

Vail shrugged again. He did not seem to care, which made his actions in the years to follow even more puzzling.

Claudia's next affair made her remember Ernest saying life was like a box of hand grenades. For the first time, despite her intelligence, she fell guardedly in love with a completely unsuitable man. He was a young "genius" director. After that she fell deeply and unguardedly in love with a man who most women in the world would have fallen in love with. Equally unsuitable.

The initial flush of ego that she could attract such primary alpha males was quickly dampened by how they treated her.

The director, an unlikable ferret of a man only a few years older than she, had made three offbeat movies that not only were critical successes but had made a goodly sum of money. Every studio wanted a relationship with him. LoddStone Studios gave him a three-picture deal and also gave him Claudia to rewrite the script he was planning to shoot.

One of the elements of the director's genius was that he had a clear vision of what he wanted. At first he condescended to Claudia because she was a woman and a writer, both inferior in the power structure of Hollywood. They quarreled immediately.

He asked her to write a scene she felt did not belong to the structure of the plot. On its own Claudia recognized that the scene would be a flashy bit that would be just a show-off scene for the director.

"I can't write that scene," Claudia said. "It does nothing for the story. It's just action and camera."

The director said curtly. "That's why they're movies. Just do it the way we discussed it."

"I don't want to waste your time and mine," Claudia said. "Just go write with your fucking camera."

The director didn't waste time even getting angry. "You're fired," he said. "Off the picture." He clapped his hands.

But Skippy Deere and Bobby Bantz made them reconcile, which was only possible because the director had become intrigued by her stubbornness. The picture was a success, and Claudia had to admit this was more because of the director's talent as a moviemaker than hers as a writer. Quite simply she had not been able to see the director's vision. They fell into bed almost by accident, but the director proved to be a disappointment. He refused to be naked, he made love with his shirt on. But still Claudia had dreams of the two of them making great movies together. One of the great director-writer teams of all time. She was quite willing to be the subordinate partner, to make her talent serve his genius. They would create great art together and become a legend. The affair lasted a month, until Claudia finished her "spec" script of *Messalina* and showed it to him. He read it and tossed it aside. "A piece of feminist bullshit with tits and ass," he said. "You're a clever girl but it's not a picture I want to waste a year of my life making."

"It's only a first draft," Claudia said.

"Jesus, I hate people taking advantage of a personal relationship to get a movie made," the director said.

In that moment Claudia fell completely out of love with him. She was outraged. "I don't have to fuck you to make a movie," she said.

"Of course you don't," the director said. "You're talented and you have your reputation of being one of the great pieces of ass in the movie business."

Now Claudia was horrified. She never gossiped about her sexual partners. And she hated his tone, as if women were somehow shameful for doing what men did.

Claudia said to him, "You have talent, but a man who fucks with his shirt on has a worse reputation. And at least I never got laid by promising someone a screen test."

That was the end of their relationship, and it had started her thinking of Dita Tommey as the director. She decided that only a woman could do justice to her script.

Well, what the hell, Claudia thought. The bastard never got totally naked and he didn't like to talk after sex. He was truly a genius in film but he had no language. And for a genius he was a truly uninteresting man, except when he talked movies.

Now Claudia was approaching the great curve of the Pacific Coast Highway that showed the ocean as a great mirror by reflecting the cliffs to her right. It was her favorite spot in the world, natural beauty that always thrilled her. It was only ten minutes to the Malibu Colony, where Athena lived. Claudia tried to formulate her plea: to save the movie, to make Athena return. She remembered that at different times in their lives they had had the same lover, and she felt a flush of pride that the man who had loved Athena could love her.

The sun was at its most brilliant now. It polished the waves of the Pacific into huge diamonds. Claudia braked suddenly. She thought one of the gliders was coming down in front of her car. She could see the glider, a young girl with one tit hanging out of her blouse, give a demure wave as she sailed onto the beach. Why were they allowed, why didn't the police appear? She shook her head and pressed the gas pedal. Traffic was loosening and the highway swerved so that she could no longer see the ocean, though in a half mile it would reappear. Like true love, Claudia thought smilingly. True love in her life always reappeared.

When she truly fell in love, it was a painful but educational experience. And it was not really her fault, for the man was Steve Stalling, a Bankable Star and idol of women all over the world. He had a fearful masculine beauty, genuine charm, and an enormous vivacity that was fueled by the prudent use of cocaine. He also had great talent as an actor. More than anything else, he was a Don Juan. He screwed everything in sight—on location in Africa, in a small town in the American West, in Bombay, Singapore, Tokyo, London, Rome, Paris. He did this in the spirit of a gentleman giving alms to the poor, an act of Christian charity. There was never any question of a relationship, no more than a beggar would be invited to a benefactor's dinner party. He was so enchanted by Claudia that the affair lasted twenty-seven days.

It was a humiliating twenty-seven days for Claudia despite the pleasure. Steve Stallings was an irresistible lover, with the help of cocaine. He was more comfortable being naked than even Claudia. The fact that he had a perfectly proportioned body helped. Often Claudia caught him inspecting himself in the mirror in much the same way as a woman adjusting her hat.

Claudia knew she was just a lesser concubine. When they had dates he would always call her to say he would be an hour late and then would arrive six hours later. Sometimes he would cancel altogether. She was only his fallback position for the night. Also, when they made love he would always insist she use cocaine with him, which was fun but turned her brain into such mush she could not work the next few days, and what she did write, she distrusted. She realized that she was becoming what she detested more than anything else in the world: a woman whose whole life depended on the whims of a man.

She was humiliated by the fact that she was his fourth or fifth choice, but she didn't really blame him. She blamed herself. After all, at this point in his fame Steve Stallings could have almost any woman in America and he had chosen her. Stallings would grow old and less beautiful, he would become less famous and use more and more cocaine. He had to cash in during his prime. She was in love and, for one of the few times in her life, terribly unhappy.

So on the twenty-seventh day when Stallings called to say he would be an hour late, she told him, "Don't bother, Steve, I'm leaving your geisha house."

There was a pause, and when he answered he did not seem surprised. "We part friends I hope," he said. "I really enjoy your company."

"Sure," Claudia said and hung up. For the first time she did not want to remain friends at the end of an affair. What really bothered her was her lack of intelligence. It was obvious that all his behavior was a trick to make her go away, that it had taken her too long to take the hint. It was mortifying. How could she have been so dumb? She wept, but in a week she found she did not miss being in love at all. Her time was her own and she could work. It was a pleasure to get back to her writing with a head clear of cocaine and true love.

After her director genius of a lover had rejected her script, Claudia worked furiously for six months on the rewrite.

Claudia De Lena wrote her original screenplay of *Messalina* as a witty propaganda piece for feminism. But after five years in the movie business she knew that any message had to be coated with more basic ingredients, such as greed, sex, murder, and a belief in humanity. She knew she had to write great parts not only for her first choice, Athena Aquitane, but for at least three other female stars in lesser roles. Good female roles were so scarce that the script would attract top-name stars. And then, absolutely essential, the great villain—charming, ruthless, handsome, and witty. Here she drew on memories of her father.

Claudia at first wanted to approach a female independent producer with clout, but most studio heads who could green-light a picture were males. They would love the script but they would worry it would turn into too overt a propaganda piece with a female producer and a female director. They would want at least one male hand in there somewhere. Claudia had already decided that Dita Tommey would direct.

Tommey would certainly accept because it would be a megabudget film. Such a film if successful would put her in the Bankable class. Even if it failed it would enhance her reputation. A huge budget film that failed was sometimes more prestigious for a director than a small budget picture that made money.

Another reason was that Dita Tommey loved women exclusively and this picture would give her access to four beautiful famous women.

Claudia wanted Tommey because they had worked together on a picture a few years ago and it had been a good experience. She was very direct, very witty, very talented. Also she was not a "writer killer" director, who called in friends to rewrite and share credit. She never filed for writing credit on a film unless she contributed her fair share, and she was not a sexual harasser as were some directors and stars. Though the term "sexual harassment" could not really be used in the movie business, where the selling of sex appeal was part of the job.

Claudia made sure she sent the script to Skippy Deere on a Friday, he only read scripts carefully on weekends. She sent it to him because, despite his betrayals, he was the best producer in town. And because she could never let go completely on an old relationship. It worked. She got a call from him on Sunday morning. He wanted her to have lunch with him that very day.

Claudia threw her computer into her Mercedes and dressed to work: blue denim man's shirt, faded blue jeans, and slip-on sneakers. She tied her hair back with a red scarf.

She took Ocean Avenue in Santa Monica. In the Palisades Park that separated Ocean Avenue from Pacific Coast Highway, she saw the homeless men and women of Santa Monica gathering for their Sunday brunch. Volunteer social workers brought their food and drink to them every Sunday in the fresh air of the park at wooden tables and benches. Claudia always took this route to watch them, to remind herself of that other world where people did not have Mercedeses and swimming pools and did not shop on Rodeo Drive. In the early years she often volunteered to serve food in the park, now she just sent a check to the church that fed them. It had become too painful to go from one world to the other, it blunted her desire to succeed. She could not avoid watching the men, so shabbily dressed, their lives in ruins, yet some of them curiously dignified. To live so without hope seemed to her an extraordinary thing, and yet it was just a question of money, that money she earned so easily writing movie scripts. What she earned in six months was more money than these men saw in their entire lives.

At Skippy Deere's mansion in the Beverly Hills canyons, Claudia was led by the housekeeper to the swimming pool, with its bright blue-and-yellow cabanas. Deere was seated in a cushioned lounge chair. Beside him was the small marble table that held his phone and a stack of scripts. He was wearing his red-framed reading glasses that he only used at home. In his hand was a tall frosted glass of Evian water.

He sprang up and embraced her. "Claudia," he said, "we have business to do fast."

She was judging his voice. She could usually tell the reaction to her scripts by the tones of voices. There was the carefully modulated praise that meant a definite "no." Then there was the joyful, enthusiastic voice that expressed an unrestrained admiration and was almost always followed by at least three reasons why the script could not be bought; another studio was doing the same subject, the proper cast could not be assembled, the studios would not touch the subject matter. But Deere's voice was that of the determined business man latching onto a good thing. He was talking money and controls. That meant "Yes."

"This could be a very big picture," he told Claudia. "Very, very big. In fact it can't be small. I know what you're doing, you're a very clever girl, but I have to sell a studio on the sex. Of course I'll sell it to the female stars on feminism. The male star we can get if you soften him a little, give him more moments as a good guy. Now I know you want to be an associate producer on this, but I call the shots. You can have your say, I'm open to reason."

"I want to have my say on the director," Claudia said.

"You, the studio, and the stars," Deere said, laughing.

"I don't sell it unless I get approval of the director," Claudia said.

"Okay," Deere said. "So first tell the studio you want to direct, then back down, and they'll be so relieved that they'll give you the approval." He paused for a moment. "Who do you have in mind?"

"Dita Tommey," Claudia said.

"Good. Clever," Deere said. "Female stars love her. The Studio too. She brings everything in on budget, she doesn't live off the picture. But you and I do the casting before we bring her on."

"Who will you bring it to?" Claudia asked.

"LoddStone," Deere said. "They go with me pretty much so we won't have to fight too much about casting and directors. Claudia, you've written a perfect script. Witty, exciting, with a great point of view on early feminism and that's hot today. And sex. You justify Messalina and all women. I'll talk to Melo and Molly Flanders about your deal and she can talk to Business Affairs at LoddStone."

"You son of a bitch," Claudia said. "You've already talked to LoddStone?"

"Last night," Skippy Deere said with a grin. "I brought the script over to them and they gave me the green light if I can put everything together. And listen, Claudia, don't shit me. I know you've got Athena in your pocket on this, that's why you're being so tough." He paused for a moment. "That's what I told LoddStone. Now let's go to work."

That had been the beginning of the great project. She could not let it go down the drain now.

. . .

Claudia was approaching the traffic light where she would have to take a left turn onto the side road that would lead her to the Colony. For the first time, she felt a sense of panic. Athena was so strong-willed, as stars must be, that she would never change her mind. No matter; if Athena refused, she would fly to Vegas and ask her brother Cross to help. He had never failed her. Not when they were growing up, not when she went to live with her mother, not when their mother died.

Claudia had a memory of the great festive occasions at the Clericuzio mansion on Long Island. A setting from a Grimm's fairy tale, mansion enclosed by walls, she and Cross playing among the fig trees. There were two groups of boys ranging from eight to twelve years old. The opposing group was led by Dante Clericuzio, grandson of the old Don who had stationed himself at an upstairs window like a dragon.

Dante was an aggressive boy who loved to fight, who loved to be a general, and the only boy who dared to challenge her brother, Cross, in physical combat. Dante had Claudia on the ground, hitting her, trying to beat her into submission, when Cross appeared. Then Dante and Cross had fought. What had struck Claudia then was how confident Cross had been in the face of Dante's ferocity. And Cross won easily.

And so Claudia could not understand her mother's choice. How could she not love Cross more? Cross was so much more worthy. Proving his worth by electing to go with his father. And Claudia never doubted that Cross had wanted to stay with his mother and her.

In the years that followed the disruption, the family still maintained a relationship of sorts. Claudia came to know, by conversations, by the body language of the people around them, that her brother Cross had to some degree achieved their father's eminence. The affection between her and her brother remained constant, though they were now completely different. She realized that Cross was part of the Clericuzio Family, she was not.

Two years after Claudia moved to L.A., when she was twenty-three, her mother, Nalene, was diagnosed with cancer. Cross, then working with Gronevelt at the Xanadu after making his bones for the Clericuzio, came to spend the last two weeks with them in Sacramento. Cross hired nurses around the clock and a cook and housekeeper. The three of them lived together for the first time since the breakup of the family. Nalene forbade Pippi to visit her.

The cancer had affected Nalene's eyesight, so Claudia read to her constantly, from magazines, from newspapers and books. Cross went out to do the shopping. Sometimes he had to fly to Vegas for an afternoon to take care of Hotel business, but he always returned at evening.

During the night, Cross and Claudia would take turns holding their mother's hand, comforting her. And though she was heavily medicated, she continually pressed their hands. Sometimes she hallucinated and thought her two children were little again. One terrible night she wept and begged forgiveness of Cross for what she had done to him. Cross had to hold her in his arms and reassure her that everything had turned out for the best.

During the long evenings when their mother was deep into a drugged sleep, Cross and Claudia told each other the details of their lives.

Cross explained that he had sold the Collection Agency and left the Clericuzio Family, though they had used their influence to get him his job at the Xanadu Hotel. He hinted at his power and told Claudia that she was welcome at the Hotel anytime, RFB—room, food, and beverage free. Claudia asked how he could do that and Cross told her with just a touch of pride, "I have the Pencil."

Claudia found that pride comical and a little sad.

Claudia seemingly felt their mother's death far more strongly than Cross, but the experience had brought them together again. They regained their childhood intimacy. Claudia frequently went to Vegas over the years and met Gronevelt and observed the close relationship the old man had with her brother. During these years Claudia saw that Cross had a certain kind of power, but that he never linked his power with the Clericuzio Family. Since Claudia had severed all ties with the Family and never attended the funerals, weddings, and christenings, she didn't know that Cross still was part of the Family social structure. And Cross never spoke of it to her. She rarely saw her father. He had no interest in her.

New Year's Eve was the biggest event in Vegas; people all over the country flocked there, but Cross always had a suite for Claudia. Claudia was not a big gambler, but one New Year's Eve she got carried away. She had brought an aspiring actor with her and was trying to impress him. She lost control and signed fifty thousand dollars in markers. Cross had come down to the suite with the markers in his hand, and there was a curious look on his face. Claudia recognized it when he spoke. It was his father's face.

"Claudia," Cross said, "I thought you were smarter than me. What the hell is this?"

Claudia felt a little sheepish. Cross had often warned her to gamble only for small stakes. Also to never increase her bets when she was losing. And to spend no more than two or three hours gambling every day, because the length of time spent gambling was the greatest trap. Claudia had violated all his advice. . . .

She said, "Cross, give me a couple of weeks and I'll pay it off."

She was surprised by her brother's reaction. "I'll kill you before I let you pay off these markers." Very deliberately he tore up the slips of paper and put them in his pocket. He said, "Look, I invite you down here because I want to see you, not to take your money. Get this through your head, you cannot win. It has nothing to do with luck. Two and two make four."

"Okay, okay," Claudia said.

"I don't mind having to tear up these markers, but I hate your being dumb," Cross said.

They had left it at that, but Claudia wondered. Did Cross have that much power? Would Gronevelt approve or would he even know about this?

There had been other such incidents, but one of the most chilling involved a woman named Loretta Lang.

Loretta had been a singing and dancing star in the Xanadu Follies show. She had an abundance of verve and a natural humorous perkiness that charmed Claudia. Cross introduced them after the show.

Loretta Lang was as charming in person as she was on the stage. But Claudia noticed that Cross was not as charmed, in fact seemed a little irritated by her vivacity.

On Claudia's next visit, she brought along Melo Stuart for an evening in Vegas where they could catch the Follies show. Melo had come merely to indulge Claudia, not expecting much. He watched appraisingly and then told Claudia, "This girl has a real shot. Not singing or dancing, but she's a natural comic. A female with that is gold."

Backstage to meet Loretta, Melo put on his game face and said, "Loretta, I loved you. Loved you. Understand? Can you come to L.A. next week? I'll arrange to have you on film to show to a studio friend of mine. But first you have to sign a contract with my agency. You know I have to put in a lot of work before I make any money. That's the business, but remember I love you."

Loretta threw her arms around Melo. There was no witty mocking of devotion here, Claudia noted. A date was set and the three of them had dinner together to celebrate, before Melo caught his early morning plane back to L.A.

During supper Loretta confessed that she was already under an airtight contract with an agency that specialized in nightclub entertainment. A contract with three years to run. Melo assured Loretta that everything could be ironed out.

But things could not be ironed out. Loretta's showbiz agency insisted on controlling her career for the next three years. Loretta frantic, astonished Claudia by asking her to appeal to her brother, Cross.

"What the hell can Cross do?" Claudia asked.

Loretta said, "He has a lot of clout in this town. He can get a deal I can live with. Please?"

When Claudia went up to the penthouse suite on the roof of the Hotel and presented the problem to Cross, her brother looked at her with disgust. He shook his head.

"What the hell's the big deal?" Claudia asked. "Just put the word in, that's all I'm asking."

"You are dumb," Cross said. "I've seen dozens of dames like her. They ride friends like you up to the top and then you're history."

"So what?" Claudia said. "She's really talented. This could change her whole life for the better."

Cross shook his head again. "Don't ask me to do this," he said.

"Why not?" Claudia asked. She was used to asking people favors for other people, it was part of the movie business.

"Because once I get in to it, I have to succeed," Cross said.

"I'm not expecting you to succeed, I'm just asking you to do your best," Claudia said. "At least then I can tell Loretta we tried."

Cross laughed. "You really are dumb," he said. "Okay, tell Loretta and her agency to come and see me tomorrow. Ten A.M. sharp. And you might as well be there too."

At the meeting the next morning, Claudia met Loretta's showbiz agent for the first time. His name was Tolly Nevans, and he was dressed in the casual Vegas style, modified by the seriousness of the meeting. That is, he wore a blue blazer over a collarless white shirt and blue denim pants.

"Cross, a pleasure to see you again," Tolly Nevans said.

"We've met?" Cross asked. He never had handled the business details of the Follies show personally.

"A long time ago," Nevans said smoothly. "When Loretta opened her first time at the Xanadu."

Claudia noted the difference between the L.A. agents who dealt with big-time film talent and Tolly Nevans, who managed the much smaller-time world of nightclub entertainment. Nevans was a little more nervous, his physical appearance not so overpowering. He did not have the complete confidence of Melo Stuart.

Loretta pecked Cross on the cheek but did not say anything to him. Indeed she showed none of her usual vivacity. She sat next to Claudia, who sensed Loretta's tension.

Cross was in a golf outfit, white slacks, a white T-shirt, and white sneakers. He wore a blue baseball cap on his head. He offered drinks from the wet bar but they all refused. Then he said quietly, "Let's get this business settled. Loretta?"

Her voice trembled. "Tolly wants to keep his percentage of everything I earn. That includes any movie work. But the L.A. agency naturally wants their full percentage of any movie work they get me. I can't pay two percentages. And then Tolly wants to call the shots on anything I do. The L.A. people won't stand for that and neither will I."

Nevans shrugged. "We have a contract. We just want her to live up to that contract."

Loretta said, "But then my film agent won't sign me up."

Cross said, "It seems simple to me. Loretta, you just buy your way out of the contract."

Nevans said, "Loretta is a great performer, she makes a lot of money for us. We've always promoted her, we always believed in her talent. We've invested a lot of money. We can't just let her go now when she's paying off."

Cross said, "Loretta, buy him out."

Loretta almost wailed, "I can't pay two percentages. It's too cruel."

Claudia tried to control the smile on her face. But Cross did not. Nevans looked hurt.

Finally Cross said, "Claudia, go get your golf gear. I want you to shoot nine holes with me. I'll meet you downstairs at the Cashier's cage when I'm finished here."

Claudia had wondered at Cross being dressed for the meeting in such a cavalier way. As if he were not taking it seriously. It had offended her and she knew it offended Loretta. But it had reassured Tolly. The man had not proposed any compromise. So Claudia said to Cross, "I'll stick around, I want to see Solomon at work."

Cross could never get angry at his sister. He laughed and she smiled back at him. Then Cross turned to Nevans. "I see you're not bending. And I think you're right. How about a percentage of her movie earnings for one year? But you have to relinquish control or it won't work."

Loretta burst in angrily, "I'm not giving him that."

Nevans said, "And that's not what I want. The percentage is okay but what if we have a great booking for you and you're tied up in a movie? We lose money."

Cross sighed and said almost sadly, "Tolly, I want you to let this girl out of her contract. It is a request. Our hotel does a lot of business with you. Do me a favor."

For the first time Nevans seemed alarmed. He said in almost a pleading tone, "I'd love to do you this favor, Cross, but I have to check with my partners at the Agency." He paused for a moment. "Maybe I can arrange a buyout."

"No," Cross said. "I'm asking a favor. No buyout. And I want your answer now so I can go out and enjoy my golf game." He paused. "Just say yes or no."

Claudia was shocked by this abruptness. Cross was not threatening or intimidating as far as she could see. In fact he seemed to be giving up the whole affair, as if he had lost interest. But Claudia could see that Nevans was shaken.

What Nevans replied was surprising. "But that's unfair," he said. He shot a reproachful glance at Loretta, she lowered her eyes.

Cross pulled his baseball cap sideways in a swaggering manner. "It's just a request," he said. "You can refuse me. It's up to you."

"No, no," Nevans said. "I just didn't know you felt so strongly, that you were such good friends."

Suddenly Claudia saw an amazing change in her brother. Cross leaned over and gave Tolly Nevans a half hug of affection. His smile warmed his face. That bastard is handsome, she thought. And then Cross said in a voice full of gratitude, "Tolly, I won't forget this. Look, you have carte blanche here at the Xanadu for any new talent you want to showcase, third billing at the least. I'll even arrange to have a special night at the Follies with all the talent from you and on that night, I want you and your partners to have dinner with me at the hotel. Call me anytime and I'll leave word you get through. Direct. Okay?"

Claudia realized two things. Cross had deliberately shown his power. And that Cross had been careful to recompense Nevans to some degree but only after he had knuckled under, not before. Tolly Nevans would have his special night, would bask in power for that one night.

Claudia realized further that Cross had allowed her to see that power to show his love for her and that that love had a material force. And she saw in his beautifully planed face, in that beauty she had envied from childhood, of the sensual lips, the perfect nose, the oval eyes, all slightly hardening as if turning into the marble of ancient statues.

...

Claudia turned off the Pacific Coast Highway and drove to the gate of the Malibu Colony. She loved the Colony, the houses right on the beach, the ocean sparkling in front of them, and far off on the water, she saw again the reflections of the mountains behind them. She parked the car in front of Athena's house.

Boz Skannet was lying on the public beach south of the Malibu Colony fence. That fence of plain wire mesh ran down the beach for about ten steps into the water. But this fence was only a formal barrier. If you went out far enough, you could swim around it.

Boz was scouting for his next attack on Athena. Today would be a probing foray and so he had driven out to the public beach, bathing suit covered with a T-shirt and tennis slacks. His beach bag, really a tennis bag, held the vial of acid wrapped in towels.

From his spot on the beach he could look through the mesh fence at Athena's house. He could see the two private security guards on the beach. They were armed. If the back was covered, certainly the front of the house was covered. He didn't mind hurting the guards but he didn't want to make it seem like a madman slaughtering a whole bunch of people. That would detract from his justified destruction of Athena.

Boz Skannet took off his slacks and T-shirt and stretched out on his blanket, staring over the sand and the blue sheet of the Pacific Ocean beyond. The warmth of the sun made him drowsy. He thought of Athena.

In college he had heard a professor lecturing on Emerson's essays and quoting, "Beauty is its own excuse." Was it Emerson, was it Beauty? But he had thought of Athena.

It is so rare to find a human being so beautiful in physical form and so virtuous in other parts of her nature. And so he thought of Thena. Everybody had called her Thena in those days of her girlhood.

He had loved her so much in his youth that he lived in a dream of happiness that she loved him. He could not believe that life could be so sweet. And little by little everything had been tarnished with decay.

How did she dare to be so perfect? How did she dare to be so demanding of love? How did she dare to make so many people love her? Didn't she know how dangerous that would be?

And Boz wondered at himself. Why had his own love turned to hate? It was simple really. Because he knew he could not possess her to the end of their lives; that one day he must lose her. That one day she would lie down with other men, that one day she would disappear from his Heaven. And never think of him again.

He felt the sun's warmth move off his face and opened his eyes. Looming above him was a very large, well-dressed man who was carrying a folding chair. Boz recognized him. It was Jim Losey, the detective who had interrogated him after he threw the water in Thena's face.

Boz squinted up at him. "What a coincidence, both of us swimming on the same beach. What the fuck do you want?"

Losey unfolded the chair and sat on it. "My ex-wife gave me this chair. I was interrogating and arresting so many surfers she said I might as well be comfortable." He looked down at Boz Skannet almost kindly. "I just wanted to ask you a few questions. One, what are you doing so close to Miss Aquitane's house? You're violating the judge's restraining order."

"I'm on a public beach, there's a fence in between us, and I'm in a bathing suit. Do I look like I'm harassing her?" Boz said.

Losey had a sympathetic smile on his face. "Hey, look," he said, "if I was married to that broad, I couldn't stay away from her either. How about if I take a look in your beach bag?"

Boz put the beach bag beneath his head. "No," he said. "Unless you have a warrant."

Losey gave him a friendly smile. "Don't make me arrest you," he said. "Or just beat the shit out of you and take the bag."

This aroused Boz. He stood up, he offered the bag to Losey, but then he held it away from him. "Try and take it," he said.

Jim Losey was startled. In his own estimation he had never met anybody tougher than himself. In any other situation he would have drawn his blackjack or his gun and beaten the man to a pulp. Perhaps it was the sand under his feet that made him uncertain, or perhaps it was the utter fearlessness of Skannet.

Boz was smiling at him. "You'll have to shoot me," he said. "I'm stronger than you. Big as you are. And if you shoot me, you won't have probable cause."

Losey admired the man's perceptiveness. In a physical struggle the issue might be in doubt. And there was no cause to draw a weapon.

"Okay," he said. He folded up his chair and started to walk away. Then he turned and said admiringly, "You're really a tough guy. You win. But don't give me a good probable cause. You see I haven't measured your distance from the house, you may be just out of range of the judge's order. . . ."

Boz laughed. "I won't give you cause, don't worry."

He watched Jim Losey walk off the beach to his car and drive away. Boz put his blanket into the beach bag and returned to his own car. He put the beach bag in the trunk, took the car key off its ring, and hid it under the front seat. Then he went back to the beach for his swim around the fence.

CHAPTER 5

ATHENA AQUITANE had earned her way to stardom in the traditional way that the public seldom appreciates. She spent long years in training: acting classes, dance and movement classes, voice lessons, extensive reading in dramatic literature, all necessary to the art of acting.

And of course the scut work. She made the rounds of agents, casting directors, mildly lecherous producers and directors, the more dinosaur-like sexual advances of studio wheels and chiefs.

In her first year she earned her living by doing commercials, and some modeling, as a skimpily clad hostess for automotive expositions, but that was only her first year. Then her acting skills began to pay off. She had lovers who showered her with gifts of jewelry and money. Some of them offered marriage. The affairs were brief and ended on friendly terms.

None of this had been painful or humiliating to her, not even when the buyer of a Rolls-Royce assumed she came with the car. She had put him off with the joke that she had the same price as the car. She was fond of men, she enjoyed sex, but only as a treat and reward for more serious endeavor. Men were not a serious part of her world.

Acting was Life. Her secret knowledge of herself was serious. The dangers of the world were serious. But acting came first. Not the tiny movie roles that enabled her to pay expenses, but the great acting parts in great plays put on by local theater groups and then the plays at the Mark Taper Forum that finally propelled her toward major film roles.

Her real life was the parts she played, she felt more alive as she brought her characters to life, carried them around inside her while living out her ordinary existence. Her love affairs were like amusements, playing golf and tennis, dining with friends, dreamlike substances.

Real life was only in the cathedral-like theater: putting on makeup, adding one splash of color to her costume, her face contorting with emotions of the lines of the play running through her head, and then, looking into that deep blackness of the audience—God finally showing his face—she pleaded her fate. She wept, fell in love, screamed with anguish, begged forgiveness for her secret sins, and sometimes experienced the redemptive joy of happiness found.

She hungered for fame and success to obliterate her past, to drown her memories of Boz Skannet, of the child they had together, of the betrayal by her beauty; a sly fairy godmother's boon.

Like any artist, she wanted the world to love her. She knew she was beautiful—how could she not, her world constantly told her so—but she knew also she was intelligent. And so from the beginning she believed in herself. What she really could not believe, at the beginning, was that she had the indispensable ingredients of true genius: enormous energy and concentration. And curiosity.

Acting and music were Athena's true loves, and to be able to concentrate on these things she used her energy to make herself expert in everything else. She learned to fix a car, became a superb cook, excelled at sports. She studied lovemaking in the literature and in life, knowing how important it was in her chosen profession.

She had a flaw. She could not bear to inflict pain on a fellow human being, and since in this life this was impossible to avoid, she was an unhappy woman. Yet she made hard-nosed decisions that furthered her place in the world. She used her power as a Bankable Star; she sometimes had a coldness that was as intense as her beauty. Powerful men beseeched her to appear in their movies, men begged to climb into her bed. She influenced, even demanded, the choosing of directors and costars. She could commit minor crimes without punishment, outrage custom, defy nearly all moralities, and who was to say who was the real Athena? She had the inscrutability of all

Bankable Stars, she was a twin, you could not separate her real life from the lives she lived on screen.

All this and the world loved her, but that was not enough. She knew her inner ugliness. There was one person who did not love her and that caused her to suffer. It is part of the definition of an actress that she will despair if she gets one hundred positive reviews and a single hateful one.

At the end of her first five years in Los Angeles, Athena got her first starring role in film and made her greatest conquest.

Like all top male stars, Steven Stallings had a veto over the female leading role of each of his pictures. He saw Athena in a Mark Taper Forum play and recognized her talent. But even more he was struck by her beauty, and so he chose Athena to costar with him in his next film.

Athena was completely surprised and flattered. She knew this was her big break, and initially she did not know why she had been chosen. Her agent, Melo Stuart, enlightened her.

They were in Melo's office, a wonderfully decorated room with Oriental bric-a-brac, gold-threaded carpets, and heavy comfortable furniture all bathed in artificial lights since the curtains were closed to cut out daylight. Melo liked an English tea in his office rather than going out for lunch and picked up the little sandwiches and popped them into his mouth as he talked. He only went out to lunch with his really famous clients.

"You deserve this break," he told Athena. "You're a great actress. But you've only been in this town a few years and despite your intelligence you're a little green. So don't take offense about what I'm going to say—here's what happened." He paused for a moment. "Usually I would never explain this, usually it's not necessary."

"But I'm so green," Athena said smiling.

"Not green exactly," Melo said. "But you're so focused on your art, you sometimes seem unaware of the social complexities of the industry."

Athena was amused. "So tell me how I got the part."

Melo said, "Stalling's agent called me. He said Stallings saw you in the Taper play and was knocked out by your performance. He definitely wants you in the picture. Then the producer called me to negotiate and we made the deal. Straight salary, two hundred grand, no points, that comes later in your career, and no strings for any other picture. That's a really great deal for you."

"Thank you," Athena said.

"I really shouldn't have to be saying this," Melo said. "Steven has a habit of falling madly in love with his costars. Sincerely, but he's a very ardent wooer."

Athena interrupted him. "Melo, don't spell it out."

"I feel I must," Melo said.

He gazed at her fondly. He himself, usually so impervious, had fallen in love with Athena at the beginning, but since she had never acted seductively, he had taken the hint and not revealed his feelings. She was, after all, a valuable piece of property that would in the future earn him millions.

"Are you trying to tell me that I'm supposed to jump on his bones the first time we're alone?" Athena said dryly. "Isn't my great talent enough?"

"Absolutely not," Melo said. "And absolutely. A great actress is a great actress, no matter what. But you know how someone becomes a great star in film? At some time they have to get the great part at exactly the right moment. And this is that great part for you. You cannot afford to miss it. And what's so hard about falling in love with Steven Stallings? A hundred million women all over the world love him, why not you? You should be flattered."

"I'm flattered," Athena said coolly. "But if I really hate him, then what?"

Melo popped another tea sandwich into his mouth. "What's to hate? He's really a sweet man, I swear to you. But at least dally with him until they've shot you enough in the picture so they can't cut you out."

"What if I'm so good they won't want to cut me?" Athena said.

Melo sighed. "To tell the truth, Steven won't wait that long. If you're not in love with him after three days, you'll be out of the picture."

"That's sexual harassment," Athena said, laughing.

"There can be no sexual harassment in the movie business," Melo said. "In one form or another you're offering your ass for sale by just going in."

"I meant the part where I have to fall in love with him," Athena said. "Straight screwing is not enough for Steven?"

"He can get all the screwing he wants," Melo said. "He's in love with you so he wants love in return. Until the shoot is over." He sighed. "Then you'll both fall out of love because you'll be too busy working." He paused for a moment. "It won't be insulting to your dignity," he said. "A star like Steven indicates his interest. The recipient, yourself, responds or shows a lack of interest in that interest. Steven will send you flowers the first day. The second day after rehearsal he invites you to dinner to study the script. There's nothing forced about it. Except, of course, that you will be cut from the picture if you don't go. With a full payoff, I can do that for you."

"Melo, don't you think I'm good enough to make it without selling my body?" Athena said with mock reproach.

"Of course you are," Melo said. "You're young, only twenty-five. You can wait two or three, even four or five years. I have absolute faith in your talent. But give it a chance. Everybody loves Steven."

It went exactly as Melo Stuart predicted. Athena received flowers the first day. They second day they rehearsed with the whole company. It was a dramatic comedy where laughter led to tears, one of the hardest things to do. Athena was impressed with Steven Stallings's skill. He read his part in a monotone with no effort to impress but still the lines came alive, and on the variations he invariably picked the one most true. They played one scene a dozen different ways and responded to each other, followed each other like dancers. At the end, he muttered, "Good, good," and smiled at her with respectful acknowledgment that was purely professional.

At the end of the day Steven finally turned on his charm.

"I think this may be a great movie because of you," he said. "How about getting together tonight and really doing a number on this script?" He paused for a moment and then said with a boyish smile that was endearing, "We were really good together."

"Thank you," Athena said. "When and where?"

Immediately Steven's face expressed a polite, playful horror. "Oh, no," he said. "Your choice."

At that moment Athena decided to accept her role and to play it as a true professional. He was the superstar. She was the newcomer. But all the choices were his and it was her duty to choose what he wanted. Ringing in her ears was Melo saying, "you wait two, three, four, five years." She couldn't wait.

"Would you mind coming to my place?" Athena asked. "I'll make dinner simple so we can work while we eat." She paused for a moment, then said, "At seven?"

Because she was a perfectionist, Athena prepared for the mutual seduction physically and mentally. Dinner would be light so it would not affect their work or their sexual performance. Though she rarely touched alcohol, she bought a bottle of white wine. The meal would show off her talent as a cook, but she could prepare while they worked.

Clothes. She understood that the seduction was supposed to be accidental, with no prior intent. But they should not be used as a signal to ward him off either. As an actor, Steven would be looking to interpret every sign.

So she wore faded blue jeans that showed her buttocks to advantage, the mottled blue and faded white invitingly cheerful. No belt. Above, a frilly white silk blouse that though it showed no cleavage, indicated the milkier color of her breasts beneath. Her ears she decorated with small round clip-ons, green to match her eyes. Still it was just a little too severe, a little standoffish. It left room for doubt. Then she had a stroke of genius. She painted her toenails a scarlet red and greeted him barefoot.

Steven Stallings arrived carrying a bottle of good red wine, not super but very good. He was also dressed for business. Baggy brown corduroy trousers, blue denim shirt, white sneakers, his dark black hair carelessly combed. Under his arm was the script with yellow note slips peeking out demurely. The only thing that gave him away was the faint scent of cologne.

They ate casually at the kitchen table. He complimented her on the food, as well he should. And as they ate they leafed through their scripts, comparing notes, changing dialogue for smoother delivery.

After dinner they moved to the living room and played out specific scenes they had targeted as trouble areas in the script. Through all this they were very conscious of each other, and it affected their work.

Athena noticed that Steven Stallings was playing his part perfectly. He was professional, respectful. Just his eyes betrayed his genuine admiration of her beauty, his appreciation of her talent as an actress, of her mastery of the material. Finally he asked her if she was too tired to play the crucial love scene in the movie script.

By that time the dinner had been comfortably digested. By that time they had become close friends, like the characters in the script. They played the love scene, Steven kissing her slightly on the lips but leaving out the body gropings. After the first chaste kiss, he looked deeply and sincerely into her eyes, and with perfect husky emotion in his voice, he said, "I wanted to do that the first time I saw you."

Athena held his eyes with her own. Then she lowered them, pulled his head down gently and gave him a chaste kiss. The necessary signal. They were both surprised by the genuine passion with which he responded. Which proved she was the better actor, Athena thought. But he was skillful. As he undressed her, his hands smoothed her skin and his fingers probed, his tongue tickled the inside of her thigh and her body responded. This wasn't so terrible, she thought as they moved into the bedroom. And Steven was so startlingly handsome, his classic face, suffused with passion, had an intensity that could not be duplicated on film, indeed on film this would be degraded into lecherousness. When he made love on screen it was far more spiritual.

Athena had now worked herself into the part of a woman overcome with mad physical passion. They were perfectly in sync and in one blinding moment rose to a simultaneous climax. Lying back in exhaustion, both wondered how the scene would have appeared on film and decided it would not have been good enough for a take. It had not revealed character as it should, or advanced the story as it should. It had lacked the inner tender emotion of true love or even true lust. There would have to be another take.

Steven Stallings fell in love, but he often did that. Athena, despite the fact that it was in some sense professional rape, felt pleased that things had turned out so well. There was no real downside except the question of free will. And it could be said of any life that the suppression of free will, judiciously exercised, was often necessary for human survival.

Steven was happy that now in the shooting of his new film he had all his ducks in a row. He had a good working partner. They would have a pleasant relationship, he wouldn't have to look around for sex. Also, he had rarely had a woman so blessed with talent and beauty as Athena, and also so good in bed. And obviously madly in love with him, which of course could be a problem later on.

What happened next cemented their love. They both jumped out of bed and said, "Let's go back to work." They picked up their scripts and, naked, perfected their readings.

However, one disconcerting note for Athena was when Steven put on his shorts. They were scalloped pink, especially designed to show off his shapely buttocks, those buns that were the source of ecstasy to his female fans. Another odd note was when he proudly told her that he had used a condom made especially for him, manufactured by a company he had invested in. You could never detect he was wearing one. They were also absolutely impregnable. And he asked her what would be the best marketing name for them: Excalibur or King Arthur. He liked King Arthur. Athena thought it over for a moment.

Then she said with mock seriousness, "Maybe a more politically correct name?"

"You're right," Steven said. "They're so expensive to make we have to sell them to both sexes. Our tag marketing line will be 'Condom of the Stars.' How about that for a name? Star Condoms."

. . .

The movie and their affair were both huge successes. Athena had successfully climbed the first rung of the ladder to stardom, and each picture she made over the next five years solidified that success.

The affair, as most star affairs go, was also a success but naturally short-lived. Steven and Athena loved each other with help from the script, but their love had the humor and detachment made necessary by his fame and her ambition. Neither could afford to be more in love than the other and this equality in love was death to their passion. Also there was the question of geography. The affair ended when the picture ended. Athena went on location to India, Steven on location to Italy. There were phone calls and Christmas cards and gifts, they even flew to Hawaii for a weekend of ecstasy. Working together on a movie was like being Knights at the Round Table. Searching for fame and fortune was looking for the Holy Grail, you had to do it on your own.

There had been speculation that they might marry. Of this there was no possibility. Athena enjoyed the affair but always saw its comic side. Though she made it her business as a professional actor to appear more in love than Steven, it was almost impossible for her not to giggle. Steven was so sincere, so perfect as an ardent and sensitive lover, that she could just as well have gone to one of his films.

His physical beauty could be enjoyed but not constantly admired. His constant use of drugs and liquor was so controlled it was impossible to pass judgment. He treated cocaine as a prescription drug, alcohol made him more charming. Even his success had not made him willful or moody.

So it was a great surprise when Steven proposed marriage. Athena refused with good humor. She knew that Steven screwed everything that moved, on location, in Hollywood, and even at the rehabilitation clinic when his drug problem got out of control. He was not a man she wanted to have as a semipermanent part of her life.

Steven took her refusal well. It had been a momentary weakness springing from an excess of cocaine. He was almost relieved.

Over the next five years, as Athena shot up to the top rank of stardom, Steven began to fade. He was still an idol to his fans, especially women, but he was unlucky or unintelligent in picking his roles. Drugs and alcohol made him more careless in his work habits. Through Melo Stuart, Steven had asked Athena for the male lead in *Messalina.* The shoe was now on the other foot. Athena had approval of her costar and she gave him the role. She said yes out of a perverse sense of gratitude and because he was perfect for the part, however with the proviso that he did not have to sleep with her.

During the last five years Athena had had short affairs. One had been with a young producer, Kevin Marrion, the only son of Eli Marrion.

Kevin Marrion was her age but a veteran of the movie business. He had produced his first major film at the age of twenty-one and it had been a hit. Which convinced him he had a genius for movies. Since that time he had produced three flops, and now only his father gave him credibility in the industry.

Kevin Marrion was extremely good-looking; after all, Eli Marrion's first wife had been one of the greatest beauties in the business. Unfortunately his looks iced out in the camera and he failed all his screen tests. As a serious artist his future was as a producer.

Athena and Kevin met when he asked her to star in his new film. Athena listened to him in rapt wonder and horror. He talked with the particular innocence of the very serious-minded.

"This is the best movie script I have ever read," Kevin said. "I must tell you in all honesty that I helped rewrite it. Athena you are absolutely the only actress that deserves this role. I could have any actress in the industry but I want you." He looked sternly at her to convince her of his sincerity.

Athena was fascinated by his pitching of the script. It was the story of a homeless woman living on the streets who is redeemed by the finding of an abandoned infant in a garbage pail and who then goes on to become the leader of the homeless in America. Half of the film consisted of her pushing the shopping cart that held all her possessions. And after surviving alcohol, drugs, near starvation, rape, and a government attempt to take away her foundling, she goes on to run for president of the United States on an independent ticket. Not winning, however—that was the class of the script.

Athena's fascination had really been horror. This was a script that would require her to be a homeless, despairing woman in a desolate background in old clothes. Visually, a disaster. The sentimentality was rank, the intelligence level of dramatic construction, idiotic. It was a bewildering, hopeless mess.

Kevin said, "If you play this part, I will die happy."

And Athena thought, Am I crazy or is this guy a moron? But he was a powerful producer. Obviously sincere, and obviously a man who could get things done. She looked despairingly at Melo Stuart, and he smiled back at her encouragingly. But she could not speak.

"Wonderful. Wonderful idea," Melo said. "Classic. Rise and fall. Fall and rise. The very essence of drama. But Kevin, you know how important it is for Athena after her breakthrough to select the proper follow-up. Let us read the script and we'll get back to you."

"Of course," Kevin said and handed both of them copies of the script. "I know you'll love it."

Melo took Athena to a small Thai restaurant on Melrose. They ordered their meal and flipped through the script.

"I'll kill myself first," Athena said. "Is Kevin retarded?"

"You still don't understand the movie business," Melo said. "Kevin has intelligence. He's just doing something he is not equipped to do. I've seen worse."

"Where? When?" Athena said.

"I can't recall offhand," Melo said. "You're a big enough star to say no but you're not big enough to make unnecessary enemies."

"Eli Marrion is too smart to back his son up on this one," Athena said. "He must know how terrible this script is."

"Sure," Melo said. "He even jokes that he has a son who makes flop commercial movies and a daughter who makes serious movies that lose money. But Eli has to make his children happy. We don't. We say no to this movie. But there's a catch. LoddStone owns the rights to a big novel that has a great role for you. If you turn Kevin down, you may not get that other part."

Athena shrugged. "This time I'll wait."

"Why not take both parts? Make it a condition you do the novel first. Then we'll find an out on making Kevin's picture."

"And that won't make enemies?" Athena asked him smiling.

"The first picture will be a big hit so it won't matter. Then you can afford to make enemies."

"Are you sure I can get out of Kevin's picture afterwards?" Athena said.

"If I don't get you out, you can fire me," Melo said. He had already made the deal with Eli Marrion, who could not give the direct no to his son and had chosen this way out of the disaster. Eli wanted to make Melo and Athena the villains. And Melo didn't mind. Part of any movie agent's job was to be the villain in the script.

Everything worked out. The first part, the film of the novel, made Athena an absolutely first-rank star. But unfortunately the consequences made her decide on a period of celibacy.

During the sham of the preproduction of Kevin's movie that would never be made, it was predictable that he would fall in love with Athena. Kevin Marrion was a relatively innocent young man for a producer, and he pursued Athena with unabashed sincerity and ardor. His enthusiasm and his social conscience were his greatest charm. One evening, in a moment of weakness compounded by the guilt she felt about betraying the picture, Athena took him to bed. It was enjoyable enough and Kevin insisted on marriage.

Meanwhile Athena and Melo had persuaded Claudia De Lena to rewrite the script. She rewrote it as farce and Kevin fired her. He was so angry that he became a bore.

For Athena the affair was convenient. It fitted in nicely with her working schedule. And Kevin's enthusiasm was pleasurable in bed. And his insistence on marriage even without a prenuptial agreement was flattering, since he would inherit LoddStone Studios one day.

But one night after listening to him talk incessantly about the movies they were going to make together, a sudden insight flashed through Athena's mind: "If I have to listen to this guy one more minute, I will kill myself." Like many kind people exasperated into being unkind, she went all the way. Knowing she would feel guilty, she made it a package. In that moment, she told Kevin that not only would she not marry him, but she would not sleep with him anymore and that also she would not appear in his movie.

Kevin was stunned. "We have a contract," he said. "And we'll enforce it. You are betraying me in every way."

"I know," Athena said. "Just talk to Melo." She was disgusted with herself. Of course, Kevin was right, but she found it interesting that he was more worried about his movies than his love for her.

It was after this affair, her film career assured, that Athena lost interest in men. She remained celibate. She had more important things to do, things in which the love of men had no part.

Athena Aquitane and Claudia De Lena became close friends solely because Claudia was persistent in her pursuit of friendship with women she liked. She first met Athena while rewriting the script of one of her early movies, when Athena was not quite yet a great star.

Athena insisted on helping her with the script, and although this was usually a scary process for the writer, she proved to be intelligent and a great help. Her instincts on character and story were always good and nearly always unselfish. She was intelligent enough to know that the stronger the characters around her, the more she would have to play with in her own role.

They often worked in Athena's home in Malibu, and it was there they discovered they had many things in common. They were athletes: strong swimmers, top amateur golfers, and very good on the tennis court. The two of them played doubles together and beat most of the male doubles on the Malibu Beach tennis courts. So when the picture finished shooting, they continued their friendship.

Claudia told Athena everything about herself. Athena told Claudia little. It was that kind of friendship. Claudia recognized this but it didn't matter. Claudia told of her affair with Steve Stallings. Athena laughed delightedly and they compared notes. They agreed, yes, Steve had been great fun, great in bed. And so talented, he was a marvelously gifted actor and a really sweet man.

"He was almost as beautiful as you," Claudia said. She generously admired beauty in others.

Athena seemed not to have heard. It was a habit she had when somebody mentioned her beauty.

"Is he a better actor though?" Athena said teasingly.

"Oh no, you're a really great actor," Claudia said. And then to provoke Athena into revealing more of herself, she added, "But he's a lot happier person than you."

"Really?" Athena said. "That may be. But someday he will be a hell of a lot unhappier than I ever will be."

"Yeah," Claudia said. "The cocaine and booze will get him. He's not going to age well. But he's intelligent, maybe he'll adapt."

"I don't ever want to become what he's going to be," Athena said. "And I won't."

"You're my hero," Claudia said. "But you're not going to beat the aging process. I know you don't drink and booze or even fool around much but your secrets will get you."

Athena laughed. "My secrets will be my salvation," she said. "My secrets are so banal they're not even worth telling. We movie stars need our mystery."

Every Saturday morning when they were not working, they went shopping together on Rodeo Drive. Claudia was always amazed at how Athena could disguise herself so that she would not be recognized by fans or the clerks in the stores. She wore a black wig and loose clothes to disguise her figure. She changed her makeup so her jaw seemed to be thicker, her lips fuller, but most interesting of all, it seemed as if she could rearrange the features on her face. She also wore contact lenses that changed her brilliant green eyes to a demure hazel. Her voice became a soft Southern drawl.

When Athena bought something, she put it on one of Claudia's charge cards and then reimbursed her with a check when they had their late lunch. It was wonderful to relax in a restaurant as complete nobodies; as Claudia joked, no one ever recognized a screenwriter.

Twice a month Claudia spent the entire weekend at Athena's Malibu beach house for swimming and tennis. Claudia had let Athena read the second draft of *Messalina,* and Athena had asked for the lead role. As if she were not a top star and Claudia should not be begging her.

...

So when Claudia arrived in Malibu to persuade Athena to go back to work on the picture, she felt some hope for success. After all, Athena would not only ruin her own career but damage Claudia's.

The first thing that shook Claudia's confidence was the tight security around Athena's house, in addition to the usual guards at the Malibu Colony gates.

Two men with Pacific Ocean Security Company uniforms were at the gate of the house itself. Two additional guards patrolled the huge garden inside. When the little South American housekeeper led her to the Ocean Room, she could see two more guards on the beach outside. All the guards had batons and holstered guns.

Athena greeted Claudia with a tight hug. "I'll miss you," she said. "In a week I'll be gone."

"Why are you being so crazy?" Claudia said. "You're going to let some jerk of a macho man ruin your whole life. And mine. I can't believe you're so chicken. Listen, I'll stay with you tonight and tomorrow we'll get gun permits and start training. In a couple of days we'll be sharpshooters."

Athena laughed and gave her another hug. "Your Mafia blood is coming out," she said. Claudia had told her about the Clericuzio and her father.

They made drinks and sat in the stuffed chairs that gave them a view of the ocean that was like looking at some deep blue-green portrait of water.

"You can't change my mind and I'm not chickenshit," Athena said. "Now, I'll tell you the secret you wanted to know and you can tell the Studio and then maybe you'll both understand."

Then she told Claudia the whole story of her marriage. Of Boz Skannet's sadism and cruelty and deliberate humiliation and of her running away. . . .

With her astute, storyteller mind, Claudia felt there was something missing in Athena's story, that she was deliberately leaving out some important elements.

"What happened to the baby?" Claudia asked.

Athena's features arranged themselves into a movie-star mask. "I can't tell you anything more about that right now, in fact what I did tell you about me having a baby is just between you and me. That's the one part you mustn't tell the Studio. I trust you with that."

Claudia knew she couldn't press Athena on this. "But why are you quitting the picture?" Claudia asked. "You'll be protected. Then you can disappear."

"No," Athena said. "The Studio will only protect me while the picture's shooting. And that won't matter. I know Boz. Nothing will stop him. If I stay, I'll never finish the picture anyway."

At that moment they both noticed a man in bathing trunks walking up from the water to the house. The two security guards intercepted him. One of the guards blew a whistle and the two guards in the garden came running around. With the odds at four to one, the man in the bathing trunks seemed to retreat slightly.

Athena was standing up, obviously shaken. "It's Boz," she said to Claudia quietly. "He's doing this just to scare me. It's not his real move." She went out onto the deck and looked down at the five men. Claudia followed her.

Boz Skannet looked up at them, his eyes squinting, his bronzed face painted by the sun. His body, in the bathing trunks, looked lethal.

He smiled and said, "Hey, Athena, how about inviting me in for a drink?"

Athena gave him a brilliant smile. "I would if I had poison. You've broken the court order—I could have you locked up."

"Nah, you wouldn't," Boz said. "We're too close, we have too many secrets together." Though he smiled, he looked savage.

Claudia was reminded of the men who came to the Clericuzio feasts in Quogue.

One of the guards said, "He swam around the fence from the public beach. He must have a car there. Or we can have him locked up."

"No," Athena said. "Take him to his car. And tell the Agency I want four more guards around my house."

Boz still had his face tilted up, his body seemed to be a great statue rooted in the sand. "See you, Athena," he said. And then the guards led him away.

"He is frightening," Claudia said. "Maybe you're right. We would have to shoot cannons to stop him."

"I'll call you before I *flee,*" Athena said, making it actressy. "We can have one last dinner together."

Claudia was almost in tears. Boz had really frightened her, had reminded her of her father. "I'm going to fly to Vegas and see my brother Cross. He's smart and knows a lot of people. I'm sure he can help. So don't leave until I come back."

"Why should he help?" Athena said. "And how? Is he in the Mafia?"

"Of course not," Claudia said indignantly. "He'll help because he loves me." She said this with pride in her voice. "And I'm the only person he really loves except for my father."

Athena looked at her with a frown. "Your brother sounds just a little shady. You're very innocent for a woman working in the movies. And, by the way, how come you sleep with so many men? You're not an actress and I don't think you're a tramp."

"That's no secret," Claudia said. "Why do men screw so many women?" Then she hugged Athena. "I'm off to Vegas," she said. "Don't move till I get back."

That night Athena sat on the deck and watched the ocean, black beneath the moonless sky. She went over her plans and thought fondly of Claudia. It was really funny that she could not see through her brother, but that's what love did.

When Claudia met with Skippy Deere later that afternoon and told him Athena's story, they both sat in silence for a while. Then Deere said, "She left some things out. I went to see Boz Skannet to buy him off. He refused. And he warned me that if we tried any funny stuff, he'd give the papers a story that would ruin us. How Athena dumped their kid."

Claudia flew into a rage. "That's not true," she said. "Anyone who knows Athena knows she couldn't do such a thing."

"Sure," Deere said. "But we didn't know Athena when she was twenty."

"Fuck you too," Claudia said. "I'm going to fly to Vegas and see my brother Cross. He has more brains and more balls than any of you guys. He'll straighten this out."

"I don't think he can scare Boz Skannet," Deere said. "We already gave it a good try." But now he saw another opportunity.

He knew certain things about Cross. Cross was looking to get into the movie business. He had invested in six of Deere's pictures and lost money overall, so Cross wasn't that smart. It was rumored Cross was "connected," that he had some influence in the Mafia. But everybody was connected with the Mafia, Deere thought. That didn't make them dangerous. He doubted that Cross could help them with Boz Skannet. But a producer always listened, a producer specialized in long shots. And besides he could always pitch Cross to invest in another picture. It was always a great help to have minor partners who had no control over the making of the picture and the finances.

Skippy Deere paused, then said to Claudia, "I'll go with you."

Claudia De Lena loved Skippy Deere despite the fact that Deere had once screwed her out of a half-million dollars. She loved Deere for his faults and the diversity of his corruption and because Skippy was always good company, all admirable qualities in a producer.

Years ago they had worked on a picture together and had been buddies. Even then, Deere had been one of the most successful and colorful producers in Hollywood. One time on a set, the star of the movie had boasted of fucking Deere's wife and Deere, listening off a ledge on the set three stories above him, had jumped and landed on the star's head and broken his shoulder in addition to then smashing his nose with a good right-hand punch.

Claudia had another memory. The two of them had been walking down Rodeo Drive and Claudia had seen a blouse in the window. It was the most beautiful blouse Claudia had ever seen. It was white with almost invisible stripes of green, so lovely it could have been painted by Monet. The store was one of those that required an appointment before you could even go in and shop, as if the owner were some great physician. No problem. Skippy Deere was a personal friend of the owner as he was a great friend of studio chiefs, the great corporate heads, the rulers of countries throughout the Western world.

When they were in the store, the clerk told them the blouse was five hundred dollars. Claudia staggered back, held her hands on her chest. "Five hundred dollars for one blouse?" she asked. "Don't make me laugh."

The clerk was staggered in his turn by Claudia's impudence. "It's of the finest fabric," he said, "handmade. . . . And the green stripe is a green like no other fabric in the entire world. The price is very reasonable."

Deere was smiling. "Don't buy it, Claudia," he said. "Do you know how much it costs to get it laundered? At least thirty bucks. Every time you wear it, thirty bucks. And you have to take care of it like a baby. No food stains, and definitely you can't smoke. If you burn a hole, bang, there goes your five hundred."

Claudia smiled at the clerk. "Tell me," she said, "do I get a free gift if I buy the blouse?"

The clerk, a beautifully dressed man, had tears in his eyes and said, "Please leave."

They walked out of the store.

"Since when can a store clerk throw a customer out?" Claudia asked, laughing.

"This is Rodeo Drive," Skippy said. "You're lucky you even got in."

The next day when Claudia arrived for work at the studio, there was a gift box on her desk. In it were a dozen of the blouses and a note from Skippy Deere: "Not to be worn except at the Oscars."

Claudia knew that the clerk at the store and Skippy Deere were both full of shit. She had later seen that same beautiful green stripe on a woman's dress and on a special hundred-dollar tennis bandanna.

And the picture she was working on with Deere was a schlock love-action film that would never come closer to an Academy Award than Deere's appointment to the Supreme Court. But she was touched.

And then there was the day that the picture they had worked on reached the magical one-hundred-million-dollar gross and Claudia had thought she would be rich. Skippy Deere invited her to dinner to celebrate. Skippy was bubbling over with good humor. "This is my lucky day," he said. "The picture goes over a hundred, I got a great blow job from Bobby Bantz's secretary, and my ex-wife got killed in a car accident last night."

There were two other producers at dinner with them and they both winced. Claudia thought Deere was making a joke. But then Deere said to the two producers, "I see your eyes green with envy. I save five hundred grand a year in alimony and my two kids inherit her estate, the settlement she got from me, so I don't have to support them anymore."

Claudia was suddenly depressed and Deere said to her, "I'm being honest, it's what every man would think but never say out loud."

Skippy Deere had paid his dues in the movie business. The son of a carpenter, he had helped his father work on the houses of movie stars in Hollywood. In one of those situations that are probable only in Hollywood, he became the lover of a middle-aged female star, who got him a job as an apprentice in her agent's company, a prelude to getting rid of him.

He worked hard, learning to control his fiery nature. Most of all, how to coddle Talent. How to beg hot new directors, fast-talk fresh young stars, become best friend and mentor to horseshit writers. He made fun of his own behavior, citing a great Renaissance cardinal pleading the Borgia Pope's cause with the King of France. When the King exposed his derriere, then defecated to show his contempt for the Pope, the Cardinal exclaimed, "Oh, the ass of an angel," and rushed to kiss it.

But Deere mastered the indispensable hardware. He learned the art of negotiation, which he simplified to "Ask for everything." He became literate, developing an eye for those novels that would make good movies. He could spot acting talent. He scrutinized the details of production, the different ways to steal money from the budget of a film. He became a successful producer, one who could put 50 percent of the script and 70 percent of the budget on the screen.

It was helpful that he enjoyed reading and also that he could screen-write. Not on a totally blank piece of paper, but he was adept at crossing out scenes and revising dialogue, and could actually create pieces of action, little set pieces, which sometimes played brilliantly but were seldom necessary to the story being told. What he prided himself on, what helped his pictures achieve financial success, was that he was especially good at endings, which were almost always triumphant, the exaltation of good over evil—and if that didn't fit, the sweetness of defeat. His masterpiece had been the ending of a film that dealt with the atom-bomb destruction of New York, in which all the characters came out as better human beings dedicated to the love of their fellow man, even the one who had exploded the bomb. He had to hire five extra writers to get that done.

All this would have been worth very little to him as a producer if he had not been especially astute about finance. He pulled investment money out of thin air. Rich men doted on his company, as did the beautiful women who hung on his arm. Stars and directors enjoyed his honest and bawdy appreciation of the good things in life. He charmed development money out of studios, and he learned that it was possible to get a green light out of some studio heads with an enormous bribe. His Christmas card and Christmas gift lists were endless, to stars, to critics on newspapers and magazines, even to high-ranking law enforcement people. He called them all dear friends and when they no longer became useful he cut them from the gift list but never from the card list.

One of the keys to being a producer was to own a property. It could be an obscure novel, unsuccessful in print, but it was something concrete you could talk about to the studio. Deere secured rights to these with five-year options at five hundred dollars a year. Or he would option a screenplay and work with the writer to shape it into something a studio would buy. That was real ditch-digging work, writers were so fragile. "Fragile" was his favorite word for people he thought jerks. It was especially useful with female stars.

One of his most successful relationships had been with Claudia De Lena, and one of the most enjoyable. He had really liked the kid, wanted to teach her the ropes. They had spent three months together working on the script. They went out to dinner together, they played golf together (Deere had been surprised when Claudia beat him). They went to the Santa Anita race track. They swam in Skippy Deere's pool with secretaries in bathing suits to take dictation. Claudia had even taken Deere to Vegas for a weekend at the Xanadu to meet her brother, Cross. They sometimes slept together, it was convenient.

The picture was a great financial success, and Claudia assumed she would earn a great deal of money on the back end. She had a percentage of Skippy Deere's percentage, and she knew that he was always positioned "upstream," as Deere liked to call gross percentage. But what Claudia did not know was that Deere had two different percentages, one on gross, the other on net. And Claudia's back end deal called for a piece of Skippy Deere's net position. Which, though the picture made over $100 million, came to nothing. The Studio's accounting procedure, Deere's percentage of the gross, and the cost of the picture easily wiped out net profits.

Claudia sued, and Skippy Deere settled for a small sum to preserve their friendship. When Claudia reproached him, Deere said, "This had nothing to do with our personal relationship, this is between our lawyers."

Skippy Deere often said, "I was human once, then I got married." More than that, he had fallen truly in love. His excuse was that he was young, and that he had married her because even then his keen eye knew she was a talented actress. In this he was correct, but his wife, Christi, did not have that magic quality on film that translated into a star. The best she could achieve was the third female lead.

But Deere really loved her. When he became a power in the movie industry, he did his best to make Christi a star. He called in favors from other producers, from directors, from studio chiefs, to get her big parts. In a few pictures he got her up to second female lead. But as she got older, she worked less. They had two children, but Christi became more and more unhappy and this took up a fair amount of Deere's work time.

Skippy Deere, like all successful producers, was insanely busy. He had to travel all over the world supervising his pictures, getting financing, developing projects. Coming in contact with so many beautiful, charming women, and needing companionship, he often had romantic liaisons, which he enjoyed with gusto, but still he loved his wife.

One day a Development girl brought him a script that she said was perfect for Christi, a foolproof star role that would exactly suit her talent. It was a dark movie, a woman who murdered her husband for love of a young poet and then had to escape the grief of her children and the suspicions of her in-laws. Then of course found redemption. It was very outrageous baloney, but it could work.

Skippy Deere had two problems: convincing a studio to make the movie and then convincing it to cast Christi in the part.

He called in all his favors. He took all his money on the back end. He persuaded a top male star to take a part that was really a featured role and got Dita Tommey to direct. Everything went like a dream. Christi played the part perfectly, Deere produced the film perfectly, that is to say, 90 percent of the budget actually got up on the screen.

During that time Deere was never unfaithful to his wife except for one night he spent in London arranging distribution, and then he fell only because the English girl was so thin he was intrigued by the logistics.

It worked. The picture was a commercial success, he made more on the sacrificial back end than he would have on a straight deal, and Christi won the Academy Award as best actress.

And, as Skippy Deere later said to Claudia, that was where the movie should have ended: Happily Ever After. But now his wife had found real self-esteem, now she sensed her true worth. The proof was that she became a vehicle star, she now received scripts delivered by messenger, with roles for beautiful, celluloid-magic personalities. Deere advised her to look for something more suited to her, the next picture would be crucial. He had never worried about her being faithful, indeed had conceded her the right to have fun when she was on location. But now in the few months after her Award—the toast of the town, invited to all the top parties, appearing in all the showbiz columns, courted by young actors struggling to get roles—she blossomed into a fresh young womanhood. She went out, openly, on dates with actors fifteen years her junior. The gossip journalists took note, the feminists among them cheering her on.

Skippy Deere seemingly took this very well. He understood the whole thing. After all, why did he himself keep screwing young girls? So why begrudge his wife equal pleasure? But then again why should he continue his extraordinary efforts to further Christi's career? Especially after she actually asked him for a role for one of her young lovers. He stopped looking for scripts for her, he stopped campaigning for her with other producers and directors and studio heads. And they, being older men, took umbrage for him in masculine brotherhood and no longer gave Christi any special consideration.

Christi made two more pictures in a starring role; both were flops because she was miscast. And so she spent the professional credit the Award had earned for her. In three years, she was back to playing third female leads.

By this time she had fallen in love with a young man who aspired to be a producer, indeed was very much like her husband, but he needed capital. So Christi sued for divorce, winning a huge settlement and $500,000 a year in alimony. Her lawyers never found out about Skippy's assets in Europe, so they parted friends. And now, seven years later, she had died in an automobile accident. By that time, although she had remained on Deere's Christmas card list, she was on his famous "Life Is Too Short" list, signifying he would not return her phone calls.

So Claudia De Lena had a twisted affection for Deere. For his exposing his true self to others, for his living his life so blatantly in his own self-interest, for his ability to look you in the eye and call you his friend while not caring that you knew he would never perform a true act of friendship. That he was such a cheerful, ardent hypocrite. And besides, Deere was a great persuader. And he was the only man she knew who could match wits with Cross. They took the next plane to Vegas.

BOOK IV

Cross De Lena
The Clericuzio

CHAPTER 6

BY THE TIME Cross reached the age of twenty-one, Pippi De Lena was impatient for Cross to follow his destiny. The most important fact in a man's life, conceded by all, was that he must make a living. He must earn his bread, put a roof over his head and clothes on his back, and feed the mouths of his children. To do that without unnecessary misery, a man had to have a certain degree of power in the world. It followed then, as night the day, that Cross must take his place in the Clericuzio Family. To do that, it was absolutely necessary he "make his bones."

Cross had a good reputation in the Family. His answer to Dante when Dante told him that Pippi was a Hammer was quoted happily by Don Domenico himself, who savored the words almost with ecstasy. "I don't know that. You don't know that. Nobody knows that. Where did you get that fuckin' hat?" What an answer, the Don exclaimed with delight. So young a man to be so discreet, and so witty, what a credit to his father. We must give this boy his chance. All this had been related to Pippi, and so he knew the time was ripe.

He started to groom Cross. He sent him out on collection assignments that were difficult and required force. He discussed the old history of the Family and how operations were executed. Nothing fancy, he stressed. But when you had to get fancy, it must be planned in extreme detail. Simple was extreme simplicity. You sealed off a small geographic area and then you caught the target in that area. Surveillance first, then car and hit man, then blocking cars for any pursuers, then going to ground for a time afterward so that you could not be immediately questioned. That was simple. For fancy, you got fancy. You could dream up anything but you had to back it up with solid planning. You only got fancy when it was absolutely necessary.

He even told Cross certain code words. A "Communion" was when the victim's body disappeared. That was fancy. A "Confirmation" was when the body was found. That was simple.

Pippi gave Cross a briefing on the Clericuzio Family. Their great war with the Santadio Family, which established their dominance. Pippi said nothing of his part in that war and was indeed scarce on details. Rather he praised Giorgio and Vincent and Petie. But most of all he praised Don Domenico for his farsightedness.

The Clericuzio had spun many webs, but its most extensive was gaming. It dominated all forms of casino and illegal gambling in the United States. It had a very subtle influence on the Native American casinos, it had a serious influence on sports betting, legal in Nevada and illegal in the rest of the country. The Family owned slot machine factories, had an interest in the manufacture of dice and cards, the supply of chinaware and silverware, the laundries for the gambling hotels. Gambling was the great jewel of their empire, and they ran a public relations campaign to make gambling legal in every state of the union.

Legal gambling all over the United States by federal law was now the Holy Grail of the Clericuzio Family. Not only casinos and lotteries but also wagering on sports: baseball, football, basketball, and all others. Sports were holy in America, and once gambling was legalized that holiness would descend on gambling itself. The profits would be enormous.

Giorgio, whose company managed some of the state lotteries, had given the Family a breakdown on the expected numbers. A minimum of two billion dollars was bet on the Super Bowl all over the United States, most of it illegally. The sports books in Vegas, legal betting alone ran up over fifty million. The World Series, depending on how many games were played, totaled about another billion. Basketball was much smaller, but the many playoff games carried another billion, and this was not counting the everyday betting during the season.

Once made legal, all this could be easily doubled or tripled with special lotteries and combination betting, except for the Super Bowl, whose increase would be tenfold and might even provide a net revenue for one day of $1 billion. The overall total could reach $100 billion, and the beauty was that there was no productivity involved, the only expenses were marketing and administration. What a great deal of money for the Clericuzio Family to rack up, a profit of at least $5 billion a year.

And the Clericuzio Family had the expertise and the political connections and pure force to control a great deal of this market. Giorgio had charts to show the complicated prizes that could be constructed based on big sports events. Gambling would be a great magnet to draw the money from the huge gold mine that was the American people.

So gambling was low-risk and had great growth potential. To achieve legal gambling, cost was no object and even greater risks were considered.

The Family was also made rich with income from drugs, but only at a very high level, it was too risky. They controlled European processing, provided political protection and judicial intervention, and they laundered the money. Their position in drugs was legally impregnable and extremely profitable. They dropped the black money in a chain of banks in Europe and a few banks in the United States. The structure of the law was outflanked.

But then, Pippi cautiously pointed out, despite all this there came times when risks had to be taken, when an iron fist must be shown. This the Family did with the utmost discretion and with terminal ferocity. And that was when you must earn the good life you led, when you truly earned your daily bread.

Shortly after his twenty-first birthday, Cross was finally put to the test.

One of the most prized political assets of the Clericuzio Family was Walter Wavven, the governor of Nevada. He was a man in his early fifties, tall and lanky, who wore a cowboy hat but dressed in perfectly tailored suits. He was a handsome man and though married had a lusty appetite for the female sex. He also enjoyed good food and good drink, loved to bet sports, and was an enthusiastic casino gambler. He was too tender of public feelings to expose these traits, or to risk romantic seductions. So he relied on Alfred Gronevelt and the Xanadu Hotel to satisfy these appetites while preserving his political and personal image of the God-fearing, steadfast believer in old-fashioned family values.

Gronevelt had recognized Wavven's special gifts early on and provided the financial base that enabled Wavven to climb the political ladder. When Wavven became governor of Nevada and wanted a relaxing weekend, Gronevelt gave him one of the prized Villas.

The Villas had been Gronevelt's greatest inspiration. . . .

Gronevelt had come to Vegas early, when it was still basically a western cowboy gambling town, and he had studied gambling and gamblers as a brilliant scientist might study an insect important to evolution. The one great mystery that would never be solved was why very rich men still wasted time gambling to win money they did not need. Gronevelt decided they did so to hide other vices, or they desired to conquer fate itself, but more than anything it was to show some sort of superiority to their fellow creatures. Therefore he reasoned that when they gambled they should be treated as gods. They would gamble as the gods gambled or the kings of France in Versailles.

So Gronevelt spent $100 million to build seven luxurious Villas and a special jewel-box casino on the grounds of the Xanadu Hotel (with his usual foresight he had bought much more land than the Xanadu needed). These Villas were small palaces, each could sleep six couples in six separate apartments, not merely suites. The furnishings were lavish: hand-woven rugs, marble floors, gold bathrooms, rich fabrics on the walls; dining rooms and kitchens staffed by the Hotel. The latest audiovisual equipment turned living rooms into theaters. The bars of these Villas were stocked with the finest wines and liquors and a box of illegal Havana cigars. Each Villa had its own outdoor swimming pool and inside Jacuzzi. All free to the gambler.

In the special security area that held the Villas was the small oval casino called the Pearl, where the high rollers could play in privacy and where the minimum bet in baccarat was a thousand dollars. The chips in this casino were also different, the black one-hundred-dollar chip was the lowest denominator; the five hundred, pale white threaded with gold; a gold-barred blue chip for the thousand; and the specially designed ten-thousand-dollar chip, with a real diamond embedded in the center of its gold surface. However, as a concession to the ladies, the roulette wheel would change hundred-dollar chips into five-dollar chips.

It was amazing that enormously wealthy men and women would take this bait. Gronevelt figured that all these extravagant RFB comps ran the Hotel fifty thousand dollars a week on the cost sheet. But these were written off on tax reports. Plus the prices of everything were inflated on paper. Figures (he kept a separate accounting) showed that each Villa made an average profit of a million dollars a week. The very fancy restaurants that served the Villas' and other important guests also made a profit as tax write-offs. On the cost sheets, a dinner for four totaled over a thousand dollars, which since the guests were comped, was written off as business expense for that amount in taxes. Since the meal cost the Hotel no more than a hundred dollars counting labor, there was a profit right there.

And so, to Gronevelt, the seven Villas were like seven crowns that he bestowed on the heads of only those gamblers who risked or made a Drop of over a million dollars on their two- or three-day stay. It didn't matter that they won or lost. Just that they gambled it. And they had to be prompt in paying their markers or they would be relegated to one of the suites in the Hotel itself, which, however plush, were not comparable to the Villas.

Of course there was a little more. These were Villas where important public men could bring their mistresses or boyfriends, where they could gamble in anonymity. And strange to say there were many titans of business, men worth hundreds of millions of dollars, even with wives and mistresses, who were lonely. Lonely for carefree feminine company, for women of exceptional sympathy. And for these men, the Villas would be furnished by Gronevelt with the proper beauty.

Governor Walter Wavven was one of these men. And he was the only exception to Gronevelt's rule of the million-dollar Drop. He gambled modestly and then with a purse supplied privately by Gronevelt, and if his markers exceeded a certain amount they were put on hold to be paid by his future winnings.

Wavven came to the Hotel to relax, to golf on the Xanadu course, and to drink and court the beauties supplied by Gronevelt.

Gronevelt played it very long with the governor. In twenty years he had never asked an outright favor, just the special access to present his arguments for legislation that would help the casino business in Vegas. Most of the time his point of view prevailed; when it did not, the governor gave him a detailed explanation of the political realities that had denied him. But the governor provided a valuable service in that he introduced Gronevelt to influential judges and politicians who could be swayed with hard cash.

Gronevelt nurtured in his secret heart the hope that, against long odds, Governor Walter Wavven might someday be the president of the United States. Then the rewards could be enormous.

But Fate foils the most cunning of men, as Gronevelt always acknowledged. The most insignificant of mortals become the agents of disaster to the most powerful. This particular agent was a twenty-five-year-old young man who became the lover of the governor's eldest child, a young woman of eighteen.

The governor was married to an intelligent, good-looking woman who was more fair, more liberal in her political views than her husband, though they worked well as a team. They had three children, and this family was a great political asset for the governor. Marcy, the eldest, was attending Berkeley, her choice and her mother's, not the governor's.

Freed from the stiffness of a political household, Marcy was entranced by the freedom of the university, its orientation toward the political left, its openness to new music, the insights offered by drugs. A true daughter of her father, she had a frankness of sexual interest. With that innocence and the natural instinct for fair play in the young, her sympathies were with the poor, the working class, the suffering minorities. She also fell in love with the purity of art. It was therefore very natural for her to hang out with students who were poets and musicians. It was even more natural that after a few casual encounters she fell in love with a fellow student who wrote plays and strummed the guitar and was poor.

His name was Theo Tatoski and he was perfect for a college romance. He had dark good looks, he came from a family of Catholics who worked in Detroit's auto factories and, with a poet's alliterative wit, always swore he would rather fuck than fit a fender. Despite this he worked part-time jobs to pay his tuition. He took himself very seriously, but this was mitigated by the fact that he had talent.

Marcy and Theo were inseparable for two years. She brought Theo to meet her family in the governor's mansion and was delighted that he was unimpressed by her father. Later in their bedroom in the state mansion, he informed her that her father was a typical phony.

Perhaps Theo had detected their condescension; the governor and his wife had both been extra friendly, extra courteous, determined to honor their daughter's choice, while privately deploring so unsuitable a match. The mother was not worried; she knew Theo's charm would fade with her daughter's growth. The father was uneasy but tried to make up for it with a more-than-common affability, even for a politician. After all, the governor was a champion of the working class, per his political platform, the mother was an educated liberal. A romance with Theo could only give Marcy a broader view of life. Meanwhile Marcy and Theo were living together, and planned to get married after they graduated. Theo would write and perform his plays, Marcy would be his muse and a professor of literature.

A stable arrangement. The young people did not seem to be heavily into drugs, their sexual relationship was no big deal. The governor even thought idly that if worse came to worst their marriage would help him politically, an indication to the public that despite his pure WASP background, his wealth, his culture, he democratically accepted a blue-collar son-in-law.

They all made their adjustments to a banal situation. The parents just wished that Theo was not such a bore.

But the young are perverse. Marcy, in her final year of college, fell in love with a fellow student who was rich and socially more acceptable to her parents than Theo. But she still wanted to keep Theo as a friend. She found it exciting to juggle two lovers without committing the technical sin of adultery. In her innocence, it made her feel unique.

The surprise was Theo. He reacted to the situation not as a tolerant Berkeley radical, but like some beknighted Polack. Despite his poetic, musical bohemianism, the teachings of feminist professors, the whole Berkeley atmosphere of sexual laissez-faire, he became violently jealous.

Theo had always been moodily eccentric, it was part of his youthful charm. In conversation, he often took the extremely revolutionary position that blowing up a hundred innocent people was a small price to pay for a free society in the future. Yet Marcy knew Theo could never do such a thing. Once when they came to their apartment after a two-week vacation, they had found a litter of newborn mice in their bed. Theo had simply put the tiny creatures out into the street unharmed. Marcy found that endearing.

But when Theo found out about Marcy's other lover, he struck her in the face. Then he burst into tears and begged her forgiveness. She forgave him. She still found their lovemaking exciting, more exciting because now she held more power with his knowledge of her betrayal. But he became progressively more violent, they quarreled often, life together was no longer such fun, and Marcy moved out of their apartment.

Her other lover faded. Marcy had a few other affairs. But she and Theo remained friends and slept together occasionally. Marcy planned to go East and do her master's in an Ivy League university, Theo moved down to Los Angeles to write plays and look for moviescript work. One of his short musical plays was being produced by a small theater group for three performances. He invited Marcy to come to see it.

Marcy flew to Los Angeles to see the play. It was so terrible half the audience walked out. So Marcy stayed over that night in Theo's apartment to console him. What exactly happened that night could never be established. What was proven was that sometime in the early morning, Theo stabbed Marcy to death, knife wounds in each eye. Then he stabbed himself in the stomach and called the police. In time to save his life, but not Marcy's.

The trial in California was, naturally, a huge media event. A daughter of the governor of Nevada murdered by a blue-collar poet who had been her lover for three years and was then dumped.

The defense lawyer, Molly Flanders, successfully specialized in "passion" murders, though this case proved to be her last criminal case before she entered entertainment law. Her tactics were classic. Witnesses were brought in to show that Marcy had at least six lovers, while Theo believed they were to be married. The rich, socially prominent, sluttish Marcy had dumped her sincere blue-collar playwright, whose mind then snapped. Flanders pleaded "temporary insanity" on her client's behalf. The most relished line (written for Molly by Claudia De Lena) was "He is forever not responsible for what he has done." A line that would have incited Don Clericuzio into a fury.

Theo looked properly stricken during his testimony. His parents, devout Catholics, had persuaded powerful members of the California clergy to take up the cause, and they testified that Theo had renounced his hedonistic ways and was now determined to study for the priesthood. It was pointed out that Theo had tried to kill himself and was therefore self-evidently remorseful, thus proving his insanity, as if the two went together. All this was varnished by the rhetoric of Molly Flanders, who painted a picture of the great contribution Theo could make to society if he was not punished for a foolish act triggered by a woman of loose morals who broke his blue-collar heart. A careless rich girl, now unfortunately dead.

Molly Flanders loved California juries. Intelligent, well-educated enough to understand the nuances of psychiatric trauma, exposed to the higher culture of theater, film, music, literature, they pulsed with empathy. When Flanders got through with them, the outcome was never in doubt. Theo was found not guilty by reason of temporary insanity. He was immediately signed to appear in his life story for a miniseries, not as the primary actor but as a minor one who sang songs of his own composition to link the story together. It was a completely satisfactory ending to a modern tragedy.

But the effect on Governor Walter Wavven, the girl's father, was disastrous. Alfred Gronevelt saw his twenty-year investment going down the drain, for Governor Wavven in the privacy of his Villa announced to Gronevelt that he would not stand for reelection. What was the point of acquiring power when any son-of-a-bitch low-life white trash could stab his daughter to death, almost cut off her head, and live his life a free man? Even worse, his beloved child had been dragged through the papers and TV as a silly cunt who deserved to be killed.

There are tragedies in life that cannot be cured, and for the governor this was one of them. He spent as much time as possible at the Xanadu Hotel but was not his old jolly self. He was not interested in showgirls, or the roll of the dice. He simply drank and played golf. Which posed a very delicate problem for Gronevelt.

He was deeply sympathetic to the governor's problem. You cannot cultivate a man for over twenty years, even out of self-interest, without having some affection for him. But the reality was that Governor Walter Wavven, resigning from politics, was no longer a key asset, had no future potential. He was simply a man destroying himself with booze. Also, when he gambled he did so distractedly, Gronevelt held two hundred grand of his markers. So now had come the time when he must refuse the governor the use of a Villa. Certainly he would give the governor a luxury suite in the Hotel, but it would be a demotion, and before doing that Gronevelt took a last stab at rehabilitation.

Gronevelt persuaded the governor to meet him for golf one morning. To complete the foursome he recruited Pippi De Lena and his son, Cross. Pippi had a crude wit the governor always appreciated, and Cross was such a good-looking and polite young man that his elders were always glad to have him around. After they played they went to the governor's Villa for a late lunch.

Wavven had lost a great deal of weight and seemed to take no pride in his appearance. He was in a stained sweatsuit and wore a baseball cap with the Xanadu logo. He was unshaven. He smiled often, not a politician smile, but a sort of shameful grimace. Gronevelt noticed that his teeth were very yellow. He was also extremely drunk.

Gronevelt decided to take the plunge. He said, "Governor, you are letting your family down, you are letting your friends down, and you are letting the people of Nevada down. You cannot go on like this."

"Sure I can," Walter Wavven said. "Fuck the people of Nevada. Who cares?"

Gronevelt said, "I do. I care about you. I'll put the money together and you must run for senator in the next election."

"Why the hell should I?" the governor said. "It doesn't mean anything in this fucking country. I'm governor of the great state of Nevada and that little prick murders my daughter and goes free. And I have to take it. People make jokes about my dead kid and pray for the murderer. You know what I pray for? That an atom bomb wipes out this fucking country and especially the state of California."

Pippi and Cross remained silent during all this. They were a little shaken by the governor's intensity. Also, both understood Gronevelt was working to a purpose.

"You have to put all of that behind you," Gronevelt said. "Don't let this tragedy destroy your life." His unctuousness would have irritated a saint.

The governor threw his baseball cap across the room and helped himself to another whiskey at the bar.

"I can't forget," he said. "I lie awake at night and dream about squeezing that little cocksucker's eyes out of his head. I want to set him on fire, I want to cut off his hands and legs. And then I want him to be alive so I can do it again and again." He smiled drunkenly at them, almost fell, they could see the yellow teeth and smell the decay in his mouth.

Wavven now seemed less drunk, his voice became quiet, he spoke almost conversationally. "Did you see how he stabbed her?" he asked. "He stabbed her through the eyes. The judge wouldn't let the jury see the photos. Prejudicial. But I, her father, could see the photos. And so little Theo goes free, with that smirk on his face. He stabbed my daughter through the eyes but he gets up every morning and he sees the sun shining. Oh, I wish I could kill them all—the judge, the jurors, the lawyers, all of them." He filled his glass and then walked around the room furiously, his speech a crazy ramble.

"I can't go out there and bullshit about what I no longer believe. Not while the little bastard is alive. He sat at my dinner table, my wife and I treated him like a human being even though we disliked him. We gave him the benefit of the doubt. Never give anybody the benefit of the doubt. We took him into our home, gave him a bed to sleep in with our daughter and he was laughing at us all the time. He was saying, 'Who gives a fuck if you're the governor? Who gives a fuck if you have money? Who gives a fuck that you are civilized, decent human beings? I will kill your daughter whenever I like and there is nothing you can do. I'll bring you all down. I'll fuck your daughter, then I'll kill her, and then I'll stick it up your ass and go free.' " Wavven staggered and Cross quickly went to hold him. The governor looked up beyond Cross, to the high mural-decorated ceiling above, all pink angels and white-clad saints. "I want him dead," the governor said and burst into tears. "I want him dead."

Gronevelt said quietly, "Walter, it will all go away, give it time. File for senator. You have the best years of your life ahead of you, you can still do so much."

Wavven shook himself away from Cross and said quite calmly to Gronevelt, "Don't you see, I don't believe in doing good anymore. I'm forbidden to tell anyone how I really feel, not even my wife. The hatred I feel. And I'll tell you something else. The voting public has contempt for me, they perceive me as a weak fool. A man who lets his daughter get murdered, then can't get him punished. Who would trust the welfare of the great state of Nevada to such a man?" He was sneering now. "That little fuck could get elected easier than me." He paused for a moment. "Alfred, forget it. I'm not running for anything."

Gronevelt was studying him carefully. He was catching something that Pippi and Cross did not. Passionate grief so often led to weakness, but Gronevelt decided to take the risk. He said, "Walter, will you run for senator if the man is punished? Will you be the man you were?"

The governor seemed not to understand. His eyes rolled slightly toward Pippi and Cross, then stared into Gronevelt's face. Gronevelt said to Pippi and Cross, "Wait for me in my office."

Pippi and Cross quickly left. Gronevelt and Governor Wavven were alone. Gronevelt said to him gravely, "Walter, you and I must be very direct for the first time in our lives. We've known each other twenty years, have you ever found me to be indiscreet? So answer. It will be safe. Will you run again if that boy is dead?"

The governor went to the bar and poured whiskey. But he did not drink. He smiled. "I'll file the day after I go to that boy's funeral to show my forgiveness," he said. "My voters will love that."

Gronevelt relaxed. It was done. Out of relief, he indulged his temper. "First, go see your dentist," he told the governor. "You have to get those fucking teeth cleaned."

Pippi and Cross were waiting for Gronevelt back in his penthouse office suite. He led them into his living quarters so that they could be more comfortable, then told them what had been said.

"The governor is okay?" Pippi asked.

"The governor was not as drunk as he pretended," Gronevelt said. "He gave me the message without really implicating himself."

"I'll fly East tonight," Pippi said. "This must get the Clericuzio OK."

"Tell them I think the governor is a man who can go all the way," Gronevelt said. "To the very top. He would be an invaluable friend."

"Giorgio and the Don will understand that," Pippi said. "I just have to lay everything out and get the OK."

Gronevelt looked at Cross and smiled, then he turned to Pippi. He said gently, "Pippi, I think it's time Cross joined the Family. I think he should fly East with you."

But Giorgio Clericuzio decided to come West to Vegas for the meeting. He wanted to be briefed by Gronevelt himself, and Gronevelt had not traveled for the last ten years.

Giorgio and his bodyguards were established in one of the Villas, though he was not a high roller. Gronevelt was a man who knew how to make exceptions. He had refused the Villas to powerful politicians, financial giants, to some of the most famous movie stars in Hollywood, to beautiful women who had slept with him, to close personal friends. Even Pippi De Lena. But he gave a Villa to Giorgio Clericuzio, though he knew Giorgio had spartan tastes and did not really appreciate extraordinary luxuries. Every mark of respect counted, mounted up, and one breach, no matter how tiny, could be remembered someday.

They met in Giorgio's Villa. Gronevelt, Pippi, and Giorgio . . .

Gronevelt explained the situation. "The governor can be an enormous asset to the Family," Gronevelt said. "If he pulls himself together, he may go all the way. First, senator, then the presidency. That happens and you have a good shot at getting sports gambling legalized all over the country. That will be worth billions to the Family and those billions will not be black money. It will be white money. I say it's something we have to do."

White money was far more valuable than black money. But Giorgio's great asset was that he was never stampeded into rash decisions. "Does the governor know you are with us?"

"Not for sure," Gronevelt said. "But he must have heard rumors. And he's not a dummy. I've done some things for him that he knows I couldn't do if I were alone. And he's clever. All he said was that he would run for office if the kid were dead. He didn't ask me to do anything. He's a great con, he wasn't that drunk when he broke down. I think he figured the whole thing out. He was sincere, but he was faking it too. He couldn't figure out his revenge but he had the idea I could do something. He is suffering, but he's also scheming." He paused for a moment. "If we come through, he'll run for senator and he will be our senator."

Giorgio prowled uneasily in the room, avoiding the statues on their pedestals, the curtained Jacuzzi whose marble seemed to shine through the fabric. He said to Gronevelt, "You promised him without our OK?"

"Yes," Gronevelt said. "It was a matter of persuasion. I had to be positive to give him a sense that he still has power. That he could, still, cause things to happen, and so make power appeal to him again."

Giorgio sighed. "I hate this part of the business," he said.

Pippi smiled. Giorgio was so full of shit. He had helped wipe out the Santadio Family with a savageness that made the old Don proud.

"I think we need Pippi's expertise on this," Gronevelt said. "And I think it's time for his son, Cross, to join the Family."

Giorgio looked at Pippi. "Do you think Cross is ready?" he asked.

Pippi said, "He's had all the gravy, it's time for him to earn his living."

"But will he do it?" Giorgio asked. "It's a big step."

"I'll talk to him," Pippi said. "He'll do it."

Giorgio turned toward Gronevelt. "We do it for the governor, then what if he forgets about us? We take the risk and it's all for nothing. Here's a man who is governor of Nevada, his daughter gets killed and he lies down. He has no balls."

"He did do something, he came to me," Gronevelt said. "You have to understand people like the governor. That took a lot of balls for him."

"So he'll come through?" Giorgio said.

"We'll save him for the few big things," Gronevelt said. "I've done business with him for twenty years. I guarantee he comes through if he's handled right. He knows the score, he's very smart."

Giorgio said, "Pippi, it has to look like an accident. This will get a lot of heat. We want the governor to escape any innuendos from his enemies or the papers and that fucking TV."

Gronevelt said, "Yes, it's important that nothing can be implied about the governor."

Giorgio said, "Maybe this is too tricky for Cross to make his bones on."

"No, this is perfect for him," Pippi said. And they could not object. Pippi was the commander in the field. He had proved himself in many operations of this kind, especially in the great war against the Santadio. He had often told the Clericuzio Family, "It's my ass on the line, if I get stuck, I want it to be my fault, not somebody else's."

Giorgio clapped his hands. "Okay, let's get it done. Alfred, how about a round of golf in the morning? Tomorrow night I go on business to L.A. and the day after I go back East. Pippi, let me know who you want from the Enclave to help, and tell me if Cross is in or out."

And with that Pippi knew that Cross would never be admitted to the inside of the Clericuzio Family if he refused this operation.

Golf had become a passion for Pippi's generation of the Clericuzio Family; the old Don made malicious jokes that it was a game for *Brugliones.* Pippi and Cross were on the Xanadu course that afternoon. They didn't use driving carts; Pippi wanted the exercise of walking and the solitude of the greens.

Just off the ninth hole there was an orchard of trees with a bench beneath. They sat there.

"I won't live forever," Pippi said. "And you have to make a living. The Collection Agency is a big moneymaker but tough to keep. You have to be in solid with the Clericuzio Family." Pippi had prepared Cross, had sent him on some tough collecting missions where he had to use force and abuse, had exposed him to Family gossip; he knew the score. Pippi had waited patiently for the right situation, for a target that would not arouse sympathy.

Cross said quietly, "I understand."

Pippi said, "That guy that killed the governor's daughter. A punk prick and he gets away with it. That's not right."

Cross was amused by his father's psychology. "And the governor is our friend," he said.

"That's right," Pippi said. "Cross, you can say no, remember that. But I want you to help me on a job I have to do."

Cross looked down the rolling greens, the flags above the holes dead still in the desert air, the silvery mountain ranges beyond, the sky reflecting the neon signs of the Strip he could not see. He knew his life was about to change and he felt a moment of dread. "If I don't like it I can always go to work for Gronevelt," he said. But he let his hand rest on his father's shoulder for a moment to let him know it was a joke.

Pippi grinned at him. "This job is for Gronevelt. You saw him with the governor. Well, we're going to give him his wish. Gronevelt had to get the OK from Giorgio. And I said you would help me out."

Far away on one of the greens, Cross could see a foursome of two women and two men shimmering cartoonlike in the desert sun. "I have to make my bones," he said to his father. He knew he had to agree or live a completely different life. And he loved the life he led, working for his father, hanging out at the Xanadu, the direction of Gronevelt, the beautiful showgirls, the easy money, the sense of power. And once he did so he should never be subject to the fates of ordinary men.

"I'll do all the planning," Pippi said. "I'll be with you all the way. There's no danger. But you have to be the shooter."

Cross rose from the bench. He could see the flags on the seven Villas flapping, though there was no breeze on the golf course. For the first time in his young life he felt the ache of a world that was to be lost. "I'm with you," he said.

In the three weeks that followed, Pippi gave Cross an indoctrination. He explained that they were waiting for a surveillance team report on Theo, his movements, his habits, recent photos. Also, an operations team of six men from the Enclave in New York were moving into place in Los Angeles where Theo was still living. The whole operation plan would be based on the report of the surveillance team. Then Pippi lectured Cross on the philosophy.

"This is a business," he said. "You take all the precautions to prevent the downside. Anybody can knock somebody off. The trick is never to get caught. That is the sin. And never think of the personalities involved. When the head of General Motors throws fifty thousand people out of work, that's business. He can't help wrecking their lives, he has to do it. Cigarettes kill thousands of people, but what can you do? People want to smoke and you can't ban a business that generates billions of dollars. Same with guns, everybody has a gun, everybody kills everybody, but it's a billion-dollar industry, you can't get rid of it. What can you do? People must earn a living, that comes first. All the time. You don't believe that, go live in the shit."

The Clericuzio Family was very strict, Pippi told Cross. "You have to get their OK. You can't go around killing people because they spit on your shoe. The Family has to be with you because they can make you jailproof."

Cross listened. He only asked one question. "Giorgio wants it to look like an accident? How do we do that?"

Pippi laughed. "Never let anybody tell you how to run your operation. They can go fuck themselves. They tell me their maximum expectations. I do what is best for me. And the best is to be simple.

Very, very simple. And when you have to get fancy, get very, very fancy."

When the surveillance reports came, Pippi made Cross study all the data. There were some photos of Theo, photos of his car showing its license plates. A map of the road he traveled from Brentwood up to Oxnard to visit a girlfriend. Cross said to his father, "He can still get a girlfriend?"

"You don't know women," Pippi said. "If they like you, you can piss in the sink. If they don't like you, you can make them the Queen of England and they'll shit on you."

Pippi flew into L.A. to set up his operations team. He came back two days later and told Cross, "Tomorrow night."

The next day, before dawn, to escape the heat of the desert, they drove from Las Vegas to Los Angeles. Driving across the desert, Pippi told Cross to relax. Cross was mesmerized by the glorious sunrise that seemed to melt the desert sand into a deep river of gold lapping at the foot of the distant Sierra Nevadas. He felt anxious. He wanted to get the job done.

They arrived in a Family house in the Pacific Palisades where the six-man crew from the Bronx Enclave was awaiting them. In the driveway was a stolen car that had been repainted and had false license plates. Also at the house were the untraceable guns that were to be used.

Cross was surprised at the luxuriousness of the house. It had a beautiful view of the ocean across the highway, a swimming pool, and a huge sundeck. It also had six bedrooms. The men seemed to know Pippi well. But they were not introduced to Cross nor he to them.

They had eleven hours to kill before the operation started at midnight. The other men, ignoring a huge TV set, started a card game on the sundeck; they were all in bathing suits. Pippi smiled at Cross and said, "Shit, I forgot about the swimming pool."

"That's OK," Cross said. "We can go swimming in our shorts." The house was secluded, shielded by enormous trees and an encircling hedge.

"We can go bare-assed," Pippi said. "Nobody can see except the helicopters and they'll be looking at all the broads sunbathing outside their Malibu houses."

Both of them swam and sunbathed for a few hours and then ate a meal prepared by one of the six-man crew. The meal was steak, cooked on the sundeck grill, and a salad of arugula and lettuce. The other men drank red wine with their food, but Cross had a club soda. He noticed that all the men ate and drank sparingly.

After the meal, Pippi took Cross on a reconnaissance in the stolen car. They drove to the western-style restaurant and coffee shop farther down the Pacific Coast Highway where they would find Theo. The surveillance reports showed that on Wednesday nights Theo, on his way to Oxnard, had made a habit of stopping at the Pacific Coast Highway Restaurant at around midnight for coffee and ham and eggs. That he would leave about one in the morning. That night a surveillance team of two men would be tailing him and would report by telephone when he was on the way.

Back at the house Pippi rebriefed the men on the operation. The six men would have three cars. One car would precede them, another would bring up the rear, the third car would park in the restaurant lot and be prepared for any emergency.

Cross and Pippi sat on the sundeck waiting for the phone call. There were five cars in the driveway, all black, shining in the moonlight like bugs. The six men from the Enclave continued their card game, playing with silver coins: nickels, dimes, and quarters. Finally at eleven-thirty the phone call came: Theo was on his way from Brentwood to the restaurant. The six men got in three cars and drove away to take up their appointed posts. Pippi and Cross got into the stolen car and waited another fifteen minutes before they left. Cross had in the pocket of his jacket a small .22 pistol, which, though it had no silencer, only gave off a sharp little pop; Pippi carried a Glock that would make a loud report. Ever since his only arrest for murder, Pippi always refused to carry a silencer.

Pippi drove. The operation had been planned in the most specific detail. No member of the operations team was to go into the restaurant. Detectives would question the help about all the customers. The surveillance team had reported what Theo was wearing, the car he was driving, the license plates. They were lucky that Theo's car was a flaming red and that it was a cheap Ford, easily identifiable in an area where Mercedeses and Porsches were commonplace.

When Pippi and Cross arrived in the parking lot of the restaurant, they could see Theo's car was already there. Pippi parked next to it. Then he turned off the car lights and ignition and sat in the darkness. Across the Pacific Coast Highway they saw the ocean shimmering, parted with streaks of gold that were the moonlight. They saw one of their team cars parked on the far side of the lot. They knew their other two teams were at their stations on the highway waiting to shepherd them back to the house, ready to cut off any pursuers and intercept any problems before them.

Cross looked at his watch. It was twelve-thirty. They had to wait another fifteen minutes. Suddenly Pippi hit his shoulder. "He's early," Pippi said. "Go!"

Cross saw the figure emerging from the restaurant, caught in the glow of the door lights. He was struck by the boyishness of the figure, slight and short, a shock of curly hair above the pale, thin face. Theo looked too frail to be a murderer.

Then they were surprised. Theo, instead of going to his car, walked across the Pacific Coast Highway, dodging traffic. On the other side, he strolled out onto the open beach to the very edge, daring the waves. He stood there gazing at the ocean, the yellow moon setting on the horizon so far away. Then he turned and came back across the highway and into the parking lot. He had let the waves reach him, and there was the squish of water in his fashionable boots.

Cross slowly got out of the car. Theo was almost on him. Cross waited for Theo to go past, then smiled politely to let Theo get into his car. When Theo was inside, Cross drew the gun. Theo, about to put his key into the ignition, his car window down, raised his eyes, aware of the shadow. At the moment Cross fired, they looked into each other's eyes. Theo was frozen as the bullet smashed into his face, which instantly became a mask of blood, the eyes staring out. Cross yanked open the door and fired two more bullets into the top of Theo's head. Blood sprayed into his face. Then he threw a pouch of drugs on the floor of Theo's car. He slammed the door shut. Pippi had started up the motor of his car just as Cross fired. Now he opened the car door, and Cross hopped in. According to plan he had not dropped the pistol. That would have made it look like a planned hit instead of a drug deal gone sour.

Pippi drove out of the lot, and their cover car pulled out behind them. The two lead cars swung into position, and five minutes later they were back at the Family house. Ten minutes after that, Pippi and Cross were in Pippi's car heading toward Vegas. The operations team would get rid of the stolen car and the gun.

When they drove past the restaurant there were no signs of police activity. Obviously Theo was still undiscovered. Pippi turned the car radio on and listened to the news broadcasts. There was nothing. "Perfect," Pippi said. "When you plan right, it always goes perfect."

They arrived in Las Vegas as the sun was coming up, the desert a sullen red sea. Cross never forgot that ride through the desert, through the darkness, through the moonlight that never seemed to end. And then the sun coming up and then, a little later, the neon lights of the Vegas strip shining like a beacon heralding safety, the awakening from a nightmare. Vegas was never dark.

At almost that exact moment, Theo was discovered, his face ghostly in a paler dawn. Publicity centered on the fact that Theo was in possession of half a million dollars worth of cocaine. It was obviously a drug deal gone sour. The governor was in the clear.

Cross observed many things from this event. That the drugs he had planted on Theo cost no more than ten thousand dollars, although the authorities had placed the value at half a million; that the governor was praised for the fact that he sent condolences to Theo's family; that in a week the media never referred to the matter again.

Pippi and Cross were summoned East for an audience with Giorgio. Giorgio commended them both for an intelligent and well-executed operation, making no mention of the fact that it was supposed to look like an accident. And Cross was aware on this visit that the Clericuzio Family treated him with the respect due the Family Hammer. The primary evidence of this was that Cross was given a percentage of the income of the gambling books, legal and illegal, in Las Vegas. It was understood that he was now an official member of the Clericuzio Family, to be called to duty on special occasions with bonuses calculated on the risk of the project.

. . .

Gronevelt, too, had his reward. After Walter Wavven was elected senator, he took a weekend retreat at the Xanadu. Gronevelt gave him a Villa and went to congratulate him on his victory.

Senator Wavven was back in his old form. He was gambling and winning, he had little dinners with the showgirls of the Xanadu. He seemed completely recovered. He made only one reference to his earlier crisis. He said to Gronevelt, "Alfred, you have a blank check with me."

Gronevelt said, smiling, "No man can afford to carry blank checks in his wallet, but thank you."

He didn't want checks that paid off all the senator's debt. He wanted a long, continuing friendship, one that would never end.

In the next five years, Cross became an expert on gambling and running a casino hotel. He served as an assistant to Gronevelt, though his primary job was still working with his father, Pippi, not only in running the Collection Agency, which he was now certified to inherit, but also as the number two Hammer for the Clericuzio Family.

By the age of twenty-five, Cross was known in the Clericuzio Family as the Little Hammer. He himself found it curious that he was so cold about his work. His targets were never people he knew. They were lumps of flesh enclosed in defenseless skin; the skeleton beneath gave them the outline of wild animals he had hunted with his father when he was a boy. He did fear the risk but only cerebrally; there was no physical anxiety. There were moments in his life's repose, sometimes when he awoke in the morning with a vague terror as if he had some terrible nightmare. Then there were times when he was depressed, when he called up the memory of his sister and his mother, little scenes from childhood and some visits after the breakup of the family.

He remembered his mother's cheek, her flesh so warm, her satin skin so porous that he imagined he could hear the blood flow underneath, contained, safe. But in his dreams the skin crumbled like ash, blood washing over the obscene breaks into scarlet waterfalls.

Which triggered other memories. When his mother kissed him with cold lips, her arms embracing him for tiny moments of politeness. She never held his hand as she did Claudia's. The times he visited and left her house short of breath, his chest burning as if bruised. He never felt her loss in the present, he only felt her lost in his past.

When he thought of his sister, Claudia, he did not feel this loss. Their past together existed and she was still part of his life, though not enough. He remembered how they used to fight in the winter. They kept their fists in their overcoat pockets and swung at each other. A harmless duel. All was as it should be, Cross thought, except that sometimes he missed his mother and his sister. Still, he was happy with his father and the Clericuzio Family.

So in his twenty-fifth year Cross became involved in his final operation as a Hammer of the Family. The target was someone he had known all his life. . . .

A vast FBI probe destroyed many of the titular Barons, some true *Brugliones,* across the country, and among them was Virginio Ballazzo, now the ruler of the largest Family on the Eastern Seaboard.

Virginio Ballazzo was a Baron of the Clericuzio Family for over twenty years and had been dutiful in wetting the Clericuzio beak. In return the Clericuzio made him rich; at the time of his fall, Ballazzo was worth over $50 million. He and his family lived in very good style indeed. And yet the unforeseen happened. Virginio Ballazzo, despite his debt, betrayed those who had raised him so high. He broke the law of *omertà,* the code that forbade giving any information to the authorities.

One of the charges against him was murder, but it was not so much fear of imprisonment that made him turn traitor; after all, New York had no death penalty. And no matter how long his penalty, if indeed he was convicted, the Clericuzio would get him out in ten years, would ensure that even those ten years would be easy time. He knew the repertoire. At his trial, witnesses would perjure themselves in his behalf, jurors could be approached with bribes. Even after he had served a few years, a new case would be prepared, presenting new evidence, showing that he was innocent. There was one famous case in which the Clericuzio had done such a thing after one of their clients had served five years. The man had gotten out and the state had presented him with over a million dollars as reparation for his "false" imprisonment.

No, Ballazzo had no fear of prison. What made him turn traitor was that the Federal Government threatened to seize all his worldly goods under the RICO laws passed by Congress to crush crime. Ballazzo could not bear that he and his children would lose their palatial home in New Jersey, the luxurious condo in Florida, the horse farm in Kentucky that had produced three also-rans in the Kentucky Derby. For the infamous RICO laws permitted the government to seize all worldly goods of those arrested for criminal conspiracy. The stocks and bonds, the antique cars might be taken. Don Clericuzio himself had been angered by the RICO laws, but his only comment was "the rich will rue this thing, the day will come when they will arrest the whole of Wall Street under this RICO law."

It was not luck but foresight that the Clericuzio had removed their old friend Ballazzo from its confidence in the last few years. He had become too flashy for their tastes. *The New York Times* had run a story on his collection of antique cars, Virginio Ballazzo at the wheel of a 1935 Rolls-Royce, a debonair visored cap on his head. Virginio Ballazzo, on the TV at the running of the Kentucky Derby, riding crop in hand, talked about the beauty of the sport of kings. There he was identified as a wealthy importer of rugs. All this was too much for the Clericuzio Family, they became wary of him.

When Virginio Ballazzo opened discussions with the United States District Attorney, it was Ballazzo's lawyer who informed the Clericuzio family. The Don, who was semiretired, immediately took charge from his son Giorgio. This was a situation that required a Sicilian hand.

A Family conference was held: Don Clericuzio; his three sons, Giorgio, Vincent, and Petie; and Pippi De Lena. It was true that Ballazzo could damage the Family structure, but only the lower levels would suffer greatly. The traitor could give valuable information but no legal proof. Giorgio suggested that if worse came to worst, they could always set up headquarters in a foreign country, but the Don dismissed this angrily. Where else could they live but in America? America had made them rich, America was the most powerful country in the world and protected its rich. The Don often quoted the saying, "Rather a hundred guilty men go free than one innocent man be punished," then added, "What a beautiful country." The trouble was that everyone got soft because of such good living. In Sicily Ballazzo would never have dared become a traitor, would never even have dreamed of breaking the law of *omertà.* His own sons would have killed him.

"I'm too old to live in a foreign country," the Don said. "I will not be driven from my home by a traitor."

A small problem in and of himself, Virginio Ballazzo was a symptom, an infection. There were many more like him, who did not abide by the old laws that had made them all strong. There was a Family *Bruglione* in Louisiana, another in Chicago, and another in Tampa, who flaunted their wealth, who showed off their power for all the world to see. And then these *cafoni* when they were caught sought to escape the punishment they had earned by their own carelessness. By breaking the law of *omertà.* By betraying their fellows. This rot must be eradicated. That was the Don's position. But now he would listen to the others; after all, he was old, perhaps there were other solutions.

Giorgio outlined what was happening. Ballazzo was bargaining with the government attorneys. He would willingly go to jail if the government promised not to invoke the RICO laws, if his wife and children could keep his fortune. And of course he was bargaining not to go to jail, for that he would have to testify in court against the people he betrayed. He and his wife would be placed in a Witness Protection Program and would live the rest of their lives under false identities. Some plastic surgery would be performed. And his children would live the rest of their lives in respectable comfort. That was the deal.

Ballazzo, whatever his faults, was a doting father, they all agreed. He had three well-brought-up children. One son was graduating from the Harvard School of Business, the daughter, Ceil, had a fancy cosmetics store on Fifth Avenue, another son did computer work in the space program. They were all deserving of their good fortunes. They were true Americans and lived the American dream.

"So," the old Don said, "we will send a message to Virginio that will make sense to him. He can inform on everyone else. He can send them all to jail or to the bottom of the ocean. But if he speaks one word about the Clericuzio, his children are forfeit."

Pippi De Lena said, "Threats don't seem to scare anybody anymore."

"The threat will be from me personally," Don Domenico said. "He will believe me. Promise him nothing for himself. He understands."

It was Vincent who spoke up then. "We'll never be able to get near him once he's in the Protection Program."

The Don spoke to Pippi De Lena. "And you, *Martèllo* of mine, what do you say to that?"

Pippi De Lena shrugged. "After he testifies, after they hide him away in the Protection Program, sure we can. But there will be a lot of heat, a lot of publicity. Is it worth it? Does it change anything?"

The Don said, "The publicity, the heat, is what makes it worth doing. We will send the world our message. In fact when it is done it should be done a *bella figura.*"

Giorgio said, "We could just let events take their course. No matter what Ballazzo says, it can't bury us. Pop, your answer is a short-term answer."

The Don pondered that. "What you say is true. But is there a long-term answer to anything? Life is full of doubts, of short-term answers. And you doubt that punishment will stop those others who will be trapped? It may or may not. It will certainly stop some. God himself could not create a world without punishment. I will talk personally to Ballazzo's lawyer. He will understand me. He will give the message. And Ballazzo will believe it." He paused for a moment and then sighed. "After the trials, we will do the job."

"And his wife?" Giorgio asked.

"A good woman," the Don said. "But she has become too American. We cannot leave a bereaved widow to shout her grief and secrets."

Petie spoke for the first time. "And Virginio's children?" Petie was the true assassin.

"Not if it's not necessary. We are not monsters," Don Domenico said. "And Ballazzo never told the children his business. He wanted the world to believe that he was a horse rider. So let him ride his horses at the bottom of the ocean." They were all silent. Then the Don said sadly, "Let the little ones go. After all, we live in a country where children do not avenge their parents."

The following day the message was transmitted to Virginio Ballazzo by his lawyer. In all these messages, the language was flowery. When the Don spoke to the lawyer he expressed his hope that his old friend Virginio Ballazzo had only the fondest memories of the Clericuzio, who would always look out for their unfortunate friend's interests. The Don told the lawyer that Ballazzo should never fear for his children where danger lurked, even on Fifth Avenue, but that the Don himself would guarantee their safety. He, the Don, knew how highly Ballazzo prized his children; that jail, the electric chair, the devils in hell, could not frighten his brave friend, only the specter of harm to his children. "Tell him," the Don said to the lawyer, "that I, personally, I, Don Domenico Clericuzio, guarantee that no misfortune will befall them."

The lawyer delivered this message word for word to his client, who responded as follows. "Tell my friend, my dearest friend, who grew up with my father in Sicily, that I rely on his guarantees with utmost gratitude. Tell him I have only the fondest memories of all the Clericuzio, so profound that I cannot even speak of them. I kiss his hand."

Then Ballazzo sang, "Tra la la . . ." at his lawyer. "I think we better go over our testimony very carefully," he said. "We do not want to involve my good friend. . . ."

"Yes," the lawyer said, as he reported later to the Don.

Everything proceeded according to plan. Virginio Ballazzo broke *omertà* and testified, sending numerous underlings to jail and even implicating a deputy mayor of New York. But not a word of the Clericuzio. Then the Ballazzos, man and wife, disappeared into the Witness Protection Program.

The newspapers and TV were jubilant, the mighty Mafia had been broken. There were hundreds of photos, live TV action shots of these villains being hauled off to prison. Ballazzo took up the whole centerfold of the *Daily News,* TOP MAFIA DON FALLS. It showed him with his antique cars, his Kentucky Derby horses, his impressive London wardrobe. It was an orgy.

When the Don gave Pippi the assignment of tracking down the Ballazzo couple and punishing them, he said, "Do it in such a way that it will get the same publicity as they are getting now. We don't want them to forget our Virginio." But it was to take the Hammer more than a year to complete this assignment.

Cross remembered Ballazzo and had fond memories of him as a jovial, generous man. He and Pippi had had dinner at the Ballazzo house, for Mrs. Ballazzo had a reputation as a fine Italian cook, particularly for her macaroni and cauliflower with garlic and herbs, a dish Cross still remembered. He had played with the Ballazzo children as a child and had even fallen in love with Ballazzo's daughter, Ceil, when they were teenagers. She had written him from college after that magical Sunday, but he had never answered. Alone with Pippi now, he said, "I don't want to do this operation."

His father looked at him and then smiled sadly. He said, "Cross, it happens sometimes, you have to get used to it. You won't survive otherwise."

Cross shook his head. "I can't do it," he said.

Pippi sighed. "OK," he said. "I'll tell them I'm going to use you for planning. I'll make them give me Dante for the actual operation."

Pippi set up the probe. The Clericuzio Family, with huge bribes, penetrated the screen of the Witness Protection Program.

The Ballazzos felt secure in their new identities, false birth certificates, new social security numbers, marriage papers, and the plastic surgery that had altered their faces so that they looked ten years younger. However, their body builds, their gestures, their voices, made them more easily identifiable than they realized.

Old habits die hard. On a Saturday night Virginio Ballazzo and his wife drove to the small South Dakota town near their new home to gamble in the small-time joint operating under the local option. On their way home, Pippi De Lena and Dante Clericuzio, with a crew of six other men, intercepted them. Dante, violating the plan, could not resist making himself known to the couple before he pulled the trigger of his shotgun.

No attempt was made to conceal the bodies. No valuables were taken. It was perceived as an act of retaliation, and it sent a message to the world. There was a torrent of rage from the press and television, the authorities promised justice would be done. Indeed, there was enough of a furor to make the whole Clericuzio Empire seem to be in jeopardy.

Pippi was forced to hide in Sicily for two years. Dante became the number one Hammer of the Family. Cross was made the *Bruglione* of the Western Empire of the Clericuzio. His refusal to take part in the Ballazzo execution had been noted. He did not have the temperament to be a true Hammer.

Before Pippi disappeared into Sicily for two years, he had a final meeting and bon voyage dinner with Don Clericuzio and his son Giorgio.

"I must apologize for my son," Pippi said. "Cross is young and the young are sentimental. He was very fond of the Ballazzos."

"We were fond of Virginio," the Don said. "I never liked a man better."

"Then why did we kill him?" Giorgio asked. "It's caused more trouble than it's worth."

Don Clericuzio gave him a stern look. "You cannot live a life without order. If you have power, you must use it for strict justice. Ballazzo committed a great offense. Pippi understands that, no, Pippi?"

"Of course, Don Domenico," Pippi said. "But you and I are of the old school. Our sons don't understand." He paused for a moment. "I wanted to thank you also for making Cross your *Bruglione* in the West while I'm gone. He will not disappoint you."

"I know that," the Don said. "I have as much trust in him as I have in you. He is intelligent and his squeamishness is that of youth. Time will harden his heart."

They were having a dinner cooked and served by a woman whose husband worked in the Enclave. She had forgotten the Don's bowl of grated Parmesan cheese, and Pippi went into the kitchen for the grater and brought the bowl to the Don. He carefully grated the cheese into the bowl and watched the Don dip his huge silver spoon into the yellowish mound, put it in his mouth, and then sip from his glass of powerful homemade wine. This was a man with a belly, Pippi thought. Over eighty years old and he could still order the death of a sinner, and also eat this strong cheese and harsh wine. He said casually, "Is Rose Marie in the house? I'd like to say good-bye to her."

"She's having one of her fucking spells," Giorgio said. "She's locked herself in her room, thank God, or else we wouldn't be able to enjoy our dinner."

"Ah," Pippi said. "I always thought she'd get better with time."

"She thinks too much," the Don said. "She loves her son Dante too much. She refuses to understand. The world is what it is, and you are what you are."

Giorgio said smoothly, "Pippi, how do you rate Dante after this Ballazzo operation? Did he show any nerves?"

Pippi shrugged and remained silent. The Don gave a little grunt and looked at him sharply. "You can be frank," the Don said. "Giorgio is his uncle and I am his grandfather. We are all of one blood and are permitted to judge each other."

Pippi stopped eating and looked directly at the Don and Giorgio. He said almost regretfully, "Dante has a bloody mouth."

In their world this was an idiom for a man who went beyond savageness, an intimation of bestiality while doing a necessary piece of work. It was strictly forbidden in the Clericuzio Family.

Giorgio leaned back in his chair and said, "Jesus Christ." The Don gave Giorgio a disapproving look for his blasphemy and then waved a hand at Pippi to continue. He did not seem surprised.

"He was a good pupil," Pippi said. "He has the temperament and the physical strength. He's very quick and he is intelligent. But he takes too much pleasure in his work. He took too much time with the Ballazzos. He talked to them for ten minutes before he shot the woman. Then he waited another five minutes before shooting Ballazzo. That's not to my taste but more important you never can tell when it might lead to danger, every minute might count. On other jobs he was unnecessarily cruel, a throwback to the old days when they thought it clever to hang a man on a meathook. I don't want to go into details."

Giorgio said angrily, "It's because that prick of a nephew is short. He's a fucking midget. And then he wears those fucking hats. Where the hell does he get them?"

The Don said good-humoredly, "The same place the blacks get their hats. In Sicily when I was growing up everybody wore a funny hat. Who knows why? Who cares? Now, stop talking nonsense. I wore funny hats, too. Maybe it runs in the family. It's his mother who put all kinds of nonsense in his head ever since he was little. She should have married again. Widows are like spiders. They spin too much."

Giorgio said with intensity, "But he's good at his job."

"Better than Cross could ever be," Pippi said diplomatically. "But sometimes I think he's crazy like his mother." He paused. "He even scares me sometimes."

The Don took a mouthful of cheese and wine. "Giorgio," he said, "instruct your nephew, repair his fault. It could be dangerous to all of us in the Family someday. But don't let him know it comes from me. He is too young and I am too old, I would not influence him."

Pippi and Giorgio knew this was a lie but also knew that if the old man wanted to hide his hand, he had a good reason. At that moment they heard steps overhead and then someone coming down the stairs. Rose Marie came into the dining room.

The three men saw with dismay that she was having one of her fits. Her hair was wild, her makeup was bizarre, and her clothing was twisted. Most serious, her mouth was open but no words were coming out. She used her body and hand flailing to take the place of speech. Her gestures were startlingly vivid, better than words. She hated them, she wanted them dead, she wanted their souls to burn in hell for eternity. They should choke on their food, go blind from the wine, their cocks should fall off when they slept with their wives.

Then she took Giorgio's plate and Pippi's plate and smashed them on the floor.

This was all permitted, but the first time, years ago, when she had her first fit, she treated the Don's plate in the same fashion and he had ordered her seized and locked in her room and then had her dispatched for three months to a special nursing home. Even now the Don quickly put the lid on his cheese bowl; she did a lot of spitting. Then suddenly it was over, she became very still. She spoke to Pippi. "I wanted to say good-bye. I hope you die in Sicily."

Pippi felt an overwhelming pity for her. He rose and took her in his arms. She did not resist. He kissed her on the cheek and said, "I wish to die in Sicily rather than come home and find you like this." She broke out of his arms and ran back up the stairs.

"Very touching," Giorgio said, almost sneering. "But you don't have to put up with her every month." He gave a slight leer with this, but they all knew that Rose Marie was far past menopause and she had the fits more than once a month.

The Don seemed the least upset by his daughter's fit. "She will get better or she will die," he said. "If not I will send her away."

Then he addressed Pippi. "I'll let you know when you can come back from Sicily. Enjoy the rest, we're all getting older. But keep your eyes open for new men to recruit for the Enclave. That is important. We must have men we can count on not to betray us, who have *omertà* in their bones, not like the rascals born in this country who want to lead a good life but not pay for it."

The next day, with Pippi on his way to Sicily, Dante was summoned to the Quogue mansion to spend the weekend. The first day Giorgio let Dante spend all his time with Rose Marie. It was touching to see their devotion to each other, Dante was a totally different person with his mother. He never wore one of his peculiar hats, he took her on walks around the estate, took her out for dinner. He waited on her like some eighteenth-century French gallant. When she broke into hysterical tears, he cradled her in his arms, and she never went into one of her fits. They spoke to each other constantly in low, confidential tones.

At supper time, Dante helped Rose Marie set the table, grate the Don's cheese, kept her company in the kitchen. She cooked his favorite meal of penne with broccoli and then roast lamb studded with bacon and garlic.

Giorgio was always struck by the rapport between the Don and Dante. Dante was solicitous, he spooned the penne and broccoli into the Don's plate and ostentatiously wiped and polished the great silver spoon he used to dip into the grated parmesan. Dante teased the old man. "Grandfather," he said, "if you got new teeth, we wouldn't have to grate this cheese. The dentists do great work now, they can plant steel in your jaw. A miracle."

The Don was playful in kind. "I want my teeth to die with me," he said. "And I'm too old for miracles. Why should God waste a miracle on an ancient like me?"

Rose Marie had prettied herself for her son, and traces of her young beauty could be seen. She seemed happy to see her father and her son on such familiar terms. It banished her constant air of anxiety.

Giorgio, too, was content. He was pleased that his sister seemed happy. She was not so nerve-racking and she was a better cook. She didn't stare at him with accusing eyes and she would not be subject to one of her fits.

When the Don and Rose Marie had both gone to bed, Giorgio took Dante into the den. It was the room that had neither phones nor TV and no communication lines to any part of the house. And it had a very thick door. Now it was furnished with two black leather couches and black studded leather chairs. It still contained a whiskey cabinet and a small wet bar equipped with a small refrigerator and a shelf of glasses. On the table rested a box of Havana cigars. Still, it was a room with no windows, like a small cave.

Dante's face, too sly and interesting for so young a man, always made Giorgio uneasy. His eyes were too cunningly bright and Giorgio didn't like it that he was short.

Giorgio made them both a drink and lit up one of the Havana cigars. "Thank God you don't wear those weird hats around your mother," he said. "Why do you wear them anyway?"

"I like them," Dante said. "And to make you and Uncle Petie and Uncle Vincent notice me." He paused for a moment and then said with a mischievous grin, "They make me look taller." It was true, Giorgio thought, that hats made him look handsomer. They framed his ferretlike face in a flattering way, his features were strangely uncoordinated when seen without his hat.

"You shouldn't wear them on a job," Giorgio said. "It makes an identification too easy."

"Dead men don't talk," Dante said. "I kill everybody who sees me on a job."

"Nephew, stop fucking me around," Giorgio said. "It's not smart. It's a risk. The Family doesn't take risks. Now one other thing. The word is getting around that you have a bloody mouth."

Dante for the first time reacted with anger. Suddenly he looked deadly. He put down his drink and said, "Does Grandfather know that? Does this come from him?"

"The Don knows nothing about it," Giorgio lied. He was a very expert liar. "And I won't tell him. You're his favorite, it would distress him. But I'm telling you, no more hats on the job and keep your mouth clean. You're the Family number one Hammer now and you take too much pleasure in the business. That's dangerous and against Family rules."

Dante seemed not to hear. He was thoughtful now and his smile reappeared. "Pippi must have told you," he said amiably.

"Yes," Giorgio said. He was curt. "And Pippi is the best. We put you with Pippi so you could learn the right way to do things. And do you know why he's the best? Because he has a good heart. It's never for pleasure."

Dante let himself go. He had a laughing fit. He rolled onto the sofa and then onto the floor. Giorgio watched him sourly, thinking he was as crazy as his mother. Finally Dante got to his feet, took a long swig from his drink, and said with great good humor, "Now you're saying I don't have a good heart."

"That's right," Giorgio said. "You're my nephew but I know what you are. You killed two men in some sort of personal quarrel without the Family OK. The Don wouldn't take action against you, he wouldn't even reprimand you. Then you killed some chorus girl you were banging for a year. Out of temper. You gave her a Communion so she wouldn't be found by the police. And she wasn't. You think you're a clever little prick, but the Family put the evidence together and found you guilty though you could never be convicted in a court of law."

Dante was quiet now. Not from fear but from calculation. "Does the Don know all this crap?"

"Yes," Giorgio said. "But you're still his favorite. He said to let it pass, that you're still young. That you will learn. I don't want to bring this bloody mouth business to him, he's too old. You're his grandson, your mother is his daughter. It would just break his heart."

Dante laughed again. "The Don has a heart. Pippi De Lena has a heart, Cross has a chickenshit heart, my mother has a broken heart. But I don't have a heart? How about you, Uncle Giorgio, do you have a heart?"

"Sure," Giorgio said. "I still put up with you."

"So, I'm the only one who doesn't have a fucking heart?" Dante said. "I love my mother and my grandfather and they both hate each other. My grandfather loves me less as I grow older. You and Vinnie and Petie don't even like me though we share family blood. You think I don't know these things? But I still love all of you though you put me down lower than that fucking Pippi De Lena. You think I don't have any fucking brains either?"

Giorgio was astonished by this outburst. He was also made wary by its truth. "You're wrong about the Don, he cares about you just as much. The same with Petie, Vincent, and me. Have we ever not treated you with the respect of family? Sure, the Don is a little remote but the man is very old. As for me, I'm just giving you a caution for your own safety. You're in a very dangerous business, you have to be careful. You cannot let personal emotions in. That's disaster."

"Do Vinnie and Pete know all this stuff?" Dante asked.

"No," Giorgio said. Which was another lie. Vincent had also spoken to Giorgio about Dante. Petie had not, but Petie was a born assassin. Yet he, too, had shown a distaste for Dante's company.

"Any other complaints about how I do my job?" Dante asked.

"No," Giorgio said, "and don't be so tough about this. I'm advising you as your uncle. But I'm telling you from my place in the Family. You do not anymore make anybody do their Communion or Confirmation without the Family OK. Got it?"

"OK," Dante said, "but I'm still the number one Hammer, right?"

"Until Pippi comes back from his little vacation," Giorgio said. "Depends on your work."

"I'll enjoy my work less if that's what you want," Dante said. "OK?" He tapped Giorgio on the shoulder affectionately.

"Good," Giorgio said. "Tomorrow night take your mother out to eat. Keep her company. Your grandfather will like that."

"Sure," Dante said.

"Vincent has one of his restaurants out by East Hampton," Giorgio said. "You could take your mother there."

Dante said suddenly, "Is she getting worse?"

Giorgio shrugged. "She can't forget the past. She holds on to old stories that she should forget. The Don always tells, 'The world is what it is and we are what we are,' his old line. But she cannot accept it." He gave Dante an affectionate hug. "Now let's just forget this little talk. I hate doing this stuff." As if he had not been specifically instructed by the Don.

After Dante left on Monday morning, Giorgio reported the whole conversation to the Don. The Don sighed. "What a lovely little boy he was. What could have happened?"

Giorgio had one great virtue. He spoke his mind when he really wanted to, even to his father, the great Don himself. "He talked too much to his mother. And he has bad blood." They were both silent for a time after this.

"And when Pippi comes back, what do we do with your grandson?" Giorgio asked.

"Despite everything, I think Pippi should retire," the Don said. "Dante must have his chance to be foremost, after all he is a Clericuzio. Pippi will be an advisor to his son's *Bruglione* in the West. If necessary he can always advise Dante. There is no one better versed in those matters. As he proved with the Santadio. But he should end his years in peace."

Giorgio muttered sarcastically, "The Hammer Emeritus." But the Don pretended not to understand the joke.

He frowned and said to Giorgio, "Soon you will have my responsibilities. Remember always that the task is that the Clericuzio must one day stand with society, that the Family must never die. No matter how hard the choice."

And so they left. But it was to be two years before Pippi returned from Sicily, the killing of Ballazzo receding into the bureaucratic mist. A mist manufactured by the Clericuzio.

BOOK V

Las Vegas Hollywood Quogue

CHAPTER 7

CROSS DE LENA received his sister, Claudia, and Skippy Deere in the executive penthouse suite of the Xanadu Hotel. Deere was always impressed by the difference between the two siblings. Claudia, not quite pretty and yet so likable, and Cross, so conventionally handsome with a slim but athletic body. Claudia, so naturally amiable, and Cross, so rigidly affable and distant. There was a difference between amiable and affable, Deere thought. One was in the genes, the other, learned.

Claudia and Skippy Deere sat on the couch, Cross sat opposite them. Claudia explained about Boz Skannet and then leaned forward and said, "Cross, please listen to me. This isn't only business. Athena is my dearest friend. And she is truly one of the best people I have ever known. She helped me when I needed help. And this is the most important favor I've ever asked you to do. Help Athena out of this fix and I'll never ask you for anything again." Then she turned to Skippy Deere. "You tell Cross the money part."

Deere always took the offensive before he asked a favor. He said to Cross, "I've been coming to your hotel over ten years, how come you never give me one of the Villas?"

Cross laughed, "They've always been full."

Deere said, "Throw somebody out."

"Sure," Cross said. "When I get a profit statement from one of your pictures and when I see you lay down a ten-grand bet at baccarat."

Claudia said, "I'm his sister and I never got one of the Villas. Stop fucking around, Skippy, and lay out the money problem."

When Deere finished, Cross, reading off a pad on which he had made notes, said, "Let me get this straight. You and the Studio lose fifty million in cash, plus the two hundred million in projected profit, if this Athena doesn't go back to work. She won't go back to work because she's so afraid of an ex-husband called Boz Skannet. You can buy him off but she still won't go back to work because she doesn't believe he can be stopped. Is that the whole thing?"

"Yeah," Deere said. "We promised her she'd be protected better than the president of the United States while she's making this picture. We have surveillance on this guy Skannet even now. We have her guarded twenty-four hours. She still won't come back to work."

"I don't really see the problem," Cross said.

"This guy comes from a powerful political family in Texas," Deere said. "And he's a really tough guy, I tried to get our security people to lean on him . . ."

"Who's your security agency?" Cross asked.

"Pacific Ocean Security," Deere said.

"Why are you talking to me?" Cross asked.

"Because your sister said you could help," Deere said. "It wasn't my idea."

Cross said to his sister, "Claudia, what made you think I could help?"

Claudia's face twisted up in discomfort. "I've seen you solve problems in the past, Cross. You're very persuasive, and you always seem to come up with a solution." She smiled her innocent grin. "Besides you're my older brother, I have faith in you."

Cross sighed and said, "Same old bullshit," but Deere noticed the easy affection between the two.

The three of them sat silently for a while, then Deere said, "Cross, we came here as a long shot. But if you're looking for another investment, I have a project coming up that's very, very good."

Cross looked at Claudia, then at Deere, and said thoughtfully, "Skippy, I want to meet this Athena and after that maybe I can solve all your problems."

"Great," Claudia said, relieved. "We can all fly out tomorrow." She hugged him.

"OK," Deere said. He was already trying to figure out how he could get Cross to take some of his loss on the *Messalina* film.

The next day they flew into Los Angeles. Claudia had talked Athena into seeing them, then Deere had taken the phone. That conversation had convinced him that Athena would never return to the picture. He was infuriated by this, but he diverted himself on the plane by scheming how he would get Cross to give him one of his fucking Villas when he visited Vegas again.

The Malibu Colony, where Athena Aquitane lived, was a section of beach that was located about forty minutes north of Beverly Hills and Hollywood. The Colony held a little over a hundred dwellings, each one of which was worth from three to six million dollars but looked very ordinary and ramshackle from the outside. Each house was enclosed by fencing and sometimes ornate entry gates.

The Colony itself could only be entered through a private road guarded by security men in a large hut who controlled the swinging barriers. The security personnel screened all visitors by phone or checklist. Residents had special car stickers that were changed every week. Cross recognized this as a "nuisance" security barrier, not a serious one.

But the Pacific Ocean Security men around Athena's house were another matter. They were uniformed, armed, and looked to be in very tough physical condition.

They entered Athena's house from the sidewalk parallel to the beach. It had its own additional security controlled by Athena's secretary, who buzzed them in from a small guest house nearby.

There were two more men with Pacific Ocean uniforms, and another at the door of the house. Passing the guest house, they walked through a long garden filled with flowers and lemon trees, which scented the salty air. They finally arrived at the main house which looked out over the Pacific Ocean itself.

A tiny South American maid let them in and led them through a huge kitchen into a living room that seemed to be filled with the ocean filtered through the huge windows. A room with bamboo furniture, glass tables, and deep-sea-green sofas. The maid led them through this room to a glass door that opened onto a terrace overlooking the ocean, a wide, long terrace that had chairs and tables and an exercise bike that glittered like silver. Beyond all of this was the ocean itself, blue-green, slanting to the sky.

Cross De Lena, when he saw Athena on that terrace, felt a shock of fear. She was far more exquisite than on film, which was very rare. Film could not capture her coloring, the depth of her eyes or their shade of green. Her body moved as a great athlete's moved, with a physical grace that seemed effortless. Her hair, cut into a rough, golden crop that would have been ugly on any other woman, crowned her beauty. She was wearing a powder-blue sweat suit that should have concealed the shape of her body but did not. Her legs were long in proportion to her torso, her feet were bare, there was no polish on her toenails.

But it was the look of intelligence on her face, the focusing of attention, that impressed him most.

She greeted Skippy Deere with the customary kiss on the cheek, embraced Claudia with a warm hug, and shook hands with Cross. Her eyes reflected the ocean waters behind her. "Claudia always talks about you," she said to Cross. "Her handsome, mysterious brother who can make the earth stop when he wants to." She laughed, a completely natural laugh, not the laugh of a woman frightened.

Cross felt a wonderful delight, there was no other word. Her voice was throaty, pitched low, a bewitching musical instrument. The ocean framed her, the fine-planed cheekbones, the lips unadorned, generous and the color of red wine, the radiating intelligence. Flashing through Cross's mind was one of Gronevelt's short lectures. *Money can make you safe in this world, from everything except a beautiful woman.*

Cross had known many beautiful women in Vegas, as many as in Los Angeles and Hollywood. But in Vegas the beauty was beauty as of itself with only a slight degree of talent; many of those beauties had failed in Hollywood. In Hollywood, beauty was married to talent and, less often, artistic greatness. Both cities attracted beauty from all over the world. Then there were the actresses who became Bankable Stars.

These were the women who in addition to their charm and beauty had a certain childlike innocence and courage. A curiosity in their craft that could be raised to an art form, which gave them a certain dignity. Though beauty was commonplace in both cities, in Hollywood Goddesses arose and received the adoration of the world. Athena Aquitane was one of those rare Goddesses.

Cross said coolly to Athena, "Claudia told me you are the most beautiful woman in the world."

Athena said, "What did she say about my brain?"

She leaned over the balcony of the deck and stuck one leg in back of her in some sort of exercise. What would be an affectation in another woman seemed perfectly natural with her. And indeed throughout the meeting she continued doing exercises, bending her body forward and backward, stretching a leg over the railing, her arms pantomiming some of her words.

Claudia said, "Thena, you'd never think we were related, right?"

Skippy Deere said, "Never."

But Athena looked at them and said, "You both look very much alike," and Cross could see she was serious.

Claudia said, "Now you know why I love her."

Athena stopped her motions for a moment and said to Cross, "They tell me you can help. I don't see how."

Cross tried not to stare at her, tried not to look at the flaming-sun gold of her hair set against the green behind her. He said, "I'm good at persuading people. If it's true that the only thing keeping you from going back to work is your husband, maybe I can talk him into a deal."

"I don't believe in Boz keeping his deals," Athena said. "The Studio has already talked a deal."

Deere said in what was for him a subdued voice, "Athena you really have nothing to worry about. I promise you." But for some reason he was unconvincing even to himself. He watched them all carefully. He knew how Athena overwhelmed men, actresses were the most charming people in the world when they wanted to be. But Deere detected no change in Cross.

"Skippy just won't accept that I can leave movies," Athena said. "It's so important to him."

"And not to you?" Deere said angrily.

Athena gave a long, cool look. "It was once. But I know Boz. I have to disappear, I have to start a new life." She gave them a mischievous smile. "I can get along anywhere."

"I can make an agreement with your husband," Cross said. "And I can guarantee that he'll abide by it."

Deere said confidently, "Athena, in the movie business, there are hundreds of cases like this, harassment of stars by crazies. We have foolproof procedures. There really is no danger."

Athena continued her exercises. One leg flew improbably above her head. "You don't know Boz," she said. "I do."

"Is Boz the only reason you won't go back to work?" Cross asked.

"Yes," Athena said. "He'll track me forever. You can protect me until I finish the picture but then what?"

Cross said. "I've never failed to make a deal. I'll give him whatever he wants."

Athena stopped her exercises. For the first time, she looked Cross directly in the eye. "I'll never believe in any deal Boz makes," she said. She turned away in dismissal.

Cross said, "I'm sorry I wasted your time."

"I didn't waste my time," Athena said cheerfully. "I did my exercises." Then she looked directly into his eyes. "I do appreciate your trying. It's just that I'm trying to look fearless like in one of my movies. Really, I'm scared to death." Then she quickly regained her composure and said, "Claudia and Skippy are always talking about your famous Villas. If I come to Vegas, would you give me one to hide out in?"

Her face was grave, but her eyes were dancing. She was showing off her power to Claudia and Skippy. She obviously expected Cross to say yes, if merely out of gallantry.

Cross smiled at her. "The Villas are usually taken," he said. He paused for a moment then said, with an utmost seriousness that startled the others, "But if you come to Vegas, I can guarantee no one will harm you."

Athena spoke to him directly. "Nobody can stop Boz. He doesn't care if he gets caught. Whatever he does he'll do in public so everybody can see."

Claudia spoke out impatiently, "But why?"

Athena said laughingly, "Because he loved me once. And because my life turned out better than his." She looked at them all a moment. "Isn't it a shame," she said, "that two people in love can grow to hate each other?"

At this moment the meeting was interrupted by the South American maid, who was leading a man onto the terrace.

The man was tall, handsome, and formally dressed with a touch-all-bases style: an Armani suit, Turnbull & Asser shirt, Gucci tie, and Bally shoes. He immediately murmured his apologies. "She didn't tell me you were busy, Miss Aquitane," he said. "I guess she got scared by my shield." He showed her the badge. "I just came to get some information on that incident the other night. I can wait. Or come back."

His words were polite but his look was bold. He glanced at the other two men and said, "Hello, Skippy."

Skippy Deere looked angry. "You can't talk to her without a PR and legal person around," he said. "You know better than that, Jim."

The detective offered his hand to Claudia and Cross and said, "Jim Losey."

They knew who he was. The most famous detective in Los Angeles, whose exploits had even been the basis of a miniseries. He also had appeared in very minor roles in films, and he was on Deere's Christmas gift and card lists. So Deere was emboldened to say, "Jim, give me a call later and I'll arrange a meeting with Miss Aquitane properly."

Losey smiled at him amiably and said, "Sure, Skippy."

But Athena said, "I may not be here much longer. Why not ask me now? I don't mind."

Losey would have been suave except for that constant wariness in his eyes, an alertness of his body that many years of crime work had planted in him.

He said, "In front of them?"

Athena's body was no longer in motion, and she had erased all her charm when she said quietly, "I trust them far more than I do the police."

Losey took that in stride. It was familiar. "I just wanted to ask you why you dropped the charges against your husband. Did he threaten you in any way?"

"Oh, no," Athena said scornfully. "He just threw water in my face in front of a billion people and yelled 'acid.' The next day he was out on bail."

"OK, OK," Losey said, and held up his arms in a placating gesture. "I just thought I could help."

Deere said, "Jim, give me a call later."

This raised an alarm bell in Cross. He looked thoughtfully at Deere, avoided looking at Losey. And Losey avoided looking at him.

Losey said, "I will." He saw Athena's handbag on one of the chairs and picked it up. "I saw this on Rodeo Drive," he said. "Two thousand dollars." He looked directly at Athena and said with a contemptuous politeness, "Maybe you can explain it to me, why anyone would pay that kind of money for something like this?"

Athena's face was like stone, she moved out of the frame of the ocean. She said, "That's an insulting question. Get out of here."

Losey bowed to her and left. He was grinning. He had made the impression he wanted.

"So you're human after all," Claudia said. She put her arm around Athena's shoulders. "Why did you get so mad?"

"I wasn't mad," Athena said. "I was sending him a message."

After the three visitors left, they drove from Malibu to Nate and Al's in Beverly Hills. Deere insisted to Cross that it was the only place west of the Rockies where you could get edible pastrami, corned beef, and Coney Island–style hot dogs.

As they ate Deere said reflectively, "Athena won't get back to work."

"I always knew that," Claudia said. "What I don't get is why she got so mad at that detective."

Deere laughed and said to Cross, "Did you get it?"

"No," Cross said.

Deere said, "One of the great legends of Hollywood is how anybody can get to fuck the stars. Now, male stars it's true, that's why you see the girls hanging around locations and the Beverly Wilshire Hotel. Female stars, not so much . . . a guy works on their house, a carpenter, a gardener, can get lucky, maybe she gets horny, it happened to me. Stunt men score good and other guys on the crew can get lucky. But that's fucking below the line and hurts female stars in their careers. Unless, of course, they are Superstars. Us old guys who run the show don't like that. Hell, doesn't money and power mean anything?" He grinned at them. "Now, you take Jim Losey. He's a big, handsome guy. He really kills tough guys, he's glamorous to people who live in a make-believe world. He knows that. He uses it. So he doesn't beg a star, he intimidates her That's why he made that crack. In fact that's why he came out. It was his excuse to meet Athena and he figured he could take a shot. That insulting question was a declaration he wanted to fuck her. And Athena froze him out."

"So she's the Virgin Mary?" Cross said.

"For a movie star," Deere said.

Cross said abruptly, "You think she's scamming the Studio, trying to get more money?"

"She would never do anything like that," Claudia said. "She's absolutely straight."

"She got any grudges she's paying off?" Cross asked.

"You don't understand the business," Deere said. "First thing, the Studio would let her scam them. Stars always do that. Second, if she has a grudge, it's right out in the open. She's just weird." He paused for a moment. "She hates Bobby Bantz and she's not crazy about me. We've both been after her ass for years but never a tumble."

"Too bad you couldn't help," Claudia said to Cross. But he didn't answer her.

All during the trip from Malibu, Cross had been thinking hard. That this was the opportunity he was looking for. It would be dangerous, but if it worked he could finally make a break from the Clericuzio.

"Skippy," Cross said, "I have a proposition I want to make to you and the Studio. I'll buy your picture right now. I'll give the fifty million you've invested, put up the money to complete it, and let the Studio distribute it."

"You've got a hundred million?" Skippy Deere and Claudia both asked in astonishment.

"I know people who have it," Cross said.

"You can't get Athena back. And without Athena, there's no picture," Deere said.

"I said I'm a great persuader," Cross said. "Can you get me a meeting with Eli Marrion?"

"Sure," Deere said, "but only if I stay on as producer of the picture."

The meeting was not so easy to arrange. LoddStone Studios, that is to say, Eli Marrion and Bobby Bantz, had to be convinced that Cross De Lena was not just another big-mouth hustler, that he had the money and the credentials. Certainly he owned part of the Xanadu Hotel in Vegas, but he had no personal recorded financial worth that indicated he could swing the deal he proposed. Deere would vouch for him, but the clincher was when Cross showed a fifty-million-dollar letter of credit.

On the advice of his sister, Cross De Lena hired Molly Flanders as his lawyer for the deal.

Molly Flanders received Cross in her cave of an office. Cross was very alert, he knew certain things about her. In the world he had lived all his life, he had never met a woman who wielded power in any way, and Claudia had told him that Molly Flanders was one of the most powerful people in Hollywood. Studio chiefs took her calls, monster agents like Melo Stuart sought her help on the biggest deals. Stars like Athena Aquitane used her in their quarrels with studios. Flanders had once stopped production of the top miniseries on TV when her star client's check had been delayed in the mail.

She was much better looking than Cross had expected. She was large but well-proportioned and dressed beautifully. But on that body was the face of an elfin blond witch, the aquiline nose, the generous mouth and fierce brown eyes that seemed to squint with intense, intelligent combativeness. Her hair was braided into snakes around her head. She was forbidding until she smiled.

Molly Flanders, for all her toughness, was susceptible to handsome men and liked Cross as soon as she saw him. She was surprised because she had expected Claudia's brother to be homely. More than the handsomeness, she saw a force that Claudia did not have. He had a look of awareness that the world held no surprises. All this, however, did not convince her that she wanted to take Cross on as a client. She had heard rumors about certain connections, she didn't like the world of Vegas, and she was dubious as to the extent of his determination to take such a horrendous gamble.

"Mr. De Lena," she said, "let me make one thing clear. I represent Athena Aquitane as a lawyer not an agent. I've explained the consequences she must bear if she persists in her course of action. I'm convinced she will persist in it. Now, if you make your deal with the Studio and Athena still doesn't go back to work, I will represent her if you pursue legal action against her."

Cross looked at her intently. He had no way he could read a woman like this. He had to put most of his cards on the table. "I'll sign a waiver that I won't sue Miss Aquitane if I do buy the picture," he said. "And I have a check for two hundred thousand dollars here if you take me on. That's just for openers. You can bill me for more."

"Let's see if I understand this," Molly said. "You pay the Studio the fifty million they invested. Right now. You put up the money to complete the picture, minimum another fifty million. So you're going to gamble a hundred million that Athena goes back to work. Plus you're gambling that the picture will be a hit. It could be a flop. That's an awful risk."

Cross could be charming when he wanted to be. But he sensed that charm would not help with this woman. "I understand that with the foreign money, video, and TV sales, the picture can't lose money even if it's a flop," he said. "The only real problem is getting Miss Aquitane back to work. And maybe you can help on that."

"No, I can't," Molly said. "I don't want to mislead you. I've tried and failed. Everybody tried and failed. And Eli Marrion doesn't ever bullshit. He'll close down the picture and take the loss, then he'll try to ruin Athena. But I won't let him."

Cross was intrigued. "How will you do that?"

"Marrion has to get along with me," she said. "He's a smart man. I'll fight him in the courts, I'll make his Studio miserable on every deal. Athena won't be able to work again but I won't let them take her to the cleaners."

"If you represent me, you can save your client's career," Cross said. From the inside of his jacket he took an envelope and handed it to her. She opened it, studied it, then picked up the phone and made some calls that established the check was good.

She smiled at Cross and said, "I'm not insulting you, I do this with the biggest movie producers in town."

"Like Skippy Deere?" Cross said, laughing. "I invested in six of his pictures, four of them were hits and still I haven't made money."

"Because you didn't have me representing you," Molly said. "Now before I agree, you have to tell me how you can get Athena back to work." She paused. "I've heard some rumors about you."

Cross said, "And I've heard about you. I remember years ago when you were a criminal defense lawyer, you got some kid off a murder rap. He killed his girlfriend and you got an insanity plea. He was walking the streets less than a year later." He paused for a moment, deliberately letting his irritation show. "You didn't worry about his reputation."

Molly looked at him coldly. "You have not answered my question."

Cross decided that a lie should carry a little charm. "Molly," he said. "May I call you Molly?" She nodded her head. Cross went on. "You know I run a hotel in Vegas. I've learned this. Money is magic, you can overcome any kind of fear with money, so I'm going to offer Athena fifty percent of any money I make from the movie. If you structure the deal right and we're lucky, that means thirty million for her." He paused for a minute and said earnestly, "Come on, Molly, would you take a chance for thirty million?"

Molly shook her head. "Athena doesn't really care about money."

"The only thing that puzzles me is why the Studio doesn't give her the same deal," Cross said.

For the first time in their meeting, Molly smiled at him. "You don't know movie studios," she said. "They worry that all the stars will pull the same stunt if they set such a precedent. But let's go on. The Studio will take your deal, I think, because they will make a great deal of money just distributing the film. They will insist on that. Also, they will want a percentage of the profits. But I'm telling you again, Athena will not take your offer." She paused, then said with a teasing smile, "I thought you Vegas owners never gambled."

Cross smiled back at her. "Everybody gambles. I do when the percentages are right. And besides I plan to sell the Hotel and make a living in the movie business." He paused for a minute, letting her look into him to see the desire to be part of that world. "I think it's more interesting."

"I see," Molly said. "So this is not just a passing fancy."

"A foot in the door," Cross said. "Once I do that, I'll need your help further on."

Molly was amused by this. "I'll represent you," she said. "But as for us doing business further on, let's see first if you lose that hundred million."

She picked up the phone. She spoke into it. Then she hung up and said to Cross, "We have our meeting with their Business Affairs people to set out the rules before then. And you have three days to reconsider."

Cross was impressed. "That was fast," he said.

"Them, not me," Molly said. "It's costing them a fortune to tread water on this picture."

"I don't have to say this, I know," Cross said. "But the offer I plan to make Miss Aquitane is confidential, between you and me."

"No, you didn't have to say it," Molly said.

They shook hands, and after Cross left, Molly remembered something. Why had Cross De Lena mentioned that long-ago case when she had gotten that kid off, that famous victory of hers. Why that particular case? She had gotten plenty of murderers off.

Three days later Cross De Lena and Molly Flanders met in her office before going to LoddStone Studios so that she could check over the financial papers that Cross was bringing to the meeting. Then Molly drove both of them to the Studio in her Mercedes SL 300.

When they had been cleared through the gate, Molly said to Cross, "Check the lot. I'll give you a dollar for any American car you see."

They passed a sea of sleek cars of all colors, Mercedeses, Aston Martins, BMWs, Rolls-Royces. Cross saw one Cadillac and pointed it out. Molly said cheerily, "Some poor slob of a writer from New York."

LoddStone Studios was a huge area on which were scattered small buildings housing independent production companies. The main building was only ten floors and looked like a movie set piece. The Studio had kept the flavor of the 1920s when it had started up, with only the necessary repairs being done. Cross was reminded of the Enclave in the Bronx.

The offices in the Studio Administration Building were small and crowded except for the tenth floor, where Eli Marrion and Bobby Bantz had their executive suites. Between the two suites was a huge conference room with a bar and bartender far off to one side and a small kitchen adjoining the bar. The seats around the conference table were plush armchairs of dark red. Framed posters of LoddStone movies hung on the wall.

Waiting for them were Eli Marrion, Bobby Bantz, Skippy Deere, the chief counsel of the Studio, and two other lawyers. Molly handed the chief counsel the financial papers, and the three opposing lawyers sat down to read them through. The bartender brought them drinks of their choice, then disappeared. Skippy Deere made the introductions.

Eli Marrion, as always, insisted that Cross call him by his first name. Then told them one of his favorite stories, which he often used to disarm opponents in a negotiation. His grandfather, Eli Marrion said, had started the company in the early 1920s. He had wanted to call the firm Lode Stone Studios, but he still had a severe German accent that confused the lawyers. It was only a ten-thousand-dollar company then and when the mistake was discovered, it didn't seem worth the trouble to change it. And here now it was a seven-billion-dollar company with a name that didn't make sense. But, as Marrion pointed out—he never told a joke that didn't make a serious point—

the printed word was not important. It was the visual image with the lodestone attracting light from every corner of the universe that made the company logo so powerful.

Then Molly presented the offer. Cross would pay the Studio the fifty million it had spent, would give the Studio distribution rights, keep Skippy Deere as producer. Cross would put up the money to finish the picture. LoddStone Studios would also get 5 percent of the profits.

They all listened intently. Bobby Bantz said, "The percentage is ridiculous, we would have to have more. And how do we know that you people and Athena are not in a conspiracy? That this isn't a stickup?"

Cross was astonished by Molly's reply. For some reason he had assumed that negotiations would be much more civil than he had been used to in his Vegas world.

But Molly was almost screaming, her witchlike face blazing with fury. "Fuck you, Bobby," she said to Bantz. "You have the fucking balls to accuse us of a conspiracy. Your insurance doesn't cover you on this, you take this meeting to get off the hook and then insult us. If you don't apologize, I'll take Mr. De Lena right out of here and you can eat shit."

Skippy Deere broke in, "Molly, Bobby, come on. We're trying to save a picture here. Let's talk this through at least. . . ."

Marrion had observed all this with a quiet smile but did not say anything. He would speak only to give a yes or no.

"I think it's a reasonable question," Bobby Bantz said. "What can this guy offer Athena to make her come back that we can't?"

Cross sat there smiling. Molly had told him to let her answer whenever possible.

She said, "Mr. De Lena obviously has something special to offer. Why should he tell you? If you offer him ten million to give you that information I'll confer with him. Ten million would be cheap."

Even Bobby Bantz laughed at this.

Skippy Deere said, "They think Cross wouldn't be risking all that money unless he had a sure thing. That makes them a little suspicious."

"Skippy," Molly said, "I've seen you lay out a million for a novel that you never made into a picture. How is this different?"

Bobby Bantz broke in. "Because Skippy gets our studio to put up the million."

They all laughed. Cross wondered about this meeting. He was losing patience. Also, he knew he must not look too eager, so it wouldn't hurt if he showed his irritation. He said in a low voice, "I'm going on a hunch. If it's too complicated, we can just forget the whole thing."

Bantz said angrily, "We are talking about a lot of money here. This picture could gross a half billion worldwide."

"If you could get Athena back," Molly shot in quickly. "I can tell you I talked with her this morning. She already cut off all her hair to show she's serious."

"We can wig her. Fucking actresses," Bantz said. Now he was glowering at Cross, trying to read him. He was pondering something. He said, "If Athena does not come back and you lose your fifty million and can't go on to finish the picture, who gets the footage already done?"

"I do," Cross said.

"Aha," Bantz said. "Then you just release it the way it is. Maybe as soft porn."

"That's a possibility," Cross said.

Molly shook her head at Cross, warning him to keep quiet. "If you agree to this deal," she said to Bantz, "everything can be negotiated on foreign, video, TV, and profit participation. There's only one deal-breaker. The agreement must be secret. Mr. De Lena only wants credit as a coproducer."

"That's OK with me," Skippy Deere said. "But my money deal with the Studio still stands."

For the first time Marrion spoke. "That's separate," he said, meaning no. "Cross, do you give your lawyer full discretion on negotiations?"

"Yes," Cross said.

"I want to go on record on this," Marrion said. "You must know we planned to scrap the picture and take the loss. We are convinced Athena will not come back. We do not represent to you that she may come back. If you make this deal and pay us fifty million, we are not liable. You would have to sue Athena and she doesn't have that kind of money."

"I would never sue her," Cross said. "I'd forgive and forget."

Bantz said, "You don't have to answer to your money people?"

Cross shrugged.

Marrion said, "That is a corruption. You can't let your personal attitude betray the money people who trust you. Just because they're rich."

Cross said, straight-faced, "I never think it's a good idea to get on the wrong side of rich people."

Bantz said in exasperation, "This is some kind of trick."

Masking his face with benign confidence, Cross said, "I've spent my whole life convincing people. In my Vegas hotel I have to convince very smart men to gamble their money against the odds. And I do that by making them happy. That means I give them what they really want. I'll do that with Miss Aquitane."

Bantz disliked the whole idea. He was sure his studio was being screwed. He said bluntly, "If we find out Athena has already agreed to work with you, we will sue. We will not honor this agreement."

"I want to be in the movie business for the long haul," Cross said. "I want to work with LoddStone Studios. There's money enough for everyone."

Eli Marrion had been studying Cross all during the meeting, trying to come to an assessment. The man was very low key, not a bluffer or a bullshit artist. Pacific Ocean Security could not establish any real link with Athena, there was no likely conspiracy. A decision had to be made, but it was not really as difficult a decision as the people in this room were pretending. Marrion was so weary now he could feel the weight of his clothing on his skeletal frame. He wanted this to be over.

Skippy Deere said, "Maybe Athena is just nuts, maybe she's gone over the edge. Then we can bail out with the insurance."

Molly Flanders said, "She's saner than anyone in this room. I can have all of you certified before you get her."

Bobby Bantz looked Cross directly in the face. "Will you sign papers that you have no agreement with Athena Aquitane at this point in time?"

"Yes," Cross said. He let his dislike for Bantz show.

Marrion, observing this, felt satisfaction. At least this part of the meeting was going according to plan. Bantz was now established as the bad guy. It was amazing how people almost instinctively disliked him, and it really wasn't his fault. It was the role chosen for him to play, though admittedly it suited his personality.

"We want twenty percent of the profits of the picture," Bantz said. "We distribute it domestic and foreign. And we will be partners in any sequel."

Skippy Deere said in exasperation, "Bobby, they are all dead at the end of the picture, there can be no sequel."

"OK," Bantz said, "rights in any prequel."

"Prequel, sequel, bullshit," Molly said. "You can have them. But you get no more than ten percent of the profits. You'll make a fortune on distribution. And you have no risk. Take it or leave it."

Eli Marrion could endure no more. He rose, standing very straight, and spoke in a measured, serene voice. "Twelve percent," he said, "We have a deal."

He paused and then looking directly at Cross, he said, "It's not so much the money. But this could be a great picture and I don't want to scrap it. Also, I'm very curious to see what will happen." He turned to Molly. "Now, yes or no?"

Molly Flanders, without even looking at Cross for a sign, said, "Yes."

Later, Eli Marrion and Bobby Bantz sat alone in the conference room. They were both silent. They had learned over the years that there were things that must not be said aloud. Finally Marrion said, "There's a moral question here."

Bantz said, "We've signed to keep the agreement secret, Eli, but if you feel we must, I could make a call."

Marrion sighed. "Then we lose the film. This man Cross is our only hope. Plus if he found out the leak came from you there might be some danger."

"Whatever he is, he doesn't dare touch LoddStone," Bantz said. "What I worry about is letting him get a foot in the door."

Marrion sipped his drink, puffed his cigar. The thin, woody-smelling smoke made his body tingle.

Eli Marrion was really tired now. He was getting too old to worry about long-term future disasters. The great universal disaster was closer.

"Don't make the call," he said. "We have to keep the agreement. And besides, maybe I'm getting into my second childhood, but I'd love to see what the magician pulls out of his hat."

Skippy Deere, after the meeting, went back to his house and made a call summoning Jim Losey to meet with him. At their meeting he swore Losey to secrecy and told him what had happened. "I think you should put a surveillance on Cross," he said. "You might find out something interesting."

But he said this only after he had agreed to sign Jim Losey to play a small part in a new movie he was making about serial murders in Santa Monica.

As for Cross De Lena, he returned to Las Vegas and in his penthouse suite pondered the new course of his life. Why had he taken the risk? Most important, the winnings could be huge: not only the money but a new way of life. But what he questioned was an underlying motive, the vision of Athena Aquitane framed by the sea-green water, her constantly moving body, the notion that one day she might come to know him and love him, not forever, but just for a moment of time. What had Gronevelt said? "Women are never more dangerous to men than when they have to be saved. Beware, beware," Gronevelt said, "of Beauty in Distress."

But he dismissed all this from his mind. Looking down on the Vegas Strip, the wall of colored light, the throngs moving through that light, ants carrying bales of money to bury in some great nest, he analyzed the whole problem for the first time in a coldly neutral way.

If Athena Aquitane was such an angel, why then was she demanding, in effect if not in words, that the price for her returning to the picture was that someone kill her husband? Surely that had to be clear to anyone. The Studio's offer to protect her while she completed the picture was worth less because she would be working toward her own death. After the picture was done and she was alone, Skannet would come after her.

Eli Marrion, Bobby Bantz, Skippy Deere, they knew the problem and knew the answer. But no one would dare speak it aloud. For people like them, the risk was too great. They had risen so high, lived so well, that they had too much to lose. For them the gain did not equal the risk. They could accommodate the loss of the picture, for them it was only a minor defeat. They could not afford the great tumble from the highest level of society to the lowest. That risk was mortal.

Also, to give them their due, they had made an intelligent decision. They were not expert in this field of endeavor; they could make mistakes. Better to treat the fifty million dollars like a loss of points in their stock on Wall Street.

So now there were two main problems. The execution of Boz Skannet in a manner that would not injure the picture or Athena in any way. Problem number two, and far more important, was winning the approval of his father, Pippi De Lena, and the Clericuzio Family. For Cross knew the whole arrangement would not remain secret to them very long.

CHAPTER 8

CROSS DE LENA pleaded for Big Tim's life for many different reasons. One, he contributed between five hundred grand and one million to the Xanadu cage every year. Second, he had a sneaking affection for the man, for his lust for life, his outrageous buffooneries.

Tim Snedden, known as the Rustler, was the owner of a string of shopping malls that stretched over the northern part of the state of California. He was also a Las Vegas high roller who usually stayed at the Xanadu. He was particularly fond of and extraordinarily lucky at sports betting. The Rustler made big bets, fifty grand on football and sometimes ten grand on basketball. Thinking he was being clever, he lost small bets but almost invariably won his big bets. Cross was on to that immediately.

The Rustler was very big, nearly six and a half feet and over three hundred fifty pounds. His appetite matched his physique, he ate everything in sight. He boasted he had had a partial stomach bypass so that food passed directly through his system and he never gained weight. He was gleeful about this as an ultimate scam on nature itself.

For the Rustler was a natural-born scam artist, which was how he earned his nickname. At the Xanadu he fed his friends free under his comp, he absolutely destroyed room service. He tried to pay his call girls and the purchases at the gift shop under his comp. And then when he lost and had a cage full of markers, he stalled payment until his next visit to the Xanadu, instead of paying them within a month as a gentleman gambler would do.

Though he was very lucky with his sports gambling, the Rustler was less fortunate with casino games. He was skillful, he knew the odds and bet correctly, but his natural exuberance carried him away, and his winnings on sports would be wiped out and more. So it wasn't because of the money but because of long-range strategic reasons that the Clericuzio took an interest.

Since the Family's ultimate goal was the legalization of sports gambling all over the United States, any gambling scandal involving sports would hurt that aim. So an inquiry into the life of Big Tim Snedden the Rustler was launched. The results were so alarming that Pippi and Cross were summoned East to the mansion in Quogue for a conference. It was Pippi's first operation after his return from Sicily.

Pippi and Cross took the flight back East together. Cross worried that the Clericuzio had already found out about his movie deal on *Messalina* and that his father would be angry he had not been consulted. For Pippi, at fifty-seven, though retired, still was consigliere to his son the *Bruglione.*

So on the plane Cross told his father about the movie and reassured him that he still valued his counsel but had not wanted to put him in a bad light with the Clericuzio. He also voiced his anxiety about being summoned back East because the Don had learned about his Hollywood plans.

Pippi listened without saying a word, then sighed with disgust. "You're still too young," he said. "It won't be about the movie deal. The Don would never show his hand this quick. He'd wait to see what happened. It looks like Giorgio runs things, that's what Vincent and Petie and Dante think. But they're wrong. The old man is smarter than all of us. And don't worry about him, he's always fair in these things. It's Giorgio and Dante you have to worry about." He paused for a moment as if reluctant to talk about the Family even with Cross.

"You notice that Giorgio and Vincent and Petie's kids know nothing about Family business? The Don and Giorgio have all planned that the children will be strictly legit. The Don planned that for Dante too, but Dante was too smart, figured everything out, and he wanted in. The Don couldn't stop him. Think of all of us—Giorgio, Vincent, and Petie, you and me and Dante—as the rear guard, fighting so that the Clericuzio clan can escape to safety. That's the Don's planning. It's his strength, what makes him great. So he may even be glad you're making your escape, it's what he hoped Dante would do. That's what it is, isn't it?"

"I think so," Cross said. Not even to his father would he confess his terrible weakness. That he was doing it for the love of a woman.

"Always play it long, like Gronevelt," Pippi said. "When the time comes, tell the Don directly and make sure the Family wets its beak on the deal. But watch out for Giorgio and Dante. Vincent and Petie won't give a shit."

"Why Giorgio and Dante?" Cross asked.

"Because Giorgio is a greedy prick," Pippi said. "And Dante, because he's always jealous of you and because you're my son. Besides, he's a fucking lunatic."

Cross was surprised. It was the first time he had heard his father criticize any of the Clericuzio. "And why won't Vincent and Petie care?" he asked.

"Because Vincent has his restaurants and Petie has his construction business and the Bronx Enclave. Vincent wants to enjoy his old age and Petie likes the action. And both of them like you and respect me. We did jobs together when we were young."

Cross said, "Pop, you're not mad I didn't clear it with you?"

Pippi gave him a sardonic look. "Don't bullshit me," he said. "You knew I would disapprove and the Don would disapprove. Now when are you going to kill this Skannet guy?"

"I don't know yet," Cross said. "It's very tricky, has to be a Confirmation so that Athena will know she doesn't have to worry about him anymore. Then she can come back to the picture."

"Let me plan it for you," Pippi said. "And what if this broad, Athena, doesn't come back to work? Then you lose fifty mil."

"She'll come back to work," Cross said. "She and Claudia are close friends and Claudia says she will."

"My darling daughter," Pippi said. "She still doesn't want to see me?"

"I don't think so," Cross said. "But you can always drop around when she's staying at the Hotel."

"No," Pippi said. "If this Athena doesn't come to work after you do the job, I'll plan her Communion for her, no matter how big a movie star she is."

"No, no," Cross said. "You should see Claudia. She's much prettier now."

"That's good," Pippi said. "She had such an ugly mug when she was a kid. Like me."

"Why don't you make up with her?" Cross asked.

"She wouldn't let me go to my ex-wife's funeral, and she doesn't like me. So what's the point? In fact, when I die I want you to bar her from my funeral. Fuck her." He paused for a moment. "She was a ballsy little kid."

"You should see her now," Cross said.

"Remember," Pippi said. "Don't volunteer anything to the Don. This meeting is about something else."

"How can you be sure?" Cross asked.

"Because he would have met with me first to see if I would give you away," Pippi said.

As it turned out, Pippi was right.

At the mansion, Giorgio, Don Domenico, Vincent, Petie, and Dante waited to greet them in the garden by the fig trees. As was the custom they all had lunch together before they got down to business.

Giorgio laid it out. An investigation had shown that Rustler Snedden was fixing certain college games in the Midwest. That he possibly shaved points in the pro football and pro basketball games. He did this by bribing the officials and certain players, a very tricky and dangerous business. If this came out, it would cause a tremendous scandal and uproar that would give a near fatal blow to the Clericuzio Family's effort to have sports gambling legalized in the United States. And it would eventually be found out.

"The cops throw more manpower into a sports fix than into a serial murder," Giorgio said. "Why, I don't know. What the hell difference does it make who wins or loses? It's a crime that hurts nobody except the bookmakers and the cops hate them anyway. If the Rustler fixed all the Notre Dame games so that they always won, the whole country would be happy."

Pippi said impatiently, "Why are we even talking about this? Just have somebody warn him off."

Vincent said, "We already tried that. This guy is a special piece of work. He doesn't know what fear is. He's been warned, he still keeps doing it."

Petie said, "They call him Big Tim, and they call him the Rustler, and he loves all that shit. He never pays his bills, he even stiffs the IRS, he fights with the California state authorities because he won't pay the sales tax of the stores he owns in his malls. Hell, he even stiffs his ex-wife and his kids on support payments. He's a thief in his heart. You cannot talk sense to him."

Giorgio said, "Cross, you know him personally from his gambling in Vegas. What do you say?"

Cross considered. "He's very late paying his markers. But he finally pays. He's smart gambling, not degenerate. He's one of those guys who is hard to like, but he's very rich so he has lots of friends that he brings to Vegas. Actually even fixing the games and winning some of our money, he is a big plus for us. Just let it go." As he said this he noticed Dante smiling, knowing something he didn't know.

"We can't let it go," Giorgio said. "Because this Big Tim, this Rustler, is fucking nuts. He's laying down some crazy scheme to fix the Super Bowl game."

Don Domenico spoke for the first time and directly to Cross, "Nephew, is that possible?"

The question was a compliment. It was the Don acknowledging that Cross was the expert in the field.

"No," Cross said to the Don. "You can't fix the Super Bowl officials because no one knows who they will be. You can't fix the players because the important ones make too much money. Also, you can never fix one game in any sport a one hundred percent sure thing. If you are a fixer you have to be able to fix fifty or a hundred games. That way if you lose three or four, you don't get hurt. And so unless you can do a lot of them it's not worth the risk."

"Bravo," the Don said. "Then why does this man, who is rich, want to do something so foolhardy?"

"He wants to be famous," Cross said. "To fix the Super Bowl he would have to do something so risky he is sure to be found out. Something so crazy I can't even think what it will be. The Rustler will think it clever. And he is a man who believes he can get out of every jam he gets in."

"I have never met a man like that," the Don said.

Giorgio said, "They grow them only in America."

"But then he is very dangerous to what we want to do," the Don said. "From what you tell me, he is a man who will not listen to reason. So there is no choice."

Cross said, "Wait. He means at least a half million dollars' profit every year to the casino."

Vincent said, "It's a matter of principle. The Books pay us money to protect them."

Cross said, "Let me talk to him. Maybe he'll listen to me. The whole thing is small potatoes. He can't fix the Super Bowl. It's not worth our taking action." But then he got a look from his father and he realized that in some way it was not proper for him to make such arguments.

The Don said with a terminal determination, "The man is dangerous. Don't talk to him, nephew. He doesn't know who you really are. Why give him the advantage? The man is dangerous because he is stupid, he is stupid as an animal is stupid, he wants to feed on everything. And then when he is caught he wants to wreak as much havoc as he can. He will implicate everyone whether true or not." He paused for a moment and then looked at Dante. "Grandson," he said, "I think you should do the job. But let Pippi do the planning on this one, he knows the territory."

Dante nodded.

Pippi knew he was on dangerous ground. If anything happened to Dante, he would be held responsible. And another thing was clear to him. The Don and Giorgio were determined some day Dante would head the Clericuzio Family. But at present they did not trust his judgment.

. . .

In Vegas Dante registered in a suite at the Xanadu. The Rustler, Snedden, was not due in Vegas for a week, and during that time Cross and Pippi indoctrinated Dante.

"Rustler is a high roller," Cross said. "But not high enough to rate a Villa. Not in the class of Arabs and Asians. His RFB is enormous, he wants everything free he can get. He puts friends on restaurant tabs, orders the best wines, he even tries to put the gift shop on his tab. We don't give that even to the Villa guys. He's a claim artist, so the dealers have to watch him. He'll claim he made a bet just before the number hit on the crap table. He'll try to make a bet in baccarat after the first card shows. At blackjack he'll claim he wanted to hit an eighteen when the next card is three. He's very late paying his markers. But he gives us a half million a year, even after we take off what he beats the sports book for. He's cute. He even draws chips for his friends and puts them on his marker so we'll think he gambles bigger than he actually does. All that chickenshit stuff like the garment center guys used to pull in the old days. But then he goes berserk when his luck goes bad. Last year he dropped two million and we made him a party and gave him a Cadillac. He bitched that it wasn't a Mercedes."

Dante was outraged. "He draws chips and money from the cage and doesn't gamble it?"

"Sure," Cross said. "A lot of guys do it. We don't mind. We like to look stupid. It gives them more confidence at the tables. They outsmart us again."

"Why do they call him the Rustler?" Dante asked.

"Because he takes things without paying for them," Cross said. "When he has girls he bites them as if he wants to take a chunk of their flesh. And he gets away with it. He's a great, great bullshit artist."

Dante said dreamily, "I can't wait to hear him."

"He could never talk Gronevelt into giving him a Villa," Cross said. "So I don't."

Dante looked at him sharply. "How come I didn't get a Villa?"

"Because it could cost the Hotel a hundred grand to a million bucks a night," Cross said.

Dante said, "But Giorgio gets a Villa."

"OK," Cross said, "I'll clear it with Giorgio." They both knew Giorgio would be outraged by Dante's request.

"Fat chance," Dante said.

"When you get married," Cross said, "you'll get a Villa for your honeymoon."

Pippi said, "My operational plan depends on Big Tim's character. Cross you have to cooperate just here in Vegas to set the guy up. You have to let Dante draw unlimited credit in the cage and then make his markers disappear. Timewise, the arrangements in L.A. are set. You have to make sure the guy gets here and doesn't cancel his reservation. So you give him a party to present him with a Rolls-Royce. Then when he's here you have to introduce him to Dante and me. After that you're through."

It took Pippi more than an hour to tell the plan in detail. Dante said admiringly, "Giorgio always said you were the best. I was pissed off when the Don put you over me on this. But I can see he was right."

Pippi took this flattery stone-faced. He said to Dante, "Remember this is a Communion not a Confirmation. It has to look as if he took it on the lam. With his record and all the lawsuits against him, that will be plausible. Dante, don't wear one of your fucking hats on this operation. People have funny memories. And remember that the Don said he would like the guy to give information about the fix, but it's not really necessary. He's the ringleader, when he's gone the whole fix will disappear. So don't do anything crazy."

Dante said coolly, "I feel unlucky without my hat."

Pippi shrugged. "Another thing, don't try to cheat on your unlimited credit. That comes from the Don himself, he doesn't want the Hotel to lose a fortune on this operation. They already have to put up the Rolls."

"Don't worry," Dante said. "My work is my pleasure." He paused for a moment and then said with a sly grin, "I hope you give me a good report on this one."

This surprised Cross. It was plain that there was some hostility between them. And he was also surprised that Dante would try to intimidate his father. That could be disastrous, grandson of the Don or not.

But Pippi seemed not to have noticed. "You're a Clericuzio," he said. "Who am I to report on you?" He clapped Dante on the shoulder. "We have a job to do together. Let's make it fun."

When Rustler Snedden arrived, Dante studied him. He was big and fat but the fat was hard, it stuck to his bones and didn't roll. His shirt was blue denim with large pockets on each breast, a white button in the middle. In one pocket he stuffed the black hundred-dollar chips, and in the other, the white-and-gold five hundreds. The red fives and green twenty-fives he stuffed into the pocket of his wide-trousered white canvas pants. On his feet were floppy brown sandals.

The Rustler played mostly craps, the best percentage game. Cross and Dante knew that he had already bet ten grand on two college basketball games and placed a five-thousand-dollar bet with the illegal books in town on a horse race in Santa Anita. The Rustler was not going to pay the taxes. And he seemed not to be worrying about his bets. He was having a grand time shooting craps.

He was the mayor of the crap table, telling other gamblers to ride with his dice, shouting good-humoredly at them not to be chicken. He was betting the blacks, stacks of them covering all the numbers, betting right all the way. When the dice came to him he hurled them vigorously so that they bounced off the opposite wall of the table and came back to his easy reach. He would then try to grab them, but the stickman was always alert to catch them in the claw of his stick and hold them so that other players could make their bets.

Dante took his place at the crap table and bet with Big Tim to win. Then he made all the ruinous side bets that would, unless he was very lucky, make him a sure loser. He bet the hard four and the hard ten. He bet the boxcars in one roll and the aces and eleven in one roll at odds of thirty and fifteen to one. He called for a twenty-thousand-dollar marker and, after signing for the black chips, spread them all over the table. He called for another marker. By this time, he had caught Big Tim's attention.

"Hey, you with the hat. Learn to play this game," Big Tim said.

Dante waved to him cheerily and continued his wild betting. When Big Tim sevened out, Dante took the dice and called for a fifty-thousand-dollar marker. He spread black chips all over the table hoping he wouldn't get lucky. He didn't. Now Big Tim was watching him with more than ordinary interest.

Big Tim the Rustler ate in the coffee shop, which was also the restaurant that served plain American fare. Big Tim rarely ate in the Xanadu's fancy French restaurant or its Northern Italian Restaurant or its authentic English Royal Pub restaurant. Five friends joined him for dinner, and Big Tim the Rustler made out Keno tickets for everybody so they could watch the numbers board while eating. Cross and Dante sat in a corner booth.

His short-cut blond hair made the Rustler resemble a Brueghel painting of a jolly German burgher. He ordered a great variety of dishes, the equivalent of three dinners, but to his credit he ate most of them while also dipping into his companions' plates.

"It's really too bad," Dante said. "I never saw a guy who enjoyed life so much."

"That's one way to make enemies," Cross said. "Especially when you enjoy it at other people's expense."

They watched Big Tim sign the check, which he did not have to pay, and order one of his companions to tip in cash. After they left, Cross and Dante relaxed over their coffee. Cross loved this huge room with glass walls showing the night lit outside by pink lamps, green from the grass and trees outside reflecting into the room, softening the chandeliers.

"I remember one night about three years ago," Cross said to Dante. "The Rustler had a great streak at the crap table. I think he won over a hundred grand. It was about three in the morning. And when the pit boss took his chips to the cage, the Rustler jumped up on the crap table and pissed all over it."

"What did you do?" Dante asked.

"I had the security guards take him to his room and charged him five grand for the piss on the table. Which he never paid."

"I would have ripped his fucking heart out," Dante said.

"If a man gives you a half million a year, wouldn't you let him piss on a table?" Cross said. "But to tell the truth, I always held it against him. In fact, if he had done that in the Villas' casino, who knows?"

The next day Cross had lunch with Big Tim to brief him on his party and the presentation of the Rolls-Royce. Pippi joined them and was introduced.

Big Tim always pushed for more. "I appreciate the Rolls but when do I get one of your Villas?"

"Yeah, you deserve it," Cross said. "The next time you come to Vegas, you get a Villa. That's a promise, even if I have to kick somebody out."

Big Tim the Rustler said to Pippi, "Your son is a much nicer man than that old prick, Gronevelt."

"He was a little funny in his last years," Pippi said. "I was maybe his best friend and he would never give me a Villa."

"Well, fuck him," Big Tim said. "Now that your son is running the Hotel, you can get a Villa whenever you want."

"Never," Cross said, "he's not a gambler." They all laughed.

But now Big Tim was on another tack. "There's a weird little guy who wears a funny hat and is the worst crapshooter I ever saw," he said. "This guy signed nearly two hundred grand in markers in less than an hour. What can you tell me about him? You know I'm always looking for investors."

"I can't tell you anything about my players," Cross said. "How would you like it if I gave out information about you? I can tell you he can get a Villa anytime, but he never asks. He likes to keep a low profile."

"Just give me an intro," Big Tim said. "If I make a deal, you'll get a piece."

"No," Cross said. "But my father knows him."

"I could use some dough," Pippi said.

Big Tim said, "Good. Give me a big buildup."

Pippi turned on his charm. "You two guys would make a great team. This guy has a lot of money but he doesn't have your flair for big business. I know you're a fair guy, Tim, so just give me what you think I deserve."

Big Tim beamed at this. Pippi would be another of his suckers. "Great," he said. "I'll be at the crap table tonight, so bring him around."

When the introductions were made at the crap table, Big Tim the Rustler startled both Dante and Pippi by snatching Dante's Renaissance cap off his head and replacing it with a Dodger baseball cap he was wearing. The result was hilarious. The Renaissance cap on Big Tim's head made him look like one of Snow White's dwarfs.

"To change our luck," Big Tim said. They all laughed but Pippi didn't like the malevolent gleam in Dante's eyes. Also, he was angry that Dante had ignored his instructions and was wearing the hat. He had introduced Dante as Steve Sharpe and had pumped Big Tim up with stories that Steve was the overlord of a drug empire on the Eastern Seaboard and had to "wash" many millions. Also that Steve was a degenerate gambler who had bet a million on the Super Bowl and had lost without batting an eye. And his markers in the casino cage were pure gold. Paid them right up.

So now Big Tim threw his massive arm over Dante's shoulders and said, "Stevie, we have to talk. Let's have a little bite in the coffee shop."

There, Big Tim took a secluded booth. Dante ordered coffee but Big Tim ordered a whole array of desserts: strawberry ice cream, napoleons, and banana cream pie plus a dish of assorted cookies.

Then he launched into an hour-long selling speech. He owned a small mall he wanted to get rid of, a long-term moneymaker, and he could arrange that the payment would be mostly under-the-table cash. There was a meat-packing plant and carloads of fresh produce that could be sold for undercover cash, then resold for a profit for white money. He had an "in" with the movie business so that he could help finance pictures that went direct to video or to porno theaters. "Great business," Big Tim said. "You get to meet the stars and fuck the starlets and turn your money white."

Dante enjoyed the performance. Everything Big Tim said was with such confidence and brio that the victim could only believe in future riches. He asked questions that betrayed his eagerness but made a show of coyness.

"Give me your card," he said. "I'll give you a call or have Pippi call you and then we can set up a dinner meeting and have a full discussion so I can make a commitment."

Big Tim gave him his card. "Let's do it real quick," he said. "I have one particular 'no lose' deal I'll cut you in on. But we would have to move fast." He paused for a moment. "It's a sports thing."

Now Dante showed an enthusiasm he had not shown before. "Jesus, that has always been my dream. I love sports. You mean maybe buy a major league baseball team?"

"Not that big," Big Tim said hastily. "But big enough."

"So when do we meet?" Dante asked.

Big Tim said proudly, "Tomorrow the Hotel is giving me a party and a Rolls. For being one of their best suckers. I go back to L.A. the day after. How about that night?"

Dante pretended to give the question some thought. "Okay," he said. "Pippi's coming to L.A. with me and I'll have him give you a call to set it up."

"Great," Big Tim said. He wondered a bit about the man's cautiousness but knew better than to queer a deal with unnecessary questions. "And tonight I'm going to show you how to shoot craps so that you have some chance of winning."

Dante made himself look sheepish. "I know the odds, I just like to fuck around. And then the word gets out and I can get a whack at the chorus girls."

"Then there's no hope for you," Big Tim said. "But you and me, we'll make some money together anyway."

The next day the party for Big Tim the Rustler was held in the great ballroom of the Xanadu Hotel, which was often used for special events: the New Year's Eve party, Christmas buffets, weddings for high rollers, presentations of special awards and gifts, Super Bowl parties, the World Series, and even political conventions.

It was a huge, high-ceilinged room, with balloons floating everywhere and two enormous buffet tables, splitting the room in half. The buffets were shaped like huge ice glaciers, and encrushed in the ice were exotic fruits of all colors. Crenshaw melons, split open to show their yellow-gold flesh, great purple grapes with their juice bursting against the skin, porcupine pineapples, kiwi and kumquat, nectarines and lichee nuts, and a huge log of watermelon. Buckets of twelve different kinds of ice cream were buried like submarines. Then there was a passageway of hot dishes: a baron of beef as big as a buffalo, a huge turkey, a white, fat-ringed ham. Then there was a tray of different pastas, sprinkled green with pesto and red with tomato sauce. And then a great red pot, as big as a garbage can, with silver handles and steaming with a "wild boar" stew that was really a pork, beef, and veal mixture. Then came bread of all kinds and rolls heavy with flour. Another bank of ice held desserts, cream puffs, whipped-cream-filled doughnuts, an assortment of tiered cakes decorated with replicas of the Hotel Xanadu. Coffee and hard liquor would be served to the guests by the best-looking waitresses at the Hotel.

Big Tim the Rustler was already wreaking havoc on these tables before the first guest arrived.

In the full center of the room, mounted on a ramp separated by ropes from the crowd, was the Rolls-Royce. Creamy, white, luxurious, with true elegance and a certain genius in design, it stood in sharp contrast to the pretensions of this Vegas world. A wall of the room had been replaced by heavy golden draperies to allow its entrance and departure. Then off in a corner of the room was a purple Cadillac that was to be awarded as a door prize to those with numbered invitations: high rollers invited to the party and casino managers of the biggest hotels. This had been one of Gronevelt's best ideas. These parties increased the Drop at the Hotel significantly.

The party was a huge success because Big Tim was so flamboyant. Attended by his two waitresses, he almost single-handedly destroyed the buffet table. He loaded up three plates and gave an exhibition of eating that nearly made Dante's mission unnecessary.

Cross made the presentation speech for the Hotel. Then Big Tim made his acceptance speech.

"I want to thank the Xanadu Hotel for this wonderful gift," he said. "That two-hundred-thousand-dollar car is now mine for nothing. It's my reward for coming to the Xanadu the last ten years, during which they treated me like a prince and emptied my wallet. I figure if they give me fifty Rolls we would be about even but what the hell, I can only drive one car at at time."

Here he was interrupted by applause and cheers. Cross grimaced. He was always embarrassed by these rituals that exposed the falseness of the Hotel's goodwill.

Big Tim threw his arms around the two waitresses flanking him. He squeezed their breasts in a friendly way. He waited like an experienced comic for the applause to die down.

"No kidding, I'm truly grateful," he said. "This is one of the happiest days of my life. Right up there with my divorce. One little thing. Who's going to give me gas money to drive this car back to L.A.? The Xanadu cleaned me out again."

Big Tim knew when to stop. As the applause and cheers broke out again, he climbed the ramp and got into the car. The golden draperies that had replaced the wall now parted, and Big Tim drove out.

The party speedily broke up after the Cadillac was won by a high roller. The festivities had lasted for four hours and everybody wanted to get back to the gambling tables.

That night Gronevelt's ghost would have been overjoyed with the results of the party. The Drop was nearly double the average. Sexual coupling could not be confirmed but the smell of semen seemed to seep out into the hallways. The great-looking call girls that had been invited to Big Tim's party had quickly snuggled into relationships with less dedicated high rollers, who gave them black chips to gamble.

Gronevelt had often remarked to Cross that male and female gamblers had different sex patterns. And that it was important for casino owners to know them.

First Gronevelt proclaimed the primacy of pussy, as he called it. Pussy could overcome anything. It could even make a degenerate gambler go straight. There had been many important men of the world who had been guests at the Hotel. Nobel Prize–winning scientists, billionaires, great religious revivalists, eminent literary icons. A Nobel Prize–winner in physics, the best brain maybe in the world, had frolicked with a whole line of chorus girls during his six-day stay. He didn't gamble much but it was an honor for the Hotel. Gronevelt himself had to give gifts to each of the girls, it had never occurred to the Nobel Prize–winner to do so. The girls had reported he was the best screw in the world, eager, ardent, and skillful, no tricks, with one of the most beautiful cocks they had ever seen. And best of all, amusing, never boring them with serious talk. As gossipy and bitchy as any of the girls. For some reason this cheered Gronevelt up. That such a brain could please the opposite sex. Not like Ernest Vail, such a great writer but a middle-aged kid with a perpetual hard-on and no small talk to go with it. Then there was Senator Wavven, a possible future president of the United States, who treated sex like a game of golf. To say nothing of the dean of Yale, the cardinal of Chicago, the leader of the Civil Rights National Committee, and the crusty Republican bigwigs. All of them reduced to children by pussy. The only possible exceptions were the gays or druggies, but after all they were not typically gamblers.

Gronevelt noted that male gamblers called for hookers *before* they set out to gamble. Women, however, preferred sex *after* they gambled. Since the Hotel had to cater to the sexual needs of everyone and there were no male hookers, just gigolos, the Hotel used barmen croupiers and junior pit boys for the women, and that was their report. So Gronevelt made a jump. Males need sex to prepare them to go into battle with confidence. Women need sex to assuage the sorrow of losing or as part of the reward for their victory.

It was true that Big Tim called for a hooker an hour before his party and then went to bed with his two waitresses in the early morning after losing a big sum of money. They were reluctant, they were straight girls. Big Tim solved the problem in his own particular way. He put up ten thousand dollars worth of black chips and told them it was theirs if they spent the night with him. Accompanied with his usual vague promise of more if they had a really good night. He loved the way they studied the chips thoughtfully before agreeing. The joke was they got him so drunk that he fell asleep, gorged with food and drink, before he got past the fondling stage. He fell asleep between the two of them, his huge frame pushing them to the edges, both girls clinging to him until finally they fell on the floor to sleep.

Late that night Cross received a call from Claudia. "Athena disappeared," she said. "The Studio is frantic and I'm worried. Except ever since I've known her Athena has disappeared at least one weekend a month. But this time I thought you should know. You better do something before she runs away forever."

"It's OK," Cross said. He didn't tell her he had his own men covering Skannet.

But that call focused his mind on Athena. That magical face, which seemed to show her every emotion; the long, beautiful stretch of her legs. And the intelligence of her eyes, the vibration from some invisible instrument of inner being.

He picked up the phone and called a chorus girl he sometimes dated called Tiffany.

Tiffany was the captain of the chorus line of the Xanadu's big cabaret show. This entitled her to extra pay and perks for keeping discipline and preventing the usual quarrels and outright fights the girls fell into. She was a statuesque beauty who had failed screen tests because she simply was too big for celluloid. Where on the stage her beauty was commanding, on film she looked huge.

When she arrived, she was surprised at the quickness of Cross's lovemaking. He simply grabbed her and stripped her of her clothes and then seemed to devour her body with kisses. He entered her quickly and came to a climax quickly. This was so different from his usual style that she said, almost ruefully, "This time it must be true love."

"It sure is," Cross said, and began to make love to her again.

"Not me, you dope," Tiffany said. "Who's the lucky girl?"

Cross was annoyed that he was so easy to read. And yet he could not stop his devotion to the flesh beside him. He could not have enough of her succulent breasts, her silky tongue, the velvet mound between her thighs, all radiating an irresistible heat. When finally, hours later, the lustful fever was gone, he could not stop thinking about Athena.

Tiffany picked up the phone and ordered room service for them both. "I pity that poor girl when you finally get her," Tiffany said.

After she left, Cross felt free. It was a weakness to be so much in love, but satisfied lust gave him confidence. At three in the morning he made his last tour of the casino.

In the coffee shop he saw Dante with three good-looking, vivacious women. Though one of them was Loretta Lang, the singer he had helped to break her contract, he did not recognize her. Dante waved him over, but he declined with a shake of his head. Up in his penthouse suite he took two sleeping pills before going to bed, but he still dreamed of Athena.

The three women at Dante's table were famous ladies of Hollywood, wives of Bankable Stars and minor stars in their own right. They had been guests at Big Tim's party, not by invitation but by having wangled their way in on their charms.

The oldest was Julia Deleree, who was married to one of the most famous Bankable Stars in the movies. She had two children, and the family often appeared in magazines as the exceptional couple that had no problems, were ecstatic with their marriage.

The second was Joan Ward. She was still very attractive, nearly fifty. She played second leads now, usually as the intelligent woman, the suffering mother of a doomed child, or in the role of a deserted woman whose tragedy leads to a second happy marriage. Or as a fiery fighter for the feminist viewpoint. She was married to the head of a studio who paid her charge cards without complaint, no matter how huge, and whose only demand on her was to be the hostess for the many social-business parties he gave. She had no children.

The third star was Loretta, who by now was first choice as the comedy lead in kooky comedies. She, too, had married well, to a Bankable Star of empty-headed action films that took him on location in other countries for the best part of the year.

These three had become friends by being cast in the same movies and by shopping on Rodeo Drive and having lunches at the Beverly Hills Hotel's Polo Lounge, where they compared notes on their husbands and their charge cards. About the cards, they had no complaints. It was like having a shovel to dig in a gold mine, and their husbands never questioned their bills.

Julia complained that her husband didn't spend enough time with her kids. Joan, whose husband was acclaimed as a discoverer of new stars, complained she was childless. Loretta complained that her husband should branch out into more serious roles. But there came a day when Loretta, with her usual vivaciousness, said, "Let's stop bullshitting ourselves. We're all happily and very suitably married to very important guys. What we really hate is that our husbands send us out on Rodeo Drive so they feel less guilty about fucking other women." The three of them laughed. It was so true.

Julia said, "I love my husband but he's been in Tahiti for a month shooting a picture. And I know he's not sitting on the beach masturbating. But I don't want to spend a month in Tahiti, so he's either screwing his leading lady or the local talent."

"Which he would be doing even if you were there," Loretta said.

Joan said wistfully, "And even though my husband hasn't the sperm of a fucking ant, his cock is like a water wand. How come most of the stars he discovers are females? He screen-tests them by finding out how much of his cock they can swallow."

They were all half tipsy by now. They believed that wine had no calories.

Loretta said crisply, "We can't blame our husbands. The most beautiful women in the world show it to them. They really have no choice. But why should we suffer? Fuck the charge cards, let's have some fun."

And so had followed their sacred once-a-month girl's night out. When their husbands were gone, which was often, they would go on overnight adventures.

Since they were recognizable to most Americans, they had to disguise themselves. This proved to be extraordinarily easy to do. They used wigs to change the style and color of their hair. They used makeup, thickened their lips or thinned them. They dressed in the style of middle-class women. They downgraded their beauty, which didn't matter because, like most actresses, they could be enormously charming. And they delighted in the role playing. They loved to listen to different kinds of men bare their hearts to them in hope of getting into bed with them, often successfully. It was a breath of real life, the characters still mysterious, not doomed to a written script. And there were delightful surprises. Sincere offers of marriage and true love; men sharing their pain because they thought they would never see them again. The admiration they received not because of their hidden status, but because of their innate charms. And they loved creating new personas for themselves. Sometimes they would be computer operators on vacation, sometimes off-duty nurses or dental technicians or social workers. They would bone up for their parts by reading about their new professions. Sometimes they would pretend to be legal secretaries in the office of a big showbiz lawyer in L.A. and spread scandal about their own husbands and other of their actor friends. They had great times but always went out of town; Los Angeles was too dangerous, they might run into friends who would easily recognize them despite their disguise. They discovered that San Francisco was also risky. Some gay men seemed to know their true identity at a glance. Their favorite place was Las Vegas.

Dante had picked them up at the Xanadu Club Lounge, where tired gamblers took a break and listened to a band, a comic, and a girl singer. Loretta had once performed there at the beginning of her career. There was no dancing. The Hotel wanted their customers to get back to the tables as soon as they were rested.

Dante was attracted to them by their vivaciousness, their natural charm. They were attracted to him because they had watched him gamble and lose enormous amounts of money with his unlimited credit. After the drinks, he took them to the roulette wheel and staked them each to a thousand dollars' worth of chips. They were charmed by his hat and the extravagant courtesy showed to him by the croupiers and the pit boss. And his sly charm, which was touched by a vicious humor. Dante was witty in a vulgar and sometimes chilling way. And the extravagance of his gambling excited them. Of course they themselves were rich, they earned enormous amounts of money, but his was hard cash and that had its own magic. Certainly they had spent tens of thousands on Rodeo Drive in one day, but they had received luxurious goods in return. When Dante signed a hundred-thousand-dollar marker, they were awed, though their husbands had bought them cars that cost more. But Dante was throwing away money.

They didn't always sleep with men they picked up, but when they went to the ladies room they conferred on which one would get Dante. Julia begged and she said she had a real yen to pee in Dante's funny hat. The others gave in.

Joan had hoped to score five or ten grand. Not that she really needed it, but it was cash, real money. Loretta was not as charmed as the others by Dante. Her life in Las Vegas cabaret had partly inured her to such men. They were too full of surprises, most of them not pleasant.

The women had a three-bedroom suite in the Xanadu. They always stuck close together on these outings, for reasons of safety and so they could gossip together about their adventures. They made it a rule not to spend the entire night with the men they picked up.

So Julia wound up with Dante, who had no say in the matter, though he preferred Loretta. But he insisted Julia go to his suite, which was just below hers. "I'll walk you up to your suite," he said coolly. "We'll just be an hour. I have to get up early in the morning." It was then Julia realized he thought they were soft hookers.

"Come up to my suite," Julia said. "I'll walk you down."

Dante said, "You got your two horny buddies up there. How do I know you won't all jump me and sodomize me? I'm just a little guy."

That amused Julia enough to go to his suite. She had missed the slyness of his smile. On their way to his room, she said jokingly, "I want to pee in your hat."

Dante said to her, stone-faced, "If it's fun for you, it's fun for me."

Once in his suite there was very little chitchat. Julia threw her purse on the sofa and then pulled down the top of her dress so that her breasts showed, they were her best feature. But Dante seemed to be the exception, a male who was not interested in breasts.

He led her into the bedroom and then pulled off her dress and underclothes. When she was naked, he shed his own clothes. She could see his penis was short, stubby, and uncircumcised. "You have to use a condom," she said.

Dante threw her on the bed. Julia was a robust woman, but he picked her up and threw her without seeming to make an effort. Then he straddled her.

"I insist you use a condom," she said. "I mean it."

In the next moment there was an explosion of light in her head. She realized he had slapped her so hard that she had almost lost consciousness. She tried to wriggle away but for so small a man he was incredibly strong. She felt two more slaps that suffused her face with a hot glow and made her teeth ache. Then she felt him enter her. His driving thrusts lasted for only a few seconds and then he slumped over her.

They lay entwined and then he began to turn her over. She could see that he still had an erection and she knew he wanted to penetrate her anally. She whispered to him, "I love that but I have to get some Vaseline from my purse."

He let her slide out from under him and she went into the living room. Dante came to the door of the bedchamber. They were both still naked and he still had an erection.

Julia fumbled in her purse and then, with a dramatic flourish, took out a tiny silver handgun. It was a prop from a movie she had worked in and she had always fantasized about using it in a real-life situation. She pointed it at Dante, took the crouch stance she had been taught in the movie, and said, "I'm going to dress and leave. If you try to stop me, I'll shoot."

To her surprise, the naked Dante burst out in a good-humored laugh. But Julia noted with satisfaction that he immediately lost his erection.

She was enjoying the situation. She was imagining that she was back upstairs with Joan and Loretta and how they would laugh about this. She tried to get up the courage to ask for his hat so she could pee in it.

But now Dante surprised her. He started walking toward her slowly. He was smiling, he said gently, "That's such a small caliber, it won't even stop me unless you get a lucky shot to the head. Never use a small gun. You can put three bullets to my body and then I'll strangle you. Also, you're holding that gun wrong, you don't need that stance, there's no kick in it. Plus the chances are you won't even hit me, those little bitty things are inaccurate. So throw it away and we'll talk this over. Then you can leave."

He continued walking toward her so she threw the gun on the sofa. Dante picked it up and looked at it, shook his head. "A fake gun?" he said. "That's the sure way to get killed." He shook his head in an almost affectionate disapproval. "Well, if you were a real hooker, this would be a real gun. So who are you?"

He pushed Julia down on the sofa and imprisoned her there with his leg, his toes pushed against her pubic hair. Then he opened her purse and spilled the contents onto the coffee table. He fished into the purse pockets and took out her wallet of credit cards and her driver's license. He studied them carefully and then grinned in pure delight. He said to her, "Take off that wig." Then he reached over with a doily from the sofa and wiped her face clean of makeup.

"Jesus Christ, you are Julia Deleree," Dante said. "I'm fucking a movie star." He gave another delighted laugh. "You can pee in my hat anytime."

His toes were searching her crotch. Then he pulled her to her feet. "Don't be scared," he said. He kissed her and then turned her around and pushed her so that she was bent over the back of the sofa, breasts hanging down, her buttocks presented, tilted up to him.

Julia said to him tearfully, "You promised to let me leave."

Dante was kissing her buttocks, his fingers probing. Then he entered her savagely and she gave a yell of pain. When he finished, he patted her buttocks tenderly.

"You can get dressed now," he said. "I'm sorry I broke my word. I just couldn't miss the chance of telling my friends that I fucked Julia Deleree up her great ass."

The next morning Cross had a wakeup call push him out of bed early. It would be a busy day. He had to pull all of Dante's markers out of the casino cage and do the necessary paperwork to make them disappear. He had to get the pit bosses' marker books out of their hands and have them redone. Then he had to make arrangements so that the papers on the Rolls for Big Tim would be revoked. Giorgio had had the legal papers prepared so that the official change of ownership would not be valid until a month in the future. That was vintage Giorgio.

In the middle of all this he was interrupted with a call from Loretta Lang. She was in the Hotel and urgently wanted to see him. Because he thought it might be something about Claudia, he had Security bring her up to the penthouse.

Loretta kissed him on both cheeks and then told him the whole story about Julia and Dante. She said the man had introduced himself as Steve Sharpe and had lost a hundred grand at the crap table. They were impressed, and Julia decided to sleep with him. The three of them had only come to relax and have a night of gambling. Now they were terrified that Steve might cause a scandal.

Cross nodded sympathetically. He was thinking, What a stupid thing for Dante to do before a big operation, and the son of a bitch was giving away black chips for his pickups to gamble with. He said to Loretta calmly, "I know the man, of course. Who are the two women with you?"

Loretta knew better than to dally with Cross. She told him the two names. Cross smiled. "Do you three do this often?"

"We have to have a little fun," Loretta said. Cross gave her a sympathetic smile.

"OK," he said. "Your friend went to his room. She undressed. She wants to scream rape? What?"

Loretta said hastily, "No, no. We just want him to keep quiet. If he talks it could be absolute disasters for our careers."

"He won't talk," Cross said. "He's a funny kind of guy. Keeps a low profile. But take my advice, don't get mixed up with him again. You girls should be more careful."

Loretta was annoyed by this last remark. The three women had decided to continue their outings. They were not going to be frightened by one mishap. Nothing really terrible had happened. She said, "How do you know he won't talk?"

Cross looked at her gravely. "I'll ask him the favor," he said.

When Loretta left, Cross called for the secret camera file that showed all the guests at the registration desk. He studied them. Now that he had the information, it was easy to penetrate the disguises of the two women with Loretta Lang. It was dumb for Dante not to have gotten that info.

Pippi came by the penthouse office to have lunch before he left for Los Angeles to check off the logistics of the Big Tim operation. Cross told him the story Loretta had told.

Pippi shook his head. "The little bastard could have ruined the whole operation by throwing the timing off. And he keeps wearing that fucking hat after I told him not to."

Cross said, "Be careful on this operation. Keep your eye on Dante."

"I planned it, he can't fuck it up," Pippi said. "And when I see him in L.A. tonight, I'll give him another briefing."

Cross told him about how Giorgio had prepared the papers on the Rolls so that Big Tim would not acquire legal ownership for a month and so that after his death, the Hotel could regain the car.

"Typical Giorgio," Pippi said. "The Don would have let the estate keep his car for his kids."

Big Tim the Rustler Snedden left Vegas two days later, owing sixty grand in markers to the Xanadu Hotel. He took the late-afternoon plane to Los Angeles, went to his office and worked for a few hours, and then drove to Santa Monica to have dinner with his ex-wife and his two children. His pockets had wads of five-dollar bills, which he gave to his kids along with a cardboard container, a quart of silver dollars. To his wife he gave the support and alimony check due, without which he would not be allowed to visit. He conned his wife with sweet talk after the children went to bed but she wouldn't give him a screw, which he didn't really want after Vegas. But he had to try, it was something for nothing.

The next day Big Tim the Rustler had a very busy day indeed. Two Internal Revenue Agents tried to frighten him into paying some disputed taxes. He told them he would go to tax court and threw them out. Then he had to visit a warehouse of canned foods and another warehouse of over-the-counter drugs, all acquired at rock-bottom prices because their expiration dates were coming up. Those expiration dates would have to be changed. At lunch he met with a supermarket-chain vice president who would accept the shipment of these goods. During lunch he slipped the executive an envelope that held ten thousand dollars.

After lunch he received a surprise call from two FBI agents who wanted to ask him about his relationship with a congressman who was under indictment. Big Tim told them to go fuck themselves.

Big Tim the Rustler had never known fear. Perhaps because of his bulk, or maybe there was a piece of his brain missing. For he not only lacked physical fear, he lacked mental fear. He had not only taken the offensive against man but against nature itself. When the doctors told him he was eating himself to death and he should seriously diet, he had opted instead for the stomach bypass operation, which was more hazardous. And it had turned out perfectly. He ate as he wished without apparent harmful effect.

He had built his financial empire the same way. He made contracts that he refused to honor when they became unprofitable, he betrayed partners and friends. Everybody sued him, but they always had to settle for less than they would have received on the original terms. It was a life of success for one who took no precautions for the future. He always thought he would win in the end. He could always collapse corporate entities, shmooze over personal animosities. With women he was even more merciless. He promised them whole malls, apartments, boutiques. Then they settled for a small piece of jewelry at Christmas, a small check on their birthdays. Significant sums but not up to the original promises. Big Tim did not want a relationship. He just wanted to make sure he could have a friendly screw when he needed it.

Big Tim loved all this rustling, it made life interesting. There had been an independent bookmaker in L.A. that he had stiffed for a seventy-grand bet on football games. The bookmaker held a gun to his head and Big Tim said, "Go fuck yourself," then offered ten grand to settle the debt. The bookmaker took it.

His fortune, his ruddy health, his imposing bulk, his lack of guilt made Big Tim successful in everything he touched. His belief that all humanity was corruptible gave him a certain air of innocence that was useful not only in a woman's bed but also in the courts of law. And his gusto for life gave him a certain charm. He was a con man who let you peek at his cards.

So Big Tim did not wonder at the mystery of the arrangement Pippi De Lena had made with him for that night. The man was a hustler like himself and could be dealt with appropriately. Big promises and small rewards.

As for Steve Sharpe, Big Tim smelled a great opportunity, a multi-year scam. The little guy had dropped at least a half million in one day at the tables that he observed. Which meant he had an enormous credit line at the casino and must be in a position to earn a great deal of black money. He would be perfect in the Super Bowl fix. Not only could he supply the betting money, but he had the confidence of bookmakers. After all, those guys didn't take mammoth bets from just anybody.

Then Big Tim daydreamed about his next visit to Vegas. Finally he would get a Villa. He pondered on who to bring with him as guests. Business or pleasure? Future scam victims or maybe all women? Finally it was time to go to dinner with Pippi and Steve Sharpe. He called his ex-wife and his two kids for a chat and then was on his way.

The dinner was at a small fish restaurant down in the L.A. dock area. There was no valet service, so Big Tim put his car in a parking lot.

In the restaurant he was greeted by a tiny maître d' who took one look at him and ushered him to a table where Pippi De Lena was waiting.

Big Tim was an expert of the *abraccio* and he took Pippi into his arms. "Where's Steve? Is he jerking me around? I haven't the time for that kind of bullshit."

Pippi turned on all his charm. He clapped Big Tim on the shoulder. "What am I, chopped liver?" he said. "Sit down and have the best fish dinner you ever ate. We'll be seeing Steve after."

When the maître d' came to take their order, Pippi told him, "We want the best of everything and the most of everything. My friend here is a champion eater and if he gets up from this table hungry, I'll talk to Vincent."

The maître d' smiled confidently; he knew the quality of his kitchen. His restaurant was part of Vincent Clericuzio's empire. When the police backtracked Big Tim's trail, they would meet a blank wall here.

They ate a progression of clams, mussels, shrimps, and then lobsters: three for Big Tim and one for Pippi. Pippi was finished long before Big Tim. He said to him, "This guy is a friend of mine and I can tell you now he is tops in drugs. If that scares you off, tell me now."

"That scares me as much as this lobster," Big Tim said, waving its huge, nibbled claws in Pippi's face. "What else?"

"He always has to launder black money," Pippi said. "Your deal will have to include that."

Big Tim was enjoying the food; all the briney spices of the ocean filled his nostrils. "Great, I know all that," he said. "But where the fuck is he?"

"He's on his yacht," Pippi said. "He doesn't want anybody to see you with him. That's to your interest. He's a very cautious guy."

"I don't give a flying fuck who sees me with him," Big Tim said. "I want to see *me* with *him*."

Finally Big Tim was finished. His dessert was fruit, with a cup of espresso. Pippi skillfully skinned a pear for him. Tim ordered another espresso. "To keep me awake," he said. "That third lobster nearly put me away."

No check was presented. Pippi left a twenty-dollar bill on the table and the two left the restaurant, the maître d' silently applauding Tim's performance at the table.

Pippi guided Big Tim to a small rental car that Tim squeezed into with difficulty. "Christ, can't you afford a bigger car?" Big Tim said.

"It's only a short distance," Pippi said soothingly. And indeed it was a five-minute ride. By that time it was really dark except for the lights of a small yacht moored to the pier.

The gangplank was down, guarded by a man almost as big as Tim. There was another man on the far deck. Pippi and Big Tim went up the gangplank and onto the deck of the yacht. Then Dante appeared on the deck and came forward to shake their hands. He was wearing his Renaissance hat, which he guarded good-naturedly from Big Tim's swipe.

Dante led them below deck to a cabin decorated as a dining room. They sat around a table in comfortable chairs screwed into the floor.

On the table was an array of liquor bottles, a bucket of ice, and a tray with drinking glasses. Pippi poured them all a brandy.

At that moment the engines started and the yacht began to move. Big Tim said, "Where the hell are we going?"

Dante said smoothly, "Just a little spin for some fresh air. Once we're out on the open sea, we can go up on the deck and enjoy it."

Big Tim was not that unsuspicious, but he had faith in himself, that he could handle anything that happened in the future. He accepted the explanation.

Dante said, "Tim, my understanding is that you want to go into business with me."

"No, I want you to go into business with *me,*" Big Tim said with boastful good humor. "I run the show. You get your money washed without paying a premium. And make a good bit extra. I have a mall I'm building outside Fresno and you can get a piece for five million or ten. I have a lot of other deals all the time."

"That sounds very good," Pippi De Lena said.

Big Tim gave him a cold stare. "Where do you shine in? I've been meaning to ask."

"He's my junior partner," Dante said. "My advisor. I have the money but he has the brains." He paused and then said sincerely, "He's told me a lot of good things about you, Tim, that's why we're talking."

The yacht was moving very swiftly now, the glasses trembled on the tray. Big Tim debated whether he should cut this guy in on the Super Bowl fix. Then he had one of his hunches, and they were never wrong. He leaned back in his chair, sipped his brandy, and gave both men a serious questioning look, which he often gave and had in fact rehearsed. The look of a man about to bestow his trust. In a best friend. "I'm going to let you guys in on a secret," he said. "But first, are we going to do business? You want a piece of the mall?"

"I'm in," Dante said. "Our lawyers will get together tomorrow and I'll put up some good faith money."

Big Tim emptied his brandy glass and then leaned forward. "I can fix the Super Bowl," he said. With a dramatic flourish he signaled to Pippi to fill his glass. He was gratified to see the look of astonishment on their faces. "You think I'm full of shit, right?" he said.

Dante took off his Renaissance hat and looked at it thoughtfully. "I think you're peeing in my hat," he said with a reminiscing smile. "A lot of people try. But Pippi is the expert on this stuff. Pippi?"

"Can't be done," Pippi said. "The Super Bowl is eight months away and you don't even know who'll be in it."

"Then fuck you," Big Tim said. "You don't want part of a sure thing, that's okay with me. But I'm telling you I can fix it. If you don't want it okay, let's do the mall. Turn this boat around and stop wasting my fucking time."

"Don't be so touchy," Pippi said. "Just tell us how the fix works."

Big Tim gulped his brandy and said in a regretful voice, "I can't tell you that. But I'll give you a guarantee. You bet ten million and we split the winnings. If anything goes wrong, I'll give you ten million back. Now is that fair?"

Dante and Pippi looked at each other with amused grins. Dante ducked his head, and his Renaissance hat made him look like a cunning squirrel. "You give me the money back in cash?" he asked.

"Not exactly," Big Tim said. "I'll make it up on another deal. Take ten million off the price."

"Do you fix the players?" Dante asked.

"He can't," Pippi said. "They make too much money. It must be the officials."

Big Tim was enthusiastic now. "I can't tell you but it's foolproof. And never mind the money. Think of the glory. It will be the biggest fix in sports history."

"Sure, they'll toast us in jail," Dante said.

"That's the beauty of me not telling you anything," Big Tim said. "I go to jail, you guys don't. And my lawyers are too good and I have too many connections."

For the first time, Dante varied Pippi's script. He said, "Are we far enough out?"

Pippi said, "Yeah, but I think if we talk a little more, Tim will tell us."

"Fuck Tim," Dante said pleasantly. "You hear that, Big Tim? Now I want to hear how the fix works and no bullshit." His tone was so contemptuous that Big Tim's face flushed red.

"You little prick," he said, "you think you can scare me? You think you're tougher than the FBI, and the IRS, and the toughest shylock on the West Coast? I'll *shit* in your hat."

Dante leaned back in his chair and banged on the wall of the cabin. A few seconds later two large, tough-looking men opened the door, then stood guard. In answer, Big Tim stood up and swept the table clean with one huge arm. Liquor bottles, the bucket of ice, and the tray of glasses crashed to the cabin floor.

"No Tim, listen to me," Pippi shouted. He wanted to spare the man unnecessary suffering. Also, he did not want to be the shooter, that was not part of the plan. But Big Tim was rushing toward the door, ready to do battle.

Then suddenly Dante was slipping inside Big Tim's arms, nestled against his huge body. They broke apart and Big Tim sagged to his knees. It was a frightening sight. Half his shirt had been sliced away and where once his hairy right breast had been there was just a huge red patch from which an enormous gush of blood poured, staining half the table.

In Dante's hand was the knife he had used, the blood crimson on its broad blade up to the hilt.

"Put him in a chair," Dante said to the guards, and then he took the cloth off the table to staunch Big Tim's bleeding. Big Tim was nearly unconscious with shock.

Pippi said, "You could have waited."

"No," Dante said. "He's a tough guy. Let's see how tough."

"I'll get things ready on the deck," Pippi said. He didn't want to watch. He had never done torture. There were really no secrets so important that justified that kind of work. When you killed a man, you merely separated him from this world so that he could do you no harm.

Up on the deck he saw that two of his men had already prepared. The steel cage was ready on its hook, the slatted bars closed. The deck was covered with a plastic sheet.

He felt the balmy air fragrant with salt, the night ocean purple and still. The yacht was slowing down and then it stopped.

Pippi gazed down at the ocean for a full fifteen minutes before the two men who had stood guard at the door appeared, carrying Big Tim's body. It was so terrible a sight that Pippi averted his eyes.

The four men put Big Tim's body into the cage and then lowered it over the water. One of the men adjusted the slats so that the cage was open for the denizens of the ocean deep to slide between the bars and feast on the body. Then the hook was released and the cage plunged to the bottom of the sea.

Before the sun rose, there would be only the skeleton of Big Tim's body swimming eternally in its cage on the ocean floor.

Dante came up on deck. He had obviously taken a shower and changed his clothes. Underneath the Renaissance hat his hair was slick and wet. There was no trace of blood.

"So he already made his Communion," Dante said. "You could have waited for me."

Pippi said, "Did he talk?"

"Oh yeah," Dante said. "The fix was really simple. Except maybe he was full of shit right up to the end."

The next day Pippi flew East to give the Don and Giorgio a full report. "Big Tim was crazy," he said. "He bribed the caterer who supplies the food and drink to the teams in the Super Bowl. They were going to use drugs to make the team they bet against weaker as the game went on. The coaches and players would notice even if the fans didn't, and the FBI, too. You were right, Uncle, the scandal would have set back our program maybe forever."

"Was he an idiot?" Giorgio asked.

"I think he wanted to be famous," Pippi said. "Rich wasn't enough."

"What about the others involved in the scheme?" the Don asked.

"When they don't hear from the Rustler, they'll be scared off," Pippi said.

Giorgio said, "I agree."

"Very good," the Don said. "And my grandson, did he perform well?"

It seemed an offhand remark, but Pippi knew the Don well enough to understand that this was a very serious question. He answered as carefully as he could but with a certain purpose.

"I told him not to wear his hat on this operation in Vegas and L.A. He did anyway. Then he didn't follow the script of the operation. We could have got the information with more talk but he wanted blood. He cut the guy to pieces. He cut off his cock and nuts and breasts. That wasn't necessary. He enjoys doing it and that is very dangerous for the Family. Somebody really has got to talk to him."

"It will have to be you," Giorgio said to the Don. "He doesn't listen to me."

Don Domenico pondered this a long time. "He's young, he'll grow out of it."

Pippi saw that the Don would not do anything. So he told them about Dante's indiscretion with the movie star the night before the operation. He saw the Don flinch and Giorgio grimace with distaste. There was a long silence. Pippi wondered if he had gone too far.

Finally, the Don shook his head and said, "Pippi, you have planned well, as always, but you can set your mind at rest. You will never have to work with Dante again. But you must understand, Dante is my daughter's only child. Giorgio and I must do our best with him. He will grow wiser."

Cross De Lena sat on the balcony of his executive penthouse suite in the Xanadu Hotel and examined the dangers of the course of action he was taking. From his vantage point he could see the full length of the Strip, the line of luxury casino hotels on either side, the crowds of people in the street. He could see the gamblers on the Xanadu golf course, superstitiously trying for a hole in one to ensure the victory at the gaming tables later.

First danger: In this Boz operation he was making a crucial move without consulting the Clericuzio Family. It was true that he was the administrative Baron of the Western District, which comprised

Nevada and the southern part of California. It was true that the Barons operated independently in many areas and were not strictly under the Clericuzio Family as long as they wet the Clericuzio beak with a percentage of earnings. But there were very strict rules. No Baron, or *Bruglione,* could embark on an operation of such magnitude without the approval of the Clericuzio. For one simple reason. If a Baron did so and got into trouble, he would receive no prosecutorial indulgence, no judicial intervention. In addition, he would receive no support against any rising chief in his own territories, and his money would not be laundered and tucked away for his old age. Cross knew he should see Giorgio and the Don for an OK.

This operation could be enormously sensitive. And he was putting up part of his 51 percent equity in the Xanadu, left to him by Gronevelt, to finance the movie deal. It was true it was his own money, but it was money allied to the hidden interest that the Clericuzio shared in the Hotel. And it was money that the Clericuzio had helped him earn. It was a peculiar and yet somehow very human quirk of the Clericuzio that they felt a proprietary interest in the fortunes of their subordinates. They would resent his investing this money without their advice. Their quirk, though it had no legal foundation, resembled a medieval courtesy: no baron could sell his castle without royal consent.

And the magnitude of the money involved was a factor. Cross had inherited Gronevelt's fifty-one points, the Xanadu was worth a billion dollars. But he was gambling fifty million, investing another fifty million for a total of a C million. The economic risk was enormous. And the Clericuzio were notoriously prudent and conservative, as indeed they had to be to survive the world they moved in.

Cross remembered another thing. Long ago, when the Santadio and Clericuzio Families were on good terms, they had gained a foothold in the movie business. But it had not turned out well. When the Santadio Empire was crushed, Don Clericuzio had ordered that all attempts to infiltrate the movie business be halted. "Those people are too clever," the Don said. "And they have no fear because the rewards are so high. We should have to kill them all and then we would not know how to run the business. It is more complicated than drugs."

No, Cross decided. If he asked permission it would be denied. And then it would be impossible to proceed. When it was done he could do penance, he could let the Clericuzio beak drown itself in his profits, success often excused the most impudent of sins. And if he failed, then most likely he would be finished anyway, approval or not. Which brought up a final doubt.

Why was he doing this? He thought of Gronevelt's "Beware of damsels in distress." Well, he had met damsels in distress before and had left them to their dragons. Vegas was full of damsels in distress.

But he knew. He yearned for the beauty of Athena Aquitane. It wasn't just for the loveliness of her face, her eyes, her hair, her legs, her breasts. He yearned to see the look of intelligence and warmth in her eyes, in the very bones of her face, in the delicate curve of her lips. He felt that if he could know her, be in her presence, the whole world would take on a different light, the sun a different heat. He saw the ocean behind her, rolling green and capped with white flume, like a halo around her head. And the thought strayed into his mind: Athena was the woman his mother had dreamed of becoming.

Astonished, he felt a well of longing to see her, to be with her, to listen to her voice, to watch her move. And then he thought, Oh shit, is this why I'm doing this?

He accepted it and was pleased that finally he knew the real reason for his actions. It made him resolute and it made him focus. At the present time the main problem was operational. Forget Athena. Forget the Clericuzio. There was the difficult problem of Boz Skannet, a problem that had to be solved quickly.

Cross knew he had put himself in too naked a position, another complication. To publicly profit if anything happened to Skannet was dangerous.

Cross resolved on the three people he needed for the planned operation. The first was Andrew Pollard, who owned Pacific Ocean Security and was already involved in the whole mess. The second was Lia Vazzi, the caretaker of the Clericuzio hunting lodge in the Nevada mountains. Lia headed a crew of men who also served as caretakers but were on call for special duties. The third man was Leonard Sossa, a retired counterfeiter on Family retainer to do odd jobs. All three came under Cross De Lena's control as the Western *Bruglione.*

It was two days later that Andrew Pollard got the phone call from Cross De Lena. "I hear you're working too hard," Cross said. "How about coming to Vegas for a little vacation? I'll comp you RFB—room, food, beverage. Bring the wife. And if you get bored pop up to my office for a chat."

"Thanks," Pollard said, "I'm pretty busy right now, but how about next week?"

"Sure," Cross said. "But then I'll be out of town, so I'll miss you."

"I'll come tomorrow then," Pollard said.

"Great," Cross said and hung up.

Pollard leaned back in his chair, pondering. The invitation had been a command. He would have to walk a very thin line.

Leonard Sossa enjoyed life as only a man reprieved from a terrible death sentence can enjoy life. He enjoyed the sunrise, he enjoyed the sunset. He enjoyed the grass growing and the cows who ate the grass. He enjoyed the sight of beautiful women and confident young men and clever children. He enjoyed a crust of bread, a glass of wine, a knob of cheese.

Twenty years before, the FBI had arrested him for making hundred-dollar bills for the now-extinct Santadio Family. His confederates had copped a plea, sold him out, and he had believed the flower of his manhood would wither in prison. Counterfeiting money was a far more dangerous crime than rape, murder, arson. When you counterfeited money, you attacked the machinery of government itself. When you committed the other crimes you were only some scavenger taking a bite out of the carcass of the huge beast that composed the expendable human chain. He expected no mercy and was given none. Leonard Sossa was sentenced to twenty years.

Sossa did only a year. A fellow inmate, overcome with admiration for Sossa's skills, his genius with ink and pencil and pen, recruited him for the Clericuzio Family.

Suddenly he had a new lawyer. Suddenly he had an outside doctor he had never met. Suddenly there was a hearing for clemency on the ground that his mental capacity had deteriorated to that of a child and he was no longer a menace to society. Suddenly Leonard Sossa was a free man and an employee of the Clericuzio Family.

The Family had a need for a first-rate forger. Not for currency, they knew that to the authorities counterfeiting was an unforgivable crime. They needed a forger for far more important tasks. In the mountains of paperwork Giorgio had to handle, juggling different national and international corporations, signing legal documents by nonexistent corporate officers, making deposits and withdrawals of vast sums of money, a variety of signatures and imitations of signatures were needed. Then, as time went on, other uses were found for Leonard.

The Xanadu Hotel used his skills very profitably. When a very rich high roller died and had markers in the cage, Sossa was brought in to sign another million dollars. Of course the dead man's estate would not pay the markers. But then the whole amount could be charged as loss on the Xanadu's taxes. This happened far more often than was natural. There seemed to be a high mortality rate in pleasure. The same was done to high rollers who reneged on their debts or settled dimes on the dollar.

For all this Leonard Sossa was paid a hundred thousand dollars a year and barred from doing any other kind of work, especially counterfeiting currency. This fit in with Family policy in general. The Clericuzio had an edict that prohibited all crime-family members from engaging in counterfeiting and kidnapping. These were the crimes that made all the Federal enforcement agencies come down with crushing force. The rewards were simply not worth the risk.

So for twenty years Sossa enjoyed life as an artist in his little house that nestled in Topanga Canyon, not far from Malibu. He had a small garden, a goat, a cat, and a dog. He painted during the day and drank at night. There was an endless supply of young girls who lived in the Canyon and were free spirits and fellow painters.

Sossa never left the Canyon except to shop in Santa Monica or when he was called to duty by the Clericuzio Family, which was usually twice a month for a period of no more than a few days. He did the work they wanted him to do and never asked questions. He was a valued soldier in the Clericuzio Family.

So when a car came to pick him up and the driver told him to bring his tools and clothes for a few days, Sossa turned his goat, dog, and cat loose into the Canyon and locked his house. The animals could take care of themselves; after all, they were not children. It was not that he was not fond of them, but animals had a short life span, especially in the Canyon, and he had gotten used to losing them. His year in prison had made Leonard Sossa a realist, and his unexpected release had made him an optimist.

Lia Vazzi, the caretaker of the Clericuzio Family's hunting lodge in the Sierra Nevada, had arrived in the United States when he was only thirty years old and the most wanted man in Italy. In the ten years since then he had learned to speak English with only a very slight accent and could read and write it to a fair degree. In Sicily he had been born to one of the most learned and powerful Families on the island.

Fifteen years before, Lia Vazzi had been the leader of the Mafia in Palermo, a Qualified Man of the first rank. But he had reached too far.

In Rome, the government had appointed an examining magistrate and given him extraordinary powers to wipe out the Mafia in Sicily. The examining magistrate had arrived in Palermo with his wife and children, protected by army troops and a horde of police. He gave a fiery speech, promising to show no mercy to those criminals who had ruled the beautiful island of Sicily for centuries. The time had come for the law to rule, for the elected representatives of the people of Italy to decide the fate of Sicily, not the ignorant thugs with their shameful secret societies. Vazzi took his speech as a personal insult.

The examining magistrate was heavily guarded day and night, as he heard the testimony of witnesses and issued arrest orders. His court was a fortress, his living quarters rimmed by a perimeter of army troops. He was seemingly impregnable. But after three months Vazzi learned the magistrate's itinerary, which had been kept secret to prevent surprise attacks.

The magistrate traveled to the big towns in Sicily to gather evidence and issue arrest warrants. He was scheduled to return to

Palermo to be given a medal for his heroic attempt to rid the island of its Mafia scourge. Lia Vazzi and his men mined a small bridge that the magistrate had to pass over. The magistrate and his guards were blown into such tiny bits that the bodies had to be brought out of the water with sieves. The government in Rome, infuriated, replied with a massive search for the culprits responsible, and Vazzi had to go underground. Though the government had no proof, he knew that if he fell into their hands he would be better off dead.

Now the Clericuzio sent Pippi De Lena to Sicily every year to recruit men to live in the Bronx Enclave and soldier for the Clericuzio Family. The bedrock of the Don's faith was that only Sicilians with their centuries-long tradition of *omertà* could be trusted not to turn traitor. The young men in America were too soft, too lightheaded with vanity, could be too easily turned into informants by the more ferocious of the district attorneys who were sending so many of the *Brugliones* to prison.

As a philosophy, *omertà* was quite simple. It was a mortal sin to talk to the police about anything that would harm the Mafia. If a rival Mafia clan murdered your father before your eyes, you were forbidden to inform the police. If you yourself were shot and lay dying, you were forbidden to inform the police. If they stole your mule, your goat, your jewelry, you were forbidden to go to the police. The authorities were the Great Satan a true Sicilian could never turn to. Family and the Mafia were the avengers.

Ten years before, Pippi De Lena had taken his son, Cross, on his trip to Sicily as part of his training. The task was not so much recruiting as screening, there were hundreds of willing men whose greatest dream was to be picked to go to America.

They went to a little town fifty miles from Palermo, into the countryside of villages built of stone, decorated with the bright flowers of Sicily. There they were welcomed into the home of the mayor himself.

The mayor was a short man with a rounded belly, the belly figurative as well as literal, for "a man with a belly" was the Sicilian idiom for a Mafia chief.

The house had a pleasant garden with fig and olive and lemon trees, and it was here that Pippi did his interviews. The garden strangely resembled the Clericuzio garden in Quogue, except for the brilliantly colored flowers and the lemon trees. The mayor was obviously a man who loved beauty, for in addition he had a comely wife and three lusciously pretty daughters who, though in their early teens, were fully developed women.

But Cross saw that his father, Pippi, was a different man in Sicily. There was none of his carefree gallantry here, he was soberly respectful to the women, his charm erased. Late that night, in the room they shared, he lectured Cross. "You have to be careful with Sicilians. They distrust men who are interested in women. You screw one of their daughters, we'll never get out of here alive."

Over the next few days men came to be interviewed and screened by Pippi. He had criteria. The men could not be older than thirty-five or younger than twenty. If they were married, they could not have more than one child. Finally, they had to be vouched for by the mayor. He explained this. If the men were too young, they might be too influenced by the American culture. If they were too old, they could not make the adjustment to America. If they had more than one child, they would be of too cautious a temperament to take the risks their duties would demand.

Some of the men who came were so seriously compromised in the eyes of the law that they had to leave Sicily. Some were simply seeking a better life in America no matter the cost. Some were too clever to rely on fate and desperately wanted to soldier for the Clericuzio, and these were the best.

At the end of the week Pippi had his quota of twenty men, and he gave his list to the mayor, who would approve them and then arrange for their emigration. The mayor crossed out one name on the list.

Pippi said, "I thought he would be perfect for us. Have I made a mistake?"

"No, no," the mayor said. "You have done cleverly as always."

Pippi was puzzled. All of the recruits would be treated very well. The single men would be given apartments, the married men with a child a small house. They would all have steady jobs. They would all live in the Bronx Enclave. And then some would be chosen as soldiers in the Clericuzio Family and make a handsome living with a bright future. The man whose name had been crossed out by the mayor had to be in very bad odor. But then why had he been cleared for an interview? Pippi sensed a Sicilian rat.

The mayor was observing him shrewdly, seeming to read his mind and pleased by what he read.

"You are too much of a Sicilian for me to deceive you," the mayor said. "The name I crossed out is a man my daughter intends to marry. I want to keep him here a year longer for my daughter's happiness, then you can have him. I could not refuse his interview. The other reason is that I have a man who I think you should take in his place. Will you do me the favor of seeing him?"

"Of course," Pippi said.

The mayor said, "I don't want to mislead you, but this is a special case and he must leave immediately."

"You know I have to be very careful," Pippi said. "The Clericuzio are particular."

"It will be to your interest," the mayor said. "But it is a little dangerous." He then explained about Lia Vazzi. The assassination of the magistrate had made world headlines, so Pippi and Cross were familiar with the case.

"If they have no proof, why is this situation so desperate for Vazzi?" Cross said.

The mayor said, "Young man, this is Sicily. The police are also Sicilians. The magistrate was a Sicilian. Everybody knows it was Lia. Never mind your legal proof. If he falls into their hands, he will be dead."

Pippi said, "Can you get him out of the country and into America?"

"Yes," said the mayor. "The difficulty is keeping him hidden in America."

Pippi said, "He sounds like he's more trouble than he's worth."

The mayor shrugged. "He's a friend of mine, I confess. But put that aside." He paused and smiled benignly to make sure that it was not put aside. "He is also an ultimate Qualified Man. He is expert in explosives and that is always a very tricky business. He knows the rope, an old and very useful skill. The knife and gun of course. Most important of all he is intelligent, a man of all parts. And steadfast.

Like a rock. He never talks. He listens and has the gift of loosening tongues. Now tell me, can you not use a man like that?"

"An answer to my prayers," Pippi said smoothly. "But still why does such a man run away?"

"Because in addition to all his other virtues," the mayor said, "he is prudent. He does not challenge fate. His days are numbered here."

"And a man who's qualified," Pippi said, "can he be happy as a mere soldier in America?"

The mayor bowed his head in a sorrowful commiseration. "He is a true Christian," he said. "He has the humility that Christ has always taught us."

"I must meet such a man," Pippi said, "if only for the pleasure of the experience. But I can guarantee nothing."

The mayor made a wide, expansive gesture. "Of course he must suit you," he said. "But there is another thing I must tell you. He forbade me to deceive you about this." For the first time the mayor was not so confident. "He has a wife and three children and they must go with him."

At that moment Pippi knew his answer would be no. "Ah," he said, "that makes it very difficult. When do we see him?"

"He will be in the garden after dark," the mayor said. "There is no danger, I have seen to that."

Lia Vazzi was a small man but with that wiry toughness that many Sicilians inherited from long-ago Arab ancestors. He had a handsome, hawklike face, a dark brown, dignified mask, and he spoke English to a degree.

They sat around the mayor's garden table with a bottle of homemade red wine, a dish of olives from the nearby trees, and bread, crusty and freshly baked that evening, round, still warm, and beside it a whole leg of prosciutto, studded with grains of whole pepper, like black diamonds. Lia Vazzi ate and drank and said nothing.

"I have received the highest recommendations," Pippi said respectfully. "But I worry. Can a man of your education and qualification be happy in America in the service of another man?"

Lia looked at Cross and then said to Pippi, "You have a son. What would you do to save him? I want to have my wife and children safe and for that I will do my duty."

"There will be some danger for us," Pippi said. "You understand that I have to think of the benefits that justify the risk."

Lia shrugged. "I can't be the judge of that." He seemed resigned to being refused.

Pippi said, "If you come by yourself, it will be easier."

"No," Vazzi said. "My family will live together or die together." He paused for a moment. "If I leave them here, Rome will make it very difficult for them. I would rather give myself up."

Pippi said, "The problem is how to hide you and your family."

Vazzi shrugged. "America is vast," he said. He offered the plate of olives to Cross and said almost mockingly, "Would your father ever desert you?"

"No," Cross said. "He is old-fashioned, like yourself." He said it gravely but with a tiny trace of a smile. Then he said, "I hear you're a farmer also."

"Olives," Vazzi said. "I have my own press."

Cross said to Pippi, "How about the Family hunting lodge in the Sierras? He could take care of it with his family and earn his keep. It's isolated. His family can help." He turned to Lia. "Would you live in the woods?" Woods as the idiom for anything not urban. Lia shrugged.

It was the personal force of Lia Vazzi that persuaded Pippi De Lena. Vazzi was not a big man, but his body put out an electric dignity. He had a chilling effect, a man who was not daunted by death, feared neither Hell nor Heaven.

Pippi said, "It's a good idea. Perfect camouflage. And we can call on you for special jobs and let you earn extra money. Those jobs will be your risk."

They could see the muscles on Lia's face loosen when he realized that he had been chosen. His voice trembled slightly when he spoke. "I want to thank you for saving my wife and children," he said, and looked directly at Cross De Lena.

. . .

Since then Lia Vazzi had more than earned the mercy that had been shown to him. He had risen from soldier to leader of all of Cross's operational crews. He supervised the six men who helped him care for the Hunting Lodge estate, on whose grounds he owned his own house. He had prospered, he had become a citizen, his children went away to the university. All this earned by his courage and good sense, and most of all, his loyalty. So when he received the message to meet Cross De Lena in Las Vegas, it was with a goodwill that he packed his suitcase in his new Buick and made the long drive to Vegas and the Xanadu Hotel.

Andrew Pollard was the first to arrive in Las Vegas. He flew from L.A. on the noon flight, relaxed by one of the Hotel Xanadu's huge pools, gambled small-time craps for a few hours, then was secretly whisked into Cross De Lena's penthouse office suite.

They shook hands and Cross said, "I won't keep you long. You can fly back tonight. What I need is all the information you have on the Skannet guy."

Pollard briefed him on everything that had happened and informed him that Skannet was now staying in the Beverly Hills Hotel. He told of his conversation with Bantz.

"So they don't really give a shit about her, they just want to get the picture done," he told Cross. "Also, the Studio doesn't take characters like that seriously. I have a twenty-man section in my company that just handles harassers. Movie stars really have to worry about people like him."

"What about the cops?" Cross asked. "Can't they do something?"

"No," Pollard said. "Not until after the damage."

"What about you?" Cross asked. "You have some good personnel working for you."

"I have to be careful," Pollard said. "I could lose my business if I get tough. You know how the courts are. Why should I stick my neck out?"

"This Boz Skannet, what kind of guy is he?" Cross said.

"He won't scare," Pollard said. "In fact he scares me. He's one of those genuinely tough guys who doesn't care about consequences.

His family has money and political power so he figures he can get away with anything. And he really enjoys trouble, you know, how some guys do. If you're going to get into this you have to be serious."

"I'm always serious," Cross said. "You have Skannet under surveillance now?"

"I sure have," Pollard said. "He is definitely capable of pulling bad shit."

Cross said, "Pull off your surveillance. I don't want anyone watching him. Understand?"

"OK, if you say so," Pollard said. He paused for a moment, then said, "Watch out for Jim Losey, he's keeping an eye out on Skannet. Do you know Losey?"

"I've met him," Cross said. "I want you to do one other thing. Lend me your Pacific Ocean Security ID for a couple of hours. You'll have it back in time to catch the midnight flight to L.A."

Pollard was worried. "You know I'll do anything for you Cross, but be careful; this is a very touchy case. I've built up a very good life out here and I don't want it to go down the drain. I know I owe it all to the Clericuzio Family, I'm always grateful, I'm always paid back. But this is a very complicated business."

Cross smiled at him reassuringly. "You're too valuable to us. One other thing, if Skannet calls up to check on men from your office talking to him, you just verify it."

At this, Pollard's heart sank. This was going to be real trouble.

Cross said, "Now tell me anything else you can about him." When Pollard hesitated, Cross added, "I'll do something for you. Later on."

Pollard thought for a moment. "Skannet claims he knows a big secret that Athena would do anything not to have anyone find out. That's why she dropped the charges against him. A terrific secret, Skannet loves that secret. Cross, I don't know how or why you're involved, but maybe knowing that secret can solve your problem."

For the first time Cross looked at him without affability and suddenly he knew why Cross had acquired his reputation. The look was cold, judging, a judging that could result in death.

Cross said, "You know why I'm interested. Bantz must have told you the story. He hired you to do a background on me. Now do you have any of this big secret or does the Studio?"

"No," Pollard said. "Nobody knows. Cross, I'm doing my best for you, you know that."

"I do know that," Cross said, suddenly gentle. "Let me make it easier for you. The Studio is hot to know how I'm going to get Athena Aquitane back to work. I'll tell you. I'm going to give her half the profits of the movie. And it's okay by me for you to tell them. You can make points, they may even give you a bonus." He reached into his desk and took out a round leather bag and put it in Pollard's hand. "Five grand of black chips," he said. "I always worry when I ask you up here on business that you'll lose money in the casino."

He need not have worried. Andrew Pollard always turned the chips into the casino cage for cash.

Leonard Sossa was just getting settled into a secured business suite at the Xanadu when Pollard's ID was brought to him. With his own equipment he carefully forged four sets of Pacific Ocean Security IDs, complete with special flap-open billfolds. They would not have passed an inspection by Pollard, but that was not necessary, Pollard would never see these IDs. When Sossa finished the job several hours later, two men drove him to the Sierra Nevada Hunting Lodge, where he was installed in a bungalow deep in the woods.

On the porch of the bungalow that afternoon, he watched a deer and bear that wandered by. At night he cleaned his tools and waited. He didn't know where he was or what he was going to do and he didn't want to know. He got his hundred grand a year and lived the life of a free man in the open air. He killed time by sketching the bear and the deer he had seen on a hundred sheets of paper and then riffling them together to give the impression of the deer chasing the bear.

Lia Vazzi was greeted in an altogether different fashion. Cross embraced him, gave him dinner in his suite. During Vazzi's years in America, Cross had been his operational chief many times. Vazzi, despite his own force of character, had never tried to usurp authority, and Cross in turn had treated him with the respect that a man gave his equal.

Over the years Cross had gone to the Hunting Lodge for weekend vacations and the two of them had gone hunting together. Vazzi told stories of the troubles in Sicily and the difference in living in America. Cross had reciprocated by inviting Vazzi and his family to Vegas, comped RFB at the Xanadu plus a credit rating of five thousand in the casino, which Lia was never asked to pay.

Over dinner they talked generally. Vazzi marveled still at his life in America. His oldest son was taking a degree at the University of California and had no knowledge of his father's secret life. Vazzi was uneasy with this. "Sometimes I think he has none of my blood," he said. "He believes everything his professors tell him. He believes women are equal to men, he believes peasants should be given free land. He belongs to the swimming team at college. In all my life in Sicily, and Sicily is an island, I have never seen a Sicilian swimming."

"Except a fisherman thrown off his boat," Cross said laughing.

"Not even then," Vazzi said. "They all drowned."

When they had finished eating, they talked business. Vazzi never really enjoyed the food in Vegas, but he loved the brandy and Havana cigars. Cross always sent him a case of good brandy and a box of thin Havana cigars once a year at Christmas.

"I have something very difficult for you to do," Cross said. "Something that must be done very intelligently."

"That is always difficult," Vazzi said.

"It must be at the Hunting Lodge," Cross said. "We will bring a certain person there. I want him to write some letters, I want him to give a piece of information." He paused to smile at Vazzi's dismissive gesture. Vazzi had often commented on American movies where the hero or villain refused to give information. "I could make them speak Chinese," Vazzi would say.

"The difficulty," Cross said, "is that there must be no mark on his body, no drugs inside his body. Also this certain person is very strong-willed."

"Only women can make a man talk with kisses," Vazzi said amiably, savoring his cigar. "It sounds to me that you are going to be personally involved in this story."

Cross said, "There is no other way. The men working will be your crew but first the Lodge must be cleared of the women and children."

Vazzi waved his cigar. "They will go to Disneyland, that blessing in happiness and trouble. We always send them there."

"Disneyland?" Cross asked, and laughed.

"I have never been," Vazzi said. "I hope to go there when I die. Will this be a Communion or a Confirmation?"

"Confirmation," Cross said.

Then they got down to business. Cross explained the operation to Vazzi and why and how it should be done. "How does it sound to you?" he asked.

"You are far more Sicilian than my son and you were born in America," Vazzi said. "But what happens if he remains stubborn and won't give you what you want."

"Then the fault will be mine," Cross said. "And his. And then we must pay. In that, America and Sicily are the same."

"True," Vazzi said. "As in China and Russia and Africa. As the Don often says, then we can all go swim in the bottom of the ocean."

CHAPTER 9

ELI MARRION, Bobby Bantz, Skippy Deere, and Melo Stuart assembled in emergency session in Marrion's home. Andrew Pollard had reported to Bantz Cross De Lena's secret scheme to get Athena back to work. This information had been corroborated by the detective Jim Losey, who refused to divulge his source.

"This is a stickup," Bantz said. "Melo, you're her agent, you're responsible for her and all your clients. Does this mean when we are in the middle of a big picture your star refuses to go to work until they get half the profits?"

"Only if you're crazy enough to pay it," Stuart said. "Let this De Lena guy do it. He won't stay in the business long."

Marrion said, "Melo, you're talking strategy, we're talking right this minute. If Athena goes back to work, then you and your client are sticking us up like bank robbers. Will you permit that?"

They were all astonished. It was rare that Marrion cut so quickly to the bone, at least since his younger days. Stuart was alarmed.

"Athena knows nothing about this," he said. "She would have told me."

Deere said, "Would she take the deal if she knew?"

Stuart said, "I would advise her to take it and then in a side letter split her half with the studio."

Bantz said crisply, "Then all her protestations of fear would be a mockery. Bullshit, in short. And Melo, you're full of shit. You think this studio would settle for half of what Athena gets from De Lena? All that money rightfully belongs to us. And she may get away rich with De Lena but it means the end of her career in the movies. No studio will ever hire her again."

"Foreign," Skippy said. "Foreign would take a chance."

Marrion picked up the phone and handed it to Stuart. "This is all to no purpose. Call Athena. Tell her what Cross De Lena is going to offer and ask if she is going to accept."

Deere said, "She disappeared over the weekend."

"She's back," Stuart said. "She often disappears on weekends." He pushed the buttons on the phone.

The conversation was very brief. Stuart hung up and smiled. "She said she has received no such offer. And no such offer would make her come back to work. She doesn't give a shit about her career." He paused for a moment and then said admiringly, "I'd like to meet this guy Skannet. Any man who can scare an actress out of her career has some good in him."

Marrion said, "It's settled then. We've recouped our loss out of a hopeless situation. But it's a pity. Athena was such a great star."

Andrew Pollard had his instructions. The first had been to inform Bantz of Cross De Lena's intention regarding Athena. The second was to pull the surveillance team off Skannet. The third was to visit Boz Skannet and offer a proposition.

Skannet was in his undershirt when he let Pollard into his Beverly Hills Hotel suite, and he smelled of cologne. "Just finished shaving," he said. "This hotel has more bathroom perfumes than a whorehouse."

"You are not supposed to be in this town," Pollard said reproachfully.

Skannet slapped him on the back. "I know, but I'll leave tomorrow. I just have a few loose ends to tie up." His malicious glee while saying this, his massive torso, would have frightened Pollard before, but now that Cross was involved it only evoked pity. But he would have to be careful.

"Athena is not surprised that you haven't left," he said. "She feels the Studio doesn't understand you but she does. So she would like to meet with you personally. She thinks that just the two of you alone can strike a deal."

When he saw the momentary rush of joy on Skannet's face, he knew that Cross had been right. This guy was still in love, he would buy the story.

Boz Skannet was suddenly wary. "That doesn't sound like Athena. She can't stand the sight of me, not that I blame her." He laughed. "She needs that pretty mug of hers."

Pollard said, "She wants to make a serious offer. A lifetime annuity. A percentage of her earnings for the rest of her life if you want. But she wants to talk to you personally and secretly. There's something else she wants."

"I know what she wants," Skannet said. Skannet had a curious look on his face. Pollard had seen that look on the faces of wistfully repentant rapists.

"Seven o'clock," Pollard said. "Two of my men will come to pick you up and bring you to the meeting place. They will stay with her to be her bodyguards. Two of my best men, armed. Just so you won't get any funny ideas."

Skannet smiled. "Don't worry about me," he said.

"Right," Pollard said and left.

When the door closed, Skannet shot his right hand up in the air. He would see Athena again with only two half-assed private detectives to protect her. And he would have proof that she initiated the meeting, he would not be violating the judge's restraining order.

For the rest of the day he dreamed of their reunion. It was really a surprise to him, and thinking about it he knew that Athena would use her body to persuade him into the bargain. He lay on his bed imagining how it would be to be with her again. The image of her body was clear. Her white skin, the gentle curve of her belly, her breasts with their pink nipples, her eyes so green they were another kind of light, her warm delicate mouth, her breath, her flaming hair like the sun turning into smoky brass under a night sky. For a moment his old love swept over him, his love of her intelligence and her brave character that he had broken down into fear. Then for the first time since he was sixteen, he was fondling himself. His mind formed clear figures of Athena urging him on, until he climaxed. For that one moment he was happy and he loved her.

And then everything turned around. He felt a sense of shame, of humiliation. He hated her again. Suddenly he was convinced it was some sort of trap. What did he really know about this guy Pollard, anyway. Skannet dressed hurriedly and studied the card Pollard had given him. The office was only a twenty-minute drive from the hotel. He rushed down to the hotel entrance and a valet brought his car.

When he entered the Pacific Ocean Security Building, he was surprised at the size and opulence of the operation. He made his way to the reception desk and stated his business. An armed security guard escorted him to Pollard's office. Skannet noticed that the walls were decorated with awards from the L.A. Police Department, the Association to Help the Homeless, and other organizations, including the Boy Scouts of America. There was even some sort of a movie award.

Andrew Pollard was regarding him with surprise, and a little concern. Skannet reassured him.

"I just wanted to tell you," he said, "I'll drive to the meeting in my car. Your men can ride with me and give me directions."

Pollard shrugged. This would be none of his business. He had done what he had been instructed to do. "Fine," he said. "But you could have called me."

Skannet grinned at him. "Sure, but I just wanted to check on your offices. Also, I want to call Athena to make sure this is on the up-and-up. I figured you can get her on the phone for me. She might not take my call."

"Sure," Pollard said agreeably. He picked up the phone. He didn't know what was going on and in his heart he hoped that Skannet would abort the meeting and he would no longer be involved in whatever Cross was planning to do. He also knew Athena would not speak to him directly.

He dialed the number and asked for Athena. He put the loudspeaker on so that Skannet could hear the call. Athena's secretary told him that Miss Aquitane was out and was not expected back until the next day. He put down the phone and raised an eyebrow to Skannet. Skannet looked happy.

And Skannet was. He had been right. Athena was planning to use her body to make the deal. She was planning to spend the night with him. The red skin of his face took on an almost bronze sheen with the rush of blood to his brain, remembering when she was young, when she had loved him, when he had loved her.

At seven that evening, when Lia Vazzi arrived at the hotel with one of his soldiers, Skannet was waiting for him and ready to go immediately. Skannet was dressed very neatly in a boyish way. He wore heavy blue jeans, a faded blue denim shirt, and a white sports jacket. He had shaved carefully, and his blond hair was combed straight back. His red skin seemed paler, his face softened by the paleness. Lia Vazzi and his soldier showed Skannet their forged Pacific Ocean Security IDs.

Skannet was not impressed by the men. Two runts, one with a slight accent he thought might be Mexican. They would give him no trouble. These private dick agencies were so full of shit, what kind of protection was this for Athena?

Vazzi said to Skannet, "I understand you want to drive your own car. I will go with you and my friend will follow in our car. Is that agreeable to you?"

"OK," Skannet said.

When they got out of the elevator and entered the lobby, they were stopped by Jim Losey. The detective had been waiting on a sofa by the fireplace and intercepted them on just a hunch. He had staked out there to keep an eye on Skannet just in case. Now he held his ID out to the three men.

Skannet looked at the ID and said, "What the fuck do you want?"

Jim Losey said, "Who are these two men with you?"

"None of your fucking business," Skannet said. Vazzi and his companion remained silent as Losey studied their faces.

"I'd like to have a few words with you in private," Losey said.

Skannet brushed him aside and Losey grabbed his arm. They were both big men. Skannet was frantic to be away. He said to Losey, his voice furious and loud, "The charges were dropped, I don't have to talk to you. And if you don't get your hands away, I'm going to kick the shit out of you."

Losey dropped his hand. He was in no way intimidated, but his mind was working. The two men with Skannet seemed strange to him, there was something going on. He stepped aside but followed them to the archway where cars were brought to hotel guests. He watched Skannet get into his car with Lia Vazzi. Somehow the other man had vanished. Losey noted this and waited to see if another car pulled out of the parking lot, but there was none.

There was no use trying to follow and there was equally no purpose to be served in putting out an alert for Skannet's car. He debated on whether to report this incident to Skippy Deere and decided against it. One thing was for certain, if Skannet got out of line again, he would regret his insults today.

It was a long drive, Skannet kept complaining and asking questions and even threatening to turn back. But Lia Vazzi was reassuring. Skannet had been told that the meeting place was a hunting lodge Athena owned in the Sierra Nevada, and the instructions were that they were to spend the night. Athena had insisted she wanted the meeting a secret from everyone, that she would settle the whole problem to everyone's satisfaction. Skannet didn't know what that meant. What could she do to dissolve the hatred that had grown over the last ten years? Was she stupid enough to think that a night of lovemaking and a bundle of cash would soften him? Did she think he was that simple? He had always admired her intelligence but maybe now she was just one of those arrogant Hollywood actresses who thought she could buy anything with her body and her money? And yet the thought of her beauty haunted him. Finally after all these years, she would smile at him, charm him, submit to him. No matter what happened he would have this coming night.

Lia Vazzi was not worried about Skannet's threats to turn back. He knew there were three cars on the road behind him as escort and he had his instructions. As a last resort he could simply have Skannet killed. But his instructions were also clear that Skannet should not suffer any injury short of death.

They drove through the open gate, and Skannet was surprised at the size of the Hunting Lodge. It looked like a small hotel. He got out and stretched his arms and legs. There were five or six cars parked alongside the lodge, which made him wonder for a moment.

Vazzi led him to the door and opened it. At that moment Skannet heard more cars pulling into the driveway. He turned thinking that Athena had arrived. What he saw were three cars parking and two men getting out of each one. Then Lia led him through the main entry of the lodge and into the living room with its huge fireplace. There, sitting on the sofa waiting for him, was a man he had never seen. The man was Cross De Lena.

What happened next was very quick. Skannet asked angrily, "Where's Athena?" then two men grabbed his arms, another two men put guns to his head, and the seemingly harmless Lia Vazzi pulled his legs out from under him so that he toppled to the floor.

Vazzi said, "You can die now if you don't do exactly as you are told. Don't struggle. Lie still."

Still another man shackled Skannet's legs together and then they pulled him to his feet so that he was facing Cross. Skannet was surprised how helpless he felt even when the men released his arms. His imprisoned feet seemed to neutralize all his physical powers. He reached out to at least punch the little bastard, but Vazzi stepped back, and though Skannet gave a little hop he could not get leverage with his arms.

Vazzi regarded him with quiet contempt. "We know you are a violent man," he said, "but now is the time to use your brain. Strength is of no use here. . . ."

Skannet seemed to take his advice. He was thinking hard. If they had wanted to kill him they would have done so. This was some process of intimidation to make him agree to something. Well and good, he would agree. And then he would take precautions in the future. One thing he was sure of. Athena was not involved in such an operation. He disregarded Vazzi and turned to the man sitting on the sofa.

"Who the hell are you?" he said.

Cross said, "I have a few things I want you to do and then you will be allowed to drive home."

"And if I don't, you'll torture me, right?" Skannet laughed. He was beginning to think this was some jerk-off Hollywood scene, some bad movie the Studio was using.

"No," Cross said simply. "No torture. No one will touch you. I want you to sit down at that table and write four letters for me. One to Lodd-Stone Studios promising never to go near their lot. One to Athena Aquitane apologizing for your previous conduct and swearing never to go near her again. Another to the police authorities admitting you purchased acid to be used in another attack on your wife, and another letter to me stating what secret you hold over your wife. Simple."

Skannet took a hobbling leap toward Cross and was pushed by one of the men so that he went sprawling onto the opposite sofa.

"Don't touch him," Cross said sharply.

Skannet used his arms to push himself to his feet.

Cross pointed to the desk where there was a stack of paper.

"Where's Athena?" Skannet said.

"She's not here," Cross said. "Everybody out of the room, except Lia," he said. The other men went out the door.

"Go sit at the desk," Cross said to Skannet. Skannet did so.

Cross said to him, "I want to talk to you very seriously. Stop trying to show how tough you are. I want you to listen. Don't do anything foolish. You have your hands free and that may give you illusions of grandeur. All I want you to do is write those letters and you'll be free."

Skannet said contemptuously, "You can go fuck yourself."

Cross turned to Vazzi and said, "No use wasting time. Kill him."

Cross had kept his voice even and yet there was something terrible in his casualness. In that moment Skannet felt a fear he had not known since he was a child. He realized for the first time the significance of all the men in the lodge, all the forces that were arrayed against him. Lia Vazzi had not yet made a move. Skannet said, "OK. I'll do it." He picked up a sheet of paper and began to write.

Cunningly, he wrote the letters with his left hand; like some good athletes, he could perform almost equally well with either hand. Cross came up behind him and watched. Skannet, ashamed of his sudden cowardice, braced his feet against the floor. Confident of his physical coordination, he switched the pen to his right hand and sprang up to stab Cross in the face, hoping to get the bastard in the eye. He exploded into action, his arm coming around, the whole torso of his body propelled, and was surprised that Cross had easily moved out of range. Still Skannet tried to move with his leg shackles.

Cross regarded him quietly and said, "Everybody is entitled to his once. You've had that. Now put down the pen and give me those sheets."

Skannet did so. Cross studied the sheets of paper and said, "You haven't told me the secret."

"I won't put it on paper. Get rid of that guy," he motioned to Vazzi, "and I'll tell you."

Cross handed the sheets of paper to Lia and said, "Take care of these."

Vazzi went out of the room.

"OK," Cross said to Skannet, "let's hear this big secret."

When Vazzi left the Hunting Lodge he ran the hundred yards to the bungalow that housed Leonard Sossa. Sossa was waiting. He looked at the two sheets of paper and said disgustedly, "This is left-handed. I can't do left-handed script. Cross knows that."

"Look at it again," Vazzi said. "He tried to stab Cross with his right hand."

Sossa studied the pages again. "Yeah," he said. "This guy is not a real lefty. He's just dicking you around."

Vazzi took the sheets and went back to the Hunting Lodge and entered the library. By Cross's face he knew something had gone wrong. Cross had a look of bewilderment, and Skannet was lying down on the sofa, his shackled legs extended over the arm, smiling happily up at the ceiling.

"These letters are no good," Vazzi said. "He wrote them left-handed and the analyst says he's a rightie."

Cross said to Skannet, "I think you're too tough for me to handle. I can't scare you, I can't make you do what I want. I give up."

Skannet rose from the sofa and said malevolently to Cross, "But what I told you is true. Everybody falls in love with Athena, but nobody knows her the way I do."

Cross said quietly, "You don't know her. And you don't know me." He went to the door and motioned. Four men came into the room. Then Cross turned to Lia. "You know what I want. If he doesn't give it to me, then just get rid of him." He walked out of the room.

Lia Vazzi gave a visible sigh of relief. He admired Cross, had been a willing subordinate all these years, but Cross was too patient. It was true that all the great Dons in Sicily excelled in patience, but they knew when to stop. Vazzi suspected that there was an American softness in Cross De Lena that would prevent his rise to greatness.

Vazzi turned to Skannet and said silkily, "You and I, we begin." He turned to the four men. "Secure his arms, but gently. Don't hurt him."

The four men pounced on Skannet. One of the men produced handcuffs, and in a moment Skannet was completely helpless. Vazzi pushed him to the floor on his knees, the other men forced Skannet to stay in place.

"The comedy is finished," Vazzi said to Skannet. His wiry body seemed relaxed, his voice was conversational. "You will scribble those letters with your right hand. Or you can refuse." One of the men produced a huge revolver and a box of bullets and handed them to Lia. He loaded the revolver, showing each of the bullets to Skannet. He went to the window and fired into the forest until the gun was empty. Then he went back to Skannet and put one bullet in. Spinning the cylinder, he put the gun under Skannet's nose.

"I don't know where the bullet is," Lia said. "You don't know where it is. If you still refuse to write the letters, I pull the trigger. Now is it yes or no?"

Skannet looked into Lia's eyes and did not answer. Lia pulled the trigger. There was just the click of an empty chamber. Lia nodded approvingly. "I was rooting for you," he said to Skannet.

He looked into the cylinder and put the bullet in the first chamber. He went to the window and fired. The explosion seemed to rock the room. Lia went back to the table, took another bullet from the box, loaded the gun with it, spinning the cylinder.

"We will try again," Lia said. He put the revolver beneath Skannet's chin. But this time Skannet flinched.

"Call back your boss," Skannet said. "I have a few more things I can tell him."

"No," Lia said, "that foolishness is over. Now answer yes or no."

Skannet looked into Lia's eyes and saw not a threat but a mournful regret. "OK," Skannet said. "I'll write."

He was immediately hauled to his feet and seated at the writing desk. Vazzi sat on the sofa while Skannet busied himself writing. He took the papers from Skannet and went to Sossa's bungalow. "Is that OK?" he asked.

"This will do fine," Sossa said.

Vazzi went back to the Hunting Lodge and reported to Cross. Then he went to the library and said to Skannet, "It's all over. I'll drive you back to L.A. as soon as I'm ready." Then Lia walked Cross out to his car.

Cross said, "You know everything you have to do. Wait until morning, I should be back in Vegas by then."

"Don't worry," Vazzi said. "I thought he would never write. What an animal." He could see that Cross was preoccupied. "What did he tell you when I was away?" Vazzi asked. "Something I should know?"

Cross said, with savage bitterness Vazzi had never seen before, "I should have killed him straight out. I should have taken my chances. I hate being so fucking clever."

"Ah well," Vazzi said, "it's done now."

He watched Cross drive through the gates. For one of the few times in ten years, he was homesick for Sicily. In Sicily men never became so distraught about a woman's secret. And in Sicily there would never have been all this fuss. Skannet would have been swimming at the bottom of the ocean a long time ago.

As dawn broke, a closed van pulled up to the Hunting Lodge.

Lia Vazzi collected the forged suicide notes from Leonard Sossa and put him into the car that would take him back to Topanga Canyon. Vazzi cleaned up the bungalow, burned the letters Skannet had written, removing all traces of occupancy. Leonard Sossa had never seen either Skannet or Cross during his stay.

Then Lia Vazzi prepared for the execution of Boz Skannet.

Six men were involved in this operation. They had blindfolded and gagged Skannet and put him in the van. Two of the men got into the van with him. Skannet was completely helpless, shackled hand and foot. Another man drove the van, and another man rode shotgun for the driver. The fifth man drove Skannet's car. Lia Vazzi and the sixth man drove another car that went in front.

Lia Vazzi watched the sun slowly rise from the shadows of the mountains. The caravan drove nearly sixty miles and then turned into a road deep in the woods.

Finally the caravan halted. Vazzi directed exactly how Skannet's car should be parked. Then he had Skannet taken out of the van. Skannet made no resistance, he seemed to have accepted his fate. Well, he's finally figured it all out, Vazzi thought.

Vazzi took the rope out of the car. He measured the length carefully and hung one end to the thick limb of a nearby tree. Two men were holding Skannet up straight so that he could slip the noose around the man's neck. Vazzi took out the two suicide notes that Leonard Sossa had forged and slipped them into Skannet's jacket pocket.

It took four of the men to lift Skannet to the roof of the van and then Lia Vazzi threw his fist out in the direction of the driver. The van shot ahead and Skannet flew off the roof and dangled in the air. The sound of his neck cracking resounded through the forest. Vazzi checked the corpse and removed the shackles from the body. The other men removed the blindfold and the gag. There were little scrapes around the mouth, but a couple of days hanging in the forest and they would not be significant. He checked the arms and legs for signs of restraint. Again, there were slight marks, but they would not be conclusive. He was satisfied. He did not know if it would work, but everything Cross ordered had been done.

Two days later, alerted by an anonymous tip, the county sheriff found Skannet's body. He had to scare off an inquisitive brown bear who was hitting the rope to make the body sway back and forth, and when the coroner and his assistants arrived, they found the body's rotting skin eaten by insects.

BOOK VI

A Hollywood Death

CHAPTER 10

TEN BARE female asses rose in harmony to greet the camera's blinking eye. Despite the picture still being in limbo, Dita Tommey was auditioning actresses on the *Messalina* soundstage for an ass to double for Athena Aquitane's.

Athena had refused to do nudes, that is, she would not show full tits and ass, an astonishing modesty in a star but not a fatal one. Dita would simply substitute tits and ass from some of the different actresses she was now auditioning.

Of course she had given the actresses full scenes with dialogue, she wouldn't demean them by posing them as if they were pornography. But the determining factor would be in the culminating sex scene, when rolling around in bed they would thrust their bare buttocks up to the camera eye. Her sex-scene choreographer was sketching out the rolls and twists with the male actor, Steve Stallings.

Watching the tests with Dita Tommey were Bobby Bantz and Skippy Deere. The only other people on the set were the necessary crew members. Tommey didn't mind Deere watching, but what the hell was Bobby Bantz doing here. She had considered briefly barring him from the set, but if *Messalina* was abandoned she would be in a very weak power position. She could use his goodwill.

Bantz asked fretfully, "What exactly are we looking for here?"

The sex-scene choreographer, a young man named Willis, who was also the head of the Los Angeles Ballet Company, said cheerfully, "The most beautiful ass in the world. But also with great muscles. We don't want sleaze, we don't want the crack open."

"Right," Bantz said, "Nothing sleazy."

"How about the tits?" Deere asked.

"They cannot be allowed to bounce," the choreographer said.

"We audition tits tomorrow," Tommey said. "No woman has perfect tits and a perfect ass, except maybe Athena, and she won't show them."

Bantz said slyly, "You should know, Dita."

Tommey forgot her weak power position. "Bobby, you're the perfect asshole, if that's what we're looking for. She won't fuck you so you assume she's a dyke."

"OK, OK," Bantz said. "I've got a hundred phone calls I have to return."

"Me too," Deere said.

"I don't believe you guys," Tommey said.

Deere said, "Dit, have a little sympathy. Bobby and I, what recreation do we get? We're too busy to play golf. Watching movies is work. We don't have the time to go to the theater or opera. We can squeeze maybe an hour a day for fun after we spend time with our families. What can you do with just one hour a day? Screw. It's the least labor-intensive recreation."

"Wow, Skippy, look at that," Bantz said. "That's the most beautiful ass I have ever seen."

Deere shook his head in wonder. "Bobby's right. Dita, that's the one. Sign her up."

Tommey shook her head in disbelief. "Jesus, you guys are morons," she said. "That's a black ass."

"Sign her up anyway," Deere said with exuberant joy.

"Yeah," Bantz said. "An Ethiopian slave girl for Messalina. But why the hell is she auditioning?"

Dita Tommey observed both men with curiosity. Here were two of the toughest men in the movie business, with over a hundred phone calls to return, and they were like two teenagers looking for their first orgasm. She said patiently, "When we send out casting calls we're not allowed to say we just want white asses."

Bantz said, "I want to meet that girl."

"Me too," Deere said.

But all this was interrupted by Melo Stuart coming on the set. He was smiling triumphantly. "We can all go back to work," he said.

"Athena is going back on the picture. Her husband, Boz Skannet, hung himself. Boz Skannet, off the picture." As he said this he clapped his hands as the crew always clapped when an actor finished work on a movie, his part finished. Skippy and Bobby clapped with him. Dita Tommey stared at the three of them with disgust.

"Eli wants the two of you right away," Melo said. "Not you, Dita," he smiled apologetically. "This will just be a business discussion, no creative decisions." The men left the soundstage.

When they were gone, Dita Tommey summoned the girl with the beautiful ass to her trailer. She was very pretty, truly black rather than tan, and she had an impudent vivacity that Dita identified as natural and not an actor's put-on.

"I'm giving you the part of an Ethiopian slave girl to the Empress Messalina," Dita said. "You'll have one line of dialogue but mainly we'll be showing your ass. Unfortunately we need a white ass to double for Miss Aquitane and yours is too black, otherwise you might steal the picture. She gave the girl a friendly smile. "Falene Fant, that's a movie name."

"Whatever," the girl said. "Thank you. For both the compliments and the job."

"One more thing," Dita said. "Our producer, Skippy Deere, thinks you have the most beautiful ass in the world. So does Mr. Bantz, the president and head of production for the Studio. You'll be hearing from them."

Falene Fant gave her a wicked grin. "And what do you think?" she said.

Dita Tommey shrugged. "I'm not into asses as much as men are. But I think you're charming and a very good actress. Good enough so that I think you can carry more than one line in this picture. And if you come to my house tonight, we can talk about your career. I'll give you dinner."

That night, after Dita Tommey and Falene Fant spent two hours in bed, Dita cooked dinner and they discussed Falene's career.

"It was fun," Dita said, "but I think from now on we should just be friends and keep this night a secret."

"Sure," Falene said. "But everyone knows you're dykey. Is it my black ass?" She was grinning.

Dita ignored the word *dykey.* That was a deliberate impudence to pay back for the seeming rejection. “It’s a great ass, black, white, green, or yellow,” Dita said. “But you have real talent. If I keep casting you in my pictures, you won’t get credit for your talent. And I only make a picture every two years. You have to work more than that. Most directors are male and when they cast somebody like you they’re always hoping for a little screw. If they think you’re dykey, they may pass.”

“Who needs directors if I have a producer and the head of a studio,” Falene said cheerfully.

“You do,” Dita said. “The other guys can get you a foot in the door, but the director can leave you on the cutting-room floor. Or he can shoot you so that you look and sound like shit.”

Falene shook her head woefully. “I have to fuck Bobby Bantz, Skippy Deere, and I’ve already fucked you. Is this absolutely necessary?” She opened her eyes wide, innocently.

Dita really felt fond of her at the moment. Here was a girl who didn’t try to be indignant. “I had a very good time tonight,” she said. “You hit exactly the right note.”

“Well, I never understood the fuss people make about sex,” Falene said. “It’s no hardship for me. I don’t do drugs, I don’t drink a lot. I have to have a little fun.”

“Fine,” Dita said. “Now, about Deere and Bantz. Deere is the better bet and I’ll tell you why. Deere is in love with himself and he loves women. He will really do something for you. He’ll find you a good part, he’s smart enough to see your talent. Now Bantz doesn’t like anybody except Eli Marrion. Also he has no taste, no eye for talent. Bantz will sign you to a studio contract and then let you rot. He does that with his wife to keep her quiet. She gets a lot of work for top dollar but never a decent part. Skippy Deere, if he likes you, will do something for your career.”

“This sounds a little cold-blooded,” Falene said.

Dita tapped her on the arm. “Don’t bullshit me. I’m a dyke but I’m a woman too. And I know actors. They will do anything, male or female, to go up the ladder. We all play for big stakes. Do you want to go to a nine-to-five job in Oklahoma or do you want to become a movie star and live in Malibu? I see by your sheet that you're twenty-three years old. How many have you fucked already?"

"Counting you?" Falene said. "Maybe fifty. But all for fun," she said in mock apology.

"So a few more won't traumatize you," Dita said. "And who knows, it may be fun again."

"You know," Falene said, "I wouldn't do it if I wasn't so sure I'd be a star."

"Of course," Dita said. "None of us would."

Falene laughed. "What about you?" she asked.

"I didn't have the option," Dita said. "I made it on sheer overwhelming talent."

"Poor you," Falene said.

At LoddStone Studios, Bobby Bantz, Skippy Deere, and Melo Stuart were meeting with Eli Marrion in his office. Bantz was enraged. "That silly prick, he scares everybody to death and then commits suicide."

Marrion said to Stuart, "Melo, your client is coming back to work I assume."

"Of course," Melo said.

"She has no further requests, she doesn't need any extra inducements?" Marrion asked in a quiet, deadly voice. For the first time, Melo Stuart became aware that Marrion was in a rage.

"No," Melo said. "She can start work tomorrow."

"Great," Deere said. "We may still come in under budget."

"I want you all to shut up and listen to me," Marrion said. And this rudeness, so unprecedented in him, made them silent.

Marrion spoke in his usual low, pleasant voice, but there was now no mistaking his anger.

"Skippy, what do we give a fuck if the picture comes in on budget? We don't own the picture anymore. We panicked, we made a stupid mistake. All of us are at fault. We do not own this film, an outsider does."

Skippy Deere tried to interrupt him. "LoddStone will make a fortune on distribution. And you get a percentage on profits. It's still a very good deal."

"But De Lena makes more money than we do," Bantz said. "That's not right."

"The point is that De Lena did nothing to solve the problem," Marrion said. "Surely our studio has some sort of legal basis to regain the picture."

"That's right," Bantz said. "Fuck him. Let's go to court."

Marrion said, "We threaten him with court and then we cut a deal. We give him his money back and ten percent of the adjusted gross."

Deere laughed. "Eli, Molly Flanders won't let him take your deal."

"We'll negotiate directly with De Lena," Marrion said. "I think I can persuade him." He paused for a moment. "I called him as soon as I got the news. He will be joining us very shortly. And you know he has a certain background, this suicide is too fortunate for him, I don't think he will care for the publicity of a court case."

Cross De Lena, in his penthouse suite at the Xanadu Hotel, read the newspaper reports of Skannet's death. Everything had gone perfectly. It was a clear case of suicide, the two farewell notes on the body clinched it. There was no possibility the handwriting experts could detect the forgery, Boz Skannet had not left any great body of correspondence and Leonard Sossa was too good. The shackles on Skannet's legs and arms had been purposely loose and had left no marks. Lia Vazzi was an expert.

The first call Cross received was expected. Giorgio Clericuzio summoning him to the Family mansion in Quogue. Cross had never deceived himself that the Clericuzio would not find out what he was doing.

The second call Cross received was from Eli Marrion asking him to come to Los Angeles and without his lawyer. Cross said he would. But before he left Las Vegas he called Molly Flanders and told her about the phone call from Marrion. She was enraged. "Those slimy bastards," she said. "I'll pick you up at the airport and we'll go in together. Never even say good morning to a studio head unless you've got a lawyer with you."

When the two of them walked into LoddStone Studios and Marrion's office they knew there was trouble. The four men waiting there had the seriously truculent look of men about to commit strong-arm.

"I decided to bring my lawyer," Cross said to Marrion. "I hope you don't mind."

"As you wish," Marrion said. "I merely wanted to save you a possible embarrassment."

Molly Flanders, stern-faced and angry, said, "This is going to be really good. You want the picture back but our contract is iron."

"You're correct," Marrion said. "But we are going to appeal to Cross's sense of fair play. He did nothing to solve the problem, whereas LoddStone Studios has invested considerable time and money and creative talent without which this movie would not have been possible. Cross will get his money back. He gets ten percent of the adjusted gross and we will be generous in determining the adjustments. He will not be at risk."

"He has already survived the risk," Molly said. "Your offer is insulting."

"Then we will have to go to court," Marrion said. "Cross, I'm sure you will find that as distasteful as I do." He smiled at Cross. It was a kindly smile that made his gorilla-like face angelic.

Molly was furious. "Eli, you go to court twenty times a year and give depositions because you're always pulling crap like this." She turned to Cross and said, "We're leaving."

But Cross knew that a long court case was something he could not afford. His buying the film followed by Skannet's opportune death would be held up to scrutiny. They would dig up everything about his background, they would paint him in such a way that he would become too much of a public figure, and that was something the old Don had never tolerated. There was no mistaking that Marrion knew all this.

"Let's stick around," Cross said to Molly. Then he turned to Marrion, Bantz, Skippy Deere, and Melo Stuart. "If a gambler comes into my hotel and plays a long shot and wins, I pay him the full odds. I don't say I'll pay him even money. That's what you gentlemen are doing here. So why don't you reconsider this?"

Bantz said with contempt, "This is business not gambling."

Melo Stuart said soothingly to Cross, "You will make conservatively ten million dollars on your investment. Surely that's fair."

"And you didn't even do anything," Bantz said.

Only Skippy Deere seemed to be on his side. "Cross, you deserve more. But what they offer is better than a court fight, the risk of losing. Let this one go and you and I will do business again without the Studio. And I promise you'll get a fair shake."

Cross knew it was important to seem nonthreatening. He smiled in resignation. "Maybe you're all right," he said. "I want to stay in the movie business on good terms with everybody and ten million profit is not a bad start. Molly, take care of the papers. Now I have to catch a plane so please excuse me." He left the room and Molly followed him.

"We can win in court," Molly told him.

"I don't want to go to court," Cross said. "Make the deal."

Molly studied him carefully, then she said, "OK, but I'll get more than ten percent."

When Cross arrived at the mansion in Quogue the next day, Don Domenico Clericuzio, his sons Giorgio, Vincent, and Petie, and the grandson, Dante, were waiting for him. They had lunch in the garden, a lunch of cold Italian hams and cheeses and an enormous wooden bowl of salad, long loaves of crispy Italian bread. There was the bowl of grated cheese for the Don's spoon. As they ate, the Don said conversationally, "Croccifixio, we hear you have become involved in the moving picture business." He paused to sip his red wine. He then took a spoonful of the grated Italian Parmesan cheese.

"Yes," Cross answered.

Giorgio said, "Is it true that you pledged some of your shares in the Xanadu to finance a movie?"

"That is within my right," Cross said. "I am, after all, your *Bruglione* in the West." He laughed.

" *'Bruglione'* is right," Dante said.

The Don shot a disapproving look at his grandson. He said to Cross, "You got involved in a very serious affair without Family consultation. You did not seek our wisdom. Most important of all, you carried out a violent action that might have severe official repercussions. On that, custom is clear, you must have our consent or go your own way and suffer consequences."

"And you used resources of the Family," Giorgio said harshly. "The Hunting Lodge in the Sierra. You used Lia Vazzi, Leonard Sossa, and Pollard with his Security Agency. Of course, they are your people in the West but they are also Family resources. Luckily everything went perfectly but what if it had not? We would all have been at risk."

Don Clericuzio said impatiently, "He knows all that. The question is why. Nephew, years ago you asked not to take part in that necessary work some men must do. I granted your request despite the fact that you were so valuable. Now you do it for your own profit. That is not like the beloved nephew I have always known."

Cross knew then that the Don was sympathetic to him. He knew he could not tell the truth, that he had been seduced by Athena's beauty; that would not be a reasonable explanation, indeed it would be insulting. And possibly fatal. What could be more inexcusable than that the attraction to a strange woman outweighed his loyalty to the Clericuzio Family. He spoke carefully. "I saw an opportunity to make a great deal of money," he said. "I saw a chance to get a foothold in a new business. For me and the Family. A business to be used to turn black money white. But I had to move quickly. Certainly I did not wish to keep it a secret and the proof is that I used Family resources which you must come to know. I wanted to come to you with the deed done."

The Don was smiling at him when he asked gently, "And is the deed done?"

Cross immediately sensed that the Don knew everything. "There is another problem," Cross said, and explained the new deal he had made with Marrion. He was surprised when the Don laughed aloud.

"You did exactly right," the Don said. "A court case might be a disaster. Let them have their victory. But what rascals they are. It's a good thing we always stayed out of that business." He paused for a moment. "At least you've made your ten million. That's a tidy sum."

"No," Cross said. "Five for me and five for the Family, that is understood. I don't think we should be discouraged so easily. I have some plans but I must have Family help."

"Then we must discuss better shares," Giorgio said. He was like Bantz, Cross thought, always pressing for more.

The Don interrupted impatiently. "First catch the rabbit then we will share it. You have the Family blessing. But one thing. Full discussion on everything drastic that is done. You understand me, nephew?"

"Yes," Cross said.

He left Quogue with a feeling of relief. The Don had shown his affection.

Don Domenico Clericuzio, in his eighties, still commanded his Empire. A world he had created with great endeavor and at great cost and so therefore felt he had earned.

At a venerable age, when most men are obsessed with sins inevitably committed, the regrets of lost dreams, and even doubts of their own righteousness, the Don was still as unshakable in his virtue as when he was fourteen.

Don Clericuzio was strict in his beliefs and strict in his judgments. God had created a perilous world, and mankind had made it even more dangerous. God's world was a prison in which man had to earn his daily bread, and his fellow man was a fellow beast, carnivorous and without mercy. Don Clericuzio was proud that he had guarded his loved ones safely in their journey through life.

He was content that, at his advanced age, he had the will to pass the sentence of death on his enemies. Certainly he forgave them, was he not a Christian who maintained a holy chapel in his own home? But he forgave his enemies as God forgives all men while condemning them to inevitable extinction.

In the world Don Clericuzio had created, he was revered. His family, the thousands who lived in the Bronx Enclave, the *Bru-*

gliones who ruled territories and entrusted their money to him and came for his intercession when they got into trouble with the formal society. They knew that the Don was just. That in time of need, sickness, or any trouble, they could go to him and he would address their misfortunes. And so they loved him.

The Don knew that love is not a reliable emotion no matter how deep. Love does not ensure gratitude, does not ensure obedience, does not provide harmony in so difficult a world. No one understood this better than Don Clericuzio. To inspire *true* love, one also had to be feared. Love alone was contemptible, it was nothing if it did not also include trust and obedience. What good was love to him if it did not acknowledge his rule?

For he was responsible for their lives, he was the root of their good fortune, and so he could not falter in his duty. He must be strict in his judgment. If a man betrayed him, if a man damaged the integrity of his world, that man must be punished and restrained even if it meant a sentence of death. There could be no excuse, no mitigating circumstance, no appeal to pity. What must be done must be done. His son Giorgio had once called him archaic. He accepted that this could not be otherwise.

Now he had many things to ponder. He had planned well over the last twenty-five years since the Santadio war. He had been farsighted, cunning, brutal when necessary, and merciful when it was safe to be so. And now the Clericuzio Family was at the height of its power, seemingly safe from any attack. Soon it would disappear into the legal fabric of society and become invulnerable.

But Don Domenico had not survived so long by being optimistically shortsighted. He could spot a malignant weed before it popped its head above the ground. The great danger now was internal, the rise of Dante, his growing into manhood in a manner not entirely satisfactory to the Don.

Then there was Cross, enriched by the Gronevelt legacy, actually making a major move without Family supervision. The young man had started so brilliantly, nearly becoming a Qualified Man, like his father, Pippi. Then the Virginio Ballazzo job had turned him finicky. And after being excused from operational duties by the Family because of his tender heart, he had gone back into the field for his own personal gain and executed that man Skannet. Without the permission of the Don himself. But Don Clericuzio excused himself for condoning these actions, for his rare sentimentalities. Cross was trying to escape his world and enter another. Though these actions were or could be the seeds of treason, Don Clericuzio understood. Still, Pippi and Cross combined would be a threat to the Family. Also, the Don was not unaware of Dante's hatred for the De Lenas. Pippi was too clever not to know this also, and Pippi was a dangerous man. An eye must be kept on him despite his proven loyalty.

The Don's forbearance sprang from a fondness for Cross and a love for Pippi, his old and faithful soldier, his sister's son. After all, they had Clericuzio blood. He was truly more worried about the danger to the Family presented by Dante.

Don Clericuzio had always been a fond and loving grandfather to Dante. The two had been very close until the boy was about ten years old and a certain disenchantment had settled in. The Don detected traits in the boy's character that troubled him.

Dante at the age of ten was an exuberant, slyly humorous child. He was a good athlete with great physical coordination. He loved to talk, especially with his grandfather, and he had long secret conversations with his mother, Rose Marie. But then, after the age of ten, he became malicious and crude. He fought with boys his own age with inappropriate intensity. He teased girls mercilessly and with an innocent lewdness that was shocking though funny. He tortured small animals—not necessarily significant with small boys, as the Don knew—but he tried once to drown a smaller boy in the school swimming pool.

Not that the Don was particularly judgmental of these things. After all, children were animals, civilization had to be drummed into their brains and backsides. There had been children like Dante who had grown up to be saints. What disturbed the Don was his loquacity, his long conversations with his mother, and most of all, his small disobediences to the Don himself.

Perhaps what disturbed the Don as well, who was in awe of the vagaries of nature, was that at the age of fifteen, Dante stopped growing. He remained at the height of five feet three inches. Doctors were consulted and agreed that at the most he would grow three more inches, and not to the usual Clericuzio family height of six feet. The Don considered Dante's short stature to be a danger signal, as he also considered twins. He claimed that while birth was a blessed miracle, twins were going too far. There had been a soldier in the Bronx Enclave who had fathered triplets, and the Don, horrified, bought them a grocery store in Portland, Oregon, a good living but a lonely one. The Don also had superstitions about left-handed people, and those who stuttered. Whatever anyone said, these could not be good signs. Dante was naturally left-handed.

But even all this would not have been enough to make the Don wary of his grandchild or lessen his affection; anyone of his blood was naturally exempt. But as Dante grew older he grew more contrary to the Don's dreams of his future.

Dante quit school in his sixteenth year and immediately pushed his nose into Family affairs. He worked for Vincent in his restaurant. He was a popular waiter and earned huge tips because of his quickness and his wit. Tiring of that, he worked for two months in Giorgio's Wall Street office but hated it and showed no aptitude, despite Giorgio's earnest attempts to teach him the intricacies of paper wealth. Finally he settled in with Petie's construction company and loved working with the Enclave soldiers. He was proud of his body, which grew more and more muscular. But in all this he acquired to some degree certain characteristics of his three uncles, which the Don noted with pride. He had Vincent's directness, Giorgio's coolness, and Petie's ferocity. Somewhere along the way, he established his own personality, what he truly was: sly, cunning, devious, but with a sense of fun that could be charming. And it was then he began wearing his Renaissance hats.

The hats—nobody knew where he got them—were made of colorful iridescent thread; some were round, some were rectangular, and they rode on his head as if they were on water. They seemed to make him taller, handsomer, and more likable. Partly because they were clownlike and disarming, partly because they balanced his two profiles. The hats suited him. They disguised his hair, jet black and ropey as with all the Clericuzio.

One day in the den, where Silvio's photo still occupied the place of honor, Dante asked his grandfather, "How did he die?"

The Don said shortly, "An accident."

"He was your favorite son, right?" Dante asked.

The Don was startled by all this. Dante was still only fifteen. "Why would this be true?" the Don asked.

"Because he's dead," Dante said with a sly grin, and it took the Don a few moments to realize that this raw youth had dared to make such a joke.

The Don also knew that Dante roamed and searched his office suite in the house when the Don was down at dinner. This did not disturb him, children were always curious about the old and the Don never had anything on paper that would divulge information of any kind. Don Clericuzio had a huge blackboard in a corner of his brain that was chalked with all necessary information, including the totals of all the sins and virtues of those dearest to him.

But as Don Clericuzio became more wary of Dante, he showed him even more affection, assuring the boy he was to be one of the heirs to his Family Empire. And rebukes and admonitions were given the boy by his uncles, primarily Giorgio.

Finally, the Don despaired of Dante joining the retreat into a legal society and gave his permission for Dante to train to be a Hammer.

The Don heard his daughter, Rose Marie, calling him to dinner in the kitchen where they ate when it was just the two of them. He went in, sat in the chair in front of the large, colorful bowl of angel hair pasta covered with tomatoes and fresh basil from his garden. She put the silver bowl of grated cheese before him, the cheese was very yellow, which proved its nutty sweetness. Rose Marie came to sit opposite him. She was gay and cheerful, and he was delighted by her good humor. Tonight there would be none of her terrible fits. She was as she had been before the Santadio War.

What a tragedy that had been, one of the few mistakes he had made, one that proved a victory was not always a victory. But who would have thought that Rose Marie would remain forever a widow?

Lovers always loved again, he'd always believed that. At that moment the Don felt an overpowering affection for his daughter. She would excuse Dante's small sins. Rose Marie leaned over and gave the Don's grizzled head an affectionate caress.

He took a huge spoonful of the grated cheese and felt its nutty heat against his gums. He sipped his wine and watched Rose Marie carve the leg of lamb. She served him three crusty brown potatoes, glossy with fat. His troubled mind cleared. Who was better than him?

He was in such a good mood that he let Rose Marie persuade him to watch television with her in the sitting room for the second time that week.

After watching four hours filled with horror, he said to Rose Marie, "Is it possible to live in such a world where everyone does what he pleases? No one is punished by God or man and no one has to earn a living? Are there such women who follow every whim? Men such foolish weaklings, who succumb to every little desire, every little dream of happiness? Where are the honest husbands who work to earn their bread, who think of the best ways to protect their children from fate and the cruel world? Where are the people who understand a piece of cheese, a glass of wine, a warm house at the end of the day is reward enough? Who are these people who yearn for some mysterious happiness? What an uproar they make of life, what tragedies they brew up out of nothing." The Don patted his daughter on the head and waved at the television screen with a dismissive hand. He said, "Let them all swim at the bottom of the ocean." Then he gave her a final piece of wisdom. "Everyone is responsible for everything he does."

That night, alone in his bedroom, the Don stepped out on his balcony. The houses in the compound were all brightly illuminated; he could hear the thwack of tennis balls on the tennis court and see the players underneath its bank of lights. There were no children playing outdoors so late. He could see the guards on the gate and around the house.

He pondered what steps he could take to prevent future tragedy. His love for his daughter and grandson washed over him, that was what made old age worthwhile. He would simply have to protect them as best he could. Then he was angry with himself. Why was he always foreseeing tragedy? He had solved all the problems in his life and he would solve this one.

Still, his mind whirled with plans. He thought of Senator Wavven. For years he had given the man millions of dollars to get legislation passed to ensure legalized gambling. But the senator was slippery. It was too bad that Gronevelt was not still alive; Cross and Giorgio did not have the necessary skill to prod him. Perhaps the gambling empire would never come to pass.

Then he thought of his old friend David Redfellow, now living so comfortably in Rome. Perhaps it was time to bring him back into the Family. It was all very well for Cross to be so forgiving of his Hollywood partners. After all, he was young. He could not know that one sign of weakness might be fatal. The Don decided he would summon David Redfellow from Rome to do something about the movie business.

CHAPTER 11

A WEEK AFTER the death of Boz Skannet, Cross received, through Claudia, a dinner invitation to Athena Aquitane's house in Malibu.

Cross flew from Vegas to L.A., rented a car, and arrived at the Malibu Colony guarded gatehouse as the sun began to fall into the ocean. There was no longer any special security, though there was still the secretary in the guest house who checked and buzzed him in. He walked through the longitudinal garden to the house on the beach. There was still the little South American maid, who led him to the sea-green living room that seemed just out of reach of the Pacific Ocean waves.

Athena was waiting for him, and she was even more beautiful than he remembered. She was dressed in a green blouse and slacks, and she seemed to melt and become part of the mist over the ocean behind her. He could not take his eyes off her. She shook his hand in greeting, not the usual Hollywood kiss on both cheeks. She had drinks ready and she handed him one. It was Evian water with lime. They sat in the large, mint green upholstered chairs that faced the ocean. The descending sun scattered gold coins of light in the room.

Cross was so aware of her beauty that he had to bow his head to avoid looking at her. The golden helmet of hair, the creamy skin, the way her long body sprawled in her chair. Some of the gold coins fell into her green eyes, fleeting shadows. He felt an urgent desire to touch her, to be closer to her, to own her.

Athena seemed unaware of the emotions she was causing. She sipped her drink and said quietly, "I wanted to thank you for keeping me in the movie business."

The sound of her voice further entranced Cross. It was not sultry or inviting. But it had such a velvet tone, it had such regal confidence and yet was so warm, that he just wanted her to keep talking. Jesus Christ, he thought, what the hell is this? He was ashamed of her power over him. His head still down, he murmured, "I thought I could get you back to work by appealing to your greed."

"That is not one of my many weaknesses," Athena said. Now she turned her head from the ocean so that she could look directly into his eyes. "Claudia told me the Studio reneged on their deal once my husband killed himself. You had to give them back the picture and take a percentage."

Cross kept his face impassive. He hoped to banish everything he was feeling about her. "I guess I'm not a very good businessman," he said. He wanted to give her the impression that he was ineffective.

"Molly Flanders wrote your contract," Athena said. "She's the best. You could have held on."

Cross shrugged. "A matter of politics. I want to get into the movie business permanently and didn't want enemies as powerful as Loddstone Studios."

"I could help you," Athena said. "I could refuse to return to the picture."

Cross felt a thrill that she would do that for him. He considered the offer. The Studio might still take him to court. Also, he could not bear to make Athena put him in her debt. And then it occurred to him that though Athena was beautiful that didn't mean she was not clever.

"Why would you do that?" he asked.

Athena got up from her chair and moved to stand close to the picture window. The beaches were gray shadows, the sun had disappeared, and the ocean seemed to reflect the mountain ranges behind her house and the Pacific Coast Highway. She gazed out toward the now blue-black water, the small waves rippling in slyly. She did not turn her head to him when she said, "Why would I do that? Simply because I knew Boz Skannet better than anybody. And I don't care if he left a hundred suicide notes, he would never kill himself."

Cross shrugged. "Dead is dead," he said.

"That's true," Athena said. She turned to face him, looked directly at him. "You buy the picture and suddenly Boz conveniently commits suicide. You're my candidate as the killer." Even stern, her face was so beautiful to Cross that his voice was not as steady as he would have wished.

"How about the Studio?" Cross said. "Marrion is one of the most powerful men in the country. What about Bantz and Skippy Deere?"

Athena shook her head. "They understood what I was asking them. Just as you did. They didn't do it, they sold the picture to you. They didn't care if I was killed after the picture was finished, but you did. And I knew you would help me even when you said you couldn't. When I heard about you buying the picture, I knew exactly what you would do, but I must say I didn't think you could be so clever."

Suddenly she came toward him and he rose from his chair. She took his hands in hers. He could smell her body, her breath.

Athena said, "That was the only evil thing I have ever done in my life. Making somebody commit murder. It was terrible. I would have been a much better person if I had done it myself. But I couldn't."

Cross said, "Why were you so sure I would do something?"

Athena said, "Claudia told me so much about you. I understood who you were but she's so naïve, she still hasn't caught on. She thinks you're just a tough guy with a lot of clout."

Cross became very alert. She was trying to get him to admit his guilt. Something he would never do even to a priest, not even to God himself.

Athena said, "And the way you looked at me. A lot of men have looked at me that way. I'm not being immodest, I know I'm beautiful, people have been telling me that since I was a child. I always knew I had power, but I could never really understand that power. I'm not really happy with it but I use it. What they call 'love.' "

Cross let go of her hands. "Why were you so afraid of your husband? Because he could ruin your career?"

For one moment there was a flash of anger in her eyes. "It wasn't my career," she said, "and it wasn't out of fear, though I knew he would kill me. I had a better reason." She paused, then said, "I can make them give you the picture back. I can refuse to keep working."

"No," Cross said.

Athena smiled and said with a brilliant, gay cheerfulness, "Then we can just go to bed together. I find you very attractive and I'm sure we'll have a good time."

His first reaction was one of anger, that she could think she could just buy him off. That she was acting a part, using her skill as a woman the same way a man would use physical force. But what really bothered him was that he could hear a faint bit of mockery in her voice. Mockery of his gallantry, and turning his true love into a simple screw. As if she was telling him that his love for her was as fake as her love for him.

He said to her coolly, "I had a long talk with Boz, trying to make a deal. He said he used to fuck you five times a day when you were married."

He was pleased that she seemed startled. She said, "I wasn't counting, but it was a lot. I was eighteen and I really loved him. Isn't it funny that now I wanted him dead?" She frowned a moment and said, casually, "What else did you talk about?"

Cross looked at her grimly. "Boz told me the terrible secret you had between you. He claims you confessed that when you ran away, you buried your baby in the desert."

Athena's face became a mask, her green eyes went dull. For the first time that night, Cross felt she could not possibly be acting. Her face had a pallor no actress could achieve. She whispered to him, "Do you really believe I murdered my baby?"

"Boz said that's what you told him," Cross said.

"I did tell him that," Athena said. "Now, I'm asking you again. Do you believe I murdered my baby?"

There is nothing so terrible as to condemn a beautiful woman. Cross knew that if he answered truthfully, he would lose her forever. Suddenly he put his arms around her very gently. "You're too beautiful. Nobody as beautiful as you could do that." The eternal worship of men for beauty against all evidence. "No," he said. "I don't believe you did."

She stepped away from him. "Even though I'm responsible for Boz?"

"You're not responsible," Cross said. "He killed himself."

Athena was gazing at him intently. He took her hands. "Do you believe I killed Boz?" he asked.

And then Athena smiled, an actress who finally realized how to play a scene. "No more than you believe I killed my baby."

They smiled, they had declared each other innocent. She took his hand and said, "Now, I'm cooking dinner for you and then we're going to bed." She led him into the kitchen.

How many times had she played this scene, Cross thought jealously. The beautiful Queen performing housewifely duties like an ordinary woman. He watched her cook. She wore no protective clothing and she was extraordinarily professional. She spoke to him as she chopped vegetables, prepared a skillet, and set the table. She gave him a bottle of wine to open, holding his hand and brushing against his body. She saw him looking with admiration when the table was laden after just a half hour.

She said, "I played a woman chef in one of my first roles, so I went to school to get everything right. And one critic wrote, 'When Athena Aquitane acts as well as she cooks, she will be a star.' "

They ate in the alcove of the kitchen so they could look at the rolling ocean. The food was delicious, little squares of beef covered with vegetables and then a salad of bitter greens. There was a platter of cheeses and warm short loaves of bread, plump as pigeons. Then there was espresso with a small, light lemon tart.

"You should have been a cook," Cross said, "My cousin Vincent would hire you for his restaurants any day."

"Oh, I could have been anything," Athena said with mock boastfulness.

All through dinner she had touched him casually in a way that was sexual, as if she were searching for some spirit in his flesh. Cross with every touch yearned to feel her body on his. By the end of the meal, he no longer could taste what he was eating. Finally they were done and Athena took him by the hand and led him out of the kitchen and up the two flights of stairs to her bedroom. She did it gracefully, almost shyly, almost blushing, as if she were an eager virginal bride. Cross marveled at her acting ability.

The large bedroom was at the very top of the house and had a small balcony that looked out over the ocean. The walls were covered with a weird, garish painting that seemed to light up the room.

They stood on the balcony and watched the room illuminate the beach sand with a spooky yellow glow, the other Malibu houses squatted along the water showing little boxes of light. Tiny birds, as if playing a game, ran in and out of the incoming waves to escape getting wet.

Athena put her hand on Cross's shoulder, around his body, the other hand reaching out to pull his mouth down to hers. They kissed for a long time as the warm ocean air washed over them. Then Athena led him inside the bedroom.

She undressed quickly, slipping out of her green blouse and slacks. Her white body flashed in the moon-ridden darkness. She was as beautiful as he had imagined. The rising breasts with their raspberry nipples seemed spun of sugar. Her long legs, the curve of her hips, the blond hair at her crotch, her absolute stillness, limned by misty ocean air.

Cross reached out for her body and her flesh was velvet, her lips filled with the scent of flowers. The sheer joy of touching her was so sweet he could not do anything else. Athena began to undress him. She did so gently, running her hands over his body as he had over hers. Then, kissing him, she gently pulled him onto the bed.

Cross made love with a passion he had never known or even dreamed existed. He was so urgent that Athena had to stroke his face to gentle him. He could not let loose of her body, even after they climaxed. They lay intertwined until they began again. She was even more ardent than before, as if it was some sort of contest, some sort of avowal. Finally they both drifted off into slumber.

Cross awoke just as the sun showed above the horizon. For the first time in his life, he had a headache. Naked, he moved onto the balcony and sat on one of the straw chairs. He watched the sun slyly rise slowly from the ocean and begin its ascent to the sky.

She was a dangerous woman. The murderer of her own child, whose bones were now filled with desert sand. And she was too skillful in bed. She could be the end of him. At that moment he decided he would never see her again.

Then he felt her arms around his neck and his face twisted around to kiss her. She was in a white fluffy bathrobe, and her hair was held in place by pins that glittered like jewels in a crown. "Take a shower and I'll make you breakfast before you go," she said.

She led him into the double bathroom, two sinks, two marble counters, two bathtubs, and two showers. It was stocked with men's toilet articles, razors, shaving cream, skin toners, brushes, and combs.

When he had finished and was out on the balcony again, Athena brought a tray with croissants, coffee, and orange juice to the table. "I can make you bacon and eggs," she said.

"This is fine," Cross said.

"When will I see you again?" Athena asked.

"I have lots of things to do in Las Vegas," Cross said. "I'll call you next week."

Athena gave him an appraising look. "That means good-bye, doesn't it?" she asked. "And I really enjoyed last night."

Cross shrugged. "You paid off your obligation," he said.

She gave him a good-humored grin and said, "And with amazing goodwill, don't you think? It wasn't begrudging."

Cross laughed. "No," he said.

She seemed to read his mind. Last night they had lied to each other, this morning the lies had no power. She seemed to know that her beauty was too much for him to trust. That he felt in danger with her, and with her confessed sins. She seemed deep in thought and ate silently. Then she said to him, "I know you're busy but I have something to show you. Can you spare this morning and catch an afternoon plane? It's important. I want to take you someplace."

Cross could not resist spending one last time with her and so he said yes.

Athena drove them in her car, a Mercedes SL 300, and took the highway south to San Diego. But just before they reached the city, she turned off into a thin road that led inland through the mountains.

In fifteen minutes they came to a compound enclosed by barbed wire. Inside the compound were six redbrick buildings separated by green lawns and connected by sky blue painted walkways. In one of the green squares, a group of about twenty children were playing with a soccer ball. On another green about ten children were flying kites. There was a group of three or four adults standing around watching them, but something seemed odd about the scene. When the soccer ball flew through the air, it seemed most of the children ran away from it, while on the other square the kites flew up, up, into the sky and never returned.

"What is this place?" Cross asked.

Athena looked pleadingly at him. "Just come with me please for now. Later, you can ask your questions."

Athena drove to the entry gate and showed a gold ID badge to the security guard. Passing through, she drove to the largest building and parked.

Once inside at the reception desk, Athena asked the attendant something in a low voice. Cross stood back, but still he heard the answer. "She was in a mood so we gave her a hug in her room."

"What the hell was that?" Cross asked.

But Athena didn't answer. She took his hand and led him through a long, shiny tile hallway to an adjoining building and into some sort of dormitory.

A nurse sitting at the entrance asked their names. When she nodded, Athena led Cross down another long hallway of doors. Finally, she opened one.

They were standing in a pretty bedroom, large and full of light. There were the same strange, dark paintings as on the wall in Athena's house, but here they were strewn on the floor. On the wall a small shelf held a row of pretty dolls dressed in starched Amish costumes. Also on the floor were several other scraps of drawings and paintings.

There was a small bed covered with a pink fuzzy blanket, the pillows white with red roses stitched all over them. But there was no child in the bed.

Athena walked toward a large box that was open at the top, its walls and base covered with a thick, soft pad colored light blue, and when Cross looked inside he saw the child lying there. She didn't notice them. She was fiddling with a knob at the head of the box, and Cross watched as she forced the pads together, almost crushing herself.

She was a small girl of ten, a tiny copy of Athena, but without emotion, devoid of all expression, and her green eyes were as unseeing as those of a porcelain doll. Yet each time she turned the controls to make the panels squeeze her tight, her face shone with complete serenity. She did not acknowledge them in any way.

Athena moved to the top of the wooden box. She switched the controls so that she could lift the child out of the box. The child seemed to weigh almost nothing.

Athena held her like an infant and bent her head to kiss the child's cheek, but the child flinched and pulled away.

"It's your mommy," Athena said. "Won't you give me a kiss?"

The tone of her voice broke Cross's heart. It was an abject pleading, but now the child was churning wildly within her arms. Finally Athena gently put her down on the floor. The child scrambled to her knees and immediately picked up a box of paints and a huge cardboard sheet. Completely absorbed, she began to paint.

Cross stood back and watched as Athena tried all her acting skill to establish a rapport with the child. First she kneeled down next to the little girl and was the loving playmate helping her daughter paint, but the child took no notice.

Athena then sat up, tried to be a confiding parent telling the child what was happening in the world. Then Athena became a fawning adult praising the child's paintings. To all this the child merely kept moving away. Athena picked up one of the brushes and tried to help, but when the child did see, she grabbed the brush away. She never said a word.

Finally Athena gave up.

"I'll come back tomorrow, darling," she said. "I'll take you for a ride and I'll bring a new paint box. See," she said, tears welling in her eyes, "you're running out of reds." She tried to give the child a farewell kiss but was held away by two small, beautiful hands.

Finally Athena rose and led Cross out of the room.

Athena gave him the keys to the car so he could drive back to Malibu, and during the ride, she held her head in her hands and wept. Cross was so stunned he could not say a word.

When they got out of the car, Athena seemed to have control of herself. She pulled Cross into the house and then turned and faced him. "That was the baby I told Boz I buried in the desert. Now do you believe me?" And for the first time Cross really believed she might love him.

Athena led him into the kitchen and made coffee. They sat in the alcove to watch the ocean. As they drank their coffee, Athena started speaking. She talked casually, no emotion in her voice or on her face.

"When I ran away from Boz, I left my baby with some distant cousins, a married couple in San Diego. She seemed a normal baby. I didn't know she was autistic then, maybe she wasn't. I left her there because I was determined to be a successful actress. I had to make money for both of us. I was sure I was talented and God knows everybody told me how beautiful I was. I always thought that when I was successful, I could take my baby back."

"So I worked in Los Angeles and visited her in San Diego whenever I could. Then I began to break through and I didn't see her that often, maybe once a month. Finally when I was ready to bring her home I went to her third birthday party with all kinds of presents, but Bethany seemed to have slipped into another world. She was a blank. I couldn't reach her at all. I was frantic. I thought maybe she had a brain tumor, I remembered when Boz had let her fall on the floor, that maybe her brain had been injured and it was now beginning to show. For months after that I brought her to doctors, she underwent a battery of tests of all kinds, I took her to specialists and they checked everything. Then someone, and I don't remember whether it was the doctor in Boston or the psychiatrist in Texas Children's Hospital, told me she was autistic. I didn't even know what that meant except that I thought it was some kind of retardation. 'No,' the doctor said. It meant she lived in her own world, was unaware of other people's existence, had no interest in them, could feel nothing for anything or anyone. It was when I brought her to the clinic here to be close to me that we found she could respond to that hugging machine you saw. That seemed to help, so I had to leave her there."

Cross sat without a word, while Athena continued. "Being autistic meant she could never love me. But the doctors told me some autistic people are talented, even geniuslike. And I think Bethany is a genius. Not only with her painting. Something else. The doctors tell me that after many years of hard training some autistic people can be taught to care for some things, then some people. A few can even live a near-to-normal life. Right now, Bethany can't stand listening to music or any noise. But at first she couldn't bear to have me touch her, and now she's learned to tolerate me, so she's better than she used to be.

"She still rejects me but not as violently. We've made some progress. I used to think it was punishment for my neglect of her because I wanted to be a success. But the specialists say that sometimes though it seems hereditary, it can be acquired, but they don't know what really makes it happen. The doctors told me it had nothing to do with Boz dropping her on her head or me deserting her, but I don't know if I believe that. They kept trying to reassure me that we were not responsible, that it was one of the mysteries of life, maybe it was preordained. They insisted nothing could have prevented it from happening and nothing can ever change it. But again something inside me refuses to believe any of that.

"Even when I first found out, I thought about it constantly. I had to make some hard decisions. I knew I would be helpless to rescue her until I made a lot of money. So I put her in the clinic and visited her at least one weekend a month and some weekdays. Finally, I got rich, I was famous and nothing that mattered before mattered any longer. All I wanted was to be with Bethany. Even if this hadn't happened, I was going to quit after *Messalina* anyway."

"Why?" Cross asked. "What were you going to do?"

"There's a special clinic in France with this great doctor," Athena explained. "And I was going to go there after the picture. Then Boz showed up and I knew he would kill me and Bethany would be all alone. That's why I sort of put a contract out on him. She has nobody but me. And well, I'll bear that sin." Athena paused now and smiled at Cross. "It's worse than the soaps, isn't it?" she said with a small smile.

Cross looked out over the ocean. It was a very bright oily blue in the sunlight. He remembered the little girl and her blank, masklike face that would never open up to this world.

"What was that box she was lying in?" he asked.

Athena laughed. "That's what gives me hope," she said. "Sad, isn't it? It's a hug box. A lot of autistic children use it when they get depressed. It's just like a hug from a person but they don't have to connect or relate to another human being." Athena took a deep breath and said, "Cross, someday I'm going to take the place of that box. That's the whole purpose of my life now. My life has no meaning except for that. Isn't that funny? The Studio tells me that I get thousands of letters from people who love me. In public people want to touch me. Men keep telling me they love me. Everybody but Bethany, and she's the only one I want."

Cross said, "I'll help you in any way I can."

"Then call me next week," Athena said. "Let's be together as much as we can until *Messalina* is finished."

"I'll call," Cross said. "I can't prove my innocence, but I love you more than anything in my life."

"And are you truly innocent?" Athena asked.

"Yes," Cross said. Now that she had been proven innocent, he could not bear for her to know.

Cross thought about Bethany, her blank face so artistically beautiful with its sharp planes, its mirror eyes; the rare human being totally free of sin.

As for Athena, she had been judging Cross. Of all the people she knew, he was the only one who had ever seen her daughter since the child had been diagnosed as autistic. It had been a test.

One of the greatest shocks of her life came when she found out that though she was so beautiful, though she was so talented (and, she thought with self-mockery, so kind, so gentle, so generous), her closest friends, men who loved her, relatives who adored her, sometimes seemed to relish her misfortunes.

It was when Boz had given her a black eye, and though everyone called Boz a "no-good bastard," she caught in all of them a fleeting look of satisfaction. At first she thought she had imagined it, was too sensitive. But when Boz had given her the second black eye, she caught those looks again. And she had been terribly hurt. For this time she had understood completely.

Of course they all loved her, she did not doubt that. But it seemed no one could resist a little touch of malice. Greatness in any form arouses envy.

One of the reasons she loved Claudia was because Claudia had never betrayed her with that look.

It was why she kept Bethany so secret from her day-to-day life. She hated the idea that people she loved would have that fleeting look of satisfaction, that she had been punished for her own beauty.

So though she knew the power of her beauty and used that power, she despised it. She longed for the day when lines would cut deep into her perfect face, each showing a path she had taken, a journey survived, when her body would fill out, soften and enlarge her to provide comfort for those she'd hold and care for, and her eyes would grow more liquid with mercy from all the suffering she'd witnessed and all the tears she'd never shed. She'd grow smile lines around her mouth from laughing at herself, and at life itself. How free she would be when she no longer feared the consequences of her physical beauty and instead delighted in its loss as it was replaced by a more enduring serenity.

And so she had kept careful watch on Cross De Lena when he met Bethany, saw his slight recoil at first but then afterward nothing. She knew he was helplessly in love with her and she saw he did not have that certain look of satisfaction when he knew of her misfortune with Bethany.

CHAPTER 12

CLAUDIA WAS DETERMINED to cash in on her sexual marker with Eli Marrion; she would shame him into giving Ernest Vail the points he wanted on his novel. It was a long shot, but she was willing to compromise her principles. Bobby Bantz was implacable on gross points, but Eli Marrion was unpredictable and had a soft spot for her. Besides, it was an honorable custom in the movie business that sexual congress, no matter how brief, demanded a certain material courtesy.

Vail's threat of suicide had been the trigger for this meeting. If carried out, the rights to his novel would revert to his former wife and her children, and Molly Flanders would drive a hard bargain. Nobody believed in the threat, not even Claudia, but Bobby Bantz and Eli Marrion, operating from their knowledge of what they would do for money, always had to worry.

When Claudia, Ernest, and Molly arrived at LoddStone, they found only Bobby Bantz in the executive suite. He looked uncomfortable, though he tried to disguise it with effusive greetings, especially to Vail. "Our National Treasure," he said and hugged Ernest with respectful affection.

Molly was immediately alert, wary. "Where's Eli?" she said. "He's the only one who can make the final decision on this."

Bantz's voice was reassuring. "Eli's in the hospital, Cedar Sinai, nothing serious, just a checkup. That's confidential. The LoddStone stock goes up and down on his health."

Claudia said dryly, "He's over eighty, everything is serious."

"No, no," Bantz said. "We do business every day in the hospital. He's even sharper. So present your case to me and I'll tell him your story when I visit."

"No," Molly said curtly.

But Ernest Vail said, "Let's talk to Bobby."

They presented their case. Bantz was amused but did not laugh outright. He said, "I've heard everything in this town but this is a beauty. I ran it by my lawyers and they say that Vail's demise does not affect our rights. It's a complicated legal point."

"Run it by your PR people," Claudia said. "If Ernest does it and the whole story comes out LoddStone will look like shit. Eli won't like that. He has more moral sense."

"Than me?" Bobby Bantz said politely. But he was furious. Why didn't people understand that Marrion approved everything he did. He turned to Ernest and said, "How would you knock yourself off? Gun, knife, out the window?"

Vail grinned at him. "Hara-kiri on your desk, Bobby." They all laughed.

"We're getting nowhere," Molly said. "Why can't we all go to the hospital and see Eli?"

Vail said, "I'm not going to a sick man's hospital bed and argue about money."

They all looked at him sympathetically. Of course in conventional terms it seemed insensitive. But men in sickbeds planned murders, revolution, frauds, studio betrayals. A hospital bed was not a true sanctuary. And they knew that Vail's protest was basically a romantic convention.

Molly said coldly, "Keep your mouth shut, Ernest, if you want to remain my client. Eli has screwed a hundred people from his hospital bed. Bobby, let's make a sensible deal. LoddStone has a gold mine in the sequels. You can afford to give Ernest a couple of gross points, for insurance."

Bantz was horrified, a hot stab went through his bowels. "*Gross points?*" he shouted incredulously. "Never."

"OK," Molly said. "How about a structured five percent of the net? No advertising charges, no interest deductions or gross points to the stars."

Bantz said contemptuously, "That's almost gross. And we all know that Ernest won't kill himself. That's too stupid and he is too intelligent." What he really wanted to say was that the guy didn't have the balls.

"Why gamble?" Molly said. "I've gone over the figures. You plan at least three sequels. That's at least a half billion in rentals including foreign but not the videos and TV. And God knows how much money you fucking thieves make in video. So why not give Ernest points, a measly twenty million. You would give that to any half-assed star."

Bantz thought it over. Then he turned on the charm. "Ernest," he said, "as a novelist you are a National Treasure. No one respects you more than me. And Eli has read every one of your books. He absolutely adores you. So we want to come to an accommodation."

Claudia was embarrassed at how Ernest obviously swallowed this bullshit, though to his credit, he shuddered a bit at the "National Treasure."

"Be specific," he said. Now Claudia was proud of him.

Bantz spoke to Molly. "How about a five-year contract at ten grand a week to write original scripts and do some rewrites and of course on the originals we only get first look. And for every rewrite he gets an additional fifty grand a week. In five years he could make as much as ten million."

"Double the money," Molly said. "Then we can talk."

At this point Vail seemed to lose his almost angelic patience. "None of you are taking me seriously," he said. "I can do simple arithmetic. Bobby, your deal is only worth two and a half. You'll never buy an original script from me and I'll never do one. You'll never give me rewrites. And what if you make six sequels? Then you make a billion." Vail began to laugh with genuine enjoyment. "Two and a half million dollars doesn't help me."

"What the fuck are you laughing about?" Bobby said.

Vail was almost hysterical. "I never dreamed in my life of even one million and now it doesn't help me."

Claudia knew Vail's sense of humor. She said, "Why doesn't it help you?"

"Because I'll still be alive," Vail said. "My family needs the points. They trusted me and I betrayed them."

They would have been touched, even Bantz, except that Vail sounded so false, so self-satisfied.

Molly Flanders said, "Let's go talk to Eli."

Vail lost his temper completely and stormed out of the door shouting, "I can't deal with you people. I won't beg a man on a hospital bed."

When he was gone, Bobby Bantz said, "And you two want to stick up for that guy?"

"Why not?" Molly said. "I represented a guy who stabbed his mother and his own three kids. Ernest is no worse than him."

"And what's your excuse?" Bantz asked Claudia.

"We writers have to stick together," she said wryly. They all laughed.

"I guess that's about it," Bobby said. "I did the best I could, right?"

Claudia said, "Bobby, why can't you give him a point or two, it's only fair."

"Because over the years he's screwed a thousand writers and stars and directors. It's a matter of principle," Molly said.

"That's right," Bantz said. "And when they have the muscle they screw us. That's business."

Molly said to Bantz with fake concern, "Eli is okay? Nothing serious?"

"He's fine," Bantz said. "Don't sell your stock."

Molly pounced. "Then he can see us."

Claudia said, "I want to see him anyway. I really care about Eli. He gave me my first break."

Bantz shrugged them off. Molly said, "You will really kick yourself if Ernest knocks himself off. Those sequels are worth more than I said. I softened him up for you."

Bantz said scornfully, "That schmuck won't kill himself. He doesn't have the balls."

"From 'National Treasure' to 'schmuck,' " Claudia said musingly.

Molly said, "The guy is definitely a little crazy. He'll croak out of sheer carelessness."

"Does he do drugs?" Bantz asked, a little worried.

"No," Claudia said, "but Ernest is full of surprises. He's a true eccentric who doesn't even know he's eccentric."

Bantz pondered this for a moment. There was some merit in their argument. And besides he never believed in making unnecessary enemies. He didn't want Molly Flanders to carry a grudge against him. The woman was a terror.

"Let me call Eli," he said. "If he gives the okay, I'll take you to the hospital." He was sure that Marrion would refuse.

But to his surprise, Marrion said, "By all means, they can all come to see me."

They drove to the hospital in Bantz's limo, which was a big stretch job but by no means luxurious. It was fitted with a fax, a computer, and a cellular phone. A bodyguard supplied by Pacific Ocean Security sat next to the driver. Another security car with two men followed behind.

The brown-tinted windows of the limo presented the city in a beige monochrome of old-time cowboy movies. As they progressed inward, the buildings became taller, as if they were penetrating a deep stone forest. Claudia was always amazed how in the short space of ten minutes she could go from a mildly bucolic small-town green to a metropolis of concrete and glass.

In Cedars Sinai, the hospital corridors seemed as vast as the halls of an airport, but the ceiling compressed like a bizarre camera shot in a German impressionist movie. They were met by a hospital coordinator, a handsome women dressed in a severe but high-couture suit who reminded Claudia of the "Hosts" in Vegas hotels.

She led them to a special elevator that took them nonstop to the top penthouse suites.

These suites had huge carved black oak doors that reached from floor to ceiling, with shiny brass knobs. The doors opened like gates, to a suite of a hospital bedroom, a larger, open-walled room with dining table and chairs, a sofa and lounge chairs, and a secretarial niche that held a computer and fax. There was also a small kitchen space and guest bathroom in addition to the bathroom for the patient. The ceiling was very high and the absence of walls between the kitchen niche, the living room area, and the business nook gave the whole room the look of a movie set.

Lying on a crisp, white hospital bed, propped up by huge pillows, was Eli Marrion. He was reading an orange-covered script. On the table beside him were business folders with budgets of movies in production. A pretty young secretary seated on the other side of the bed was taking notes. Marrion always liked pretty women around him.

Billy Bantz kissed Marrion on the cheek and said, "Eli, you look great, just great." Molly and Claudia also kissed him on the cheek. Claudia had insisted on bringing flowers, and put them on the bed. Such familiarities were excused because the great Eli Marrion was ill.

Claudia was noting all the details as if researching a script. Medical dramas were almost financially foolproof.

In fact, Eli Marrion was not looking "great just great." His lips were ridged with blue lines that seemed drawn with ink, he gasped for air when he spoke. Two green prongs grew from his nostrils, the prongs attached to a thin plastic tube that ran to a bubbling bottle of water that was plugged into the wall, all connected to some oxygen tank hidden there.

Marrion noted her gaze. "Oxygen," he said.

"Only temporary," Bobby Bantz said hurriedly. "Makes it easier for him to breathe."

Molly Flanders ignored them. "Eli," she said, "I've explained the situation to Bobby and he needs your OK."

Marrion seemed to be in good humor. "Molly," he said, "you were always the toughest lawyer in this town. Are you going to harass me on my deathbed?"

Claudia was distressed. "Eli, Bobby told us you were okay. And we really wanted to see you." She was so obviously ashamed that Marrion raised his hand with acceptance and benediction.

"I understand all the arguments," Marrion said. He made a motion of dismissal to the secretary and she left the room. The private duty nurse, a handsome, tough-looking woman, was reading a book at the dining room table. Marrion gestured to her to leave. She looked at him and shook her head. She resumed reading.

Marrion laughed, a low wheezing laugh. He said to the others, "That is Priscilla, the best nurse in California. She's an intensive care nurse, that's why she's so tough. My doctor recruited her especially for this case. She's the boss."

Priscilla acknowledged them with a nod of her head and resumed reading.

Molly said, "I'll be willing to limit his points to a maximum of twenty million. It will be insurance. Why take the risk? And why be so unfair?"

Bantz said angrily, "It's not unfair. He signed a contract."

"Fuck you, Bobby," Molly said.

Marrion ignored them. "Claudia, what do you think?"

Claudia was thinking many things. Obviously Marrion was sicker than anyone was admitting. And it was terribly cruel to put pressure on this old man who had to make such an effort to even speak. She was tempted to say that she was leaving, then she remembered that Eli would never have let them come except for some purpose of his own.

"Ernest is a man who does surprising things," Claudia said. "He is determined to provide for his family. But Eli, he's a writer and you always loved writers. Think of it as a contribution to art. Hell, you gave twenty million to the Metropolitan Museum. Why not do it for Ernest?"

"And have all the agents on our ass?" Bantz said.

Eli Marrion took a deep breath, the green prongs seemed to go deeper into his face. "Molly, Claudia, we will have to keep this our little secret. I'll give Vail two gross points to a max of twenty million. I'll give him a million up front. Will that satisfy you?"

Molly thought it over. Two gross points on all the pictures should yield a minimum of fifteen million but maybe more. It was the best she could do, and she was surprised that Marrion had gone so far. If she haggled he was quite capable of withdrawing the offer.

"That's wonderful, Eli, thank you." She leaned over to kiss him on the cheek. "I'll send your office a memo tomorrow. And Eli, I do hope you get well soon."

Claudia could not restrain her emotion. She clasped Eli's hand in hers. She noticed the brown specks that mottled the skin, the hand chilly with approaching death. "You saved Ernest's life."

At that moment Eli Marrion's daughter came into the room with her two small children. The nurse, Priscilla, rose from her chair like a cat scenting mice and moved toward the children, interposing herself between them and the bed. The daughter had been twice divorced and did not get on with her father, but she had a production company on the LoddStone lot because Eli was so fond of his grandchildren.

Claudia and Molly took their leave. They drove to Molly's office and called Ernest to tell him the good news. He insisted on taking them out to dinner to celebrate.

Marrion's daughter and two grandchildren stayed only a short time. But long enough for the daughter to get her father to promise to buy her a very expensive novel for her next movie.

Bobby Bantz and Eli Marrion were alone. "You're a soft touch today," Bantz said.

Marrion felt the weariness in his body, the air being sucked into it. He could relax with Bobby, he never had to act with him. They had been through so much together, used power together, won wars, traveled and schemed through the wide world. They could read each other's minds.

"That novel I'm buying for my daughter, will it make a movie?" Marrion asked.

"Low-budget," Bantz said. "Your daughter makes quote-unquote 'serious' movies."

Marrion made a weary gesture. "Why do we always have to pay for other people's good intentions? Give her a decent writer but no stars. She'll be happy and we won't lose too much money."

"Are you really going to give Vail gross?" Bantz asked. "Our lawyer says we can win in court if he dies."

Marrion said smilingly, "If I get well. If not, it will be up to you. You'll be running the show."

Bantz was astonished at this sentimentality. "Eli, you'll get well, of course you will." And he was absolutely sincere. He had no desire to succeed Eli Marrion, indeed he dreaded the day that inevitably had to come. He could do anything as long as Marrion approved it.

"It's going to be up to you, Bobby," Marrion said. "The truth is that I'm not going to make it. The doctors tell me I need a heart transplant and I've decided not to get one. I can live maybe six months, maybe a year, maybe much less with this lousy heart I have. And besides, I'm too old to qualify for a transplant."

Bantz was stunned. "They can't do a bypass?" he asked. When Marrion shook his head, Bantz went on. "Don't be ridiculous, of course you'll get a transplant. You built half the hospital, they have to give you a heart. You have another good ten years." He paused for a moment. "You're tired, Eli, we'll talk about this tomorrow." But Marrion had dozed off. Bantz left to check with the doctors and then to tell them to start all procedures to harvest a new heart for Eli Marrion.

Ernest Vail, Molly Flanders, and Claudia De Lena celebrated by having dinner at La Dolce Vita on Santa Monica. It was Claudia's favorite restaurant. She had memories of herself as a little girl being brought there by her father and being treated like royalty. She had memories of the bottles of red and white wine being stacked in all the window alcoves, on the back rails of banquettes, and in every vacant space. The customers could reach out and pluck a bottle as if they were grapes.

Ernest Vail was in good spirits, and Claudia wondered again how anybody could believe he would commit suicide. He was bubbling over with glee that his threat had worked. And the very good red wine put them all into a merry mood that was slightly boastful. They were very pleased with themselves. The food itself, robustly Italian, fueled their energy.

"Now what we have to think about," Vail said, "is two points good enough or should we push for three?"

"Don't get greedy," Molly said. "The deal is made."

Vail kissed her hand movie-star style and said, "Molly you're a genius. A ruthless genius, true. How could you two browbeat a guy sick on his hospital bed?"

Molly dipped bread into tomato sauce. "Ernest," she said, "you will never understand this town. There is no mercy. Not when you're drunk, or on coke, or in love, or broke. Why make an exception for sick?"

Claudia said, "Skippy Deere once told me that when you're buying, take people to a Chinese restaurant, but when you're selling, take them to an Italian restaurant. Does that make any sense?"

"He's a producer," Molly said. "He read it someplace. It doesn't mean anything without a context."

Vail was eating with the gusto of a reprieved criminal. He had ordered three different kinds of pasta just for himself but gave small portions to Claudia and Molly and demanded their opinions. "The best Italian food in the world outside Rome," he said. "About Skippy, it makes a certain kind of movie sense. Chinese food is cheap, it brings the price down. Italian food can put you to sleep and make you less sharp. I like both. Isn't it nice to know that Skippy is always scheming?"

Vail always ordered three desserts. Not that he ate all of them, but he wanted to taste many different things at one dinner. In him it did not seem eccentric. Not even the way he dressed, as if clothes were to shield skin from wind or sun, or the way he carelessly shaved, one sideburn cut lower than the other. Not even his threat to kill himself seemed illogical or strange. Nor his complete and childish frankness, which often hurt people's feelings. Claudia was not unused to eccentricity. Hollywood abounded with eccentrics.

"You know, Ernest, you belong to Hollywood. You're eccentric enough," she said.

"I am not an eccentric," Vail said. "I'm not that sophisticated."

"You don't call wanting to kill yourself over a dispute about money eccentric?" Claudia said.

"That was an extremely cool-headed response to our culture," Vail said. "I was tired of being a nobody."

Claudia said impatiently, "How can you think that? You've written ten books, you've won the Pulitzer. You're internationally famous."

Vail had polished off his three pastas and was looking at his entrée, three pearly slices of veal covered with lemon. He picked up a fork and knife. "All that means shit," he said. "I have no money. It took me fifty-five years to learn that if you have no money, you're shit."

Molly said, "You're not eccentric, you're crazy. And stop whining because you're not rich. You're not poor either. Or we wouldn't be here. You're not suffering too much for your art."

Vail put down his knife and fork. He patted Molly's arm. "You're right," he said. "Everything you say is true. I enjoy life from moment to moment. It's the arc of life that gets me down." He drank his glass of wine and then went on matter-of-factly. "I'm never going to write again," he said. "Writing novels is a dead end, like being a blacksmith. It's all movies and TV now."

"That's nonsense," Claudia said. "People will always read."

"You're just lazy," Molly said. "Any excuse not to write. That's the real reason why you wanted to kill yourself." They all laughed. Ernest helped them to the veal on his dish and then to the extra desserts. The only time he was courtly was over dinner, he seemed to take pleasure in feeding people.

"That's all true," he said. "But a novelist can't make a good living unless he writes simple novels. And even that is a dead end. A novel can never be as simple as a movie."

Claudia said angrily, "Why do you put movies down? I've seen you cry at good movies. And they are art."

Vail was enjoying himself. After all, he had won his fight against the Studio, he had his points. "Claudia, I really agree," he said. "Movies are art. I complain out of envy. Movies are making novels irrelevant. What's the point of writing a lyrical passage about nature, painting the world in red heat, a beautiful sunset, a mountain range coated with snow, the awe-inspiring waves of great oceans." He was declaiming, waving his arms. "What can you write about passion and the beauty of women? What's the use of all that when you can see it on the movie screen in Technicolor? Oh, those mysterious women with full red lips, their magical eyes, when you can see them bare-assed, tits as delicious-looking as beef Wellington. All much better than real life even, never mind prose. And how can we write about the amazing deeds of heroes who slay their enemies by the hundred, who conquer great odds and great temptation, when you can get it all in gouts of blood before your eyes, tortured, agonized faces on the screen. Actors and cameras doing all the work without processing through the brain. Sly Stallone as Achilles in the Iliad. Now the one thing the screen can't do is get into the minds of their characters, it cannot duplicate the thinking process, the complexity of life." He paused for a moment, then said wistfully, "But you know what's worst of all? I'm an elitist. I wanted to be an artist to be something special. So what I hate is that movies are such a democratic art. Anybody can make a movie. You're right, Claudia, I've seen movies that moved me to tears and I know for a fact that the people who made them are moronic, insensitive, uneducated, and with not an iota of morality. The screenwriter is illiterate, the director an egomaniac, the producer a butcher of morality and the actors smash their fists into the wall or a mirror to show the audience they are upset. But then the movie works. How can that be? Because a movie uses sculpture, painting, music, human bodies, and technology to form itself, while a novelist only has a string of words, black print on white paper. And to tell the truth that's not so terrible. That's progress. And the new great art. A democratic art. And art without suffering. Just buy the right camera and meet with your friends."

Vail beamed at the two women. "Isn't it wonderful, an art that requires no real talent? What democracy, what therapy, to make your own movie. It will replace sex. I go to see your movie and you come to see mine. It's an art that will transform the world and for the better. Claudia, be happy that you are in an art form that is the future."

"You are a condescending prick," Molly said. "Claudia fought for you, defended you. And I've been more patient with you than any murderer I've defended. And you buy us dinner to insult us."

Vail seemed genuinely astonished. "I'm not insulting, I'm just defining. I am grateful and I love you both." He paused for a moment and then said humbly, "I'm not saying I'm better than you."

Claudia burst out laughing. "Ernest, you're so full of shit," she said.

"Just in real life," Vail said amiably. "Can we talk business a little bit? Molly, if I were dead and my family regained all the rights, would LoddStone pay five points?"

"At least five," Molly said. "Now you're going to kill yourself over extra points? You lose me entirely."

Claudia was looking at him, troubled. She distrusted his high spirits. "Ernest, are you still unhappy? We got you a wonderful deal. I was so thrilled."

Vail said fondly, "Claudia, you have no idea what the real world is all about. Which makes you perfect to do screenplays. What the hell difference does it make if I'm happy? The happiest man who ever lived is going to have terrible times in his life. Terrible tragedies. Look at me now. I've just won a great victory, I don't have to kill myself. I'm enjoying this meal, I'm enjoying the company of you two beautiful, intelligent, compassionate women. And I love it that my wife and children will have economic security."

"Then why the fuck are you whining?" Molly asked him. "Why are you spoiling a good time?"

"Because I can't write," Vail said. "Which is no great tragedy. It's not really important anymore but it's the only thing I know how to do." As he was saying this, he was finishing the three desserts with such evident enjoyment that the two women burst out laughing. Vail grinned back at them. "We sure bluffed out old Eli," he said.

"You take writer's block too seriously," Claudia said. "Just take some speed."

"Screenwriters don't have writer's block because they don't write," Vail said. "I cannot write because I have nothing to say. Now let's talk about something more interesting. Molly, I've never understood how I can have ten percent of the profit of a picture that grosses one hundred million dollars and costs only fifteen million to make, and then never see a penny. That's one mystery I'd like to solve before I die."

This put Molly in good spirits again; she loved to teach the law. She took a notebook out of her purse and scribbled down some figures.

"It's absolutely legal," she said. "They are abiding by the contract, one you should not have signed in the first place. Look, take the one-hundred-million gross. The theaters, the exhibitors, take half, so now the studio only gets fifty million, which is called rentals.

"OK. The studio takes out the fifteen million dollars the picture costs. Now there's thirty-five million left. But by the terms of your contract and most studio contracts, the studio takes thirty percent of the rentals for distribution costs on the film. That's another fifteen mil in their pockets. So you're down to twenty mil. Then they deduct the cost of making prints, the cost for advertising the picture, which could easily be another five. You're down to fifteen. Now here's the beauty. By contract, the studio gets twenty-five percent of the budget for studio overhead, telephone bills, electricity, use of soundstages etc. Now you're down to eleven. Good, you say. You'll take your piece of eleven million. But the Bankable Star gets at least five percent of the rentals, the director and producer another five percent. So that comes to another five million. You're down to six million. At last you'll get something. But not so fast. They then charge you all the costs of distribution, they charge fifty grand for delivering the prints to the English market, another fifty to France or Germany.

And then finally they charge the interest on the fifteen million they borrowed to make the picture. And there they lose me. But that last six million disappears. That's what happens when you don't have me for a lawyer. I write a contract that really gets you a piece of the gold mine. Not gross for a writer but a very good definition of net. Do you understand it now?"

Vail was laughing. "Not really," he said. "How about TV and video money?"

"TV you'll see a little," Molly said. "Nobody knows how much money they make in video."

"And my deal with Marrion now is straight gross?" Vail asked. "They can't screw me again?"

"Not the way I'll write the contract," Molly said. "It will be straight gross all the way."

Vail said mournfully, "Then I won't have a grievance anymore. I won't have an excuse for not writing."

"You really are so eccentric," Claudia said.

"No, no," Vail said. "I'm just a fuckup. Eccentrics do odd things to distract people from what they do or are. They are ashamed. That's why movie people are so eccentric."

Who would have dreamed that dying could be so pleasant, that you could be so at peace, that you could be so without fear? That best of all you had solved the one great common myth?

Eli Marrion, in the long hours of the sick at night, sucked oxygen from the tube in the wall and reflected on his life. His private duty nurse, Priscilla, working a double shift, was reading a book by the dim lamp on the other side of the room. He could see her eyes dart quickly up and then down, as if checking him after every line she read

Marrion thought how different this scene was from how it would be in a movie. In a movie there would be a great deal of tension because he was hovering between life and death. The nurse would be crouched over his bed, doctors would be coming in and out. There should sure as hell be a lot of noise, a lot of tension. And here he was in a room absolutely quiet, the nurse reading, Marrion easily breathing through his plastic tube.

He knew this penthouse floor held only these huge suites for very important people. Powerful politicians, real estate billionaires, stars who were the fading myths of the entertainment world. All kings in their own right and now, here in the night in this hospital, vassals to death. They lay helpless and alone, comforted by mercenaries, their power scattered. Tubes in bodies, prongs in nostrils, waiting for surgeon's knives to scour the debris from their failing hearts or, like himself, for a completely edited heart to be inserted. He wondered if they were as resigned as he.

And why that resignation? Why had he told the doctors he would not have a transplant, that he preferred to live only the short time his failing heart would give him. He thought that, thank God, he could still make intelligent decisions devoid of sentiment.

Everything was clear to him, like making a deal on a film: figuring the cost, the percentage of return, the value of subsidiary rights, the possible traps with stars, directors, and cost overages.

Number one: He was eighty years old and not a robust eighty. A heart transplant would disable him for a year, at the very best. Certainly he would never run LoddStone Studies again. Certainly most of his power over his world would vanish.

Number two: Life without power was intolerable. After all, what could an old man like himself do even with a fresh new heart? He could not play sports, run after women, take pleasure from food or drink. No, power was an old man's only pleasure, and why was that so bad? Power could be used for the good. Had he not granted mercy to Ernest Vail, against all prudent principles, against all his lifelong prejudices? Had he not told his doctors that he did not want to deprive a child or some young man the chance to have a new life by taking a heart? Was that not a use of power for the higher good?

But he had had a long life of dealing with hypocrisy and recognized it now in himself. He had declined a new heart because it was not a good deal; a bottom-line decision. He had granted Ernest Vail his points because he desired the affection of Claudia and the respect of Molly Flanders, a sentimentality. Was it so terrible that he wanted to leave an image of goodness?

He was satisfied in the life he had lived. He had fought his way from poverty to riches, he had conquered his fellow man. He had enjoyed all the pleasure of human life, loved beautiful women, lived in luxurious homes, worn the finest silks. And he had helped in the creation of art. He had earned enormous power and a great fortune. And he had tried to do good for his fellow man. He had contributed tens of millions to this very hospital. But most of all he had enjoyed struggling against his fellow man. And what was so terrible about that? How else could you acquire the power to do good? Even now he regretted the last act of mercy to Ernest Vail. You could not simply give the spoils of your struggle to your fellow man, especially under threat. But Bobby would take care of that. Bobby would take care of everything.

Bobby would plant the necessary publicity stories featuring his refusal of a heart transplant so that someone younger could have it. Bobby would recover all the gross points that existed. Bobby would get rid of his daughter's production company, which was a losing proposition for LoddStone. Bobby would take the rap.

Far off he could hear a tiny bell, then the snakelike rattling of the fax machine transmitting the box office receipts compiled in New York. The stuttering making a refrain for his failing heart.

The truth now. He had enough of life at its best. It was not his body that had ultimately betrayed him but his mind.

The truth now. He was disappointed in human beings. He had seen too many betrayals, too many pitiful weaknesses, too much greed for money and fame. The falseness between lovers, husbands, and wives, fathers, sons, mothers, daughters. Thank God for the films he had made that gave people hope and thank God for his grandchildren and thank God he would not see them grow up into the human condition.

The fax machine stilled its stutter, and Marrion could feel the fluttering of his failing heart. Early morning light filled his room. He saw the nurse flick off her lamp and close her book. It was so lonely to die with only this stranger in this room when he was loved by so many powerful people. Then the nurse was prying open his eyelids, putting her stethoscope to his chest. The huge doors to his hospital suite opened like the great door of some ancient temple and he could hear the rattling of dishes on the breakfast trays. . . .

Then the room filled with bright lights. He could feel fists thumping his chest and wondered why they were doing this to him. A cloud was forming in his brain, filling it with mist. Through that mist voices were screaming. A line from a movie penetrated his oxygen-starved brain. "Is this how the Gods die?"

He felt the electric shocks, the pummeling, the incision made to massage his heart with bare hands.

All of Hollywood would mourn but none more than the night duty nurse, Priscilla. She had done a double shift because she supported two small children, and it displeased her that Marrion had died on her shift. She prided herself on her reputation as one of the finest nurses in California. She hated death. But the book she had been reading had excited her and she had been planning how to talk with Marrion about making it into a movie. She would not be a nurse forever, she was a screenwriter on the side. Now she did not give up hope. This top floor of the hospital with its huge suites received the greatest men of Hollywood and she would stand guard for them against death forever.

But all this had happened in Marrion's mind before he died, a mind saturated with thousands of movies he had watched.

In reality, the nurse had gone to his bed some fifteen minutes after he was dead, so quietly had he died. She debated for maybe thirty seconds about calling an alert to try to bring him back to life. She was an old hand with death and more merciful. Why try to revive him to all the torture of reclaiming life? She went to the window and watched the sun rise and the pigeons strutting lustfully on the stone ledges. Priscilla was the final power deciding Marrion's fate . . . and his most merciful judge.

CHAPTER 13

SENATOR WAVVEN had great news, and it would cost the Clericuzio five million dollars. So said Giorgio's courier. That demanded a mountain of paperwork. Cross would have to extract five million from the casino cage and leave a long record to account for its disappearance.

Cross also had a message from Claudia and Vail. They were in the Hotel occupying the same suite. They wanted to see him as soon as possible. It was urgent.

There was also a call from Lia Vazzi in the Hunting Lodge. He requested to see Cross personally as soon as possible. He did not have to say it was urgent, any request from him had to be urgent or he would not call, and he was already on his way.

Cross started on the paperwork for the transfer of the five million dollars to Senator Wavven. The cash itself would have too much bulk for a suitcase or large overnight bag. He called the Hotel gift shop; he remembered an antique Chinese trunk for sale that was big enough to hold the money. It was dark green decorated with red dragons and superimposed false green gems, and it had a strong locking mechanism.

Gronevelt had taught him how to make the paper trail that legitimized money skimmed from the Hotel casino. It was long and laborious work that involved transfers of money to different accounts, the payment of different suppliers for liquor and food, special training projects and publicity stunts, and a roster of players who did not exist as debtors to the cage.

Cross worked an hour on this. Senator Wavven was not due in until the next day, a Saturday, and the five million had to be put in his hands before he left early Monday morning. Finally his concentration began to wander and he had to take a break.

He called down to Claudia and Vail's suite. Claudia picked up the phone. She said, "I'm having a terrible time with Ernest. We have to talk to you."

"OK," Cross said. "Why don't the two of you go down and gamble and I'll pick you up in the dice pit an hour from now." He paused. "Then we can go for dinner and you can tell me your troubles."

"We can't gamble," Claudia said. "Ernest went over his credit limit and you won't give me credit anymore except for a lousy ten grand."

Cross sighed. That meant Ernest Vail owed the casino a hundred grand that was just so much toilet paper. "Give me an hour and then come up to my suite. We'll have dinner here."

Cross had to make another phone call, to Giorgio to confirm the payment to the senator, not that the courier was suspect but it was one of the built-in routines. This they did with verbal code already established. The name was in arbitrary prearranged numbers, the money designated in arbitrary prearranged alphabetical letters.

Cross tried to continue his paperwork. But again his mind wandered. For five million, Senator Wavven was going to have something important to say. For Lia to make the long drive to Vegas, he had to have serious trouble.

There was a ring at the doorbell, Security had brought Claudia and Ernest to the penthouse. Cross gave Claudia an extra warm hug because he didn't want her to think he was mad at her for losing in the casino.

In the living room of his suite, he handed them the room service menu and then ordered for them. Claudia sat stiffly on the sofa, Vail slouched back disinterestedly.

Claudia said, "Cross, Vail is in terrible shape. We have to do something for him."

Vail didn't look so bad to Cross. He seemed truly relaxed, his eyes half closed, a pleased smile on his lips. This irritated Cross.

"Sure, first thing I'll do is cut off all his credit in this town. That will save money, he's the most incompetent gambler I've ever seen."

"It's not about gambling," Claudia said. And she told him the whole story about Marrion promising to give Vail gross on all the sequels to his book, and then dying.

"So?" Cross asked.

"Now Bobby Bantz won't honor that promise," Claudia said. "Since Bobby became head of LoddStone Studios, he's gone crazy with power. He's trying his best to be like Marrion but he just hasn't got the intelligence or the charisma. So Ernest is out in the cold again."

"Just what the hell do you think I can do?" Cross asked.

"You're partners with LoddStone in *Messalina,*" Claudia said. "You must have some clout with them. I want you to ask Bobby Bantz to keep Marrion's promise."

It was at times like this that Cross despaired of Claudia. Bantz would never give way, that was part of his job and his character.

"No," Cross said. "I've explained to you before. I can't take a position unless I know the answer will be yes. And here there's no chance."

Claudia frowned. "I never understood that," she said. She paused for a moment. "Ernest is serious, he will kill himself so that his family can get back the rights."

At this, Vail took an interest. He said, "Claudia, you dumbbell, don't you understand about your brother? If he asks somebody for something and they say no, then he has to kill them." He gave Cross a big grin.

Cross was enraged that Vail would dare to speak that way in front of Claudia. Luckily, at that moment room service arrived with their rolling tables and set dinner up in the living room. Cross controlled himself as they sat down to eat, but he couldn't help saying, with a cold smile, "Ernest, you can solve everything if you knock yourself off, as I understand it. Maybe I can help. I'll move your suite up to the tenth floor and you can just step out the window."

Now Claudia was angry. "This is not a joke," she said. "Ernest is one of my best friends. And you're my brother who always claims to love me and will do anything for me." She was in tears.

Cross got up and went over to hug her. "Claudia, there's nothing I can do. I'm not a magician."

Ernest Vail was enjoying his dinner. No man looked less likely to kill himself. "You're too modest, Cross," he said. "Look, I haven't got the nerve to jump out of a window. I have too much imagination, I'd die a thousand deaths on the way down thinking how I would look splattered all over the place. And I might even land on some innocent person. I'm too chicken to cut my wrists, I can't stand the sight of blood and I'm scared to death of guns and knives and traffic. I don't want to end up a vegetable with nothing accomplished. I don't want that fuckin' Bantz and Deere laughing at me and keeping all my money. There is one thing you can do: Hire somebody to kill me. Don't tell me when. Just get it done."

Cross began laughing. He gave Claudia a reassuring pat on the head and went back to his chair. "Do you think this is a fuckin' movie?" he said to Ernest. "You think killing somebody is sort of a joke?"

Cross left the table and went to his office desk. He unlocked the drawer and took out a purse of black chips. He threw the purse at Ernest and said, "Here's ten grand. Take your last shot at the tables, maybe you'll get lucky. Just stop insulting me in front of my sister."

Vail was cheerful now. "Come on Claudia," he said. "Your brother is not going to help." He put the purse of black chips into his pocket. He seemed anxious to get started gambling.

Claudia seemed abstracted. She was adding up everything in her head but refused to come to a sum total. She looked at the serene handsome face of her brother. He could not be what Vail was saying he was. She kissed Cross on the cheek, and said, "I'm sorry, but I'm worried about Ernest."

"He'll be all right," Cross said. "He likes to gamble too much to die. And he is a genius, isn't he?"

Claudia laughed. "So he always says, and I agree," she said. "And he's such a terrible coward." But she reached out to touch Vail affectionately.

"Why the hell do you stick with him?" Cross said. "Why are you sharing a suite with him?"

"Because I'm his best and last friend," Claudia said angrily. "And I love his books."

. . .

After the two left, Cross spent the rest of the night completing the plan to transfer the five million to Senator Wavven. When he finished, he called the casino manager, a high-ranking member of the Clericuzio Family, and told him to bring the money to his penthouse suite.

The money was brought up in two huge sacks by the manager and two security guards who were also of the Clericuzio. They helped Cross stack the money into the Chinese trunk. The casino manager gave Cross a little grin and said, "Nice trunk."

After the men left, Cross took the huge quilt from his bed and wrapped it around the trunk. Then he ordered room service to bring two breakfasts. Within a few minutes, Security called to tell him Lia Vazzi was waiting to see him. He gave the OK to bring him up.

Cross embraced Lia. He was always delighted to see him.

"Good news or bad news?" Cross asked him after room service delivered breakfast.

"Bad," Lia said. "That detective who stopped me in the lobby of the Beverly Hills Hotel when I was with Skannet. Jim Losey. He showed up at the Hunting Lodge and asked me questions about my relationship with Skannet. I brushed him off. The bad part is how he knew who I was and where I was. I'm not in any police file, I've never been in trouble. So that means there's an informer."

That startled Cross. A turncoat was rare in the Clericuzio Family and was always mercilessly rooted out.

"I'll report it to the Don himself," Cross said. "How about you? Do you want to take a vacation down in Brazil until we find out what it's all about?"

Lia had eaten very little. He helped himself to the brandy and Havana cigars Cross put out.

"I'm not nervous, not yet," Lia said. "I'd just like your permission to protect myself against this man."

Cross was alarmed. "Lia, you can't do that," he said. "It's very dangerous to kill a police officer in this country. This is not Sicily. So I have to tell you something you shouldn't know. Jim Losey is on the Clericuzio pad. Big money. I think he's just nosing around to claim a bonus for laying off you."

"Good," Vazzi said. "But it remains a fact. There must be an informer."

"I'll take care of it," Cross said. "Don't worry about Losey."

Lia puffed on his cigar. "He's a dangerous man. Be careful."

"I will," Cross said. "But no preemptive strikes on your part, OK?"

"Of course," Lia said. He seemed to relax. Then he said casually, "What's under that quilt?"

"A little gift to a very important man," Cross said. "Do you want to spend the night in the Hotel?"

"No," Lia said. "I'll go back to the Lodge and you can tell me what you learn at your leisure. But my advice would be to get rid of Losey right now."

"I'll talk to the Don," Cross said.

Senator Warren Wavven and his entourage of three male aides were checked into their Xanadu Villa at three in the afternoon. As usual, he had traveled in an unmarked limo and without any sort of escort. At five, he summoned Cross to his Villa.

Cross had two of the security guards put the quilt-wrapped trunk in the back of a motorized golf cart. One of the guards drove and Cross sat in the passenger seat keeping an eye on the trunk, which rested in the cargo space that usually held golf clubs and ice water. It was only a five-minute run through the grounds of the Xanadu to the separately secured compound that held the seven Villas.

Cross always loved the sight of them, the sense of power. Small palaces of Versailles, each with a diamond-shaped emerald swimming pool, and in the center a square holding the pearl-shaped private casino for the Villa occupants.

Cross carried the trunk into the Villa himself. One of the senator's aides led him into the dining room where the senator was enjoying a sumptuous array of cold food and iced jugs of lemonade. He no longer drank alcohol.

Senator Wavven was as handsome and affable as ever. He had risen high in the political councils of the nation, was the head of several important committees, and was a dark horse in the next presidential race. He sprang up to greet Cross.

Cross whipped the quilt off the trunk and put it on the floor.

"A little gift from the Hotel, Senator," he said. "Have a pleasant stay."

The senator clasped Cross's hand with both of his. His hands were smooth. "What a delightful present," he said. "Thank you, Cross. Now, could I have a few confidential words with you?"

"Of course," Cross said and gave him the key to the trunk. Wavven slipped it into his trouser pocket. Then he turned to his aides and said, "Please put the trunk in my bedroom and one of you stay with it. Now, let me have a few moments alone with my friend Cross."

They left and the senator began to pace the room. He frowned, "I have good news naturally, but I also have bad news."

Cross nodded and said amiably, "That's usually the case." He thought that for the five mil the good news had to be a hell of a lot better than the bad.

Wavven chuckled. "Isn't that the truth? The good news first. And very good news it is. I've devoted my attention in the last few years to passing legislation that would make gambling legal all over the United States. Even the provision to make sports gambling legal. I think I finally have the votes in the Senate and the House. The money in the trunk will swing some key votes. It is five, isn't it?"

"It's five," Cross said. "And money well spent. Now, what's the bad news?"

The senator shook his head sadly. "Your friends won't like this," he said. "Especially Giorgio, who is so impatient. But he's a fabulous fellow, truly fabulous."

"My favorite cousin," Cross said dryly. Of all the Clericuzio he liked Giorgio least, and it was obvious the senator felt the same way.

Then Wavven delivered the bombshell. "The president has told me he will veto the bill."

Cross had been feeling jubilant over the final success of Don Clericuzio's master plan. To build a legitimate empire based on legal gambling. Now, he was confused. What the hell was Wavven babbling about?

"And we don't have enough votes to overcome a veto," Wavven said.

Just to give himself time to recover his composure, Cross said, "So the five mil is for the president?"

The senator was horrified. "Oh, no, no," he said. "We're not even in the same party. And besides, the president will be a very rich man when he retires into private life. Every board of directors of every big company will want him. He has no need for petty cash." Wavven gave Cross a satisfied smile. "Things work differently when you are the president of the United States."

"So we're nowhere unless the president drops dead," Cross said.

"Exactly," Wavven said. "He is a very popular president, I must say, though we are in opposing parties. He will surely be reelected. We must be patient."

"So we have to wait five years and then hope to get a president who won't veto?"

"That's not exactly true," the senator said, and here he faltered a bit. "I must be honest with you. In five years the composition of the Congress may change, I may not have the votes I have now." He paused again. "There are many factors."

Cross was completely bewildered now. What the hell was Wavven really saying? Then the senator tipped his hand. "Of course if something happens to the president, the vice president will sign the bill. So, as malicious as it sounds, you have to hope that the president has a heart attack or his plane crashes, or he has an incapacitating stroke. It could happen. All of us are mortal." The senator was beaming at him and then suddenly it all became clear to Cross.

He felt a flash of anger. This bastard was giving him a message for the Clericuzio: The senator had done his part, now they had to kill the president of the United States to get the bill passed. And he was so slick and so sly, he had not implicated himself in any concrete way. Cross was sure the Don would not go for it, and if he did, Cross would refuse to be part of the Family ever after.

Wavven was going on with an affable smile. "It looks pretty hopeless but you never know. Fate may take a hand and the vice president is a very close friend of mine, even though we're from different parties. I know for a fact, he will approve my bill. We just have to wait and see."

Cross could scarcely believe what the senator was saying. Senator Wavven was the personification of the virtuous All-American politician, though admittedly with a weakness for women and innocent golf. His face was honorably handsome and his voice patrician. He presented himself as one of the most likable men on earth. Yet he was implying that the Clericuzio Family assassinate his own president. This is a piece of work, Cross thought.

The senator was now picking at the food on the table. "I'm only staying for one night," he said. "I hope you have some girls in your show who would like to have dinner with an old geezer like me."

Back in his penthouse suite Cross called Giorgio and told him he would be in Quogue the next day. Giorgio told him the Family driver would pick him up at the airport. He didn't ask any questions. The Clericuzio never talked business on the phone.

When Cross arrived at the Quogue mansion, he was surprised to find a full attendance. Assembled in the windowless den were not only the Don, but also Pippi, and the Don's three sons, Giorgio, Vincent, and Petie, and even Dante, wearing a sky-blue Renaissance hat.

There was no food in the den, dinner was to come later. As usual the Don made everyone look at the photos of Silvio and the christening of Cross and Dante on the mantelpiece. "What a happy day," the Don always said. They all settled in on chairs and sofas, Giorgio handed out drinks, and the Don lit up his twisted black Italian cheroot.

Cross gave a detailed report: how he had delivered the five million to Senator Wavven and then, word for word, his conversation with him.

There was a long silence. None of them needed Cross's interpretation. Vincent and Petie looked the most concerned. Now that Vincent had his chain of restaurants, he was less inclined to take risks. Petie, though he was head of the soldiers in the Bronx Enclave, had his enormous construction business as his primary concern. They did not relish such a terrible mission at this stage of their lives.

"That fucking senator is crazy," Vincent said.

The Don said to Cross, "Are you sure that was the message the senator was sending us? That we should actually assassinate the leader of our country, one of his colleagues in government?"

Giorgio said dryly, "They're not in the same political party, the senator says."

Cross answered the Don. "The senator would never incriminate himself. He just presented the facts. I think he assumes we will act on it."

Dante spoke up. He was excited by the idea, by the glory, by the profit. "We can get the whole gambling business, legal. That would be worth it. That's the biggest prize."

The Don turned to Pippi. "And what do you think, *Martèllo* of mine?" he asked affectionately.

Pippi was obviously angry. "It can't be done and it shouldn't be done."

Dante said in a taunting voice, "Cousin Pippi, if you can't do it, I can."

Pippi looked at him contemptuously. "You're a butcher, not a planner. You couldn't plan something like this in a million years. This is too big a risk. This is too much heat. And the execution is too difficult. You cannot get away free."

Dante said arrogantly, "Grandfather, give me the job. I'll get it done."

The Don was respectful to his grandson. "I'm sure you could," he said. "And the rewards would be very great. But Pippi is right. The aftermath would be too risky for our Family. One can always make mistakes, but never make a fatal mistake. Even if we were successful and achieved our aim, the deed would hang over us forever. It is too great a crime. Also, this is not a situation that endangers our existence, it is simply one that achieves a purpose. A purpose that can be achieved with patience. Meanwhile, we sit in a pretty position. Giorgio, you have your seat on Wall Street, Vincent, you have your restaurants, Petie, you have your construction business. Cross, you have your hotel and Pippi, you can retire and spend your last years in peace. And Dante, my grandson, you must have patience, some day you will have your gambling empire, that shall be your legacy. And when you do, it will be without the shadow of a terrible deed hanging over your head. So—let the senator swim to the bottom of the ocean."

Everyone in the room relaxed, the tension broken; except for Dante, all were happy with the decision. And all agreed with the Don's curse that the senator should drown. That he had dared to put them in this dangerous dilemma.

Only Dante seemed to disagree. He said to Pippi, "You've got a lot of balls, calling me a butcher. What are you, a fucking Florence Nightingale?"

Vincent and Petie laughed. The Don shook his head disapprovingly. "Another thing," Don Clericuzio said. "I think we for now should continue all our ties with the senator. I don't begrudge him the extra five million, but I take it as an insult that he thinks we would kill the president of our country to further a business venture. Also, what other fish does he have to fry? How does this act benefit him? He seeks to manipulate us. Cross, when he comes to your hotel, build up his markers. Make sure he has a good time. He is too dangerous a man to have as an enemy."

Everything was settled. Cross was hesitant about bringing up another sensitive problem. But he told the story of Lia Vazzi and Jim Losey. "There could be an informer inside the Family," Cross said.

Dante said coolly, "That was your operation, that's your problem."

The Don shook his head decisively. "An informer cannot be," he said. "The detective found something by accident and he wants a bonus to stop. Giorgio, take care of it."

Giorgio said sourly, "Another fifty grand. Cross, that's your deal. You'll have to pay it out of your hotel."

The Don relit his cigar. "Now that we are all here together, are there any other problems? Vincent, how is your restaurant business?"

Vincent's granite features softened. "I'm opening three more," he said. "One in Philly, one in Denver, and another in New York City. High class. Pop, would you believe I charge sixteen dollars for a plate of spaghetti? When I make it at home, I figure out the cost is half a buck a plate. No matter how hard I try, I can't make it more than that. I even put in the cost of the garlic. And meatballs, I'm the only high-class Italian restaurant that serves meatballs, I don't know why, but I get eight dollars for them. And not big ones. They cost me twenty cents."

He would have gone on but the Don cut him off. He turned to Giorgio and said, "Giorgio, how goes your Wall Street?"

Giorgio said cautiously, "It goes up and down. But the commissions we get for trading are as good as the shylocks get on the streets if we churn it enough. And with no risk of deadbeats or jail. We should forget about all our other business, except maybe gambling."

The Don was enjoying these recitals, success in the legitimate world was dear to him. He said, "And Petie, your construction business? I hear you had a little trouble the other day . . ."

Petie shrugged. "I got more business than I can handle. Everybody's building something and we have a lock on the highway contracts. All my soldiers are on the payroll and make a good living. But a week ago, this eggplant shows up on my biggest construction job. He's got a hundred black guys behind him with all kinds of civil rights banners. So I take him into my office and all of a sudden he's charming. I just have to put ten percent blacks on the job and pay him twenty grand under the table."

That tickled Dante. "We're getting strong-armed?" he said with a giggle. "The Clericuzio?"

Petie said, "I tried to think like Pop. Why shouldn't they make a living? So I gave the eggplant his twenty grand and told him I'd put five percent on the job."

"You did well," the Don told Petie. "You kept a small problem from becoming a big problem. And who are the Clericuzio not to pay their share in the advancement of the other people and civilization itself?"

"I would have killed the black son of a bitch," Dante said. "Now, he'll come back for more."

"And we will give him more," the Don said. "Just so long as they are reasonable." He turned to Pippi and said, "And what troubles do you have?"

"None," Pippi said. "Except that now the Family is nearly nonoperational and I'm out of a job."

"That is your good fortune," the Don said. "You've worked hard enough. You've escaped many perils, so now enjoy the flower of your manhood."

Dante didn't wait to be questioned. "I'm in the same boat," he said to the Don. "And I'm too young to retire."

"Play golf like the *Brugliones,*" Don Clericuzio said dryly. "And don't worry, life always provides work and problems. Meanwhile, be patient. I fear your time will come. And mine."

CHAPTER 14

ON THE MORNING OF Eli Marrion's funeral, Bobby Bantz was screaming at Skippy Deere.

"This is fucking crazy, this is what's wrong with the movie business. How the fuck can you allow this to happen?" He was waving a stapled bundle of pages in Deere's face.

Deere looked at it. It was the transportation schedule for a picture shooting in Rome. "Yeah, so what?" Deere said.

Bantz was in rage. "Everyone in the picture is booked first class on the flight to Rome . . . the crew, the bit players, the fucking cameo roles, the gofers, the interns. There is only one exception. You know who that is? The LoddStone accounting officer we sent there to control the spending. He flew economy."

"Yeah, again, so what?" Deere said.

Bantz became deliberate in his anger. "And the picture has on budget a school to be set up for the children of everybody on the picture. The budget has the renting of a yacht for two weeks. I just read the script carefully. There are twelve actors and actresses who have maybe two, three minutes in the film. The yacht is listed for just two days' shooting. Now explain to me how you allowed this."

Skippy Deere was grinning at him. "Sure," he said. "Our director is Lorenzo Tallufo. He insists his people travel first class. The bit players and cameo roles were written into the script because they were screwing the vehicle stars. The yacht is booked for two weeks because Lorenzo wants to visit the Cannes Film Festival."

"You're the producer, talk to Lorenzo," Bantz said.

"Not *me,*" Deere told him. "Lorenzo has four one-hundred-million-dollar-grossing pictures, he has two Academy Awards. I'll kiss his ass when I help him onto the yacht. You talk to him."

There was no answer to this. Technically, in the hierarchy of the industry, the head of the Studio outranked everybody. The producer was the person who got all the elements together and oversaw the budget and script development. But the reality was that once the picture started shooting, the director was the supreme power. Especially if he had a record of successful movies.

Bantz shook his head. "I can't talk to Lorenzo, not when I don't have Eli to back me up. Lorenzo would tell me to go fuck myself and we'd lose the picture."

"And he'd be right," Deere said. "What the hell, Lorenzo always steals five million off a picture. They all do it. Now calm down so we can show ourselves at the funeral."

But Bantz was now looking at another cost sheet. "On your picture," he said to Deere, "there's a charge of five hundred thousand dollars for Chinese take-out food. Nobody, *nobody,* not even my wife can spend a half million dollars on Chinese food. French food maybe. But Chinese? Chinese take-out?"

Skippy Deere had to think fast, Bobby had him there. "It's a Japanese restaurant, the food is sushi. That's the most expensive food in the world."

Bantz was suddenly calm. People were always complaining about sushi. The head of a rival studio had told him about taking a Japanese investor to dinner at a restaurant that specialized in sushi. "A thousand bucks for two people for twenty fucking fish heads," he had said. Bantz was impressed.

"OK," Bantz said to Skippy Deere, "but you have to cut down. Try to get more college interns on your next picture." Interns worked for free.

The Hollywood funeral of Eli Marrion was more newsworthy than even that of a Bankable Star. He had been revered by studio heads, producers, and agents, he had even been respected and sometimes loved by Bankable Stars, directors, and even screenplay writers. What had inspired this was his civility and an overpowering intelligence that had solved many problems in the movie business. He also had had the reputation of being fair, within reason.

In his later years, he was an ascetic, did not wallow in power, did not command sexual favors from starlets. Also, LoddStone had made more great movies than any other studio, and there was nothing more precious to people who actually made movies.

The president of the United States sent his chief of staff to give a brief eulogy. France sent its minister of culture, though he was an enemy of Hollywood movies. The Vatican sent a papal envoy, a young cardinal, handsome enough to receive offers for cameo roles. A Japanese group of business executives magically appeared. The highest executives of movie corporations from the Netherlands, Germany, Italy, and Sweden did Eli Marrion honor.

The eulogies began. First a male Bankable Star, then a female Bankable Star, then an A director; even a writer, Benny Sly, gave Marrion tribute. Then the president's chief of staff. Then, just so the show would not be judged pretentious, two of the movie's greatest comics made jokes about Eli Marrion's power and business acumen. Finally, Eli's son, Kevin, and his daughter, Dora, and Bobby Bantz.

Kevin Marrion extolled Eli Marrion as a caring father, not only to his own children, but to everyone who worked at LoddStone. He was a man who carried the torch of Art on a film. A torch, Kevin assured the mourners, that he would pick up.

Eli Marrion's daughter, Dora, gave the most poetic speech, written by Benny Sly. It was eloquent, spiritual, and addressed Eli Marrion's virtues and accomplishments with a humorous respect. "I loved my father more than any man I have ever known," she said, "but I'm glad I never had to negotiate with him. I only had to deal with Bobby Bantz and I could outsmart him."

She got her laugh and it was Bobby Bantz's turn. Secretly he resented Dora's joke. "I spent thirty years building LoddStone Studios with Eli Marrion," he said. "He was the most intelligent, the kindest man I have ever known. Under him, my service of thirty years has been the happiest time of my life. And I will continue to serve his dream. He showed his faith in me by leaving me in control of the Studio for the next five years and I will not fail him. I cannot hope to equal Eli's achievements. He gave dreams to billions of people all over the world. He shared his wealth and love with his family and all the people of America. He was indeed a lodestone."

The assembled mourners knew that Bobby Bantz had written the speech himself, because he had given an important message to the whole movie industry. That he was to rule LoddStone Studios for the next five years and that he expected everyone to give him the same respect they had given Eli Marrion. Bobby Bantz was no longer a Number Two man, he was a Number One.

Two days after the funeral, Bantz summoned Skippy Deere to the studio and offered him the job of head of production of LoddStone, the job he had held himself. Now he was moving up to Marrion's job as chairman. The rewards he offered Deere were irresistible. Deere would get a share of profits of every movie made by the Studio. He would be able to green-light any picture budgeted for less than thirty million dollars. He would be able to fold his own production company into LoddStone as an independent, and name the head of that company.

Skippy Deere was astounded by the richness of the offer. He analyzed this as a mark of insecurity on Bantz's part. Bantz knew he was weak on the creative side and counted on Deere to cover him.

Deere accepted the offer and appointed Claudia De Lena to head his production company. Not only because she was creative, not only because she really knew movie making, but because he knew she was too honest to undercut him. With her, he would not have to watch his back. In addition, and this was no small thing in making movies, he always enjoyed her company, her good humor. And their sex thing had been gotten out of the way a long time ago.

It gave Skippy Deere a glow to think of how rich they would all become. For Deere had been around long enough to know that even Bankable Stars sometimes came to old age in semipoverty. Deere was already very wealthy, but he thought that there were ten levels of being rich and he was only on the first level. Certainly he could live in luxury the rest of his life, but he could not have his own private jet, he could not have five homes and keep them up. He could not keep a harem. He could not afford to be a degenerate gambler. He could not afford another five divorces. He could not afford to keep a hundred servants. He could not even afford to finance his own pictures over any period of time. And he couldn't afford an expensive collection of art, a major Monet or Picasso, as Eli had done. But now someday he would move up from the first level to perhaps as high as the fifth level. He would have to work very hard and be very cunning, and most important, study Bantz very carefully.

Bantz outlined his plans, and Deere was surprised at how daring they were. Obviously Bantz was determined to take his place in the world of power.

For starters, he was going to make a deal with Melo Stuart so that Melo would give LoddStone preferential access to all the Talent in his agency.

"I can handle that," Deere said. "I'll make it clear to him that I'll give him the green light on his favorite projects."

"I'm particularly interested that we have Athena Aquitane do our next picture," Bobby Bantz said.

Aha, Deere thought. Now that Bantz controlled LoddStone, he hoped to get Athena into bed. Deere thought that as head of production he had a shot, too.

"I'll tell Claudia to work on a project for her right away," Deere said.

"Great," Bantz said. "Now remember I always knew what Eli really wanted to do but couldn't because he was too soft. We are going to get rid of Dora and Kevin's production companies. They always lose money and besides I don't want them on the lot."

"You have to be careful on that one," Deere said. "They own a lot of stock in the company."

Bantz grinned. "Yeah, but Eli left me in control for five years. So you're going to be the fall guy. You will refuse to green-light their projects. I figure that after a year or two, they'll leave in disgust and blame you. That was Eli's technique. I always took the rap for him."

"I think you'll have a hard time moving them off the lot," Deere said. "It's their second home, they grew up on it."

"I'll try," Bantz said. "Another thing. The night before he died, Eli agreed to give Ernest Vail gross with some money up front on all the pictures we made from his shitty novel. Eli made that promise because Molly Flanders and Claudia nagged him on his deathbed, which was really a lousy thing to do. I've notified Molly in writing that I'm not bound legally or morally to keep that promise."

Deere pondered the problem. "He'll never kill himself but he could die a natural death in the next five years. We should ensure ourselves against that."

"No," Bantz said. "Eli and I consulted our lawyers and they say Molly's argument would lose in the courts. I'll negotiate some money but not gross. That's sucking our blood."

"So, has Molly answered?" Deere asked.

"Yeah, the usual bullshit lawyer letter," Bantz said. "I told her to go fuck herself."

Bantz picked up the phone and called his psychoanalyst. His wife had insisted for years that he go into therapy to become more likable.

Bantz said into the phone, "I just wanted to confirm our appointment for four P.M. Yes, we'll talk about your script next week." He hung up the phone and gave Deere a sly smile.

Deere knew that Bantz had a rendezvous with Falene Fant at the Studio's Beverly Hotel Bungalow. So Bobby's therapist served as his beard because the Studio had taken an option on the therapist's original screenplay about a serial murder psychiatrist. The joke was that Deere had read the script and thought it would make a nice low-budget movie, although Bantz thought it was shit. Deere would make the movie and Bantz would believe Deere was just doing him a favor.

Then Bantz and Deere chatted about why spending time with Falene made them so happy. They both agreed that it was childish for important men like themselves. They also agreed that sex with Falene was so pleasurable because she was so much fun, and because she made no claims on them. Of course there were implied claims, but she was talented and when the right time came she would be given her chance.

Bantz said, "The thing that worries me is that if she becomes some sort of half-assed star our fun may be over."

"Yeah," Deere said. "That's the way Talent reacts. But what the hell, then she'll make us a lot of money."

The two of them went over the production and release schedules. *Messalina* would be finished in two months and would be the Locomotive for the Christmas season. A Vail sequel was in the can and would be released in the next two weeks. These two LoddStone pictures combined might gross a billion dollars worldwide, including video. Bantz would see a twenty-million-dollar bonus, Deere probably five million. Bobby would be hailed as a genius in his first year as successor to Marrion. He would be acknowledged as a true Number One exec.

Deere said thoughtfully, "It's a shame we have to pay Cross fifteen percent of the adjusted gross on *Messalina.* Why don't we just pay him back his money with interest and if he doesn't like it, he can sue. Obviously, he's leery about going to court."

"Isn't he supposed to be Mafia?" Bantz asked. And Deere thought, This guy is really chickenshit.

"I know Cross," Deere said. "He's not a tough guy. His sister Claudia would have told me if he was truly dangerous. The one I worry about is Molly Flanders. We're screwing two of her clients at the same time."

"OK," Bobby said. "Christ, we really did a good day's work. We save twenty mil on Vail and maybe ten on De Lena. That will pay our bonuses. We'll be heroes."

"Yeah," Deere said. He looked at his watch. "It's getting close to four o'clock. Shouldn't you be on your way to Falene?"

At that moment the door to Bobby Bantz's office burst open and there stood Molly Flanders. She was in fighting garb, trousers, jacket, and white silk blouse. And in flat heels. Her beautiful complexion was a blushing red with rage. There were tears in her eyes and yet she had never looked more beautiful. Her voice was filled with gleeful malice.

"OK, you two cocksuckers," she said. "Ernest Vail is dead. I've got an injunction pending to prevent you from releasing your new sequel to his book. Now are you two fuckheads ready to sit down and make a deal?"

Ernest Vail knew his greatest problem in committing suicide was how to avoid violence. He was far too cowardly to use the most popular methods. Guns frightened him, knives and poisons were too direct and not foolproof. Head in a gas oven, death in his car by carbon monoxide, again left too much uncertainty. Slitting his wrists involved blood. No, he wanted to die a pleasurable death, quick, certain, leaving his body intact and dignified.

Ernest prided himself that his was a rational decision that would benefit everyone except LoddStone Studios. It was purely a matter of personal financial gain and the restoration of his ego. He would be regaining control of his life; that made him laugh. Another proof of sanity: He still had his sense of humor.

Swimming out into the ocean was too "movies," throwing himself in front of a bus was also too painful and somehow demeaning, as if he were some homeless bum. One notion appealed to him for a moment. There was a sleeping pill, no longer popular, a suppository, which you just slipped into your rectum. But again, it was too undignified and was not completely certain.

Ernest rejected all these methods and searched for something that would give him a happy certain death. This process cheered him up so much that he almost abandoned the whole idea. So did writing rough drafts of suicide notes. He wanted to use all his art not to sound self-pitying, accusatory. Most of all he wanted his suicide to be accepted as a completely rational act and not one of cowardice.

He started with the note to his first wife, whom he thought of as his only true love. The first sentence he tried to make objective and practical.

"Get in touch with Molly Flanders, my lawyer, as soon as you get this note. She will have important news for you. I thank you and the children for the many happy years you've given me. I do not want you to think that what I've done is a reproach to you in any way. We were sick of each other before we parted. Please do not think my action is because of a diseased mind, or any unhappiness. It is completely rational, as my lawyer will explain. Tell my children that I love them."

Ernest pushed the note aside. It would need a lot of rewrite. He wrote notes to his second and third wives, which sounded cold even to him, informing them that they were being left small portions of his estate and thanking them for the happiness they had given him and reassuring them they also were in no way responsible for his action. It seemed he was not really in a loving mood. So he wrote a short note to Bobby Bantz, a simple "Fuck you."

Then he wrote a note to Molly Flanders that read, "Go get the bastards." This put him in a better mood.

To Cross De Lena, he wrote, "I finally did the right thing." He had sensed De Lena's contempt for his waffling.

Finally his heart opened up when he wrote to Claudia. "You gave me the happiest times of my life and we weren't even in love. How do you figure that? And how come everything you did in life was right and everything I did was wrong? Until now. Please disregard everything I've said about your writing, how I demeaned your work, that's just the envy of an old novelist as out of date as a blacksmith. And thank you for fighting for my percentage even though finally you failed. I love you for trying."

He stacked up the notes, which he had written on yellow second sheets. They were terrible but he would rewrite them, and rewriting was always the key.

But composing the notes had stirred his subconscious. Finally he thought of the perfect way to kill himself.

Kenneth Kaldone was the greatest dentist in Hollywood, as famous as any Bankable Star within that small milieu. He was extremely skillful in his profession, he was colorful and daring in his private life. He detested the portrayal in literature and movies of dentists as extremely bourgeois and did everything to disprove it.

He was charming in dress and manner, his dental office was luxurious and had a rack of a hundred of the best magazines published in

America and England. There was another, smaller rack for magazines in foreign languages, German, Italian, French, and even Russian.

First-rate modern art hung on the walls of the waiting room, and when you went into the labyrinth of treatment rooms, the corridors were decorated with autographed pictures of some of the greatest names in Hollywood. His patients.

He was always bubbly with cheerful good humor and vaguely effeminate in a way that was strangely misleading. He loved women but did not understand in any way a commitment to women. He regarded sex as no more important than a good dinner, a fine wine, wonderful music.

The only thing Kenneth believed in was the art of dentistry. There, he was an artist, he kept up with all technical and cosmetic developments. He refused to make removable bridges for his clients, he insisted on steel implants to which an artificial series of teeth could be attached permanently. He lectured at the dental conventions, he was such an authority that he had once been summoned to treat the teeth of one of the royal bloods of Monaco.

No patient of Kenneth Kaldone's would be forced to put his teeth in a water glass at night. No patient would ever feel pain in his elaborately outfitted dental chair. He was generous in his use of drugs and especially in the use of "sweet air," the combination of nitrous oxide and oxygen inhaled by patients though a rubber mask, which remarkably killed any pain to the nerves and transported his patient into a semiconsciousness as nearly pleasurable as opium.

Ernest and Kenneth had become friends on Ernest's first visit to Hollywood almost twenty years before. Ernest had suffered an excruciating toothache at the dinner of a producer who was courting him for the rights to one of his books. The producer had called Kenneth at midnight, and Kenneth had rushed to the party to drive Ernest to his office to treat the infected tooth. Then he had driven Ernest to his hotel, instructing him to come back to the office the next day.

Ernest later commented to the producer that he must have a lot of clout for a dentist to make a house call at midnight. The producer said no, Kenneth Kaldone was just that kind of a guy. A man with a toothache was to him like a man drowning, he had to be rescued. But also Kaldone had read all of Ernest's books and loved his work.

The next day when Ernest visited Kenneth in his office, he was effusively grateful. Kenneth stopped him with an upraised hand and said, "I'm still in your debt for the pleasure your books have given me. Now let me tell you about steel implants." He gave a long lecture that argued it was never too early to take care of your mouth. That Ernest would soon lose some other teeth, and steel implants would save him from putting his teeth in a water glass at night.

Ernest said, "I'll think about it."

"No," Kenneth said, "I can't treat a patient who disagrees with me about my work."

Ernest laughed. "It's a good thing you're not a novelist," he said. "But OK."

They became friends. Vail would call him for dinner whenever he came to Hollywood and sometimes he made a special trip to L.A. just to be treated with sweet air. Kenneth spoke intelligently about Ernest's books, he knew literature almost as well as he knew dentistry.

Ernest loved sweet air. He never felt pain and he had some of his best ideas while he was in the semiconscious state it induced. In the next few years he and Kenneth built a friendship so strong it resulted in Ernest having a new set of teeth with roots of steel, which would accompany him to the grave.

But Ernest's main interest in Kenneth was as a character for a novel. Ernest had always believed that in every human being there was one startling perversity. Kenneth had revealed his, and it was sexual but not in the usual pornographic style.

They always chatted a bit before a treatment, before Ernest was given sweet air. Kenneth mentioned that his primary girlfriend, his "significant other," was also having sex with her dog, a huge German shepherd.

Ernest, just beginning to succumb to the sweet air, took the rubber mask off his face and said without thinking, "You're screwing a woman who screws her dog? Don't you worry about that?" He meant the medical and psychological complications.

Kenneth did not grasp what was implied. "Why should I worry?" he said. "A dog is no competition."

At first Ernest thought he was joking. Then he realized Kenneth was serious. Ernest put his mask back on and submerged himself in the dreaminess of the nitrous oxide and oxygen, and his mind, stimulated as usual, made a complete analysis of his dentist.

Kenneth was a man who had no conception of love as a spiritual exercise. Pleasure was paramount, similar to his skills in killing pain. Flesh was to be controlled while indulged.

They had dinner together that night, and Kenneth more or less confirmed Ernest's analysis. "Sex is better than nitrous," Kenneth said. "But like nitrous, you must have at least thirty percent oxygen mixed in." He gave Ernest a sly look. "Ernest, you really like sweet air, I can tell. I give you the maximum—seventy percent—and you tolerate it well."

Ernest asked, "Is it dangerous?"

"Not really," Kenneth said. "Unless you keep the mask on for a couple of days and maybe not even then. Of course, pure nitrous oxide will kill you in fifteen to thirty minutes. In fact about once a month I have a little midnight party in my office, carefully selected 'beautiful people.' All my patients, so I have their blood work. All healthy. The nitrous turns them on. Haven't you felt sexual under the gas?"

Ernest laughed. "When one of your technicians goes by I want to grab her ass."

Kenneth said with wry humor, "I'm sure she'd forgive you. Why don't you come by the office tomorrow at midnight? It's really a lot of fun." He saw Ernest looking scandalized and said, "Nitrous is not cocaine. Cocaine makes women sort of helpless. Nitrous just loosens them up. Just come as you would go to a cocktail party. You're not committed to any action."

Ernest thought maliciously, Are dogs allowed? Then he said he would drop in. He excused himself by thinking it would only be research for a novel.

He did not have any fun at the party and did not really participate. The truth was, the nitrous oxide made him feel more spiritual than sexy, as if it were some sacred drug only to be used to worship a merciful God. The copulation of the guests was so animal-like that for the first time he understood Kenneth's casualness about his significant other and the German shepherd. It was so devoid of human content that it was boring. Kenneth himself did not participate, he was too busy operating the controls on the nitrous.

But now, years later, Ernest knew he had a way of killing himself. It would be like painless dentistry. He would not suffer, he would not be disfigured, he would not be afraid. He would float from this world to the other in a cloud of benign reflections. As the saying goes, he would die happy.

The problem now was how to get into Kenneth's office at night and how to figure out how the controls operated. . . .

He made an appointment with Kenneth for a checkup. While Kenneth was studying his X rays, Ernest told him that he was using a dentist as a character in his new novel and asked to be shown how the controls for the sweet air worked.

Kenneth was a natural-born pedagogue and showed him how to work the controls on the tanks of nitrous oxide and oxygen, stressing the safe ratios, lecturing all the while.

"But couldn't it be dangerous?" Ernest asked. "What if you got drunk and screwed up? You could kill me."

"No, it's automatically regulated so that you always get at least thirty percent oxygen," Kenneth explained.

Ernest hesitated a moment, trying to look embarrassed. "You know I enjoyed that party years ago. Now I have a beautiful girlfriend who is acting a little coy. I need some help. Could you let me have the key to your office so I could bring her here some night? The nitrous would just tip the balance."

Kenneth studied the X rays carefully. "Your mouth is in terrific shape," he said. "I'm really a great dentist."

"The key?" Ernest said.

"A really beautiful girl?" Kenneth asked. "Tell me which night and I'll come and work the controls."

"No, no," Ernest said. "This is a really straight girl. She wouldn't do even the nitrous if you were around." He paused for a moment. "She really is old-fashioned."

"No shit," Kenneth said and looked directly into Ernest's eyes. Then he said, "I'll just be a minute," and he left the treatment room.

When he returned, he had a key in his hand. "Take this to a hardware store and get it duplicated," Kenneth said. "Make sure you let them know who you are. Then come back and give me my key."

Ernest was surprised. "I don't mean right now."

Kenneth packed away the X rays and turned to Ernest. For one of the few times since Ernest had known him, the cheerfulness in his face was gone.

"When the cops find you," Kenneth said, "dead in my chair, I don't want to be implicated in any way. I don't want my professional status jeopardized, or my patients deserting me. The cops will find the duplicate and track it down to the store. They will assume trickery on your part. I assume you're leaving a note?"

Ernest was stunned and then ashamed. He had not thought of harming Kenneth. Kenneth was looking at him with a reproachful smile tinged with sadness. Ernest took the key from Kenneth, then in a rare show of emotion, he gave Kenneth a tentative hug. "So you understand," he said. "I'm being completely rational."

"Sure I do," Kenneth said. "I've often thought about it for myself in my old age or if things go bad." He smiled cheerfully and said, "Death is no competition." They both laughed.

"You really know why?" Ernest asked.

"Everybody in Hollywood knows," Kenneth said. "Skippy Deere was at a party and someone asked if he was really going to do the picture. He said, 'I will try until Hell freezes over or Ernest Vail commits suicide.' "

"And you don't think I'm crazy?" Ernest said. "Doing it for money I can't spend . . ."

"Why not?" Kenneth said. "It's smarter than killing yourself for love. But the mechanics are not that simple. You have to disconnect this hose in the wall that supplies the oxygen, that disables the regulator and you can make the mixture more than seventy percent. Do it on Friday night after the cleaning people leave so you won't be discovered until Monday. There's always a chance you can be revived. Of course if you use pure nitrous oxide you'll be gone in thirty minutes." Again he smiled a little sadly. "All my work on your teeth wasted. What a shame."

Two days later, on a Saturday morning, Ernest woke very early in his Beverly Hills Hotel room. The sun was just coming up. He showered and shaved and dressed in a T-shirt and comfortable jeans. Over that he wore a tan linen jacket. His room was strewn with clothes and newspapers, but it would be pointless to tidy up.

Kenneth's office was a half-hour walk from the hotel, and Ernest stepped out feeling a sense of freedom. Nobody walked in L.A. He was hungry but was afraid to eat anything because it might make him throw up when he was under the nitrous.

The office was on the fifteenth floor of a sixteen-story building. There was only a single civilian guard in the lobby and no one in the elevator. Ernest turned the key in the door of the dental suite and entered. He locked the door behind him and put the key in his jacket pocket. The suite of rooms was ghostly still, the receptionist's window glinted in the early morning sun and her computer was ominously dark and silent.

Ernest opened the door that led to the work area. As he walked down the corridor, he was greeted by the photos of Bankable Stars. There were six treatment rooms, three on each side of the corridor. At the end was Kenneth's office and conference room where they had chatted many times. Kenneth's own treatment room was attached, with his special hydraulic dental chair, where he cared for his high-ranking patients.

That chair was extra luxurious, the padding thicker and the leather softer. On the mobile table beside the chair was the sweet air mask. The console, with its hose linked to the hidden nitrous oxide and oxygen tanks, had its two control knobs turned to zero.

Ernest adjusted the dials so that he would get half nitrous oxide and half oxygen. Then he sat in the chair and put the mask over his face. He relaxed. After all, Kenneth would not be sticking knives into his gums now. All the aches and pains left his body, his brain roamed over the entire world. He felt wonderful, it was ridiculous to think of death.

Ideas for future novels floated through his head, insights into many people he knew, none of them malicious, which was what he loved about nitrous. Shit, he had forgotten to rewrite the suicide notes, and he realized how, despite his good intentions and language, they were in essence insulting.

Ernest was now in a huge, sailing colored balloon. He floated over the world he had known. He thought about Eli Marrion, who had followed his destiny, achieved great power, was regarded with awe for his ruthless intelligence in using that power. And yet, when Ernest's best book came out and was bought for the movies, the one that earned him the Pulitzer, Eli had come to the cocktail party his publishers gave him.

Eli had put out his hand and said, "You are a very fine writer." His coming to the party was sensational Hollywood gossip. And the great Eli Marrion had shown him the final and absolute mark of respect, he had given him gross. No matter that Bantz had taken it away after Marrion died.

And Bantz was not a villain. His relentless pursuit of profit was a result of his experience in a special world. If truth be told, Skippy Deere was worse, because Deere, with his intelligence, his charm and his elemental energy, and his instinctive moves to betrayal in a personal sense, was more lethal.

Another insight came to Ernest. Why was he always knocking Hollywood and films, sneering at them? It was jealousy. Film was now the most revered art form, and he himself loved movies, good ones anyway. But he envied more the relationships in making a movie. The cast, the crew, the director, the Bankable Stars and even the "Suits," those crass execs, seemed to come together in a close if not ever-loving family, at least until the picture was finished. They gave each other presents then and kissed and hugged and swore eternal devotion. What a wonderful feeling that must be to have. He remembered when he wrote his first script with Claudia, he thought he might be admitted to this family.

But how that could be with his personality, his malicious wit, his constant sneering? But under the sweet nitrous oxide, he could not even judge himself harshly. He had a right, he had written great books (Ernest was an oddity among novelists because he really loved his books), and he had deserved to be treated with more respect.

Benignly saturated with forgiving nitrous, Ernest decided he really didn't want to die. Money was not that important, Bantz would relent or Claudia and Molly would find a way out.

Then he remembered all his humiliation. None of his wives had ever truly loved him. He had always been the mendicant, never enjoyed requited love. His books had been respected but never aroused the adoration that made a writer rich. Some critics had reviled him and he had pretended to take it in good sport. After all, it was wrong to get angry with critics, they were only doing their job. But their remarks hurt. And all his male friends, though they sometimes enjoyed his company, his wit and honesty, never became close, not even Kenneth. While Claudia was truly fond of him, he knew Molly Flanders and Kenneth felt pity for him.

Ernest reached over and turned off the sweet air. It took just a few minutes for his head to clear and then he went to sit in Kenneth's office.

His depression came back. He tilted back in Kenneth's lounge chair and watched the sun rise over Beverly Hills. He was so angry at the studio screwing him out of his money that he couldn't enjoy anything. He hated the dawning of a new day; at night he took sleeping pills early and tried to sleep as long as he could. . . . That he could be humiliated by such people, people he held in contempt. And now he could no longer even read, a pleasure that had never before betrayed him. And of course, he could no longer write. That elegant prose, so often praised, was now false, inflated, pretentious. He no longer enjoyed writing it.

For a long time now, he had awakened every morning dreading the coming day, too tired to even shave and shower. And he was broke. He had earned millions and had pissed it away on gambling, women, and booze. Or given it away. Money had never been important until now.

The last two months he had not been able to send his kids their support payments or his wives their alimony. Unlike most men, sending those checks made Ernest happy. He had not published a book for five years, and his personality had become less pleasant even to himself. He was always whining about his fate. He was like a sore tooth in the face of society. And this image itself depressed him. What kind of soapy metaphor was this for a writer of his talent? A wave of melancholy swept over him; he was completely powerless.

He sprang up and walked into the treatment room. Kenneth had told him what he must do. He pulled out the cable that held the two plugs, one for oxygen and one for the nitrous oxide. Then he plugged back only one. Nitrous. He sat in the dental chair, reached over and turned the dial. At that moment he thought that there must be some way to get at least a ten percent oxygen flow so that death would not be so certain. He picked up the mask and put it over his face.

The pure nitrous hit his body and he experienced a moment of ecstasy, a washing away of all pain and a dreamy content. The nitrous hit and scrubbed out the brain in his skull. There was one last moment of pure pleasure before he ceased to exist, and in that moment, he believed there was a God and a Heaven.

Molly Flanders savaged Bobby Bantz and Skippy Deere; she would have been more careful if Eli Marrion was still alive.

"You have a new sequel to Ernest's book coming out. My injunction will stop that. The property now belongs to Ernest's heirs. Sure, maybe you can override the injunction and release the picture but then I sue. If I win, Ernest's estate will own that picture and most of what it earns. And for a certainty we can prevent you from making other sequels based on the characters in his books. Now, we can save all that and years of trouble in court. You pay five million up front and ten percent of the gross of each picture. And I want a true and certified account of the money on home video."

Deere was horrified and Bantz enraged. Ernest Vail, a writer, would have a greater percentage of the profit on the pictures than anyone except a Bankable Star ever got, and that was a fucking outrage.

Bantz immediately called Melo Stuart and the chief counsel for LoddStone Pictures. They were in the meeting room within a half hour. Melo was necessary to the meeting because he was the packager of the sequels and earned a commission on the Bankable Star, the director, and the rewriter, Benny Sly. This was a situation that could require him to give up some points.

The chief counsel said, "We studied the situation when Mr. Vail made his first threat against the Studio."

Molly Flanders broke in angrily. "You call killing himself a threat to the Studio?"

"And blackmail," the chief counsel said smoothly. "Now we've completely researched the law in this situation, which is very tricky, but even then I advised the Studio we could fight your claim in court and win. In this particular case, the rights to the property do not revert back to the heirs."

"What can you guarantee?" Molly asked the counsel. "To a ninety-five percent certainty?"

"No," the counsel said. "Nothing is that certain in the law."

Molly was delighted. She would retire with the fee she earned when she won this case. She got up to go and said, "Fuck you all, I'll see you in court."

Bantz and Deere were so terrified they could not speak. Bantz wished with all his heart that Eli Marrion were still alive.

It was Melo Stuart who rose and restrained Molly with an affectionate and imploring hug. "Hey," he said, "we're just negotiating. Be civilized."

He led Molly back to her chair, noticing there were tears in her eyes. "We can make a deal, I'll give up some points in the package."

Molly said quietly to Bantz, "Do you want to risk losing everything? Can your counsel guarantee that you will win? Of course he can't. Are you a fucking businessman or some degenerate gambler? To save a fucking lousy twenty to forty mil, you want to risk losing a billion?"

They cut the deal. Ernest's estate got four million up front and 8 percent of the gross on the picture about to be released. He would get two million and 10 percent of adjusted gross on any other sequels. Ernest's three ex-wives and his children would be rich.

Molly's parting shot was, "If you think I was tough, wait until Cross De Lena hears how you screwed him."

Molly savored her victory. She remembered how one night she had taken Ernest home from a party. She was pretty drunk and extremely lonely and Ernest was witty and intelligent and she thought it might be fun to spend a night with him. Then when they arrived at her home, sobered up by the drive, and she took him to her bedroom, she had looked around despairingly. Ernest was such a shrimp and so obviously sexually shy and he was really a homely man. At that point he was tongue-tied.

But Molly was too fair a person to dismiss him at such a critical time. So she got drunk again and they went to bed. And really, in the dark, it hadn't been too bad. Ernest enjoyed it so much that she was flattered and brought him breakfast in bed.

He gave her a sly grin. "Thank you," he said. "And thank you again." And she perceived that he understood everything she had felt the previous night and was thanking her not only for bringing him breakfast but also as his sexual benefactress. She had always been regretful that she had not been a better actress, but what the hell, she was a lawyer. And now she had performed for Ernest Vail an act of requited love.

Dottore David Redfellow received Don Clericuzio's summons while attending an important meeting in Rome. He was advising the prime minister of Italy on a new banking regulation that would impose severe penal sentences on corrupt bank officials, and naturally he was advising against it. He immediately wound up his arguments and flew to America.

In the twenty-five years of his exile in Italy, David Redfellow had prospered and changed beyond his wildest dreams. At the beginning, Don Clericuzio helped him buy a small bank in Rome. With the fortune he had made in the drug trade and deposited in Swiss banks, he bought more banks and television stations. But it was Don Clericuzio's friends in Italy who helped guide him and build his empire, helped him to acquire the magazines, the newspapers, the TV stations, in addition to his string of banks.

But David Redfellow was pleased also by what he had done on his own. A complete transformation of character. He acquired Italian citizenship, an Italian wife, Italian children, and the standard Italian mistress as well as an honorary doctorate (cost, two million) from an Italian university. He wore Armani suits, spent an hour every week at his barber, acquired a circle of all-male cronies at his coffee bar (which he bought), and entered politics as advisor to the cabinet and the prime minister. Still, once a year he made his pilgrimage to Quogue to fulfill any wishes of his mentor, Don Clericuzio. So this special summons filled him with alarm.

Dinner was waiting for him at the Quogue mansion when he arrived, and Rose Marie had outdone herself because Redfellow was always rapturous about the restaurants of Rome. Assembled to honor him was the entire Clericuzio clan: the Don himself; his sons, Giorgio, Petie, and Vincent; his grandson, Dante; and Pippi and Cross De Lena.

It was a hero's welcome. David Redfellow, the college-dropout drug king, the louche dresser with an earring in his ear, the hyena riding the kills of sex, had transformed himself into a pillar of society. They were proud of him. Even more, Don Clericuzio felt he was in Redfellow's debt. For it was Redfellow who had taught him a great lesson in morality.

In his early days Don Clericuzio had suffered a strange sentimentality. He had believed that the forces of law could not be generally corrupted in the matter of drugs.

David Redfellow was a twenty-year-old college student in 1960 when he first started dealing drugs, not for profit but simply so he and his friends could have a steady cheap supply. An amateur endeavor, just cocaine and marijuana. In a year it had grown so big he and his classmate partners owned a small plane that brought goods over the Mexican and South American borders. Quite naturally they soon ran afoul of the law, and that was where David first showed his genius. The six-man partnership was earning vast amounts of money, and David Redfellow laid on such massive bribes that he soon had on his payroll a roster of sheriffs, district attorneys, judges, and hundreds of police along the Eastern seaboard.

He always claimed it was quite simple. You learned the official's yearly salary and offered him five times that amount.

But then the cartel of Colombians appeared on the scene, wilder than the wildest of the Old West movie Indians, not just taking scalps but whole heads. Four of Redfellow's partners were killed, and Redfellow made contact with the Clericuzio Family and asked for protection, offering 50 percent of his profits.

Petie Clericuzio and a crew of soldiers from the Bronx Enclave became his bodyguards, and this arrangement lasted until the Don exiled Redfellow to Italy in 1965. The drug business had become too dangerous.

Now, gathered together over dinner, they congratulated the Don on the wisdom of his decision many years before. Dante and Cross heard the story of Redfellow for the first time. Redfellow was a good storyteller and he praised Petie to the skies. "What a fighter," he said. "If it wasn't for him I would never have lived to go to Sicily." He turned to Dante and Cross and said to them, "It was the day you both were christened. I remember you both never flinched when they almost drowned you in Holy Water. I never dreamed that someday we would be doing business together, as grown men."

Don Clericuzio said drily, "You will not be doing business with them, you will do business only with me and Giorgio. If you need help you can call on Pippi De Lena. I have decided to go on with the business I spoke to you about. Giorgio will tell you why."

Giorgio told David the latest developments, that Eli Marrion was dead and Bobby Bantz had taken over the Studio, that he had taken away all the points Cross owned in *Messalina,* and returned his money with interest.

Redfellow enjoyed that story. "He is a very clever man. He knows you will not go to court so he takes away your money. That's good business."

Dante was drinking a cup of coffee, and he eyed Redfellow with distaste. Rose Marie, who was sitting beside him, put her hand on his arm.

"You think that's funny?" Dante said to Redfellow.

Redfellow studied Dante for a moment. He made his face very serious. "Only because I know that in this instance it is a mistake to be so clever."

The Don observed this exchange and it seemed to amuse him. In any case he was frivolous, a rare occurrence, which his sons always recognized and enjoyed.

"So Grandson," he said to Dante, "how would you solve this problem?"

"Send him swimming to the bottom of the ocean," Dante said, and the Don smiled at him.

"And you, Croccifixio? How would you solve this situation?" the Don asked.

"I'd just accept it," Cross said. "I'd learn from it. I just got outfoxed because I didn't believe they'd have the balls."

"Petie and Vincent?" the Don asked.

But they refused to answer. They knew the game he was playing.

"You can't just ignore it," the Don said to Cross. "You will be known for a fool and men all over the world will refuse you any respect."

Cross was taking the Don seriously. "Eli Marrion's house still holds his paintings and they're worth about twenty or thirty million. We could hijack them and hold them for ransom."

"No," the Don said. "That would expose you, reveal your power, and no matter how delicately handled, could lead to danger. It is too complicated. David, what would you do?"

David puffed on his cigar, thoughtfully. He said, "Buy the Studio. Do a civilized businesslike thing. With our banks and communications companies, buy LoddStone."

Cross was incredulous. "LoddStone is the oldest and richest film studio in the world. Even if you could put up the ten billion, they wouldn't sell it to you. That's simply not possible."

Petie said in his joker's voice, "David my old buddy, you can get your mitts on ten billion? The man whose life I saved? The man who said he could never repay me?"

Redfellow waved him away. "You don't understand how big money works. It's like whipped cream, you get a small amount and whip it up into a big froth with bonds, loans, stock shares. Money is not the problem."

Cross said, "The problem is how to get Bantz out of the way. He controls the Studio and whatever his faults, he is loyal to Marrion's wishes. He would never agree to selling the Studio."

"I'll go out there and give him a kiss," Petie said.

Now the Don made his decision. He said to Redfellow, "Carry out your plan. Get it done. But with all caution. Pippi and Croccifixio will be at your command."

"One more thing," Giorgio said to Redfellow. "Bobby Bantz, by the terms of Eli Marrion's will, has total command over the Studio for the next five years. But Marrion's son and daughter have more stock in the company than Bantz. Bantz can't get fired but if the Studio is sold, the new owners will have to pay him off. So that's the problem you have to solve."

David Redfellow smiled and puffed on his cigar. "Just like the old days. Don Clericuzio, the only help I need is yours. Some of those banks in Italy may be reluctant to gamble on such a venture. Remember, we will have to pay a big premium over the actual worth of the Studio."

"Don't worry," the Don said. "I have a lot of money in those banks."

Pippi DeLena had watched all this with a wary eye. What disturbed him was the openness of this meeting. By procedure only the Don, Giorgio, and David Redfellow should have been present. Pippi and Cross could have been given orders separately to help Redfellow. Why had they been let in on these secrets? Even more important, why were Dante, Petie, and Vincent brought into the circle? All this was not like the Don Clericuzio he knew, who always kept his plans as secret as possible.

Vincent and Rose Marie were helping the Don up the stairs to go to bed. He had stubbornly refused to have a lift chair installed on the railings.

As soon as they were out of sight, Dante turned to Giorgio and said furiously, "And who gets the Studio when we own it? Cross?"

David Redfellow interrupted coolly. "I will own the Studio. I will run it. Your grandfather will have a financial interest. This will be documented."

Giorgio agreed.

Cross said laughing, "Dante, neither one of us can run a movie studio. We're not ruthless enough."

Pippi studied all of them. He was good at scenting danger. That's why he had lived so long. But this he couldn't figure out. Maybe the Don was just getting old.

Petie drove Redfellow back to Kennedy Airport where his private jet waited. Cross and Pippi had used a chartered jet from Vegas. Don Clericuzio absolutely forbade the owning of a jet by the Xanadu or any of his enterprises.

Cross drove their rented car to the airport. During the drive, Pippi said to Cross, "I'm going to spend some time in New York City. I'll just keep the car when we get to the airport."

Cross saw that his father was worried. "I didn't do well in there," he said.

"You were OK," Pippi said. "But the Don was right. You can't let anybody screw you twice."

When they arrived at Kennedy, Cross got out and Pippi slid across the seat to get behind the wheel. Through the open window, they shook hands. In that moment Pippi looked up at his son's handsome face and felt an enormous wave of affection. He tried to smile as he slapped Cross gently on the cheek and said, "Be careful."

"Of what?" Cross asked, his dark eyes searching his father's.

"Everything," Pippi said. Then, startling Cross, he said, "Maybe I should have let you go with your mother but I was selfish. I needed you around."

Cross watched his father drive away and for the first time he realized how much his father worried about him, how much his father loved him.

CHAPTER 15

MUCH TO HIS OWN DISMAY, Pippi De Lena decided to get married, not for love but for companionship. True, he had Cross, he had the cronies at the Xanadu Hotel, he had the Clericuzio Family and a vast network or relatives. True, he had three mistresses and he ate with good and sincere appetite; he enjoyed his golf and was down to a ten handicap, and he still loved to dance. But as the Don would say, he could go dancing to his coffin.

So in his late fifties, robust in health, sanguine in temperament, rich, semiretired, he longed for a settled home life and perhaps a new batch of kids. Why not? The idea appealed to him more and more. Surprisingly, he yearned to be a father again. It would be fun to raise a daughter, he had loved Claudia as a child, though they no longer spoke. She had been so cunning and so forthright at the same time, and she had made her way in the world as a successful screenplay writer. And who knows, maybe someday they would make up. In some ways she was as stubborn as he was, so he understood her and he admired the way she stood up for what she believed in.

Cross had lost the gamble he had taken in the movie business, but one way or another his future was assured. He still had the Xanadu and the Don would help him recover from the risk he had taken with his new venture. He was a good kid, but he was young and the young must take risks. That's what life was all about.

After dropping off Cross at the airport, Pippi drove to New York City to spend a few days with his East Coast mistress. She was a good-looking brunette, a legal secretary with a sharp New York wit, and a great dancer. True, she had a tongue that lashed out, she loved to spend money, she would be an expensive wife. But she was too old, over forty-five. And she was too independent, a great quality for a mistress but not for the kind of marriage that Pippi would demand.

It was a pleasurable weekend with her, though she spent half the Sunday reading the *Times.* They ate in the finest restaurants, went dancing in the nightclubs, and had great sex in her apartment. But Pippi needed something more placid.

Pippi flew to Chicago. His mistress there was the sexual equivalent of that brawling city. She drank a little too much, she partied too exuberantly, she was happy-go-lucky and a lot of fun. But she was a little lazy, a little too messy, Pippi liked a clean home. Again, she was too old to start a family, at least forty, she said. But what the hell. Was he up to running around with a really young broad? After two days in Chicago, Pippi crossed her off the list.

With both, he would have a problem settling them in Vegas. They were big-city women, and Vegas, Pippi knew in his heart, was really a hick cow town where casinos took the place of cattle. And there was no way that Pippi would live in any place but Vegas, for in Vegas nighttime did not exist. Electric neon banished all ghosts, the city shone like a rosy diamond in the desert at night, and after dawn the hot sun burned away all the wraiths that had escaped the neon.

His best shot was his mistress in Los Angeles, and Pippi was pleased that he had geographically positioned them so neatly. There could be no accidental confrontations, no mental struggles in choosing between them. They served a certain purpose and they could not interfere with any temporary love affairs. Indeed, looking back, he was pleased at how he had conducted his life. Daring but prudent, brave but not foolhardy, loyal to the Family and rewarded by them. His only mistake had been in marrying a woman like Nalene, and even there, what woman could have given him more happiness for eleven years. And what man could boast of having made only one mistake in his lifetime? What was it the Don always said, It was OK to make mistakes in life as long as it was not a fatal mistake.

He decided to go directly to L.A. and not stop in Vegas. He called to notify Michelle that he was on his way and refused her offer to pick him up at the airport. "Just be ready for me when I get there," he told her. "I've been missing you. And I've got something important to tell you."

Michelle was young enough, thirty-two, and she was more tender, more giving, more easy on the nerves, maybe because she had been born and raised in California. She was also good in bed, not that the others were not, for this was a primary qualification for Pippi. But she had no sharp edges, she wouldn't be trouble. She was a little kooky, she believed in New Age crap called channeling and being able to talk to spirits, and talked about all the past lives she had lived, but she could also be fun. Like many California beauties, she had dreamed of being an actress, but that had been knocked out of her head. She was completely wrapped up in yoga and channeling now, in physical health, running and going to the gym. And besides, she always complimented Pippi on his karma. For of course none of these women knew his true vocation. He was simply an administrative officer of the hotel association in Vegas.

Yes, with Michelle, he could stay in Vegas, they could keep an apartment in L.A. and when they got bored they could make the forty-minute flight to L.A. for a couple of weeks. And maybe to keep her busy, he would buy her a gift shop in the Hotel Xanadu. It could really work out. But what if she said no?

Something struck his memory: Nalene reading *Goldilocks and the Three Bears* when the children were small. He was just like Goldilocks. The New York woman was too hard, the Chicago woman was too soft, and the L.A. woman was just right. The thought gave him pleasure. Of course, in real life nothing was "just right."

When he deplaned in L.A., he breathed in the balmy air of California, not even noticing the smog. He rented a car and drove first to Rodeo Drive, he loved to bring his women little gifts as a surprise and enjoyed walking down the street of fancy shops that held the luxuries of the world. He bought a gaudy wristwatch in the Gucci store; a purse in Fendi's, though he thought it ugly; a Hermès scarf; and some perfume in a bottle that looked like an expensive sculpture. When he bought a box of expensive lingerie, he was in such good spirits that he kidded the saleswoman, a young blonde, that it was for himself. The girl gave him one look and said, "Right . . ."

Back in the car, three thousand dollars poorer, he headed for Santa Monica, the goodies in the passenger seat, gifts crammed into a gaily colored Gucci shopping bag. In Brentwood, he stopped in the Brentwood Mart, a favorite place. He loved the food stores that boxed an open square studded with picnic tables where you could have a cold drink and eat. The food on the plane had been terrible, and he was hungry. Michelle never kept food in the refrigerator because she was always dieting.

In one store he bought two roast chickens, a dozen barbecued spareribs, and four hot dogs with all the trimmings. In another shop, he bought fresh baked white and rye bread. At an open stand he bought a huge glass of Coke and sat down at one of the picnic tables for a final moment of solitude. He ate two of the hot dogs, half of one of the roast chickens, and some French fries. He had never tasted anything so good. He sat in the golden light of the late afternoon sun in California, the sweet balmy air washed his face clean. He hated to leave but Michelle was waiting. She would be bathed and scented and a little tipsy and she would take him to bed immediately before he could even brush his teeth. He would propose to her before they started.

The shopping bag holding the food was decorated with type telling some fable about food, an intellectual shopping bag as befitted the intellectual clientele of the Mart. When he put it into the car, he read only the beginning line, "Fruit is the oldest product of human consumption. In the Garden of Eden . . ." Jesus, Pippi thought.

He drove to Santa Monica and stopped in front of Michelle's condo, which was in a two-story-high series of Spanish-looking bungalows. When he got out of the car he carried the two bags automatically in his left hand, leaving his right hand free. Out of habit, he surveyed the street up and down. It was lovely, no cars parked, the Spanish styles provided commodious driveways and a mildly religious benignity. The runners along the curbs were hidden by flowers and grass, the heavy-branched trees made a canopy against the descending sun.

Pippi now had to walk down a long alleyway whose wooden, green-painted fences were draped with roses. Michelle's apartment was in the back, a relic of the old Santa Monica, which was still bucolic. The buildings themselves were of seemingly old wood, and each separated swimming pool was adorned by white benches.

Outside the alleyway, far down the other end, Pippi heard the growling motor of a stationary vehicle. It alerted him, he was always alert. At the same moment he caught sight of a man rising from one of the benches. He was so surprised that he said, "What the fuck are you doing here?"

The man's hand did not come out to greet him and in that instant everything was clear to Pippi. He knew what was going to happen. His brain processed so much information that he could not react. He saw the gun appear, so small and inoffensive, saw the tension on the killer's face. Understood for the first time the look on the faces of men he had put to death, their supreme astonishment that life was at an end. And he understood that finally he would have to pay the price for living his life. He even thought briefly that the killer had planned badly, that this was not how he would have done it.

He tried his best, knowing there was no mercy. He dropped the shopping bags and lunged forward, at the same time reaching for his gun. The man came forward to meet him, and Pippi in exultation reached for him. Six bullets carried his body into the air and flung it into a pillow of flowers at the foot of the green fence. He smelled their fragrance. He looked up at the man standing over him and said, "You fucking Santadio." Then the final bullet crashed into his skull. Pippi De Lena was no more.

CHAPTER 16

EARLY ON THE DAY Pippi De Lena was to die, Cross picked up Athena at her Malibu home and they drove to San Diego to visit Athena's daughter, Bethany.

Bethany had been prepared by the nurses, she was dressed to go out. Cross could see she was a blurry reflection of her mother, and tall for her age. There was still the blankness in her face and eyes, and her body was too slack. Her features did not seem to have real definition, as if partially dissolved, like a bar of used soap. She still wore the red plastic apron that she used to protect her clothes when she was painting. She had been painting on the wall since early that morning. She didn't acknowledge seeing them, and she received her mother's hug and kisses with a shrinking away of her body and face.

Athena disregarded this and hugged her even harder.

The day was to be a picnic at a wooded lake nearby. Athena had packed a lunch basket.

On the short drive, Bethany sat between them, with Athena driving. Athena frequently brushed back Bethany's hair and caressed her cheek while Bethany stared straight ahead.

Cross thought of how when the day was done he and Athena would be back in Malibu making love. He was imagining her naked body on the bed and him standing over her.

Suddenly Bethany spoke, and it was to him. She had never acknowledged him before. She stared at him with her flat green eyes and said, "Who are you?"

Athena answered, and her voice was perfect, as if it was the most natural thing in the world for Bethany to ask. She said, "His name is

Cross and he's my very best friend." Bethany seemed not to hear and retired into her world again.

Athena parked the car a few yards from a dazzling lake nestled in the forest, a tiny blue gem in a vast cloth of green. Cross took the basket of food, and Athena unpacked it onto a red cloth she spread over the grass. She also put out crisp green napkins and forks and spoons. The cloth was embroidered with musical instruments that caught Bethany's attention. Then Athena spread out a pile of different sandwiches, glass bowls of potato salad, and sliced fruits. Then a plate of sweet cakes oozing cream. And a platter of fried chicken. She had prepared everything with the care of a catering professional because Bethany loved food.

Cross went back to the car and took a case of soda from the trunk. There were glasses in the basket and he poured soda for them. Athena offered her glass to Bethany, but Bethany struck her hand aside. She was watching Cross.

Cross stared into her eyes. Her face was so rigid it could have been a mask instead of flesh, but her eyes were now alert. It was as if she was trapped in some secret cave, that she was being smothered but could not call for help, that her flesh was blistered and she could not bear to be touched.

They ate, and Athena took on the role of the insensitive chatterbox, trying to make Bethany laugh. Cross marveled at how skillful she was, affectedly irritating and boring, as if the autistic behavior of her child was perfectly natural, treating Bethany as a fellow gossip though the girl never answered. It was an inspired monologue she created to ease her own pain.

Finally it was time for dessert. Athena unwrapped one of the creamy cakes and offered it to Bethany, who refused it. She offered one to Cross and he shook his head. He was getting very nervous because, though Bethany had consumed an enormous amount of food, it was obvious she was very angry with her mother. He knew that Athena sensed it, too.

Athena ate the pastry and exclaimed enthusiastically about how delicious it was. She unwrapped another two and set them before Bethany. The girl usually loved sweets. Bethany took them off the tablecloth and put them on the grass. In a few minutes they were covered with insects. Then Bethany picked up the two cakes and shoved one into her mouth. She handed the other to Cross. Without a moment's hesitation, Cross put the pastry into his mouth. There was a tickling sensation all across his palate and on the sides of his gums. He quickly gulped some soda to wash it down. Bethany looked at Athena.

Athena had the studied frown of an actress planning to do a difficult scene. Then she laughed, a wonderfully infectious laugh, and clapped her hands. "I told you it was delicious," she said. She unwrapped another pastry, but Bethany refused and so did Cross. Athena threw the pastry onto the grass and then took her napkin and wiped Bethany's mouth and then did the same to Cross. She was enjoying herself, it seemed.

On the drive back to the hospital, she spoke to Cross with some of the same inflections she used with Bethany. As if he, too, were autistic. Bethany watched her carefully and then turned to stare at Cross.

When they dropped the child off at the hospital, Bethany took Cross by the hand for a moment. "You're beautiful," she said, but when Cross tried to kiss her good-bye, she turned her head away. Then she ran.

Driving back to Malibu, Athena said excitedly, "She responded to you, that's a very good sign."

"Because I'm beautiful," Cross said dryly.

"No," Athena said, "because you can eat bugs. I'm at least as beautiful as you are and she hates me . . ." She was smiling joyfully, and as always her beauty made Cross dizzy and alarmed him.

"She thinks you're like her," Athena said. "She thinks you're autistic."

Cross laughed, he enjoyed the idea. "She may be right," he said. "Maybe you should put me in the hospital with her."

"No," Athena said, smiling. "Then I couldn't have your body whenever I wanted it. Besides, I'm going to take her out after I finish *Messalina*."

When they arrived at her Malibu house, Cross went in with her. They had planned for him to spend the night. By this time he had learned to read Athena: The more vivacious she acted, the more disturbed she was.

"If you're upset, I can go back to Vegas," he said.

Now she looked sad. Cross wondered how he loved her most, when she was naturally exuberant, when she was stern and serious, or when she was melancholy. Her face changed so magically in its beauty that he always found his feelings matching hers.

She said to him fondly, "You've had a terrible day and you shall have your reward." There was a mocking tone to her voice, but he understood it was a mockery of her own beauty, she knew her magic was false.

"I didn't have a terrible day," Cross said. And it was true. The joy he felt that day, with the three of them alone by the lake in the vast forest, reminded him of his childhood.

"You love ants on your pastry . . ." Athena said sadly.

"They weren't bad," Cross said. "Can Bethany get better?"

"I don't know but I'll keep searching until I find out," Athena said. "I have a long weekend coming up when they won't need to shoot *Messalina.* I'm going to fly to France with Bethany. There's a great doctor in Paris and I'm going to take her for another evaluation."

"What if he says there's no hope?" Cross said.

"Maybe I won't believe him. It doesn't matter," Athena said. "I love her. I'll take care of her."

"Forever and ever?" Cross asked.

"Yes," Athena said. Then she clapped her hands together, her green eyes shining. "Meanwhile, let's have some fun. Let's take care of ourselves. We'll go upstairs and shower and jump into bed. We'll make mad passionate love for hours. Then I'll cook us a midnight supper."

For Cross, he was a child again waking up with a day of pleasure before him, the breakfast his mother prepared, the playing of games with his friends, the hunting trips with his father, then supper with his family, Claudia, Nalene, and Pippi. The card games afterward. It was that innocent a feeling. Before him was making love to Athena in the twilight, watching the sun disappear over the Pacific from the balcony, the sky painted with marvelous reds and pinks, the touch of her warm flesh and silky skin. Her beautiful face and lips to kiss. He smiled and led her up the stairs.

The phone in the bedroom rang, and Athena ran up ahead of Cross to answer it. She covered the mouthpiece and in a startled voice said, "It's for you. A man named Giorgio." He had never received a phone call at her house before.

This could only be trouble, Cross thought, and so he did something he never thought he was capable of doing. He shook his head.

Athena said into the phone, "He's not here. . . . Yes, I'll tell him to call you when he comes." She hung up the phone and asked, "Who's Giorgio?"

"Just a relative," Cross said. He was stunned by what he had done, and why: because he could not give up a night with Athena. That was a grievous crime. And then he wondered how Giorgio knew he would be here and what Giorgio wanted. It must be something important, he thought, but still it could wait until morning. More than anything else he was desperate for the hours of making love to Athena.

It was the moment they'd been waiting for all day, all week; they were stripping off their clothes before showering together but he couldn't resist embracing her, their bodies still sweaty from the picnic. Then she took his hand and led him under the spraying water.

They dried each other with the large orange towels and, wrapped in them, stood on the balcony to watch the sun slide gradually behind the horizon. Then they went inside to lay on the bed.

When Cross made love to her, it seemed that all the cells of his brain and body flew out and he was left in some feverish dream; he was a ghost whose wisps were filled with ecstasy, a ghost who entered her flesh. He lost all his caution, all his reason, he didn't even study her face to see if she was acting, if she truly loved him. It seemed to go on forever, until they fell asleep in each other's arms. When they woke they were still entwined, lit by a moon whose light seemed brighter than the sun's. Athena kissed him and said, "Did you really like Bethany?"

"Yes," Cross said. "She's part of you."

"Do you think she can get better?" Athena asked. "Do you think I can help her get better?"

At that moment Cross felt as though he would give up his life to make the girl well. He felt the urge to sacrifice for the woman he loved, which many men feel but which until that time had been completely alien to him.

"We can both try to help," Cross said.

"No," Athena said, "I have to do it by myself."

They fell asleep again, and when the phone rang the air was misty with the newly born dawn. Athena picked up the phone, listened, and then said to Cross, "It's the guard at the gate. He says four men in a car want to come and see you."

Cross felt a shock of fear. He took the phone and said to the guard, "Put one of them on the phone."

The voice he heard was Vincent's. "Cross, Petie is with me. We got some really bad news."

"OK, put the guard on," Cross said, and then, to the guard, "They can come in."

He had completely forgotten about Giorgio's call. That's what love does, he thought contemptuously. I won't live a year if I keep this up.

He slipped on his clothes quickly and ran downstairs. The car was just pulling up to the front of the house, the sun, still half hidden, threw its light from over the horizon.

Vincent and Petie were getting out of the back of a long limousine. Cross could see the driver and another man in front. Petie and Vincent walked the long garden path to the door and Cross opened it for them.

Suddenly Athena was standing beside him, clad in slacks and a pullover, nothing beneath. Petie and Vincent were staring at her. She had never looked more beautiful.

Athena led them all into the kitchen and started making coffee, and Cross introduced them as his cousins.

"How did you guys get here?" Cross asked. "Last night you were in New York."

"Giorgio chartered us a plane," Petie said.

Athena was studying them as she made the coffee. Neither of them showed any emotion. They looked like brothers, both were big men, but Vincent was pale as granite, while Petie's leaner face was tanned red with weather or drink.

"So what's the bad news?" Cross said. He expected to hear that the Don had died, that Rose Marie had really gone crazy, or that Dante had done something so terrible that the Family was in crisis.

Vincent said with his usual curtness, "We have to talk to you alone."

Athena poured them coffee. "I tell you all my bad news," she said to Cross. "I should hear yours."

"I'll just leave with them," Cross said.

"Don't you be so fucking condescending," Athena said. "Don't you dare leave."

At this Vincent and Petie reacted. Vincent's granite face flushed with embarrassment, Petie gave Athena a speculative grin, as if she was someone to be watched. Cross, seeing this, laughed and said, "OK, let's hear it."

Petie tried to soften the blow. "Something happened to your father," he said.

Vincent broke in savagely, "Pippi got shot by some punk eggplant mugger. He's dead. So is the mugger, a cop named Losey shot him as he was running away. They need you in L.A. to identify the body and do the paperwork. The old man wants him buried in Quogue."

Cross lost his breath. He wavered for a moment, trembling in some dark wind, then he felt Athena holding his arm with both her hands.

"When?" Cross asked.

"About eight last night," Petie said. "Giorgio called for you."

Cross thought, While I was making love, my father was lying in the morgue. He felt an extraordinary contempt for his moment of weakness, an overwhelming shame. "I have to go," he said to Athena.

She looked at his stricken face. She had never seen him so.

"I'm sorry," she said. "Call me."

. . .

In the backseat of the limousine, Cross heard the other two men offering condolences. He recognized them as soldiers from the Bronx Enclave. As they moved through the Malibu Colony gate and then onto the Pacific Coast Highway, Cross detected a sluggishness of movement. The car they were riding in was armored.

Five days later the funeral of Pippi De Lena was held in Quogue. The Don's estate held its own private cemetery as the mansion held its own private chapel, and Pippi was buried in the grave next to Silvio, to show the Don's respect.

Only the Clericuzio clan and the most valued soldiers of the Bronx Enclave attended. Lia Vazzi came from the Hunting Lodge in the Sierras at the request of Cross. Rose Marie was not present. On hearing of Pippi's death, she had one of her fits and was taken to the psychiatric clinic.

But Claudia De Lena was there. She flew in to comfort Cross and to say good-bye to her father. What she had not been able to do when Pippi was alive, she felt she must do after his death. She wanted to claim a part of him for herself, to show the Clericuzio that he was as much her father as he was part of their Family.

The lawn in front of the Clericuzio mansion was decorated with a huge floral wreath the size of a billboard, and there were buffet tables and waiters and a bartender at a makeshift table to serve the guests. It was strictly a day of mourning, and no Family business was discussed.

Claudia cried bitter tears for all the years she'd been forced to live without her father, but Cross received condolences with a quiet dignity and showed no signs of grief.

The next night he was on the balcony of his suite in the Xanadu Hotel watching the riot of colors on the neoned Strip. Even this far up he could hear the sounds of music, the buzz of gamblers crowding the Strip looking for a lucky casino. But it was quiet enough for him to analyze what had happened in the last month. And to reflect on the death of his father.

Cross did not believe for a moment that Pippi De Lena had been shot down by a punk mugger. It was impossible for a Qualified Man to meet such a fate.

He reviewed all the facts he had been told. His father had been shot by a black mugger named Hugh Marlowe. The mugger was twenty-three years old, with a record as a drug dealer. Marlowe had been killed while fleeing the scene by Detective Jim Losey, who had been trailing Marlowe in a drug case. Marlowe had a gun in his hand and pointed it at Losey who had therefore shot him down, a clean shot through the bridge of his nose. When Losey investigated, he discovered Pippi De Lena, and immediately called Dante Clericuzio. Before he notified even the police. Why would he do so even if he was on the Family payroll? A great irony—Pippi De Lena, the ultimate Qualified Man, the Clericuzio Number One Hammer for over thirty years, murdered by a raggedy drug-dealing mugger.

But then why had the Don sent Vincent and Petie to transport him with an armored car and guarded him until the funeral? Why had the Don taken such elaborate precautions? During the funeral he had asked the Don. But the Don said only that it was wise to be prepared until all the facts were known. That he had made a full investigation and it seemed all the facts were true. A petty thief had made a mistake and a foolish tragedy had ensued, but then, the Don said, most tragedies were foolish.

There was no doubting the Don's grief. He had always treated Pippi as one of his sons, had indeed given him some preference, and had said to Cross, "You shall have your father's place in the Family."

But now Cross on his balcony overlooking Vegas pondered the central issue. The Don never believed in coincidence and yet here was a case bursting with coincidence. Detective Jim Losey was on the Family payroll and out of the thousands of detectives and policemen in Los Angeles, it was he who stumbled on the killing. What were the odds on that? But put that aside. Even more important, Don Domenico Clericuzio well knew it was impossible for a street mugger to get that close to Pippi De Lena. And what mugger fired six shots before fleeing? Never would the Don believe such a case.

So the question came. Had the Clericuzio decided that their greatest soldier was a danger to them? For what reason? Could they disregard his loyalty and devotion as well as their own affection for him? No, they were innocent. And the strongest evidence in their favor was that Cross himself was still alive. The Don would never allow that if they had killed Pippi. But Cross knew that he himself must be in danger.

Cross thought about his father. He had truly loved him, and Pippi was hurt that Claudia had refused to speak to him while he was alive. Yet she went to the funeral. Why? Could it be that she had finally remembered how good he was to both of them before their family fell apart?

He thought of that terrible day when he had chosen to go with his father because he realized what his father really was, knew that he could really kill Nalene if she took both children. But he had stepped up and taken his father's hand, not because of love but because of the fear in Claudia's eyes.

Cross had always thought his father was protection against the world they lived in, always thought his father invulnerable. A giver of death, not a receiver. Now he himself would have to guard against his enemies, even perhaps the Clericuzio. After all, he was rich, he owned half a billion worth of the Xanadu, his life was now worth taking.

And that made him think of the life he was now leading. To what purpose? To grow old like his father, taking all risks and then still to be killed? True, Pippi had enjoyed his life, the power, the money, but now to Cross it seemed to have been an empty life. His father had never known the happiness of loving a woman like Athena.

He was only twenty-six years old; he could make a new life. He thought of Athena and that he would see her tomorrow working for the first time, observe her make-believe life and see all the masks she could wear. How Pippi would have loved her, he loved all beautiful women. But then he thought of the wife of Virginio Ballazzo. Pippi had been fond of her, eaten at her table, hugged her, danced with her, played boccie with her husband, then planned the killing of them both.

He sighed and rose to go back into his suite. Dawn was breaking, and its light misted the neon that hung like a great theater curtain over the Strip. He could look down and see the flags of all the great casino hotels, the Sands, Caesars, the Flamingo, the Desert Inn, and the shooting volcano of the Mirage. The Xanadu was greater than them all. He watched the flags flying over the Xanadu Villas. What a dream he had lived in, and now it was dissolving, Gronevelt dead and his father murdered.

Back in his room he picked up the phone and called Lia Vazzi to come up and have breakfast with him. They had traveled from the funeral in Quogue to Vegas together. Then he called for breakfast for both of them. He remembered that Lia was fond of pancakes, an exotic dish to him still after all his years in America. The security guard arrived with Vazzi the same time as breakfast did. They ate in the kitchen of the suite.

"So what do you think?" Cross asked Lia.

"I think we should kill this detective Losey," Lia said. "I told you that a long time ago."

"So you don't believe his story?" Cross asked.

Lia was cutting his pancakes into strips. "It's a disgrace, that story," he said. "There is no way a Qualified Man like your father would let a rascal get that close to him."

"The Don thinks it's true," Cross said. "He investigated."

Lia reached for one of the Havana cigars and the glass of brandy Cross had set out for him. "I would never contradict Don Clericuzio," he said. "But let me kill Losey just to make sure."

"And what if the Clericuzio were behind him?" Cross asked.

"The Don is a man of honor," Lia said. "From the old days. If he killed Pippi, he would have killed you. He knows you. He understands you will avenge your father and he is a prudent man."

"But still," Cross said, "who would you choose to fight for? Me or the Clericuzio?"

"I don't have a choice," Lia said. "I was too close to your father and I'm too close to you. They won't let me live if you go down."

Cross for the first time had brandy with Lia for breakfast. "Maybe it's just one of those foolish things," he said.

"No," Lia said. "It's Losey."

"But he has no reason," Cross said. "Still, we'll have to find out. Now I want you to form a crew of six men, those most loyal to you, none from the Bronx Enclave. Have them ready and wait for my orders."

Lia was unusually sober. "Forgive me," he said. "I have never questioned your orders. But on this I beg you to consult with me on the overall plan."

"Good," Cross said. "Next weekend I plan to fly to France for two days. Meanwhile find out all you can about Losey."

Lia smiled at Cross. "You're going with your fiancée?"

Cross was amused by his politeness. "Yes, and with her daughter."

"The one with the quarter of her brain missing?" Lia asked. He did not mean to be offensive. It was an idiom in Italian that also included brilliant people who were forgetful.

"Yes," Cross said. "There is a doctor there who may help her."

"Bravo," Lia said. "I wish you all the best. This woman, does she know about Family matters?"

"God forbid," Cross said, and they both laughed. And Cross was wondering how Lia knew so much about his private life.

CHAPTER 17

FOR THE FIRST TIME Cross was going to watch Athena work on a movie set, to see her act out false emotions, to be someone other than herself.

He met Claudia in her office at the LoddStone lot, they would watch Athena together. There were two other women in the office, and Claudia introduced them. "This is my brother Cross and this is the director, Dita Tommey. And Falene Fante, who is working today in the picture."

Tommey gave him a searching look, thinking he was handsome enough to be in the business except that he showed no fire, no passion, he would be stone cold dead on the screen. She lost interest. "I'm just leaving," she said as she shook his hand. "I'm very sorry about your father. By the way, you're welcome on my set, Claudia and Athena vouch for you even though you're one of the producers."

Cross became aware of the other woman. She was sort of dark chocolate with an outrageously insolent face and a terrific body, which her clothes flaunted. Falene was far less formal than Tommey.

"I didn't know Claudia had such a handsome brother—and rich, too, from what I hear. If you ever need somebody to keep you company at dinner, give me a call," Falene said.

"I will," Cross said. He was not surprised by the invitation. Plenty of the showgirls and dancers at the Xanadu had been just as direct. This was a girl who was naturally flirtatious, aware of her beauty, and not about to let a man she liked the looks of escape because of social rules.

Claudia said, "We were just giving Falene a little more to do in the film. Dita thinks she's talented and so do I."

Falene gave Cross a big grin. "Yeah, now I shake my ass ten times instead of six. And I get to say to Messalina, 'All the women of Rome love you and hope for your victory.' " She paused for a minute and said, "I hear you're one of the producers. Maybe you can get them to let me shake my ass twenty times."

Cross sensed something in her, something she was trying to hide, despite her vivaciousness.

"I'm just one of the money men," Cross said. "Everybody has to shake their ass at some time or another." He smiled and said with charming simplicity, "Anyway, I wish you luck."

Falene leaned over and kissed him on the cheek. He could smell her perfume, which was heavy and erotic, and then he felt the grateful hug for his goodwill. Then she leaned back. "I have to tell you and Claudia something but in secret. I don't want to get into trouble, especially now."

Claudia, sitting at her computer, frowned and did not answer. Cross took a step away from Falene. He did not like surprises.

Falene noticed these responses. Her voice faltered a little. "I'm sorry about your father," she said. "But there's something you should hear about. Marlowe, the guy who supposedly mugged him, was a kid I grew up with and I knew him really well. Supposedly that detective Jim Losey shot Marlowe who supposedly shot your father. But I know Marlowe never had a gun. He was scared shitless of guns. Marlowe did small-time drugs and played the clarinet. And he was such a sweet coward. Jim Losey and his partner, Phil Sharkey, used to pick him up sometimes and ride him around so that he could spot dealers for them. Marlowe was so scared of jail, he was a police informant. All of a sudden he's a mugger and a murderer. I know Marlowe, he wouldn't harm a soul."

Claudia was silent. Falene waved to her and went out the door, then came back. "Remember," she said, "it's a secret between us."

"It's all gone and forgotten," Cross said with his most reassuring smile. "And your story won't change anything."

"I just had to get it off my chest," Falene said. "Marlowe was such a good kid." She left.

"What do you think?" Claudia said to Cross. "What the hell could that be about?"

Cross shrugged. "Druggies are always full of surprises. He needed dope money and he does a stickup and he gets unlucky."

"I guess," Claudia said. "And Falene is so good-hearted she'll believe anything. But it is an irony, our father dying like that."

Cross looked at her stone-faced. "Everybody gets unlucky once."

He spent the rest of the afternoon watching scenes being shot. One scene showed the hero, unarmed, defeating three armed men. This offended him, it was ridiculous. A hero should never be put in such a hopeless position. All it proved was that he was too dumb to be a hero. Then he watched Athena do a love scene and a quarrel scene. He was a little disappointed, she seemed to do little acting, the other actors seemed to outshine her. Cross was too inexperienced to know that what Athena was doing would register much more forcefully on film, that the camera would work its magic for her.

And he did not discover the real Athena. The acting she did was only for a few short snippets of time, and then there were long intervals in between. You could not see any of the electricity that would flash across the screen. Athena even seemed less beautiful when she was acting before the camera.

He said nothing of this when he spent the night with her that night in Malibu. After they had made love and she was cooking their midnight supper, she said, "I wasn't very good today, was I?" She gave him her catlike grin, which always sent a shock of pleasure through him. "I didn't want to show you my best moves," she said. "I knew you'd be standing there trying to figure me out."

He laughed. Always he was delighted by her perception of his character. "No, you weren't much," he said. "Would you like me to fly with you to Paris Friday?"

Athena was surprised. He knew she was surprised by her eyes. Her face never changed, she was in control. She thought it over. "That could be a big help," she said. "And we could see Paris together."

"And we'll be back Monday," Cross asked.

"Yes," Athena said. "I have to shoot Tuesday morning. We have only a few weeks to go on the picture."

"And then?" Cross asked.

"Then I'll retire and take care of my daughter," Athena said. "Besides, I don't want to keep her a secret much longer."

"The doctor in Paris is the final word?" Cross asked.

"Nobody's the final word," Athena said. "Not on this stuff. But he's close."

On Friday evening they flew to Paris on a specially chartered plane. Athena was disguised in a wig, and her makeup veiled her beauty in such a way as to make her even look homely. She wore loosely fitting clothing that hid her figure entirely and in some ways made her look matronly. Cross was amazed. She even walked differently.

On the plane Bethany was fascinated to find herself looking down on the earth. She roamed the plane looking out all the different windows. She seemed a little startled, her usually blank expression became almost normal.

They went from the plane to a small hotel off Georges-Mandel Avenue. They had a suite with two separate bedrooms, one for Cross and one for Athena and Bethany, the sitting room between them. It was ten in the morning; Athena removed her wig and makeup and changed her clothes. She could not bear to be homely in Paris.

At noon the three of them were in the doctor's office, a small chateau set on its own grounds and enclosed by an iron fence. There was a guard at the gate, and after checking their names he let them in.

They were met at the door by a maid who led them into a huge sitting room, which was densely furnished. There the doctor awaited them.

Dr. Ocell Gerard was a huge, heavy man, carefully dressed in a beautifully cut suit of brown pin stripes, a white shirt, and a dark brown silk tie to match. He had a round face, which should have had a beard to hide his heavy jowls. His thick lips were a dusky red. He introduced himself to Athena and Cross but ignored the child. Both Athena and Cross felt an immediate aversion to the man. He did not look like a doctor suitable to the sensitive profession he practiced.

There was a table set for tea and pastries. A maid attended to them. They were joined by two nurses, young women clad in strict professional attire, white caps and ivory-colored blouses and skirts. The two nurses watched Bethany intensely all during the meal.

Dr. Gerard addressed Athena. "Madame, I would like to thank you for your very generous contribution to our Medical Institute for Autistic Children. I have observed your request for complete confidentiality, which is why I'm conducting this examination here in my own private center. Now tell me exactly what you expect of me." His voice was a mellow bass, it was magnetic. It attracted Bethany's attention, and she stared at him, but he ignored her.

Athena was nervous, she really didn't like the man. "I want you to evaluate. I want her to have some sort of normal life if possible and I will give up everything to achieve that. I want you to accept her into your Institute, I am willing to live in France and help in her schooling."

She said this with enchanting sadness and hope, with such an air of self-abnegation, that the two nurses gazed at her almost adoringly. Cross was aware she was using all her acting skills to convince the doctor to take Bethany into the Institute. He saw her reach her arm out to clasp Bethany's hand with a caressing gesture.

Only Dr. Gerard seemed unimpressed. He did not look at Bethany. He addressed himself directly to Athena. "Do not deceive yourself," he said. "All your love will not help this child. I have examined her records and there is no doubt she is genuinely autistic. She cannot return your love. She does not live in our world. She does not even live in the world of animals. She lives on a different star, absolutely alone."

He continued, "You are not at fault. Nor, I believe, is the father. This is one of those mysterious complexities of the human condition. Here is what I can do. I will examine and test her more thoroughly. Then I will tell you what we at the Institute can and cannot do. If I cannot help, you must take her home. If we can, you will leave her with me in France for five years."

He spoke to one of the nurses in French, and the woman left and returned with a huge book containing photographs of famous paintings. She gave the book to Bethany, but it was too big to fit on her lap. For the first time Dr. Gerard spoke to her. He spoke to her in French. She immediately put the textbook on the table and began to turn the pages. Soon she was lost in studying the pictures.

The doctor seemed ill at ease. "I don't mean to be offensive," he said. "But this is in the best interest of your child. I know Mr. De Lena is not your husband, but is it possible he is the father of your child? If so, I would want to test him."

Athena said, "I did not know him when my daughter was born."

"Bon," the doctor said. He shrugged. "Such things are always possible."

Cross laughed. "Maybe the doctor sees some symptoms in me."

The doctor's thick red lips pursed as he nodded and smiled amiably. "You do have certain symptoms. So do we all. Who knows? A centimeter either way, all of us could be autistic. Now I must make a thorough examination of the child and run some tests. It will take at the very least four hours. Why don't the two of you take a stroll through our lovely Paris. Mr. De Lena, your first time?"

"Yes," Cross said.

Athena said, "I want to remain with my daughter."

"As you wish, madame," he said and then spoke to Cross. "Enjoy your stroll. I detest Paris myself. If a city could be autistic, it would be Paris."

A taxi was called, and Cross went back to the hotel room. He had no desire to see Paris without Athena and he needed rest. Besides, he had come to Paris to clear his head, to think things out.

He pondered what Falene had told him. He remembered that Losey had come to Malibu alone, detectives usually worked in pairs. Before leaving Paris he had asked Vazzi to look into it.

At four, Cross was back in the doctor's sitting room. They were waiting for him. Bethany was poring over the book of paintings, Athena was pale, the only physical sign that Cross knew could not be acting. Bethany was also gobbling a plate of pastries, and the doctor took it away from her, saying something in French. Bethany did not protest. A nurse came then to take her to the playroom.

"Forgive me," the doctor said to Cross. "But I must ask you some questions."

"Whatever you like," Cross said.

The doctor rose from his chair and strode about the room. "I will tell you what I have told madame," the doctor said. "There are no miracles in these cases, absolutely none. With long training there could be enormous improvement, in some cases, not many. And with Mademoiselle, there are certain limits. She must stay in my institution in Nice for five years at least. We have teachers there who can explore every possibility. In that time we will know whether it is possible for her to live a nearly normal life. Or whether she must be institutionalized forever."

Here Athena began to weep. She held a small blue silk handkerchief to her eyes and Cross could smell its perfume.

The doctor looked at her impassively. "Madame has agreed. She will join the Institute as a teacher. . . . So."

He sat directly across from Cross. "There are some very good signs. She has genuine talent as a painter. Certain senses alert, not withdrawn. She was interested when I spoke French, a language she cannot understand but intuits. That is a very good sign. Another good sign: The child showed some signs of missing you this afternoon, she has some feeling for another human being and that may be extended. It is highly unusual, but can be explained in not so mysterious a way. When I explored this with her she said you were beautiful. Now, you must not be offended, Mr. De Lena. I ask this question only for medical reasons to help the child, not accuse you. Have you sexually stimulated the girl in any way, perhaps unintentionally?"

Cross was so startled he burst out laughing. "I didn't know she responded to me. And I never gave her anything to respond to."

Athena's cheeks were red with anger. "This is ridiculous," she said. "He was never alone with her."

The doctor persisted. "Have you at any time given her physical caresses? I don't mean clasping her hand, patting her hair, or even kissing her cheek. The girl is nubile, she would respond simply out of physicality. You would not be the first man tempted by such innocence."

"Maybe she knows about my relationship with her mother," Cross said.

"She doesn't care about her mother," the doctor said. "Forgive me, madame, that is one of the things you must accept—nor her mother's beauty or her fame. They literally do not exist for her. It is you who she extends herself to. Think. Perhaps an innocent tenderness, something inadvertent."

Cross looked at him coolly. "If I did it I would tell you. If that would help her."

"Do you feel tenderness for this girl?" the doctor asked.

Cross considered for a moment. "Yes," he said.

Dr. Gerard leaned back and clasped his hands. "I believe you," he said. "And that gives me great hope. If she can respond to you, she may be helped to respond to others. She may tolerate her mother someday and that will be enough for you, am I right, madame?"

"Oh, Cross," Athena said. "I hope you're not angry."

"It's OK, really," Cross said.

Dr. Gerard looked at him carefully. "You are not offended?" he said. "Most men would be extremely upset. One patient's father actually struck me. But you are not angry. Tell me why."

He could not explain to this man, or even to Athena, how the sight of Bethany in her hugging machine affected him. How it reminded him of Tiffany and all the showgirls he had made love to who had left him feeling empty. How his relationships with all the Clericuzio and even with his father left him with feelings of isolation and despair. And finally how all the victims he had left behind seemed the victims of some ghostly world that became real only in his dreams.

Cross looked the doctor directly in the eye. "Maybe because I'm autistic too," he said. "Or maybe because I have worse crimes to hide."

The doctor leaned back and said in a satisfied voice, "Ah." He paused and smiled for the first time. "Would you like to come in for some tests?" They both laughed.

"Now, madame," Dr. Gerard said. "I understand you catch a plane back to America tomorrow morning. Why not leave your daughter with me now. My nurses are very good, and I can assure you the girl will not miss you."

"But I'll miss her," Athena said. "Could I keep her tonight and bring her back tomorrow morning? We have a chartered plane so I can leave when I like."

"Certainly," the doctor said. "Bring her here in the morning. I will have my nurses escort her down to Nice. You have the phone number of the Institute and you can call me as often as you like."

They got up to go. Athena impetuously kissed the doctor on the cheek. The doctor flushed, he was not insensible to her beauty and fame, despite his ogreish appearance.

Athena, Bethany, and Cross spent the rest of the day strolling the streets of Paris. Athena bought new clothes for Bethany, a full wardrobe. She bought painting supplies and a huge suitcase to hold all the new things. They sent everything to the hotel.

They had dinner in a restaurant on the Champs Elysées. Bethany ate greedily, especially the pastries. She had not spoken a word all day or responded to any of Athena's gestures of affection.

Cross had never seen such a show of love as that Athena showed Bethany. Except when as a child he saw his own mother, Nalene, brushing Claudia's hair.

During dinner Athena held Bethany's hand, brushed the crumbs off her face, and explained that she would return to France in a month to stay with her at the school for the next five years.

Bethany paid no attention.

Athena was enthusiastic when she told Bethany how they could learn French together, go to museums together and see all the great paintings, and how Bethany could spend as much time as she wanted on her own paintings. She described how they would travel all over Europe, to Spain, to Italy, to Germany.

Then Bethany spoke the first words of the day. "I want my machine."

As always Cross was stricken by a sense of holiness. The beautiful girl was like a copy of a great portrait painting but without the soul of the artist, as if her body had been left empty for God.

It was after dark when they walked back to their hotel. Bethany was between them, and they swung her hands so that she lifted up in the air, and for once she allowed it, in fact seemed to delight in it so much that they continued past the hotel.

It was at this moment that Cross had the precise feeling of happiness he had had at the picnic. And it consisted of nothing more than the three of them linked together, holding hands. He was filled with wonder and horror at his sentimentality.

Finally they returned to the hotel. After Athena had helped Bethany to bed, she came into the sitting room of the suite, where Cross was waiting for her. They sat side by side on the lavender sofa holding hands.

"Lovers in Paris," Athena said, smiling at him. "And we never got to sleep together in a French bed."

"Are you worried about leaving Bethany here?" Cross asked.

"No," Athena said. "She won't miss us."

"Five years," Cross said, "is a long time. And you're willing to give up five years and your profession?"

Athena got up from the sofa and walked up and down the room. She spoke passionately. "I glory in being able to do without acting. When I was a kid I dreamed of being a great heroine, Marie Antoinette going to the guillotine, Joan of Arc burning at the stake, Marie Curie saving mankind from some great disease. And of course, also giving up everything for the love of a great man, most ridiculous of all. I dreamed of living a heroic life and knew I'd surely go to Heaven. That I would be pure in mind and body. I detested the idea of doing anything that would compromise me, especially for money. I was determined that under no circumstance would I ever harm another human being. Everyone would love me, including myself. I knew I was smart, everyone told me I was beautiful, and I proved to be not only competent but talented.

"So what did I do? I fell in love with Boz Skannet. I slept with men not out of desire but to further my career. I gave life to a human being who may never love me or anyone. Then I very cleverly maneuver or request the murder of my husband. Not so subtly I ask who will murder this husband of mine who is such a threat to me now." She pressed his hand. "And for this I thank you."

Cross said to reassure her, "You didn't do any of those things. It was just your destiny, as we say in my family. As for Skannet, he was a stone in your shoe, another family saying, so why shouldn't you get rid of him?"

Athena kissed him briefly on the lips. "Now I have," she said. "My knight errant. The only trouble is you don't stop at killing dragons."

"After five years, if the doctor says she can't improve, then what?" Cross asked.

"I don't care what anyone says," Athena said. "There's always hope. I'll be with her the rest of my life."

"And you won't miss your work?" he asked.

"Of course I'll miss it, and I'll miss you," Athena said. "But finally I'll do what I believe is right, not just be a heroine in a movie." Her voice was amused. Then she said with a flat tone, "I want her to love me, that's all I want."

They kissed each other good night and went into their separate bedrooms.

The next morning they took Bethany to the doctor's office. Athena had a difficult time saying good-bye to her daughter. She hugged the girl and wept, but Bethany would have none of it. She pushed her mother away and got ready to repulse Cross, but he did not move to embrace her.

Cross was momentarily angry with Athena for being so helpless with her daughter. The doctor, observing this, said to Athena, "When you return, you will need a great deal of training to cope with this child."

"I'll be back as quickly as I can," Athena said.

"You needn't hurry," the doctor said. "She lives in a world where time does not exist."

On the plane back to L.A., Cross and Athena agreed that he would go on to Vegas and not accompany Athena to Malibu. There had only been one terrible moment on the whole trip. For a full half hour Athena had doubled over in her grief, wordlessly crying. Then she became calm.

When they parted Athena said to Cross, "I'm sorry we never got to make love in Paris." But he understood she was being kind. That at this particular time, she was repulsed by the thought of them making love. That like her daughter, she was now separated from the world.

Cross was met at the airport by a big limo driven by a soldier from the Hunting Lodge. Lia Vazzi was in the back. Lia closed the glass partition so that the driver couldn't hear their conversation.

"Detective Losey was up to see me again," he said. "The next time he comes will be his last."

"Be patient," Cross said.

"I know the signs, trust me on this," Lia said. "Something else. A crew from the Bronx Enclave has moved into place in Los Angeles, I don't know by whose orders. I would say you need bodyguards."

"Not yet," Cross said. "You have your six-man crew together?"

"Yes," Lia said. "But they are men who will not act directly against the Clericuzio."

When they got to the Xanadu, Cross found a memo from Andrew Pollard, a complete file on Jim Losey, that made for interesting reading. And a piece of information that could be acted on immediately.

Cross drew a hundred grand from the casino cage, all in C notes. He told Lia they were going to L.A. Lia would be his driver and he wanted no one else with them. He showed him Pollard's memo. They flew to L.A. the next day and rented a car to drive to Santa Monica.

Phil Sharkey was mowing the lawn in front of his house. Cross got out of the car with Lia and identified himself as a friend of Pollard's who was in need of information. Lia carefully studied Sharkey's face. Then he went back to the car.

Phil Sharkey was not as impressive-looking as Jim Losey, but he looked tough enough. He also looked as if his years of police work had burned out his confidence in his fellow human beings. He had that alert suspiciousness, that seriousness of manner, that the best cops have. But he was obviously not a happy man.

Sharkey ushered Cross into his house, which was really a bungalow, the insides dreary and worn; it had the forlorn look of a womanless and childless dwelling. The first thing Sharkey did was call Pollard and confirm the identity of his visitor. Then without offering any courtesy, a seat, or a drink, he said to Cross, "Go ahead, ask."

Cross opened his briefcase and took out a packet of hundreds. "There's ten grand," he said. "That's just for letting me talk. But it will take a little time. How about a beer and a place to sit?"

Sharkey's face broke into a grin. It was curiously affable, the good cop in the partnership, Cross thought.

Sharkey shoved the money casually into his trouser pocket. "I like you," Sharkey said. "You're smart. You know it's money that talks, not bullshit."

They sat at a little round table on the back porch of the bungalow, which overlooked Ocean Avenue to the sandy beach and water beyond, as they drank their beers out of the bottle. Sharkey patted his pocket to make sure the money was still there.

Cross said, "If I hear the right answers, there's another twenty grand for you right after. Then, if you keep your mouth shut about me being here, I'll come around to see you in two months with another fifty grand."

Sharkey gave his grin, but now there was a hint of mischief in it. "In two months you won't care who I tell, is that it?"

"Yes," Cross said.

Sharkey was serious now. "I'm not telling you anything that gets anybody indicted."

"Hey, then you don't know who I really am," Cross said. "Maybe you better call Pollard again."

Sharkey said curtly, "I know who you are. Jim Losey told me I should always treat you right. All the way." And then he put on his sympathetic listening style that was part of his profession.

Cross said, "You and Jim Losey were partners for the last ten years and you were both making good money on the side. And then you retired. I'd like to know why."

"So, it's Jim you're after," Sharkey said. "That's very dangerous. He was the bravest and the smartest cop I ever knew."

"How about honest?" Cross asked.

"We were cops, and in Los Angeles," Sharkey said. "Do you know what the fuck that means? If we do our real job and kick the shit out of the spics and blacks, we could get indicted and lose our jobs. The only ones we could arrest without getting into trouble were the white schmucks who had money. Look, I got no prejudice, but why should I throw white guys in jail when I can't throw the other kind in jail? That's not right."

"But I understand Jim got a chest full of medals," Cross said. "You got some too."

Sharkey gave him a dismissive shrug. "You can't help being a hero cop in this town if you have just a little bit of balls. A lot of those guys didn't know they could do business if they talked nice. And some of them were out-and-out killers. So we had to defend ourselves and we got some medals. Believe me, we never looked for a fight."

Cross was doubting everything Sharkey was saying. Jim Losey was a natural-born strong-arm guy despite his fancy clothes.

"Were you two partners in everything?" Cross asked. "Did you know everything that was going on."

Sharkey laughed. "Jim Losey? He was the boss always. Sometimes I didn't even know exactly what we were doing. I didn't even know how much we were getting paid. Jim handled all that and he gave me what he said was my fair share." He paused a moment. "He had his own rules."

"So how did you make money?" Cross asked.

"We were on the pad for some of the big gambling syndicates," Sharkey said. "Sometimes a payoff for the drug guys. There was a time when Jim Losey wouldn't take drug money but then every cop in the world started taking it, so we did."

"Did you and Losey ever use a black kid named Marlowe to finger big shot drug dealers?" Cross asked.

"Sure," Sharkey said. "Marlowe. A nice kid scared of his own shadow. We used him all the time."

Cross said, "So when you heard Losey shot him running away from a mug-murder, you were surprised?" Cross asked.

"Hell, no," Sharkey said. "Druggies graduate. But they are so fucked up, they always botch it. And Jim, in that situation, never gives the warning we're taught to give. He just shoots."

"But wasn't it a strange coincidence," Cross said, "their paths crossing like that?"

For the first time Sharkey's face seemed to lose its toughness, grow sad. "It's fishy," he said. "The whole thing is fishy. But now I guess I have to give you something. Jim Losey was brave, women loved him and men held him in high regard. I was his partner and I felt the same way. But the truth is he was always a fishy guy."

"So it could have been some sort of setup," Cross said.

"No, no," Sharkey said. "You have to understand. The job makes you take graft. But it doesn't make you a hit man. Jim Losey would never do that. I'll never believe that."

"So why did you take your retirement after that?" Cross asked.

"It was just that Jim was getting me nervous," Sharkey said.

"I met Losey out at Malibu not long ago," Cross said. "He was alone. Does he often operate without you?"

Now Sharkey gave his grin again. "Sometimes," he said. "That particular time he went to take a shot at the actress. You'd be surprised how often he made a score with big stars in that business. Sometimes he had lunches with people and he didn't want me around."

"One other thing," Cross said. "Was Jim Losey a racist? Did he hate blacks?"

Sharkey gave him a look of amused astonishment. "Of course he did. You're one of those bullshit liberals, right? You think that's terrible? Just go out and put a year in on the job. You'll vote to put them all in the zoo."

"I have another question," Cross said. "You ever see him with a short guy wearing a funny hat?"

"An Italian guy," Sharkey said. "We had lunch and then Jim told me to get lost. Spooky guy."

Cross reached into his briefcase and took out another two packets of money. "Here's twenty grand," he said. "And remember, you keep your mouth shut and you get another fifty grand. OK?"

"I know who you are," Sharkey said.

"Sure you do," Cross said. "I instructed Pollard to tell you who I am."

"I know who you really are," Sharkey said with his infectious grin. "That's why I don't take your whole briefcase right now. And why I'll keep quiet for two months. Between you and Losey, I don't know who'll kill me faster."

Cross De Lena realized he had enormous problems. He knew Jim Losey was on the Clericuzio Family "pad." That he received fifty thousand a year as a salary, and bonuses for special jobs, but none of these had included murder. It was enough for Cross to make a final judgment. Dante and Losey had killed his father. It was an easy judgment for him to make, he was not bound by the legal laws of evidence. And his whole training with the Clericuzio helped him make the verdict of guilty. He knew his father's competence and character. No mugger could get close to him. He also knew Dante's character and competence and Dante's dislike for his father.

The big question was this: Had Dante acted on his own or had the Don commanded the killing? But the Clericuzio had no reason; his father had been loyal for over forty years and an important factor in the Family ascension. He had been the great general in the war against the Santadio. And Cross wondered, not for the first time, why no one had ever told him the details of that war, not his father, not Gronevelt, not Giorgio or Petie or Vincent.

The more he thought about it, the more Cross was sure of one thing: The Don had no hand in the killing of his father. Don Domenico was a very conservative man of business. He rewarded loyal service, he did not punish it. He was extremely fair-minded, to the point of cruelty. But the clinching argument was this: He would never have let Cross live if he had killed Pippi. That was the proof of the Don's innocence.

Don Domenico believed in God, he sometimes believed in Fate, but he did not believe in coincidence. The coincidence of Jim Losey being the cop who shot the mugger who shot Pippi would be absolutely rejected by the Don. He had surely made his own investigation and discovered Dante's connection with Losey. And he would not only know Dante's guilt but his motive.

And what about Rose Marie, Dante's mother? What did she know? When she had heard of Pippi's death, she had had her most serious fit, screaming unintelligibly, weeping incessantly, so that the Don had sent her to the East Hampton psychiatric clinic he had funded many years ago. She would be there for at least a month.

Visitors to Rose Marie in the clinic had always been forbidden by the Don, except for Dante, Giorgio, Vincent, and Petie. But Cross often sent flowers and baskets of fruit. So what the hell was Rose Marie so upset about? Did she know about Dante's guilt, understand his motive? At that moment Cross thought about the Don saying that Dante would be his heir. That was ominous. Cross decided he would visit Rose Marie at the clinic, despite the Don's interdiction. He would go with flowers, and fruit, and chocolates and cheeses, with true affection, but with the purpose of tricking her into betraying her son.

Two days later, Cross entered the lobby of the psychiatric clinic in East Hampton. There were two guards at the door, and one escorted him to the reception desk.

The woman at the reception desk was middle-aged and well dressed. When he stated his business, she gave him a charming smile and said he would have to wait a half hour because Rose Marie was undergoing a minor medical procedure. She would notify him when it was done.

Cross sat down in the waiting room of the reception area, just off the lobby, where there were tables and soft armchairs. He picked up a copy of a Hollywood magazine. Reading it, he came across an article on Jim Losey, the detective hero of Los Angeles. The article detailed his heroic achievements, capped by his killing the mugger-murderer Marlowe. Cross was amused by two things. That his father was referred to as the owner of a financial service agency and a typical helpless victim of a brutal criminal. And by the tag line of the article, which asserted that if there were more cops like Jim Losey, street crime would be under control.

A nurse tapped him on the shoulder. She was an impressively strong-looking woman, but she said with a pleasant smile, "I'll bring you up."

Cross picked up the box of chocolates and the flowers he had brought and followed her up a short flight of stairs and then down a long corridor spaced by doors. At the last door the nurse used a master key and opened it. She motioned Cross inside and closed the door after him.

Rose Marie, clad in a gray robe, her hair neatly braided, was watching a small TV. When she saw Cross she jumped up from the couch and flew into his arms. She was weeping. Cross kissed her cheek and gave her the chocolates and flowers.

"Oh, you came to see me," she said. "I thought you hated me for what I did to your father."

"You didn't do anything to my father," Cross said, and led her back to the couch. Then he turned off the TV. He kneeled beside the couch. "I was worried about you."

She reached out and stroked his hair. "You were always so beautiful," she said. "I hated that you were your father's son. I was glad to see him dead. But I always knew terrible things would happen. I filled the air and the earth with poison for him. Now you think my father will let this pass?"

"The Don is a just man," Cross said. "He will never blame you."

"He has fooled you as he has tricked everyone else," Rose Marie said. "Never trust him. He betrayed his own daughter, he betrayed his grandson and he betrayed his nephew Pippi. . . . And now he will betray you."

Her voice had risen to a loud pitch and Cross was afraid she would go into one of her fits.

"Quiet down, Aunt Roe," Cross said. "Just tell me what upset you so that you had to come back here." He stared into her eyes and thought how pretty she must have been as a young girl, the innocence still in her eyes.

Rose Marie whispered, "Make them tell you about the Santadio War, then you will understand everything." She looked past Cross and then covered her head with her hands. Cross turned. The door opened. Vincent and Petie were standing there silently. Rose Marie jumped off the couch and ran into the bedroom and slammed the door shut.

Vincent's granite face showed pity and despair. "Jesus Christ," he said. He went to the bedroom door and knocked, then said through it, "Roe, open the door. We're your brothers. We won't hurt you . . ."

Cross said, "What a coincidence to meet you here. I was visiting Rose Marie too."

Vincent never had any time for bullshit. "We're not here to visit. The Don wants to see you in Quogue."

Cross appraised the situation. Obviously the receptionist had called somebody in Quogue. Obviously, it was a planned procedure. And just as obviously, the Don did not want him talking to Rose Marie. That Petie and Vincent had been sent meant that it was not a hit, they would not be so carelessly exposed.

This was confirmed when Vincent said, "Cross, I'll go with you in your car. Petie can go in his." A hit in the Clericuzio Family would never be one on one.

Cross said, "We can't leave Rose Marie like this."

"Sure we can," Petie said. "The nurse will just shoot her up."

Cross tried to make conversation while he drove. "Vincent, you guys sure got here fast."

"Petie drove," Vincent said. "He's a fucking maniac." He paused for a moment and then said in a worried voice, "Cross, you know the rules, how come you visit Rose Marie?"

"Hey," Cross said, "Rose Marie was one of my favorite aunts while I was growing up."

"The Don doesn't like it," Vincent said. "He's very pissed off. He says it's not like Cross. He knows."

"I'll straighten it out," Cross said. "But I was really worried about your sister. How's she doing?"

Vincent sighed. "This time it may be for keeps. You know she was sweet on your old man when she was a kid. Who could figure Pippi being killed would throw her so much?"

Cross caught the false note in Vincent's voice. He knew something. But Cross only said, "My father was always fond of Rose Marie."

"In the past years she wasn't so fond of him," Vincent said. "Especially when she got into one of her fits. You should hear the things she said about him then."

Cross said casually, "You were in the Santadio War. How come you guys never talk about it to me?"

"Because we never talk about operations," Vincent said. "My father taught us it served no purpose. You just go on. There's plenty of trouble in the present to worry about."

"My father was a big hero though, right?" Cross said.

Vincent smiled for just a moment, his stone face almost softened. "Your father was a genius," Vincent said. "He could plan an operation like Napoleon. Nothing ever went wrong when he planned it. Maybe once or twice because of bad luck."

"So he planned the war against the Santadio," Cross said.

"Ask the Don these questions," Vincent said. "Now talk about something else."

"OK," Cross said. "Am I going to be knocked off like my father?"

The usually cold and stone-faced Vincent reacted violently. He grabbed the steering wheel and forced Cross to park on the side of the highway. His voice choked with emotion when he said, "Are you crazy? Do you think the Clericuzio Family would do such a thing? Your father had Clericuzio blood. He was our best soldier, he saved us. The Don loved him as much as any of his sons. Jesus Christ, why do you ask something like that?"

Cross said meekly, "I just got scared, you guys popping up."

"Get back on the road," Vincent said disgustedly. "Your father and me and Giorgio and Petie fought together during really rough times. There is no way we could go against each other. Pippi just got unlucky, a crazy jigaboo mugger."

They rode the rest of the way in silence.

At the mansion in Quogue, there were the usual two guards at the gate and one man sitting on the porch. There did not seem to be any unusual activity.

Don Clericuzio, Giorgio, and Petie were awaiting them in the den of the mansion. On the bar was a box of Havana cigars and a mug filled with twisted black Italian cheroots.

Don Clericuzio sat in one of the huge brown leather armchairs. Cross went to greet him and was surprised when the Don pushed himself up to stand, with an agility that belied his age, and embraced him. After which he motioned Cross to the huge coffee table on which various dishes of cheeses and dried meats were spread.

Cross sensed that the Don was not yet ready to speak. He made himself a sandwich of mozzarella cheese and prosciutto. The prosciutto was thin slabs of dark red meat fringed with very tender white fat. The mozzarella was a white ball so fresh it was still sweating milk. It was tied off on top with a thick salty knob like the knot in a rope. The closest that the Don had ever come to boasting was that he never ate a mozzarella that was more than thirty minutes old.

Vincent and Petie were also helping themselves to food, while Giorgio served as bartender, bringing wine to the Don and soft drinks to the others. The Don only ate the dripping mozzarella, letting it melt inside his mouth. Petie gave him one of the twisted cheroots and lit it for him. What a wonderful stomach the old man had, thought Cross.

Don Clericuzio said abruptly, "Croccifixio, whatever you seek now from Rose Marie, I will tell you. And you suspect something amiss about your father's death. You are wrong. I have had inquiries made, the story is true as it stands. Pippi was unlucky. He was the most prudent of men in his profession but such ludicrous accidents happen. Let me set your mind at rest. Your father was my nephew and a Clericuzio, and one of my dearest friends."

"Tell me about the war with the Santadio," Cross said.

BOOK VII

The Santadio War

CHAPTER 18

IT IS DANGEROUS to be reasonable with stupid people," Don Clericuzio said, as he sipped from his wine glass. He put his cheroot aside. "Pay strict attention. It's a long story and everything was not what it seemed to be. It was almost thirty years ago . . ." He motioned to his three sons and said, "If I forget something important, help me." His three sons smiled at the idea that he would forget something important.

The light in the den was a soft golden haze tinged with cigar smoke, and even the smell of the food was so sharply aromatic that it seemed to affect the light.

"I became convinced of that after the Santadio . . ." He paused a moment to sip his wine. "There was a time when the Santadio were our equal in power. But the Santadio made too many enemies, they drew too much attention from the authorities and they had no sense of justice. They created a world without any values and a world without any sense of justice cannot continue to exist.

"I proposed many arrangements with the Santadio, I made concessions, I wanted to live in a world of peace. But because they were strong, they had a sense of power that violent people have. They believe that power is all. And so it came to war between us."

Giorgio interrupted. "Why does Cross have to know this story? How can it benefit him or benefit us?"

Vincent looked away from Cross, Petie stared at him, his head tilted back, appraising. None of the three sons wanted the Don to tell the story.

"Because we owe it to Pippi and Croccifixio," said the Don. And then he spoke directly to Cross. "Make of this story what you will but I and my sons are innocent of the crime you suspect. Pippi was a son to me, you are to me as a grandchild. All of Clericuzio blood."

Giorgio said again, "This can do all of us no good."

Don Clericuzio waved his arm impatiently, then said to his sons, "It's true, what I've said so far?"

They nodded and Petie said, "We should have wiped them out from the beginning."

The Don shrugged and said to Cross, "My sons were young, your father was young, none of them yet thirty. I didn't want to waste their lives in a great war. Don Santadio, God have mercy on his soul, had six sons but he thought of them more as soldiers than as sons. Jimmy Santadio was the oldest and he worked with our old friend Gronevelt, God have mercy on him as well. The Santadio then had half the Hotel. Jimmy was the best of the lot, the only one who saw that peace was the best solution for all of us. But the old man and his other sons were hot for blood.

"Now it was not to my interest for the war to be bloody. I wanted time to use reason, to convince them of the good sense of my proposals. I would give them all of the drugs, and they would give me all of the gambling. I wanted their half of the Xanadu and in return they would control all drugs in America, a dirty business that required a violent and firm hand. A very sensible proposal. There was far more money in drugs and it was a business that did not involve long-term strategy. A dirty business with a lot of operational work. All this added to the Santadio strength. I wanted the Clericuzio to control all of gambling, not as risky as drugs, not as profitable, but, managed cleverly, more valuable in the long term. And this added to the Clericuzio strength. I always aimed to finally be a member of society, and gambling could become a legal gold mine with none of the everyday risk and dirty work. In this, time has proved me justified.

"Unfortunately, the Santadio wanted everything. Everything. Think of it then, nephew, it was a very dangerous time for us all. By then the FBI knew we Families existed and cooperated with each other. The government, with its resources and technology, brought many Families down. The wall of *omertà* was cracking.

"Young men, born in America, were cooperating with the authorities to save their own skins. Luckily, I established the Bronx Enclave, and brought new people from Sicily to be my soldiers.

"The only thing I have never been able to understand is how women can cause so much trouble. My daughter, Rose Marie, was eighteen years old at this time. How did she become besotted over Jimmy Santadio? She said they were like Romeo and Juliet. Who were Romeo and Juliet? Who in Christ's name were those people? Certainly not Italians. When I was told of this, I reconciled myself. I reopened negotiations with the Santadio Family, I lowered my demands so that the two Families could exist together. In their stupidity, they read this as a sign of weakness. And so began the whole tragedy that has lasted all these years."

Here the Don broke off. Giorgio helped himself to a glass of wine, a slice of bread, and a chunk of the milky cheese. Then he stood behind the Don.

"Why today?" Giorgio asked.

"Because my great nephew here is worried about how his father died and we must dispel any suspicions he may have of us," the Don said.

"I have no suspicions of you, Don Domenico," Cross said.

"Everyone has suspicions of everything," the Don said. "That's human nature. But let me continue. Rose Marie was young, she had no knowledge of worldly affairs. She was heartbroken when at first both Families opposed the match. But she had no real idea why. And so she decided to bring everyone together, she believed love would conquer all, she later informed me. She was very loving then. And she was the light of my life. My wife died young, and I never remarried because I could not bear to share Rose Marie with a stranger. I denied her nothing and I had high hopes for her future. But a marriage with the Santadio, I could not bear. I forbade it. I was young then too. I thought my orders would be obeyed by my children. I wanted her to go to college, marry someone from a different world. Giorgio, Vincent, and Petie had to support me in this life, I needed their help. And I had hopes that their children could also escape to a better world. And my youngest son,

Silvio." The Don pointed to the photograph on the mantelpiece of the den.

Cross had never really taken a close look at the photo, he had not known its history. The photo was of a young man of twenty who looked very much like Rose Marie, only more gentle, his eyes grayer and more intelligent. It was a face that showed such a good soul that Cross wondered if it had been retouched.

The air in the windowless room was becoming more pungent with cigar smoke. Giorgio had lit a huge Havana.

Don Clericuzio said, "I doted on Silvio even more than on Rose Marie. He had a better heart than most people. He had been accepted to the university with a scholarship. There was every hope for him. But he was too innocent."

Vincent said, "He had no street smarts. None of us would have gone. Not like he did, without protection."

Giorgio took up the story. "Rose Marie and Jimmy Santadio were shacked up in this Commack Motel. And Rose Marie came up with the idea that if Jimmy and Silvio talked, they could bring the two Families together. She called Silvio and he went to the motel without telling anybody. The three of them discussed strategies. Silvio always called Rose Marie 'Roe.' His last words to her were, 'Everything is going to be okay, Roe. Dad will listen to me.' "

But Silvio was never to speak to his father. Unfortunately, two of the Santadio brothers, Fonsa and Italo, were doing a guardian-like surveillance on their brother Jimmy.

The Santadio with their violent paranoia suspected that Rose Marie was leading their brother Jimmy into a trap. Or at least luring him into a marriage that would lessen their own power in their Family. And Rose Marie was offensive to them with her ferocious courage and determination to marry their brother. She had even defied her own father, the great Don Clericuzio. She would stop at nothing.

Recognizing Silvio, when he left the motel they trapped him on the Robert Moses Causeway and shot him dead. They stripped him of his wallet and watch to make it look like a robbery. It was typical of the Santadio mentality, their act was one of savagery.

Don Clericuzio was not deceived for a moment. But then Jimmy Santadio came to the wake, unguarded and unarmed. He requested a private audience with the Don.

"Don Clericuzio," he said, "my sorrow is nearly equal to yours. I place my life in your hands if you think the Santadio are responsible. I talked to my father and he gave no such order. And he authorizes me to say to you that he will reconsider all your proposals. He gave me permission to marry your daughter."

Rose Marie had come to hold Jimmy's arm. And there was such a pitiful look on her face that for the moment the Don's heart melted. Sorrow and fear gave her a tragic beauty. Her eyes were startling, so dark and bright with tears. And there was a stunned, uncomprehending look on her face.

She turned from the Don and looked at Jimmy Santadio with such love that Don Clericuzio for one of the few times in his life thought of mercy. How could he bring sorrow to such a beautiful daughter?

Rose Marie said to her father, "Jimmy was so horrified that you might think his family had anything to do with it. I know they didn't. Jimmy promised me that his family would come to an agreement."

Don Clericuzio had already convicted the Santadio Family of the murder. He did not require any proof. But mercy was another matter.

"I believe and accept you," the Don said, and indeed he believed in Jimmy's innocence, though that would make no difference. "Rose Marie, you have my permission to marry but not in this house, nor will any of my family be present. And Jimmy, tell your father that we will sit down together and discuss business after the marriage."

"Thank you," Jimmy Santadio said. "I understand. The wedding will be in our Palm Springs house. In one month all my family will be there and all your family will be invited. If they choose not to come then it's their decision."

The Don was offended. "So quickly after this?" He gestured toward the coffin.

And then Rose Marie collapsed into the Don's arms. He could sense her terror. She whispered to him, "I'm pregnant."

"Ah," the Don said. He smiled at Jimmy Santadio.

Rose Marie whispered again. "I'll name him after Silvio. He'll be just like Silvio."

The Don patted her dark hair and kissed her cheek. "Good," he said. "Good. But I still will not attend the wedding."

Now Rose Marie had recovered her courage. She lifted her face to his and kissed him on the cheek. Then she said, "Dad, somebody has to come. Somebody has to give me away."

The Don turned to Pippi who was standing beside him. "Pippi will represent the Family at the wedding. He's a nephew and he loves to dance. Pippi, you will give your cousin away and then you can all dance to the bottom of the ocean."

Pippi bent to kiss Rose Marie's cheek. "I'll be there," he said with false gallantry, "and if Jimmy doesn't show up, we'll run away together."

Rose Marie gratefully raised her eyes and came into his arms.

A month later Pippi De Lena was on the plane from Vegas to Palm Springs to attend the wedding. That month had been spent with Don Clericuzio in the Quogue mansion, and in meetings with Giorgio, Vincent, and Petie.

The Don clearly instructed that Pippi was to be in charge of the operation. That his orders were to be treated as orders from the Don himself, no matter what the orders might be.

Only Vincent dared to question the Don. "What if the Santadio didn't kill Silvio?"

The Don said, "It doesn't matter, but it reeks of their stupidity, which will endanger us in the future. We will only have to fight them at another time. Of course, they are guilty. Ill will itself is murder. If the Santadio are not guilty then we must agree that Fate itself is against us. Which would you rather believe?"

For the first time in his life, Pippi noted that the Don was distraught. He spent long hours in the chapel in the basement of his house. He ate very little, and drank more wine, which was unusual for him.

And he put Silvio's framed photo in his bedroom for a few days. One Sunday he asked the priest saying Mass to hear his confession.

On the last day, the Don had a meeting with Pippi alone.

"Pippi," the Don said, "this is a very tricky operation. There may be a situation when the question comes up if Jimmy Santadio is to be spared. Do not. But no one is to know this is my order. That deed must be on your head. Not on mine, not Giorgio or Vincent or Petie. Are you willing to take the blame?"

"Yes," Pippi said. "You don't want your daughter to hate you or reproach you. Or her brothers."

"A situation may arise where Rose Marie is at risk," the Don said.

"Yes," Pippi said.

The Don sighed. "Do everything to safeguard my children," he said. "You must make the final decisions. But I never gave you the order to kill Jimmy Santadio."

"And if Rose Marie discovers it was . . ." Pippi asked.

The Don looked directly at Pippi De Lena. "She is my child and the sister of Silvio. She will never betray us."

The Santadio mansion in Palm Springs had forty rooms on just three floors, built in the Spanish style to harmonize with the surrounding desert. It was separated from that enormous field of sand by an encircling wall of redstone. The compound within held not only the house but a huge swimming pool, a tennis court, and a boccie alley.

On this wedding day there was a massive barbecue pit, a platform for the orchestra, and a wooden dance floor, laid over the lawn. This floor was surrounded by long banquet tables. Parked by the huge bronzed gates of the compound were three large catering trucks.

Pippi De Lena arrived early Saturday morning with a suitcase filled with wedding clothes. He was given a room on the second floor, the bright golden light of the desert sun pouring in the windows. He started to unpack.

The church ceremony would be held in Palm Springs only a half hour away. The religious rites would begin about noon. Then the guests would return to the house for the celebration.

There was a knock on the door and Jimmy Santadio came in. His face was shiny with happiness and he gave Pippi a vigorous hug. He was not yet dressed in his wedding clothes and looked very handsome in loose white slacks and a gray-and-silver silk shirt. He held Pippi's hands in his to show his affection.

"It's great you came," Jimmy said, "and Roe is thrilled you're giving her away. Now before everything starts, the old man wants to meet you."

Still holding his hand, he led Pippi down to the first floor and down a long corridor to Don Santadio's room. Don Santadio lay in bed clad in blue cotton nightclothes. He was far more decrepit than Don Clericuzio but he had the same sharp eyes, the alert listening manner; his head was round as a ball and bald. He beckoned Pippi close to him and held out his arms so that Pippi could embrace him.

"How just it is that you came," the old man said, his voice was hoarse. "I count on you to help our two Families embrace each other as we two have done. You are the dove of peace we must have. Bless you. Bless you." He sank back on the bed and closed his eyes. "How happy I am this day."

There was a nurse in the room, a stout middle-aged woman. Jimmy introduced her as a cousin. The nurse whispered that they should leave, the old Don was conserving his strength to join the celebration later in the day. For a moment Pippi reconsidered. It was obvious that Don Santadio did not have long to live. Then Jimmy would become the head of his Family. Perhaps things still could be worked out. But Don Clericuzio could never accept the murder of his son, Silvio; there never could be real peace between the two Families. In any case, the Don had given him strict instructions.

Meanwhile two of the Santadio brothers, Fonsa and Italo, were searching Pippi's room for weapons and communications equipment. Pippi's rental car had also been thoroughly checked.

The Santadio had prepared lavishly for the wedding of their prince. Huge woven baskets filled with exotic flowers were scattered all over the compound. There were colorful pavilions stocked with bartenders pouring champagne. There was a jester in a medieval costume doing magic tricks for the children, and music blasted out of speakers strung along the compound. Each guest was given a lotto ticket for a prize of twenty thousand dollars that was to be drawn later. What could be more splendid?

Huge gaily colored tents had been pitched all over the manicured lawn to protect the guests from the desert heat. Green tents over the dance floor, red over the orchestra. Blue tents over the tennis court, which held the wedding gifts. These included a silver Mercedes for the bride and a small private plane for the groom, from Don Santadio himself.

The church ceremony was simple and short, and the guests returned to the Santadio compound to find the orchestra playing. Food counters and three separate bars were put in their own tents, one decorated with scenes of hunters pursuing wild boars, another filled with highball glasses containing fruity tropical drinks.

The wedding couple danced the first dance in lonely splendor. They danced in the shade of the tent, the red desert sun peeked into the corners and bronzed their happiness as they ducked their heads into the patches of sunlight. They were so obviously in love that the crowd cheered and clapped. Rose Marie had never looked so beautiful, nor Jimmy Santadio so young.

When the band stopped playing, Jimmy plucked Pippi out of the crowd and presented him to the more than two hundred guests.

He said, "This is Pippi De Lena who gave the bride away, and he represents the Clericuzio Family. He is my dearest friend. His friends are my friends. His enemies are my enemies." He raised his glass and said, "We all drink to him. And he gets the first dance with the bride."

As Pippi and Rose Marie danced, she whispered to him, "You'll bring the Families together, won't you Pippi?"

"It's a cinch," Pippi said, and whirled her around.

Pippi was the marvel of the celebration, never had there been a more convivial wedding guest. He danced every dance, and was lighter on his feet than any of the younger men. He danced with Jimmy and then with the other brothers, Fonsa, Italo, Benedict,

Gino, and Louis. He danced with the children and the matrons. He waltzed with the orchestra leader, and sang with the band, rowdy songs in Sicilian dialect. He ate and drank with such abandon that his tux was spotted with tomato sauce and the fruity juice of the cocktails and the wine. He hurled the boccie balls with such élan that the court became the center of the wedding for an hour.

After boccie, Jimmy Santadio drew Pippi aside. "I'm counting on you to make everything work," he said. "Our two Families together, nothing can stop us. Me and you." It was Jimmy Santadio at his charming best.

Pippi mustered every ounce of sincerity for his answer. "We will. We will." And he wondered if Jimmy Santadio was as honest as he seemed. By now he must know that somebody in his Family had committed the murder.

Jimmy seemed to sense this. "I swear to you, Pippi, I had nothing to do with it." He took Pippi's hand in his. "We had nothing to do with Silvio's death. Nothing. I swear on the head of my father."

"I believe you," Pippi said and pressed Jimmy's hands. He had a moment of doubt, but it didn't matter. It was too late.

The red desert sun faded to twilight, and lights came on all over the compound. This was the signal for a formal dinner to be served. And all the brothers, Fonsa, Italo, Gino, Benedict, and Louis, proposed a toast to the bride and groom. To the happiness of the marriage, to the special virtues of Jimmy, to Pippi De Lena, their great new friend.

Old Don Santadio was too ill to leave his bed but sent his heartiest good wishes in which he mentioned the plane he had given his son, at which everybody cheered. Then the bride herself cut a huge slice of the wedding cake and brought it to the old man's bedroom. But he was asleep, so they gave it to his nurse, who promised to feed it to him when he woke up.

Finally, toward midnight, the party broke. Jimmy and Rose Marie retired to their bridal chamber, saying they would leave on their honeymoon to Europe the next morning and they needed their rest. At which the guests hooted derisively and made vulgar remarks. All in high spirits and good humor.

The hundreds of cars left the compound and sped off into the desert. The catering trucks were packed, the personnel pulled down the tents and assembled the tables and chairs, then pulled up the platform and even hastily policed the grounds to be certain there was no garbage. Finally they were through; they would finish it up the next day.

At Pippi's request, a ceremonial meeting had been arranged with the five Santadio brothers, to be held after the guests had left. They would exchange gifts to celebrate the new friendship of the two Families.

At midnight they gathered together in the huge dining room of the Santadio mansion. Pippi had a suitcase full of Rolex watches (genuine, not knockoffs). There was also a large Japanese kimono studded with hand-painted sexual scenes of Oriental lovemaking.

Fonsa shouted out, "Let's bring it up to Jimmy right now."

"Too late," Italo said cheerily. "Jimmy and Rose Marie are on their third round."

And they all laughed.

Outside, the desert moon isolated the compound in an icy white light. Chinese lanterns hanging on compound walls made red circles in the white moonbeams.

A large truck, the word CATERING limned in gold paint on its side, rumbled up to the gates of the Santadio compound.

One of the two guards approached the truck, and the driver told him they had come back to pick up a forgotten generator.

"This late?" the guard said.

As he spoke the driver's helper got out of the truck and moved toward the other guard. Both guards were sluggish with the food and drink from the wedding.

In one synchronized movement two things happened: The driver reached down between his legs and showed a gun with a silencer, then fired three times directly into the first guard's face. The driver's helper grabbed the other guard in a stranglehold and with a large, sharp knife in one swift motion cut his throat.

They were dead on the ground. The soft hum of a motor sounded as the large metal platform on the rear of the truck quickly descended and twenty soldiers of the Clericuzio sprang out. Stocking masked, dressed in black, armed with silenced guns, led by Giorgio, Petie, and Vincent, they spilled all over the compound. A special crew cut through the telephone lines. Another crew spread out to command the compound. Ten of the masked men with Giorgio, Petie, and Vincent crashed into the dining room.

The Santadio brothers held their wine glasses to toast Pippi, he stepped away from them. No words were spoken. The invaders opened fire and the five Santadio brothers were torn apart by a hail of bullets. One of the masked men, Petie, stood over them and gave all five the coup de grace, a bullet under the chin. The floor glittered with broken glass.

Another masked man, Giorgio, handed Pippi a mask and black trousers and sweater. Pippi quickly changed and threw his discarded clothes into a bag held by another masked invader.

Pippi, still unarmed, led Giorgio, Petie, and Vincent down the long corridor to the bedroom of Don Santadio. He pushed open the door.

Don Santadio had finally woken and was eating the bridal cake. He took one look at the four men, made the sign of the cross, and put a pillow over his face. The dish holding the cake slipped to the floor.

The nurse was reading in the corner of the room. Petie was on her like a great cat, gagging her and then tying her to the chair with thin nylon rope.

It was Giorgio who advanced to the bed. He reached out gently and pulled the pillow from Don Santadio's head. He hesitated a moment and then fired two shots, the first in the eye, the second, lifting up the round bald head, upward from under the chin.

They regrouped. Vincent finally armed Pippi, he handed over a long silver rope.

Pippi led them from the room down the long corridor and then up to the third floor, which held the bridal chamber. The corridor was littered with flowers and baskets of fruit.

Pippi pushed against the bridal chamber door. It was locked. Petie took off one of his gloves and produced a pick. With this he easily opened the door and pushed it back.

Rose Marie and Jimmy were sprawled on the bed. They had just finished making love, and their bodies were almost liquid with released sensuality. Rose Marie's see-through negligee was bunched above her waist, and the straps had slipped down, exposing her breasts. Her right hand was on Jimmy's hair, the left on his stomach. Jimmy was completely naked, but he sprang up as soon as he saw the men and pulled a bedsheet to use as a robe. He understood everything. "Not here, outside," he said, and advanced toward them.

Rose Marie, for a fraction of a second, was still uncomprehending. As Jimmy moved toward the door, she clutched at him but he evaded her. He went through the door surrounded by the masked Giorgio, Petie, and Vincent. And then Rose Marie said, "Pippi, Pippi, please don't." It was only when the three men turned to look at her that she realized that they were her brothers. "Giorgio, Petie, Vincent. Don't. Don't."

This was the most difficult moment for Pippi. If Rose Marie talked, the Clericuzio Family was doomed. His duty was to kill her. The Don had not specifically instructed him on this; how could he condone the killing of his daughter? Would her brothers obey him? And how did she know it was them? He made the decision. He closed the door behind him and was out in the corridor with Jimmy and Rose Marie's three brothers.

Here the Don had been explicit. Jimmy Santadio was to be strangled. It was perhaps the mark of mercy that there should be no penetrations of his body for his loved ones to weep over. It was perhaps from some tradition of not shedding a loved one's blood while consecrating him to death.

Suddenly Jimmy Santadio let the bedsheet drop, and his hands reached out and ripped Pippi's mask from his face. Giorgio grabbed one of his arms, Pippi the other. Vincent dropped to the floor and grabbed Jimmy's legs. Now Pippi had his rope around Jimmy's neck and bent him to the floor. Jimmy had a twisted smile on his lips, curiously pitying as he stared into Pippi's face: that this act would be avenged by Fate or some mysterious God.

Pippi pulled the cord tight, Petie reached to help with the pressure, and they all sank to the floor of the corridor, where the white bedsheet received Jimmy Santadio's body like a shroud. Inside the bridal chamber, Rose Marie began to scream . . .

The Don had finished speaking. He lit up another cheroot and sipped his wine.

Giorgio said, "Pippi planned the whole thing. We got away clean and the Santadio were wiped out. It was brilliant."

Vincent said, "It solved everything. We haven't had any trouble since."

Don Clericuzio sighed. "It was my decision and it was wrong. But how were we to know Rose Marie would go mad? We were in crisis and this was our only opportunity to strike a decisive blow. You must remember that at that time, I was not yet sixty, I thought too much of my power and intelligence. I thought then certainly it would be a tragedy for my daughter but widows do not grieve forever. And they had killed my son Silvio. How could I forgive that, daughter or no daughter? But I learned. You cannot come to a reasonable solution with stupid people. I should have wiped them out at the very beginning. Before the lovers met. I would have saved my son and daughter." He paused for a moment.

"So, you see, Dante is Jimmy Santadio's son. And you, Cross, shared a baby carriage with him when you were infants, your first summer in this house. All those years I have tried to make up to Dante for the loss of his father. I tried to help my daughter recover from her grief. Dante was brought up as a Clericuzio and he will, with my sons, be my heir."

Cross tried to understand what was happening. His whole body quivered with revulsion toward the Clericuzio and the world they lived in. He thought of his father, Pippi, playing the role of Satan, seducing the Santadio to their death. How could such a man be his father? He thought then of his beloved aunt, Rose Marie, living all those years with her heart and her mind broken, knowing that her husband had been murdered by her father and her brothers. That her own family had betrayed her. He even thought of Dante with some pity, now Dante's guilt was established. And then he wondered about the Don. Surely he did not believe the story of Pippi's mugging. Why did he seem to accept it, a man who had never believed in coincidence. What was the message here?

Cross could never read Giorgio. Did he believe in the mugging killing? It was obvious that Vincent and Petie believed it. But now he understood the special bond between his father and the Don and his three sons. They had been soldiers together in the massacre of the Santadio. And his father had spared Rose Marie.

Cross said, "And Rose Marie never talked?"

"No," the Don said, sardonically. "She did even better. She became crazy." There was just a hint of pride in his voice. "I sent her to Sicily and brought her back in time for Dante to be born on American soil. Who knows, someday he might be president of the United States. I had dreams for the little boy but the combination of Clericuzio and Santadio blood was too much for him.

"And you know the most terrible thing?" the Don said. "Your father, Pippi, made a mistake. He should never have spared Rose Marie, though I loved him for it." He sighed. He took a sip of wine and, looking Cross full in the face, he said, "Be aware. The world is what it is. And you are what you are."

On the flight back to Vegas, Cross pondered the riddle. Why had the Don finally told him the story of the Santadio War? To prevent him from visiting Rose Marie and hearing a different version? Or was he warning him off, telling him not to avenge his father's murder because Dante was involved. The Don was a mystery. But of one thing Cross was sure. If it was Dante who killed his father, then Dante must kill him. And surely Don Domenico Clericuzio knew that, too.

CHAPTER 19

DANTE CLERICUZIO did not have to hear this story. His mother, Rose Marie, had whispered it into his tiny ear from the time he was two years old: whenever she had one of her fits, whenever she felt her grief for the lost love of her husband and her brother Silvio, whenever her terror of Pippi and her brothers overcame her.

It was only when Rose Marie had her worst fits that she accused her father, Don Clericuzio, of the death of her husband. The Don always denied giving the order, as he denied that his sons and Pippi had carried out the massacre. But after she accused him two times, he packed her off to the clinic for a month. After that, she only ranted and raved, and never accused him directly again.

But Dante remembered her whisperings always. As a child he loved his grandfather and believed in his innocence. But he schemed against his three uncles though they always treated him tenderly. Especially, he dreamed of vengeance on Pippi, and though these were fantasies, he thought them for his mother's sake.

When Rose Marie was normal she took care of the widower Don Clericuzio with the utmost affection. To her three brothers she showed sisterly concern. With Pippi, she was distant. And because in those times she had such a sweet visage, it was difficult for her to express malice convincingly. The structure of the bones in her face, the curve of her mouth, and the gentle eyes of liquid brown denied her hate. To her child Dante she showed her overwhelming need to love, which she could no longer feel for any man. She showered him with gifts out of that affection, as did his grandfather and his uncles out of something less pure, a love muddied with guilt. When Rose Marie was normal, she never told Dante the story.

But in her fits she was foul-mouthed, full of curses, even her face could turn into an ugly mask of fury. Dante was always bewildered. When he was seven years old, a doubt entered his mind. "How did you know it was Pippi and my uncles?" he asked her.

Rose Marie cackled with glee. She seemed to Dante a witch out of his fairy-tale books. She told him, "They think they are so clever, that they plan for everything with their masks and special clothes and hats. Do you want to know what they forgot? Pippi was still wearing his dancing shoes. Patent leather and black string bows. And your uncles always grouped themselves together in a particular way. Giorgio always to the front, Vincent a little behind, and Petie always to the right. And the way they looked at Pippi to see if he would give the order to kill me. Because I had recognized them. The way they wavered, almost shrank back. But they would have killed me, they would have. My own brothers." She would then burst into such great weeping that Dante would be terrified.

Even as a small child of seven, he would try to comfort her. "Uncle Petie would never hurt you," he said. "And Grandpa would have killed them all if they did." He wasn't certain of his Uncle Giorgio or even Uncle Vinnie. But in his child's heart, it was Pippi he could never forgive.

By the time Dante was ten years old, he had learned to watch for his mother's fits, and so when she beckoned him to her to tell the Santadio story again, he would quickly take her away into the safety of her bedroom so his grandfather and his uncles would not hear.

By the time Dante grew into manhood, he was too clever to be fooled by all the disguises of the Clericuzio Family. He was of so humorously malicious a nature that he showed his grandfather and his uncles that he knew the truth. And he could perceive that his uncles were not that fond of him. Dante had been designated to join the legal social world, to perhaps take Giorgio's place and learn the financial complexities, but he showed no interest. He had even taunted his uncles that he had no interest in the sissy side of the Family. Giorgio listened to this with a coolness that for a moment frightened the sixteen-year-old Dante.

Uncle Giorgio said, "OK, you won't." There was sadness in his voice and some anger, too.

When Dante quit high school in his senior year, he was sent to work in Petie's construction company in the Bronx Enclave. Dante was a hard worker and developed huge muscles from the hard, grueling work on the building sites. Petie put him on crews of soldiers from the Bronx Enclave. When Dante was old enough, the Don decreed the boy would be a soldier under Petie.

The Don had come to his decision only after reports from Giorgio on Dante's character, and some acts committed by Dante. The young boy was accused of rape by a pretty high school classmate and of assault with a small knife by another fellow student, a boy his own age. Dante had begged his uncles not to let his grandfather know and they had promised him, but of course they had reported to the Don immediately. These charges were settled by large sums of money before Dante could be prosecuted.

And it was during his teenage years that his jealousy of Cross De Lena increased. Cross had grown into a tall, extraordinarily handsome youth with a mature courtesy. All the women in the Clericuzio clan adored him, fussed over him. His female cousins flirted with him, something they never did with the Don's grandson. Dante, wearing his Renaissance hats, with his sly humor and his short and hugely muscular body, was frightening to these young girls. Dante was too clever not to observe all this.

When Dante was taken to the Hunting Lodge in the Sierras, he enjoyed trapping more than shooting. When he fell in love with one of the female cousins, as was perfectly natural in the close-knit Clericuzio clan, he was too direct in his advances. And he was too familiar with the daughters of the Clericuzio soldiers who lived in the Bronx Enclave. Finally Giorgio, who had the role of an instructive, punitive parent, enrolled him with the owner of a New York City high-class bordello to quiet him down.

But Dante's enormous curiosity, his cunning cleverness, made him the only one of his generation of the Clericuzio who really knew what the Family did. So it was finally decided he would be given operational training.

As time went on, Dante felt a growing separation from his Family. The Don was as fond of him as ever and made clear to him that he was an heir to the Empire, but he no longer shared his thoughts with his grandson, no longer gave him his insights, his secret little pearls of wisdom. And the Don did not support Dante's suggestions and ideas on strategy.

His uncles, Giorgio, Vincent, and Petie, were not as warm in their affection as when he was a child. Petie, it was true, seemed more of a friend, but then he had been trained by Petie.

Dante was clever enough to think that maybe the fault was his, because he had betrayed his knowledge of the massacre of the Santadio and his father. He even asked questions of Petie about Jimmy Santadio, and his uncle told him how much they had respected his father and how sad they had been about his death. It was never said openly, never admitted, but Don Clericuzio and his sons understood that Dante knew the true story, that Rose Marie, in her fits, had disclosed the secret. They wanted to make amends, they treated him as a child prince.

But what most formed Dante's character was his pity and love for his mother. In her fits she inflamed in him a hatred for Pippi DeLena; she exonerated her father and brothers.

All these things helped Don Clericuzio make his final decision, for the Don could read his grandson's mind as easily as he could read his prayer book. The Don judged that Dante could never take part in the final retreat to the cloak of society. His Santadio and (the Don was a fair man) Clericuzio blood was too ferocious a mixture. Therefore Dante would join the society of Vincent and Petie, of Giorgio and Pippi De Lena. They would all fight the final battle together.

And Dante proved to be a good soldier, though an irrepressible one. He had an independence that made him flout the Family rules, and indeed he sometimes did not comply with specific orders. His ferocity was useful when a confused *Bruglione* or an undisciplined soldier stepped over the Family line and had to be dispatched to a less complex world. Dante was not subject to control except by the Don himself, and mysteriously the Don refused to chastise him personally.

Dante feared for his mother's future. That future depended on the Don, and as her fits occurred more often, Dante could see the Don becoming more impatient. Especially when Rose Marie would make a grand exit by drawing a circle with her foot and then spitting in the middle while screaming she would never enter the house again. That was when the Don would ship her off to the clinic again for a few days.

So Dante would coax her out of her fits, restore her to her natural sweetness and affection. But there was always the dread that finally he could not protect her. Unless he became as powerful as the Don himself.

The only person in the world Dante feared was the old Don. It was a feeling that came from his experiences with his grandfather as a child. And it sprang, too, from his sense that the sons feared Don Clericuzio as much as they loved him. Which was amazing to Dante. The Don was in his eighties, he no longer had physical strength, he rarely left his mansion, and his height was diminished. Why fear him?

True, he ate well, he made an imposing appearance, the only physical disarray time had done was to soften his teeth so that his diet was reduced to pasta, grated cheese, stewed vegetables, and soups. Meats were simmered to shreds in tomato sauces.

But the old Don had to die soon, so there would be shifts of power. What if Pippi became Giorgio's right-hand man? What if Pippi seized power by sheer force? And if that happened, Cross would ascend, especially since he had acquired so much wealth with his share of the Xanadu.

So there were practical reasons, Dante assured himself, not his hatred of Pippi, who dared to criticize him to his own Family.

Dante had made his original contact with Jim Losey when Giorgio decided that Dante should have some points of power and designated him to deliver Losey's salary from the Family.

Of course precautions had been taken to protect Dante if Losey should ever turn traitor. Contracts were signed that showed Losey to be working for a Family-controlled security corporation as a consultant. The contract specified confidentiality and that Losey be paid in cash. But in the security corporation's tax filings, the money was reported as expenses, with Losey using a corporation dummy as recipient.

Dante had made special payments to Losey over several years before he initiated a more intimate relationship. He was not intimidated by Losey's reputation, he sized him up as a man who was at a juncture where he was thinking of accumulating a very large nest egg for his old age. Losey had a hand in everything. He was protecting drug dealers, taking Clericuzio money to protect gambling, was even dabbling in strong-arming certain high-powered retail merchants into paying extra protection fees.

Dante exerted all his charm to make a good impression on Losey; both his sly and vicious sense of humor and his disregard for accepted moral principles appealed to Losey. Dante reacted particularly well to Losey's bitter tales of his war against the blacks who were destroying Western civilization. Dante himself had no racial prejudices. Blacks had no influence on his life, and if they did they would be mercilessly removed.

Dante and Losey had a powerful common urge. They were both dandies interested in their looks, and they both had a similar sexual drive for the domination of women. Not so much erotic but as an expression of power. They took to spending time together when Dante was in the West. They went to dinner together and cruised the nightclubs. Dante never dared to bring him to Vegas and the Xanadu, and it was not to his purpose.

Dante loved to tell Losey of how he was first the abject extravagant courter of women, and the women were imperious in the power of their beauty. And then how he enjoyed the imperiousness by maneuvering them into a position where they could not escape the unwilling giving of sex. Losey, a little contemptuous of Dante's trick, would tell how he would break women down from the very beginning with his extraordinary macho presence, and then humiliate them.

Both of them declared that they would never force a woman to have sex who did not respond to their courtship. They both agreed that Athena Aquitane would be a grand prize if she ever gave them an opening. When they roved around the L.A. clubs together and picked up women, they would compare notes and laugh at those vain women who thought they could go to the utmost limit and then refuse the final act. Sometimes the protests would be too vehement, and then Losey would show his shield and tell the women he would bust them for prostitution. Since many of them were soft hookers, the threat worked.

They spent evenings of camaraderie, orchestrated by Dante. Losey, when not telling the "nigger" stories, tried to define the varieties of hookers.

There were first the out-and-out prostitutes who held one hand out for money and grabbed your cock with the other. Then there was the soft hooker who was attracted to you and gave you a friendly screw and then, before you left in the morning, asked you for a check to help pay the rent.

Then there was the soft hooker who loved you but loved others too and established a long-term relationship studded with gifts of jewelry for every holiday, including Labor Day. Then there were the freelance nine-to-five secretaries, airline stewardesses, shop clerks in fancy boutiques, who invited you up to their apartment for coffee after an expensive dinner and then tried to throw you out on your ass to freeze in the street without even a hand job. These were their favorites. Sex with them was exciting, fraught with drama, tears, and subdued cries for forbearance and patience, which produced a sex that was better than love.

One night after they had dinner at Le Chinois, a restaurant in Venice, Dante suggested they take a stroll along the boardwalk. They sat on a bench and watched the human traffic go by, beautiful young girls on Rollerblades, pimps of all colors pursuing them and shouting endearments, the soft hookers selling T-shirts decorated with sayings incomprehensible to the two men. Hare Krishnas with begging bowls, bearded groups of singers with guitars, family groups with cameras, and reflecting them, the black ocean of the Pacific, on whose sandy beaches isolated twosomes crouched under blankets they believed disguised their fornication.

"I could lock up everybody here for probable cause," Losey said, laughing. "What a fucking zoo."

"Even those pretty young kids on skates?" Dante asked.

"I'd just bust them for carrying pussies as a dangerous weapon," Losey said.

"Not many eggplants here," Dante said.

Losey stretched out on the beach, and when he spoke it was with a fair imitation of a Southern accent.

"I think I've been too hard on my black brethren," he said. "It's like the liberals always say, it all springs from their having been slaves."

Dante waited for the punch line.

Losey linked his hands behind his head and pulled back his jacket to let his gun holster show to scare off any reckless punks. Nobody paid attention, they had spotted him for a cop by his first step on the boardwalk.

"Slavery," Jim Losey said. "Demoralizing. It was too easy a life for them so it made them too dependent. Freedom was too hard. On the plantations they were taken care of, three meals a day, free rent, they were clothed and they were given good medical attention because they were valuable property. They weren't even responsible for their children. Imagine. The plantation owners fucked their daughters and gave those children jobs for the rest of their lives. Sure they worked but they were always singing, so how hard could they be working? I'll bet five white guys could do the work of a hundred niggers."

Dante was tickled. Was Losey serious? It didn't matter, he was expressing an emotional view not a rational one.

They were enjoying themselves, it was a balmy night, the world they observed gave them a comfortable feeling of security. These people were never a danger to them.

Then Dante said, "I've got a really important proposition to put to you. Do you want the rewards first or the risks first?"

Losey smiled at him. "Rewards first, always."

Dante said, "Two hundred grand cash up front. A year later, a job as head of security at the Xanadu Hotel. With a salary five times what you get now. Expense account. Big car, room, board, and all the pussy you can eat. You get to do all the background checks on the hotel showgirls. Plus bonuses like you make now. And you don't have the risk of being the primary shooter."

"Sounds too good," Losey said. "But somebody has to get shot. That's the risk, right?"

"For me," Dante said. "I'm the shooter."

"Why not me?" Losey asked. "I have the badge to make it legal."

"Because you wouldn't live six months after it," Dante said.

"And what do I do?" Losey asked. "Tickle your ass with a feather?"

Dante explained the whole operation. Losey whistled to express his admiration for the daring of the idea.

"Why Pippi De Lena?" Losey asked.

"Because he's about to turn traitor," Dante said.

Losey was still looking doubtful. It would be the first time he committed the crime of cold-blooded murder. Dante decided to give it something extra.

"You remember that Boz Skannet suicide?" he said. "Cross made that hit, not personally, but with a guy named Lia Vazzi."

"What does he look like?" Losey asked. When Dante had described Vazzi he realized it was the man accompanying Skannet when he had stopped him in the hotel lobby. "Where can I find this Vazzi guy?"

For a long moment Dante considered. He was doing something that broke the only really holy law of the Family. Of the Don. But it might get Cross out of the way, and Cross would be someone to fear after Pippi's death.

"I'll never tell anybody where it came from," Losey said.

Dante for a moment reconsidered, then he said, "Vazzi lives in a hunting lodge my family owns up in the Sierras. But don't do anything until we finish with Pippi."

"Sure," Losey said. He would do what he liked. "And I get my two hundred grand right up front, right?"

"Right," Dante said.

"Sounds good," Losey said. "One thing. If the Clericuzio come after me, I'll sell you down the river."

"Don't worry," Dante said amiably. "If I hear that, I'll kill you first. Now we just have to work out the details."

It all went as they planned.

When Dante fired the six shots into Pippi De Lena's body and when Pippi whispered, calling him a "fucking Santadio," Dante felt an exultation he had never felt before.

CHAPTER 20

LIA VAZZI, for the first time, deliberately disobeyed the order of his boss, Cross De Lena.

It was unavoidable. Detective Jim Losey had made another visit to the Hunting Lodge and had again asked questions about Skannet's death. Lia denied all knowledge of Skannet and claimed he had just happened to be in the hotel lobby at that particular time. Losey patted him on the shoulder, then lightly slapped him across the face. "OK, you little guinea prick," he said, "I'll get you soon."

In his mind Lia signed a death warrant for Losey. No matter what else happened, and he knew his future was in peril, he would make sure of Losey's fate. But he had to be very careful. The Clericuzio Family had strict rules. You never harmed a police officer.

Lia remembered driving Cross to the meeting with Phil Sharkey, Losey's retired partner. He had never believed that Sharkey would remain quiet on the promise of a future fifty grand. Now he was sure that Sharkey had informed Losey of that meeting and probably had seen Vazzi waiting in the car. If this was true, there would be a great danger to Cross and himself. In essence he distrusted the judgment of Cross, police officers stuck together like Mafioso. They had their own kind of *omertà*.

Lia recruited two of his soldiers to drive him down from the Hunting Lodge to Santa Monica, the home of Phil Sharkey. He was confident that just by talking to Sharkey he would know if the man had informed Losey of the visit by Cross.

The outside of Sharkey's house was deserted, the lawn empty except for an abandoned mower. But the garage door was open, a car in it, and Lia walked up the cement path to the door and rang the bell. There was no answer. He kept ringing. He tested the knob, the door was not locked, now there was a choice to be made. Did he go in or leave immediately? He wiped his prints off the knob and bell with the tail of his tie. Then he went through the door into the small hallway and called Sharkey's name in a shout. There was no answer.

Lia moved through the house; the two bedrooms were bare, he looked into the closets and under the beds. He went through the living room, looking under the sofa and through the cushions. Then he went into the kitchen and to the patio table where there was a container of milk and a paper plate that held a partially eaten cheese sandwich, white bread with dehydrated yellow mayo on the edges.

There was a slatted brown door in the kitchen, and Lia opened it to reveal a shallow basement only two wooden steps down, sort of a dropped room with no windows.

Lia Vazzi descended the two steps and looked behind a mound of used bicycles. He opened a closet with huge doors. In it was a policeman's uniform hanging all by itself, on the floor was a pair of thick black shoes, and resting on the shoes was a braided street policeman's cap. That was all.

Lia went to the one trunk on the floor and pulled up the lid. It was surprisingly light. The interior was filled to the top with neatly folded gray blankets.

Lia went back up the stairs and stood on the patio staring at the ocean. Burying a body in the sand was foolhardy, so he dismissed the idea. Maybe somebody had come by and picked Sharkey up. But for an assassin there would be a risk of being seen. Also, Sharkey would be a dangerous man to kill. So, Lia reasoned, if the man was dead he had to be in this house. Immediately he went back down to the basement and threw all the wool blankets out of the trunk. And sure enough, there at the bottom was first the large head, and then the lean body. There was a hole in Sharkey's right eye and over it a thin cake of blood like a red coin. The facial skin, waxy with long death, was pockmarked with black dots. Lia, as a Qualified Man, knew exactly what that meant. Someone trusted had been allowed to come very close to shoot point blank into the eye; those dots were powder marks.

Carefully, Lia folded the blankets, put them back over the body, and then exited the house. He had not left any fingerprints but was aware that fragments of the blankets must have adhered to his clothing. He would have to destroy the clothes thoroughly. His shoes, too. He had his soldiers drive him to the airport, and while he was waiting for a plane to take him to Vegas, he bought a change of clothing including new shoes in one of the stores in the airport mall. Then he bought a carry-on bag and put his old clothes into it.

In Vegas he checked into the Xanadu and left a message for Cross. Then he showered thoroughly and dressed again in his new clothes. He waited for Cross to call.

When the call came, he told Cross he would be up to see him. He brought the bag of his old clothing, and the first thing he said to Cross was "You just saved yourself fifty grand."

Cross looked at him and smiled. Lia, usually a natty dresser, had bought a flowery shirt, blue canvas pants, and a light jacket, also blue. He looked like a low-caste casino hustler.

Lia told him about Sharkey. He attempted to make excuses for his actions, but Cross dismissed them. "You're in this with me, you have to protect yourself. But what the hell does this mean?"

"Simple," Lia said. "Sharkey was the only one who could tie Losey with Dante. Otherwise it's just your say-so. Dante made Losey kill his partner."

Cross said, "How the hell could Sharkey be that dumb?"

Lia shrugged. "He figured he could get money from Losey and then get the fifty from you anyway. He knew that Losey must be playing for big stakes because of the money you gave him. After all, he was a detective for twenty years, he could figure these things out. And he never dreamed Losey would kill him, his old partner. He didn't figure on Dante."

"They were extreme," Cross said.

"In this situation you cannot allow an extra player," Lia said. "I must say I'm surprised that Dante could see that particular danger. He must have convinced Losey, who really would not want to kill an old partner. We all have our sentimentalities."

"So now Dante is controlling Losey," Cross said. "I thought Losey was tougher than that."

"You're talking about two different classes of animal," Lia said. "Losey is formidable, Dante is crazy."

"So Dante knows I know about him," Cross said.

"Which means I have to act very quickly," Lia said.

Cross nodded. "It will have to be a Communion," he said. "They will have to disappear."

Lia laughed. "Do you think that will deceive Don Clericuzio?" he said.

"If we plan it right, nobody can blame us," Cross said.

Lia spent the next three days with Cross going over plans. During that time he burned his old clothes in the hotel incinerator with his own hands. Cross exercised by shooting a lone eighteen holes of golf, with Lia accompanying him to drive the golf cart. Lia could not understand the popularity of golf in all the Families. To him it was a quaint aberration.

On the night of the third day they sat on the balcony of the penthouse. Cross had laid out the brandy and Havana cigars. They watched the crowds on the Strip below.

"No matter how clever they are, my death so soon after my father's would compromise Dante with the Don," Cross said. "I think we can wait."

Lia puffed on his cigar. "Not too long. Now they know you spoke with Sharkey."

"We have to get them both at the same time," Cross said. "Remember, it will have to be a Communion. Their bodies must not be found."

Lia said, "You're putting last things first. And first we have to be sure we can kill them."

Cross sighed. "It's going to be very difficult. Losey is a dangerous man and careful. Dante can fight. We have to isolate them in one place. Can it be done in Los Angeles?"

"No," Lia said. "That is Losey's territory. He is too formidable there. We will have to do it in Vegas."

"And break rules," Cross said.

"If it's a Communion then nobody will know where they were killed," Lia said. "And we are already breaking the rule by killing a police officer."

"I think I know how to get them to Vegas at the same time," Cross said. He explained the scheme to Lia.

"We will have to use more bait," Lia told Cross. "We have to make sure Losey and Dante come when we want them here."

Cross drank another brandy. "OK, here's some more bait." He told Lia, and Lia nodded in agreement. "Their disappearance will be our salvation," Cross said. "And it will deceive everyone."

"Except Don Clericuzio," Lia said. "He is the only one to fear."

BOOK VIII

Communion

CHAPTER 21

VERY LUCKILY Steve Stallings did not die until his final close-up scene in *Messalina* was shot. It could have cost millions of dollars in reshooting.

The last scene to be shot was a battle scene that actually took place in the middle of the film. A desert town had been erected fifty miles from Vegas to denote the base of the Persian army that was to be destroyed by the Emperor Claudius (Steve Stallings) accompanied by his wife, Messalina (Athena).

At the end of the day, Steve Stallings retired to his hotel suite in the small town. He had his cocaine and his booze and two female companions for the night, and he was going to kick everybody's ass, he was pissed off. For one thing, his part in the picture had been cut to a character part, not a star. He realized he was shifting into a secondary career, an inevitable fate for aging stars. Another thing, Athena had been distant from him all during the shoot, he had hoped for more. Also—and this was, he himself felt, a little childish—at the wrap party and showing of the rough cut, he was not getting star treatment; he had not been given one of the Xanadu Hotel's famous Villas.

After his long years in the movie business, Steve Stallings knew how the power structure worked. When he was a Bankable Star, he could override everyone. Theoretically, the studio chief was boss, he gave the green light for a picture. A powerful producer who brought a "property" to the studio was also the boss, he got the elements together—i.e., stars, director, screenplay—supervised the development of the script, and raised independent money from people who were given a credit as associate producers but had no power. For that period he was the boss.

But once the picture started shooting, it was the director who was the boss. Providing he was an A director or the even more powerful Bankable Director (that is, one who would assure an audience in the film's opening weeks and attract Bankable Stars to appear in the movie).

The director had complete charge over the picture. Everything had to go through him. The costumes, music, sets, how the actors played their parts. Also, the Directors Guild was the most powerful union in the movie business. No name director would accept the job of replacing another director.

But all these people, powerful as they were, had to bow to the Bankable Star. A director who had two Bankable Stars in the same movie was like a man riding two wild horses. His balls could be scattered to the four winds.

Steve Stallings had been such a star and knew he no longer was.

The day's shoot had been physically taxing and Steve Stallings needed relaxation. He showered, ate a big steak, and when the two girls came up, local talent and not bad looking at all, he fed them cocaine and champagne. For once he relaxed his prudence, after all his career was entering its twilight years, and he didn't really have to be careful anymore. He went heavy on the coke.

The two girls were wearing T-shirts emblazoned with STEVE STALLINGS ASS KISSERS, in tribute to his buttocks, admired by fans all over the world, male and female. They were properly awe-stricken, and it was only after the cocaine that they peeled off their T-shirts and bundled in with him. This cheered him up somewhat. He took another snort of cocaine. The girls were caressing him, stripping off his shorts and shirt. Stallings daydreamed as they fiddled, their fiddling putting him at ease.

Tomorrow at the wrap party, he would see all his conquests. He had screwed Athena Aquitane, he had screwed Claudia who had written the movie, he had even screwed Dita Tommey long ago, when she wasn't yet fully convinced of her true sexual orientation. He had screwed Bobby Bantz's wife and, though she no longer counted because she was dead, Skippy Deere's wife. It always gave him a feeling of virtuous fulfillment when at a dinner party he looked around and tallied up all the women who were now sitting so placidly with their husbands and lovers. He was an intimate of them all.

There was a distraction. One of the girls was sticking a finger up his ass and that always annoyed him. He had hemorrhoids. He rose from the bed to snort some more cocaine and take a full swig of champagne, but the wine upset his stomach. He felt nauseous and then disoriented. He didn't quite know where he was.

Suddenly, he was aware of a great fatigue: his legs sagged, the glass fell from his hand. He was bewildered. Very far away he heard one of the girls scream and he was furious with her for screaming, and then the very last thing he felt was a lightning bolt exploding in his head.

What happened next could only have happened with a combination of stupidity and malice. One girl had screamed because Steve Stallings had toppled over her onto the bed and had lain there, mouth open and eyes staring, so obviously dead that both girls panicked and just kept screaming. The screaming attracted the hotel personnel and a number of people who were gambling in the tiny hotel casino, which held only slots, a dice table, and a large, round poker setup. These people followed the screaming and came upstairs.

There were, outside Stalling's hotel room, with its now-open door, several people staring at his naked body sprawled out on the bed. In what seemed just a few minutes, an additional crowd gathered from the town, hundreds of them. They crowded into the room to touch his body.

At first there were just reverent touches for the man who had made women all over the world fall in love with him. Then some women kissed him, other women touched his testicles, his penis, one women took out a pair of scissors from her purse and cut off a great thatch of glossy black hair to expose the underlying fuzz of gray on his skull.

The malice came in because Skippy Deere had been one of the first to arrive and had failed to call the police immediately. He watched the first wave of women approach Steve Stallings's body. He had a clear view. Stallings's mouth was open as if he had been caught in the act of singing and there was a look of astonishment on his face.

The first woman who reached him—Deere saw her clearly—gently closed his eyes and pushed his mouth shut before she softly kissed him on the forehead. But she was pushed aside by the next wave who were not so restrained. And Deere felt the malice within him, the horns Stallings had given him years ago seemed to tingle, and he let the invasion continue. Stallings often boasted that no women could resist him and he was certainly on the mark. Even dead, women were caressing his body.

Only when a piece of Stallings's ear vanished and he had been turned sideways to show his famous buttocks, his whole body deathly pale, did Deere finally call the police and take command of the situation and solve all the problems. That was what producers did. That was their forte.

Skippy Deere made all the arrangements for the body to be autopsied immediately and then shipped to Los Angeles, where the funeral would be held three days later.

The autopsy showed that Stallings had died of a cerebral aneurysm which, when it exploded, sent all his blood rushing through his head.

Deere hunted down the two young girls who had been with him and promised them they would not be prosecuted for cocaine use and that they would be signed for small parts in a new movie he was producing. He would pay them a thousand a week for two years. However, there was a moral turpitude clause that would end the contract if they talked to anyone about Stallings's death.

Then he took the time to call Bobby Bantz in L.A. and explain what he had done. He also called Dita Tommey to give her the news and have her tell all the *Messalina* personnel, above the line and below the line, to be sure to attend the showing in Vegas and the wrap party. Then, shaken more than he would admit, he took two Halcions and went to sleep.

CHAPTER 22

THE DEATH OF Steve Stallings did not affect the showing and wrap party in Vegas. That was Skippy Deere's expertise. And the emotional structure of movie making. It was true that Stallings had been a star, but he had ceased to be a Bankable Star. It was true that he had made love to many women in their bodies, and millions more in their minds, but his love had never been more than reciprocal pleasure. Even the women in the picture, Athena, Claudia, Dita Tommey, and the three other featured female stars, were less grieved than would be imagined by romantics. Everyone agreed that Steve Stallings would want the show to go on, nothing would distress him more than to have the wrap party and screening canceled because of his death.

In the film industry you said good-bye to most of your lovers at the end of a picture as politely as you did in the old days to your dancing partner at a ball.

Skippy Deere claimed it was his idea to hold the wrap party at the Xanadu Hotel and to show a very rough cut of the picture that same night. He knew that Athena would be leaving the country in the next few days and wanted to make sure that Athena did not have to reshoot any scenes.

But, in reality, it was Cross who proposed the idea of a wrap party and showing of the film at the Xanadu Hotel. He asked it as a favor.

"It will be great publicity for the Xanadu," Cross told Deere. "And here's what I'll do for you. I'll comp everybody on the picture and anybody you invite for one night—room, food, beverage. I'll give you and Bantz a Villa. I'll give Athena a Villa. I'll provide security so nobody gets to see the rough cut—like the press—that you don't want to. You've been screaming for years you wanted a Villa."

Deere pondered this. "Just for publicity?"

Cross grinned at him. "Also you get hundreds of people loaded with big cash. The casino will get a good part of it."

"Bantz doesn't gamble," Deere said. "I do. You'll get my money."

"I'll give you fifty grand in credit," Cross said. "If you lose we won't press for payment."

That convinced Deere. "OK," he said. "But it has to be my idea or I can't sell it to the Studio."

"Certainly," Cross said. "But Skippy, you and I have done a lot of things together. And I've always come out on the short end. This time it's different. This time you have to come through." He smiled at Deere. "This time you can't disappoint me."

For one of the few times in his life Deere felt a thrill of apprehension and did not quite know why. Cross was not making a threat. He seemed genial, he seemed to be just stating a fact.

"Don't worry," Skippy Deere said, "We finish shooting in three weeks. Make your plans for then."

Then Cross had to make sure that Athena would agree to come to the wrap party and showing of the rough cut. "I really need it for the Hotel and a chance to see you again," he said to her.

She agreed. Now Cross had to make sure that Dante and Losey would come to the party.

He invited Dante to come to Vegas to talk about LoddStone's and Losey's plan to make a picture based on Losey's adventures in the police department. Everybody knew that Losey and Dante were now good buddies.

"I want you to put in a word for me with Jim Losey," Cross told Dante. "I want to be a coproducer on his film and I'm willing to invest half the budget."

Dante was amused by this. "You're really serious about this movie business," he said, "Why?"

"Big money," Cross said. "And broads."

Dante laughed. "You've got big money and broads already," he said.

"Class. Big money and class broads," Cross said.

"How come you don't invite me to this party?" Dante asked. "And how come I never get a Villa?"

"Put the word in for me with Losey," Cross said, "and you'll get both. Bring Losey along. Plus if you're looking for a date I can fix you up with Tiffany. You've seen her show."

To Dante, Tiffany was the ultimate personification of pure lust, her breasts so full, her smooth, elongated face with its thick lips and wide mouth, her height and long, shapely legs. For the first time Dante was enthusiastic. "No shit," he said. "She's twice as big as me. Imagine? You've got a deal."

It was a little too obvious, but Cross was counting on the fact that the interdiction on violence in Vegas by all the Families would make Dante confident.

Then Cross added casually, "Even Athena is coming. And she's the main reason I want to stay in the movie business."

Bobby Bantz, Melo Stuart, and Claudia flew to Vegas on the Studio jet. Athena and the rest of the cast arrived from the shoot in their personal trailers, as did Dita Tommey. Senator Wavven would represent the state of Nevada, as would Nevada's governor, who had been handpicked for the job by Wavven himself.

Dante and Losey would have two apartments in one of the Villas. Lia Vazzi and his men would occupy the other four apartments.

Senator Wavven and the governor and their entourages would occupy another Villa. Cross had arranged a private dinner for them with selected showgirls. He hoped that their presence would help take the heat off any investigation of what was to happen. That they would use their political influence to smother any publicity and legal pursuit.

Cross was breaking all the rules. Athena had a Villa, but Claudia, Dita Tommey, and Molly Flanders also had apartments in that Villa. The remaining two apartments held a four-man crew of Lia Vazzi's men, to guard Athena.

A fourth Villa was assigned to Bantz and Skippy Deere and their entourages. The remaining three Villas were occupied by twenty of Lia's men, who would replace the usual security guards. However, none of the Vazzi crews were to be involved in the real action, they did not know Cross's true purpose. Lia and Cross were to be the only executioners.

Cross shut down the Villas' Pearl Casino for the two days. Most of the Hollywood personnel, no matter how successful, could not afford to play the casino's stakes. Those superrich guests who had already booked were informed that the Villas were undergoing repairs and renovations and could not accommodate them.

In their plan Cross and Lia Vazzi had determined that Cross would kill Dante and that Lia would kill Losey. If the Don decided on their guilt and determined that Lia had actually done the job on Dante, he might wipe out Lia's whole family. If the Don found the truth, he would not extend his vengeance to Claudia. She, after all, had Clericuzio blood.

Also, Lia had a personal vendetta against Jim Losey, he hated all representatives of government, and why not mix a little personal pleasure in with such a dangerous business.

The real problem was how to isolate the two men and make the bodies disappear. It had always been the rule of all the Families all over America that no execution could be carried out in Vegas, in order to preserve the public acceptance of gambling. The Don was a strong enforcer of that rule.

Cross hoped Dante and Losey would not suspect a trap. They did not know that Lia had discovered Sharkey's body and therefore knew of their intentions. The other problem was how to prepare for Dante's strike against Cross. And then Lia established a spy in Dante's camp.

Molly Flanders flew in early on the day of the party, she and Cross had business. She brought with her a justice of the Supreme Court of California and a monsignor of the Catholic Diocese of Los Angeles. They would serve as witnesses when Cross signed the will she had also prepared and brought. Cross knew that his chances of remaining alive were small, and he had carefully considered where his half of the Xanadu Hotel should go. His interest was worth $500 million, and that was nothing to be sneezed at.

The will left Lia's wife and children a comfortable pension for life. The rest he divided between Claudia and Athena, with Athena's portion held in trust for her daughter, Bethany. It struck him that there was no one else in the world he cared enough about to leave his money to.

When Molly, the judge, and the monsignor arrived in the penthouse suite, the judge congratulated him on his good sense for making a will at so young an age. The monsignor calmly surveyed the luxury of the suite as if to weigh the wages of sin.

They were both good friends of Molly's, who had done pro bono work for them. She had called in her markers at the special request of Cross. He wanted witnesses who could not be corrupted or intimidated by the Clericuzio.

Cross gave them drinks, and the signing of the will was completed. The two men left; though they had been invited, they did not want their reputations sullied by attending a movie wrap party in the gambling hell of Las Vegas. They were, after all, not elected officials of the state.

Cross and Molly were alone in the suite. Molly gave him the original of the will. Cross said, "You have a copy for yourself, right?"

"Of course," Molly said. "I must say I was surprised when you gave me your instructions. I had no idea you and Athena were so close. And besides she's pretty rich in her own right."

"She may need more money than she has," Cross said.

"Her daughter?" Molly said. "I know about her. I'm Athena's personal attorney. You're right, Bethany may need that money. I had you figured differently."

"You did?" Cross said. "How so?"

Molly said quietly, "I had the idea that you took care of Boz Skannet. I had you figured as a Mafia guy with no mercy. I remember about that poor kid I got off from a murder rap. And that you mentioned him. And that he was killed supposedly in some drug deal."

"And now you see how wrong you were," Cross said, smiling at her.

Molly looked at him coldly. "And I was very surprised when you let Bobby Bantz screw you out of your profit share in *Messalina.*"

"That was small potatoes," Cross said. He thought of the Don and David Redfellow.

"Athena is going to France the day after tomorrow," Molly said. "For quite a while. Are you going with her?"

"No," Cross said. "I have too many things here."

"OK," Molly said. "I'll see you at the movie screening and the wrap party. Maybe the rough cut of the film will give you an idea of the fortune Bantz gypped you out of."

"It doesn't matter," Cross said.

"You know, Dita put in a card at the beginning of the rough cut. Dedicated to Steve Stallings. Bantz will be really pissed off at that."

"Why?" Cross asked.

"Because Steve screwed all the women Bantz couldn't," Molly said. "What shits men are," she added. Then she left.

Cross went to sit on his balcony. The Vegas street below him was crowded, people sifting into the hotel casinos that lined the strip on either side. The neon marquees flashed their signs: Caesars, the Sands, the Mirage, the Aladdin, the Desert Inn, the Stardust—purples, reds, and greens, a mixed rainbow to which there was no end until you lifted your eyes to the desert and mountains that lay beyond. The blazing afternoon sun could not subdue them.

The *Messalina* people would not begin to arrive until three, and then he would see Athena for the last time if things went wrong. He picked up the balcony phone and called the Villa where he had housed Lia Vazzi and told him to come up to the penthouse suite so that they could go over their plans one more time.

Messalina wrapped at noon. Dita Tommey had wanted the last shot of the rising sun illuminating a terrible slaughter of the Roman battlefield. Athena and Steve Stallings looking down. She shot a double for Stallings and used a shadow over his face for disguise. It was nearly three in the afternoon before the camera truck, the huge mobile trailers that served as homes on the set, the mobile catering kitchens, the wardrobe trailers and vehicles carrying weapons of the time before Christ, rolled into Vegas. Many others came as well, because Cross had treated this occasion in the Old Vegas style.

He had comped everyone who worked on *Messalina,* above the line and below the line, with room, food, and beverage. LoddStone Studios had supplied the list of over three hundred names. Certainly it was generous, certainly it created goodwill. But these three hundred people would leave a substantial part of their wages in the casino drop. This he had learned from Gronevelt. "When people feel good, when they want to celebrate, they gamble."

The rough cut of the movie *Messalina* would be played at ten P.M., but without music and special effects. After the screening would come the wrap party. The huge Xanadu ballroom where the party for Big Tim had been held was cut into two parts. One to show the film, the other, larger part for the buffet and orchestra.

By four in the afternoon, everybody was in the Hotel and the Villas. It was not to be missed by anyone: everything free in the convergence of two glamorous worlds, Hollywood and Las Vegas.

The press was infuriated by the tight security. Access was barred to the Villas and the ballroom. It was not even possible to photograph the players in this glamorous event. Not the stars of the film, the director, the senator and the governor, the producer and the head of the Studio. They could not even get into the screening of the rough cut of the film. They prowled around the casino and offered huge bribes to the gamblers below the line for their IDs to get into the ballroom. Some were successful.

Four crew members, two cynical stuntmen, and two women from the catering team sold their IDs to reporters for a thousand dollars apiece.

Dante Clericuzio and Jim Losey were enjoying the luxury of their Villa. Losey shook his head in wonderment. "A burglar could live for a year on just the gold from the bathroom," he said aloud.

"No, he couldn't," Dante said. "He'd be dead in six months."

They were sitting in the living room of Dante's apartment. They hadn't called room service because the huge kitchen refrigerator was stuffed with trays of sandwiches and caviar canapés, bottles of imported beer and the finest wines.

"So we're all set," Losey said.

"Yep," Dante said, "and when we're done, I'll ask my grandfather for the Hotel. Then we'll be set for life."

"The important thing is that we get him here alone," Losey said.

"I'll do that, don't worry," Dante said. "Worse comes to worst, we'll drive him out to the desert."

"How do you get him here in this Villa?" Losey said. "That's the important thing."

"I'll tell him Giorgio flew in secretly and wants to see him," Dante said. "Then I do the job and you clean up after me. You know crime scenes, what they'll look for."

He said musingly, "The best way is to drop him into the desert. They may never find him." He paused for a moment. "You know Cross ducked Giorgio the night Pippi died. He won't dare do it again."

"But what if he does?" Losey asked. "I'll be waiting here all night jerking off."

"Athena's Villa is next door," Dante said. "You just tap on it and get lucky."

"Too much heat," Losey said.

Dante said with a grin. "We can take her out into the desert with Cross."

"You're crazy," Losey said. And he realized this was true.

"Why not?" Dante said. "Why not have some fun? The desert is big enough to dump two bodies."

Losey thought of Athena's body, her lovely face, her voice, her regal air. Oh, he and Dante would have fun. He was already a murderer, he might as well be a rapist. Marlowe, Pippi De Lena, and his old partner, Phil Sharkey. He was a three-time murderer and too shy to commit rape. He was turning into one of those morons he had arrested all his life. And for a woman who sold her body to the whole world. But this little prick before him with the funny hat was really a piece of work.

"I'll give it a shot," Losey said. "I'll invite her in for a drink and if she comes, she's asking for it."

Dante was amused by Losey's rationalization. "Everybody asks for it," he said. "We ask for it."

They went over the details, and then Dante went back to his apartment. He ran a bath; he wanted to use the expensive scents in the Villa. As he lay in the hot, perfumey water, his black, horselike Clericuzio hair soaped into a white, heavy topknot, he thought about what his fate would be. After he and Losey dumped the body of Cross into the desert, miles from Vegas, the toughest part of the operation would begin. He would have to convince his grandfather that he was innocent. If worse came to worst, he could confess to Pippi's death also, and his grandfather would forgive him. The Don had always showed him a special love.

Also, now, Dante was the Family Hammer. He would apply for appointment as *Bruglione* of the West and the overlordship of the Xanadu Hotel. Giorgio would oppose him, but Vincent and Petie would be neutral. They were content to live on their legal enterprises. And the old man could not live forever, Giorgio was a white-collar guy. There would come a time when the warmaker would become the emperor. He would not retreat into society. He would lead the Family back to its glory. He would never give up the power over life and death.

Dante left the bath and showered to get all the soap out of his ropy hair. He anointed his body with the colognes from their fancy bottles, sculpted his hair from delicate tubes of aromatic gels, reading the directions carefully. Then he went to the suitcase that held his Renaissance hats and chose one encrusted with precious jewels that had the shape of a custard. Its threads were gold and purple. Lying there it looked ridiculous, but when he put it on his head, Dante was enchanted. It made him look like a prince. Especially the row of studded green gems sewed along the front. This was how Athena would see him tonight, or failing that, Tiffany. But the two could wait if necessary.

As he finished dressing, Dante thought of what his life would come to be. He would live in a Villa, as luxurious as any palace. He would have an inexhaustible supply of beautiful women, a self-supporting harem dancing and singing in the Xanadu Hotel showroom. He could eat in six different restaurants with six different national cuisines. He could order the death of an enemy, reward a friend. He would be as close to being a Roman emperor as modern times allowed. Only Cross stood in the way.

Jim Losey, finally alone in his apartment, was contemplating the course his life had taken. He had been, for the first half of his career, a great cop, a true knight defending his society. He'd had an intense hatred for all criminals, especially blacks. And then gradually he had changed. He resented the charges in the media that cops were brutal. The very society he was defending from scum was attacking him. His superiors, with their gold-braided uniforms, sided with the politicians who talked shit to the people. All that bullshit about how you couldn't hate blacks. What was so bad about that? They committed most of the crimes. And wasn't he a free American who could hate whoever he wanted to hate? They were the cockroaches who would eat away all civilization. They didn't want to work, they didn't want to study, burning the midnight oil was a joke to them unless it meant shooting basketball under the light of the moon. They mugged unarmed citizens, they turned their women into whores, and they had an intolerable disrespect for the law and its enforcers. It was his job to protect the rich from the malice of the poor. And his own desire was to become rich. He wanted the clothing, the cars, the food, the drink, and above all, the women the rich could afford. And surely that was American.

It had started with bribes to protect the gambling, then some frame-ups of drug dealers to make them pay protection. He had been proud of his "hero cop" status, the recognition he received for the courage he had shown, but there was no monetary reward. He was still buying cheap clothes, he still had to be very careful with his money to make his paycheck stretch out. And he, who guarded the rich against the poor, received no reward, indeed was one of the poor. But the final straw was that in public esteem he was lower than the criminal. Some of his friends, law enforcers, had been prosecuted and sent to jail for doing their duty. Or fired from their jobs. Rapists, burglars, lethal muggers, armed robbers in broad daylight, had more rights than cops.

Over the years, Losey sold himself his story in his head. The press and TV reviled law enforcers. The fucking Miranda rights, the fucking ACLU; let those fucking lawyers do patrol for six months, they'd grow a lynching tree.

After all, he used the tricks, the beatings, and the threats to get some scumbag to confess his crime and to put him away from society. But Losey could not sell himself completely, he was too good a cop. He could not sell himself on having become a murderer.

Forget all that; he would be rich. He would fling his badge and his bravery citations into the face of the government and the public. He would be security chief for the Xanadu Hotel at ten times the salary, and from this Paradise in the desert, he would watch with pleasure as Los Angeles crumbled under the assault of criminals he would no longer fight. Tonight he would see the movie *Messalina* and go to the wrap party. And maybe get a shot at Athena. Here his mind cringed, even as he felt his body ache with the thought of exercising such sexual power. At the party, he'd pitch a feature film to Skippy based on his career, the greatest hero cop in the LAPD. Dante had told him that Cross wanted to invest, which was really funny. Why kill off a guy who would invest in his movie? That was simple. Because he knew Dante would kill him if he backed out. And Losey, tough as he was, knew he could not kill Dante. He knew the Clericuzio too well.

For a flash he thought of Marlowe, a good nigger, really sweet, always so cheerful and cooperative. He had always liked Marlowe, and his murder was the one thing he felt sorry about.

Jim Losey still had hours to wait before the screening and the party. He could go gamble in the main casino, but gambling was a mug's game. He decided against it. He had a big night ahead. First the movie and the party, then at three in the morning he would have to help Dante kill Cross De Lena and bury him in the desert.

Bobby Bantz invited the above-the-line principals of *Messalina* to his Villa for celebratory drinks at five that evening: Athena, Dita Tommey, Skippy Deere, and as a courtesy, Cross De Lena. Only

Cross declined, claiming pressure of duties at the Hotel on this special night.

Bantz had brought his latest "conquest," a seemingly fresh young girl named Johanna, discovered by a talent scout in a small town in Oregon. She was signed to a five-hundred-dollar-a-week contract for two years. Beautiful but completely untalented, she gave off such a virginal air that the innocence was a separate attraction. And yet with a shrewdness beyond her years, she had refused to sleep with Bobby Bantz until he promised to bring her to Vegas for the showing of *Messalina*.

Skippy Deere, with an adjoining apartment in Bantz's Villa, chose to be a squatter in Bantz's place, and so prevented Bantz from getting in a quick screw with Johanna, which made Bantz irritable. Skippy was pitching an idea for a feature film that he really was crazy about. Being crazy for a property was a legitimate part of a producer's job.

Deere was telling Bantz about Jim Losey, the greatest hero cop in the LAPD, a big, handsome son of a bitch, who might even be able to play the title role himself, since it would be a story about his life. One of those great "true" life stories where you could invent anything bizarre.

Deere and Bantz both knew that Losey playing himself was a fantasy, invented to con Losey so that he would sell his story cheap, and also for public hype.

Skippy Deere outlined the story with great enthusiasm. Nobody could sell a nonexistent property better. In a moment of pure exhilaration, he picked up the phone and, before Bantz could protest, invited the detective to the five P.M. cocktail party. Losey asked if he could bring a friend, and Deere assured him he could, assuming it was a girlfriend. Skippy Deere, as a producer of films, liked to mix different worlds together. You never knew what miracle might emerge.

Cross De Lena and Lia Vazzi were in the Xanadu penthouse suite reviewing the details of what they would do that night.

"I have all the men in place," Lia said. "I control the Villa compound. None of them know what you and I will do, they will have no part in that. But I have word that Dante has a crew from the Enclave digging your grave in the desert. We have to be careful tonight."

"After tonight is what I worry about," Cross said. "Then we have Don Clericuzio to deal with. Do you think he'll buy the story?"

"Not really," Lia said. "But that is our only hope."

Cross shrugged. "I have no choice. Dante killed my father and so now he has to kill me." He paused for a moment and then said, "I hope the Don was not on his side from the beginning. Then we have no chance."

Lia said cautiously, "We could abort everything and lay our troubles in front of the Don. Let him decide and act."

"No," Cross said. "He can't decide against his grandson."

"You're right, of course," Lia said. "But still, the Don has gone a little soft. He let those Hollywood people cheat you, and that in his youth he would never have allowed. Not the money, the disrespect."

Cross poured more brandy into Lia's glass and lit his cigar. He did not tell him about David Redfellow. "How do you like your room?" he said jokingly.

Lia puffed on his cigar. "What nonsense. So beautiful. To what purpose? Why does anyone have to live like that? It is too much. It takes away your strength. It arouses envy. It's not clever to insult the poor like that. Why then would they not want to kill you? My father was a rich man in Sicily but never did he live in luxury."

"You don't understand America, Lia," Cross said. "Every poor man who sees the inside of that Villa rejoices. Because he knows in his heart someday he will live in just such a place."

At that moment the private phone in the penthouse rang. Cross picked it up. His heart gave a little jump. It was Athena.

"Can we meet before the movie shows?" she asked.

"Only if you come to my suite," Cross said. "I really can't leave here."

"How gallant," Athena said coolly. "Then we can meet after the wrap party, I'll leave early and you can come to my Villa."

"I really can't," Cross said.

"I'm leaving in the morning for L.A.," Athena said. "Then the day after, I fly to France. We won't meet in private until you come there . . . if you come."

Cross looked at Lia, who shook his head and frowned. So Cross said to Athena, "Can you come to me here, now? Please?"

He waited for a long time before she said, "Yes, give me an hour."

"I'll send a car and security for you," Cross said. "They'll be waiting outside your Villa." He hung up the phone and said to Lia, "We have to watch out for her. Dante is crazy enough to do anything."

The cocktail party in Bantz's Villa was graced by beauty.

Melo Stuart brought a young actress with a great stage reputation that he and Skippy Deere planned to cast as the female lead in the Jim Losey Story. She had a strong Egyptian beauty, bold features, an imperious manner. Bantz had his new find, Johanna, last name not decided, the innocent virgin. Athena, who had never looked so radiant, was surrounded by her friends: Claudia, Dita Tommey, and Molly Flanders. Athena was unusually quiet, but still Johanna and the stage actress, Liza Wrongate, looked at her almost in awe and envy. Both came to Athena, the Queen they hoped to replace.

Claudia asked Bobby Bantz, "Didn't you invite my brother?"

"Sure," Bantz said. "He was too busy."

"Thanks for giving Ernest's family his points," Claudia said, grinning.

"Molly robbed me," Bantz said. He had always liked Claudia, maybe because Marrion had liked her, so he didn't mind her kidding. "She held a cannon to my head."

"But you could have made it tough," Claudia said. "Marrion would approve."

Bantz stared at her blankly. He felt suddenly tearful. Never would he be the man Marrion had been. And he missed him.

Meanwhile Skippy Deere had cornered Johanna and was telling her about his new film, which had a great cameo of an innocent young girl grossly raped and killed by a drug dealer. "You look perfect for the part. You don't have much experience but if I can get it past Bobby, you can come and test." He paused for a moment and then said in a warm, confidential manner, "I think you should change your name. Johanna is too square for your career." Implying the stardom that lay ahead.

He noted how her face flushed; really it was touching how young girls believed in their beauty, desired to be stars, as passionately as Renaissance girls wanted to be saints. When Ernest Vail's cynical smile appeared before him, Deere thought: Laugh as much as you like, still it was a spiritual desire. In both instances it would lead more often to martyrdom than glory, but that was part of the deal.

Johanna went off predictably to talk to Bantz. Deere joined Melo Stuart and his new girlfriend, Liza. Though she was talented on stage, Skippy had doubts about her future on the movie screen. The camera was too cruel for her kind of beauty. And her intelligence would make her unfit for many roles. But Melo had insisted she be the female lead in the Losey picture, and there were times when Melo could not be denied. And the female lead was just a bullshit, carry-the-water-bag part.

Deere kissed Liza on both cheeks. "I saw you in New York," he said. "Marvelous performance." He paused for a moment and said, "I'll hope you take the part in my new movie. Melo thinks it will be your breakthrough on film."

Liza gave him a cold smile. "I have to see the script," she said. Deere felt that flash of resentment he always felt. She was getting the break of her life and she wanted to see a fucking script. He could see Melo smiling with amusement.

"Of course," Deere said. "But believe me I would not send you a script that was not worthy of your talent."

Melo, never as ardent a lover as he was a businessman, said, "Liza, we can guarantee you the leading female role in an A feature. The script is not a sacred text as in the theater. It can be changed to please you."

Liza gave him a slightly warmer smile. She said, "You believe that crap too? Stage plays are rewritten. What do you think we do when we try them out of town?"

Before they could answer, Jim Losey and Dante Clericuzio entered the apartment. Deere rushed over to greet them and introduce them to the others at the party.

Losey and Dante were an almost comical pair. Losey, tall, handsome, impeccably tailored—full shirt and tie, despite the intense July heat of Vegas. And Dante beside him, his hugely muscled body bulging out of a T-shirt, his brightly jeweled Renaissance cap crowning his black ropy hair, and so short. All the others in the room, experts in make-believe worlds, knew these two were not make-believe, despite their weirdness. Their faces were too blank and cold. That could not be duplicated with shadows.

Losey immediately addressed Athena and told her how he looked forward to seeing her in *Messalina.* He abandoned his intimidating style and was almost fawning. Women had always found him charming, could Athena be an exception?

Dante helped himself to a drink and sat on the sofa. No one came near him except Claudia. They had not seen each other more than three times over the years, all they had in common were childhood memories. Claudia kissed him on the cheek. When they were children he had tormented her, but she always remembered him with a certain fondness.

Dante reached up to give her a hug. "*Cugina,* you look beautiful. If you looked like that when we were kids I would never have beaten you up so much."

Claudia plucked his Renaissance hat from his head. "Cross told me about your hats. They make you look cute." She put the hat on her head. "Even the Pope doesn't have a hat this cute."

"And he has a lot of hats," Dante said. "Now who would have thought you'd become such a big wheel in the movie business."

"What do you do these days?" Claudia asked.

"I run a meat company," Dante said. "We supply the hotels." He smiled, then asked, "Listen, could you introduce me to your beautiful star?"

Claudia brought him over to Athena, who was still cornered by Jim Losey putting on his charm. Athena smiled at Dante's Renaissance hat. Dante made himself look disarmingly comical.

Losey continued on with his flattery. "I know your movie will be great," he told her. "After the wrap party maybe you'll let me be your bodyguard back to the Villa, then we can have a drink together." He was playing the good cop role.

Athena was at her best refusing an advance. She smiled at him sweetly. "I'd love to," she said. "But I'm only going to stay a half hour at the party and I wouldn't want you to miss it. I have to catch an early plane tomorrow, then I fly to France. I simply have too many things to do."

Dante was admiring her. He could see she loathed Losey and that she was afraid of him. But she had made Losey think he could somehow have a shot at her.

"I can fly with you to L.A.," Losey said. "What time is your flight?"

"You are nice," Athena said. "But it's a small private charter and all the seats are full."

When she was safely back in her Villa, she called Cross and told him that she was on her way over.

The first thing Athena was aware of was the security. There were guards on the elevator to the penthouse suite of the Xanadu Hotel. There was a special key to unlock the elevator. The elevator itself had security cameras in the ceiling, and its doors opened up into an anteroom that held five men. One was at the elevator door to greet her. Another man was at the lone desk that held a bank of TV screens, and there were two other men playing cards in the corner of the room. Another was seated at the sofa reading *Sports Illustrated.*

They all looked at her with a special appraising, slightly astonished look she had encountered many times, acknowledging that her beauty was of a special variety. But it had long since failed to rouse her vanity; now it only made her aware of some danger.

The man at the desk pushed a button that opened the door to Cross's suite, and she went in, the door swinging shut behind her.

She was in the office part of the suite. Cross met her and led her into the living quarters. He kissed her briefly on the lips and then led her into the bedroom. Without saying a word, they both undressed and held each other naked. For Cross it was such a relief to hold her flesh, to look into her radiant face, that he sighed. "I'd rather just look at you than do anything else in the world."

In reply, she caressed him, made him kiss her, drew him down on the bed. She felt that this was a man who truly loved her, would do anything she commanded, and in return she would give him his every wish. For the first time in a very long time, she responded both physically and mentally. She truly loved him and loved making love to him. Yet she always knew he was dangerous, even to her, in some way.

After an hour they dressed and went out onto the balcony.

Las Vegas was showered in neon lights, the late sun baked the streets and gaudy hotels in a great band of gold. Beyond was the desert and the mountains. Here in time, they were isolated; the green flags of the villas hung limply in the air.

Athena held his hand tightly. "Will I see you at the movie and the wrap party?" she asked.

"I'm sorry, I can't," Cross said. "But I'll see you in France."

"I've noticed it's very hard to get to see you," Athena said. "The locked elevator and all those guards."

Cross said, "It's just for the next few days, too many strange people in town."

"I met your cousin, Dante," Athena said. "That detective seems to be a buddy of his. They make a charming pair. Losey was very interested in my welfare, and my schedule. Dante offered his help too. They were so worried about my getting to L.A. safely."

Cross pressed her hand. "You will," he said.

"Claudia said you and Dante are cousins," Athena said. "Why does he wear those funny hats?"

"Dante is a nice guy," Cross said.

"But Claudia told me the two of you were enemies since you were kids," Athena said.

"Sure," Cross said amiably, "but that doesn't make him a bad person."

They were silent, the streets below were clogged with vehicles and walking people migrating to different hotels for dinner and gambling. Dreaming of pleasure fraught with risk.

"So this is the last time we will see each other," Athena said and pressed his hand as if to nullify what she said.

"I said I'll meet you in France," Cross said.

"When?" Athena asked.

"I don't know," Cross said. "If I don't come, you'll know I'm dead."

"Things are that serious?" Athena said.

"Yes," Cross said.

"And you can't tell me anything about it?" Athena asked.

Cross didn't answer for a moment. "You'll be safe," he said. "And I think I'll be safe. I can't tell you any more than that."

"I'll wait," Athena said. She kissed him and then walked out of the bedroom and out of the suite. Cross watched and then went out to the balcony to see her emerge from the Hotel and onto the colonnade. He saw the car with his security guards drive her to her Villa. Then he picked up the phone and called Lia Vazzi. He told Vazzi to tighten security around Athena even more.

By ten P.M. the theater section of the ballroom of the Xanadu Hotel was full. The audience was gathered waiting for the first rough cut showing of *Messalina.* There was a premiere seating section that consisted of soft armchairs with a telephone console in the middle. There was one empty seat with a wreath of flowers bearing Steve Stalling's name. The other seats held Claudia, Dita Tommey, and Bobby Bantz and his companion, Johanna. Melo Stuart and Liza. Skippy Deere immediately took possession of the phone.

Athena was the last to arrive and was cheered by the crew and stunt men below the line. The above-the-line people, the supporting cast, and all the people seated in the armchairs applauded and kissed her on the cheek as she made her way to the center armchair. Then Skippy Deere picked up the phone and told the projectionist to begin.

Against the black background the line "Dedicated to Steve Stallings" appeared, and the audience applauded in a muted, respectful fashion. The insertion had been opposed by Bobby Bantz and Skippy Deere, but Dita Tommey vetoed them, God only knew why, Bantz said. But what the hell, it was only a rough cut, and besides, the sentimentality would create some press.

Then the picture came on the screen . . .

Athena was mesmerizing, she had even more sexuality on screen than she had in real life and a wit that was no surprise to anyone who knew her well. Indeed Claudia had written lines specifically to show off this quality in her. No cost had been stinted, and the crucial sex scenes were done in good taste.

There was no question that *Messalina,* after all its troubles, would be a major hit. And that, without final music and special effects. Dita Tommey was ecstatic, she was finally a Bankable Director. Melo Stuart was calculating how much he would ask for Athena's next picture; Bantz, looking not too happy, was worrying about the same thing. Skippy was counting the money he would make; finally he could own his own jet.

Claudia was more thrilled than any of them. Her creation was up on the screen. She had sole credit and it was an original screenplay. Thanks to Molly Flanders, she had *gross* points. Of course, there had been a little rewrite by Ben Sly but not enough for a credit.

Everybody was clustered around Athena and Dita Tommey, congratulating them. But Molly had her eye on one of the stunt men. Stunt men were crazy bastards, but they had hard bodies and were great in bed.

The wreath for Steve Stallings had been brushed to the floor, and people were trampling it. Molly could see that Athena had detached herself from the crowd to pick it up and place it back on the chair. Athena caught Molly's eye and they both shrugged, Athena giving a shy smile as if to say, That's movies.

The crowd moved to the other side of the ballroom. A small band was playing, but everyone rushed the buffet tables. Then the dancing began. Molly went up to the stunt man, who was glowering around; it was at these parties they were most vulnerable. They felt their work was not appreciated, and they resented like hell when the flabby male star was allowed to punch them out on screen when they could kill the faggot bastard in real life. Just like a stunt man, his cock is already hard, Molly thought, as he led her onto the dance floor.

Athena only spent an hour at the party. Receiving everyone's congratulations, she was gracious, and yet she observed herself being gracious and she hated it. She danced with the "best boy" and other members of the crew and then with a stunt man whose aggressiveness made her decide to leave.

The Xanadu Rolls was waiting for her with an armed driver and two security guards. When she got out of the Rolls at her Villa, she was surprised to see Jim Losey coming out of the adjoining Villa. He approached her. "You were great in that movie tonight," he said. "I've never seen a better body on a woman. Especially that ass."

Athena would have been wary except that the driver and both security guards were already out of the car, positioned. It was part of her theatrical training, the blocking out of the stage where actors position themselves. She noted that they placed themselves so that none of the lines of fire would jeopardize any of them. She also noticed that Losey viewed them with a mild contempt.

"That was not my ass," Athena said, "but thank you anyway." She smiled at him.

Suddenly Losey was holding her hand. "You're the greatest-looking woman I ever met," he said. "Why don't you try a real guy instead of those phony actor faggots."

Athena took her hand away. "I'm an actor too, and we're not phonies. Good night."

"Can I come in for a drink?" Losey asked.

"I'm sorry," Athena said, and rang the bell to the Villa. The door was opened by a butler Athena had never seen before.

Losey took a step to go in with her, and then to her surprise, the butler walked outside and quickly pushed her into the Villa. The three security guards formed a barricade between Losey and the door.

Losey looked at them with contempt. "What the fuck is this?" he said.

The butler remained outside the door. "Miss Aquitane's security," he said. "You will have to leave."

Losey took out his police ID. "You see who I am," he said. "I'll kick the shit out of all of you, and then I'll lock you up."

The butler looked at the ID. He said, "You're Los Angeles. No jurisdiction." He pulled out his own ID. "I'm Las Vegas County."

Athena Aquitane had remained just inside the doorway. She was surprised her new butler was a detective, but now she was beginning to understand. "Don't make a big deal out of it," she said, and closed the door against all of them.

Both men put their IDs back into their jackets.

Losey gave each in turn a hard stare. "I'll remember you guys," he said. None of the men reacted.

Losey turned away. He had more important fish to fry. In the next two hours Dante Clericuzio would be bringing Cross De Lena to their Villa.

Dante Clericuzio, Renaissance hat perched on his head, was having a great time at the wrap party. He used fun to prepare himself for serious action. A girl in the catering crew had caught his attention, but she gave him no encouragement because she had focused on one of the stunt men. The stunt man had given Dante threatening looks. Lucky for him, Dante thought, I have business to do tonight. He looked at his watch, maybe good old Jim had managed to snare Athena. Tiffany had never showed, though she had been promised. Dante decided to start a half hour early. He called Cross, using the private number with the operator.

Cross answered.

"I have to see you right away," Dante said. "I'm in the ballroom. Great party."

"So, come up," Cross said.

"No," Dante said. "These are orders. Not on the phone and not in your suite. Come on down."

There was a long pause. Then Cross said, "I'll be down."

Dante stationed himself so that he could observe Cross making his way through the ballroom. There seemed to be no security around him. Dante patted down his hat and thought back to their childhood together. Cross had been the only boy who had made him fearful, and he had fought him often because of that fear. But he loved the way Cross looked, had often been envious. And he envied his cousin's confidence. It was just too bad . . .

Once he killed Pippi, Dante had known he could not let Cross remain alive. Now, after this, he would have to confront the Don. But Dante had never doubted that his grandfather loved him, he had always shown his love. The Don might not like this, but he would never invoke his awful power to punish his beloved grandson.

Cross was standing before him. Now he had to get Cross to the Villa where Losey was waiting. It would be simple. He would shoot Cross, and then they would drive his body out into the desert and bury him. Nothing fancy, as Pippi De Lena had always preached. The car was already parked behind the Villa for transport.

Cross said to him abruptly, "So what is it?" He did not look suspicious or even wary. "Nice new hat," he said and smiled. Dante had always envied that smile, as though the guy knew everything Dante was thinking.

Dante played it very slow, very low-voiced. He took Cross by the arm and led him outside, in front of the huge colored marquee that had cost the Xanadu Hotel ten million dollars. The flashing blue, red, and purple bathed their figures in cold light blanched by the desert moon. Dante whispered to Cross, "Giorgio flew in, he's at my Villa. Top secret. And he wants to see you right away. That's why I couldn't say anything on the phone."

Dante was delighted that Cross looked concerned. "He told me not to tell you anything, but he's pissed off. I think he found out something about your old man."

At this Cross gave Dante a somber look, almost one of displeasure. Then he said, "OK, let's go." And he led Dante through the grounds of the Hotel to the Villa compound.

The four guards at the compound gates recognized Cross and waved them through.

Dante opened the door with a flourish and doffed his Renaissance hat. He said, "After you," and smiled slyly, which gave his face a puckish humor.

Cross walked in.

. . .

Jim Losey was filled with cold rage when he turned away from Athena's guards and walked back to his own Villa. Yet there was a part of his brain that assessed the situation, gave out a warning signal. What were all those guards doing around? But, shit, she was a movie star and that experience with Boz Skannet must have scared the hell out of her.

He used his key to get into the Villa, it seemed to be deserted, everyone was at the party. He had more than an hour to get ready to receive Cross. He went to his suitcase and unlocked it. There was his Glock, gleaming, wiped clean of oil. He opened his other suitcase, which had a secret pocket. In there was the bullet-filled magazine. He put them together, put on a shoulder holster and tucked the gun inside. He was all set. He noted that he was not nervous, he was never nervous in these situations. That was what made him a good cop.

Losey left the bedroom and walked into the kitchen. There were sure a lot of hallways in this Villa. From the refrigerator, he took a bottle of imported beer and a tray of canapés. He crumbled one with his teeth. Caviar. He gave a little sigh of pleasure, he had never tasted anything so delicious. This was the way to live. This was his for the rest of his life, the caviar, the showgirls, maybe some day Athena. He just had to do his job tonight.

Carrying the tray and bottle, he went into the huge living room.

The first thing that startled him was that the floor and the furniture were covered with plastic sheeting, giving the whole room a ghostly white glow. And then, seated in a plastic-covered armchair, was a man smoking a thin cigar and holding a glass of peach brandy. It was Lia Vazzi.

Losey thought, What the fuck is this? He put the tray and bottle on the coffee table and said to Lia, "I've been looking for you."

Lia puffed his cigar, took a sip of brandy. "And now you've found me," he said. He stood up. "Now you can slap me again."

Losey was too experienced a man not to be alert. He was putting things together. He had wondered why the other apartments in the Villa were vacant, it had struck him as strange. He casually unbuttoned his jacket and grinned at Lia. More than a slap this time, he thought. It would be an hour before Dante arrived with Cross, he could work while waiting. Now that he was armed, he had no fear of being one-on-one with Lia.

Suddenly there was a flood of men in the room. They seeped in from the kitchen, the connecting foyer, from the video/TV room. They were all bigger than Jim Losey. Only two of them had drawn guns.

Losey said to them, "You know I'm a cop?"

"We all know that," Lia said in a reassuring voice. He stepped closer to Losey. At the same time, the two men pressed their guns against Losey's back.

Lia flipped his hand inside Losey's jacket and came out holding the Glock. He handed it to one of the men and then gave Losey a quick pat-down.

"Now," Lia said, "you always had so many questions to ask. Here I am. Ask."

Losey still had no real fear. He was just worried that Dante would arrive with Cross. He could not believe that a man like himself, who had had the great good fortune to remain alive in so many dangerous situations, could finally be overcome.

"I know you set that guy Skannet up," Losey said. "And I'll get you for it sooner or later."

"It will have to be sooner," Lia said. "There's no later. Yes, you are right and now you can die happy."

Losey still could not believe that anyone would dare to murder a police officer in cold blood. Sure, drug dealers would exchange bullets, and sure, some crazy nigger would blow you away because you showed a badge, as would fleeing bank robbers, but no mob guy would have the balls to execute a police officer. It would be too much heat.

He reached out to shove Lia away, to achieve a dominance over the situation. But suddenly there was a shocking line of fire slashing through his stomach and his legs trembled. He started to crumble to his knees. Something thick slapped against his head and his ear was on fire and he could not hear. He sank to his knees and the rug felt like an enormous cushion. He looked up. Standing over him was Lia Vazzi, and in his hands was a thin silk rope.

Lia Vazzi had spent two whole days sewing together the two body bags he would have to use. They were of dark brown canvas with a drawstring at the head. Each bag could contain a large body. There was no possible leakage of blood from the bag, and once you drew the string, you could sling it over your shoulder like an army duffel bag. Losey had not noticed the two bags lying on the sofa. Now the men stuffed his body into one, and Lia drew the string tight. He left the bag leaning upright against the sofa. He gave orders to the men that they were to surround the Villa but were not to appear until he summoned them explicitly. They knew what they were to do after that.

Cross and Dante strolled from the compound gates toward Dante's Villa. The night air was oppressive with the cauldron of heat spewed from the day's desert sun. They were both perspiring. Dante noted that Cross was dressed in slacks, open shirt, and buttoned jacket, that he could be armed . . .

The seven Villas, their green flags waving slightly, made a magnificent sight under the desert moon. They looked like edifices from another century with their balconies, their frilled green awnings over the windows, their huge white doors decorated with gold. Dante held Cross by the arm. "Look at that," he said. "Isn't it beautiful? I hear you're fucking that great-looking broad in the movie. Congratulations. When you get tired of her let me know."

"Sure," Cross said amiably. "She sort of likes you and your hat."

Dante took off his hat and said eagerly, "Everybody likes my hats. Did she really say she likes me?"

"She's enchanted by you," Cross said dryly.

"Enchanted," Dante said musingly. "That's really classy." He wondered for a moment if Losey had been able to get Athena into their Villa for a drink. That would be the icing on the cake. He was tickled that he had distracted Cross, he had noticed the slight irritation in his cousin's voice.

They were at the door of the Villa. There seemed to be no security guards around. Dante pressed the bell, waited, and then rang again. When there was no answer, he took out his key and opened the door. They entered Losey's suite.

Dante was thinking, Maybe Losey was in the sack with Athena. Which was a hell of a way to run an operation, but he would have done the same thing.

Dante led Cross into the living room and was astonished to see the walls and furniture covered with clear plastic sheets. Leaning against the sofa was a huge brown duffel bag standing upright. On the sofa was an empty duffel bag of the same kind. All under plastic. "Jesus Christ, what the hell is this?" Dante said.

He turned to face Cross. Cross was holding a very small gun in his hand. "To keep the blood off the furniture," Cross said. "I have to tell you, I never thought your hats were cute and I never believed that a mugger killed my father."

Dante was thinking, Where the hell is Losey? He called out to him, meanwhile thinking that such a small-caliber gun could never stop him.

Cross said, "All your life you were a Santadio."

Dante whirled sideways to give a smaller target and flung himself on Cross. His strategy worked; the bullet hit him in the shoulder. He had a fraction of a second of joy, that he would win, and then the bullet exploded, taking away half of his arm. And he realized there was no hope. Then he really surprised Cross. With his good arm, he began pulling up the plastic sheeting from the floor. Blood pouring from his body, his arms filled with plastic sheeting, he tried to stagger away from Cross, then held up the sheets of plastic as a silvery shield.

Cross stepped forward. Very deliberately he fired through the plastic, then fired again. The bullets exploded, and Dante's face was almost covered with tiny bits of plastic turned red. Dante's left thigh seemed to separate from his body as Cross fired again. Dante fell, the white rug now held concentric circles of scarlet. Cross knelt beside Dante and wrapped his head with plastic and fired again. The Renaissance cap still on his head exploded upward into the air but remained attached. Cross saw that the hat was secured to the head by some sort of clip but now it rested on an open skull. It seemed to float.

Cross stood up and put the gun in the holster in the small of his back. At that moment Lia came into the room. They looked at each other.

"It's done," Lia said. "Wash off in the bathroom and go back to the Hotel. And get rid of your clothes. I'll take the gun and clean up."

"And the rugs and the furniture?" Cross asked.

"I'll take care of everything," Lia said. "Wash up and go to that party."

When Cross left, Lia helped himself to a cigar that was on a marble-topped table and looked for bloodstains while he was at it. There were none. But the sofa and the floor were soaked. Well, that was it.

He wrapped Dante's body in the plastic sheeting and, with the help of two of his men, stuffed it into the empty canvas bag. Then he gathered all the plastic sheeting in the room and stuffed it into the same bag. When he had finished, he drew the strings tight. First, they carried the bag containing Losey into the Villa garage and threw it into the van. They made another trip with Dante's body bag.

The van had been modified by Lia Vazzi. It had double floors with a space between the two. Lia and his men squeezed the two bags into the hollow space and then rejoined the floor strips.

As a Qualified Man, Lia had prepared for everything. In the van were two cans of gasoline. He himself carried them back into the Villa and poured them over the floors and furniture. He set a fuse that would give him five minutes to get away. Then he got into the van and started the long drive to L.A.

Before him and after him were the members of his crew.

It was early morning before he pulled onto the pavement in front of the yacht that was waiting for him. He unloaded the two bags and brought them aboard. The yacht pulled away from shore.

It was nearly noon when, far out at sea, he watched the iron cage holding the two bodies slowly descend into the ocean. They had made their final Communion.

Molly Flanders disappeared with her stunt man, to his room in the Hotel rather than to the Villa, because Molly, despite her affection for the less worldly in power, had a tiny trace of the old Hollywood snobbism, she didn't want it known she was screwing below the line.

The wrap party began to filter out just as dawn appeared, the sun rising ominously clad in red, a thin trail of blue smoke rising to meet it.

Cross had changed his clothes and showered and then had gone to the party. He was seated with Claudia, Bobby Bantz, Skippy Deere, and Dita Tommey celebrating the sure success of *Messalina.* Suddenly there were shouts of alarm from outside. The Hollywood group ran out and Cross followed them.

A thin pillar of fire rose triumphantly over the neon lights of the Vegas Strip. It mushroomed into a great pillow of plum and rosy clouds against the sandy mountains.

"Oh my God," Claudia said, holding Cross tightly by the arm. "It's one of your Villas."

Cross was silent. He watched the green flag over the Villa being consumed by smoke and fire, heard the fire engines screaming down the Strip. Twelve million dollars going up in flames to hide the blood he'd shed. Lia Vazzi was a Qualified Man who spared no expense, courted no risks.

CHAPTER 23

BECAUSE HE WAS on official leave, Detective Jim Losey's disappearance wasn't noted until five days after the fire at the Xanadu. The vanishing of Dante Clericuzio was, of course, never reported to any authorities.

The investigation led to the police finding Phil Sharkey's body. Suspicion focused on Losey, and it was assumed he had fled to escape interrogation.

L.A. detectives came to interview Cross because Losey was last seen at the Xanadu Hotel. But there was nothing to show any connection between the two men. Cross explained he had only seen him briefly on the night of the party.

But Cross was not worried about the law. He was waiting to hear from Don Clericuzio.

Surely the Clericuzio knew that Dante was missing, surely they knew he had been at the Xanadu when last seen. Why then had they not contacted him for information. Could the whole matter be passed over so easily? Cross did not believe that for a moment.

He continued to run the Hotel day by day, busy with plans to rebuild the burned-out Villa. Lia Vazzi had certainly taken care of the bloodstains.

Claudia came to visit him. She was brimming over with excitement. Cross arranged for dinner to be brought up to his suite so they could talk in private.

"You're not going to believe this," she said to Cross. "Your sister is going to be head of LoddStone Studios."

"Congratulations," Cross said, giving her a brotherly hug. "I always said you were the toughest of the Clericuzio."

"I went to our father's funeral for your sake. I made that clear to everyone," Claudia said with a frown.

Cross laughed. "You certainly did, and you pissed everybody off except the Don himself who said, 'Let her go make pictures and God bless her.' "

Claudia shrugged. "I don't care about them. But let me tell you what happened because it is so strange. When we all left Vegas in Bobby's jet, everything seemed perfect. But when we landed in L.A., all hell broke loose. Detectives arrested Bobby. For guess what?"

"Making lousy movies," Cross teased.

"No, listen, this is weird," Claudia said. "Remember that girl Johanna that Bantz had with him at the wrap party? Do you remember what she looked like? Well, it turns out she was only fifteen years old. They got Bobby on statutory rape and white slavery because he took her across the state border." Claudia's eyes were wide with excitement. "But it was all a setup. Johanna's mother and father were there screaming bloody murder that their poor daughter had been raped by a man forty years older."

"She sure didn't look fifteen," Cross said. "Though she did look like a good hustler."

"It would have made a terrible scandal," Claudia said. "But good old Skippy Deere took charge. He got Bantz off the hook for that moment. He kept him from being arrested and the whole thing getting into the media. So everything seems squared away."

Cross was smiling. Apparently good old David Redfellow had lost none of his skills.

"It's not funny," Claudia said reproachfully. "Poor Bobby was *framed.* The girl swore that Bobby forced her to have sex in Vegas. The father and mother swore they cared nothing for money but wanted to stop all future rapists of young and innocent girls. The whole Studio was in an uproar. Dora and Kevin Marrion were so upset that they talked about selling the Studio. Then Skippy took charge again. He signed the girl to star in a low-budget film, the script to be written by her father. For very good money. Then he got Benny Sly to rewrite the script in one day for a lot of money. Not bad, by the way, Benny is some kind of genius. We're all set. And then the district attorney of Los Angeles insists he's going to prosecute. The DA that LoddStone got elected, the DA who was treated like a king by Eli Marrion. Skippy even offered him a job at the Studio in Business Affairs at a million a year for five years and he turned it down. He insisted Bobby Bantz be fired as head of the Studio. Then he would make a deal. Nobody knows why he was being so hard-nosed."

"An unbribable public official," Cross said with a shrug. "It happens."

He thought of David Redfellow again. Redfellow would violently disagree that there was any such animal. And Cross envisioned how Redfellow had managed everything. Redfellow probably said to the DA, "I'm bribing you to *do* your duty?" And as for the money, Redfellow would have immediately gone to the limit. Twenty, Cross figured. On a ten-billion buy of the Studio, what the hell was twenty million? And with no risk for the DA. He would be acting strictly according to law. It was really elegant.

Claudia was still talking, fast. "Anyway, Bantz had to step down," she said. "And Dora and Kevin were happy to sell the Studio. Plus the deal for five green lights on their own movies, a billion dollars cash in their pockets. And this little Italian guy appears at the Studio, calls a meeting and announces he will be the new owner. And then right out of the blue, he makes me head of the Studio. Skippy was pissed. Now, I'm his boss. Is this crazy?"

Cross just watched her with amusement, then he smiled.

Suddenly, Claudia stood back and looked at her brother. And her eyes were darker, sharper, more intelligent than he had ever seen before. But she had a good-natured smile on her face when she said, "Just like the boys, right, Cross? Now, I'm doing it just like the boys. And I didn't even have to fuck anybody. . . ."

Cross was surprised. "What's the matter, Claudia?" he asked. "I thought you were happy."

Claudia smiled. "I am happy. I'm just not dumb. And because you're my brother, and I love you, I want you to know that I haven't been fooled."

She walked over and sat on the couch next to him. "I lied when I said I went to Daddy's funeral just for you. I went because I wanted to be part of something that he was part of, that you were part of. I went because I couldn't stay away any longer. But I do hate what they stand for, Cross. The Don as well as the others."

"Does that mean you don't want to run the Studio?" Cross asked.

Claudia laughed aloud. "No, I'm willing to admit I'm still a Clericuzio. And I want to make good movies and make a lot of money. Movies are great equalizers, Cross. I can make a good movie about great women. . . . Let's see what can happen when I use the Family talents for good instead of evil." They both laughed.

Then Cross took her in his arms. He kissed her on the cheek. "I think it's great, really great," he said.

And he meant it for himself as well as for her. For if Don Clericuzio had made her head of the Studio, he did not connect Cross with the disappearance of Dante. The whole scheme had worked.

They had finished dinner and had been talking for hours. When Claudia rose to leave, Cross took a purse of black chips from his desk. "Take a shot at the tables on the house," he said.

She gave him a soft slap on the cheek and said, "Only if you're not going to get into that big brother thing again and talk to me like a child. That last time I wanted to deck you."

He hugged her, it felt good to feel her so close. In a moment of weakness, he said, "You know, I left a third of my estate to you in case anything happens. And I'm very rich. So you can always tell the Studio to fuck off if you want to."

Claudia eyes were shining when she said, "Cross, I appreciate you worrying about me, but I can tell the Studio to fuck off anyway, without your estate . . ." Then suddenly she looked worried. "Is anything wrong? Are you sick?"

"No, no," Cross said. "I just wanted you to know."

"Thank God," Claudia said. "Now that I'm in, maybe you can get out. You can break away from the Family. You can be free."

Cross laughed. "I am free," he said. "I'm going away very soon, to live with Athena in France."

...

On the afternoon of the tenth day, Giorgio Clericuzio appeared at the Xanadu to see him, and Cross felt a sinking sensation in his stomach that he knew would lead to panic if he did not control it.

Giorgio left his bodyguards outside the suite with Hotel Security. But Cross was under no illusions, his own bodyguards would follow any order Giorgio gave. And he was not reassured by Giorgio's appearance. Giorgio seemed to have lost weight, and his face was very pale. It was the first time that Cross had seen him look as though he was not in complete control.

Cross greeted him effusively. "Giorgio," he said, "this is an unexpected pleasure. Let me call down and get a Villa ready for you."

Giorgio gave him a tired smile and said, "We can't locate Dante." He paused for a moment. "He's gone off the map and the last time he was seen was here at the Xanadu."

"Jesus," Cross said, "that's serious. But you know Dante, he was not always under control."

Now Giorgio didn't bother to smile. "He was with Jim Losey and Losey is gone too."

"They were a funny combo," Cross said. "I wondered about that."

"They were pals," Giorgio said. "The old man didn't like it but Dante was the guy's paymaster."

"I'll help any way I can," Cross said. "I'll check all the Hotel employees. But you know Dante and Losey weren't officially registered. We never do that for anyone in the Villas."

"You can do that when you get back," Giorgio said. "The Don wants to see you personally. He even chartered a plane to bring you back."

Cross paused for a long moment. "I'll pack a bag," he said. "Giorgio, is it serious?"

Giorgio looked him squarely in the face. "I don't know," he said.

On the chartered plane to New York, Giorgio studied a briefcase full of papers. Cross did not impose himself, though this was a bad sign. In any case Giorgio would never give him any information.

The plane was met by three closed cars and six Clericuzio soldiers. Giorgio got into one car and motioned Cross into another. Again a bad sign. Dawn was breaking when the cars rolled through the security gates of the Clericuzio compound in Quogue.

The door of the house was guarded by two men. Other men were scattered around the compound, but there were no women or children to be seen.

Cross said to Giorgio, "Where the hell is everybody, in Disneyland?" But Giorgio refused to acknowledge the joke.

The first thing Cross saw in the Quogue living room was a circle of eight men, and inside that circle two men were talking in a very amiable way. His heart gave a jump. They were Petie and Lia Vazzi. Vincent was watching them and he looked angry.

Petie and Lia seemed to be on the best of terms. But Lia was dressed only in slacks and a shirt, no jacket or tie. Lia usually dressed formally, so this meant he had been searched and disarmed. And indeed he looked like a cheerful mouse surrounded by merry, menacing cats. Lia gave Cross a sad nod of acknowledgment. Petie never glanced his way. But when Giorgio led Cross into the back den, Petie broke off and followed, as did Vincent.

There, Don Clericuzio was waiting for them. Seated in a huge armchair, he was smoking one of his crooked cigars. Vincent went to him and handed him a glass of wine from the bar. Cross was offered nothing. Petie remained at the door, standing. Giorgio sat down on the sofa next to the Don and motioned to Cross to sit with him.

The Don's face, drawn thin with age, had no trace of emotion. Cross kissed him on the cheek. The Don looked at him and his face softened as if with sadness.

"So Croccifixio," the Don said, "it was all cleverly done. But now you must explain your reasons. I am Dante's grandfather, my daughter is his mother. The men here are his uncles. You must answer to all of us."

Cross tried to keep his composure. "I don't understand," he said.

Giorgio said harshly, "Dante. Where is he?"

"Christ, how should I know?" Cross said as if surprised. "He never reported to me. He could be down in Mexico having a good time."

Giorgio said, "You don't understand. Don't fuck around. You are already judged guilty. Where did you dump him?"

At the bar, Vincent turned away as though he could not look into his face. Behind him Cross could hear Petie coming closer to the sofa.

"Where's the proof?" Cross said. "Who says I killed Dante?"

"I do." It was the Don who spoke. "Understand: I have pronounced you guilty. There is no appeal from that judgment. I brought you here to make your plea for mercy, but you must justify the killing of my grandson."

Hearing that voice, the measured tone, Cross knew that everything was over. For him and Lia Vazzi. But Vazzi already knew. It had been in his eyes.

Vincent turned to Cross, his granite face softened. "Tell my father the truth, Cross, it's your only chance."

The Don nodded. He said, "Croccifixio, your father was more than my nephew, of Clericuzio blood, as you are. Your father was my trusted friend. And so I will listen to your reasons."

Cross prepared himself. "Dante killed my father. I judged him guilty as you judged me guilty. And he killed my father out of revenge and ambition. He was a Santadio in his heart."

The Don did not respond. Cross went on. "How could I not avenge my father? How could I forget my father was responsible for my life? And I had too much respect for the Clericuzio, as my father had, to suspect your hand in the killing. Yet, I think you must have known Dante was guilty and did nothing. So how could I come to you to redress the wrong?"

"Your proof," Giorgio said.

"A man like Pippi De Lena could never be surprised," Cross said. "And Jim Losey at the other end is too much of a coincidence. There is not a man in this room who believes in coincidence. All of you know Dante was guilty. And Don, you yourself told me the story of the Santadio. Who knows what Dante planned after he killed me, as he surely knew he must. Next, his uncles." Cross did not dare to mention the Don. "He counted on your affection," he said to the Don.

The Don had laid his cigar aside. He face was inscrutable but held a touch of sadness.

It was Petie who spoke. Petie had been the closest to Dante. "Where did you dump the body?" Petie asked again. And Cross could not answer him, could not get the words out of his mouth.

There was a long silence and then finally the Don raised his head to all of them and spoke. "Funerals are wasted on the young," he said. "What have they done to celebrate them? How have they inspired great respect? The young have no compassion, no gratitude. And my daughter is already crazy, why should we compound her grief and erase hopes for her recovery. She will be told her son has fled and it will take years for her to know the truth."

And now it seemed that everyone in the room relaxed. Petie came forward and sat on the sofa beside Cross. Vincent, behind the bar, raised a glass of brandy to his lips in what could have been a salute.

"But justice or no, you have committed a crime against the Family," the Don said. "There must be a punishment. For you, money, for Lia Vazzi, his life."

Cross said, "Lia had nothing to do with Dante, for Losey, yes. Let me ransom him. I own half the Xanadu. I will transfer half that ownership to you as payment for me and Vazzi."

Don Clericuzio seemed to ponder this. "You are loyal," he said. He turned to Giorgio and then Vincent and Petie. "If you three agree, I will agree." They did not answer.

The Don sighed as if in regret. "You will sign over half your interest but you must move out of our world. Vazzi must return to Sicily with his family, or not, as he pleases. That is as far as I can go. You and Vazzi must never speak together again. And I order my sons, in your presence, never to avenge their nephew's death. You will have a week to arrange your affairs, to sign the necessary papers for Giorgio." Then the Don spoke in a less harsh voice. "Let me assure you that I had no knowledge of Dante's plans. Now, go in peace and remember I always loved your father like a son."

When Cross left the house, Don Clericuzio got out of his chair and said to Vincent, "To bed." Vincent helped him up the stairs, for the Don now had a certain weakness in his legs. His age was finally beginning to ravage his body.

EPILOGUE

Nice, France
Quogue

ON HIS LAST DAY in Vegas, Cross De Lena sat on his penthouse balcony and looked down on the sun-drenched Strip. The great hotels—Caesars Palace, the Flamingo, the Desert Inn, the Mirage, and the Sands—blazed their neon marquees to challenge the sun.

Don Clericuzio had been specific in his banishment: Cross was never to return to Las Vegas. How happy his father, Pippi, had been here, and Gronevelt had built the city into his own Valhalla, but Cross had never really enjoyed their ease. True, he had enjoyed the pleasures of Vegas, but those pleasures always held the cold flavor of steel.

The green flags of the seven Villas dropped in the desert stillness, but one hung from the burned building, a black skeleton, the ghost of Dante. But he would never see all of this again.

He had loved the Xanadu, he had loved his father, Gronevelt, and Claudia. And yet he had in some sense betrayed them. Gronevelt, by failing to be faithful to the Xanadu; his father, by not being true to the Clericuzio; and Claudia, because she believed in his innocence. Now he was free of them. He would begin a new life.

What could he make of his love for Athena? He had been warned of the dangers of romantic love by Gronevelt, by his father, and even by the old Don. That was the fatal flaw of great men who would control their worlds. Then why was he now ignoring their advice? Why was he placing his fate at the mercy of a woman?

Quite simply, the sight of her, the sound of her voice, the way she moved, her happiness and her sorrow, all made him happy. The world became dazzlingly pleasurable when he was with her. Food became delicious, the sun's heat warmed his bones, and he felt that sweet hunger for her flesh that made life holy. And when he slept with her he never feared those nightmares that preceded the dawn.

It was now three weeks since he had last seen Athena, but he had heard her voice just this morning. He had called her in France to tell her he was coming, and he had caught the happiness in her voice because now she knew he was still alive. It was possible she loved him. And now, in less than twenty hours he would see her.

Cross had faith that someday she would truly love him, that she would reward him for his love, that she would never judge him, and that like some angel she would save him from Hell.

Athena Aquitane was perhaps the only woman in France who put on her makeup and clothes to try to destroy her beauty. Not that she tried to look ugly, she was not a masochist, but she had come to regard her physical beauty as too dangerous for her inner world. She hated the power it gave her over other people. She hated the vanity that still spoiled her spirit. It interfered with what she knew would be her life's work.

On the first day of work at the Institute for Autistic Children in Nice, she wanted to look like the children, to walk like them. She was overcome with the sense of identification. That day, she relaxed her facial muscles to their soulless serenity and limped in the weird, lopsided way of some of the children who had motor damage.

Dr. Gerard observed this and said sardonically, "Oh, very good but you're going in the wrong direction." Then he took her hands in his and said gently, "You must not identify with their misfortune. You must fight against it."

Athena felt rebuked and ashamed. Again her actress vanity had misled her. But she felt herself at peace caring for these children. It did not matter to them that her French was imperfect, they did not grasp the meaning of her words anyway.

Even the distressing realities did not discourage her. The children were sometimes destructive, did not recognize the rules of society. They fought each other and their nurses, they smeared their feces on the walls, they urinated where they pleased. Sometimes they were truly frightening in their ferocity, their repulsion of the outside world.

The only time Athena felt helpless was at night in the small apartment she had rented in Nice, when she studied the literature of the Institute. They were reports on the progress of the children and they were frightening. Then she would crawl into bed and weep. Unlike the movies she had lived in, these reports had mostly unhappy endings.

When she received the call from Cross that he was coming to see her, she felt a surge of happiness and hope. He was still alive and he would help her. Then she had some trepidation. She consulted Dr. Gerard.

"What do you think would be best?" she asked.

"He could be of great assistance to Bethany," Dr. Gerard said. "I would very much like to see how she relates to him over a period of time. And it might be very good for you. Mothers must not be martyrs for their children." She thought about his words on her way to pick up Cross at the Nice airport.

At the airport, Cross had to walk from the plane to the low-slung terminal. The air was balmy and sweet, not the scorching sulfurous heat of Vegas. Along the borders of the concrete reception plaza grew masses of luxurious red and purple flowers.

He saw Athena waiting for him on that plaza, and he marveled at her genius in transforming her appearance. She could not completely hide her beauty, but she could disguise it. Gold-framed tinted glasses turned her eyes from brilliant green to gray. The clothes she was wearing made her look thicker and heavier. Her blond hair was tucked under a country-brimmed hat of blue denim that overlapped the side of her face. He felt a thrill of possession that he was the only one who knew how beautiful she really was.

As Cross approached, Athena took off her glasses and put them in the pocket of her blouse. He smiled at her irrepressible vanity.

Less than an hour later they were in the suite of the Negresco Hotel where Napoleon had bedded Josephine. Or so the hotel brochure on the door still claimed. A waiter knocked and brought in a tray with a bottle of wine and a delicate plate of tiny sandwiches. He left it on the balcony table that overlooked the Mediterranean.

At first they were awkward with each other. She held his hand trustingly yet as if she were in command, and the touch of her warm flesh gave him a rush of desire. But he could see she was not quite ready.

The suite was beautifully furnished, more opulent than any of the Xanadu Villas. The bed had a canopy of dark red silk, the matching drapes were studded with golden fleur-de-lis. The tables and chairs had an elegance that could never have existed in the Vegas world.

Athena led Cross out to the balcony, and as she did so Cross blindly kissed her on the cheek. And then she couldn't help herself, she picked up a wet cotton napkin that was wrapped around the wine bottle and scrubbed her face free of all the disfiguring cosmetics. Her face glistened with drops of water, the skin radiant and pink. She put one hand on his shoulder and kissed him gently on the lips.

From the balcony they could view the stone houses of Nice, tinted the faded greens and blues of paint from hundreds of years ago. Below, the citizens of Nice strolled on the Promenade des Anglais, on the stony beach young men and women, almost nude, splashed into the blue-green water while little children dug themselves into the pebbly sand. Farther out, hawkish white yachts, strung with lights, patrolled the horizon.

Cross and Athena had taken their first sip of wine when they heard the faint roar. From the stone seawall, from what looked like the mouth of a cannon but was really the great eastern pipe of the sewers, a great wave of deep brown water gushed into the pristine blue of the sea.

Athena turned her head away. She said to Cross, "How long will you be here?"

"Five years if you let me," he said.

"That's silly," Athena said frowning. "What will you do here?"

Cross said. "I'm rich, maybe I'll buy a small hotel."

"What happened to the Xanadu?" Athena asked.

"I had to sell my interest," he said. He paused for a moment. "We won't have to worry about money."

"I have money," Athena said. "You have to understand. I'm going to stay here for five years and then I'm going to bring her home. I don't care what they say, I will never put her back in an institution, I'll take care of her for the rest of her life. And if anything happens to her, my life will be with children like her. So you see we can never have a life together."

Cross understood her perfectly. He took a long time to consider his answer.

His voice was strong and determined when he said, "Athena, the only thing I'm sure about now is that I love you and Bethany. You have to believe that. It's not going to be easy, I know that, but we'll try our best. You want to help Bethany, not be a martyr. For that we have to take a final jump. I'll do everything I can to help you. Look, we'll be like gamblers in my casino. The odds are stacked against us, but there's always that chance to beat the odds."

Cross saw her weakening so he pressed on. "Let's get married," he said. "Let's have other children and live our lives like normal people. With our children let's try to make right what seems wrong with our world. All families have some misfortune. I know we can overcome it. Will you believe me?"

Finally Athena looked at him directly. "Only if you believe I truly love you," she said.

In the bedroom when they made love, they took each other on faith; Athena believed that Cross would truly help her save Bethany, and Cross, that Athena truly loved him. When finally she turned her body toward him, she murmured, "I love you. I really do."

Cross bowed his head to kiss her. She said it again, "I truly love you," and Cross thought, What man on earth could disbelieve her?

Alone in his bedroom, the Don pulled the cool sheets up to his neck. Death was approaching, and he was too wily not to detect its nearness. But everything had worked out according to his plans. Ah, how easy it is to outwit the young.

During the last five years he had seen Dante as the great danger to his master plan. Dante would resist the folding of the Clericuzio Family into society. And yet, what could he himself, the Don, do?

Order the killing of his daughter's son, his own grandson? Would Giorgio, Vincent, and Petie obey such an order? And if they did, would they think him some kind of monster? Would they then fear him more than they loved him? And Rose Marie, what would remain of her sanity then, for surely she would sense the truth.

But when Pippi De Lena was killed, the die was cast. The Don immediately knew the truth of the matter, investigated Dante's relationship with Losey and made his judgment.

He had sent Vincent and Petie to guard Cross, armored car and all. And then, to forewarn Cross, told him the story of the Santadio War. How painful it was to set the world straight. And when he was gone, who would there be to make these terrible decisions? He decided now, once and for all, the Clericuzio would make its final retreat.

Vinnie and Petie would deal strictly with their restaurants and construction businesses. Giorgio would buy companies on Wall Street. The withdrawal would be complete. Even the Bronx Enclave would not be replenished. The Clericuzio would finally be safe and fight against the new outlaws who were rising all over America. He would not blame himself for past mistakes, the loss of his daughter's happiness and the death of his grandson. And after all, he had set Cross free.

Before he fell asleep, the Don had a vision. He would live forever, the Clericuzio blood would be part of mankind forever. And it was he, himself, alone who had created this lineage, his own virtue.

But, oh, what a wicked world it was that drove a man to sin.

Mario Puzo

THE LAST DON

THE DARK ARENA

THE DARK ARENA

For Erika

"Fathers and teachers, I ponder 'What is hell?' I maintain that it is the suffering of being unable to love."

"Oh, there are some who remain proud and fierce even in hell, in spite of their certain knowledge and contemplation of the absolute truth; there are some fearful ones who have given themselves over to Satan and his proud spirit entirely. For such, hell is voluntary and ever consuming; they are tortured by their own choice. For they have cursed themselves, cursing God and life. They live upon their vindictive pride like a starving man in the desert sucking blood out of his own body. But they are never satisfied, and they refuse forgiveness, they curse God Who calls them. They cannot behold the living God without hatred, and they cry out that the God of life should be annihilated, that God should destroy Himself and His own creation. And they will burn in the fire of their own wrath forever and yearn for death and annihilation. But they will not attain to death . . ."

THE BROTHERS KARAMAZOV

THE DARK ARENA

1

WALTER MOSCA felt a sense of excitement and the last overwhelming loneliness before a homecoming. The few ruins outside of Paris were remembered and familiar landmarks, and now on the last leg of his journey he could hardly wait to come to his final destination, the heart of the ruined continent, the destroyed city that he had never thought he would see again. The landmarks leading into Germany were more familiar to him than the approaches to his own land, his own city.

The train rocked with speed. It was a troop train with replacements for the Frankfort garrison, but half the car was taken by civilian employees recruited from the States. Mosca touched his silk tie and smiled. It felt strange to him. He would feel more at home with the G.I.'s at the other end, and, he thought, so would most of the twenty or so civilians with him.

There were two dim lights, one at each end of the car. The windows were boarded up, as if the car had been built so that its occupants would not be able to see the vast ruins through which they would travel. The seats were long wooden benches, leaving only one very narrow aisle along one side.

Mosca stretched out on his bench and put the blue gym bag under his head for a pillow. In the bad light he could hardly recognize the other civilians.

They had all traveled on the same Army ship together, and like himself, they all seemed excited and eager to reach Frankfort. They talked loudly to be heard over the roar of the train, and Mosca could hear Mr. Gerald's voice dominating the rest. Mr. Gerald was the highest ranking civilian in the shipment. He had with him a set of golf clubs, and on board the ship had let everyone know that his civilian grade was equal to the rank of Colonel. Mr. Gerald was happy and cheerful, and Mosca had a vision of him playing golf over the ruins of a city, the long drive above flattened and level streets, the approach to a rounded heap of rubble, and putting carefully into the top of a decaying skull.

The speed of the train slackened as it moved into a small deserted station. Outside it was night, and in the blind railroad car it was very dark. Mosca dozed, hearing only vaguely the voices of the others. But as the train picked up speed leaving the station it shook him fully awake.

The civilians were talking more quietly now, and Mosca sat up to watch the soldiers at the other end of the car. Some were sleeping on the long benches, but there were three circles of light surrounding three card games, giving their end of the car a friendly glow. He felt a faint nostalgia for the life he had led so long and left just a few months ago. By the light of their candles he could see them drinking from their canteens, not water he felt sure, and breaking out K-rations to munch chocolate bars. A G.I. was always prepared, Mosca thought with a grin. Blankets on his back, candles in his pack, water or something better in his canteen, and a rubber in his wallet at all times. Ready for good luck or bad.

Mosca stretched out again on the bench and tried to sleep. But his body was as stiff and unyielding as the hard wood beneath it. The train had picked up speed and was going very fast now. He looked at his watch. It was nearly midnight, and it was still a good eight hours to Frankfort. He sat up, took a bottle from the small, blue gym bag and, resting his head against the boarded window, kept drinking until his body relaxed. He must have fallen asleep, for when he looked down again to the soldiers' end of the car, there was only one circle of candlelight; but in the darkness behind him he could still hear the voices of Mr. Gerald and a few other civilians. They must have been drinking for Mr. Gerald's voice was patronizing, condescending, and he was boasting of his coming power, how he would put his paper empire on an efficient basis.

Two candles detached themselves from the circle at the other end of the car, their flares wavering unevenly down the aisle. As they passed him, Mosca was startled out of his drowsiness. The G.I. carrying the candles had on his face a look of malevolent and stupid hatred. The bright, yellow glow of the candles dyed the already drink-flushed face a dark red and gave the sullen eyes a dangerous, senseless look.

"Hey, soldier," the voice of Mr. Gerald called out, "how about leaving us a light?"

The candle obediently came to rest near Mr. Gerald and his group of civilians and the sound of their voices rose, as if they had taken courage from the flickering light. They tried to include the G.I. in their conversation, but he, his candles resting on the bench, his own face in darkness, refused to answer. They forgot about the soldier and spoke of other things; only once Mr. Gerald, leaning into the candlelight as if to show himself with absolute trust, said condescendingly but with real kindness to the G.I., "We were all of us in the Army too, you know." And then with a laugh to the others. "Thank God that's over."

One of the other civilians said, "Don't be too sure, we still have the Russians."

They forgot about the G.I. again until suddenly over and above their voices, above the noise of the train running so blindly across the continent, the silent G.I. shouted loudly and in drunken arrogance, yet as if in some panic, "Shut up, shut up, don't talk so much, shut your goddamn mouths."

There was a moment of surprised, embarrassed silence, and then Mr. Gerald leaned his head into the candlelight again and said to the G.I. quietly, "You had better get to your end of the car, son." There was no answer from the G.I., and Mr. Gerald continued to speak, picking up where he had been interrupted.

Suddenly he was standing up, fully lit by the flaring candles, his voice cut off. And then he said quietly, without alarm but with almost terrified disbelief, "My God, I've been hurt. That soldier did something to me."

Mosca sat up straight and other dark figures rose from the benches, one of them knocking out a candlelight as he brushed it to the floor. Mr. Gerald, still standing but not so brightly lit, said in a quiet horrified voice, "That soldier stabbed me," and fell out of the light into the darkness of his bench.

Two men from the G.I. end of the car hurried down the aisle. By the light of the candles they carried, Mosca could see the glint of officer bars.

Mr. Gerald was saying over and over again, "I've been stabbed, that soldier stabbed me." In his voice the terror was gone, it was surprised, incredulous. Mosca could see him sitting upright on the bench and then, lit up by the full power of the three candles, could see the rent in the trouser leg, high up on the thigh, the dark stain flowing over and around it. The Lieutenant bent over, holding his candle close and gave an order to the soldier with him. The soldier ran down to the other end of the car and returned with blankets and a first-aid kit. They spread the blankets on the floor and made Mr. Gerald lie down. The soldier started to cut off the trouser leg, but Mr. Gerald said, "No, roll it up; I can get it mended." The Lieutenant looked at the wound.

"It's nothing much," the Lieutenant said. "Wrap him in a blanket." There was no sympathy in his young, blank face or in his voice, only an impersonal kindness. "We'll have an ambulance waiting in Frankfort, just in case. I'll wire at the next stop." Then he turned to the others and asked, "Where is he?"

The drunken G.I. had disappeared; Mosca, peering into the darkness, saw a form huddled in the corner of the bench before him. He said nothing.

The Lieutenant went to his end of the car and returned wearing his pistol belt. He threw the beam of his flashlight around the car until he saw the huddled form. He prodded it with his flashlight, at the same time drawing his pistol and hiding it behind him. The G.I. didn't move.

The Lieutenant poked him roughly. "Get up, Mulrooney." The G.I. opened his eyes, and when Mosca saw the dumb, sullen animal glare, he felt a sudden pity.

The Lieutenant kept the beam of his flashlight in the soldier's eyes, blinding him. He made Mulrooney stand up. When he saw that his hands were empty, he slipped his pistol back into its holster. Then he turned the G.I. around with a rough shove and searched him. He didn't find anything, so he threw the light of his flash on the bench. Mosca saw the bloodstained knife. The Lieutenant picked it up and pushed the G.I. ahead of him to the other end of the car.

The train began to slow down and gradually came to a halt. Mosca walked to the end of the car, opened the door and looked out. He saw the Lieutenant going to the station to wire ahead for the ambulance; otherwise there was no one. The French town behind the station was dark and still.

Mosca went back to his bench. Mr. Gerald's friends were bending over him, reassuring him, and Mr. Gerald was saying impatiently, "I know it's a scratch, but why did he do it, why did he do such a crazy thing?" And when the Lieutenant came back into the car and told them the ambulance would be waiting at Frankfort, Mr. Gerald said to him, "Believe me, Lieutenant, I did nothing to provoke him. Ask any of my friends. I did nothing, nothing, to make him do such a thing."

"He's just crazy, that's all," the Lieutenant said. And then added, "You're lucky, sir, if I know Mulrooney he was aiming at your balls."

For some reason this seemed to cheer them up, as if the seriousness of intent made the event more interesting, made the scratch on Mr. Gerald's thigh important. The Lieutenant brought his bed roll back and fixed Mr. Gerald on it. "In a way you did me a favor. I've been trying to get rid of Mulrooney since the first day he came into the platoon. He'll be safe for a couple of years now."

Mosca couldn't sleep. The train had begun to move, and he walked down to the door again, rested against it and looked at the black, shadowy countryside pass by. He remembered the same, nearly the same, land going by so slowly, from the back of trucks, tanks, on foot, crawling on the ground. He had believed he would never see this country again, and he wondered now why everything had turned out so badly. He had dreamed for so long about going home, and now he had left again. In the darkened train, he remembered his first night at home.

The large square sticker on the door had read "Welcome Home Walter," and Mosca noticed that similar stickers with different names were pasted on two of the other apartment doors. The first thing he saw when he entered the apartment was the picture of himself taken just before he went overseas. Then his mother and Gloria swarmed over him, and Alf was shaking his hand.

They all stood away from each other, and there was just one moment of awkward silence.

"You've gotten older," his mother said, and they all laughed. "No, I mean more than three years older."

"He hasn't changed," Gloria said. "He hasn't changed a bit."

"The conquering hero returns," Alf said. "Look at all those ribbons. Did you do something brave, Walter?"

"Standard," Mosca said, "most of the WACs got the same set." He pulled off his combat jacket and his mother took it from him. Alf went into the kitchen and came out with a tray of drinks.

"Christ," Mosca said, startled, "I thought you lost a leg." He had completely forgotten his mother writing about Alf. But his brother had obviously been waiting for this moment. He drew up his trouser leg.

"Very pretty," Mosca said. "Tough luck, Alf."

"Hell," Alf said, "I wish I had two of 'em. No athlete's foot, no ingrown toenails—you know."

"Sure," Mosca said. He touched his brother's shoulder and smiled.

"He put it on especially for you, Walter," his mother said. "He doesn't usually wear it around the house even though he knows I hate to see him without it."

Alf raised his drink. "To the conquering hero," he said, and then with a smile, turning to Gloria. "To the girl who waited for him."

"To our family," Gloria said.

"To all my children," his mother said affectionately. Her glance included Gloria. They all looked at Mosca expectantly.

"Let me drink this one, and then I can think of something."

They all laughed and drank.

"And now for supper," his mother said. "Help me set the table, Alf." The two of them went into the kitchen.

Mosca sat down in one of the armchairs. "A long, long trip," he said.

Gloria went over to the mantel and picked up the framed photo of Mosca. With her back to him she said, "Every week I'd come here and look at the picture. I'd help your mother get supper, we'd eat together and then sit here in this room, looking at this picture and talking about you. Every week, for three years, like people visiting a cemetery, and now that you're back it doesn't look a bit like you."

Mosca got up and went over to Gloria. Putting his arm on her shoulder he looked at the picture, wondering why it irritated him.

The head was thrown back in a laugh, and he had obviously stood so that the black and white diagonal stripes of his division would show clearly. The face was youthful and full of an innocent good nature. The uniform was nattily fitted. Standing there in the heat of the southern sun he had been a typical G.I. getting himself photoed for an adoring family.

"What a jerky grin," Mosca said.

"Don't make fun of it. That was all we had for a long time." She was silent for a moment. "Ah, Walter," she said, "how we cried over it sometimes, when you didn't write, whenever we heard rumors about a troop ship being sunk or a big battle being fought. On D Day we didn't go to church. Your mother sat on the couch, and I sat here by the radio. We just sat here all day. I didn't go to work. I kept turning the radio to different stations; as soon as one news bulletin was finished I'd try to get another station, even though it would say the same thing. Your mother just sat there with a handkerchief in her hand, but she didn't cry. I slept here that night, in your room, in your bed, and I took the picture with me. I put it on the dresser and said good night to it, and then I dreamed that I would never see you again. And now here you are, Walter Mosca, in the flesh, and you don't look a bit like the picture." She tried to laugh, but she was crying.

Mosca was embarrassed. He kissed Gloria gently. "Three years is a long time," he said. And he thought: On D Day I was in an English town getting drunk. I was giving a little blonde what she claimed was her first drink of whiskey and her first lay. I was celebrating D Day but even more celebrating that I wasn't in it. He had a strong desire to tell Gloria the exact truth, that he hadn't thought of them that day, or of any thing that they had thought of, but all he said was, "I don't like the picture . . . And besides when I came in you said I hadn't changed a bit."

"Isn't it funny," Gloria said, "when you came in the door you looked exactly like your picture. But when I kept looking at you it seemed as if your whole face had changed."

His mother called from the kitchen, "It's ready," and they went into the dining room.

All his favorite foods were on the table, the rare roast beef with the small roasted potatoes, a green salad and a slab of yellow cheese. The tablecloth was snowy white, and when he was finished he noticed the napkin untouched beside his plate. It had been good but not as good as he had dreamed it would be.

"Ah," Alf said, "a big difference from G.I. chow, hey, Walter?"

"Yeah," Mosca said. He took from his shirt pocket a short, fat, dark cigar and was about to light it when he noticed they were all looking at him with amusement, Alf, Gloria and his mother.

He grinned and said, "I'm a big boy now," and lit the cigar, exaggerating his pleasure. They all four of them burst out laughing. It seemed as if the last awkwardness, the strangeness of his coming home so different in face and manner, had been swept away. Their surprise, and then amusement at their surprise when he had taken out the cigar had broken down the barrier between them. They went into the living room, the two women with their arms around Mosca's waist, Alf carrying the tray with the whiskey and ginger ale. The women sat close to Mosca on the sofa, and Alf handed them all drinks and then sat down opposite them in one of the soft armchairs. The floor lamp sent a gentle yellow glow over the room and Alf said in the benign and half-joking tone he had used all evening, "The story of Walter Mosca will now be told."

Mosca drank. "First, the presents," he said. He went to his blue gym bag still lying by the door, took out three small boxes wrapped in brown paper and handed one to each of them. While they were opening the packages he took another drink.

"Christ," Alf said, "what the hell are these?" He held up four enormous silver cylinders.

Mosca laughed. "Four of the best cigars in the world. Specially made for Hermann Goering."

Gloria opened her package and then gasped. In a black velvet box was a ring. Small diamonds were set around a square, dark green emerald. She got up and flung her arms around Mosca and then turned to show the ring to his mother.

But his mother was fascinated by roll after roll of tightly packed wine-red silk falling to the floor in large folds. His mother held it up.

It was an enormous, square flag, and in the middle, superimposed on a white, circular background, rested the spider-black swastika. They were all silent. In the quiet of this room they had seen for the first time the symbol of the enemy.

"Hell," Mosca said, breaking the silence, "it was just a gag. You were supposed to see this." He picked up the small box lying on the floor. His mother opened it, and seeing the blue-white diamonds she raised her eyes and thanked him. She folded the huge flag into a tight little square, then rose and picked up Mosca's blue gym bag, saying, "I'll unpack this."

"They are lovely presents," Gloria said, "where did you get them?"

Mosca grinned and said, "Loot," emphasizing the word comically so that they would laugh.

His mother came back into the room with a large bundle of photos in her hand.

"These were in your bag, Walter. Why didn't you show

them to us?" She sat on the sofa and started looking at the photos one by one. She passed them on to Gloria and Alf. Mosca helped himself to a drink as they exclaimed over the different pictures and asked questions about where they had been snapped. Then he saw his mother turn pale, staring hard at one of the photos. For a moment Mosca had a feeling of panic, wondering if the really obscene pictures he had picked up were still there. But he was sure he had sold them all on the boat. He saw his mother pass the photos on to Alf, and he was angry with himself that he had felt any kind of fear.

"Well, well," Alf said, "what's this?" Gloria went over and looked at the picture. He saw the three pairs of eyes turned to him, waiting.

Mosca leaned toward Alf and when he saw what it was, he felt a surge of relief. He remembered now. He had been riding on the back of a tank when it happened.

In the photo was the huddled figure of a German bazooka man lying crumpled in the snow, a dark line running black from his body to the end of the print. Over the body stood himself, Mosca, staring straight into the camera, his M–1 slung over his shoulder. He, Mosca, looked curiously misshapen in his winter combat clothing. The blanket, in which he had cut holes for his head and arms, hung like a skirt beneath his combat jacket. He seemed to stand there like a successful hunter, ready to carry home the fallen game.

And not in the picture were the burning tanks on the covered plain. Not in the picture were the charred bodies sprinkled across the whitened field like rubbish. The German had been a good bazooka man.

"My buddy took that picture with a Leica the kraut

had." Mosca turned to his drink and turning back saw them still waiting.

"My first victim," he said, trying to make it sound like a joke. And yet it was if he had said the Eiffel Tower or the Pyramids, explaining a background against which he had been standing.

His mother was studying the other photos. "Where was this taken?" she asked. Mosca sat down beside her and said. "That was in Paris on my first leave." He put his arm around his mother's waist.

"And this?" his mother asked.

"That was in Vitry."

"And this?"

"That was in Aachen."

And this? And this? And this? He named the towns and told funny little stories. The drinks had put him into a good mood, but he thought: This was in Nancy where I waited two hours on line to get laid, this was in Dombasle where I found the dead naked German with his balls swollen big as melons. The placard on the door had said, "Dead German Inside." And it hadn't lied. He wondered even now why someone had troubled to write it, even as a joke. And this was in Hamm, where he got his first piece in three months and his first dose. And this and this and this were the countless towns where the Germans, men, women and children rested in their shapeless, rubbled tombs and gave out an overpowering stench.

And in all these the background against which he stood was like a man being photographed on a desert. He, the conqueror, stood on the flattened, pulverized remains of factories, homes, human bones—the ruins stretching away like rolling sand dunes.

Mosca sat back on the sofa. He puffed on his cigar. "How about some coffee?" he asked. "I'll make it." He went into the kitchen, Gloria following him, and together they set out the cups, cut the whipped-cream cake she took from the frigidaire. And while the coffee boiled on the stove, she clung to him and said, "Darling, I love you, I love you."

They brought the coffee into the living room, and it was their turn to tell Mosca stories. How Gloria had never gone out on a date in three years, how Alf had lost his leg in a truck crash in a southern Army camp, and how his mother had gone to work again, clerking in a large department store. They had all had their adventures, but thank God the war was over, the Moscas had come through safely, a leg lost, but as Alf said, with modern transportation what did legs mean, and now here they all were, safe in this little room.

The enemy so far away, so utterly crushed, could no longer give them fear. The enemy was surrounded, occupied, starving and melting away with disease, with no physical and moral strength ever to threaten them again. And when Mosca fell asleep in his chair, they, who all loved him, watched for a few minutes with a quiet, and almost tearful pleasure, almost not believing that he had traveled so far in time and place, and by some miracle had returned, found his way back to safety unharmed.

It was the third night before Mosca could get Gloria alone. The second night had been spent at her house where his mother and Alf had settled details for the wedding with Gloria's sister and father, not really out of meddlesomeness but because of their joy and enthusiasm that everything had come out right. They had all decided that the wedding would be as soon as possible but that it must wait until Walter had a steady job. Mosca had gone along more than willingly with the idea. And Alf had surprised Mosca. The timid Alf had grown into a confident, assured, sensible man and played the family head to perfection.

On that third night his mother and Alf had gone out and Alf had grinned and said, "Watch the clock, we'll be home at eleven." His mother had pushed Alf out of the door and said, "If you go out with Gloria don't forget to lock the door."

Mosca had been amused at the note of doubt in her voice, as if the thought of leaving him and Gloria alone in the house was against her better judgment. Good Christ, he thought, and he stretched out on the sofa.

He tried to relax but was too tense and had to get up and pour himself a drink. He stood at the window and smiled, wondering how it would be. He and Gloria had spent evenings together in a small hotel room the few weeks before he had gone overseas, but he could hardly remember now. He went to the radio and turned it on and then went into the kitchen to look at the clock. It was nearly eight-thirty. The bitch was a half-hour late. He went to the window again but it was too dark now to see anything. As he turned away there was a knock on the door, and Gloria came into the apartment.

"Hello, Walter," she said, and Mosca noticed that her voice trembled slightly. She took off her coat. She had on a blouse with just a few large buttons, and with this a wide pleated skirt.

"Alone at last," he said with a grin and stretched back on the sofa. "Fix a couple of drinks." Gloria sat on the sofa and leaned over to kiss him. He put his hands on her breast, and they kissed for a long time. "Drinks coming up," she said, and pulled away from him.

They drank. The radio was playing softly and a floor lamp cast its soft yellow glow over the room. He lit two cigarettes and gave her one. They smoked and when he stubbed out his cigarette he saw that she still held on to hers. He took it away from her and carefully crushed it in the ash tray.

Mosca pulled Gloria down so that she lay across his body. He unbuttoned her blouse so that he could slip his hand inside her brassiere and then kissed her. He moved his hand down under her skirt.

Gloria sat up and pushed away from him. Mosca was surprised and instantly alert.

"I don't want to go all the way," Gloria said. The girlish phrase irritated him and he reached for her impatiently. She stood up and away from him.

"No, I really mean it," she said.

"What the hell," Mosca said, "the two weeks before I went overseas were fine. What's wrong now?"

"I know," Gloria smiled at him tenderly, and he felt a quick anger. "But then it was different. You were going away and I loved you. If I did it now it would only make you think less of me. Don't be mad, Walter, but I've talked with Emmy about it. You were so different when you came back that I had to talk to somebody. And we both thought it would be best."

Mosca lit a cigarette. "Your sister's stupid."

"Please don't say things like that, Walter. I won't do what you want because I really love you."

Mosca choked on his drink and tried hard not to laugh. "Look," he said, "if we hadn't slept together that last two weeks I wouldn't have remembered you or written. You wouldn't have meant anything to me."

He saw her face get red. She went over to the armchair facing him and sat down.

"I loved you before that," she said. He saw that her mouth was quivering, and he tossed her the pack of cigarettes, then sipped his drink and tried to reason everything out.

His desire was gone, and he actually felt a sense of relief. Why, he didn't know. There was no doubt in his mind that he could talk or threaten Gloria into doing what he wished. He knew that if he said, "This is the way it has to be or else," she would yield. He knew that he had been too abrupt and that with some patience and a little finesse the evening would end pleasantly. But he found with surprise that the effort was too much trouble for him to take. He was completely without desire.

"It's O.K. Come over here."

She came obediently. "You're not angry?" she asked in a low voice.

He kissed her and smiled. "No, it doesn't matter," he said, and it was true.

Gloria put her head on his shoulder. "Let's just stay here like this tonight and talk. We've never really had a chance to talk together since you've come back."

Mosca pulled away and went to get her coat. "We're going to the movies," he said.

"I want to stay here."

Mosca said with a deliberate, brutal carelessness. "It's either go to the movies or get laid."

She stood up and looked at him steadily. "And you don't care which."

"That's right."

He expected her to put on her coat and walk out of the apartment. But she waited submissively until he had combed his hair and knotted his tie. They went to the movies.

It was nearly noon, a month later, that Mosca, coming into the apartment, found Alf, his mother, and Gloria's sister, Emmy, drinking coffee in the kitchen.

"Do you want some coffee?" his mother asked.

"Yeah, just let me wash up a bit." Mosca went into the bathroom and smiled grimly as he wiped his face dry before going back to the kitchen.

They all sipped coffee, and then Emmy opened the attack.

"You're not treating Gloria right. She waited three years for you, she never had a date and she missed a lot of chances."

"A lot of chances for what?" Mosca asked. Then he laughed. "We're getting along O.K., it takes time."

Emmy said, "You had a date with her last night, you didn't show up. You get home now. It isn't right what you're doing."

His mother saw that Mosca was getting angry and said placatingly, "Gloria waited here until two in the morning; you should have called up."

"And we all know what you're doing," Emmy said. "You leave a girl who waited for you three years to go out with the neighborhood chippie, a girl who's had three abortions and God knows what else."

Mosca shrugged. "I can't see your sister every night."

"No, you're too important for that." He saw with surprise that she really hated him.

"It was everybody's idea that we wait until I get a steady job," Mosca reminded her.

"I didn't know what a bastard you'd turn out to be. If you don't want to get married, tell Gloria. Don't worry, she can find somebody else."

Alf spoke up. "That's silly. Of course Walter wants to marry her. Let's be sensible about this. He's finding things a bit strange, he'll get over it. The thing for us to do is help him."

Emmy said sarcastically, "If Gloria slept with him everything would be fine. You'd be readjusted, wouldn't you, Walter?"

"This is getting stupid," Alf said. "Let's get down to fundamentals. You're angry because Walter is having an affair and isn't bothering to hide it, which is the least he could do. All right. Gloria is too crazy about Walter to give him the air. I think the best thing to do is to set a marriage date."

"And my sister keeps working while he runs around with all the little whores like he did in Germany?"

Mosca looked at his mother coldly, and she dropped her eyes away from his. There was a silence. "Yes," Emmy said quietly, "your mother told Gloria about the letters you get from that girl in Germany. You should be ashamed, Walter, honestly you should."

"Those letters don't mean a thing," Mosca said. And he could see the look of relieved belief on their faces.

"He'll get a job," his mother said, "and they can live here until they find an apartment."

Mosca sipped his coffee. He had been angry for a moment but now he was impatient to be out of this room, away from them. All this crap had gone far enough.

"But he'll have to quit running around with these little chippies," Emmy said.

Mosca broke in gently. "There's only one goddamn thing wrong. I'm not ready to set a date."

They all looked at him with surprise. "I'm not sure I want to get married," he added with a grin.

"What," Emmy was screaming incoherently, "what?" She was so angry she couldn't speak any further.

"And don't give me the three-year crap. What the hell difference does it make to me that she didn't get screwed for three years? Do you think that kept me awake nights worrying? What the hell, did it grow gold because she didn't use it? I had other things to worry about."

"Please, Walter," his mother said.

"Ah, shit," Mosca said. His mother left the table and went to the stove, and he knew she was crying. They were all suddenly standing and Alf, supporting himself against the table, shouted with anger, "All right, Walter, this readjusted crap can be overdone."

"And I think you've been babied too damn much since you've been home," Emmy said with contempt.

There was nothing to say to all this except to tell them exactly how he felt. "You can kiss my ass," he said, and although he spoke to Emmy, his glance included them all. He rose to leave but Alf, holding on to the table, moved in front of him and shouted with rage. "Goddamn you, that's going too far. Apologize, do you hear, apologize."

Mosca pushed him out of the way and saw too late that Alf's false leg was not there. Alf toppled over and his head struck against the floor. Both women screamed. Mosca bent over quickly to lift Alf. "Are you O.K.?" he asked. Alf nodded but kept his face covered with his hands and remained sitting on the floor. Mosca left the apartment.

He always remembered his mother standing by the stove, crying, wringing her hands.

The last time he entered the apartment Mosca found his mother waiting for him—she had not gone out at all that day.

"Gloria called you up," she said.

Mosca nodded in acknowledgment.

"Are you going to pack now?" his mother asked timidly.

"Yeah," Mosca said.

"Do you want me to help?"

"No," he said.

He went into his bedroom and took out the two new suitcases he had bought. He stuck a cigarette in his mouth and looked through his pockets for a match and then went into the kitchen for one.

His mother was still sitting in the chair. She had a handkerchief covering her face and was weeping silently.

He took the matches and started to leave the kitchen.

"Why do you treat me like this?" his mother said. "What have I done?"

He had no pity and the tears stirred no emotion, but he didn't want hysterics. He tried to talk quietly, to keep the irritation out of his voice.

"You haven't done anything, I'm just leaving, it's nothing to do with you."

"Why do you always talk to me like that as if I were a stranger?"

The words touched him, but he could make no gesture of affection. "I'm just nervous," he said. "If you're not going out, help me pack."

She went into the bedroom with him and carefully folded his clothes before he put them into the suitcases.

"Do you need any cigarettes?" his mother asked.

"No, I'll get them on the ship."

"I'll just run down and get some, you never can tell."

"They're only a nickel a pack on the ship," he said. He didn't want her to give him anything.

"You can always use extra cigarettes," his mother said and left the apartment.

Mosca sat on his bed and stared at the picture of Gloria that hung on the wall. He felt no emotion. It hasn't worked out, he thought. It's too bad. And he wondered at their patience, realizing how hard they had tried and what little effort he had made. He searched in his mind for something he could say to his mother, to show her there was nothing she could do to help, that his actions had sprung from another root which neither he nor she could control.

In the living room the phone began to ring, and he went to it. Gloria's voice, impersonal, yet friendly, answered him.

"I hear you're leaving tomorrow. Should I come over tonight to say good-bye or just say it now over the phone."

"Suit yourself," Mosca said, "but I have to go out around nine."

"I'll come before then," she said. "Don't worry, it's just to say good-bye." And he knew that it was true, that she no longer cared for him, that he was no longer what she had loved, and she wished to say good-bye with a friendliness that was really curiosity.

When his mother came back he had made up his mind. "Mom," he said, "I'm leaving now. Gloria called. She's coming over tonight and I don't want to see her."

"You mean now. This minute?"

"Yes," Mosca said.

"But at least you can spend your last night home," she

said. "Alf will be home soon, you could at least wait to say good-bye to your brother."

"So long, Mom," he said. He leaned over and kissed her cheek.

"Wait," his mother said, "you've forgotten your gym bag." And, as she had so many times before when he had left the house to play basketball and finally when he had left for the Army, she took the small, blue gym bag and began to fill it with what he would need. Only again now, instead of the satin-covered shorts, the leather kneeguards and sneakers, she put in his shaving kit, a fresh change of underwear, towel and soap. Then taking a piece of string from one of the bureau drawers she tied the gym bag to the handle of a suitcase.

"Ah," she said, "I don't know what all the people will say. They'll think it's my fault, that I haven't made you happy. And at least after the way you treated Gloria, you could see her tonight, see her and say good-bye and be nice to her so she won't feel so badly."

"It's a tough world for everybody," Mosca said. He kissed her again, but before he could walk out of the apartment she held on to him.

"Are you going back to Germany because of that girl?" And Mosca realized that if he said yes, his mother's vanity would be soothed, that she would know then it was not her fault that he left. But he couldn't lie.

"I don't think so," he said. "She probably has another G.I. by now." And saying it out loud, in all sincerity, he was surprised that it should sound so false, as if the truth he told were a lie to hurt his mother.

She kissed him and let him go. In the street he looked up and saw her at the closed window, the white spot of a handkerchief to her face. He set the suitcases on the ground and waved to her and saw that she had left the window. Afraid that she would come down to make a scene in the street, he picked up his suitcases and walked quickly to the main avenue where he could catch a taxi.

But his mother was sitting on the sofa, weeping, with shame, grief, humiliation. Deep inside her knowing that if her son had died on an unknown beach, buried in a foreign land, the white cross over his body mingled with thousands of others, her grief would have been perhaps greater. But there would have been no shame, and she would have been, in a later time, reconciled, in some measure, proud. There would not have been this festering sorrow, this knowledge that he was irrevocably gone, that if he died, she could never weep over his body, bury him, bring flowers to his grave.

On the train taking him back to the land of the enemy, Mosca, dozing, swayed from side to side with the movement of the car. Sleepily he walked back to his bench and stretched out on it. But lying there he heard the moans of the wounded man, the chattering of teeth, the sleeping body only now protesting against the insane rage of the world. Mosca rose and walked down to the G.I. half of the car. Most of the soldiers were asleep, and there was only a small halo of light, the flaring of three closely grouped candles. Mulrooney, crumpled up on a bench, was snoring, and two G.I.'s, their carbines lying beside them, were playing rummy and drinking from a small bottle.

Mosca asked in a low voice, "Can one of you guys lend me a blanket, that guy's cold."

One of the G.I.'s threw him a blanket. "Thanks," Mosca said.

The G.I. shrugged. "I have to stay up and guard this joker anyway."

Mosca glanced at the sleeping Mulrooney. The face was blank. The eyes opened slowly, stared at him like a dumb animal, and in that moment, before the eyes closed, Mosca felt a sense of recognition and thought, "You poor stupid bastard."

He walked back down the car, threw the blanket over Mr. Gerald and stretched out again on his bench. This time he fell asleep easily and quickly. He slept dreamlessly until the train reached Frankfort and somebody shook him awake.

2

THE MORNING SUN of early June lit every corner of the roofless terminal, turning it into a vast outdoor stadium, and as Mosca stepped off the train he drew a great breath of spring air, smelling already a faint, acrid dust that rose from the debris and ruins of the city beyond. Along the length of the train he could see groups of O.D.-clad soldiers forming into platoons. With the other civilians, he followed a guide to the bus waiting outside.

They moved through the crowd like conquerors, as in an earlier time the rich passed through the poor, looking neither to right nor left, knowing that a path would appear before them. The conquered, their clothes worn, their bodies and faces thin, looked like masses of men and women accustomed to living in flophouses, eating in the soup kitchens of charity, and they made way sullenly, obediently, staring with envious eyes at the well-clad, well-fed Americans.

They came out of the station into a large square. Opposite them was the Red Cross club, G.I.'s in olive drab already lounging on the steps. Walling the square stood rebuilt hotels that housed the occupation troops and administrators. Streetcars crisscrossed each other, and military buses and taxis filled the wide streets. Even this early, G.I.'s were sitting on the benches around the station, and each had beside him a *Fräulein* with her inevitable little suitcase. It was all the same, Mosca thought, it hasn't changed. The G.I.'s met the incoming trains as suburban wives meet their commuting husbands, picked out a pretty girl and made their propositions with varying degrees of crudity. To spend a night in a cold, dirty station sleeping on a bench, waiting for a morning train; or a good dinner, liquor, cigarettes, a warm bed. He might give her a good deal of pleasure, at worst, if one were careful, a few moments of annoyance during the night. Usually the sensible choice was made.

On all the streets bounding the square stood the sharpers, the black-market operators, the children laying their trap for wary G.I.'s, who emerged from the PX with cartons full of candy, cigarettes, soap, and with eyes watchful as old prospectors carrying sacks of gold dust.

Mosca, waiting to enter the bus, felt a hand on his shoulder. Turning, he saw a dark, bony face topped by the cap of the Wehrmacht that was the standard headgear for German men.

The young man said in a low, urgent voice. "You have American dollars?" Mosca shook his head, turned away and again felt the hand on his shoulder.

"Any cigarettes?"

Mosca started to enter the bus. The hand grasped his shoulder more urgently. "Anything, you have anything you wish to sell?"

Mosca said curtly in German, "Get your hands away quick."

The man stepped back, startled, and then into his eyes came a look of proud contempt, hatred. Mosca went into the bus and sat down. He saw the man looking at him through the window, at his gray gabardine suit, the white richness of his shirt, the streak of color that was his tie.

And feeling the man's look of contempt, he wished for a moment that he was again in the olive drab of his uniform.

The bus moved slowly away from the railroad station and took one of the many exits out of the square. It moved them through another world. Outside that central square which stood like a fortress in a wilderness, the ruins stretched away as far as the eye could see, with only a flora of building remnants, a still-standing wall, a door leading into the open air behind it, a steel skeleton reaching to the sky with pieces of brick, mortar and glass clinging to it like fragments of torn flesh.

The bus unloaded most of the civilians on the outskirts of Frankfort, then continued with Mosca and a few officers to the Wiesbaden airfield. Mosca was the only one of the civilians, beside Mr. Gerald, who had been given his permanent assignment in the States. The others had to wait in Frankfort for definite orders.

When, finally, his documents were checked at the airfield, he had to wait until after lunch for the plane to Bremen. And when the plane left the field he had no feeling of rising from the earth, no sense that the plane could run off the edges of the continent, or even that it was possible to fall. He watched the earth tilt, slanting toward him so that it seemed to be coming up to form a wall of green and brown before his eyes and then as the plane banked away the continent was an endless and depthless valley. And then all the mystery was gone as the plane flew level, and they looked down as from a balcony to the flat, checkered, tableclothed fields.

Now that he was so near his final destination, that this return was so nearly completed, he thought about his few months at home and felt an uncomfortable, vague guilt at the patience his family had shown. But there was no desire to see any of them again, and feeling now a mounting impatience with the plane's slowness, its seeming suspension in the boundless spring-clear sky, he realized that the truth he had told his mother had been a lie, that he was going back because of that German girl, as his mother had said, but going back with no expectation of finding her, with no real hope of their lives coming together after these months of separation, but because he had to return to this continent in any case. He no more expected to find her waiting for him than if he had left her in a trackless jungle, disabled, with no means of sustenance, weaponless against the wild beasts. And thinking so he felt a sickness inside him, a poison of shame and sorrow flowing into his blood and mouth. He saw clearly her body, her face, the color of her hair, thought of her fully in his mind, consciously, for the first time in the months he had left her, and finally, clearly and concretely, as if he had spoken it aloud, he thought of her name.

The police presidio had blown up just a little before noon that hot summer morning nearly a year ago and Mosca, sitting in his jeep in the Hoch Allee, felt the earth shake. The officer he had been waiting for, a young Lieutenant fresh from the States, came out a few minutes later and they drove back to Military Government headquarters on the Contrescarpe. Someone shouted the news and they drove to the police building. The military police had already sealed off the area, their jeeps and white helmets blocking streets leading to the square. The Lieutenant with Mosca showed his identification, and they passed through.

The massive, dark-green building stood on a small rise of ground at the top of the Am Wald Strasse. It was large and square, with an inner courtyard for vehicle parking. German civilians were still streaming out of the main entrance, their faces and clothing covered with dust. Some of the women were weeping hysterically with shock. A crowd was being pushed away from the building, but the building itself seemed silent, untouched.

Mosca followed the Lieutenant to one of the small side entrances. It was an archway packed almost to the ceiling with debris. They crawled through to the inner courtyard.

The great inner square was filled now with a mountain of rubble. Vehicle tops, jeeps and trucks, could be seen sticking above it in some spots like masts of sunken ships in shallow water. The walls to a height three stories high had been hacked away by the explosion, and naked to their view were the desks, chairs and wall clocks of the offices above them.

Mosca heard a sound he had never heard before, a sound which had become a commonplace in the great cities of that continent. For a moment it seemed to come from all sides, a low, steady, monotonous animal scream, not recognizable as human. He located it, and half-walking, half-crawling over the rubble made his way to the right side of the square; saw the fat, red neck encircled by the green collar of the German police uniform. The neck and head in their rigidity were lifeless, the scream came from beneath the body. Mosca and the Lieutenant tried to clear away the brick but rubble kept sliding down over the dead man. The Lieutenant crawled back through the archway to get help.

And now from the many archways and descending the rubbled walls, rescuers began to fill the courtyard. Army doctors from the base hospitals, still in their dress pinks;

G.I.'s; German litter bearers and laborers to dig the bodies out. Mosca crawled back through the archway.

In the street the air was pure. Ambulances were drawn up in a long line, and opposite them the German fire engines stood in readiness. Laborers were already clearing the entrances leading into the courtyard, the rubble being loaded onto waiting trucks. On the sidewalk opposite the building a table had been set up as a command post and he saw his Colonel standing there waiting patiently, a group of his junior officers around him. Mosca noticed with amusement that they were all wearing steel helmets. One of the officers beckoned to him.

"Go up and guard our Intelligence office," he said. He handed Mosca his pistol belt. "If there's another explosion get out of there as quick as you can."

Mosca went in the building through the main entrance. The stairway was a hill of ruins and he climbed it slowly, gingerly. He walked down the corridor with one eye on the ceiling, taking care not to pass under places where it sagged.

The Intelligence office was halfway down the corridor and opening the door he saw that now it was only half a room, the other half part of the rubble in the courtyard. There was nothing left to guard, only one locked file cabinet. But he had a fine view of the drama being played beneath him.

Settling comfortably in a chair, he pulled a cigar from his pocket and lit it. His foot struck something on the floor and looking down he saw with surprise two bottles of beer lying on their sides. He picked one up, it was crusted with mortar and bits of brick. Mosca opened the bottle on the door lock and settled in his chair again.

Below him in the courtyard the scene was static, and in the dust-laden air, almost dreamlike. Beside the body he had found, the German laborers were now picking away bricks carefully in slow motion. Looming above them an American officer stood patiently still, his pink trousers and green blouse turning white with dust. By his side stood a Sergeant, holding in his hands before him the round cylinder containing blood plasma. And this scene had been copied all over the courtyard, as if from a master print. Over them all the dust from the pulverized concrete hung in the sunlit air, then fell gently to dye their hair and clothing white.

Mosca drank his beer and smoked his cigar. He heard someone stumbling along the corridor and went out of the room.

Down the long hall which ended and disappeared where floor and ceiling almost met, staggering out of the dark, inner recesses of the building, came a small file of German men and women. They went past him, not seeing him, blind and weak with shock and terror. The last one in the file was a slight girl in khaki ski pants and woolen blouse. She stumbled and fell and when none of the others turned to help her, Mosca stepped from the room and raised her to her feet. She would have gone on but Mosca stretched out his arm, the bottle of beer at the end of it, and stopped her.

She lifted her head and Mosca saw that her face, her neck, were dead white and her eyes dilated with shock. She said in German, tearfully, "Please let me get out, please." Mosca let his arm fall and she went past him down the corridor. But she went only a few steps and crumpled against the wall.

Mosca bent over and saw that her eyes were open. Not

knowing what else to do he put the bottle of beer to her mouth but she pushed it away.

"No," she said in German, "I'm just too scared to walk." He heard the note of shame, just barely understanding. He lit a cigarette and stuck it between her lips, then lifted the thin body and carried her to a chair in the room.

Mosca opened the other bottle of beer and this time she drank a little. Below them the scene had increased its tempo. The doctors bent over, their hands busy; the men holding the plasma containers knelt on the rubble. Litter bearers made their way slowly over the ruins; the corpses, flattened, dust-covered bodies, making their exits through the many archways.

The girl moved from her chair. "I can walk now." She started to leave but Mosca blocked the door.

In his awkward German he said, "Wait for me outside." She shook her head. "You need a drink," he said, "schnapps, real schnapps, warm." She shook her head again. "No monkey business," he said in English, "honest, cross my heart." And he mockingly held the bottle of beer over his breast. She smiled and brushed past him. He watched her thin figure going slowly but steadily down the corridor to the rubbled staircase.

That was how it began; the dead, conqueror and enemy alike, being carried away below them, the brick dust settling on their eyelids, and he, Mosca, moved to pity and a strange tenderness by her fragile body and thin face. At night in his room they listened to the small radio, finished off a bottle of peppermint liqueur, and when she tried to leave he had kept her there with one pretext or another until it was after curfew and she had to stay. She hadn't let him kiss her the whole evening.

She undressed underneath the bed covers, and he, smoking a last cigarette and drinking the last of the liqueur, had finally joined her. She turned to him with a passionate intensity that surprised and delighted him. Months later she told him that she hadn't been with a man for nearly a year, and he had laughed, and she had said with a rueful smile, "If a man says that everyone pities him; they laugh at a woman."

But he had understood that first night and understood more. That she had been afraid of him, he the enemy, but the radio's soft music, the warm liqueur, the precious and nerve-soothing cigarettes, the fat sandwiches he had bought from the Mess Sergeant . . . these luxuries she had not known for so long, had all combined with her bodily desire, and they had played a game, spinning out time until they knew it would be too late for her to leave. It had all been impersonal, and understanding this hadn't spoiled it, perhaps because physically they were suited to each other, and the night became a long darkness of sensual pleasure, and in the gray morning before the real dawn, she sleeping, he smoking, Mosca thought, "I'll have to keep this steady," and thought with pity, tenderness and some shame how he had punished her fragile body and met there an unexpected, tensile strength.

When Hella woke later in the morning she was frightened, not remembering for a moment where she was, and then she was ashamed that she had surrendered so easily, so casually, and to the enemy. But her legs tangled with Mosca's in the narrow bed filled her whole body with a warm sensuousness. She rose on one elbow, to look at Mosca's face, realizing with recurring shame that she did not really have a clear image of him in her mind, did not know what he really looked like.

The mouth of the enemy was thin and almost ascetic,

the face narrow and strong, not relaxed in sleep. He slept stiffly, his body rigid on the narrow bed, and he slept so silently, scarcely breathing, that she wondered if he were shamming, watching her watch him.

Hella left the bed as quietly as she could and dressed. She was hungry and seeing Mosca's cigarettes on the table she took one and lit it. It tasted very good. Looking out the window, hearing no sound in the street below, she realized it was still early. She wanted to leave but was hoping that he had a tin of food in the room and would offer it to her if he ever woke up. She thought, with rueful shame and pleasure, that she had certainly earned it.

She glanced at the bed and was startled to see that the American's eyes were open and he was studying her quietly. She stood up, felt a ridiculous shyness, and stretched out her hand to say good-bye. He laughed, reached out and pulled her down to the bed. He said mockingly, in English, "We're too good friends for that."

She didn't understand but she knew he was making fun of her and she was angry. She said, in German, "I have to leave." But he didn't let her hand go.

"Cigarette," he said. She lit one for him. He sat up in bed to smoke, the covers falling away from his body, and she saw the white jagged scar running from his groin to the nipple of his breast. She asked in German. "The war?"

He laughed, pointed to her and said, "You." It seemed to Hella for a moment that he was accusing her personally, and she turned her head so that she could not see.

He tried his bad German. "Are you hungry?" he asked. She nodded. He jumped out of bed, naked. With a modesty that seemed to Mosca very funny, she averted her eyes while he dressed.

Ready to leave, he kissed her gently and then said in

German, "Go back to bed." She made no sign that she understood but he knew that she had and for some reason would not do so. He shrugged and left, running down the stairs and out to the motor pool. He drove to the mess hall, picked up a canteen of coffee and some fried egg sandwiches. Back in the room he found her sitting by the window, still dressed. He gave her the food, and they both drank from the canteen. She held out one of the sandwiches to him, but he shook his head. He noticed with amusement that after a hesitant gesture she did not offer it a second time.

"You'll come tonight?" he asked in German.

She shook her head. They looked at each other, he with no trace of emotion on his face. She saw that he would not ask again, that he was ready to erase her from his mind and memory, make the night they had spent together completely nothing. And because her vanity was aroused and he had been a considerate lover, she said, "Tomorrow," and smiled. She took one last drink of coffee, leaned over to kiss him, and left.

She had told him all this in the time after. Had it been three months, four months? A long time of contentment, ease, physical pleasure and comfort. And one day, coming into the room, he had found her in the classical, wifely pose, mending a great, twisted bundle of socks.

"Ah," he said in German, "the good *Hausfrau*."

Hella smiled shyly and looked at him as if she were trying to penetrate into his mind, trying to see what impression the scene had made. That had been the beginning of the campaign to make him not want to leave her, to stay in the land of the enemy with her, also the enemy, and yet though he understood, it was not offensive to him.

And then later, the tried and tested frontal assault, the

lethal weapon of pregnancy, but he had felt no contempt, no pity; just annoyance.

"Get rid of it," he said. "We'll go see a good doctor."

Hella shook her head. "No," she said, "I want to have it."

Mosca shrugged. "I'm going home, nothing can stop me."

"All right," she said. She made no entreaties. She gave herself to him completely in every thing and in every way until one day, though he knew he lied he couldn't help saying, "I'll come back." She watched him intently, knew that he lied and he saw that she knew. And that had been the mistake, starting it. Because in the time that followed he kept repeating the lie, sometimes with drunken fervor, so that they had finally both come to believe in it, she with an inborn, stubborn faith, a stubbornness she had in many things.

The final day he came back to his room and found she had already packed his duffel bag. It stood upright near the window, like a stuffed green dummy. It was after lunch, and the cold lemon-colored sunlight of October filled the room. The truck for the embarkation area would leave after supper.

He dreaded the time he would have to spend with her and said, "Let's go for a walk." She shook her head.

She motioned him to her, and they both undressed. He saw the slight bulge of the coming child. He had no desire but forced himself onward until desire came and was ashamed at her urgent passion. When it was time for supper he dressed and helped her dress.

"I want you to leave now," he said. "I don't want you to wait for the truck."

"All right," she said submissively, and she gathered her clothes together into a bundle and put them into her small suitcase. Before she left he gave her all the cigarettes and German money he had and they left the building together. On the street he said, "Good-bye," and kissed her. He saw she couldn't speak, that the tears were running down her face, but she walked straight down the street, down the Contrescarpe to the Am Wald Strasse, not seeing anything, not turning around.

He watched her until she was out of sight, believing it was the last time he would ever see her, feeling a vague relief that it was all over, and so easily, with no fuss. And then he remembered what she had told him a few nights before and it had been impossible to doubt her sincerity. "Don't worry about me or the baby," she had said. "Don't feel guilty about it, if you don't come back, the baby will keep me happy, will always make me think how happy we were together. And don't come back for me, if you don't want to."

He was angered by what he thought was the false nobility of her speech but then she went on. "I'll wait for you at least a year, maybe two years. But if you don't come I'll be happy. I'll find another man and make my life, that's the way people are. And I'm not afraid, not afraid of having the baby or taking care of it alone. Do you understand that I'm not afraid?" And he had understood. That she was not afraid of any pain or sorrow he might give her, or the cruelty and lack of tenderness that was now part of him, but most of all what she did not understand herself he envied most, that she had no fear of her own inner being, that she accepted the cruelty and rage of the world around her and kept her belief in the giving of love, and that she felt more sorrow for him than for herself.

A brown-green wall tilted before his eyes, blocking off his vision, and as if on a level before him but lying on their sides, were groups of buildings and small oblongs that were people. The plane leveled off and Mosca could see the neat outlines of the airfield, the small groups of buildings that were aircraft hangars and the long, low administration building, gleaming white in the sun. Far away he could see a ragged outline formed by the few tall buildings that were still standing in Bremen. He felt the wheels meet the earth, gingerly, distrustfully, and there swept over him an impatient eagerness to be out of the plane, to stand waiting for Hella outside a door. At that moment, when he was ready to leave the plane, he was sure he would find her waiting for him.

3

MOSCA LET a German porter carry his suitcases out of the plane, and he saw Eddie Cassin coming down the ramp of the airfield to meet him. They shook hands, and Eddie Cassin said in the quiet, carefully modulated voice, vibrant with a sincerity that he always used when he felt unnatural, "It's good to see you again, Walter."

"Thanks for fixing up the job and the papers to come here," Mosca said.

"That was nothing," Eddie Cassin said. "It's worth it to me to have one of the old gang back. We had some great times together, Walter." He picked up one of Mosca's suitcases, and Mosca took the other and the blue gym bag and they walked up the ramp, off the flying area.

"We'll go to my office and have a drink and meet some of the guys," Eddie Cassin said. He put his free arm across Mosca's shoulder for a moment and said in a natural voice, "You old bastard, I'm really glad to see you, you know that?" And Mosca felt what he had not felt in his previous homecoming, a sense of true arrival, of reaching a final destination.

They followed a wire fence to a small brick building that stood some distance away from the other installations of the base. "Here I'm lord and master," Eddie said. "Civilian Personnel Office, and I'm the Assistant to the Civilian Personnel Officer who spends all his time flying. Five hundred krauts think I'm God and a hundred and fifty of them are women. How about that for living, Walter?"

The building was a one-story affair. There was a large outer office filled with German clerks scurrying to and fro, a patient horde of other Germans waiting to be interviewed for jobs as mechanics in the motor pool, kitchen help in the mess halls, PX attendants. There were rough-looking men, old women, young men and a great many young girls, some very pretty. Their eyes followed Eddie as he went by.

Eddie opened the door to the inner office. Here there were two desks face to face, so that their occupants could look each other in the eye. One desk was absolutely bare except for a lettered green-and-white shingle which read, "Lt. A. Forte, CPO," and a small neat bundle of papers waiting for signature. On the other desk there were two double-decked baskets overflowing with paper. Almost swamped by other papers scattered over the desk was a small shingle which read "Mr. E. Cassin, Asst. CPO." In the corner of the room was a desk at which a tall and very ugly girl was typing, stopping in her work long enough to say, "Good afternoon, Mr. Cassin. The Colonel called, he wants you to call him back."

Eddie winked at Mosca and picked up the telephone. While he was speaking, Mosca lit a cigarette and tried to relax. He made himself not think of Hella and looked at Eddie. Eddie hadn't changed, he thought. There was the gray, wavy hair framing the delicate, yet strong features. The mouth was as sensitive as a girl's yet the nose was long and imperial, the set of his jaw determined. The eyes were hooded as if with sensuality and the grayness of his abundant hair seemed to have tinged his skin. Yet the impression was one of youthfulness, a frank warmth of expression that was almost naïve. But Mosca knew that when Eddie

Cassin was drunk the sensitive and delicately cut mouth twisted into an ugly line, the whole face grayed and went old and vicious. And since that viciousness had no real strength behind it and because men would laugh at it as Mosca often had, the viciousness, in words and physical action, was vented on the woman who was his companion or mistress of the moment. He had one set opinion of Eddie Cassin, a crazy bastard about women and a lousy drunk, but otherwise a really nice guy who would do anything for a friend. And Eddie had been smart enough never to make a pass at Hella. He wanted to ask Eddie now whether he had seen Hella or knew what had happened to her but he could not bring himself to do so.

Eddie Cassin put down the phone and opened a drawer of his desk. He took out a bottle of gin and a tin of grapefruit juice. Turning to the typist he said, "Ingeborg, go wash the glasses." She took some glasses, empty containers of cheese spread, and left the office. Eddie Cassin went to a door that led to a smaller office behind them. "Come on, Walter, I want you to meet a couple of friends of mine."

In the next office a short, stout, pasty-faced man in the same olive green Eddie wore was standing by his desk, his foot on the rung of a chair and his body bent over so that his paunch rested on his thigh. He held in his hand a *Fragebogen* or questionnaire and was studying it. Before him, standing stiffly at attention, was a short squat German, the inevitable gray-green Wehrmacht cap under his arm. By the window sat a long-looking American civilian with the long jaw and square small mouth of a weatherbeaten American farmer, and with his air of self-centered strength.

"Wolf," Eddie said to the pudgy man, "this is an old buddy of mine, Walter Mosca. Walter, Wolf here is our security man. He clears the krauts before they can get a job on the base."

After they had shaken hands, Eddie went on. "That guy by the window is Gordon Middleton. He's the man without a job, so he's detailed to help out down here. The Colonel is trying to get rid of him, that's why he hasn't anything special to do." Middleton didn't get up from his chair to shake hands, so Mosca nodded, and the other waved a long scarecrow arm in acknowledgment.

Wolf jerked his thumb at the door and told the German, still standing at attention, to wait outside. The German clicked his heels, bowed, and left hurriedly. Wolf laughed, threw the *Fragebogen* on the desk with a contemptuous gesture.

"Never in the Party, never in the SA, never in the Hitler Youth. Christ, I'm dying to meet a Nazi."

They all laughed. Eddie shook his head wisely. "They all say the same thing. Walter here is a guy after your own heart, Wolf. A rough character with krauts when we were in Mil Gov together."

"Is that so?" Wolf raised a sandy eyebrow. "That's the only way to be."

"Yeah," Eddie said, "we had a big problem in Mil Gov. The krauts would make the coal deliveries to all the German installations, but when it came time to deliver to those Jewish refugee camps up at Grohn on Saturday either the trucks would break down or the kraut coal administrator would say there was no coal left. My boy solved the problem."

"This I'd like to hear," Wolf said. He had an easy, ingratiating way of speaking that was almost oily and had a trick of nodding his head up and down to assure the speaker of his complete comprehension.

Ingeborg brought in the glasses, the bottle and the fruit juice. Eddie fixed four drinks but one without gin. He gave this to Gordon Middleton. "The only guy in the occupation who doesn't gamble, drink or chase women. That's why the Colonel wants to get rid of him. He gives the krauts a bad impression."

"Let's hear the story," Gordon said. His low, drawling voice was a reproach but a gentle one; patient.

"Well," Eddie said, "it got so that Mosca would have to ride way the hell out to the camp every Saturday to make sure the coal got there. One Saturday he was in a crap game and let the trucks go alone. No coal. He really got chewed out. I'll never forget. I drove him out to where the trucks had broken down and he gave the drivers a little speech."

Mosca rested against the desk, lit a cigar and puffed on it nervously. He remembered the incident and knew the kind of story Eddie would make out of it. Build him up to be a real hard guy and it hadn't been that way at all. He had told the drivers that if they did not wish to drive he would see to their release without prejudice. But if they wanted to stay on the job they had better get the coal to the DP camp even if they had to carry it on their backs. One driver had quit, and Mosca had taken his name and passed cigarettes all around. Eddie was making it sound as if he had knocked the hell out of six of them in a free-for-all.

"Then he went to the coal administrator's house and had a little talk in English that I understood. That kraut was really shitting when he got through. After that he shot crap Saturday afternoon and the coal got to the camp. A real executive." Eddie shook his head admiringly.

Wolf kept nodding his head up and down with understanding and approbation. "That's the kind of stuff we need around here," he said. "These krauts get away with murder."

"You couldn't do that now, Walter," Eddie said.

"Yeah, we're teaching the krauts democracy," Wolf said, so wryly that Mosca and Eddie laughed, and even Middleton smiled.

They sipped their drinks, and then Eddie got up to look out the window at a woman passing by on her way to the exit gate. "There's some nice gash," he said, "how would you like to cut a piece of that?"

"That's a question for the *Fragebogen,*" Wolf said, and as he was about to add something else, the door leading to the corridor was flung open and a tall, blond boy was shoved into the room. His wrists were handcuffed and he was crying. Behind him were two short men in dark sack suits. One of the men stepped forward.

"Herr Dolman," he said, "we have the person who has been stealing the soap." Wolf burst out laughing.

"The soap bandit," he explained to Eddie and Mosca. "We've been missing a lot of Red Cross soap bars we were supposed to give the German kids. These men are detectives from the city."

One of the two men started to unlock the handcuffs. He held his forefinger under the boy's nose, the gesture almost fatherly, and said, "No dumb tricks, eh?" The boy nodded his head.

"Leave them on," Wolf said sharply. The detective stepped back.

Wolf walked close to the boy and shoved the blond head up with his hand. "Did you know this soap was for German children?"

The boy let his head fall and didn't answer.

"You worked here, you were trusted. You'll never work for the Americans again. However, if you'll sign a paper admitting what you've done, we will not prosecute. Do you agree to that?"

The boy nodded his head.

"Ingeborg," Wolf called. The German typist came in. Wolf nodded to the two men. "Take him in there to the other office, the girl knows what to do." He turned to Eddie and Mosca. "Too easy," and smiled his friendly smile. "But it saves everybody a lot of trouble and the kid will get his six months."

Mosca, not really caring, said, "Hell, you promised to let him off."

Wolf shrugged. "Right, but the German cops get him for making a black market. The Chief of Police in Bremen is an old friend of mine, and we co-operate."

"Justice at work," Eddie murmured. "So what if the kid stole some soap, give him a break."

Wolf said briskly, "Can't do it, they'd steal us blind." He put on his cap. "Well, I've got a busy night ahead of me. Have to make a full-scale search on all the kitchen workers before they leave the base. There's something." He grinned at them. "We get a woman cop from Bremen to search the female workers and she comes out with a big pair of rubber gloves and a bar of G.I. soap. You should see where those women hide a stick of butter. Phew." He spit. "I hope I never get that hungry."

When Wolf had left Gordon Middleton stood up and said in his deep, laconic voice. "The Colonel likes him." He smiled at Mosca, good-naturedly, as if it were something that amused him and which he did not resent. Before he left the office he said to Eddie, "I think I'll catch an early bus home," and to Mosca, simply and in a friendly tone, "See you around, Walter."

It was the end of the working day. Through the windows Mosca could see the German laborers massing at the exit gate, waiting to be searched and checked by the military police before they could leave the air base. Eddie went to the window and stood beside him.

"I guess you want to get to town and look for your girl," Eddie said and smiled, a smile almost womanly in its sweetness, in the hesitancy of the delicately cut mouth. "That's the reason I took all the trouble to fix a job here when you wrote. I figured it had to be the girl. Right?"

"I don't know," Mosca said. "Partly, I guess."

"Do you want to fix up about your billet in town first and then look her up? Or go see her now?"

"Let's fix up the billet first," Mosca said.

Eddie laughed outright. "If you go now you'll catch her home. By the time the billet is arranged you won't get to her until at least eight. Maybe she'll be out by then." He watched Mosca carefully when he said this.

"My tough luck," Mosca said.

They each picked up a suitcase and went out of the building to where Eddie had parked his jeep. Before Eddie started the motor he turned to Mosca and said. "You won't ask, but I'll tell you anyway. I've never seen her around the officer or enlisted-men clubs or with any G.I.'s. I've never even seen her." After a pause he added slyly, "And I didn't think you'd want me to look her up."

4

AS THEY PASSED through the Neustadt, then over the bridge into Bremen proper, Mosca saw his first remembered landmark. It was a church steeple and tower, the body like a face eaten away by disease, a slim thread of stone and plaster holding the spire toward the sky. Then they were going by the massive police presidio, the white scars of the explosion still showing on its dark, green walls. They traveled on the Schwachhauser Heer Strasse to the other side of Bremen, in what had once been the fashionable suburbs, the houses almost untouched and now used as billets and homes for the occupation forces.

Mosca was thinking about the man beside him. Eddie Cassin wasn't a romantic guy. As far as Mosca knew he was the opposite. He remembered when they had been G.I.'s, Eddie had found in the city a very young, very developed Belgian girl, pretty as a Dresden doll. He had established her in a small, windowless room in the billet and thrown a party. The girl had serviced the thirty-odd G.I.'s in the billet, not leaving the room for three days. The men played cards in the anteroom, a kitchen, waiting their turn. The girl was so pretty and good-natured that the men had pampered her as husbands pamper pregnant wives. They scrounged eggs, bacon and ham and took turns preparing her breakfast tray. They brought packages of food from the mess hall for her lunch and supper. She laughed and joked as she sat up naked in bed to eat from the tray. There was always someone in her room at any hour of the day and she seemed to have a real affection for everyone. She was difficult about only one thing. Eddie Cassin had to visit her once a day for at least an hour. She always called him Daddy.

"She was just too pretty to keep to myself," Eddie had said. But Mosca always remembered a note of mean satisfaction in his voice.

They turned from the Kurfürsten Allee into the Metzer Strasse and drove in late-afternoon shade cast by the long rows of wide and leafy trees. Eddie parked in front of a four-story, new-looking brick building that had a small lawn. "This is it," he said, "the best bachelor billet for Americans in Bremen."

The summer sun dyed the brick a dark red, and the street fell into deep shadows. Mosca took both suitcases and the gym bag, and Eddie Cassin went before him up the walk. They were met at the door by the German housekeeper.

"This is Frau Meyer," Eddie Cassin said and put his arm around her waist. Frau Meyer was a woman of nearly forty, an almost platinum blonde. She had a superb figure molded by years of service as swimming teacher in the *Bunddeutscher Maedel.* Her face had a friendly but dissipated look accentuated by large, very white buck teeth.

Mosca nodded and she said, "I'm very pleased to see you, Mr. Mosca. Eddie has told me so much about you."

They went up the stairs to the third floor, and Frau Meyer unlocked the door to one of the rooms and gave the key to Mosca. It was a very large room. In the corner was a narrow bed and in another corner a huge, white, painted wardrobe. Two large windows let in the dying sun and the first beginnings of the long summer twilight. The rest of the room was bare.

Mosca put the two suitcases on the floor and Eddie sat on the bed. Eddie said to Frau Meyer, "Call Yergen."

Frau Meyer said, "I'll get the sheets and blankets, too." They could hear her going up the stairs.

"It doesn't look so good," Mosca said.

Eddie Cassin smiled. "We have a magician in the house. This guy Yergen. He'll fix everything." And while they waited, Eddie told Mosca about the billet. Frau Meyer was a good housekeeper, saw to it there was aways hot water, that the eight maids were thorough in their cleaning, and (by special arrangement with Frau Meyer) the laundry perfectly done. She lived herself in two comfortably furnished rooms in the attic. "I spend most of my time up there," Eddie went on, "but I think she screws Yergen on the side. My room is on the floor below this one so we can't keep a real close check on one another, thank God."

Mosca, becoming more and more impatient as the twilight deepened, listened to Eddie go on about the billet as if he owned it. Yergen was indispensable, Eddie said, to the Americans billeted in the Metzer Strasse. He could fix the house water pump so that even people on the top floor could take baths. He made up boxes for the chinaware Americans sent home, and packed so skillfully that the grateful relatives in America never complained of breakage. They made a good team, Yergen and Frau Meyer. Only Eddie knew that during the day they would carefully loot the rooms. From one it would be a pair of shorts, another a pair of socks, here a few towels or some handkerchiefs. The Americans were careless and kept no close check on their possessions. From the room of those extraordinarily careless it would be a pack or half-filled pack of cigarettes. All this was done with discretion. The maids who cleaned the rooms were kept honest by strict discipline.

"For Christ sake," Mosca said, "you know I want to get out of here. Get those krauts on the ball."

Eddie went to the door and yelled, "Hey, Meyer, snap it up." And then to Mosca. "She probably knocked off a quickie with Yergen. She loves it." They could hear her coming down the stairs.

She came in with an armful of bedclothing and behind her came Yergen. In his hand was a hammer and in his mouth some nails. He was a short, slender German of vigorous middle age, dressed in overalls and an American Army khaki shirt. There was an air of quiet competence and dignity about him that would have inspired trust and confidence if it had not been for the bunched and wrinkled skin beneath his eyes which gave him an air of shrewd cunning.

He shook hands with Eddie Cassin and then extended to Mosca the same greeting. Mosca shook hands to be polite. The occupation was getting real friendly, he thought.

"I am the 'jack of all trades' here," Yergen said. He brought out the phrase with a stilted relish. "Times you want anything fixed just call on me."

"I'll need a bigger bed," Mosca said, "some furniture, a radio, some other stuff I'll think of later."

Yergen unbuttoned the pocket of his khaki shirt and took out a pencil. "Of course," he said briskly, "they furnish these rooms very badly. Regulations. But I have helped other of your comrades. A small or large radio?"

"How much?" Mosca asked.

"Five to ten cartons."

"Money," Mosca said. "I have no cigarettes."

"American dollars or scrip?"

"Money orders."

"I tell you," Yergen said slowly, "I think you need here a radio, some table lamps, four or five chairs, a couch and a large bed. I get you all these things, we talk about the price later. If you have no cigarettes now, I can wait. I'm a businessman, I know when to give credit. And besides you are a friend of Mr. Cassin."

"That's fine," Mosca said. He stripped to the waist and opened the blue gym bag for a soap and towel.

"And if you want someone to do your laundry, please let me know. I'll give the order to the maid." Frau Meyer smiled at him. She liked his long torso with its white ornamental scar that she guessed ran to his groin.

"What does it cost?" Mosca asked. He had opened a suitcase and was laying out a fresh change of clothing.

"Oh, please, no payment. Give me a few bars of chocolate a week, and I'll see to it that the maids are happy."

"O.K., O.K.," Mosca said impatiently. And then to Yergen. "See if you can get that stuff in here tomorrow."

After the two Germans left, Eddie Cassin shook his head sadly in mock reproof. "Times have changed, Walter," he said. "The occupation has entered into a new phase. We treat people like Frau Meyer and Yergen with respect, shake their hands and always, always, give them a cigarette to smoke when we talk business to them. They can do us favors, Walter."

"Screw 'em," Mosca said. "Where's the washroom?"

Eddie Cassin led him down the hall. The bathroom was an enormous one, with three sinks, the biggest bathtub Mosca had ever seen, and a toilet bowl beside which stood a small table littered with magazines and Stateside newspapers.

"Real class," Mosca said. He began to wash and Eddie sat on the toilet bowl to keep him company.

"You going to move your girl friend in here?" Eddie asked.

"If I find her and she wants to come back," Mosca said.

"You going out to see her tonight?"

Mosca wiped himself dry and fixed a blade in the razor. "Yeah," he said and glanced at the partly open window. The last light of evening was melting away. "I'll try it tonight."

Eddie got up and went to the door. "If it doesn't click, come up to Frau Meyer's rooms when you get back and have a drink." He gave Mosca a pat. "If everything works out, then I'll see you tomorrow morning at the air base." He went out and down the hall.

Alone, Mosca felt an overpowering urge not to finish shaving, to go back to his room and go to bed, or go up to Frau Meyer's and spend the evening drinking with Eddie. He felt a strange reluctance to leave this building to go and find Hella, thinking of her name again now, consciously, but he made himself finish shaving and then he combed his hair. He walked over to the bathroom window and opened it wide; the side street was nearly empty. But down along the ruins he saw a woman in black, a dark mass in the failing light, pulling out the grass that grew here and there in the rubble. She had a great armful of it. And nearer to him, almost underneath his window, he saw a family of four, a man, his wife and two small boys, building a wall that was as yet no more than a foot high. The boys carried from a small handcart the broken bricks they had salvaged from the rubbled city and the man and woman hacked and scraped until the bricks fitted into the wall. The skeleton of the house framed them and etched them into Mosca's mind. The last light of the day vanished, and the whole street and the people were now just dark masses moving through a deeper and more massive darkness. Mosca went back to his room.

He took a bottle out of his suitcase and had a long drink. He was careful about dressing, thinking, "It's the first time she'll see me without my uniform." He put on a light gray suit and a white open shirt. He left everything as it was in the room—the suitcases open but unpacked, the soiled clothing on the floor, the shaving kit thrown carelessly on the bed. He had one last long drink, then ran downstairs and went out into the warm and heavy summer night.

He caught a streetcar, and the ticket taker asked for a cigarette, spotting him for an American immediately. Mosca gave it to him and then kept a watchful eye on each streetcar going by in the opposite direction, thinking that perhaps she had already left her room to go some place for the evening. Every so often he became tense and nervous, thinking he had seen her, that the back or profile of some girl looked like hers, but he could never be sure.

When he left the trolley and walked down the remembered street, he wasn't sure of the house and had to check the list of names that was posted on the door of each building. He made only one mistake, for the second list he read did have her name. He knocked, waited a few minutes and knocked again.

The door opened, and in the dim light of the hallway he recognized the old woman who owned the house. Her gray hair neatly pinned around her head, the old black dress, the threadbare shawl, all gave her the universal look of sorrow of aged women everywhere.

"Yes," she asked, "what is it?"

"Is Fräulein Hella at home?" Mosca was surprised at the ease and fluency of his German.

The old woman did not recognize him or realize that he was not a German. "Please come in," she said, and he followed her down the dimly lit hall to the room. The old woman knocked and said, "Fräulein Hella, you have a visitor, a man."

Finally he heard her real voice, quietly, but on a note of surprise. "A man?" And then "Wait one moment, please." Mosca opened the door and went into the room.

She was sitting with her back to him, hastily pushing clips into her just washed hair. On the table beside her stood a gray loaf of bread. Against the wall was a narrow bed, a night table beside it.

As he watched, Hella finished pinning the hair around her head and snatched up the loaf and slice of bread to take them to the wardrobe. Then she turned; her eyes met Mosca standing by the door.

Mosca saw the white, bone-ridged, almost skeletal face, the body even more fragile than he had remembered it. Her hands emptied as the gray bread fell to the wooden, buckled floor. Her face showed no surprise, and for a moment he thought the look was one of annoyance and slight displeasure. Then the face dissolved into a mask of sorrow and grief. He walked over to her, and her face seemed to crumple and fold, the tears following the many creases down to where his hand held the pointed chin. She let her head fall and pressed it against his shoulder.

"Let me see you," Mosca said, "let me look at you." He tried to lift her face, but she kept it against him. "It's all right," he said, "I wanted to surprise you." She kept sobbing, and all he could do was wait, looking around the room, the narrow bed, the old-fashioned wardrobe, and on the dresser, enlarged, framed, the photos he had given her. The light from the single table lamp was dim, a depressing, weak yellow, the walls and ceiling sagged inward from the weight of the ruins above them.

Hella lifted her face—she was half-laughing, half-crying. "Ah, you, you," she said. "Why didn't you write? Why didn't you let me know?"

"I wanted to surprise you," he said again. He kissed her gently, and lying against him, she said in a weak, incoherent voice, "When I saw you I thought you were dead or I was dreaming or crazy, I don't know, and I look so terrible, I just washed my hair." She looked down at the shapeless, faded housedress and then lifted her face to him again.

He saw now the dark circles under her eyes, as if the pigment from the rest of her face had been drained and held there to stain the skin almost black. The hair under his hand was lifeless, still wet, her body against him hard and angular.

She smiled and he saw the gap along the side of her mouth. He caressed her cheek and asked, "And this?"

Hella looked embarrassed. "The baby," she said, "I lost two teeth." She smiled at him, asked like a child, "Do I look very ugly?"

Mosca shook his head slowly. "No," he said, "no." And then remembering. "What about the baby, did you get rid of it?"

"No," Hella said, "it was born too soon, it only lived a few hours. I just left the hospital a month ago."

And then, because she knew his disbelief, his lack of

faith, she went to the dresser and pulled out a bundle of papers tied together with old string. She leafed through it and gave him four official documents.

"Read them," she said, not hurt or angry, knowing that in the world and time in which they lived, she had to give proof, that there was no absolute trust.

The official stamps and seals of the different bureaus dispelled his doubt. Almost regretfully he accepted the fact that she had not lied.

Hella went to the wardrobe and took out a pile of clothing. She held each one up, the little undershirts, blouses, the small trousers. Some of the materials and colors were familiar to Mosca. And then he understood that because there was nothing else to be had, she had cut up her dresses, even her underclothing, and sewed them together to fit a smaller body.

"I knew it would be a boy," she said. And then suddenly Mosca was very angry. He was angry that she had given the color from her face, the flesh along her hips and shoulders, the teeth, the clothing so cleverly cut and fitted together and that she had received nothing in return. And he knew that what had brought him back was his own need and not hers.

"That was silly," he said, "that was goddamn silly."

Mosca sat on the bed and Hella sat beside him. For a moment they were both embarrassed and stared at the bare table, the only chair, the indented walls and sagging ceiling, and then moving slowly, as if taking part in an ancient tribal ritual, like heathens cementing their relationship with a vague and fearful god, not knowing if the ceremony would bring disaster or good fortune, they stretched out on the narrow bed and came together, he finally with a passion inspired by drink, guilt, remorse, and she with love, tenderness and an absolute faith that this consummation was good, that it would bring happiness to them both. And she accepted the pain given to her not-yet-healed body, the cruelty of his passion, his lack of faith in her and in himself and in all things, knowing the final truth that, of all the human beings that he had known, he had need of her, her faith, her body, her belief and love for him.

5

THAT SECOND SUMMER of peace went by quickly for Mosca. The work at the air base was so light, it seemed as if he were there only to keep Eddie Cassin company, listen to his stories and cover up for him when he was too drunk to come in and work. Eddie Cassin didn't have much to do. Lieutenant Forte came in for a few minutes each morning to sign papers and then went up to the Operations Office to sweat out a flight and pass the day talking to his fellow pilots. After work Mosca had supper with Wolf and Eddie and sometimes Gordon at the Rathskellar, the official mess for American officers and civilians in Bremen.

Evenings he and Hella kept to their room, lying together on the couch reading, the radio tuned to a German station that played soft music. When the last of the warm summer twilight died away they would look at each other and smile and go to bed. They would let the radio play until very late.

The floor on which they lived was quiet, but on the floors below parties went on night after night. In the summer evenings the sound of radios filled the Metzer Strasse, and jeeps loaded with Americans in their olive-green civilian uniforms, pretty, barelegged German girls on their laps, stopped in front of the building with a screaming of brakes and shrilling cries of the young women. The laughter and clinking of glasses carried out to passersby who turned their heads curiously and cautiously as they went on down the street. Later they might hear Eddie Cassin cursing drunkenly as he fought with one of his girl friends outside the building. Sometimes the parties would break up early, and a late summer night breeze, its freshness tainted with the smell of rubble, would rustle leaves and branches of the trees that lined the street below.

On Sundays Hella and Frau Meyer prepared dinner in Meyer's attic apartment, usually a rabbit or duck that Eddie and Mosca drove out to a nearby farm to trade for, and with it garden vegetables from the same farm. Then gray German bread topped off with PX coffee and ice cream. When they had finished eating, Hella and Mosca would leave Eddie and Frau Meyer to their drinking and go for a long walk through the city, and beyond it to the flat, green countryside.

Mosca smoking his cigar, Hella wearing one of his starched, white shirts, sleeves rolled neatly up above the elbow, they would go up past the police building, its massive, green-colored concrete showing gray scars chipped out by the explosion and past the Glocke Building, a little farther on, which now housed the American Red Cross Club. In the square before it, children waited and begged for cigarettes and chocolate. Stubble-cheeked men in Wehrmacht caps and torn, dyed Army jackets picked up the butts as soon as one of the olive-drab G.I.'s leaning against the building flicked it away. The G.I.'s lounged easily, eyeing the women, picking out the *Fräuleins* who passed by slowly as if walking on a treadmill, and who a short time later, circling the building, passed by again, and then again and again until it was like watching someone known riding a merry-go-round, the familiar face appearing inevitably before the watchful, expectant and amused onlookers. In the warm summer afternoon the square was like a gay, thriving market place, making the day seem not like Sunday, taking away the Sunday atmosphere of quiet and suspended motion.

Great olive-drab Army buses and mud-covered trucks poured into the square every few minutes, bringing occupation troops from the hamlets surrounding Bremen and some from as far away as Bremerhaven. The G.I.'s were natty in pressed olive drabs, the trouser legs tucked neatly into polished, mahogany-colored combat boots. There were English troops sweltering in their heavy woolens and beretlike headgear. American merchant mariners, wild looking in raggedy trousers and dirty sweaters and occasionally with bushy, full-grown beards, waited sullenly for MP's to check their papers before they could enter the building.

Sporadically the German police in their dyed, soldier-like uniforms cleared the square, shooing the child beggars down the many side streets, pushing the haggard-looking butt snipers to the far corner of the square and then letting them rest on the steps of the German Communications Building. The *Fräuleins* on their merry-go-round speeded up the tempo slightly but were never molested.

Mosca would pick up sandwiches in the Red Cross, and they would go on, mingling with the stream of people on their way to Burger Park.

The enemy on Sunday still took their traditional afternoon strolls. The German men walked with the dignity of family chiefs, some with unfilled pipes in their mouths. Their wives pushed baby carriages and children gamboled sedately and somewhat tiredly before them. The summer sun caught the loose dirt raised by the light afternoon breeze that swept through the ruins, imprisoned it, flooded it, so that over the whole city hung an almost imperceptible veil of golden dust.

And then, finally, after they had crossed a great, reddish prairie of ruins, an earth of leveled homes, a soil of crushed brick and dust and iron, they would come out into the countryside, and walking until they were tired, would come to rest in a green and heavily grown field. They would rest and sleep and eat the sandwiches they had brought, and if the spot were secluded enough, make love peacefully in the empty world which seemed to surround them.

When the sun faced them across the sky, they walked back into the city. Over the prairie of ruins dusk would fall, and coming into the square they could see the G.I.'s leaving the Red Cross Building. The victors had had their fill of sandwiches, ice cream, Cokes, ping-pong and the professional, sterilized friendliness of the hostesses. In the street the soldiers would lounge just as if they were on the street corners back home. The lines of *Fräuleins* passing up and down would thin out, enemy and conqueror disappearing together down the rubble-filled side streets to half-destroyed rooms in shattered buildings, or if time pressed, to cavelike cellars. In the square, black and almost still, there were only a few hopeful beggars, a child, tired and now stationary girls. As from a dying carnival, the blurring music would filter out of the building and wash gently over the silent figures in the darkened square, sift through the ruins down to the Weser, as if following them to the quiet river, and as Mosca and Hella walked along the bank, they left the music behind and gazed across the water to the moonlit skeletal city on the other side.

In the Metzer Strasse Frau Meyer and Eddie Cassin

would have tea and cookies waiting for them; sometimes Eddie would be in a drunken stupor on the couch but come alive when he heard their voices. They would drink their tea and talk quietly, feeling the new raw peace of the gentle summer night and the slow, rising drowsiness that would lead to safe and dreamless sleep.

6

IN THE BILLET, the room next to Mosca's was occupied by a short, heavy-framed civilian wearing the usual olive-green uniform. But on it was a blue-and-white patch stitched with the letters "AJDC." They saw him rarely, and no one in the billet knew him, but late at night he could be heard moving around his room, the radio playing softly. One evening he gave Mosca a lift in his jeep. They were both going to the Rathskellar for supper. His name was Leo, and he worked for the American Joint Distribution Committee, a Jewish relief organization. The initials were also painted on his jeep in great white letters.

As they were driving through the streets, Leo asked Mosca in a high voice with an English accent, "Have I met you some place, you look familiar to me?"

"I used to be with Mil Gov right after the war," Mosca said. He was sure they had never met.

"Ah, ah," Leo said, "you came up to Grohn with the coal trucks, eh?"

"That's right," Mosca said surprised.

"I was an inmate there, a DP," Leo grinned. "You didn't do such a good job. Many a week end we went without hot water."

"We had trouble for a while," Mosca said. "It got straightened out."

"Yes, I know," Leo smiled. "A fascist method but perhaps necessary."

They had supper together. Leo in ordinary times would have been fat. He had a hawk-nosed, big-boned face, the left side of which twitched spasmodically. He moved nervously and quickly but with the awkwardness and lack of co-ordination of one who had never participated in any kind of athletics. He was ignorant of almost all sports.

Over their coffee Mosca asked, "What do you people do?"

"It is UNRRA work," Leo said. "Distribute supplies to the Jews who are in the camps waiting to leave Germany. I was myself eight years in Buchenwald."

A long time ago, a time that was no longer real, Mosca thought, that was one of the big reasons he had enlisted, to fight against concentration camps, but that hadn't been him, that was the guy in the photo, the one Gloria and his mother and Alf cared so much about. But remembering this aroused a strange emotion in him, of embarrassment and shyness because he no longer gave a damn.

"Yes," Leo said. "I went in when I was thirteen." He rolled up his sleeve and on his arm as if printed there with purple ink was a six-digit number with a smeared letter before it. "My father was there with me. He died a few years before the camp was liberated."

"You speak English pretty well," Mosca said. "Nobody'd think you were German."

Leo looked at him with a smile and said in his quick, nervous voice, "No, no, I am not a German. I am a Jew." He was silent for a moment. "I was a German, of course, but Jews cannot any longer be Germans."

"How come you haven't left?" Mosca asked.

"I have a very good job here. I have all the privileges Americans have and I earn good money. And then I must make up my mind whether to go to Palestine or the United States. It is very difficult to decide."

They talked for a long time, Mosca drinking whiskey and Leo coffee. At one point Mosca found himself trying to explain different sports to Leo, really trying to tell how it felt because the other had spent his childhood and his youth in the concentration camp, had it stolen, irretrievably lost.

Mosca tried to explain how it felt to go up for a shot in basketball, the thrill of faking a guard out of position and rising easily in the air to float the ball through the basket, the quick whirling and running on the warm wooden floor of the gym, the soaking, sweaty tiredness and the magical refreshment of the warm shower afterward. Then walking down the street, his whole body relaxed, carrying the blue gym bag, and the girls waiting for them in the ice-cream parlor. Later the peaceful and complete oblivion of perfect sleep.

Riding back to the billet, Leo said, "I am always on the ways, my job makes me travel a great deal. But with the cold weather coming I will spend more time in Bremen. We'll get to know each other better, eh?"

"I'll show you how to play baseball," Mosca said with a smile, "get you ready for the States. And don't say 'on the ways.' That's German. Say 'on the road,' or 'traveling.' "

After that he would come to their room some nights and drink tea and coffee, and Mosca taught him how to play cards—poker, casino and rummy. Leo never talked about the time he had spent in the camps and never seemed depressed, but he never had the patience to stay in one place long and their quiet life was not appealing to him. They became good friends, Leo and Hella, and he claimed that she was the only girl who had been able to teach him how to dance properly.

And then when autumn came and the trees dropped their leaves on the bicycle paths and laid a speckled brown-and-green carpet along the shaded streets, the freshened air stirred Mosca's blood and lifted him out of his summer lethargy. He became restless, ate more often at the Rathskellar, went drinking at the Officers' Club—all places where Hella was not allowed to enter because she was the enemy. Returning late to the billet, a little drunk, he would eat the thick, canned soup Hella warmed up for him on the electric plate and then sleep fitfully through the night. On many mornings he would wake at dawn and watch the gray clouds being swept across the sky by the early October wind. He watched the German workers walking briskly to the corner where they could catch a *Strassenbahn* to the heart of the city.

One morning as he stood by the window, Hella rose and stood by him. She was in the undershirt she used for bedclothing. She put her arm around him, and they both looked down at the street below.

"Can't you sleep?" she murmured drowsily. "You're always up so early."

"I guess we'll have to start getting out more. This home life is too much for me."

Mosca watched the russet blanket of leaves being rolled up Metzer Strasse, covering the dirt bicycle path underneath the trees.

Hella leaned against him. "We need a baby, a wonderful baby," she said softly.

"Christ," Mosca said, "the *Führer* really drummed that crap into your heads."

"Children were loved before that." She was angry that he could laugh at what she wanted so much. "I know it's thought stupid to want children. In the *Flak* the Berlin girls used to laugh at us farmers because we cared about babies and talked about them." She pushed away from him. "All right, go to work," she said.

Mosca tried to reason with her. "You know we can't get married until they lift the ban. Everything we do here is illegal, especially your being here in the billet. When the kid comes we'll have to move to German quarters and that's illegal for me. There's a million things I'd have to do that they could ship me back to the States for and no way to take you with me."

She smiled at him and there was a trace of sadness in it. "I know you won't leave me here again." Mosca was surprised and shocked that she should know this. He had already decided to go underground with false papers if some trouble should come.

"Ah, Walter," she said, "I don't want to be like the people downstairs; drink, dance at the club, go to bed and never have anything to keep us together except ourselves. The way we live, that's not enough." She stood there, the undershirt reaching just over her hipbone and navel, without dignity and without shame. He wanted to smile.

"It's no good," he said.

"Listen to me. When you went away I was happy I was going to have a baby. I thought I had such very good luck. Because even if you didn't come back there would be another human being in the world I could love. Do you understand that? From my whole family I only have one sister left, and she is far away. Then you came and you left and I had no one. In all the world there was no one that it would be pleasure for me to bring pleasure to, no one that was part of my life. There's nothing more terrible."

Below them some Americans came out of the building into the cold street, unlocked the security chains on their jeeps and warmed up the motors, the rising and falling throb coming faintly through the closed windows.

Mosca put his arm around her. "You're not well enough." He looked down at the thin, naked body. "I don't want anything to happen to you." And as he said the words a wave of fear swept over him that she would leave for some reason, and that in the gray winter mornings he would stand alone at the window, the room empty behind him, and that the fault in some unforeseen way would be his. Turning to her suddenly, he said in a gentle voice. "Don't be mad at me. Wait a bit."

She rested in his arms and then quietly she said, "You're afraid really of yourself. I think you know that. I see how you are with other people and how you are with me. Everyone thinks you're so unfriendly, so"—she searched for a word that would not make him angry—"so rough. I know you're not that way, not really. I could never want a better man, in everything. Sometimes Frau Meyer and Yergen, when I say something nice about you, they look at each other. Oh, I know what they think." Her voice was bitter, the bitterness of all women speaking in defense of their own against a world that does not comprehend the reason for their love. "They don't understand."

He picked her up, put her on the bed and drew the blanket over her. "You'll catch a cold," he said. He leaned over to kiss her before he left for work. "You can have anything you want," he said, then smiled. "Especially something that easy. And don't worry about them ever making me leave, no matter what."

"I won't," she said laughing. "I'll be waiting for you tonight."

7

A BAND was playing fast dance music when they entered the German night club. It was a long rectangular room bare of ornament and bleak with white, unshaded light. The walls were roughly calcimined and the high, domed ceiling gave it a vast cathedral-like air. It had been a school auditorium, but the rest of the building had been blown away.

The chairs were of the hard, folding variety, the tables were equally bare and stern. There were no decorations. The room was full, people jammed together, so that the waiters in many instances could not serve a table directly and had to ask intervening couples to pass the drinks on. Wolf was known here, and they followed his portly figure to a table near the wall.

Wolf offered his cigarettes all around and said to the waiter, "Six schnapps." At the same time he slipped the rest of the cigarettes in the pack into the waiter's hand. "The clear stuff." The waiter bowed and hurried off.

Frau Meyer turned her blonde head to look at the room. "It's not very nice here," she said.

Eddie patted her hand. "Baby, this is for people who lost the war."

Mosca smiled at Hella. "Not too bad is it?" She shook her head. "It's a change," she said. "I should see how my fellow Germans enjoy themselves." Mosca missed the slight guilt in her voice, but Eddie understood and his delicate mouth curved into a smile. One weapon found, he thought, and felt a sudden elation, a sudden passion.

"There's a good story about this place," Wolf said. They had to bribe the Education Officer at Mil Gov to certify it as unfit for any school activities and then bribe the Fine Arts Officer as O.K. for entertainment purposes. Nobody knows whether it's really safe." He added, "Not that it matters, it'll be closed up in a couple of days anyway."

"Oh, why?" Hella asked.

"Wait and see," Wolf said, smiling with a knowing air.

Leo said with his usual good humor, "Look at them," he gestured around the room. "I never saw sadder looking people in my life. And they are paying to have such a bad time?" They all laughed. The waiter brought their drinks.

Eddie raised his glass. His handsome face settled into a mock seriousness. "Happiness to our two friends, a perfectly matched couple. Look at them. One, a princess so sweet and fair. The other, a scowling brute. She will mend his socks and have his slippers ready each evening and for a reward she will receive some well-chosen hard words and a blow. My friends, this marriage will be perfect. It will last a hundred years if he doesn't kill her first." They drank, Mosca and Hella smiling at each other as if they possessed an answer, a secret no one at the table could guess.

The two couples went out to dance on the small floor before the raised stage at the other end of the room. Wolf and Leo were left alone. Wolf looked around with a practiced eye.

Cigarette smoke rose over the mass of people to the high, domed ceiling. The patrons were a curious mixture, old couples who had perhaps sold a piece of good furniture and decided on one night out to relieve the dull monotony of their lives; young black-market operators, good friends of American mess sergeants and PX officers, sat at tables with young girls who wore nylon stockings and smelled of perfume; older men who trafficked in diamonds and furs, automobiles and other valuables, sat with girls not richly dressed, sedate mistresses of long standing, a salaried relationship.

The densely packed room was not noisy, the general conversation not loud in volume. The drinks were ordered at long intervals, and there was no food of any kind in sight. The band tried its best to play American tunes jazz style, the drummer's square head shaking from side to side in a strained but reserved imitation of American performers helpless with inner rhythm.

Wolf nodded to some people at other tables, black-market operators he had done business with for cigarettes. They had been spotted for Americans as soon as they came in, he thought, and curiously enough more because of the ties they wore than anything else. The other people here were just as well dressed but for some reason the black market could not supply ties, the people here wore dull, ragged pieces of cloth for neckwear. Wolf stored this away in his mind. Another way to make an easy dollar.

The music ended, and everyone went back to the tables. Eddie, flushed with dancing and the contact with Frau Meyer's body, watched Hella intently as she sat down and then leaned over on Mosca's chair, her hand resting on his shoulder. In his mind he saw the hard, white body on a brown Army blanket, spreading, spreading, his face close to her neat and passive head. In a moment he felt sure of his success—how it would happen he did not know—and then the image shattered as from the rose-colored circle of light under which the band played, the only friendly color in the room, came three short, commanding blasts of a trumpet.

The small hum quieted, the white bright lights dimmed, and the room became cavernous, the high, domed ceiling invisible in the darkness above them.

On the auditorium stage a line of girls came out dancing so badly that when they exited there was not even a polite smattering of applause. They were followed by a juggler and then by acrobats. And then a girl singer with a robust figure and a high, weak voice.

"Christ," Mosca said, "let's get the hell out."

Wolf shook his head. "Wait a bit."

The audience was still attentive, still expectant. The trumpet gave out another flourish, and the lights dimmed almost to darkness; the stage at the end of the room became a luminous, yellow square, and into it, strolling nonchalantly from the outside darkness of the wings, came a small, dapper man with the full, round, rubberlike face of the born comedian. He was greeted with a storm of applause.

He began to talk to the audience conversationally, as if there were no barrier between them.

"I must apologize that part of my famous act cannot be performed tonight. My dog, Frederick, is not to be found anywhere." He paused, his face sorrowful, and then in simulated anger: "It's a shame, really a shame. Ten dogs I have trained and always they disappear. In Berlin—gone. In Düsseldorf—gone, and now here. Always the same." A girl came rushing out on the stage. She whispered in his ear. The comedian nodded his head and turned briskly to the audience. "My friends, the management has asked me to announce that meat sandwiches will be available right after this performance." He winked. "No ration card necessary but at an exorbitant price of course. Now as I was saying—" He stopped. On his face a look so comical in its wonder, dismay and then complete understanding shattered the audience into a great wave of laughter. "Frederick, my Frederick," he shrieked, and rushed off the stage. He came strolling back into the light munching a sandwich. As the laughter subsided he said sadly, "Too late. But he is a good friend to the last. A truly tasty sandwich." And with an enormous bite he made most of it disappear.

Waiting for the applause to die, he wiped his mouth and then took a piece of paper from his pocket.

Raising a hand for silence he began, "Today everyone worries about calories. I read here that we need 1300 calories to stay alive and that we get 1550 calories in the ration established by Military Government. No criticism of the authorities intended, but I wish to point out tonight how careful we must be with our extra two hundred calories. Now, a few simple rules."

He told all the old jokes about calories but so expertly that one ripple of laughter followed another. He was interrupted by a scantily clad girl who came dancing on the stage and whirled around him. He watched her with a greedy and appraising eye and then from his pockets drew out a carrot, a small head of lettuce and a handful of green beans. He counted on his fingers and shook his head. Then shrugged and said, "She will take a thousand calories at least."

The girl pushed against him. He explained to her in pantomime what the trouble was. She reached between her breasts and drew out a small bunch of grapes. He pantomimed; not enough. She started to reach into her shorts, but he, with a look of noble abnegation said loudly: "Please, I couldn't." As the girl exited sadly from the stage he thrust out with his arm and said, "If I had only a hot beefsteak." The laughter rose to the high-domed ceiling.

On the stage the comedian's rubbery face was exalted and flushed with the power he held over them. Exuberantly he did quick imitations: Rudolph Hess, drooling, raving insanely, escaping in a plane to England; Goebbels explaining a night out to his wife with the most ridiculous and outrageous lies; Goering promising that no bombs would ever fall on Berlin as he dived underneath a table to escape the falling debris. When the comedian made his exit there was a tremendous applause. It continued until he reappeared. The audience gasped and was still.

His hair was combed over his eyes and there was a smudge on his upper lip that could be a short, small mustache. He had screwed up his rubbery face into a startling Hitlerian mask. He stood near the wings, the look on his face half-parody, half-earnest. He radiated power and magnetism. He held the audience with his glance and in a loud voice that rang to the high-domed ceiling asked: "Do you want me back?"

There was a moment of shocked silence and as he stood there, slowly on that white-floured face appeared the deadly smile of a successful anti-Christ. The audience understood.

The room exploded. Some men leaped onto chairs and tables and shouted, "Yah, Yah." The women clapped furiously. Some stomped on the floor with their feet, and others banged tables with their fists. The din filled the room, crashed against the walls and reverberated against the ceiling.

Wolf was on his feet looking across the crowd at the stage with a grim smile on his face. Mosca had understood and leaned back in his chair sipping his drink. Frau Meyer was looking down at the table trying to restrain a smile of pleasure. Eddie was asking her, "What goes on, what the hell goes on?" Frau Meyer said, "Nothing, nothing."

Hella looked at Leo across the table. His face was rigid, but the tic on the left side was out of control. She flushed and unconsciously shook her head from side to side as if to disclaim any responsibility, any share in what was going on. But Leo turned his eyes away from her and stared again at the stage.

The comedian's rubbery face was normal now and he had brushed his hair back as he bowed. The illusion was gone, and he accepted the applause as if it were his due, given for the pleasure his art afforded.

The band struck up a tune. Wolf sat down nodding his head as if he understood many things. People moved out to dance. There were many glances at their table. Two young men seated nearby had the girls with them almost hysterical with their murmured wit.

Leo stared down at the table, feeling his face twitching. He was angry, with a hurt and helpless despair. He hoped one of the others would suggest leaving.

Mosca, watching him, understood and said to Wolf and the others, "Let's get out." As he stood up he saw that one of the young men had turned his chair so that he faced their table and could stare at Leo with an amused grin. The front of his head was bald, his face heavy, the features thick and forceful.

Mosca said to Wolf with a nod of his head, "Let's take that guy with us."

Wolf studied Mosca as if he saw something he had guessed and hoped for. "O.K. I'll use my Intelligence card to get him outside. You got a weapon, just in case?"

"One of those small Hungarian things," Mosca said.

Leo raised his head. "No, I don't want to do anything like that. Let us just leave."

Hella took Mosca's arm. "Yes, let's leave," she said. The others rose. Wolf was shaking his head up and down again as if he understood something. He glanced at Leo with a look of pity and contempt. He saw that Mosca had frowned and shrugged and was on his way out. As Wolf went past the other table he leaned over and put his face close to the young German's and looked into his eyes. "A loud laugh can be very unhealthy, do you understand me?" He flashed his Intelligence card, knowing the German would be able to read it. As he followed the others, he smiled, and no laughter followed their retreat.

They drove back to Mosca's room for a drink. Hella began to prepare bacon sandwiches on the electric plate which stood on a footlocker.

They all sat around the large, square table, except Eddie who stretched out in the stuffed chair in one corner of the room. Mosca unlocked the white painted wardrobe and took out liquor and cigarettes.

Eddie from his chair asked, "How do the bastards get away with it?"

"They won't," Wolf said. "He's pulled some raw stuff, but tonight he went too far. How do you like the reception he got, though?" Wolf shook his white, heavy face up and down in amused wonder. "These krauts never learn. You'd think that if they just took a walk down the street they'd never want to fight again. But they're rarin' to go. Just in their blood."

Mosca said jokingly to Leo, "Looks like you'd better make up your mind where you're going, Palestine or the States."

Leo shrugged and sipped his coffee.

Wolf asked, "Can you go to the States?"

"Oh, yes," Leo said. "I can go there."

"Then go." Wolf studied him. "If tonight's any indication, you're too soft for that pioneer stuff."

Leo put his hand up to the left side of his face.

"Leave it lay," Mosca said.

"No. Don't misunderstand me, Leo, when I say the trouble with your race has always been that they never fight back. Some people think they're cowards. I think it's a matter of being too civilized. They don't believe in force. Like tonight. If we'd taken that guy outside and knocked him around, it would have helped, in a small way. If you people ever get a country of your own, thank your terrorist organizations. Terror and force are great weapons. Organizations in every country use them and never underestimate their power. I'm surprised you don't know that after what you've been through."

Leo said slowly, "I'm not afraid to go to Palestine, and in some ways I know it is my duty. But I think, too, how it will be a hard time. I want now—pleasure. That is the only way I can think of it. And yet I am ashamed that I think this way. But I will go away."

"Don't put it off too long," Wolf said. "These krauts will never change. It's in their blood. You can see it every day."

Leo went on as if he had not heard. "As for terror and force, I don't believe. My father was in camp with me, he was a German, by the way, my mother was a Jew. My father was a political prisoner, he went before me."

The tic on Leo's face went into motion again and he put up his hand to hold it still. "He died there but taught me before he died. He told me that one day I would be free and that the most terrible thing that could happen to me was to become like the people who kept us there. I believe him still. It is a little hard, but I believe him still."

Wolf shook his head. "I know. I know people like your father." His voice was expressionless.

Hella and Frau Meyer passed hot bacon sandwiches around. Leo refused his. "I'm going to bed," he said. He left and they could hear him in the next room, his radio tuned to a German station playing soft string music.

Frau Meyer went over to Eddie and pushed him playfully. "Stop dreaming," she said.

Eddie smiled, his handsome, delicate face soft with a sleepy tenderness. As Hella knelt by the electric plate, he watched her over his glass and thought, "It will be in this room," and every piece of furniture stood out clearly as if there were no people there. He was always doing this, his mind always creating scenes with women he had not even approached.

Wolf munched on his bacon sandwich. "It's funny the ideas people get." His voice lowered. "The men who ran Leo's camp were probably ordinary guys like you and me. Just following orders. During the war when I was in counter-intelligence, we'd get some prisoners, and the Major would look at his watch and say, 'I want such and such information by two o'clock.' We got it." Wolf accepted a cigar from Mosca and puffed on it. "I got back to the States for a leave before I started on this job and saw some of those war movies. You know, the hero gets tortured but dies of pain before he gives in and talks." Wolf waved his cigar in exasperation at the memory. "Of course, they can't even hint what's really done." He paused and looked at Mosca intently. "They're ashamed to admit it. A man can't control himself if the right things are done to him. Not one goddamn one."

Mosca filled the glasses, everybody was sleepy except Wolf. Frau Meyer sat curled in Eddie's lap, and Hella had stretched out on the couch against the wall opposite the bed.

Wolf smiled. "I had a special technique. I'd never ask a question until I gave them a little punishment first. Like that old gag about the newly married couple. The husband raps her in the mouth as soon as they're alone and says 'That's for nothing, watch what you do.' Same idea." He grinned disarmingly, his dead-white face filled with cheerful good humor. "I know what you think, here's a no-good son of a bitch. But somebody has always had to do that kind of work. You can't win wars without it. Believe me, I don't get any of this sadistic kind of pleasure like in the movies. But it's necessary. Hell, I even got a decoration out of it." He added hastily and sincerely, "But of course we never were as rough as the Germans."

Eddie yawned. "All very interesting, but I think I'll go down to my room."

Wolf laughed defensively. "I guess it *is* too late for a lecture." He let Eddie and Frau Meyer leave before him. He finished his drink and said to Mosca, "Come on downstairs, I want a talk with you." They went down to the street and sat in Wolf's jeep.

"All that Eddie thinks of is gash," Wolf said in an angry, contemptuous voice.

"He was just sleepy," Mosca said.

"How come you carry a weapon?" Wolf asked.

Mosca shrugged. "Used to having one, I guess. And the war isn't over long."

Wolf nodded. "I don't like to be out at night without one either."

There was another moment of silence, and Mosca moved restlessly.

Wolf puffed on his cigar. "I wanted to get you alone because I have an idea about making ourselves a pile of dough. I guess everybody in the occupation has a little hunk of gravy. Now I got a lot of contacts, diamonds for cigarettes, all that kind of stuff. I can fix you up."

"Hell," Mosca said impatiently, "I can't get my hands on that many cigarettes."

Wolf hesitated and then went on. "You know, some day you may need a lot of dough. For instance, if they catch Hella in your room it'll be your ass, you'll get sent back to the States." He held up his hand. "I know, you'll go underground, a lot of guys have done it. But you'll need money. Or, say it came to a pinch, and you had to take her out of Germany. You can get phony papers, but they cost an arm and a leg. And wherever you go, Scandinavia, France, any other place, living comes high. Ever think of it?"

"No, I haven't," Mosca said slowly.

"Well, I got an idea. I need help and that's why I'm asking you. I'm no philanthropist. You interested?"

"Go ahead," Mosca said.

Wolf paused again, puffing on his cigar. "You know the money we use, the Army scrip? The black-market operators break their necks to get it. Then they trade it back to G.I.'s for money orders. But they have to make it pretty slow. We can change all the scrip we can get our hands on into money orders, something we couldn't do with the old occupation marks."

"So?" Mosca said.

"Now here's the thing. The last couple of weeks the

German operators seem to have a hell of a lot of scrip. I'm making a nice bit of change turning it into money orders for them. I'll cut you in on that, by the way. Now here's the angle. I got curious and started snooping around, and I heard a terrific story. When the scrip money was shipped from the States the boat docked in Bremerhaven. And even though everything was top-secret, something slipped and a case of scrip, over a million bucks, disappeared. The Army keeps quiet because it makes them look stupid as hell. How do you like that?" In telling the story Wolf became excited. "A million bucks," he repeated.

Mosca grinned at the pure hunger in Wolf's voice. "A lot of money," he said.

"Now here's my idea. The money is probably split up all over the country, but there must be a gang here with a big chunk. If we could only find them, that's the thing. It's a long shot."

Mosca said, "How do we find it and how do we take it?"

"Finding the money is my job," Wolf said, "but you help. It's not as hard as it sounds and remember, I'm a trained man. I have a lot of contacts. I'll take you around and introduce you as a big Post Exchange wheel who's looking to dump cigarettes at three or four bucks a carton. They'll jump at the price. We'll get rid of twenty or thirty cartons that way. I can get the butts. The word'll get around. Then we'll say we have to get rid of five thousand cartons in one lump. A big deal. We'll make up a story. If everything works out somebody'll come to us, and we'll close the deal. They show up with twenty thousand bucks worth of scrip. We take it. They can't go to the police, theirs or ours. They're screwed." Wolf stopped, took a last nervous puff and threw his cigar into the street. Then he said quietly, "It'll be hard work, tramping around town a couple of nights a week. And the final business takes guts."

"Real cops and robbers," Mosca said and Wolf smiled. Mosca looked out into the dark street and over the ruins. Far away, as if separated from them by a lake or prairie, he could see a lone streetcar with its yellow light moving slowly through the blackness of the city.

Wolf said slowly, seriously. "We have to prepare for our future. Sometimes I feel that my life before now was just a dream, nothing serious, maybe you feel the same. Now we have to get ready for our real life, and it's going to be tough, real tough. This is our last chance to fix ourselves up."

"O.K.," Mosca said, "but it sounds complicated as hell."

Wolf shook his head. "It may not work out. But meanwhile I'll throw you some of this exchange business. You'll make a good few hundred anyway, no matter what happens. If we're lucky, just a little lucky, we'll split fifteen or twenty thousand. Maybe more."

Mosca got out of the jeep as Wolf raced the motor, then watched him drive away. Looking up he saw Hella's dark head in the pane of light that was his window. He waved to her and then entered the building and ran up the stairs.

8

MOSCA SLOUCHED DOWN in the parked jeep, trying to escape the cold October wind of late afternoon. The frozen metal of the floor chilled his whole body.

Farther on up the street was an important intersection, streetcars swinging to the right and left, and military vehicles pausing momentarily for drivers to read the long row of white shingles that directed them to different headquarters in the city. Ruins stretched away on four sides like rough pasture land, and beyond the crossroads, where little houses began to stand, a small German movie theatre opened its doors, and a long waiting line moved slowly inside.

Mosca was hungry and impatient. He watched three covered trucks filled with German prisoners of war go by and stop at the intersection. Probably war criminals, he thought. A jeep with two armed guards followed dutifully behind. Leo appeared in the door of the tailor shop and Mosca straightened up in his seat.

They both saw the woman across the street start to run before she screamed. She left the sidewalk and ran awkwardly, wildly toward the intersection. She waved one arm frantically and screamed continuously a name that her emotion made unintelligible. From the last truck of prisoners a figure waved to the woman in return. The truck picked up speed, the jeep at its heels like a shepherd dog.

The woman saw there was no hope and stopped. She fell to her knees and then collapsed her full length on the street, blocking traffic.

Leo climbed into the jeep. The roaring and shaking of the motor gave them an illusion of warmth. They waited until the woman had been carried to the sidewalk, then Leo put the jeep in motion. They didn't say anything about what they had seen. It was none of their concern, but far back in Mosca's mind a vague, familiar image began to stir and form and shape itself.

Just before the war's end he had been in Paris and found himself caught in an immense throng. Trying to escape from it had been like a nightmare, and against his will he had been carried to the center, the focal point. There, inching slowly through the crowd which filled the streets, the sidewalks, the cafés, were a string of open trucks filled with Frenchmen; freed prisoners of war, slave laborers, men given up for dead. The cheering and shouting from the crowd drowned the jubilant cries of the men in the trucks. But they jumped up and down and leaned out over the sides of their trucks to be kissed, to accept the white flowers offered and thrown to them. Suddenly one of the men had flung himself from the truck, slithered off the heads of people he landed on and fell to the ground. A woman fought her way to the man and caught him to her in a fierce, possessive embrace. From the truck someone flung a crutch and shouted obscene congratulations that at any other time would make a woman blush. But she had laughed with the rest of the crowd.

The pain, the shock, the guilt Mosca had felt then he felt now.

When Leo stopped the jeep in front of the Rathskellar

Mosca got out. "I don't feel like eating," he said. "I'll see you at the house later."

Leo, busy putting the padlock on the jeep's security chain, lifted his head in surprise. "What's wrong?" he asked.

"Just a headache, I'll walk it off."

He felt cold and lit a cigar; the heavy tobacco smoke warmed his face. He took the small, quiet side streets, impassable to vehicles because of the rubble which had overflowed the ruins and sidewalks, picking his way over the loose stones and bricks, careful in the gathering dusk not to fall.

When he entered his room he felt really ill, his face hot and feverish. Without turning on the light he undressed and flung his clothes over on the couch and went to bed. Under the covers he was still cold and could smell the stale cigar butt he had left lying on the table edge. He huddled and curved his body together for warmth but the chill shook him continuously. His mouth was dry, and the pounding in his head became a slow monotonous beat, barely painful.

He heard a key turn in the door and Hella moving into the room. The light flashed on. She came to the bed and sat on it.

"Aren't you well?" she asked with concern. It gave her a queer shock to see him so.

"Just a chill," Mosca said. "Get me some aspirin and throw that cigar out."

She went to the bathroom for a glass of water and when she gave it to him she brushed her hand over his head and murmured, "It's funny to see you ill. Shall I sleep on the couch?"

"No," Mosca said. "I'm cold as hell. Come in here with me."

She put out the light and came to the bed to undress. Dimly in the blackness of the room he could see her hanging her clothes over the back of a chair. He felt his body burning with fever and desire, and when she came into bed he pressed against her. Her breasts and thighs and mouth were cool, her cheeks cold, and he held her as tightly as he could.

When he rested back against the pillow he could feel the sweat between his thighs and rolling down his back. The headache was gone but his very bones seemed to hurt. He reached over her body to the night table for water.

Hella ran her hand over his burning face. "Darling, I hope that didn't make you worse."

"No, I feel better," Mosca said.

"Do you want me to sleep on the couch now?"

"No, stay here."

He reached over for a cigarette but after a few puffs crushed it against the wall and watched the red shower of sparks fall on the blanket.

"Try to sleep," she said.

"I can't sleep. Anything special happen today?"

"No, I was just having supper with Frau Meyer. Yergen saw you come into the building and came up to tell me. He said you didn't look well, and he thought I might want to come right down. He's a very kind man."

"I saw something funny today," Mosca said and told her about the woman.

In the blackness of the room he could feel the silence. Hella was thinking, If I had been in the jeep surely I would have taken her and followed, set her mind at rest about what she had seen. Men were harder, she thought, there was less pity in them.

But she said nothing. Slowly, as in other dark nights, she ran her fingertips over his body, over the scar that cut down the whole trunk of his frame. She ran her fingers over the bumpy seam as a child runs a toy back and forth over a welt in the sidewalk, the slight rise and fall almost hypnotic.

Mosca sat up straight so that his shoulders rested against the wooden headrest of the bed. He folded his hands behind his neck as a cushion and said quietly, "I was lucky I got that where nobody sees it."

"I see it," Hella said.

"You know what I mean. It would be different if it were on my face."

She kept her fingers moving over the scar. "Not to me," she said.

The fever in his body made Mosca uncomfortable. The fingers moved soothingly over him, and he knew she would accept what he had done.

"Don't fall asleep," he said. "I always meant to tell you something but I never thought it important enough." Mockingly he gave his voice the singsong inflection of one about to tell a fairy tale to a child. "I'll tell you a little story," he said. He groped for a cigarette on the night table.

The ammunition dump stretched for miles and miles, the shells stacked in clusters like black cordwood. He, Mosca, sat in the cab of the bullet-shaped truck and watched the prisoners load the vehicles in front of him. The prisoners wore green twill fatigues and on their heads floppy hats of the same material. They would have blended easily into the forest around them if it had not been for the large, white letter "P" painted heavily on their backs and on each trouser leg.

From somewhere in the forest three blasts of a whistle sounded recall. Mosca jumped out of the cab of the truck and yelled, "Hey Fritz, c'mere."

The prisoner he had made straw boss over his three truckloads of workers came to him.

"We got time to finish this load before we start back?"

The German, a small man of forty, with a curiously wrinkled, old-young face, stood before Mosca without obsequiousness, shrugged his shoulders and said in broken English, "We be late for chow."

They grinned at each other. Any of the other prisoners would have assured Mosca that the load could be finished, merely to remain in favor.

"O.K., dump what you got," Mosca said. "We'll let the bastards squawk." He gave the German a cigarette and the German shoved it into the pocket of his green twill jacket. It was against regulations to smoke in the dump area though, of course, Mosca and the other G.I. guards did so.

"Get the rest of the Fritzes loaded and give me a count." The German left him and the prisoners began to pile into the trucks.

They moved slowly over the dirt road through the forest. Where other roads intersected more vehicles joined the procession, until, finally, the long line of open trucks, in single file, left the shade of the forest and entered the open countryside, the lemon-colored sunlight of very early spring. For guards and prisoners alike the war was very far away. They were safe, between them the issue had been settled. They moved in quiet and seeming content from the forest land of the ammunition dump to the barracks enclosed in barbed wire.

The G.I. guards, men who had been wounded too badly to be returned for line duty, had had enough of war. The prisoners regretted their fate only in the evening when they saw their guards pile into jeeps for a trip to the nearby town. The prisoners' faces behind their barbed wire had the wistful envy of children watching parents prepare to leave their homes for an evening out.

Then, in the very early morning light, they would ride out together to the forest. During the morning breaks, the prisoners would scatter around on the grass munching pieces of bread they had saved from breakfast. Mosca gave his crew more time than was usual. Fritz sat with him on a pile of shells.

"Not too bad a life, eh, Fritz?" Mosca asked.

"It could be worse," the German said, "it's peaceful here." Mosca nodded. He liked the German though he never took the trouble to remember his real name. They were friendly, but it was impossible to forget the relationship of the conqueror and conquered. Even now Mosca held his carbine in his hand as a symbol. There was never a bullet in the chamber and sometimes he forgot to put a magazine in its slot.

The German was in one of his depressed moods. Suddenly he began to pour out a flooding speech in his native tongue which Mosca understood imperfectly.

"Isn't it queer that you stand here, seeing that we do not move as we wish? What a duty for human beings. And how we kill each other and hurt each other. And for what? Tell me, if Germany had kept Africa and France, would I personally have earned another penny thereby? Me, myself, do I help myself if Germany conquers the world? Even if we win, I win only a uniform for the rest of my life. When we were children how it used to thrill us to read of our country's golden age, how France or Germany or Spain ruled Europe and the world. They build statues to men who give death to millions of their fellows. How is this? We hate each other, we kill each other. I could understand if we gained something. If afterward they said: Here, here is an extra piece of land we took from the French, everyone gets a little piece of cake. And you, we already know you are the winners. And do you think you will win anything?"

In the warm sun the other prisoners rolled on their backs, slept in the cool grass. Mosca listened only half understanding, vaguely displeased, not reached. The German spoke as one of the vanquished, without authority. He had walked the streets of Paris and Prague, the cities of Scandinavia, with cheerful pride; a sense of justice came only behind barbed wire.

For the first time the German put his hand on Mosca's arm. "My friend," he said, "people like you and me meet face to face and kill each other. Our enemies are behind us." He let his hand fall. "Our enemies are behind us," he repeated bitterly, "and commit the crimes for which we die."

But most of the time the German was cheerful. He had shown Mosca a picture of his wife and two children, and a picture of himself taken with comrades outside the factory in which they had worked. And he would talk about women.

"Aha," the German would say with an almost wistful zest. "When I was in Italy," or "When I was in France, the women they were wonderful. I must admit it, I like them better than German women, let the *Führer* say what he likes. Women never let politics interfere with more important things. It's been that way through the centuries."

His blue eyes twinkled in the lined, old-young face. "I'm always sorry we did not get to America. Those beautiful girls with the long legs, like marzipan the color. Really unbelievable. I remember them from your movies and magazines. Yes it is too bad."

And Mosca playing the game would say, "They wouldn't even look at you krautheads."

The German would shake his head slowly but with decision. "Women are hardheaded," he would say. "Do you think they starve because they should not use their bodies with the enemy. In these things women think clearly. They have more fundamental values. Ah, yes, occupation duty in New York would have been wonderful."

Mosca and the German would grin at each other and then Mosca would say, "Get the rest of the Fritzes to work."

On the final evening, when the recall whistle blew, the prisoners milled together quickly from all over the clearing in which they were working, and the trucks were loaded in a few minutes. The drivers started their motors.

Mosca almost fell for the ruse. Mechanically his eyes looked for Fritz. Still unsuspecting, he took a few steps toward the nearest of the three vehicles and then seeing the strained look on some of the prisoners' faces sensed immediately what had happened.

He ran to the beginning of the dirt road and signaled the drivers out of the cabs of their trucks. As he ran he worked the bolt of the carbine, throwing a cartridge into the chamber. Then taking from his pocket the whistle he had never used, he blew six short blasts. He waited a moment and blew six more.

While he waited he made all the prisoners dismount

from the trucks and sit in a close-packed circle on the grass. He stood a distance away, watching them, though he knew none would try to escape.

The security jeep came directly through the woods, and he could hear it crashing through the underbrush before it entered the clearing. The Sergeant in it had long, handle-bar mustaches in the English style and was very big and heavy. When he saw the orderly scene he left the jeep slowly and walked over to Mosca. The other two G.I.'s sauntered to opposite sides of the clearing. The driver took his submachine gun from its jeep scabbard and sat behind the wheel, one foot dangling out of the vehicle and touching the ground.

The Sergeant stood before Mosca, waiting. Mosca said, "There's one guy missing that I know about. My straw boss. I didn't make a count."

The Sergeant was in natty O.D.'s and wore a pistol and webbed cartridge belt around his broad middle. He moved among the prisoners and ordered them to form in ranks of ten. There were five ranks and two men for an incomplete sixth. The two men who formed their own rank had an air of guilt, as if they were to blame for the missing men.

"What does that make it?" the Sergeant asked Mosca.

"Four missing, altogether," Mosca said.

The Sergeant looked down on him. "A nice trick your ass-hole buddy pulled." And for the first time since he had learned of the escape Mosca felt a sense of shame and some fear. But he could not feel angry.

The Sergeant sighed. "Well it was a good racket while it lasted. There'll be a hell of a shakeup, the chicken shit will really fly." He said to Mosca in a gentler voice, "Your ass'll be back up in the line, you know that?" They both stood there thinking of the easy life they had led, no reveille, no formation, no inspections, no fear—almost civilian.

The Sergeant straightened angrily. "Let's see what we can do with these bastards. *Achtung,*" he shouted, and walked up and down in front of the Germans standing rigidly at attention. He said nothing for a few minutes and then began to speak to them quietly in English.

"All right. We know where we stand. The honeymoon is over. You men were all treated well. You were given good food, a good place to sleep. Did we ever work you too hard? You didn't feel well we let you stay in barracks. Who has a complaint? Step forward any man." The Sergeant paused as if one of them might really do so, then went on. "O.K., let's see if you appreciate it. Some of you know when these men left and where they went. Speak up. We'll remember it. We'll appreciate it." The Sergeant stopped walking up and down and faced them. He waited as they murmured among themselves, some explaining to the others what the Sergeant had said. But after they were still, none of the green-twilled prisoners stepped forward.

The Sergeant said in a different tone, "All right, you bastards." He turned to the jeep and said to the driver, "Go back to the barracks and draw twenty picks and twenty shovels. Get four men and another jeep. If no officer hears about this we might get through. And if that jerky Supply Sergeant squawks about the shovels tell him I'll come in and break his goddamn head." He motioned the driver on his way.

Then he signaled the prisoners to sit on the grass.

When the jeeps returned with the extra men and a trailer loaded with tools the Sergeant lined up the prisoners in two ranks facing each other. He issued the tools and since there were not enough to go around he made the extra men go to the other side of the clearing and lie in the grass on their faces.

No one spoke. The prisoners worked steadily digging the long trench. The rank with picks would hack at the earth, then rest. The men with shovels lifted the loose dirt away. They worked very slowly. The guards around the clearing leaned against the trees, seemingly indifferent and unalert.

The Sergeant winked at Mosca and said in a low voice, "A good bluff always works. Watch this."

He let them dig for a short time more, then he called a halt. "Does anyone here wish to speak?" He gave them a grim smile.

No one answered.

"O.K." The Sergeant waved an arm. "Keep digging."

One of the Germans let his shovel fall. He was young and rosy cheeked. "Please," he said. "I wish to tell you something." He walked away from his fellow prisoners into the open space that separated him from the guards.

"Spit it out," the Sergeant said.

The German stood there wordless. He looked back uneasily at his fellow prisoners. The Sergeant understood. He took the German by the arm and led him over to the jeep. They stood there talking earnestly in low voices, watched by prisoners and guards alike. The Sergeant listened with his head thrust forward intently, his great body bent over, one arm thrown familiarly over the prisoner's shoulder. Then he nodded. He motioned the informer into the jeep.

The prisoners were loaded onto the three trucks and the caravan moved through the now-deserted forest, the other roads crossing theirs empty of life. In the jeep bringing up the rear the Sergeant drove, his long mustaches waving in the breeze. They left the forest, and as they entered the open countryside it was strange to see the familiar land bathed in a different light, the riper and reddish sun of late afternoon.

Turning his head for a moment the Sergeant spoke to Mosca. "Your buddy planned this for a long time. But he's out of luck."

"Where is he?" Mosca asked.

"In town. I know the house."

The caravan entered the camp, and then the two jeeps swung in a wide arc away from the trucks and raced toward the town. Then close together, as if coupled, they went down the main street, and on the corner on which stood the church, turned right. They halted by a small stone house. Mosca and the Sergeant went to the front door. Two of the men in the other jeep moved slowly to the rear of the house. The other men stayed in the jeeps.

The door was opened before they could knock. Fritz stood there before them. He wore old, crumpled blue serge trousers, a white collarless shirt and a dark jacket. He gave them an uncertain smile. "The rest are upstairs," he said. "They are afraid to come down."

"Call them," the Sergeant said. "Go up and tell them they won't be hurt."

Fritz went to the foot of the stairs and called up in German. "All is in order. Come down. Don't be afraid."

They heard a door open above them, and the three other prisoners came slowly down the stairs. They were dressed in ragged civilian clothes. On their faces was a sheepish, almost guilty look.

"Go out to the jeeps," the Sergeant said. Then he asked Fritz, "Whose house is this?"

The German raised his eyes. For the first time he looked at Mosca. "A woman I used to know. Let her go, she did it for—you know—she was lonely. It has nothing to do with the war."

"Get out there," the Sergeant said.

They all left. The Sergeant whistled for the two men behind the house. As the jeeps pulled away, a woman came down the street carrying a large bundle in brown wrapping paper. She saw the prisoners in the jeep, turned, and walked back in the direction from which she had come. The Sergeant gave Mosca a sour grin. "Goddamn women," he said.

On a lonely stretch of road nearly halfway back to camp the Sergeant's lead jeep pulled to the side and stopped. The other jeep halted close behind. On one side of the road was a rough stony pasture leading into the dark line of the forest two hundred yards away.

"Get those men out of the jeeps," the Sergeant said. They all dismounted and stood awkwardly, ill at ease in the deserted road. The Sergeant stood for some moments, deep in thought. He felt his mustaches and said, "A couple of you guys can bring these krauts back to camp. Empty the tools out of that trailer and bring it back." He pointed to Fritz. "You stay here."

"I'll go back," Mosca said quickly.

The Sergeant looked him up and down, slowly, with insolent contempt. "Listen, you son of a bitch, you're staying here. If it wasn't for me your ass'd be up in the line. By Christ, I'm not going to chase krauts all over the country whenever they get a bug up their ass. You stay here."

Two of the guards moved off silently with the three prisoners. They got into the jeep and disappeared down the road. Fritz turned his head to watch them go.

The four men in their olive drab stood facing the lone German and the stony pasture beyond him. The Sergeant stroked his mustache. The German's face was gray, but he stood stiffly, as if at attention.

"Start running," the Sergeant said. He pointed across the pasture to the forest.

The German did not move. The Sergeant gave him a shove. "Run," he said, "we'll give you a good start." He pushed the German onto the pasture grass, spinning him so that he faced the forest. The sun was gone, and there was no color on the earth, only the grayness of falling twilight. The forest was a long dark wall, far away.

The German turned, facing them again. His hand went to his collarless shirt as if searching for some dignity. He looked at Mosca, then at the others. He took a step toward them, off the grass and stone. His legs trembled, and his body wavered for a moment, but his voice was steady. He said, "Herr Mosca, *Ich hab' eine Frau und Kinder.*"

On the Sergeant's face came a look of rage and hatred. "Run, you bastard, run." He rushed to the German and struck him in the face. As the German began to fall he lifted him and shoved him toward the pasture. "Run, you kraut bastard." He shouted it three or four times.

The German fell and rose and turned to face them again, and again he said, not pleading this time but as if in explanation, *"Ich hab' eine Frau und Kinder."* One of the guards stepped forward quickly and struck him in the groin with the butt of his carbine and then, letting the weapon dangle in one hand, smashed the German's face with the other.

The lines in the wrinkled face sprang leaks of blood. And then, before he began to walk across the stony pasture toward the dark wall of the forest he gave them one last look. It was a look of lost hope and more than fear of death. It was a look of horror, as if he had seen some terrible and shameful thing in which he had never believed.

They watched him walk slowly across the pasture. They waited for him to run, but he walked very slowly. Every few steps he turned his body around to watch them, as if it were some game, breeding a childish distrust. They could see the white of his collarless shirt.

Mosca saw that every time the German turned to watch them and then turned back again his course veered a little to the right. He saw the slight, rocky rise of ground that led to the forest. The trick was obvious. The men knelt on the dirt road and raised the carbines to their shoulders. Mosca let his hang barrel downward to the dirt road.

As the German made his sudden dash for the gully the Sergeant fired and the body had begun its fall as the other shots rang out. The fall carried his body over the slight ridge, but the legs remained in view.

In the silence that followed the sharp, scattered reports of the carbines, under the gray wisps of smoke that spiraled above their heads, the living men froze in the positions from which they had fired. The acrid smell of powder floated away on the evening air.

"Go in," Mosca said. "I'll wait for the trailer. You guys go in." No one had noticed his not firing. He turned from them and walked a few steps down the road.

He could hear the roar of the jeep as it moved away, and he leaned against a tree, staring across the stony pasture, and over the danglings legs to the black, impenetrable wall of the forest. In the coming night, it seemed very near. He lit a cigarette. He felt no emotion, only a slight physical nausea and internal looseness. He waited, hoping the trailer would arrive before it became really dark.

In the now complete blackness of the room Mosca reached over Hella's body for the glass of water on the night table. He drank and leaned back.

He wanted to be completely honest. "It doesn't bother me," he said. "It's just when I see something like today, that woman chasing the truck. I remember what he said, he said it twice. 'I have a wife and children.' It didn't mean anything then. I can't explain it, but it's like the way we spent all our money whenever we could, because saving it didn't mean anything." He waited for Hella to speak.

He went on. "I tried to figure it out after, you know. I was afraid of going back into combat, and I guess I was afraid of that Sergeant. And he was a German, and Germans had done a hell of a lot worse. But the main thing was, I didn't feel any pity, when he was hurt, when he begged, when he was killed. Afterward, I was ashamed and surprised, but I never felt pity and I know that's bad."

Mosca reached down toward Hella's face and tracing along the cheek felt the wetness in the hollows beneath her eyes. For a moment he felt the nausea, and then the fever in his body burned it out. He wanted to tell her how it was, how it was like nothing else ever known, how it was like a dream, like magic, the fear all around. In the strange, deserted towns the dead people lay, the fighting went on over their rubbled graves, black flowers of smoke grew through skull-like homes, and then later the white tape lay everywhere, around the charred enemy tank, to show that it had not been demined, outside the doors of houses as in a child's game, a chalkmark over which you cannot step, and then more and more like a witch's spell, the white tape around the church, around the dead bodies in the square, around the casks of wine in the farmer's barn, and then in the open fields the sign with its skull and crossbones marking the dead animals, the cows, the heavy plow horses, all blown upside down by the land mines, their bellies torn open for the sun. And how one morning, the new strange town was so quiet, so still, and how for some reason he had been afraid, though the fighting was still some miles away. And then suddenly, far off, the church bells tolled, and they could see the square filled with people, and he knew it was Sunday. On that same day, the fear gone, in some place where the skull and crossbones were not seen, where some child had forgotten to make his white mark in chalk, where by some human error the magic white tape was not where it should be, he had suffered the first violation of his flesh and bone and come to know the meaning, the terror of annihilation.

He said nothing. He could feel Hella turning over on her stomach and bury her face in the pillow. He shoved her roughly and said, "Go sleep on the couch." He moved over against the wall, feeling its coolness against his body draw the heat of fever. He pressed against it.

In his dream the trucks moved through many lands. The countless women sprang from the earth, stood on tiptoe in the streets, searched with hungry faces. The emaciated men danced like scarecrows in their joy, and then, as the women before them began to weep, bowed their heads and bodies to be kissed. The white tape circled them, the trucks, the men, the women and the world. The sick terror born of guilt was everywhere. The white flowers withered and died.

Mosca woke. The room was shot through with shadows, the last ghosts of night, and he could make out a vague outline of the wardrobe. The air was cold, but the fever and chill had left his body. He felt a gentle tiredness that was pleasant. He was very hungry, and he thought for a moment how good breakfast would taste later in the morning. He reached out and felt Hella's sleeping body. Knowing that she had never left him, he put his cheek against her warm back and fell asleep.

9

GORDON MIDDLETON watched the children march down the street past his house in a neat column of two's. They swung their paper lanterns in time to the slow chant that came faintly to Gordon's ears through the closed window. Then the two files marched inward on its front and became a group, the lit yellow-red lanterns like a cluster of fireflies in the cold and pale October dusk. Gordon felt a pang of homesickness for the dying New Hampshire village he had left so long ago, the cold, bare beauty of its countryside, the night air lit only with fireflies, and where it seemed, there as here, that everything was dying as winter came.

Without turning his head, Gordon asked the Professor, "What are they singing, the children with the lanterns?"

The Professor sat by the chess table, surveying with satisfaction the ruin he had brought to his opponent. In the leather brief case beside him were the two sandwiches he would take home with him and the two packs of cigarettes that were his weekly tuition fee for giving lessons in German to Gordon Middleton. The cigarettes he would save for his son, when he could visit him in Nuremberg. He must again ask permission to visit. After all, if the great men could have visitors, why not his son?

"They are singing a song for the October *Fest,*" the Professor said absently. "To show that the nights are getting longer."

"And the lanterns?" Gordon Middleton asked.

"Really, I don't know, an ancient custom. To light the way." The Professor suppressed his irritation. He wanted to summon the American back to the game, complete the slaughter. But though the American never presumed on his position as conqueror, the Professor never forgot his place as one of the conquered or, far back in his mind, his own secret shame about his son.

Gordon Middleton opened the window, and floating up the street from the lanterns, filling the room with a crystal-clear tone, like the October air, came the children's sing-song voices. He listened intently, testing his newly acquired German, and the simplicity of the words and the clarity with which they sang made understanding easy. They sang:

Brenne auf mein Licht
Brenne auf mein Licht
Aber nur meine liebe Laterne nicht

"You'd think their parents would have more important things to worry about instead of making lanterns." Gordon waited, listening to the song again.

Da oben leuchten die Sterne
Hier unten leuchten wir

and then on a long note without sadness but sounding so in the falling light.

Mein Licht ist aus, wir geh' nach Haus
Und kommen Morgen wieder

Gordon Middleton saw Mosca crossing the Kurfürsten Allee, walking through the cluster of lanterns and still-singing children, scattering the light.

"My friend is coming," Gordon said to the Professor. Gordon walked over to the chess table and with his fore-finger toppled over his king.

The Professor smiled at him and said out of politeness,

"It was yet possible to win." The Professor was afraid of all young men—the hard, sullen German youths with their years of warfare and defeat—but even more of all these young, drunken Americans who would beat or kill without provocation, purely out of drunken malice and the knowledge that they were safe from retaliation. But any friend of Middleton would surely not be dangerous. Herr Middleton had assured him of this, and Herr Middleton was himself reassuring. He was almost a caricature of the Puritan Yankee with his tall, awkward, loosely knit frame, prominent Adam's apple, long bony nose and square mouth. And in his little New England town a schoolteacher. The Professor smiled thinking how in the past these little grade-school teachers had fawned on the Herr Professor, and now in this relationship his learning and title meant nothing. He was the courter.

The bell rang and Gordon went to the door. The Professor stood up and nervously straightened his coat, the frayed tie. He pulled his short body with its swollen potato stomach to an erect position and faced the door.

The Professor saw a tall, dark boy, not more than twenty-four, certainly not older than his own son. But this boy had serious brown eyes and a grave, almost sullen face that just missed being ugly. He was dressed very neatly in officer green and had the white-and-blue patch denoting his civilian status sewed on his lapels and left sleeve. He moved with an athletic carelessness that would have been contemptuous if it had not been so impersonal.

When Gordon made the introduction, the Professor said, "I am very happy to meet you," and thrust out his hand. He tried to keep his dignity but realized that he had said the words obsequiously and betrayed his nervousness with his smile. He saw the boy's eyes go hard and noticed the quick withdrawal after their hands touched. The knowledge that he had offended this youth made the Professor tremble, and he sat down to arrange the chess pieces on the board.

"Do you care to play?" he asked Mosca and tried to suppress the apologetic smile.

Gordon waved Mosca toward the table and said, "See what you can do, Walter, he's too good for me."

Mosca sat in the chair opposite the Professor. "Don't expect too much, Gordon taught me this game just a month ago."

The Professor nodded his head and murmured, "Please take the white pieces." Mosca made the opening move.

The Professor became absorbed in the game and lost his nervousness. They all used the simple opening, these Americans, but where the little schoolteacher had played a cautious game, sound but uninspired, this one played with all the impetuosity of youth. Not without talent, the Professor thought, as with a few expert moves he broke the force of the headlong attack. Then swiftly and ruthlessly he swooped on the unprotected rooks and bishop and slaughtered the pawns standing forward without support.

"You're too good for me, Professor," the boy said, and the Professor noted with relief that there was no rancor in the voice.

Then without any transition Mosca said abruptly in German, "I'd like you to give English lessons to my fiancée twice a week. What does it cost?"

The Professor flushed. It was humiliating, this common bargaining, as if he were a shopkeeper. "Whatever you wish," he said stiffly, "but you speak quite a good German, why not teach her yourself?"

"I have," Mosca said, "but she wants to learn the structure, grammar and all that. A pack of cigarettes for every two lessons O.K.?"

The Professor nodded.

Mosca borrowed a pencil from Gordon and wrote on a slip of paper. He gave it to the Professor and said, "Here's a note in case anyone in the billet questions you. The address is there too."

"Thank you," the Professor almost bowed. "Will tomorrow evening be suitable?"

"Sure," Mosca said.

Outside the house a jeep horn began a steady honking. "That must be Leo," Mosca said. "We're going over to the officers' club. Feel like coming, Gordon?"

"No," Gordon said. "Is that the boy that was in Buchenwald?" And when Mosca nodded, "Have him come in for just a second, I'd like to meet him."

Mosca went to the window and pushed it open and the horn stopped. "Come on in," Mosca shouted. It was very dark now, the children and their lanterns out of sight.

When Leo came in he shook hands with Gordon and said to the Professor stiffly, *"Angenehm."* The Professor bowed, picked up his brief case and said to Gordon, "I must go." Gordon took him to the outer door, and they shook hands in farewell. Then Gordon went to the kitchen in the rear of the house.

His wife was sitting at the table with Yergen, haggling over the price of some black-market goods. Yergen was polite, dignified and firm; they both knew she was getting a good bargain. Yergen believed in quality. On a chair beside the table was a foot-high stack of rich-looking, rusty-colored woolen material.

"Isn't this lovely stuff, Gordon?" Ann Middleton asked in a pleased voice. She was a plump woman, her features good-natured and kind despite the determined chin and shrewd eyes.

Gordon in his slow, deliberate way made a sound of assent and then said, "If you're through here I'd like you to come and meet some friends." Yergen hurriedly gulped the cup of coffee before him and began to fill his leather brief case with the round tins of fats and meats that rested on the table. "I must go," he said.

"You won't forget the material for my husband's coat next week?" Ann Middleton asked warningly.

Yergen made a gesture of protest. "Dear lady, no. Next week at the latest."

When she had locked the back entrance after Yergen, Ann Middleton unlocked a cupboard and took out a bottle of whiskey and some bottles of Coca-Cola. "It is a pleasure to do business with Yergen, he never wastes your time with anything shoddy," she said. They went into the living room together.

After the introductions Gordon rested in one of the armchairs, not listening to the usual small talk his wife made. He felt almost painfully the alien atmosphere of the requisitioned home, living with belongings which had no memories, no associations, not knowing who had picked out the pictures on the wall, the furniture scattered through the rooms, who had played the piano which rested against the far wall. But these feelings were traitorous to his intellect and not new. He had felt it most keenly on his visit home to his parents before he entered the Army. In that home, surrounded by furniture from ancestors long dead, as he kissed the dry cheeks of his mother and father, cheeks dried out and tough by the vigorous northern climate, he had known that he would never go back, as others would not, the young people who had gone to war and to the factories; and that this land, glacial in its stark and wintry beauty, would be inhabited only by old people, their hair white as the snow which covered the bony hills. And in his bedroom the large picture of Marx that his mother had thought was just a painting. How proud he had been of his cleverness and a little contemptuous of her ignorance. It was probably still hanging there.

His wife had prepared drinks, weak ones, since whiskey was rationed and since she sometimes used it to trade on the black market. Gordon asked Leo, "Wasn't it in your camp that some prisoners were killed by an Allied air raid?"

"Yes," Leo answered, "I remember. We did not resent it, believe me."

"I read that Thälman, the Communist leader, was killed in that raid. Did you know him?" For once Gordon's voice had lost its calmness. There was a vibrant note in it.

"That was a curious thing," Leo said. "Thälman was brought to the camp two days after the raid in which he was supposed to have been killed. Then he was taken away in a short time. We heard about the announcement of his death; of course it was a joke among us."

Gordon took a deep breath. "Did you meet him?"

"No," Leo said. "I remember because many of the *kapos,* the trusties, were Communists. They were the first ones sent to the camps and naturally they had the good jobs. Anyway, I heard that they had managed to secure some delicacies and even liquor and planned to welcome Thälman with a secret banquet. But it never came off. He was always under special guard."

Gordon was nodding his head with a solemn, sad pride. He said to his wife with quiet anger, "You see who were the real enemies of fascism?"

Leo said with irritation, "The Communists were not

bargains. One, a *kapo,* had great pleasure beating old men to death. He did many other things I cannot say before your wife."

Gordon became so angry that it showed on his usually well-controlled face, and his wife said to Mosca, "Why don't you come over for dinner some night with your girl. And Leo too." They settled details, giving Gordon time to recover. Suddenly Gordon said to Leo, "I don't believe the man was a Communist. He may have been at one time. But he was either a renegade or an impostor." At this Ann and Leo burst out laughing but Mosca turned his sharp, dark face toward Gordon and said, "The guy was in camp for a long time. Don't you know what that means, for Christ's sake?" And Leo said almost comfortingly, "Yes, he was one of the oldest inmates."

In a room above them a baby began to cry, and Gordon went upstairs and brought down a great big healthy boy who looked much larger than his six months. Gordon changed the diaper, proudly showing off his skill.

"He's better than I am," Ann Middleton said, "and he enjoys doing it which I'm sure I don't."

"Why don't you fellows spend the evening here instead of going on to the club?" Gordon asked.

"Yes," Ann said, "please do."

"We can stay a little while," Mosca said, "but we have to meet Eddie Cassin at the club about ten o'clock. He went to the opera."

Ann Middleton sniffed, "I'll bet he's at the opera."

"And besides," Mosca said, "it's stag night at the club and the show should be terrific. Leo here never saw a stag show. He can't miss it."

When Gordon went to the door with them he said to Mosca, "We never use up all our allowance on our commissary card. Any time you need some groceries and want to use it, just let me know."

Gordon locked the door and went back to the living room. Ann said to him, "Really that was quite shameful, you were downright rude to Leo." Gordon, knowing that this from her was a stern rebuke, said without defiance but resolutely, "I still think the man was an impostor."

This time his wife did not smile.

The soft, rose-colored lights went out. Eddie Cassin leaned forward in his seat, applauded with the rest as the old, white-haired conductor entered the pit and tapped the music stand sharply with his baton. The curtain went up.

As the music started slowly, yet with passion, Eddie Cassin forgot the school auditorium he was in, the Germans all around him, the two monstrous Russian officers almost blocking his view. The familiar figures on the stage were now all his life, and he gripped his jaw and mouth with his hands to control the emotional workings of his face.

On the stage the man and woman who at the beginning had sung of their love for each other, now sang of their hate. The man in his peasant costume cried with anger in hard beautiful tones, rising and ascending, the orchestra playing beneath the voice, rising and falling with it, as a wave might, yet falling completely away when need be. The woman's voice, shrill, cut through his, mingled, the orchestra circling what they said. The man threw the woman away from him with so much force that as she spun away she fell to the floor, really slamming against the wood of the stage. She was up on her feet instantly, screaming reproaches, yet musically, and as the man threatened her and she denied his accusations, suddenly the man's voice, the voices of the chorus, the orchestra, all fell away and the woman's voice found itself alone, admitted her guilt, hurled back defiance, and falling to a lower and sweeter tone sang of death and sorrow and a bodily love that led all men and women. Before Eddie Cassin's eyes the man took the woman by the hair and thrust into her body with a dagger. On a loud clear note she called for help, and her lover died with her; the horns and violins rose to a high, crescending wave, and the man's voice made its final utterance, a long clean note of revenge, passion and inconsolable grief. The curtain came down.

The Russian officers in their green-and-gold uniforms clapped enthusiastically, seeming to lead the applause. Eddie Cassin pushed his way out of the auditorium and into the fresh night air. He leaned against his jeep, feeling exhausted and yet content. He waited until everyone had left, waited until the woman who had died on the stage came out. He saw that she was plain, with heavy German features, dressed all in black, loosely; lumpy as a fifty-year-old housewife. He waited until she was out of sight and then got into the jeep and drove across the bridge into the Altstadt, Bremen proper, and as always the ruins rising up to meet him awakened a feeling of kinship. Mingled with this was the remembrance of the opera and how closely this physical world resembled—with the same element of the ridiculous—that interior make-believe world he had seen on the stage. Now that he was free of the music's spell, he was ashamed of the easy tears he had shed, tears for a tragedy so simple, so direct, a child's story of guiltless and unfortunate animals come to disaster, and his own tears a child's tears he would never understand.

The officers' club had been one of the finest private homes in Bremen. What had been its lawn was now a

parking lot for jeeps and command cars. The garden in the rear supplied flowers for the homes of the higher ranking officers.

When Eddie entered the club the dance floor was empty, but ringed around it, seated on the floor and leaning against the wall, the officers were three rows deep. Others watched from the barroom, standing on chairs so that they could look over the crowd before them.

Someone brushed past Eddie and went on to the dance floor. It was a girl, stark nakedness exposed on tiny, silvery platforms of ballet slippers. Her pubic hair had been shaved to an inverted triangle, dark red on her body like a shield. In some way she had fluffed out the hair so that it was a formidably thick and matty bush. She danced without skill, coming close to the officers seated on the floor, almost thrusting the triangle of hair into their faces so that some of the young officers started involuntarily and turned their crew-cut heads away. She laughed when they did this and laughed and danced away when some of the older officers made a half-joking grab. It was an exhibition curiously unsexual, with no element of lust. Someone threw a comb out on the floor, the girl continued to dance like a draft horse trying to gallop. The officers began to shout jokes she did not understand, and humiliation made her face and dance more strained, ludicrous, until everyone was laughing, throwing combs, handkerchiefs, butter knives, olives from their drinks, pretzels. One officer shouted "Hide this," and it became a refrain. The club officer came out on the floor holding an enormous pair of scissors, clicking the shears suggestively. The girl ran off the dance floor, past Eddie back to the dressing room. Eddie went to the bar. At one corner he saw Mosca and Wolf and went over to them.

"Don't tell me Leo missed the show," Eddie said. "Walter, you guaranteed he wouldn't."

"Hell," Mosca said, "he already latched onto one of the dancers. He's in."

Eddie grinned and turned to Wolf. "Find the gold mine?" He knew Wolf and Mosca went out nights and traded in the black market.

"Business is tough," Wolf said, his dead-white face shaking dolefully from side to side.

"Don't kid me," Eddie Cassin said. "I hear your *Fräulein* wears diamonds on her pajamas."

Wolf was indignant. "Now where the hell would she get pajamas?"

They all laughed.

The waiter came and Eddie ordered a double whiskey. Wolf nodded toward the dance floor and said, "We expected you in the front row tonight."

"Nah," Eddie Cassin said. "I'm cultured, I went to the opera. Anyway the broads there are better looking."

From the other room officers flooded into the bar, the show was over. The room became crowded. Mosca stood up and said, "Let's go up to the dice table and play a little."

The dice table was almost completely surrounded. It was a crudely constructed affair with four unpainted wooden joists for legs and a green cloth stretched over the wooden top. Boards half a foot high formed a rectangle to confine the dice.

The Colonel himself, a small, plump man with a blond mustache, extremely neat, was rolling the dice awkwardly, the square cubes slipping clumsily from his clenched hand. All the other players were officers, mostly flyers. On the Colonel's right stood the Adjutant, watchful, not taking any part in the game while the Colonel played.

The Adjutant, a young Captain, was an ingenuous-looking man with a bland face and a smile that was attractive when not meant to menace. He gloried in his position as Adjutant, the petty power that enabled him to select the officers who would perform the more irksome duties on the base, especially on week ends. The Colonel relied on him, and the Adjutant did not forget an affront easily. But he was fair, and only vindictive when the affront was one to his position, not to himself personally. The rigidity of Army life and Army procedure was his religion, and any breach of it sacrilegious and blasphemous. Anyone who tried to get something done without going through channels—those straight and narrow paths clearly defined in Army regulations—would suddenly find himself a very busy man, and no matter how hard he worked, busy for a few months at least. He brought to his religion the fanaticism of the young; he was no older than Mosca.

A white-jacketed waiter stood behind a small bar in the corner of the room. When the players called out for a drink he set it up, and whoever had called would step over for the glass and take his drink back to the game, resting it on the wooden ledge made by enclosing boards.

Wolf, who did not gamble, sat in one of the easy chairs, and Eddie Cassin and Mosca squeezed into places around the table. When Eddie's turn to shoot came, Mosca bet with him. Eddie, a cautious gambler, slipped the one-dollar bills from his metal clip almost regretfully. He had a good roll and made five passes before he sevened out. Mosca had made even more money than Eddie.

Since they were standing beside each other, it was Mosca's turn to shoot, the dice going around the circle clockwise. Already ahead and feeling confident, he put twenty dollars worth of scrip on the green felt. Four different officers took five dollars each. Mosca threw the great square cubes backhanded. They came up seven. "Shoot it," he said. He was sure now, and exhilarated. The forty dollars was faded by the same four officers. Eddie Cassin said, "And ten goes with him."

The Colonel said, "I'll take that." They laid the money on the table.

Mosca threw the dice as hard as he could against the side of the table. The cubes bounced off the wooden board, tumbled over the green felt and spun like two red tops; then the edges caught in the felt and they stopped dead. It was another seven. "Shoot the eighty bucks," Mosca said.

"And the twenty goes with him." Eddie Cassin left the money on the table. The Colonel covered it.

This time Mosca released the dice gently, as if turning loose a pet animal, so that they bounced off the wall and rolled a few inches coming up square red and enormous in the middle of the green felt. It was another seven and one of the officers said, "Rattle those dice." He said it without malice, a superstitious prayer against Mosca's luck. Mosca grinned at the officer and said, "The hundred and sixty goes."

The Adjutant still stood with a drink in his hand, watching Mosca and the dice. Eddie Cassin said cautiously, "Ten goes with him." And picked up the other thirty dollars he had won.

The Colonel said, "I'll bet you twenty." Eddie reluctantly laid down another ten-dollar bill, and catching Mosca's look, shrugged his shoulders.

Mosca picked up the dice, blew on them, and slammed them backhanded against the opposite wooden board. The red dice with their white dots came up a four.

One of the officers said, "I'll lay ten to five he doesn't."

Mosca took the bet and several others. He let the dice lay on the table and, unconsciously arrogant, sure of his luck, held his sheaf of bills ready to cover any bets. He was happy, he enjoyed the excitement of the game, and it was rare that he gambled with luck. "I'll take a hundred to fifty," he said, and when no one answered he picked up the dice.

Just before he threw, the Colonel said, "I'll bet twenty you don't make it." Mosca threw down a ten-dollar bill and said, "I'll take that."

"You only put down ten dollars," the Colonel said.

Mosca stopped rattling the dice and leaned against the table. He couldn't believe that the Colonel, an old Army man, didn't know the proper odds in dice. "You have to lay two to one against a four point, Colonel," he said and tried to keep the anger out of his voice.

The Colonel turned to one of the officers beside him and asked, "Is that right, Lieutenant?"

"That's right, sir," the officer said, embarrassed.

The Colonel threw down twenty dollars. "All right, shoot."

The red cubes slammed against all four sides of the table, raced swiftly across the green felt and stopped with a surprising suddenness, each red square framing two little white dots. Mosca looked at them for a moment before picking up the money and spoke his mind aloud, "I never saw a prettier sight."

There was no sense pushing his luck too far, he thought. He threw a couple of bills on the table and after a few rolls he sevened out. He continued to play with mediocre luck. When the Colonel picked up the dice to shoot, Mosca faded him. The Colonel threw a point and then sevened out on the second roll. Mosca picked up the money. The

Colonel said without rancor, "You're too lucky for me," and smiled, then walked out of the room and they could hear him going down the stairs. Mosca realized that he had been wrong, that the Colonel really hadn't known the correct odds, hadn't been trying to pull rank.

The atmosphere around the table became more relaxed, the conversation of the officers more natural. The waiter was busy with the many shouted orders for drinks. The Adjutant went over to the bar, sat on one of the stools until his glass was filled, tasted it, and then called, "Mosca, come here for a minute." Mosca looked over his shoulder. Eddie Cassin already had the dice and it was his turn next. "After my shot," he said.

Eddie had a good roll, but Mosca sevened out quickly and then went over to the patiently waiting Adjutant.

The Adjutant looked him in the eye with a calm, level glance and said, "Where do you come off telling the Colonel what the odds are?"

Mosca was surprised and a little confused. "Hell," he said, "the guy wanted a bet. Nobody'd bet him even money on a four."

The Adjutant, in a quiet voice, as if he were addressing a stupid child, said, "There were at least ten officers at the table. They didn't tell him the odds, and if they had they would have done so in a more courteous manner. Why do you think they didn't tell him?"

Mosca could feel himself flushing. For the first time he realized that there was no sound of dice, the men around the table were listening. He felt a familiar uneasiness that reminded him of his first months in the army. He shrugged. "I figured he didn't know so I told him."

The Adjutant stood up. "You may think because you're a civilian you can get away with that sort of thing. You showed pretty plainly that the Colonel was trying to use his rank to cheat you out of ten dollars. Now just remember one thing; we can ship you back to the States pretty damn quick if we really want to, and I understand you have reasons for not wanting that to happen. So watch yourself. If the Colonel doesn't know something, his fellow officers can tell him. You insulted the Commanding Officer and every officer in this room. Don't let anything like that happen again."

Unconsciously Mosca hung his head, the shame and anger washing over him. He could see Eddie Cassin watching him, and Eddie had a little smile of pleasure on his face. Mosca through the fog of anger heard the Adjutant say in a contemptuous voice, "If I had my way I wouldn't let you civilians into an officers' club. You don't know what Army means."

Without thinking Mosca lifted his head. He saw the Adjutant's face very distinctly, the gray candid eyes, the bland earnest face, stern now.

"How many battle stars you got, Captain?" Mosca asked. "How many landings you make?" The Adjutant had sat down on his stool again, sipping his drink. Mosca almost raised his arm when the Adjutant spoke.

"I don't mean that. Some of those officers there are bigger war heroes than I imagine you ever were and they didn't do what you did or take your attitude." The Adjutant's voice was dead calm, cold with reasonableness that was not conciliatory.

Mosca relinquished his anger and adopted the other's cold calm, as if imitating him as they imitated each other in age and height and bearing. "O.K.," he said, "I was wrong telling the Colonel, I apologize. But don't *you* give me that civilian shit."

The Adjutant smiled, no personal insult reaching him, the priest suffering for his religion. "As long as you understand about the other thing," he said.

Mosca said, "O.K., I understand." And despite all he could do the words were a submission, and when he went back to the dice table he felt his face burning with shame. He saw Eddie Cassin suppressing another smile, winking at him to cheer him up. The officer rolling the dice, a big easy-going southerner, said in his soft drawling voice, loud enough for the Adjutant to hear, "It's a good thing you didn't win another ten bucks, we'd have to take yuh out and shoot yuh." The officers around the table laughed, but Mosca did not. Behind him he could hear the Adjutant talking easily and occasionally laughing, drinking with his friends as if nothing had happened.

10

MOSCA AND GORDON MIDDLETON stopped working to eavesdrop; through the slightly ajar door of Eddie's office they could hear a young girl's voice. "Eddie, I wanted to see you for just a minute, it is very important." Her voice was a little shaky.

Eddie's voice, cold and formally polite said, "Sure, go ahead."

The girl said hesitatingly, "I know you told me I was not to come to your office, but you never visit me any more."

Gordon and Mosca grinned at each other. Gordon shook his head. They listened.

The girl said, "I need a carton of cigarettes."

There was a silence. Then Eddie asked with cold sarcasm, "What brand?" But the girl did not catch the inflection, the implied rejection.

"Oh, you know that doesn't matter," she said. "I need them for the doctor. That is his price."

Eddie's voice was polite, impersonal, "Are you ill?"

The girl laughed coyly. "Oh, Eddie, you know very well. I am going to have a baby. For a carton of cigarettes my doctor will help me lose it." Then reassuringly, as if anxiety for her welfare might make him refuse, "There is no danger."

Mosca and Gordon nodded at each other, laughing noiselessly, not at the girl but at Eddie, at what they imagined to be his embarrassment and the fact that this liaison would cost him a carton of cigarettes. Eddie's next words wiped their smiles away.

The voice was still cold, polite, but there was a horrible note of joyous hatred in it. "Tell your German boy friend to help. You won't get any cigarettes from me. And if you come to this office again you will not be working on this Air Base. Now get back to your job."

The girl was crying. Finally she protested in a weak voice, "I have no boy friend. It is your child. It is three months, Eddie."

"That's all," Eddie Cassin said.

The girl had regained her courage and drawn some anger from his contempt. "You didn't come to me for a whole month. I didn't know if you would come again. That man just took me to some dances. I swear it. You know you were the one. What is a carton of cigarettes to you?"

Gordon and Mosca could hear Eddie pick up the phone and ask the operator for the base Provost Marshal. Then the girl's voice with a note of terror in it said, "Help me, Mr. Cassin, please help me." They then could hear the hall door open and slam shut and Eddie saying, "Never mind," to the operator.

Eddie Cassin pushed through the door to their room and his delicate pale-gray face wore a pleased smile. "Did you enjoy our little scene?" he asked.

Mosca leaned back in his chair and said contemptuously, "You're a real prick, Eddie."

Gordon Middleton said, "I'll give you the cigarettes for her, Eddie." He said it with none of the contempt Mosca had shown, simply as a statement of fact, as if the only reason Eddie had refused was because of the value he would lose.

Eddie looked them both over with a derisive smile. "Gee, what nice guys. Willing to help a poor kid like that. Listen. That little tramp had a guy on the side all the time. He smoked the cigarettes I gave her, ate the chocolate bars and food I meant for her." He laughed with real good humor. "Besides, I've been through this before. And I know that the black-market fee for abortions is only half a carton."

The door of the office opened and Wolf came in. He said, "Hi ya fellas." He put his brief case on the desk and sat down with a weary sigh. "What a bunch of cheerful bums." He grinned at them, his pasty-white face lit with genuine happiness. "Caught two krauts stealing coffee. You know that soup the mess officer lets them take home in their little pots? Well they put the ground coffee on the bottom, sand over that, then the soup over. Don't ask me how they get the sand out later."

For some reason this soured Eddie. He said gloomily, "Wolf Tracy always gets his man. Tell us how you do it, Wolf."

Wolf grinned. "Hell, who would ever figure it out? Same as usual. Stool pigeon."

Middleton rose. "Guess I'll go home early. O.K., Eddie?"

"Sure," Eddie said.

Wolf raised his hand. "Wait a minute, Gordon." Gordon stopped by the open door. "Don't say I told you, and you other guys keep it quiet. But you'll be getting your shipping orders back to the States in about a week. O.K.?"

Gordon lowered his head to stare at the floor. Wolf said kindly, "Hell, you expected it, didn't you, Gordon?"

Gordon raised his head and smiled slowly. "I guess so," he said. "Thanks, Wolf." He went out the door.

Eddie said quietly to Wolf, "That security check came back from the States?"

"Yeah," Wolf said.

Eddie Cassin began to clear off his desk. Twilight darkened the windows of the personnel office. He opened his brief case and filled it with two bottles of gin, a large tin of grapefruit juice and some chocolate bars he took from a desk drawer.

Wolf said, "Why don't you give me your cigarettes and booze, Eddie. You'll wind up with money in the bank instead of a dose."

Eddie put the brief case under his arm and went to the door. "I'm living," he said. "Wish you scavengers luck. I'm off to tame a gorilla."

During supper Wolf said to Mosca, "You know, I must have been the first to spot Gordon. I gave him a lift to town one day and on the road he told me to stop. He got out of the jeep and walked back. Then he picks up a jagged hunk of metal that my wheel had just missed. He throws it off into the bushes and says with that nice, quiet smile, a little embarrassed, 'Save a guy a flat tire.' Now, you say that's a nice thing to do, and sure Gordon is a nice guy. But that's going to a little too much trouble. He puts himself out too much. So when my boss told me he had to keep an eye out for Gordon because he was a Party member I wasn't surprised. They eat up guys like that. Poor stupid bastard."

Mosca lit up a cigar and took a sip of coffee. "He's got balls," he said.

Wolf swallowed the food in his mouth. "Wrong attitude. Use your head now. How many times a day do we get Germans that want to join our Army? They want to fight the Russians. How many times there been rumors Russian troops invaded the British and American sectors? I see the secret reports. It won't be long now, I give it two years before everything blows up. So guys like Gordon have to get the ax. Right here." He made a chopping motion at his throat. "And me I'm going back to the States. I won't wear that PW in Siberia."

Mosca said slowly, "I hope I can get out of here before then."

Wolf wiped his mouth and leaned back to let a waiter pour coffee. "Don't worry," he said. "I got some inside dope they have to lift the marriage ban so we can make honest dames out of the *Fräuleins*. Lots of pressure from the churches back home. Don't want anybody screwing dames without a fighting chance of getting hooked."

They left the mess hall and went out to Wolf's jeep. Outside the wire fence of the air base they took the turn in the road that led away from town and to a far end of the Neustadt. It was only a short ride, and Wolf pulled up in front of an isolated house that was extraordinarily narrow, as if it consisted of one strict line of rooms from front to back. There were three other jeeps parked nearby, a few German Opel cars with wood-burning motors and tin smokestacks. Some bicycles were chained to an iron bar cemented into the stone steps.

Wolf rang the bell, and when the door opened Mosca was startled. The tallest and largest German he had ever seen stood before them. "We have an appointment with Frau Vlavern," Wolf said. The giant stood aside to let them enter.

The room was almost full. Two G.I.'s sat close together with a stuffed green duffel bag between them. There were three officers, each of them with a bulging brief case of shiny pigskin. There were five Germans with empty flaccid brief cases of black leather. They all waited patiently; everyone went in turn, Germans and Americans alike. There were no conquerors here.

The giant took them one by one into the next room and also took care of the door as more officers and G.I.'s and Germans arrived. Some Mosca recognized as base personnel, crew chiefs, a Mess Sergeant, the PX officer. All acted as if they did not know each other after the first nod of greeting.

The windows were heavily shuttered but the sound of jeep motors starting and dying to a halt could be heard in that room. When someone disappeared with the giant, they never returned. At the other end of the house was a door that served as exit.

Their turn came, and the giant took them into the next room. He indicated they were to wait. The room was empty save for two wooden chairs and a small table on which was an ash tray. When they were alone Mosca said, "That's a big guy."

"Her protection," Wolf said, "but if she has the scrip that won't mean nothing. That giant is nearly a moron. She keeps him here to scare people, like drunken G.I.'s and krauts. But for the real McCoy he can't do much." He smiled at Mosca.

After a short wait the giant came in again. He said, in German, in a huskily soft voice that did not fit his body, "Would you care to see something I personally wish to sell?" He took out a band of gold in which was fastened a large diamond. He gave it to Mosca. "Only ten cartons."

Mosca handed it over to Wolf and said, "That looks like a good buy. A carat at least."

Wolf turned it over and smiled. "It's not worth anything," he said. "See, it's flat backed. I told you this guy was a moron." He threw the ring to the giant who snatched at it clumsily but missed and had to stoop down from his great height to pick it up from the floor. Then determinedly he gave the ring to Mosca again. "Ten cartons, a bargain, but do not tell the old Frau." He put a huge finger, childlike, on his lips.

Mosca tried to give the ring back to him but the giant refused to take it. "Ten cartons, keep it for ten cartons," he said over and over again. Mosca put the ring on the table. Slowly, sadly, the giant picked it up.

Then he motioned them to follow and opened the door to the next room. He stood by the door to let them pass, first Mosca, then Wolf. But as Wolf went by he gave a malicious push that sent the American hurtling to the center of the room. Then the giant closed the door and stood by it.

A small, stout, gray-haired woman sat in a wide wicker chair, beside her a desk on which stood an open ledger. There were stacks of PX goods against one wall, hundreds of cartons of cigarettes, yellow boxes of chocolate bars, bars of toilet soap and other toilet goods with bright wrappers. A small German man was arranging the goods neatly into piles. The pockets of his black, ill-fitting jacket bulged with German currency, and when he turned to watch them a bundle of it fell to the floor.

The woman spoke first and she spoke in English. "I am very sorry," she said. "Once in a great while Johann takes a dislike to someone and does such a thing. There is nothing to be done."

Wolf had been taken by surprise and stood in momentary bewilderment. But now his heavy dead-white face turned crimson. The woman's insolent tone angered him even more. He saw Mosca smiling at him and that Mosca had stepped to a wall where he could command everyone in the room if he showed a weapon. Wolf shook his head, then turned to the old woman and saw the glint of amusement in her shrewd eyes.

"It is a small thing," Wolf said calmly. "You know what I have come for. Can you help us?"

The woman looked him up and down and still speaking English said, "My dear man, your story has a stink to it. I don't know of this million dollars in scrip. If I did I would be very careful in my dealings with you and your friend. Really, you insult my intelligence."

Wolf kept his smile. Business before pleasure, he thought. He said, "If you make a contact and deliver that contact to me it may well mean a small fortune for you. For such a little thing."

There was contempt in the woman's voice and disdain in her puffy, fat cheeks. "I am a woman of business and will have no part in such affairs. And make certain I will warn my friends against you." She gave a snort of laughter. "*You* have five thousand cartons."

Wolf was still smiling. He asked, "Can either of these two men understand English? It is important."

The woman, surprised by the unexpected question, said, "No, they do not."

The smile faded from Wolf's face and into it, as if it were a mask he had always ready, came the look of power, a confident quiet sternness.

He put his brief case on the table and leaned over it to look directly into the old woman's circled eyes.

"You are too clever and too proud," he said with measured harshness. "You think you have some power, that you are safe, that your age and your men protect you. I don't like insolent Germans. You don't understand Americans, you and your giant." The woman was alert now, her eyes a beady, flashing black. The little German with his bulging coat had a frightened look. The giant at the door moved toward Wolf. Mosca drew the Hungarian pistol from his brief case and clicked off the safety catch. They all turned to him.

He didn't point the gun, held it down to the floor. In German he said to the giant, "Turn around." The giant moved toward him. Mosca took a step forward and the old woman seeing his face called out a sharp command to the giant. He gave her a bewildered look, then retreated to the far wall and turned his back.

Wolf leaned toward the woman again. "Do you like my friend?" he asked her.

She didn't answer. She kept her eyes on Mosca. The little German, without a command, joined the giant against the wall. Wolf went on. "My friend is a very prideful and irritable man. If your giant had pushed him instead of me there would be no speeches, you would be very sad people here. There would be no words, words I speak so calmly. Now listen. I am reasonable. I hold no grudge for this incident. But if on my rounds I learn you have given information about me, then you can see the other side of my face."

He stopped and looked into the old woman's eyes. There was no fear in them. She was regarding him quite calmly, without compliance. But this was in his province, this was his life work, this challenged the genius he knew he had. He understood that look as no one else could. That words meant nothing, threats no hindrance or persuasion to the human will. He smiled because he knew the answer. He went over to the giant and pushed and turned him around.

"You lump, take off your belt and stand before your mistress," he said. The giant did so. Wolf stepped away.

He drew his gun from his brief case, for effect really, and said to the woman. "Tell him to give you three hard strokes on your back." He made his voice malignant. "If you cry out I'll kill the three of you. Now. Tell him three strokes."

The old woman was still calm. "You do not understand," she said. "If I order him he will take me quite seriously and injure me terribly. He will strike with all his power."

Wolf said good humoredly, "I understand that perfectly."

Her fat cheeks creased with a faint doubtful smile. "You have made your point, it is not necessary to go any further. I will say nothing, I promise. Now, please, I have many people waiting."

Wolf paused for a long moment, and then with a deliberately cruel smile he said, "One stroke. To seal our bargain."

For the first time the woman seemed frightened. Her face sagged, there was a quaver in her voice. "I shall scream for help," she said.

Wolf didn't answer her. He spoke to Mosca, slowly, so that the woman would be sure to understand. "When the woman goes down, kill the big man." He swung the gun up to the woman's face. She turned her head away. She said to the giant in German, "Johann give me one hard stroke across the back." She sat on the chair with her head bowed on the table, her rounded fat shoulders hunched for the blow. The giant swung his belt down and when it hit, they could hear a terrible crackling split of skin and meat beneath cloth. The woman raised her head. Her face was bloodless with pain and fright and shock. Wolf looked at her with cold, emotionless eyes. "Now you understand," he said. Then, mimicking her insolent voice and manner,

"There is nothing to be done." He walked to the door and said, "Come on, Walter," and they went through the rooms they had come by and out the front door.

In the jeep going back to town, Wolf laughed and said to Mosca, "Would you have shot that big guy if I gave the word?"

Mosca lit a cigarette. He was still tense. "Hell, I knew it was an act. I got to hand it to you, Wolf, you put on a hell of a show."

Wolf said in a satisfied voice, "Experience, boy. Some of our officers were too chicken to use real pressure on prisoners. So we had to use the scare technique. And you looked real mean there on the wall."

"I was surprised," Mosca said. "When that big guy pushed you and the old dame was so snotty, I figured a trap. Then I was mad. Christ, don't they know some of these G.I.'s would butcher the whole crew for a stunt like that?"

Wolf said slowly, "I'll tell you how people are, Walter. This old dame, she thinks she's clever. And she has this big giant and all these officers and G.I.'s treat her with respect because she can make their fortune. Now get this: She forgets. She forgets what it is to be afraid. That one stroke she got was the key. Remember that. Without that one stroke she couldn't be afraid. People are like that."

They went across the bridge and into the Bremen town. In a few minutes they were before the billet.

They smoked a cigarette together in the parked jeep.

Wolf said, "In a week or so we make the most important contacts. We'll have to stay out most of the night. So be ready for a call any time. O.K.?" He slapped Mosca on the back.

Mosca stepped out of the jeep, took a last puff on his cigarette. "You think she'll squawk to her friends?"

Wolf shook his head. "This is the one thing I know about. She'll never open her mouth to anybody." He grinned at Mosca. "She'll never forget that stripe she wears on her back."

11

WALTER MOSCA, dressed in civvies, stared out of the window of the Civilian Personnel Office. He watched the people of the base going by, the airplane mechanics in their green fatigues and fur-lined leather jackets, natty flying officers in dark greens and violet overcoats, the German laborers in their old clothing, all hunched against the sharp November wind. Behind him Eddie Cassin said, "Walter." Mosca turned around.

Eddie Cassin leaned back in his chair. "I got a job for you. I had an idea and the Lieutenant thinks it's pretty good. We're having a food conservation drive all over the European Theatre, you know, try to tell the chowhounds that they shouldn't eat themselves sick. Not to starve but not to load up their trays, then leave a lot of stuff that has to be thrown out. Now here's the idea. We want a picture of a G.I. with a big heaping tray of food and caption it 'Stop This.' Next to it we want a photo of two little German kids sniping butts in the street and the caption, 'And You Stop This.' How does it sound?"

"It sounds like real shit to me," Mosca said.

Eddie grinned at him. "All right. But it looks clever as hell. Real public-relations stuff. Headquarters will eat it up. Maybe *Stars and Stripes* will print it. Who knows? It could turn out big.

"For Christ's sake," Mosca said.

"O.K.," Eddie Cassin said, a little annoyed. "Just get a picture of kids sniping butts. The jeep is outside and you can pick up that photographer, the Corporal, at the lab."

"O.K.," Mosca said. He went out and watched the afternoon flight from Wiesbaden come down out of the sky, as if appearing by magic from nothing but air. Then he got into the jeep.

It was late afternoon before he drove the jeep over the bridge into Bremen proper. The Corporal had been goofing around the hangars, and it had taken Mosca an hour to track him down.

The streets of the city were full of hurrying Germans and the Strassenbahns clanged their way through dense traffic, passengers hanging on to the step poles. Mosca parked the jeep in front of the Glocke.

In the gray workaday afternoon all was still. The front of the Red Cross Club was empty of beggars, streetwalkers and children; activity would begin after the supper hour. Two German policewomen strolled slowly up and down the sidewalk, slowly as if bemused by the melodious clanging of streetcar bells.

Mosca and the Corporal waited in their jeep for some begging children to appear, smoking cigarettes but not talking. Finally the Corporal said, "What goddamn luck. This is the first time I didn't see some kraut kids hangin' around."

Mosca got out of the jeep. "I'll take a look," he said. It was very cold and he turned up the collar of his jacket. He walked around the corner and seeing no children, continued to walk until he was in the rear of the Glocke Building.

Serenely perched on a great hill of rubble, looking down

on half the great city that lay in ruins before them, were two small boys. They were wrapped in coats reaching to their shoes and on their heads were caps that came down almost over their ears. Through their bare hands they strained the loose dirt out of the rubble they scooped up, and then threw stones and fragments of brick out across the prairie and valley of ruins below them; throwing at nothing in particular and not hard enough to lose balance on top of the hill.

"Here," Mosca called in German, "do you two want to earn some chocolate?"

The children looked down at him gravely, judging him, recognizing him as one of the enemy, despite his civilian clothes, then slid down the hill, not afraid. They followed him, leaving their vast, silent, empty playground, clasping each other's hand when they came into the busy square before the Glocke.

The Corporal was out of the jeep, waiting for them. He slipped a plate into his camera and adjusted the range finder. When he was set he said to Mosca, "O.K., tell them what to do." The Corporal could speak no German.

"Pick up those cigarette butts," Mosca told the boys. "Now look up so that man can take your picture." They bent obediently but their long, peaked caps shadowed their faces.

"Push their caps back," the Corporal said. Mosca did so, exposing two grinning gnomelike faces to the camera.

"Those butts are too small," the Corporal said. "They won't show up." Mosca took out some whole cigarettes and threw them into the gutter.

The Corporal had made a few shots but was not satisfied. He was preparing for another when Mosca felt someone's hand on his arm and he was spun around.

Before him were the two policewomen, the one who had spun him around nearly as tall as he, her hand still on his arm. He gave her a push that was nearly a blow, feeling the soft breast beneath the rough, blue wool of her uniform. She staggered back, her hand falling away from his arm, then said defensively, "That is not allowed here." She turned to the boys and said in a warning voice, "You two leave here instantly."

Mosca grabbed the children by their coats. "Stay here," he said. He turned on the two women, his lean, dark face ugly and vicious with anger. "Do you see that uniform?" pointing to the Corporal. He held out his hand. "Give me your identification." The two women began to stutter explanations, that it was their job to keep the children away, keep them from begging. A German man going by stopped, the boys edged away from the quarrel, and the man said something to them in an angry, scolding voice which frightened them, and they began to run. Mosca caught them again as the Corporal let out a warning shout. The man began to walk away quickly to get to the throng of fellow Germans waiting on the corner for a streetcar. Mosca ran down the street after him and when the German heard the pounding feet he turned around, his eyes blinking with fright.

"Did you tell those children to leave?" Mosca shouted at him.

The German said quietly, apologetically, "I did not understand. I thought they were begging."

"Give me your identity pass," Mosca said. He held out his hand. The German, trembling with nervousness and shock, reached into his jacket pocket and pulled out the usual enormous wallet stuffed with papers. He fumbled unseeingly, trying to watch Mosca at the same time until Mosca took the papers out of his hand and found the blue card himself.

Mosca handed the wallet back. "Come to the police station in the morning for your pass," he said, and turned to walk back to the jeep.

Across the street, on the other side of the square, he saw in the failing November light a dark, silent mass of Germans watching him; tall, giantlike, black as the outline of a forest. For one moment he knew fear and terror as if they could see into his heart and mind, and then his anger flared up again. He walked slowly, calmly, to the jeep. The two boys were still there but the policewomen had disappeared.

"Let's go," he said to the Corporal. He drove down to the Metzer Strasse and got out. He said to the Corporal, "Take the jeep back to the base for me."

The Corporal nodded and said quietly, "I think those shots will be enough." And Mosca realized that he had forgotten to renew the taking of pictures and had left the children standing in front of the Glocke, not given them the chocolate he had promised.

When Mosca entered the room, Hella was warming soup on the electric plate, a red-labeled empty can open on the table. A pan full of bacon waited its turn. Leo sat on the couch reading.

The room was warm with the smell of food, comfortable in its well-filled largeness. The bed and its night table in one corner, on the table a lamp and small radio; the great white wardrobe in the corner near the door, and in the middle a great round table surrounded by wicker chairs. Along one wall the enormous, empty china closet helped give the room a coziness that was not crowded, that yet gave plenty of space to move around in. A hell of a big room, Mosca always thought.

Hella looked up from her cooking. "Oh, you're home early," she said and rose to kiss him. Her face always changed when she saw him, he could see the happiness there, giving him always a sense of guilt and fear because she built so much of her life on him. As if she did not know the many dangers he felt in the world around them.

"I had something to do in town and didn't go back to the base," Mosca said. Leo raised his head and nodded to him, then continued to read. Mosca reached into his pocket for a cigarette, and his fingers touched the German's identity card.

"How about giving me a lift to the police station after we eat?" Mosca asked Leo. He threw the card on the table.

Leo nodded and said, "What have you there?" Mosca told them what had happened. He noticed that Leo was watching him with a curious, amused smile. Hella poured the hot soup into cups and said nothing. Then she put the bacon on the electric plate.

They drank the soup carefully, dipping crackers into it. Hella lifted the blue identity card from the table. Holding the cup in one hand she flipped the card open with the other. "He's married," she said. "He has blue eyes and brown hair and works as a printer. That is a good job." She studied the picture. "He doesn't look like a bad man, I wonder if he has children."

"Doesn't it say on the pass?" Mosca asked.

"No," Hella said. "He has a scar on his finger." She let the card drop back onto the table.

Leo tilted his head back and drank the last of his soup,

then leaned over the table, the tic in his face working a little. "Tell me," he said, "why didn't you go to the police station with the man right away? It was close by."

Mosca smiled at him. "I just wanted to scare the guy, I'm not going to do anything. I guess I just wanted to scare the son of a bitch."

"He'll have a very bad night," Hella said.

"He deserves it," Mosca said angrily, defensively. "Where does that bastard come off putting his two cents in a deal like that."

Hella lifted her pale, gray eyes to him. "He was ashamed," she said, "and I think he felt it his fault that these children beg and pick up cigarettes in the streets."

"Ah hell, let him sweat," Mosca said. "How about some bacon before you burn the hell out of it?"

Hella put the bacon and a loaf of gray German bread on the table. When they had finished eating the grease-soaked sandwiches Leo and Mosca rose, Leo searching for his jeep keys on the trunk. Hella picked up the identity card and looked at the address. "See," she said eagerly, "he lives on Rubsam Strasse. That is closer than the police station."

Mosca said curtly, "Don't wait up for me. We're going to the club after." Then he smiled at her as she leaned her head to be kissed, her thin, closely drawn light-brown hair like a helmet. The sentimental action always endeared her to him though he smiled at it and never made the first move himself. "Do you want me to bring some ice cream?" She nodded. As he went out the door she called after him, "It's on the way to the club."

In the jeep Leo said to him, "Where do we go?"

"O.K., for Christ's sake, take me to the guy's house." Mosca shook his head. "You and her give me a big pain in the ass."

"I don't give a damn," Leo said, "but it is on the way to the club. And besides I know what it is to 'sweat,' as you say. That is a very accurate word." He turned his big-boned face to Mosca and smiled with a touch of sadness.

Mosca shrugged. "I don't even want to see the bastard. How about you going in the house, Leo?"

"Not me," Leo said with a grin. "You took it away from him? You give it back."

They had no trouble finding the house, a private, two-family home cut up into a tenement to provide much-needed housing. On the vestibule door was a list of all the tenants, including every member of the family, and what apartments they occupied. Mosca looked at the identity pass and compared names. Then he went up to the second floor. He knocked sharply and the door was opened immediately. He realized that he had been seen from the window and his knock waited for. The man at the door had the same bullet head and stern features but his face was set in a constrained mask and softened by the now naked baldness of his skull. The German stood aside and Mosca went in.

He had interrupted the evening meal. The table in the large room held four dishes filled with black gravy in which floated dark, shredded vegetables and large pasty white potatoes. In one corner was a bed, further along the wall a sink hung awkwardly, above it a great framed painting in dark greens and browns. A woman, light hair drawn against her skull, was trying to bring two small boys through the door to the other room of the apartment. But as she turned to see Mosca she let the children escape her. They all looked at Mosca and waited.

He handed the German the blue identity card. The man took it and said falteringly, "Yes?"

Mosca said, "You don't have to go to the police station. Forget about everything."

The blunt, stern face turned ghastly white. The relief from fear, the shock of the day, the jeep screaming to a stop in front of his house, all combined now—a poison disintegrated his blood. He trembled visibly and his wife hurried to his support, helped him to one of the four empty wooden chairs surrounding the table. Mosca, alarmed, said to the woman, "What's the trouble, what's the matter with him?"

"Nothing," the woman said, her voice dead, completely empty of emotion or any life. "We thought you came to take him away." Her voice wavered slightly.

One of the children began to cry with quiet fright, as if the strength and walls of his world had been destroyed. Mosca, thinking to quiet him, took a few steps forward and brought out a bar of chocolate. The child was terrified and began to scream great hysterical screams, so high pitched they were barely audible. Mosca stopped and looked at the woman helplessly. She was bringing her husband a small glass of schnapps. As the man drank, the woman ran over to the child, slapped him full in the mouth and then picked him up in her arms. The child was still. The father, still terribly agitated said, "Wait, please wait," and almost ran to the cupboard for a bottle of schnapps and a small water glass.

He poured Mosca a drink and forced it into his hands. "It was all a mistake, you see, all a mistake, I thought the children were annoying you. I did not mean to interfere." And Mosca remembered the man's angry tone when he had scolded the two boys in front of the Glocke, the angry shame and guilt, as if its owners were himself the cause of the children's degradation.

"It's all right," Mosca said. He tried to leave the drink on the table but the German kept hold of his arm and forced the drink on him again.

Forgetting his wife and children watching him, as if he were pleading for his life, the father went on feverishly, "I was never a Nazi. I joined the Party to keep my job, all printers must join. But I paid my dues. No more. I was never a Nazi. Drink. It's good stuff. Drink it. I save this for when I feel ill." Mosca drank and broke away for the door but the German caught him, shook his hand, "I am very grateful for your kindness. That is from the heart. I will never forget this. I have always said the Americans were good. They are kindhearted, we Germans are fortunate." He wrung Mosca's hand for the last time, his head shaking up and down with nervousness and passionate relief.

At that moment Mosca felt an almost uncontrollable urge to strike him down, to make the blood flow from that bald skull and twitching face, and turned his head away to hide his contempt and disgust.

Framed against the brown door, in the room beyond, Mosca saw the wife's face. The flesh was drawn tight around the separate and distinctly seen bones. The skin was dead white and her head was slightly lowered, the shoulders hunched by the weight of the child in her arms. Her gray eyes, almost black now, were dark pools of unforgetting hatred. Her hair, too, seemed dark beside the child's golden one and her gaze did not flinch as it met Mosca's. Not one muscle of her face moved.

As the door closed behind him, Mosca heard her voice, quiet but sharp, speaking to her husband. Out in the street, by the light of the lamp-lit room, he could see her looking down at him, the child still in her arms.

12

WOLF ATE his cold supper German-peasant fashion, picking up the long, blood-red wurst and slicing off a thick, glutinous chunk with his pocketknife. Then he cut a block of dark bread from the enormous loaf resting before him. The German girl he lived with, Ursula, and her father, took the bread and wurst in their turn. Each had a can of American beer beside their plates with which they filled small wine glasses when necessary.

"When do you have to go?" Ursula asked. She was a small, dark girl with an ungovernable temper. Wolf had taken pleasure in taming her. He had already put in his marriage papers, and it was with this understanding that he had been allowed to move into the father's house to live with her. There were other considerations.

"I have to meet Mosca at the Rathskellar in about an hour," Wolf said, looking at the watch he had taken from the Polish refugee after the war. The dead Polack, Wolf thought.

"I don't care for that man," Ursula said. "He has no manners. I don't know what that girl sees in him."

Wolf cut another slice of wurst and said jokingly, "The same thing you see in me."

As he knew she would, Ursula flared up. "You damn Americans think we'll do anything for your goods. Try treating me as your Ami friends treat their girls. See if I keep you. Out the house you go."

The father, munching on the hard bread, said placatingly, "Ursula, Ursula," but he said it out of habit, thinking of something else.

When Wolf had finished supper he went into the bedroom and stuffed his large, brown leather brief case with cigarettes, chocolate and a few cigars. He took these from a locked wardrobe to which he had the only key. As he was about to leave Ursula's father came in.

"Wolfgang, before you leave. A word if I may." The father was always polite and respectful, always remembering the lover of his daughter was an American. Wolf liked this in him.

The father led Wolf to their cold storeroom in the back of the basement apartment. The father threw open the door and in a dramatically concerned voice said, "Look."

From the wooden beams hung bare bones of hams with tiny shreds of dark meat clinging to them, small ends of salamis, and a white cheese like a thin quarter moon.

"We have to do something, Wolfgang," the father said, "our supplies are very low. Very, very low."

Wolf sighed. He wondered what the old bastard had done with all that stuff. They both knew damn well it hadn't been eaten. A regiment couldn't have done such damage. As always when the old man had outgeneraled him he thought grimly, wait until Ursula and me get back to the States. I'll teach them both a lesson. The old man would expect packages. Balls he'd get. Wolf nodded his head as if he had been thinking over the problem.

"All right," he said. They went back to the bedroom and he gave the father five cartons of cigarettes. "These are the last I can give for a few months," Wolf said warningly. "I have a very big deal ready."

"Don't worry," the father said, "this will last a long time. My daughter and I get along as sparingly as we can, you know that, Wolfgang." Wolf nodded his head reassuringly, and also in admiration of the man's nerve, thinking, the old robber will make his fortune out of me yet.

Before he left the room, Wolf took the heavy Walther pistol from his bureau drawer and slipped it into the jacket of his coat. This always captured the father's attention, made him more respectful, and this also pleased Wolf.

As they left the room together the older man threw his arm in a confidential, fatherly way around Wolf's shoulders. "Next week I am getting a great supply of brown and gray gabardine. I'll have some beautiful suits made for you, as a present. And if any of your friends wish to buy I will give them a special price. As a favcr to you."

Wolf nodded gravely. As he went cut the door Ursula called out, "Be careful." He left the basement and walked up a few steps to the street. Then he strode briskly in the direction of the Rathskellar. It was only fifteen minutes away, he would be in plenty of time. As he walked he marveled over the father. A load of gabardine. *His* gabardine really. And then he was supposed to sell it without commission. He'd fix that. He'd make himself a little something. He'd give Mosca, Cassin and Gordon a good break, maybe even the Jew, but still earn a little something. But he should be able to sell a lot of it. At a nice cut for himself. Well, that was chicken feed, but every bit helped.

In the Rathskellar, the great underground restaurant that before the war had been one of Germany's finest, he found Eddie Cassin and Mosca at a table by the giant wine casks.

These huge barrels reaching to the ceiling formed a shadow over the two men, cutting them off from the rest of the olive-drab officers and the few women who spotted the vast, cavernous room. A string orchestra played quietly, the lights were dim, and small white-clothed tables stretched out as far as the eye could see; then clustered in white eddies like foam; in alcoves and small private dining rooms.

"Wolf, the living cigarette tree," Eddie Cassin shouted. His voice rose above the music and rose to the almost invisible ceiling high above them and became lost there. No one paid any attention. He leaned over the table and whispered, "What you two hustlers got planned tonight?"

Wolf sat down. "Just making a little trip around town. See if we can pick up any bargains. Stop using your butts for gash, and I'll make you a few pennies." Though he joked, Wolf was worried. He could see Mosca was nearly as drunk as Eddie and he was surprised. He had never seen Mosca drunk before. He wondered if he should cancel the whole deal for this night. But it was all set up, this was the first night they would hit the big black-market wheels, they might even get a lead on who had the dough. Wolf ordered a drink, watching Mosca to see if he would be O.K.

Mosca noticed this and smiled. "I'll be all right, a coupla minutes fresh air. I'll be O.K." He tried to enunciate carefully but the words slurred together. Wolf shook his head with an impatient disgust he could not hide.

Eddie shook his head in drunken mimicry. "The trouble with you, Wolf, is you think you're clever. You wanna be a millionaire. Wolf, you'll never make it. Never in a million years. One, you got no brains, just a little cunning. Two, you havn't got real guts. You can slap kraut prisoners around but that's all. That's all, that's all."

"How can you stand this gash hound?" Wolf asked Mosca, his voice deliberately quiet, insulting. "He's had so many dames sitting on his head, his brain's gone soft."

Eddie jumped up angrily and shouted, "You lousy butt hustler—" Mosca pulled him down to the chair. Some of the people at the other tables turned around. "Take it easy, Eddie, he's only kidding. You too, Wolf. He's drunk. When he's drunk he hates everybody. And besides, his wife wrote him she's leaving England with the kid and coming here, and he can't stand giving up all his dames."

Eddie turned on Mosca with drunken reproachfulness and said, "That's not so, Walter, I really gave her some raw deals." He shook his head dolefully.

Mosca, to cheer him up, said, "Tell Wolf about your gorilla."

Wolf drank his whiskey down, and some of his good humor returned. He grinned at Eddie Cassin.

Eddie said solemnly, almost reverently, "I'm screwing a gorilla." He waited for Wolf's reaction.

"I'm not surprised," Wolf said and laughed with Mosca. "What's the deal?"

"I'm screwing a real honest-to-God gorilla," Eddie insisted.

Wolf looked questioningly at Mosca. "It's a dame," Mosca said, "he claims she looks just like a gorilla, she's that homely."

Eddie looked down at the table and then turned earnestly to Mosca. "I got a confession to make, Walter, she's really a gorilla, I was ashamed to admit it. But she's a real gorilla. I lied to you. She lives right near the air base and she works for Military Government. She's an interpreter." He smiled at them and Wolf, his spirits completely restored, laughed so heartily that the people at the nearby tables turned around again.

"How about bringing her around and giving us a break?" Wolf asked jokingly.

Eddie shuddered. "Christ, I never go out in the street with her even. I sneak into the house when it's dark."

"It's time for us to leave, Walter," Wolf said briskly, "this is the big night and it's going to be a long one." Mosca leaned over Eddie and asked, "You all right? Can you get home O.K.?" Eddie mumbled that he was and as they walked to the door they could hear him shouting to the waiter for another drink.

Wolf waited for Mosca to get ahead of him, noticing the unsteady walk. Going up the steps he could not help saying, "You picked a hell of a night to get stewed."

The cold winter air sliced through Mosca's cheek bones, freezing the red pulp of his gums and palate, flesh already raw from too much alcohol and cigarettes. He lit a cigarette to warm his mouth and throat and thought, "Screw you, Wolf," and thought if this son of a bitch makes another crack I'll rap him or walk away. He could feel the cold working through his coat and below it, freezing his knees and thighs, feeling his whole torso itch with the beginning chill as if it were glazed with frost, and he felt nausea as the frozen air hit the souring whiskey in his belly, sending it spinning up to his brain. He wanted to vomit but knotted his stomach muscles, held it down, not wanting Wolf to see him so. Knowing that Wolf was right, it was a hell of a night to get stewed. But for the first time he'd had a real quarrel with Hella, not the kind of an argument that made you mad or resentful but one in which neither could understand the other. Just depressing and sad.

The street Wolf and Mosca followed led down a hill

from the Rathskellar, past the area of light shed by the Red Cross Club, the music from it trailing after them like a ghost through the ruins. Past the Police Building with its searchlight that imprisoned the jeeps in a white blinding pool of light cut from the surrounding darkness, and then descending the hill, steep as a well, they left the heart of the city and became part of the black night, and though they must have walked for some time it seemed almost a moment to Mosca before Wolf had knocked on a door, and they were inside some place, out of the cold.

In the room there was a large table, four chairs around it. These were the only pieces of furniture. Against the walls were stacks of merchandise over which brown Army blankets had been hastily thrown. There were no windows, and the room was hazy with smoke.

Mosca could hear Wolf saying something, introducing him to the little almost dwarflike German before him, and though the closeness of the room brought the nausea back he made an effort to listen, bring everything into focus.

"You know what he is interested in," Wolf was saying. "Money, only money. American scrip."

The German shook his head. "I have asked, I have asked all around. No one has the amount you say. That I know. I can buy a few hundred dollars, but that is the most possible.

Mosca broke in, enunciating slowly what he had been taught to say. "I am interested in selling a great quantity at one time. Five thousand cartons minimum."

The little German looked at him with respect and awe and his voice was filled with envious greed. "Five thousand cartons, OH OH OH." He thought of it dreamily and then said with a brisk, businesslike air, "However, I will keep an eye out, have no fear. A drink before you go?

Friedl," he called. A woman opened an inner door and peered out. "Schnapps," the German shouted as if he were calling a dog's name, bringing it to heel. The woman disappeared and reappeared a few minutes later with a thin, white bottle and three small water glasses. Behind her came a small boy and girl, golden-haired but with dirty, red-splotched faces.

Wolf crouched on his haunches, "Ah, what beautiful children," he exclaimed. From his brief case he took four bars of chocolate and extended a pair to each.

The father stepped between them and reaching out took the chocolate into his own hands. "No," he said, "it is too late for them to eat candy." He went to one of the footlockers resting against the wall and when he turned to face them his hands were empty. "Tomorrow, my children," he said. The boy and girl turned away sullenly. As Wolf and Mosca lifted their drinks the woman said something sharply in a dialect they could not understand. The man gave her a warning and threatening look, "Tomorrow, I have said. Tomorrow."

Mosca and Wolf left, and in the dark street, lit only by a single yellow window pane they could hear the shrill voices of man and wife, voices raised in menacing anger, fear and hate.

The white, homemade potato schnapps, almost as strong and raw as alcohol, warmed Mosca but added to the blackness of the winter night. He was unsteady and stumbled often. Finally Wolf stopped and held his arm and asked in a concerned voice, "You wanta call it off for tonight, Walter, and go home?" Mosca shook his head at Wolf's pasty-white face, luminous and cold as death in the darkness before him. They started to walk again, Wolf slightly ahead, Mosca following, straining against the cold wind and the physical nausea in his body. He thought of how Hella had said the same words to him that afternoon.

She had been wearing one of the dresses he had given her for the Christmas just past. Ann Middleton had let him use her clothing card at the Army store. Hella had watched him take the little Hungarian pistol from the wardrobe and slip it into the pocket of his short coat. Then she asked him quietly, "Don't you want to go home?"

He knew what she meant. The marriage ban against Germans had been lifted a few days before Christmas and now more than a month later he had done nothing about putting in his papers for permission to marry. And she knew that this was because once they were married they would have to leave Germany and go back to the States. And he answered, "No, I can't right now, I have six months to go on my job contract."

She had been hesitant, almost fearful, and when she came to kiss him good-bye, as she always did when he left her, even for a few hours, she said, "Why don't you read the letters from your family? Why don't you answer them with more than a little note?"

Against his own body he could feel the slight swelling of her rounded stomach and filling breasts. "We have to leave here sometime," she said. And he knew that this was true. But he couldn't tell her why he couldn't go home now. That he had no real feeling for his mother or Alf, and reading their letters would be like hearing their voices crying out. That the sight of the ruined city pleased him, the gaping wounds left in streets by destroyed buildings, the ragged and torn skyline as if a great, jagged ax had chopped off the top of the city's skull. That when he was home the solid, unending, wall-like streets, unmarred, secure, had made him angry, uneasy.

"We have time," he said. "After the baby comes in June, we'll get the papers and marry."

Hella stood away from him. "I'm not worried about that. But you shouldn't treat your family so, you should at least read their letters." He had flared up at her and said, "Look, don't keep trying to make me do things I don't want to do." And she had kissed him and said, "Be careful tonight," and he knew she would wait up for him though he had told her not to.

He could hear Wolf's voice say, "Here we are," and see the white face before him. There was a high stoop and they were standing in a pool of light formed by a naked bulb fastened into the face of the house. Its yellow light weakly stained the fabric of night. Mosca climbed the steps warily, holding fast to the iron rail.

"This guy is a long shot," Wolf said as he rang the bell. "But I want you to know him. He's a jeweler, and if you want something for your girl, he'll be a right guy."

A window above their heads, above the nakedly lit bulb, was thrown open. Wolf tilted his head back and said, "Ah, Herr Furstenberg, good evening."

"Please, just one moment, Herr Wolfgang." The voice was mellow with sadness and age, and a despair that came natural to it.

When the door opened a small bald-headed man, dark and with enormous black eyes waited to greet them, and when Wolf introduced Mosca the German clicked his heels and bowed. "Please come up," he said, and they climbed the stairs and went through a door to a large living room with many pieces of furniture which included two large sofas, three or four stuffed chairs and a grand piano. There was a large table in the center of the room and several smaller ones against the walls. On one of the sofas two young girls not more than sixteen were sitting, not close to each other but with a space between them. Herr Furstenberg sat in this space.

"Please," he said, motioning to the empty chairs nearest him. Wolf and Mosca sat down.

"I wanted you to meet the man I have spoken about," Wolf said. "He is a very good friend of mine and I know you will treat him well if he should ever need your help."

Herr Furstenberg, his arms around both girls' waists, bowed his bald head courteously and said with equal formality and graveness, "There can be no question of that." Then turning his great, black hollow eyes directly to Mosca he said, "Please come to me any time if I can help you."

Mosca nodded and sank back into the comfortable chair, feeling his legs quiver with fatigue. Idly, hazily through the fog of his tired mind, he noticed that the two young girls were fresh looking, without make-up, and wore heavy woolen stockings that rose to their kneecaps. They sat soberly beside Herr Furstenberg in daughterly fashion, and one had pigtails braided down each side of her shoulder, long golden ropes which piled into her rough, woolen-skirted lap and coiled into Herr Furstenberg's waiting hand.

"In that other matter," the German said, turning to Wolf again, "I am truly sorry, but I cannot help you. None of my friends have heard of such a thing, this theft of a million dollars of scrip. It is a fantastic story." He smiled kindly at them both.

"No," Wolf said firmly, "the story is true." He rose, extended his hand. "I'm sorry I disturbed you at so late an hour. If some information should come, please let me know."

"Of course," Herr Furstenberg said. He rose, bowed to

Mosca and shook his hand, saying to him, "Please come to me any time." The two girls rose from the sofa and Herr Furstenberg put his arms around their waists as a fond father might, and the three of them walked Mosca and Wolf to the staircase. One of the girls, not the one with long hair, ran down the steps and showed them out. They could hear the door being bolted behind them. Then the naked bulb above the stoop went out and they were in total darkness.

Mosca, dead tired, disgusted at leaving the comfortable room, asked Wolf curtly, "Do you think we'll ever find these bastards?"

"I'm just looking for a lead tonight," Wolf said, "and letting these people look you over. That's the big thing."

Now in the darkened streets they passed other hurrying forms, saw jeeps parked in front of deserted-looking houses. "Everybody is on the hunt tonight," Wolf said. He waited for a moment and then asked, "How did you like Furstenberg?"

The wind had died away and they could talk easily. "He seems like a nice guy," Mosca said.

"He's damn nice for a Jew especially," Wolf said. "No offense against your buddy." He waited for Mosca to say something and then went on. "Furstenberg did his time in a concentration camp. His wife and kids are in the States. He thought he was going to join them, but he has TB so bad they won't let him in. And he got it in the camp. Funny, huh?" Mosca didn't answer. They crossed a well-lighted avenue, coming back to the heart of the city.

"He's gone a little crazy," Wolf almost shouted. The wind had started up again and they were walking into it, tripping over rubble. They turned a corner and the wind was gone again. "You see those two girls? He gets them fresh from the country, new ones every month or so. His agent told me the story, we do business together. Furstenberg goes along for weeks living with the girls, they have their own room. And then, bang, after treating them like daughters all this time, one night he goes into their room and humps their ass off. Next day he ships them away with some real valuable presents and a week later he gets a fresh set. These are new ones, I haven't seen them before. That must be a nice little scene when he slips them the business. Real wild. Like a guy chasing chickens to cut off their heads."

Another guy, Mosca thought. Everybody going off their nuts. And he wasn't much better. So they wouldn't let the poor bastard in because he had TB. That was a law for the books. Sensible, all laws were sensible. But they always screwed somebody. But screw that son of a bitch Furstenberg, that heel-clicking prick. He had his own troubles. And that's what he had wanted to tell Hella this afternoon. That every day he lived he broke a law. Having her with him in the billet, buying clothes for her with Middleton's Army card, sleeping with her, and he could be sent to jail for loving her. And he wasn't complaining, that was the world, he wasn't indignant. But when they pulled all the other shit with this and tried to make you feel ashamed and tried to say it was right, justice, then it was shit. When they wanted him to act as if everything the world told him was so, then he just said fuck you in his mind. He couldn't stand listening to his mother, and Alf and Gloria. He couldn't stand reading the newspapers, they made him puke. They said this is good today and tomorrow they said you're evil, a murderer, a wild animal, and they made you believe it so much you helped hunt yourself down. He could get away with murdering Fritz but go to jail for taking care of a woman he wanted. And a week ago he had watched them shoot the Polacks against the wall, the handball court behind the air base, the three brave Polacks who had massacred a small German village, men, women and children, but those poor bastard Polacks had made a mistake, they murdered a few days after the occupation had begun instead of a few days before, and instead of receiving their medals from the General as brave guerrillas, the top half of their bodies had been shrouded in brown cord sacks, and they were tied to wooden stakes driven into cracks in the cement, and the firing squad stood almost on top of them, shooting down into the slumped bodies a few feet away. And you could say it any way you wanted, you could prove a million times how necessary it was, the murdering, backwards and forwards, and he didn't give a shit about the whole business anyway. Didn't he eat a good breakfast after watching the Polacks?

But he couldn't tell Hella why he practically hated his mother, his girl, his brother now and why he loved her. Maybe because she had been afraid as he had been afraid, that she was as frightened of death as he was, and maybe really it was because she had lost everything as he had except that he had lost everything inside himself and she hadn't. That he hated all the mothers and fathers and sisters and brothers, sweethearts and wives that he saw in the newspapers, the newsreels, in brightly colored magazines, receiving medals for their dead sons, their dead heroes, the proud smiles, the proud weeping, the brave dress for the occasion showing real grief, painful but sweet in its very release of pain, and all the stern faces of the bestowing dignitaries in their blazing-white shirts and black ties, and he could imagine them all over the world the loved ones of the enemies too receiving the same medals for their dead sons and heroes weeping and smiling bravely, accepting in exchange the beribboned metal disc in its satin-lined box—and suddenly wriggling into his throbbing brain came an image of all the monstrously sated worms raising their pulpy white heads to bow in thanks to the dignitaries, the mothers, the fathers, the brothers, the sweethearts.

But you couldn't blame them because our cause was just; that's true, he thought, but how about Fritz? That was an accident, really an accident. And everybody would forgive him, his own dignitaries, his mother, Alf and Gloria. They would all say you couldn't help what you did. The worms would forgive him. Hella had wept but she accepted because there was nothing else she had left. And he couldn't blame any of them but don't try to tell me what's wrong, don't say I should read their letters, don't say the world shouldn't come to an end because men are holy and have immortal souls, don't say I should smile and be polite to every son of a bitch who does me a favor and says hello. All of Hella's hints about being nicer to Frau Meyer and Yergen and my own friends and answer and read my family's letters. It's all mixed up and it's nobody's fault and why blame them for being alive?

He had to stop walking, he felt really ill, his head was spinning, and he could not feel his own legs move. Wolf was holding his arm, and he rested against Wolf's shoulder until his head cleared so he could walk again.

White streaks and shadows ran through the night and Mosca, following them, raised his head and saw for the first time the cold and distant winter moon, and saw that they were in the Contrescarpe park, skirting around the little lake. Icy moonbeams glinted over water and webbed the black trees with frosted light, and as he watched, great dark-blue shadows raced across the sky and drowned the moon, its light, and now he couldn't see anything at all. Then Wolf spoke to him saying, "You looked real bad, Walter, keep going a few minutes, and we'll make a stop where I can fix you up."

They came suddenly into the city and to a square on a little rise of ground. On one corner stood a church, the great wooden doors barred shut. Wolf led the way to a side entrance and they climbed a narrow staircase to the steeple, and flush with the top step was a door which seemed to be cut out of the very wall. Wolf knocked, and through his nausea, Mosca still felt a shock to see that it was Yergen and thought, Wolf knows Yergen won't believe I have the cigarettes. But he was too sick to care.

The closeness of the room made him lean against a wall and then Yergen was giving him a green pill and hot coffee, shoving the pill into his mouth and holding a burning cup to his lips.

The room, Yergen and Wolf sprang into focus. The nausea left Mosca's body, and he could feel the cold sweat over his whole body running down between his thighs. Wolf and Yergen were watching him with little knowing smiles on their faces and Yergen patted him on the shoulder and said kindly, "You're all right now, eh?"

The room was cold. It was large, square, with a very low ceiling and one corner had been made into a cubicle by a wooden partition painted pink and covered with illustrations cut from a book of fairy tales. "My daughter is sleeping behind there," Yergen said, and as he spoke they could hear the little girl moaning, then wake and begin to cry softly, as if she were alone and the sound of her own fear would frighten her. Yergen went behind the partition and came back out carrying his little daughter in his arms. She was wrapped in an American Army blanket, and she looked at them gravely with her wet eyes. She had jet-black hair, a sad, mature face.

Yergen sat on the couch against one wall and Wolf sat beside him. Mosca drew up the only other chair in the room.

"Can you go out with us tonight?" Wolf asked. "We're going over to Honny's place. He is the man I am counting on."

Yergen shook his head. "I can't tonight." He rubbed his cheek against his daughter's wet one. "My little girl had a fright earlier this evening. Someone came up and kept knocking on the door, and she knew it wasn't me because we have a special signal. I have to leave her so much alone and the woman who takes care of her goes home at seven. When I came she was so frightened and in such shock I had to give her one of the pills."

Wolf shook his head. "She is too young. That should not be done often. But I hope you don't think we came. You know I respect your wishes and come only by appointment."

Yergen held his daughter closely. "I know, Wolfgang, I know you are dependable. And I know I should not give her drugs. But she was in such a state that I was frightened." Mosca was surprised to see the look of love on Yergen's proud face, and the sadness and despair.

"Do you think Honny has some news yet?" Wolf asked. Yergen shook his head. "I don't think so, but, forgive me for saying this. I know you and Honny are very good friends. But if he does have news I am not so sure that he will tell it immediately."

Wolf smiled. "I know that. So I'm bringing Mosca to see him tonight, to convince him I have a man with five thousand cartons."

Yergen looked into Mosca's eyes and for the first time Mosca realized that Yergen was their accomplice, a partner. And he saw that in Yergen's eyes was a look of fascinated fear as if he were looking at someone he knew would perform an act of murder. For the first time he realized concretely the exact role his two partners had given him. He stared back at Yergen until Yergen bowed his head.

They left. Out in the street the blackness of the night had become thinner as if the moon had spread itself against the sky and diluted the shadows without giving light. Mosca felt refreshed, alert, and the cold wind cleared his head. He walked briskly beside Wolf. He lit a cigarette and the smoke was mellow and warm on his tongue. They were silent. Once Wolf said, "This is a long walk, but one more stop will end the night and we'll get treated good. Combine business with pleasure."

They took short cuts through ruined buildings until Mosca lost all sense of direction, and then suddenly they were in a street that seemed cut off from the rest of the city, a little village surrounded by a desert of rubble. Wolf stopped at the last house at the end of the street and gave a quick series of raps on the door.

It opened, and facing them stood a short, blond man, the front of his head completely bald, the golden hair covering the back and top of his head like a skullcap. He was very neatly dressed.

The German grasped Wolf's hand and said, "Wolfgang, just in time for a midnight snack." He let them in and bolted the door. He put his arm around Wolf's shoulder and hugged him. "Ah, it is good to see you. Come in." They went into a living room that was luxurious, with a china closet stuffed full of cut glass and tableware, the floor covered by rich, dark-red rugs. There was a wall of books and glowing yellow lamps and soft armchairs, and in one of the armchairs, her feet over a yellow hassock, sat a thick-bodied, thick-lipped woman with bright-red hair. She was reading a brightly covered American fashion magazine. The blond man said to her, "Here is our Wolfgang and the friend he told us about." She extended a limp hand to both of them. She let the magazine fall to the floor.

Wolf peeled off his coat and put his brief case on the chair beside him.

"So," he said to the blond man. "Any luck, Honny?"

"Ah," the woman said, "I think you are making a little joke with us. We have been able to find out nothing." She spoke to Wolf, but she looked at Mosca. Her voice was peculiarly sweet, softening the meaning of everything she said. Mosca lit a cigarette, feeling his face tighten with the desire she aroused in him with her look, the complete frankness of her eyes and the memory of her hand which had been burning hot when it touched his. And yet now, raising his eyes, watching her through the cigarette smoke, he saw that she was ugly; despite her careful disguise with make-up she could not hide her voracious mouth, the cruel tiny blue eyes.

"It is a true story," Wolf was saying. "I know. I need only to make contact with the right people. Whoever helps me with that contact will earn a pretty reward."

"And this really is your rich friend?" the blond man asked with a smile. Mosca noticed that his face was covered with large freckles, giving him a boyish look.

Wolf laughed and said, "There sits a man with five thousand cartons," burlesquing it but making his voice sound really envious. Mosca, enjoying himself, gave the two Germans a smile as if he already had a truck loaded with cigarettes outside the house. They smiled back at him. He thought, you kraut bastards, smile later.

The sliding door to the next room opened and there was another German, slight, in a dark business suit. Behind him Mosca could see a dining table set with snowy white tablecloth and napkins, gleaming silver, and tall, beautifully cut drinking glasses.

The blond man said, "Please join us in our late supper. On your business, Wolfgang, I cannot help. But surely, a man with such a fortune in cigarettes as your friend can give me a little business for other items besides scrip."

Mosca said gravely, "That is very possible." He smiled, and the others laughed as if he had made a very clever joke. They went into the dining room.

The servant brought in a platter on which was a large, dark-red ham such as was sold in American Army commissaries. On a silver dish there were evenly cut slices of fresh white American Army bread. It was still warm. Wolf buttered a piece, raised his eyebrows in complimentary astonishment and said, "I see yours is delivered even before it gets to the American commissary." The blond man made a gesture of delight, laughing meanwhile. The servant brought several bottles of wine and Mosca, very thirsty from the long walking and feeling much better, drank his glass down in one gulp. The blond man was amused and pretended to be pleased.

"Ah," he said, "a man to my taste. Not like you, Wolfgang, a cautious sipper and plodder. Now you see why he has five thousand cartons and you do not."

Wolf smiled back at him and said banteringly, "Superficial psychology, my friend, very superficial. You forget how I eat." And he started to help himself from the ham platter and then the long dish on which lay a dozen sticks of different kinds of wurst. From the cheese and salad dish he treated himself liberally and then looked at the blond man, saying, "Well, Honny, now what do you think? What can you say now?" Honny, his blue eyes sparkling with pleasure in his freckled face, almost shouted with great good humor, "I can only say one thing. Good appetite."

The red-haired woman laughed as did the rest of them and bent down to feed the huge dog lying beneath the table. She fed him an enormous slice of ham, and then from the servant took a large wooden bowl into which she poured a whole liter bottle full of milk. As she was bending, she let her hand slide carelessly along Mosca's leg and then pressed his thigh to lift herself again to a sitting position. She did it casually with no attempt at concealment.

"You're too fond of that dog," Honny said. "You really need children. They would be an interest."

"My dear Honny," she said, looking him straight in the face, "then you must change your tastes in love-making." But the sweetness of her voice flooded the words.

Honny murmured, "And that is too high a price to pay." He winked at Wolf. "Every man to his tastes, eh, Wolfgang?" Wolf nodded, continuing to chew on the enormous sandwich he had made for himself.

They ate and drank. Mosca, watchful, ate more and drank less. He felt fine. There was a long silence, then the woman snapped out of her moody trance and said with sudden verve, excitement, "Honny, shall we show them our treasure? Please?"

Wolf's face appeared alertly, comically, from behind his

sandwich. Honny laughed and said, "No, no, Wolfgang, there is no profit in this. And besides it is very late and perhaps you are too tired."

Trying not to sound eager, Wolf said cautiously, "Tell me what it is."

The blond man smiled at him. "There is no gain involved. This is a curiosity. In our back yard I am building a little garden. The house from the other side of the street is destroyed and part of it flowed over my property. I started to clear it away and I was enjoying the exercise. But then I found something very strange. I found a hole in the rubble and underneath it the basement is intact and the rest of the house has fallen into it. Now. This is interesting. By some freak some beams have fallen in such a way as to hold up the building and form a great room underneath." He smiled and the red freckles stood out like blood on his face. "I assure you it is unique. Would you care to go?"

"Sure," Mosca said and Wolf nodded his head with indifferent consent.

"You won't need your coats. It is just across the garden and once underneath it is very warm." But Wolf and Mosca took their belongings from the other room, not wanting to go out defenseless and not wanting Honny to know they carried weapons. Honny shrugged. "Wait till I get my flashlight and some candles. Will you come, Erda?" he asked the woman.

"Of course," the woman said.

The four of them went through what was to be the garden, the blond man using his flashlight to show the way. The garden was a square piece of hard ground bordered by a brick wall so low they could step over it with ease. They climbed a little hill of rubble and could see over the top of the house behind them, but a cloud hung veil-like before the moon, the city below was invisible. They descended into the valley formed by two mounds of shale and fragmented brick and came to the wall which supported and hedged in another heap of ruins.

The blond man crouched down. "Through here," he said, and showed a hole in the wall that looked as dark and opaque as a deep shadow. They entered in single file, the blond man first, then the woman, Wolf and Mosca.

Unexpectedly, when they had taken a few steps inside, they were going down steps. Honny called out a warning behind him.

At the end of the steps Honny waited. The woman lit two candles and gave one to Mosca.

By yellow candlelight they could see before them, below them, breaking away from the concrete on which they stood as the sea breaks away from cliffs, a great subterranean room, their candles lighting it as a lighthouse the ocean, leaving great depths of shadows. There was a shifting floor and sloping walls of rubble. Another staircase in the middle of the room led upward and disappeared, blotted out by the ruins which had fallen into it, as if someone had built stairs running blindly into a ceiling.

"This was an SS billet when they made a hit, your bombers. Just before the war ended," Honny said. "They have been buried now over a year. How glorious."

"There may be something valuable," Wolf said, "have you searched?"

"No," Honny said.

They dropped off the ledge, their feet sinking into the floor. The woman remained by the wall, resting against the end of a huge wooden beam, one end of which had fallen and jammed into the floor, the other end wedged against the ceiling. She held the candle high, and the three men spread out into the enormous room.

They moved cautiously, their feet dragging through a treacherous shale of glass, dirt and pulverized brick, like men wading through a swiftly moving stream. Sometimes when they hit a soft spot and sank alarmingly into the rubble their frantic scrambling was like treading water.

Before him Mosca saw a shiny, black boot. He picked it up, it was unexpectedly heavy. He realized there was a leg inside it, the top sealed off by a cover of pressed brick and stone glued together with blood and marrow of crushed bone. He let the boot drop and went to the farthest corner, sometimes sinking down through the rubble halfway to the knee. Near the wall he stumbled over a long body trunk with no head or neck or legs or arms. He pressed against it with his fingers, the black cloth unrecognizable, and inside it he felt flesh out of which all the fat and blood had been squeezed by the enormous pressure of the falling building. The flesh felt very firm against the bone, but he could feel the bonelike rock underneath. The two extremities of the trunk were sealed off in the same way as the boot.

There was nothing horrible in these remnants of human beings. No sight of blood or flesh. They had been so crushed that the clothing they wore had been pressed into the place of skin. The blood had been absorbed by the tons of brick turned to blotting dirt. Mosca kicked the rubble around a bit and, when his other foot began to sink, moved away hastily. Wolf was busy alone in a far corner, without illumination, almost invisible.

Suddenly Mosca felt oppressively warm. A hot dust rose in the air and a curious smell, like charred flesh, came from that dust, as if under the shifting floor, underground fires were raging all through the city, hidden by similar ruins.

"Give me a light," Wolf said from his corner. His voice was like a great hollow whisper. Mosca threw his lit candle across the room. It made a great arc of yellow flame and landed beside Wolf. He let it rest there.

They could see Wolf's shadow fumbling with a torso. The quiet voice of Honny said conversationally, "It is very curious that these bodies have no heads. There are six or seven I have found, some have a leg or arm, but none have heads. And why have they not decomposed?"

"Here," Wolf said, his voice reverberating now from the far corner, "I have something." He lifted up a leather holster in which hung a pistol. He drew the gun out of its holster and parts of it crumbled away and fell into the shale of the floor. Wolf flung the holster away from him and resumed his poking around, meanwhile speaking to the blond man.

"Like the mummies, those old mummies," he said. "All the stuff pressed into them. And maybe they were sealed off and the building just shifted so we could get in. And their heads were crushed right into the floor, into little bits, shreds, part of the floor we walk on here. I've seen that before." He had worked himself away from the candle and was now deep in the far corner and he said again, "Give me some light." The woman at the wall lifted her candle high and Wolf held something aloft so that the weak yellow ray would fall on it. At the same moment the blond man swung his flashlight toward him.

Wolf's scream was short, more one of surprise, the woman's hysterical, trilling off to a sob. Caught in the light of the flashlight and candle, was a gray hand, tremendously elongated fingers patinaed with paintlike dirt. The light of the candle fell away from it almost in the instant Wolf flung the hand away. They were silent, all now feeling the heat of the room, the oppressiveness of the air from the dust they had stirred from the shifting floor. Then Mosca said to Wolf teasingly, "Aren't you ashamed?"

The blond man laughed softly, but it echoed through the room. Wolf said apologetically, "I thought the goddamn thing was a rat."

The woman by the ledge said, "Let's go quickly, I need air," and as Mosca started to move toward her and the light, part of the wall shifted.

A wave of rubble swept him off his feet. His head fell against one of the torsos. His lips touched it and that touch told him there was no cloth over the body, but skin burned and charred hard as leather. Underneath that skin the body was hot as if already burning in hell. He pushed away with his hands and when he tried to rise a great black wave of vomit gushed out of his mouth. He heard the others moving to help and almost screamed, "Stay away from me. Stay away." He knelt, clutching great handfuls of the sharp fragments of glass and brick and bone and vomited out everything, the putrified food, the alcohol turned to bile. He could feel his hand stinging as the rubble cut into his flesh.

He was empty of everything. He rose. The woman helped him up to the ledge out of the room. By the light of the candle she held, he could see on her face a strangely distraught look of excitement and pleasure. She held on to the back of Mosca's short coat as they went up the stairs.

They came out into the cold night air and breathed deeply. "It is good to be alive," the blond man said. "That, below, that is the after death."

They climbed the little hill of rubble from the defile

they were standing in. The moon was out across the city and made it like a gray deserted fairyland, with wisps of fog and dust interlacing, spinning cobwebs to form a room above the earth, as if everyone were sleeping in a living death. Up the slope of the hill on which stood the *Polizeihaus* they could see the yellow light of a streetcar climbing slowly, and they could hear lightly on the winter air the soft, muted tone of its bell, cold and crystal clear. Mosca realized they must be quite close to his billet in the Metzer Strasse for he had seen this streetcar often at night, climbing the same hill, hearing the same bell.

The woman clung to the blond man as they stood there on the rubble heap and asked, "Will you come in for a drink?"

"No," Mosca said and to Wolf said, "Let's go home." He felt lonely and afraid, afraid of the people he was with including Wolf, afraid that something had happened to Hella alone in the billet. Now, completely sober, it seemed a very long time ago that he had left Eddie Cassin drunk and alone in the Rathskellar and started the long walking through the streets with Wolf.

He wondered if Eddie had made it home all right, and how late it was, surely long after midnight. And Hella would be waiting up for him, alone, reading on the couch. He thought for the first time with emotion of his mother and Alf and Gloria, of their letters that he hadn't read. For the first time he knew that the safety he imagined they felt, they did not feel; they dreamed in their own terror. Suddenly he felt they were all in danger, everyone that he knew, and that there was nothing he could do about it. He remembered his mother going to church and knew what he wanted to say to her that would explain everything and make him accept everything, because it was true. "We are not made in God's image," and that was all of it, and now he could go on living, trying hard to make himself happy and Hella too.

Tiredness washed everything out of his mind. He started down the hill of rubble his chin buried in the collar of his coat, feeling the cold, the ache in his bones, and as he and Wolf walked through the streets, the pale flooding light of the moon showed the wounds of the city as cruelly as the sun, but without color or pity, bloodlessly; as if it were a light shed by some lifeless and metal instrument, mirroring its own image in the earth, its own arid craters and lifeless scars.

13

THE BRILLIANT MORNING SUN of early spring washed the ruined city in colors of bright yellow and gold, glinting off smashed red brick; a light-blue sky curtained maimed and disfigured buildings on the horizon.

Yergen's daughter pushed the cream-colored baby carriage, her sad little face proud and happy, yet concerned; her pretty blue dress matched the sky. Yergen walked beside her, watching her, enjoying her happiness, sensing the coming alive of the great city after a long, terrible winter.

Coupled *Strassenbahnen* made a great clanging as they went through the streets, filling the golden morning air with a sound of bells. Turning into the Metzer Strasse, Yergen saw far down the street Mosca and his friends working on a jeep. Then he saw Hella standing under a tree. Coming closer he saw that Mosca, Leo and Eddie were loading the jeep with Mosca's possessions. There were suitcases and Val-packs full of clothing, a wooden box full of tinned food and a small coal stove which he, Yergen, had procured for them.

Yergen touched his daughter's shoulder. "Giselle, push the wagon right under their noses, surprise them." The little girl smiled happily and pushed faster. Hella saw them first and Yergen could hear her squeal of delight before she took a few awkward running steps to meet them.

"How do you like it?" Yergen asked with pride. "Isn't it every bit as good as I promised?"

"Oh, it is wonderful, Yergen, it's beautiful," Hella exclaimed. The thin, serene face had such a look of joy that Yergen was really and truly touched. He looked at the carriage again and saw that it was beautiful, low slung with lines like a racer, its lovely, creamy paint, framed by the green earth on which it rested and the light-blue sky above them.

"My daughter Giselle," Yergen said, "she wanted to bring it herself." The shy little girl bowed her head. Hella knelt clumsily, the loose overcoat she wore folding around her onto the earth. "Thank you very much," she said and kissed the little girl on the cheek. "Will you help me bring it to my new home?" The child nodded.

Mosca came over from the jeep. He was dressed in old, wrinkled sun tans. "I'll pay you later, Yergen," he said, barely glancing at the carriage. "We're moving over to Kurfürsten Allee. Why don't you walk over there with Hella and the carriage. We'll be there soon as we get loaded."

"Of course, of course," Yergen said. In high spirits he lifted his hat to Hella and said in German, "Dear lady, may I accompany you?" She smiled at him and took the arm he offered. They let the child go before them.

They walked into a spring breeze that smelled of flowers and grass, and Hella buttoned her coat. Yergen could see it stretch tight across the front of her stomach and felt an unaccountable content mixed with sadness. His own wife dead, his daughter without a mother, and now walking beside the mistress of the enemy, he thought of how it would be if Hella belonged to him, her tenderness and love given to him and his child and carrying a new life within her that would belong to both of them. How sweet it would be on this sweet morning, how the sadness and fear would wash away inside himself and how Giselle too would be safe. And as he thought this, Giselle turned her head to give them both a smile.

"She looks much better now," Hella said.

Yergen shook his head. "I am bringing her away to the country this very day. For a month. On the doctor's advice." Yergen slowed his walk so that Giselle would not hear what he said next. "I think she is very ill. It was a bad winter for her."

Giselle was far ahead of them now, pushing the carriage through a great patch of sunlight. Hella slipped her arm into Yergen's again. He said, "I must get her away from the ruins, anything that makes her think of her mother's death, away from Germany." He hesitated and then matter of factly, casually, as if repeating something he did not even remotely believe, "The doctor says she may become insane."

Giselle was waiting for them where the shade of the street began again, as if afraid of walking alone among the shadows of a tree. Hella walked ahead of Yergen so that she would come first to the little girl and said to her gaily, "Do you want to ride in the carriage?" Giselle nodded and Yergen helped her into it, letting her long legs dangle over the side. Hella pushed, saying laughingly, "Oh, what a big baby I have," tickling the child under the chin. Then she tried to run to make an impression of speed, but she was too awkward. Giselle didn't laugh, but she was smiling and making little sounds that were the shadows of laughter.

They came to a long row of white stone houses beaded along the Kurfürsten Allee. Hella stopped by the first house, by a little gate that barred a cemented path leading to the door. Hella called out, "Frau Saunders," and a woman appeared at the open window. She had a sad, stern face with the hair severely done, and they could see from the upper part of her body visible to them that she was wearing a plain black dress.

"Forgive me for calling out," Hella said smilingly. "I walk so badly now. Could you throw me the key, they will be here in a few minutes." The woman disappeared and then reappeared to drop the keys into Yergen's waiting hand. Then she disappeared again into the house.

"Oh. Oh," Yergen said, "you may have some trouble in that quarter. She looks very respectable." And then realizing what he had said, embarrassed, he paused, but Hella laughed and said, "She's very nice, she'll understand. She recently lost her husband with cancer. That's how she has two empty rooms. They had special privileges because of his illness."

"And how were you fortunate enough to find them?" Yergen asked.

"I went to the housing officer of the district and inquired," Hella said. "But first I offered a little present of five packs of cigarettes." They smiled at each other.

Yergen saw the loaded jeep coming down the Allee. Leo parked as he always did, bumping against a tree on the sidewalk. Mosca jumped down and Eddie and Leo got out of the front seats. They began to carry stuff into the house, Hella showing them the way. When Hella came out again, she had a large brown parcel which she handed to Yergen. "Ten cartons," she said, "is that right?" Yergen nodded. Hella went to Giselle who was now leaning against the carriage. She took from her coat pocket a handful of chocolate bars and gave them to the child, saying, "Thank you for bringing me such a beautiful carriage. Will you come to see me when the baby comes?" Giselle nodded her head and handed the chocolate to Yergen. He took one and broke it into small pieces so that she could hide them in her hand as she ate. Then as Hella watched them walk down the Kurfürsten Allee she saw Yergen stop to pick up his daughter, she holding the brown parcel balanced on his shoulder. Hella went back into the house and climbed the flight of stairs to the second floor.

The floor consisted of a four-room apartment; a bedroom, a living room, then another bedroom and a small room that was to be made into a kitchen. Mosca and Hella, it was understood, were to have the small bedroom and the kitchen and were to be allowed to use the living room on special occasions. Frau Saunders had her bedroom and a stove in the living room to do her cooking.

Hella found Mosca, Leo and Eddie waiting for her. There were two bottles of Coke and two glasses of whiskey on the small table. The bedroom was cluttered with suitcases and everything else they had brought. Hella noticed that Frau Saunders had hung pretty blue-flowered curtains on both windows.

Mosca lifted his glass, Hella and Leo lifted their bottles of Coke. Eddie was already sipping his whiskey, but then waited for them.

"To our new home," Hella said. They all drank together. Eddie Cassin watched Hella take one sip from her Coke and then open the suitcases to put her clothes away in a great mahogany dresser.

He had never made his play for Hella, though he had been in Mosca's room alone with her many times. He wondered why and he realized that partly she had never given him the opportunity. She had never moved close to him, or given him any sort of opening, verbally or physically. She had no coquetry. And all in a very natural manner that was not provoking. He realized that it was partly his fear of Mosca, and trying to analyze that fear, he thought it was grounded in his knowledge of Mosca's carelessness of other people and the stories he had heard about Mosca from some other men in the outfit, a fight he had had with a Sergeant for which he had been transferred to Military Government and for which he had just escaped court-martial. The Sergeant was so badly hurt that he was sent back to a hospital in the States. But it was a queer story, hushed up, and just rumors. Basically it was the carelessness, a lack of interest so complete that it was frightening. His friends, Eddie thought, myself, Leo, Wolf, Gordon, we think we're his buddies. If we were all killed tomorrow he wouldn't give a good goddamn.

"The carriage," Hella exclaimed suddenly, "where did you put the carriage?"

They all laughed. Leo clapped his hands to his head and said in German, "My God, I left the wagon in the street." But Mosca said quickly, "It's in the small room, Hella, the kitchen." And Eddie Cassin thought, he can't even stand to see her anxious as a joke.

Hella went into the other room. Leo finished up his Coke. "The next week I leave for Nuremberg," he said. "They want me to testify about those people who were guards and officials at Buchenwald. At first I said no, but then they told me a certain doctor was among the defendants. He is the one who used to tell us, 'I am not here to cure your aches and pains. I am not even here to keep you alive. My job is to see that you are able every day to work.' That bastard I will testify against."

Mosca filled the glasses again and gave Leo a fresh bottle of Coke. "If I were in your shoes I'd want to kill those bastards."

Leo shrugged. "I don't know. I have only contempt but no hatred any more. I don't know why. I just want to get out of here." He took a long slug from his Coke.

"We'll miss you at the billet, Walter," Eddie said. "How do you think you'll like living kraut style?"

Mosca shrugged. "It's all the same." He filled Eddie's glass, then said. "Scram, Eddie, after that one. I don't want you scaring the hell out of my new landlady. No more drinks."

"I've reformed," Eddie Cassin said. "My wife is coming from England with the kid." He looked at them with mock pride. "My family is coming to join me."

Mosca shook his head. "Poor dame, I thought she gave up when you were in the Army. What the hell are all your chippies going to do?"

"They'll get along," Eddie said. "Don't worry about them, they always get along." Suddenly, unreasonably, he was angry. "I'd like to give 'em all a boot in the ass." He took his jacket and left.

Eddie Cassin went down the Kurfürsten Allee, walking slowly. The curved, tree-shaded avenue was pleasant in the warmth of the early spring afternoon. He decided to take a shower in the billet and then go on for supper at the Rathskellar. He glanced across the Allee before he turned into the Metzer Strasse, a flash of color attracting his eye, and there he saw a young girl standing underneath a wide, green tree, four little children dancing around her. Across the broad avenue he could see the delicate lines of her face, the purity of youth in them. As he watched, she lifted her head to the yellow light of the afternoon sun and turning away from the children looked directly at Eddie Cassin.

He saw on her face that smile which, in its innocence and instinctive knowledge of sexual power, always excited him. It was a smile of youth, Eddie thought, a smile they wear when being flattered, and yet innocent, curious, wondering what the power really was that they possessed, and a little excited. To Eddie Cassin it denoted virginity, a virginity of mind, of body too, but primarily a mental innocence which he had seen and corrupted before, the struggle and courtship sweeter to him than the actual taking.

Now staring across the street, he was moved to a sadness that was sweet, and also a wonder that this young girl in her white blouse could move him so. He hesitated to go to her; he was unshaven, dirty, and he could smell his own sweat. Hell, I can't screw 'em all, he thought, knowing that across the broad avenue, even in the bright sunlight, she could only see the delicate cut of his features and not the fine lines of age. What would seem to her old age, decay.

She had turned to the children, and that graceful, youthful motion of her head and body, the picture they made as they all sat on the green carpet of grass, burned into his brain. Under that dark-green tree, the young girl in her white shirt, the white sleeves rolled up nearly to her shoulder, the two bulges of white cloth that were her breasts, her golden head bending over the seated children, these were not to be borne. He strode quickly away down the Metzer Strasse and into the billet.

Eddie showered and shaved and found himself hurrying, but he paused long enough to put a great deal of sweet-smelling talcum powder over his body and face. He combed his hair carefully, regretting its grayness on the sides, and in his room put on his olive-green officer's uniform with the civilian patch, knowing that he would not appear as old in her eyes in these as he would in civilian clothing.

There was a knock on the door and Frau Meyer came in. She was in a bathrobe. It was an old trick of hers. When she knew Eddie was bathing she would bathe also, and smelling sweetly of perfume come to the room as he was dressing. Usually it would work.

"Have you a cigarette for me, Eddie?" she asked and sat on the bed and crossed her legs. Eddie, tying his shoelaces, motioned toward the table. She took a cigarette, lit it, and sat again on the bed.

"You look very handsome, are you seeing someone?"

Eddie stopped for a moment, surveyed the almost-perfect body, the pleasant, buck-toothed face. It was known. He lifted her off the bed, carried her out of the room and set her down in the hall. "Not today, baby," he said and ran down the stairs and out of the building. There was a tremendous excitement and exultation in him, a quivering of the heart. He trotted up the Metzer Strasse, slowing to a quick walk as he came to the corner and, puffing a little, turned into the Kurfürsten Allee.

As far as he could see, the trees along the Allee stood all alone, no children underneath them. The strip of grass was a continuous green line with no foreign body to mar its harmony with the trees above it. His eye singled out the exact spot in the row opposite him and it was as if it were a picture hanging on his wall, familiar, known every day, out of which the human figures he had always seen had magically faded. Eddie Cassin crossed the Allee and went to the nearest house. He knocked on the door and inquired in bad German about the girl taking care of four children, but no one knew anything about her, in that house or the others. The last house was an apartment billet for American civilians and the man who answered the door Eddie recognized as someone he had seen often at the Rathskellar. "No," the man said, "she doesn't come from this street. The guys in here are laying all the dames in the block, and I know them all. I felt like going out myself. You're out of luck, fella." And he grinned sympathetically at Eddie Cassin.

He stood in the center of the Allee, not knowing which way to go. The spring evening fell upon him, fresh breezes blowing away the afternoon heat. On the other side of the Allee and beyond it, he could see the gardens with their newly sprouting green, the even patches and the mottled brown wooden and paper huts in which the gardeners kept their tools and in which some of them lived. He could see some men working in that small, farmlike area, and he could smell the river behind the hill which rose above the gardens. Patched through the rubble and from the sides of ruined houses he could see wild little streaks of dark green. He knew he would never see the girl again and would not recognize her if he did, but suddenly the exhilaration returned and he started the long walk down the whole length of the Kurfürsten Allee until it ended where the city ended and he could see the country unmarked, the slightly rolling, restful hills, the moist green of spring over them like fresh-grown skin; and where no blemish of gray and blackened ruins could mar the beauty of the day.

That evening Hella tacked the woodcut illustrations of fairy tales on the walls. She had bought them for the coming child, she said, but Mosca felt that it was some sort of superstition, a magic that would make everything go well. When she finished she said, "I think we should go in to see Frau Saunders."

"Christ, I'm too tired tonight," Mosca said. "We did a hell of a lot of work."

Hella sat still on the bed, her hands folded, inspecting the almost square room. The cream-colored carriage rested against one light blue flowered curtain, looking like a picture on a wall. There was a blue cloth on a small round table, and the two chairs were upholstered in light gray. On the floor was a maroon rug, faded with age. Bed and dresser were both mahogany, and on each wall there was a small painting of a country scene in light greens, violets, blues and the white silvers of running streams. A great surge of joy went through her body. Then she noticed Mosca's face set, strained, and she knew he felt uneasy. She took his hand and held it in her lap. "Now it seems really true, that we'll always be together."

"Let's go in and pay our respects to the landlady," Mosca said.

All the rooms had doors that opened on the hall, and the hall itself had a door that locked the floor off from the stairs. To go from one room to the other they had to go out in the hall and knock on the door of the living room. They heard a voice telling them to come in.

Frau Saunders was sitting on the sofa reading a newspaper. She stood up when Hella introduced them and shook Mosca's hand. Mosca saw that she was not as old as he had thought from the glimpse he had had of her. The hair was severely done and her face was lined, but there was a curious youthfulness in the movements of her lanky body, in its straight flowing black.

"I hope you will feel free to use the living room whenever you wish," Frau Saunders said. She had a low, sweet voice but she said the words out of politeness.

"Thank you," Hella said. "I wanted to thank you for the curtains and the extras you put in the rooms. If there is anything we can help you in, please tell us."

Frau Saunders hesitated. "I hope only that there will be no trouble with the authorities." She gave Mosca a doubtful glance as if she wished to say something else.

Hella guessed what it was. "We're very quiet people, he's not one of these wild Americans always giving parties." She smiled at Mosca but he did not smile in return. "We just came in for a few minutes," Hella went on, "we had a hard day, so—" She rose and they said good night awkwardly, Mosca giving a polite smile, Frau Saunders giving the same smile in return, and in that moment Mosca realized that this woman was shy despite her age, and that she was a little frightened by the thought of the enemy living in her home.

As they undressed in their room Mosca told Hella a bit of news he had almost forgotten. "Orders finally came in to ship the Middletons back to the States. They leave next week."

Hella was surprised. "Oh, that is too bad," she said.

"Don't worry," Mosca said, "I can get some other people's commissary cards, and we can trade out in the country like real Germans."

In bed Hella said, "So that is why you looked so worried today." Mosca didn't say anything. After she had fallen asleep he lay awake for a long time.

He felt strange that now, finally, as if this had been the purpose behind everything, he lived as one of the enemy. The house was full of Germans and the houses in the streets around him; in his bed, carrying his child. He missed the sound of parties that went on in the billet, the throbbing of jeep motors, radios tuned to the Armed Forces Network giving out American music. Here all was still. The bathroom in the hall gave a small sudden roar of water. Frau Saunders, he thought, and then had to get up and go himself, waiting a little to give the woman plenty of time to get back to her own room. Then he stood by the curtained window, smoking a cigarette, trying to see in the darkness outside. He tried to think back to when he had been given his first weapon, his first steel helmet, his first combat orientation lecture to protect himself against the enemy. But that now too seemed unreal and unimportant. What finally was real was this room, the carriage, the woman in the bed.

14

THE EVENING before the Middletons were to leave Germany, Hella and Mosca went for a walk through the city before visiting them. Leaving the house on the Kurfürsten Allee, Hella stopped to say good evening to the women in their doorways. Mosca stood by her patiently, a polite smile on his face.

They began the walk to the center of town. "Let's get Frau Saunders some ice cream from the Red Cross Club," Hella said. Mosca looked at her.

"You two sure became awful good buddies in a week," he said. "What goes on anyway? I know you give her part of your meals and some of the sugar and coffee we have. When the Middletons leave you'll have to get stingy, baby. That stuff will be hard to get."

She gave him an amused smile. "If I thought you really cared I wouldn't do it. I know it's just that you want me to have everything. But I can't do it, Walter. When I cook some meat the smell fills the whole hall, and I think of her in the living room with just dry potatoes. Besides I'm too fat. Look at me."

"That's not from eating," Mosca said. She laughed and gave him a push. He grinned at her and said. "But you're pretty big. At least now you can't wear my shirts any more." She had on a blue maternity dress Ann Middleton had given her.

They walked along, Mosca holding her arm when they had to climb over rubble that overflowed onto the walk. The trees were all heavy with leaves and the rays of the setting sun only occasionally glanced over them. Hella said thoughtfully, "Frau Saunders is really fine. You wouldn't think it to look at her, but she is a lot of fun to talk to and she does nearly all my work for me. And not because I give her things, she really wants to help. Will you get her some ice cream?"

Mosca laughed and said, "Sure."

She had to wait outside while he went in to the Red Cross Club. On the way back they went by the *Polizeihaus* and on the outskirts of the Contrescarpe park below they were blocked off by a small crowd listening to a man standing on a park bench. He was lecturing, waving his arms, shouting. They paused. Mosca shifted the cold box of ice cream to his right hand and Hella leaned on his shoulder.

"The guilt is on every one of us," the man was shouting. "This godless age, this godless land. Who thinks of Christ, of Jesus? We accept his blood as our salvation and do not believe. But I tell you, I tell you, his blood has washed away so many sins, that blood is weary, the Lord God is weary of our ways. How much longer will he be patient? How much longer will the blood of Jesus save us?" He paused and his voice became soft, pleading. "The love of Jesus is no longer enough, the blood of Jesus is no longer enough. Please believe me. Save yourselves and me and our children and our wives, our mothers, our fathers, sisters, brothers and our country." His voice became calm, factual, reasonable, and his body relaxed. He spoke conversationally.

"You see this land in ruins, the continent, and Christ sees further than we, he sees a destruction of soul universal, evil triumphant, Satan looking over the world in glee, seeing with his laughing eyes the death of man and everything man has done since the beginning of time."

A plane passed overhead on its way to the air base. The roar of the motor made him stop. He was a small man with a pouter-pigeon chest accentuated by the way he threw back his head to glare with his rolling, brilliant, birdy eyes. He went on.

"Picture to yourself a world innocent of life. In the polar regions the snow and ice everywhere untracked, unmoved upon. In Africa, in the jungles, where the sun gives, from God, innumerable and diverse forms of creation, there everything is still." The voice now was madly rhetorical, pompous, the brilliant eyes bulging from his small head. "The carcasses of dead beasts lie putrifying in the rotting vegetation. On China's plains, by the fertile rivers, not even the crocodile lifts his grinning head to return the leer of Satan. And in our cities, in the many hearts of what is known as civilization, there is nothing but ruins. Hills of stone out of which no life will ever grow, a soil of broken glass. For eternity."

He stopped and waited for a sign of approval but instead a surprising shout rose from different parts of the crowd. "Where is your permit? Where is your permission from Military Government?" Three or four male voices could be heard shouting this. The preacher was stunned.

Hella and Mosca found themselves standing now almost in the middle of the crowd, a pile of people bunched up behind them. On their left was a young man dressed in a blue, washed-out shirt and heavy working trousers. He carried in his arms a pretty girl of six or seven whose eyes were curiously blank and whose sleeve on the side facing them was pinned to her flowered frock. On their right was an old worker puffing a stubby pipe. The young man was shouting with the others, "Where is your permit, where is your permission from Military Government?" Then he turned to Mosca and the old worker and said, "We're bawled out by everybody now that we've lost, even by swine like this." Mosca, in civilian clothes, smiled at Hella, amused that he had passed as German.

Now the preacher pointed his arm slowly toward the sky and said in a great solemn voice, "I have permission from our Creator." The sun, red with its last, dying fire bathed the upraised arm with crimson light. The sun began to sink below the earth, and gray in the soft summer twilight, springing up on the horizon like a great ragged circle of spears, the ruins of the city rose like magic before their eyes. The preacher bowed his head in thanksgiving.

He raised his head to the sky. He embraced them all with a sweep of his arms. "Come back to Jesus Christ," he shouted, "Come Back to Jesus. LEAVE YOUR SINS BEHIND. LEAVE THE DRINKING. LEAVE THE FORNICATION. RENOUNCE THE GAMBLING, THE PRIDE FOR WORLDLY SUCCESS. BELIEVE IN JESUS AND BE SAVED. BELIEVE IN JESUS AND BE SAVED. YOU HAVE BEEN PUNISHED FOR YOUR SINS. THE PUNISHMENT IS BEFORE YOUR EYES. REPENT BEFORE IT IS TOO LATE. SIN NO MORE."

The deafening voice stopped for breath. The crowd was stunned, rolled back by the great volume of sound from that little man. He returned to a normal shout.

"Each one of you, think of the lives you led before the war, are you not to believe that the suffering, the ruin you see is God's punishment for the sins you committed then?

"And now the young girls fornicate with enemy soldiers,

the young men beg for cigarettes. Puff Puff." He blew out imaginary smoke with maniacal hatred. "On our Sabbath people go to the country to steal or bargain for food. The house of the Lord is empty. We invite destruction. Repent, I say again. Repent. Repent." The words began to run together, hysterically. "Believe in the Lord Jesus Christ Believe in the Lord the one and only God Believe in the One Lord Believe in Christ."

He paused and then in a threatening and scolding voice shouted at them. Harshly. Accusingly. "You are all sinners, you are all condemned to everlasting hell. I see some of you smile. You pity yourselves. Why should God make us suffer so? You ask that?"

Someone in the crowd shouted mockingly, "It wasn't God, it was the Ami bombers." The crowd laughed. The man on the bench waited for them to be still and then peering through the failing light, savagely, vindictively, he pointed to a woman wearing black. "You, woman, do you laugh at God? Where is your husband, your children?" He pointed to the young man beside Mosca. "Look," he said to the crowd and they all turned and followed that pointing finger. "There is another scoffer, one of the young men, the hope of Germany. For HIS sins his child is mutilated and he laughs at the wrath of God. Wait, scoffer, in your child's face I see another punishment. Wait. Look at your child and wait." With spite and malice he pointed out other members of the crowd.

The young man with the child set her down and said to Hella, "Please look after her." Then they could see him push through to where the preacher stood on his bench, break through to the open space. With one violent blow he struck the little preacher to the ground. He knelt on the preacher's chest, grabbed a handful of hair and slammed the bird-shaped head against the cement walk. Then he rose.

The crowd dispersed. The young man picked up his child and walked into the Contrescarpe park. As if by magic most of the people had disappeared. The preacher lay still and alone in the falling twilight.

Some men helped him up. There was blood running out of his thick curly hair, many tiny rivers flowed down his forehead to form a red mask over his face. Hella had turned away and Mosca took her arm and walked her down the street. He saw that she looked ill, the sight of blood, he thought. "You'd better stay home with Frau Saunders tonight." And then, as if he owed her an excuse for not interfering, he said, "It's not our business."

Mosca, Leo and Eddie Cassin sat around the Middleton living room. The household furniture belonged to the requisitioned house so there were still chairs to sit on. Everything else was packed in wooden crates lined against the wall.

"So you're really going to the Nuremberg trials tomorrow?" Gordon asked Leo. "What time are you leaving?"

"Oh, in the evening," Leo said. "I would rather drive at night."

"Give it to the bastards when you get there," Ann Middleton said. "Lie if you have to but make sure they all get what's coming to them."

"I won't have to lie," Leo said. "My memory is very good."

"I want to apologize about the way I acted the last time you were here," Gordon Middleton said. "I'm afriad I was very rude."

Leo waved his hand. "No, I understand. My father was

a political prisoner, a Communist. My mother was Jewish, that is why I was sent away. But my father was a political. Of course, after the Stalin-Hitler pact he lost his faith. He realized one was no better than the other."

The Professor, who was sitting in a corner by the chess table and had a polite smile of interest on his face, became frightened by this tactless remark. He saw, with panic and embarrassment, the anger rising in Gordon Middleton and did not wish to witness a scene of verbal violence. All violence distressed him. "I must go," he said. "I have an appointment to give a lesson." He shook hands with Gordon and Ann. "Allow me to wish you a good trip to America and good fortune. I have been very happy to know you."

Gordon escorted him to the door and said earnestly, "I hope you won't forget to write me, Professor. I'm depending on you to tell me what happens to Germany." The Professor nodded his head. "Certainly, certainly." He had already decided not to communicate in any way with Gordon Middleton. Any tie with a Communist, however innocent, could in the unpredictable future do him great harm.

"Wait a minute, wait a minute," Gordon led the Professor back into the room. "Leo, I just remembered the Professor is going to Nuremberg the end of the week. Can you give him a lift or would that be against your outfit's regulation?"

"No, no," the Professor said in great agitation. "That is not necessary, please."

"It's no trouble," Leo said.

"No," the Professor said, and now he was almost hysterically frightened. "I have my train tickets, everything is arranged. Please, I know it would be too much trouble for you."

"O.K., Professor, O.K.," Gordon said soothingly, and took him to the door.

When Gordon came back into the room, Mosca asked, "What the hell did he get so excited about?"

Gordon glanced at Leo. "He's a very correct man. His son is under arrest as a minor war criminal, I don't know exactly what, except that he's being tried by a German court, not the occupation so it can't be too bad. I guess he was horrified that Leo might find out and think it was something to do with the concentration camps, which of course it couldn't be. You don't mind do you, Leo?"

"No," Leo said.

"I'll tell you what," Gordon said. "I'll go to his place tomorrow, I'll have time. I'll say you'll pick him up tomorrow night. Once he knows you know, he'll be willing. Is that O.K.?"

"Sure," Leo said, "it is very nice you should worry so about that old man."

Ann Middleton looked at him sharply, but there was no irony on Leo's hawklike face. He was sincere. She smiled. "Gordon always takes care of his converts," she said.

"I haven't converted him, Ann," Gordon drawled in his slow, even voice, "but I think I've put a few ideas in his head. He listens." Gordon paused and in a calm tone in which there was a gentle reproof he said. "I don't think 'convert' is the right word to use." They were all silent.

"When do you think you'll be back," Mosca asked Leo.

Leo grinned at him. "Don't worry, I won't miss it."

"Miss what?" Ann Middleton asked.

"I'm going to be a godfather," Leo said. "I already have the present."

"It's a shame I won't be here to see the child when it

comes," Ann said. "Too bad Hella couldn't be here tonight. I hope she isn't too ill."

"No," Mosca said. "She just took too long a walk this evening. She wanted to come but I told her she'd better not."

"After all, we're not that important, Walter," Ann said jokingly but with a touch of malice. Eddie Cassin in his corner armchair opened his eyes. He had dozed off. Visiting married couples was something he hated. He nearly always detested wives when they were with their husbands and in their own homes. And he disliked Ann Middleton. She was plain, she was strong willed, and she treated him with contempt.

Mosca was grinning at her. "You know damn well I'm right."

"It just irritates her that you aren't concerned about other people," Gordon said. "I wish I could be like that sometimes."

Mosca said, "Gordon, maybe I'm being out of line but I'll take a chance. Everybody around the base knows that you're being sent home because you held a Communist party card. I don't know anything about politics. I was a kid when I went into the Army. I guess in some ways I still am. What I'm trying to say is this. I have a lot of respect for you because you have guts. You know things are screwed up. I think you're wrong because I wouldn't trust anybody who can make me do what he wants, no matter what the reason is. That includes the United States Army, the Communist party, Russia, that fat bastard of a Colonel, right on down the line." He turned to Eddie Cassin. "What the hell am I trying to say?"

Eddie said dryly, "That you like him even if you didn't let Hella come." They all laughed.

Gordon didn't. His long Yankee face expressionless, he said to Mosca. "Since you've spoken maybe I can say somethink I've always wanted to say to you before, Walter." He paused a moment, rubbed his great, bony hands together. "I know how you feel or think I do, and maybe you can't help yourself. You say I'm wrong, but I have a belief I can hold no matter what happens. I believe in the human race, that life on earth can be extraordinarily beautiful. I believe that this can be accomplished through the efforts of the Communist party. You build everything on a few people you care about. Believe me that is a fallacious way of life."

"Yeah? Why?" Mosca bowed his head and when he raised it to look at Gordon there were dark-red spots of anger on his face.

"Because those people and you yourself are controlled by forces that you refuse to concern yourself with. You exercise no free will when you fight on your level, in your narrow circle, your little, personal, arena. When you do that you put those people you care about in terrible danger."

Mosca said, "This talk about controlling forces that affect my life. Christ, don't you think I know about it? I don't believe anything can help. But nobody is going to move me around, make me think one thing one day, and then, all of a sudden, bang on the other side we go. I don't care if it's right or wrong. Every day some kraut at the air base or in the billet or working in the Rathskellar tells me how happy he'll be when we march together against the Russians and expects me to give him a cigarette. And on the other side I guess it's the same. You know what I'm glad about?" He leaned over the table at Gordon, his face flushed with excitement and liquor. "That this time there's a good chance of everything going up in smoke. Everybody gets it up the ass."

"Hey, hey," Ann Middleton applauded, clapping her hands. Eddie Cassin was laughing and said, "Jesus Christ, what a speech." Leo seemed shocked. Mosca burst out laughing and said to Gordon. "Look what you made me do."

Gordon had been smiling too, thinking how he always forgot how young Mosca was, and was always surprised when that youthful, immature sincerity flashed through Mosca's reserve. And trying to help he said, "How about Hella, then, and your kid?"

Mosca didn't answer. Ann got up to fill their glasses. Leo said, "He doesn't mean what he says." And then Mosca, as if he had not heard, said to Gordon, "I make myself responsible." And only Eddie Cassin felt that he had said these words as dogma, something he would have to live by. Mosca smiled at them and said it jokingly this time. "I make myself responsible." He shook his head. "Who can do better than that?"

"And how is it you don't feel that way?" Ann Middleton asked Leo.

"I don't know," Leo said. "I went to Buchenwald when I was quite young, and I met my father there and we were for a long time together. And people are different. Besides Walter is changing. I caught him bowing, actually bowing good evening to his German neighbors."

The others laughed, but Mosca said impatiently, "How a guy can spend eight years in a concentration camp and come out the way you did I'll never understand. If I were you and a kraut looked at me crosswise I'd send him to the hospital. And every time he gave me an answer I didn't like I'd kick him in the balls."

"Please, please," Ann said in mock horror.

"Too bad about you," Mosca said, but he grinned at her. She had used worse language cursing black-market operators who had cheated her.

Leo said slowly. "You forget I am part German. And the things the Germans did, they did not because they were Germans but because they were human beings. My father told me that. And then I am having a good time, I live a new life, it would poison that life if I were cruel to other people."

"You're right, Leo," Gordon said. "We need a more intellectual approach, not emotional reactions. We have to reason, to change the world by logical action. The Communist party believes in that."

There was no doubting his sincerity, the purity of his belief.

Leo gave him a long look. "I know one thing only about communism. My father was a Communist. The camps could never crush his spirit. When the word came into the camp that Hitler and Stalin had signed a pact, my father died easily afterward."

"And if that pact was necessary to save the Soviet Union?" Gordon asked. "If that pact was necessary to save the world from the Nazis?"

Leo bowed his head and put his hand up to his face to hold the muscles tight and stop the tic. "No," he said, "if my father had to die that way the world isn't worth saving. That is emotional, I know, not your intellectual approach the party favors."

In the silence that followed they could hear the baby crying upstairs. "I'll go change him," Gordon said. His wife gave him a grateful smile.

When he had left Ann said, "Don't mind him," to Leo,

keeping the tone of her voice absolutely without inflection so that she could not be thought disloyal. She went out into the kitchen to make coffee.

When the evening ended everyone shook hands all around. Ann said, "I'll drop around tomorrow to say goodbye to Hella." And Gordon said to Leo, "Don't forget the Professor, Leo, will you?" Leo nodded. Gordon added slowly and sincerely. "I wish you luck."

Gordon locked the door behind them and went back into the living room. He found Ann sitting thoughtfully in her chair. "I want to talk to you, Gordon," she said.

Gordon smiled at her. "Well, here I am, talk." He felt a sharp pang of fear. But he could talk to Ann without becoming angry when they discussed politics, even though she never agreed with him.

Ann got up and walked nervously up and down the room. Gordon watched her face. He loved the broad, honest planes, the blunt nose and the pale-blue eyes. She was a pure Saxon type, he thought, and yet she looked almost Slavic. He wondered if there were any connection. He would have to read up on it.

Her words smashed against his mind. She said, "You'll have to give it up, you will just have to give it up."

"Give up what?" Gordon asked innocently.

"You know what," she said. And the shock of understanding, the pain that she should say such a thing, was so great that there was no anger in him, only a sinking in his stomach, a despairing hopelessness. When she saw his face she came and knelt beside his chair, and it was only when they were alone that she relinquished her strength, that she was tender, supplicating. She said, "I'm not angry you lost this job because you were a Communist. But what are we going to do? We have to think of our child. You have to be able to work and earn money, Gordon. And the way you lose all your friends when you get so angry about politics. We can't live like this, darling, we just can't."

Gordon rose from his chair and moved away from her. He was profoundly shocked, not so much that she was capable of saying such a thing but that she knew him so little, the human being closest to him. That she could think he would leave the party as one would give up tobacco or a special food. But he had to answer her.

"I'm thinking of our child," Gordon said. "That's why I'm a Communist. How would you like to have him grow up and suffer what Leo went through or become someone like Mosca who cares nothing for his fellow human beings? I didn't like the way he talked in front of you, but he doesn't care about that though he professes to be fond of me. I want our son to grow up in a healthy society that won't send him to wars or concentration camps. I want him to grow up in a moral society. That's what I'm fighting for. And you know that our society is corrupt, Ann, you know it."

Ann rose to face him. She was no longer tender or supplicating. She spoke to him factually. "You don't believe anything bad that has been written about Russia. I believe some of it, enough of it. They won't make my son safe. I have faith in my own country, as people have faith in their brothers and sisters. You always say that is nationalistic. I don't know. You're prepared to make sacrifices for what you believe in, but I'm not prepared to have our child suffer for your beliefs. And Gordon if I thought you fitted in with them I wouldn't try to make you stop. But what happened to Leo's father is exactly what will happen to you. I felt that when he told us, and I felt he told us for that reason, to warn you. Or even worse, you'll become corrupt.

You have to quit, you just have to quit." Her broad-planed face was stubborn and he knew that stubbornness to be invincible.

"Let me see if we understand each other," Gordon said slowly. "You want me to get a good job, live like a good middle-class citizen and not place my future in jeopardy by remaining in the party. Is that correct?"

She didn't answer and he went on. "I know your motives are irreproachable. Basically we both agree. We want to do the best thing for our son. We disagree on method. The security you want for him is only a temporary one, a security at the mercy of the capitalists who run the country. My way, we fight for a permanent security, a security that can't be shattered by a few members of the ruling class. Don't you see?"

"You'll have to give it up," Ann said stubbornly. "You'll just have to give it up."

"And if I can't?"

"If you don't promise to give it up—" Ann paused and composed herself to say the words, "I'll go back to England with the baby instead of to America."

They were both frightened by what she had finally said, then Ann went on in a low voice close to tears. "I know you'll keep your promise once you've made it. You see, I trust you." And for the first time since they had been together Gordon was truly angry with her, because he knew her faith was justified; he had never lied to her, never broken a promise. His New England conscience had always functioned in personal relationships. And now she was using his honesty to trap him.

"Let me get this straight," Gordon said deliberately. "If I don't promise to leave the party, you'll take our son and go to England. You'll leave me." He kept the pain and anger out of his voice. "If I do promise, you will come to the States with me." Ann nodded her head.

"You know that's not a fair thing to do," Gordon said, and he couldn't hide the pain. He walked over to the chair and sat down again. Calmly and patiently he sorted out everything in his mind. He knew Ann meant what she said. He knew he never could give up the party, that he would only grow to hate her if he did, and he knew he could not give her and the child up, possibly her but not the baby.

"I promise," he said, and he knew he lied. And when she came to him, her face flooding with tears of relief, and knelt and put her head in his lap, he felt for her pity and compassion and felt also a sense of dread for what he had done. For he had full knowledge of his deed, that once in America it would take her some time to discover his deception, and once she had discovered it she would not have the money or the will to go back to England. Their roots in each other would be too strong. He knew that for both of them their lives would now be mixed with hate and distrust and contempt and that for the rest of their years there would be a struggle between them. But there was nothing he could do. He stroked her coarse and heavy hair, which always excited him, as did her sturdy peasant body. He turned her heavy-planed almost Slavic face upward so that he could kiss it through the tears.

He thought, there was nothing I could do, and the kiss he gave her was painful to him.

15

IN TWILIGHT, the ruins of Nuremberg had a quiet grandeur, as if all this destruction was a thing of long ago, and by forces of nature—fire, earthquakes, centuries of rain and sun—and parts of it were tarry black as if the earth had been bled, and caked lava had formed enormous mounds.

Leo drove through it and for the first time found pleasure in the sight of this desolation. In the suburbs he stopped in front of a little, square white-painted house absolutely identical with the houses beside it. He hoped the Professor was ready; he was anxious to leave Nuremberg, glad to leave the trial behind him. He had given his testimony honestly, factually, against the guards and the *kapos* he had known. He had met some of his old friends, old inmates, and shared their grim satisfaction in this long-awaited vengeance. But curiously enough he had disliked being with his former comrades, as if they had not been victims but had all participated in some shameful act in which they all now felt an equal guilt. He tried to reason this out and knew that he did not wish to be with people who remembered and shared the degradation, the terror, the hopeless misery of his life in that time. And just a face associated with that life made it real again. He pressed the horn of his jeep and shattered the evening stillness.

Almost immediately he saw the Professor's small, slight

figure leave the house and come down the walk toward the jeep. He had a little surprise for the Professor, Leo thought grimly, but he made an effort to be polite. "Did you have a good visit with your son?" he asked.

"Yes, yes," the Professor said, "a very nice visit." He said the words politely, listlessly. He looked ill, dark circles pouched beneath his eyes, an almost bloodless mouth and gray skin.

Leo drove slowly so that they could talk, the slight breeze pleasant against his face. Later he would go at the fullest speed and then because of the rushing night wind they would not be able to speak. He took a pack of cigarettes from his shirt pocket with his right hand, controlling the wheel with his left. He gave one to the Professor, and the Professor lit a match, cupped it in his hand and leaned over to light Leo's cigarette, then lit his own. After a few puffs Leo said, "I know about your son, one of my friends testified against him last month." He saw the Professor's hand shake as it brought the cigarette up to the mouth but the old man said nothing.

"If I had known about him I would never have taken you here," Leo said, and wondered why then he was taking the man back to Bremen.

The Professor said nervously, excitedly, holding tightly to the open side of the jeep, "I did not want you to help me. I knew it was not proper. But Herr Middleton said he explained everything to you, that you understood."

"When will they execute your son?" Leo asked cruelly and then felt ashamed.

"In a few weeks," the Professor said. He had lost the cigarette and his hands were tugging at each other in nervous spasms. "This was my last visit." He sat and waited for pity, hoping that Leo would not question him.

Leo was silent. They were in the open country, the smell of fresh grass and growing trees untainted by dust. The jeep was moving very slowly. Leo turned his head toward the old man. He spoke slowly. "He was convicted by a German court, your son, for killing a fellow German, not for his crimes as a camp guard. That is ironic. You will never be able to think in your heart that the damn Jews killed him. That hatred can never be your consolation. What a pity."

The Professor bowed his head and watched his hands. "I never thought such things," he said. "Truly, I am an educated man."

"Your son deserves to die," Leo said. "He is a monster. If ever a man deserved to have his life taken away, that monster does. Do you know the things he did? An evil creature, the world will be better without him. I say that with a clear conscience. Do you know the things he did?" The hate in his voice and in his heart made him stop the jeep on the side of the road and turn for an answer.

But the Professor did not answer. He had buried his head in his arms as if to hide as much of himself as he could. His whole body was shaking. There was no sound coming from the old man, but his small body was weaving backward and forward, continuously, aimlessly, as if severed from the motor of his brain.

Leo waited for it to end, and as pity and compassion began to wash away the hate, he thought *no no* and called to his mind the image of his own father, the tall emaciated figure, head shaven, walking down the gravel path and Leo in his own uniform walking to meet him, not knowing him, and his father suddenly stopping and saying, "What are you doing here?" and Leo at that time remembering, and remembering now, how in an even earlier time he had been caught by his father in the Tiergarten when he was supposed to have been in school and his father saying in the salfsame tone, *"Was machst Du hier?"* Only now here along the gravel path with its white-painted stones, the barbed wire ringing the horizon all around them, now the father saying these words was weeping, stooping down to his son, the red stripe of the political prisoner across his breast, the boy with the green diagonal denoting his race. And Leo in the jeep, remembering this, only now knowing what his father must have suffered at that time ten years ago, felt only contempt for this old man before him paying for his father's grief with his own. This man, well educated, knowing right from wrong, who out of fear, cowardice, impotence, did not come to the help of his father. Slept warm in his bed, ate well, and earned it all with a helpless shrug, an easy resignation. Leo looked away from the Professor and across the road and down into a green valley growing black with the falling night. He knew he could never remain in Germany, that he could never live with these people, could not even hate them, they who had kept his youth behind barbed wire, burned a number into his arm that he would carry to his grave, killed his father, made his mother flee into the night thousands of miles away, robbing her mind of the co-ordination necessary to live so that finally a time had come when she had died because she could not sleep, literally could not sleep.

And now in this land, and with this people, he lived in peace and did not rage with fire and sword. Slept with their daughters, gave chocolate bars to their children, gave them cigarettes, drove them around the countryside. With his contempt for himself Leo drove out the last pity he felt for the old man. He put the jeep in motion, making it go at top speed, wanting to get back to Bremen. The Professor had wiped his face with a handkerchief and sat passively, bracing his feet against the floor, his body rigid, fighting the swaying of the jeep.

In the early morning hours, the countryside becoming shadowy with the first beginning light, Leo stopped at one of the coffee-and-snack bars the Americans had set up on the *Autobahn*. He took the Professor in with him, and they sat at a long wooden table. Along it some G.I. truck drivers were sleeping, their heads pillowed on their arms.

They drank their first cup of coffee in silence but when Leo returned with the cups filled a second time and a handful of doughnuts the Professor began to talk, slowly at first, then more quickly, his hands trembling as he hurriedly sipped coffee.

"You don't know yet how a father feels, Leo, a father is helpless. I know all about my son, and he confessed to me something else. When his mother was dying he was on the Russian front, and I managed to get him leave—he was a hero, he had courage, many decorations, but he never came. He wrote that his leave was canceled. Now he told me everything, that he went on through to Paris. That he wanted a good time. He explained to me that he could feel no pity, no love for his mother. And after that was when everything went bad, and he began to do all those terrible things. But," the Professor paused as if bewildered and then more intensely, "but how is that, a son not weep for his mother's death? He was never unnatural, he was like all the other boys, perhaps more handsome, more intelligent. I taught him to be generous, to share his things with his little playmates, to believe in God. We both loved him, his mother and I, we never spoiled him. He was a good son. Now, even now, I can't believe the things he's done, but he confesses, he confessed to me." The pouched eyes filled with tears. "He told me these things, and last night he cried in my arms and said 'Poppa, I'm glad to die, I'm glad to die.' We talked all week about our lives together, and then last night he cried as he used to when a child." The Professor stopped suddenly and Leo realized that his face must be showing the mixture of repulsion and pity that he felt.

The Professor began again but now his voice was calm, reasonable, and slightly apologetic as if showing his grief had been the extreme of bad manners. He spoke very slowly. "I go over our life together and try to find out where did it start? I can't find it. I can see nothing. It all happened by itself that he became a monster. It's terrifying to think that. That makes you stop. You called him that, Leo, and it is true. Your son could be such a monster." The Professor smiled to show that this was impersonal, mere theorizing, and this smile was so ghastly in that grief-masked face, the bloodless lips twisted so unnaturally, that Leo had to bow his head over his coffee not to see.

And this smile taking all of his strength the old man became more intense. "I say these things to you because you are the victim. My son and I, I too, we were the ones who did these things to you. What can I say? That it was an accident, as if I drove a car and was careless and ran you down. Without malice. My son caught a terrible fever, as if he lived in a swamp, do you understand that? He must die of this illness, I know that. But I believe he is good in spite of everything, I believe he is good." The Professor began to weep and said loudly, hysterically, "God have pity on him, God have pity on him."

One of the G.I.'s lifted his head from the table and said, "Pipe down for Chrissake." The Professor became silent.

Leo said, "Sleep a little and then we'll go on, first smoke

a cigarette." When they had finished they both pillowed their heads on their arms and the Professor fell asleep immediately, but not Leo.

He raised his head again and stared at the brown-skinned doughnuts scattered on the dirty wooden table. A black pool of coffee in its tin mess kit caught a few golden glints from the weak yellow bulbs in the room. He felt no pity for the old man; he could not. His own suffering rose in his blood as antidote. But he knew now his mother and father's grief on his account, a cruel suffering. Sleepily his mind made a circle around a half-formed dream of countless evil men put to death with perfect justice and that death spreading like a disease to countless more innocent. There was no other way, but before his head dropped onto the wooden table he thought hazily of a wonderful solution, at every execution a drug be given to the loved ones, a drug of forgetfulness, and in a full dream he dipped a great steel needle into the black pool of coffee, drew the golden glints up into the glass tube with the black liquid and finally in the back of the Professor's head with its little fleshy neck he stabbed until the steel hit bone and watched the needle empty itself. The Professor turned his face up to him, humbly, gratefully.

It was almost dawn when they woke, and they made the long ride to Bremen without further conversation than was necessary. The afternoon sun had just begun its voyage west when they rode through the outskirts of Bremen, and Leo stopped the jeep at the house where the Professor had his room.

Leo raced the motor to drown out the old man's polite gratitude. He drove away quickly. He felt cold, fatigued, but not ready for sleep. He drove through the town, past the *Polizeihaus* and down the Schwachhauser, then made the turn into the Kurfürsten Allee. He drove slowly down the long, curved tree-lined avenue, the sunlight and warm afternoon breeze giving him new strength. As he approached Mosca's house he took his foot off the gas pedal and bumped over the curb so that the jeep was tilted, one side on the street and one on the walk. He steered into the tree to stop the slowly rolling jeep but he had been going faster than he thought and the shock of contact snapped his head back. He cursed, leaned against the cushion and lit a cigarette, then honked the jeep horn three times.

The window went up quickly, but instead of Hella it was Frau Saunders who put her head out. She called down to him, "Frau Mosca is not here. She was taken this morning to the hospital. The child came early."

Leo in his excitement stood up in the jeep. "Ah, no, is she all right?"

"She's fine," Frau Saunders said. "The child is a boy. Everything went well. Herr Mosca is there now."

Leo didn't wait to answer her. He roared the jeep into action and made the turn that would take him to the city hospital. On the way he stopped by the officers' club and gave a German servant a pack of cigarettes for a great bouquet of flowers.

16

MOSCA HEARD Inge calling him to the phone in the outer office. He went in, picked up the receiver and said hello. A woman's voice answered in German. "Herr Mosca, here is Frau Saunders. They took your wife to the hospital an hour ago. I think it is the baby."

Mosca paused, looking at Inge and Eddie, as if they could hear the voice over the phone. They were both busy, bent over their desks.

"But it's two weeks early," Mosca said and saw Eddie look up and Inge turn around to watch him.

"I think it is the baby," Frau Saunders was saying. "She had pains this morning after you left. I called the hospital and they sent an ambulance."

"O.K.," Mosca said, "I'll go right away."

"Will you telephone me when you find out?" Frau Saunders asked.

"All right," Mosca said and then before he hung up he heard Frau Saunders say, "She told me to tell you not to be worried."

Eddie Cassin raised his eyebrows when Mosca told him the news. Eddie picked up the phone and ordered a vehicle from the motor pool.

When the jeep came Eddie said, "I'll meet you at the Rathskellar for supper if you can make it. Give me a ring if anything happens."

"It may not even be the baby," Mosca said, "she's not too rugged."

"She'll be O.K.," Eddie said reassuringly. "It's the baby all right. They come early and they come late. I've gone through all that." He put out his hand to shake Mosca's and said, "Here's luck."

On the drive to town, Mosca became anxious, really worried. Without warning a great wave of fear flooded over him, so powerful that he was sure that she was ill and said to the driver, "Go faster."

The driver said, "I have my orders, the regulations." Mosca threw his half-full pack of cigarettes into the German's lap. The jeep leaped forward.

The city hospital was a group of red brick buildings scattered over a great area of tree-lined walks and green lawns, and all encircled by an iron fence crawling with ivy to hide the defending spikes. Along the perimeter of the fence were little iron doors. The main entrance for visitors, however, was an enormous gateway through which entered vehicles and pedestrians. The jeep went through this gate, moving slowly through eddies of German men and women.

"Find out where the maternity ward is," Mosca said. The jeep stopped. The driver leaned out and spoke to a passing nurse, then put the jeep in motion. Mosca leaned back and tried to relax as they rolled slowly through the hospital grounds.

Now he was in a German world. Here there were no uniforms, no military vehicles except the one he rode in. The people around him were all the enemy; their clothes, their speech, the way they walked, the very atmosphere. As they rode, he could see from time to time the iron spears enclosing this world. Near the fence was the maternity building.

Mosca went in and found a small office in which sat an elderly nurse. Against the wall stood two men wearing American Army fatigues but on their heads the peaked caps of the Wehrmacht. These were ambulance drivers.

"I'm looking for Hella Broda, she entered here this morning," Mosca said. The nurse consulted a record book on her desk. For a moment Mosca was afraid she would say no and his fears would be realized. She looked up at him and smiled. "Yes," she said. "Wait, I'll call up about her." As she spoke over the phone one of the ambulance drivers said to Mosca, "We brought her here," and both men smiled at him. He smiled back politely and then saw they were hoping for cigarettes as a reward. He reached in his pocket; he had given his driver the last pack. He shrugged and waited for the nurse to finish.

She hung up the phone. "You have a baby boy," she said to him.

Mosca said impatiently, "Is my wife all right?" Then he was self-conscious about the word wife.

"Yes, of course," the nurse said. "If you wish you can wait and see her in about an hour. She's sleeping now."

"I'll wait," Mosca said. He went out and sat on the wooden bench that ran along the ivy-covered building.

He could smell flowers from a nearby garden, a burning sweetness mixed with the reddish light of the burning midday sun. White-clad nurses and doctors passed to and fro, crossed over green lawns and entered blood-red brick buildings fastened squarely and without visible scars in the fresh, living earth. Filling the air was a muted trilling of insects and new-born birds. He felt a sense of absolute peace, a quiet restfulness, as if the iron fence were a barrier to the noise and ruin and dust of the city on the other side.

The two ambulance drivers came out and sat near him. The bastards never give up, Mosca thought. He was dying for a smoke himself. He turned to one of the men and asked, "Have you a cigarette?" They were stunned, the one nearest him actually gaped, his mouth open. Mosca grinned. "I have none with me. I'll leave a few packs for you both when I come again."

The nearest man took out a dark-colored pack of German cigarettes and extended it to Mosca, saying, "If you really wish to smoke one of these—?"

Mosca lit one up and choked on his first breath. The two ambulance drivers burst out laughing and one said, "These take getting used to." But after that first puff, it tasted good to Mosca. He lay back on the bench, letting the afternoon sun strike his face, resting. He felt tired.

"How was she when you brought her?" He spoke with his eyes closed.

"Fine, like all of them," the driver who had given him the cigarette said. He had a face that was perpetually set in an expression of good humor, a half-smile that was formed by the very structure of facial bone. "We've had hundreds like her, no trouble."

Mosca opened his eyes to look at him. "Not nice work, carrying women around every day, listening to them cry and scream." He realized as he spoke that he felt resentment toward these two men because they had seen Hella defenseless, that for a period of time she had been helpless in their hands.

The same driver said, "It's nice carrying around people who can make noise. In the war I was with a burial squad. We used to take a truck out and pick up the dead. In the winter they were stiff, we had to pack them in carefully, like cordwood, in neat stacks, sometimes you could bend their arms a little and there was a nice little trick of hooking arms in one pile to arms in another so you could stack them higher."

The other driver left the bench and went back into the building. "He's heard these stories before," the German continued. "And he was with the Luftwaffe; they empty a can of garbage, they have nightmares for weeks. Anyway, as I was telling you. In the summer, terrible. Terrible. I used to pack fruit before the war, maybe that is why the Army gave me the burial squad. I used to pack oranges, sometimes they were rotten, we have to import them you know, so I'd repack them. The bad ones I'd squeeze into small boxes to take home. In summers that was the way with dead men. They would be all squashy, we'd press them in against one another. It would be like a big pile of garbage in the truck. So this job is fine. The other one, winter or summer, we had no conversation, nothing interesting, you understand." He gave Mosca a huge grin.

Mosca thought, how about this bastard. He felt a genuine liking for the man, recognized the intended kindliness.

"I like conversation," the man went on, "so I didn't care for my Army work. Now here, it is a pleasure. I sit with the woman, and when she screams I say go ahead and scream, nobody will hear. When they cry, like your wife, I say, Cry, it will do you good. Anybody who has children must get used to tears. My little joke. I don't always say things the same. I think of something new usually and it is almost always true. I don't talk much, just enough so they won't feel alone, as if I were their husband."

Mosca closed his eyes. "Why did my wife cry?"

"Man, it is a painful business." The German tried to give him a reproachful look but only succeeded in making a kindly grimace, the bones of his face working against him. "The pain made her cry but that means nothing because you could see she was very happy. I thought then, her husband is a lucky man. I didn't say anything to her, I couldn't think of anything to say. I wiped her face with a wet towel because the pain made her sweat, and she cried a great deal. But when she got out of the ambulance she smiled at me. No, she was fine, there was nothing for me to say."

A tap on the window behind them made the driver turn; the nurse was motioning for him to come in. The German left and a few moments later both drivers came out. The German shook Mosca's hand. "All the best, don't forget our cigarettes when you come again." They got into their ambulance and drove slowly toward the main gate.

Mosca closed his eyes, leaned back, and the heat of the June sun made him doze off. It seemed as if he slept for a long time, even dreamed, and then he was awake. There was a tapping on the windowpane behind him. He turned his head and saw the nurse motioning him to enter.

She gave him the floor and room number and he ran up the two flights of stairs. When he came to the room he saw outside a long table on rollers and on the table nearly twenty small white-clothed bundles from which came an overwhelming din. One of them might be his and he stopped to look for a moment. A nurse came out of the room and started to wheel the table away. "You can go in," she told him. He pushed open the door and stepped into a large, square, green-walled room in which were six high hospital beds filled with women, none of them Hella. Then in one corner he saw a bed so low it was nearly level with the floor.

She was lying flat, her eyes open, watching him, and

she was more beautiful than he had ever seen her. Her mouth was the dark redness of blood and her face very white except for two crimson spots on her cheeks. Her eyes were shining and alive and except for her body, which was curiously lifeless and immobile, she did not look as if she had had a child only a few hours before. Conscious of the other women in the room, he went to her and bent down to kiss her cheek, but she twisted her head so that her mouth met his. "Are you happy?" she whispered. Her voice was peculiarly hoarse, as if she had a heavy cold. Mosca smiled down at her and nodded.

"It's a beautiful baby, so much hair," she whispered. "Like yours." He didn't know what to say and stood there wondering how all this could make her so happy and leave him so untouched.

A nurse came in and said, "That's all, please, you can come back tomorrow, in the regular visiting hours." Mosca leaned down to Hella and said, "I'll see you tomorrow, O.K.?" She nodded and tilted her head for him to kiss her again.

Outside the nurse asked if he would like to see the baby and he followed her down a long corridor to where it ended in a glass wall. There were some men looking through this wall at babies held up in turn by a small, pert-looking nurse who obviously enjoyed her work and the antics of the visiting, newly made fathers. She opened a small pane in the glass wall and the nurse with Mosca said, "The Broda child." The nurse disappeared into a room behind the glass wall and came out with a small bundle. She took the cloth away from its face, holding up the baby proudly.

Mosca was shocked by the baby's ugliness. It was the first time he had ever seen a new-born infant. The face was wrinkled, puckered up sourly, the small black eyes almost closed but still emitting malignant gleams toward the new and hostile world, and over its head like an untidy shawl, a great shock of black hair gave it an animal-like appearance.

Beside Mosca a small, bald-headed German man was going into ecstasies over another baby held by another nurse behind the glass wall. Mosca saw with relief that this baby looked almost exactly like his own. The German was exclaiming and cooing, "Oh, what a sweet child, what a lovely child," making sucking noises with his mouth and twisting his face into extraordinary grimaces to get a reaction from the infant. Mosca watched curiously and then stared at his own child, trying to feel some emotion, then signaled to the nurse to take it away. The nurse gave him a long, angry look; she had been waiting impatiently for his performance. Mosca thought, Screw you, sister.

He ran down the steps and walked through the hospital grounds toward the gate. He saw Leo driving slowly against the waves of Germans going out. He stopped in front of the jeep and climbed up over the hood, stepped over the windshield and into the jeep. He saw the great bouquet of flowers in Leo's lap, and as their sweet, cool fragrance hit his face, he was suddenly free of tension and felt extraordinarily happy.

When, finally, they met Eddie at the Rathskellar, Eddie was already drunk. He said, "You son of a bitch, why didn't you call? I had Inge phone the hospital and they gave me the dope. Then your landlady called and I told her the news."

"Christ, I forgot," Mosca said with a foolish smile.

Eddie threw an arm around his shoulders. "Congratulations. Now, tonight we celebrate."

They ate and then went to one of the tables in the bar.

"Do we buy the drinks or does Walter?" Leo asked as if this were a very serious point.

Eddie gave them both an amused, paternal look. "Tonight I'll buy everything. If I know Walter he won't even give out cigars. Look at that sad face."

"Jesus," Mosca said, "how the hell can I act like a bigwheel father. We're not even married. They kept calling the kid by Hella's last name. That made me feel funny. I was thinking I'll put in the marriage papers."

"Let's see," Eddie said. "You can figure three months. But then thirty days after you're married, back to the States. You going to leave all this gravy?"

Mosca thought it over. "I figure I can get the papers and hold off the marriage for a while. But I'd like to have everything set, just in case."

"You could do that," Eddie said, "but you have to go back sometime. Especially now the Middletons are gone, you can't get the right food for a wife and kid." He gave Mosca a strange, peering look. "You sure you want those papers, Walter, you ready to go back?"

Mosca said to Leo. "How about you, you made up your mind yet, U. S. A. or Palestine?"

"I'm doing well here," Leo said. He thought of the Professor. "But soon I must decide."

"You ought to come back with me," Mosca said. "You could stay with me and Hella until you get set. That is, if I can get a place myself."

Eddie asked curiously, "What will you do when you get back to the States?"

"I don't know," Mosca said. "I figure I'll go to school maybe. I'm an ignorant guy, I went right from high school into the Army." He grinned at them. "You wouldn't think it but I used to be a good student. But I enlisted, you know that, Eddie, you used to break my balls about it when we were G.I.'s. Now I want to learn what goes on." He stopped, trying to think of how he could put it into words. "Sometimes I wanta fight like hell against everything around me, but I don't know what to fight. It seems like I can't get out of a straight line to a trap. Like now. I want to do something but I'm not allowed. My own personal business. I can't marry a kraut and I can see why the Army makes it tough. I don't give a crap about the Germans but that stops me. All right, screw it." He took another drink.

"You know, when I was a kid I thought everybody was wonderful. I had definite ideas and now I can't even remember them. In a street fight when I was a kid I always used to fight like I was a hero in the movies, always fight fair, never hit the other guy when he slipped or was off balance. A real jerk. But that wasn't for real. Now it seems like that life before I got into the Army was never really real. Like you could never believe the war would end. You knew you would go on to Japan, and then they would find somebody new to fight, the Russians maybe. Then after that maybe the men on Mars. But always somebody new so that you could never go home. Now for the first time I believe that it is over, that I'll have to go back to that dream life or whatever it was. I can start by going back to school."

Leo and Eddie were embarrassed. It was the first time Mosca had ever spoken to them about his feelings, and they were surprised by the boyishness of the emotions behind the lean, dark, almost cruel-looking face. Leo said, "Don't worry, Walter, when you lead a normal life with a wife and children everything will be O.K."

"What the hell do you know?" Eddie demanded in drunken anger. "Eight years in a concentration camp without dames. What the hell do you know?"

Leo said with a quiet contempt, "I know one thing. You'll never leave here." This stunned Eddie.

"You're right," he said. "Goddamn if you're not right. I wrote my wife again that she gotta come and bring the kid or I'll never leave this goddamn continent. That's my only hope. But she's screwing for her boss, she thinks I don't know about it. But I've got her figured all the way."

Leo said to Mosca, "Maybe I will come with you, who knows what will happen by that time? I can't stay here forever. Maybe we can go into a business together with our black-market profits and you could go to school too, how would that be?"

"That's right," Eddie said. "Go into business with Leo and you can't lose, Walter." He smiled at them and saw that neither of them had understood or perhaps had not heard because the liquor was twisting the words as they came out of his loose mouth and also perhaps because about that, they had always trusted him. He felt ashamed. "You guys are dreaming," he said and realized that he was angry because they were making plans together and leaving him out, with no malice, assuming that he would never leave here. He felt, suddenly, concern for both of them. Leo for his innocence of the real world, Mosca for what he sensed was an endless struggle that raged behind that seemingly indifferent, dark proud face; a struggle to hold to the world with the help of one thin thread. And he felt an overwhelming drunken sorrow for himself. To the amazement of Leo and Mosca, he put his head down on the table and began to cry. Then he fell asleep.

17

WOLF EASED his pudgy body down the basement steps and sighed wearily, glad to be out of the hot summer sun. He was tired, as there had been a lot of work to catch up after a month's vacation. He had taken his wife to visit a sister in Bavaria, a last visit before they went to the States. Now he went directly to the kitchen where Ursula was preparing supper. "They have a baby boy," he said.

Ursula turned around and exclaimed happily, "Isn't that wonderful, just what she wanted. Is she back from the hospital yet? I must go to see her."

"It happened the day after we left," Wolf said. "The baby came early. So she's been home three weeks now." And he thought, they barely know each other and yet Ursula is happy. Something about children being born always touched him too. He wanted kids of his own, when he was all set. That was one thing you were sure of and he could teach them how to take care of themselves. They'd be the sharpest kids in the neighborhood, they'd know what the score was.

"Have you heard anything about our marriage papers?" Ursula asked.

"They haven't come back from Frankfort," Wolf said. This was a lie. The papers were now in his desk at the air base. But if Ursula knew she would insist on getting married immediately and he would have to leave Germany within thirty days after the ceremony. He wanted to remain a few months longer and complete a few deals.

Ursula's father spoke behind him. "Ah, Wolfgang, home at last." Wolf swung around. "You had a telephone message. You must get in touch with a man named Honny, at once." The father had just come in from the storeroom and carried a great ham which he now put on the kitchen table. He took a large carving knife and lovingly cut off medium-thick slices to be fried with their potatoes.

One thing, Wolf thought wryly, the old man always made himself useful around the house. He asked, "Did the man say anything else?"

"No," Ursula's father said, but he kept repeating that it was very important.

Wolf went into his bedroom and dialed the number. When someone picked up the phone and said hello, he recognized Honny's voice and said, "Here is Wolfgang."

Honny's voice, very excited and effeminate in its higher register said, "Wolfgang, it is good you called so quickly. That contact you were looking for during the winter. I have it."

"Are you sure?" Wolf asked.

Honny's voice became lower, more guarded. "I saw enough of the evidence to think so." He stressed the word "evidence."

"Ah so," Wolf said, "very well. I will be there in about an hour. Can you have him there then?"

"In two hours," Honny said.

"All right," Wolf said and hung up. He called out to Ursula that he would not be eating supper and hurried out of the house. He heard her exclamation of surprise and disappointment before he closed the door. He walked quickly down the street and arrived just in time to catch a *Strassenbahn,* making it on the run.

Wolf was excited. He had given up hope on the whole deal, hadn't even thought about it for several months except when Mosca had kidded him. And now everything was breaking just right. The marriage papers were all set, he could get plane tickets, the hell with free government transportation. And it would be a perfect out on the old-man deal. Ursula and her father had been breaking his balls about taking the old man with them to the States, and he had almost laughed in their faces. But you had to lie to women all the time, he had promised Ursula he would try his best. And he wouldn't mind if the old man was on the ball. But the father had taken a nice shellacking when he had tried to put over a swindle on some black-market operators. He spent a week in the hospital recovering. Since then the father had stayed in the basement apartment like a mole, eating a whole twenty-pound ham in less than a week, three or four ducks at a sitting, almost an entire goose during the course of a Sunday. He must have gained forty pounds in the last two months. The wrinkles of his skin had been filled out with layer on layer of lard and he had let out his prewar suits to contain a great, new paunch.

He must be the only fat kraut in Bremen, Wolf thought, the only one who could pose for those posters and travel folders showing the tremendous, jolly German who illustrated the good living of his country. In his basement he had the fattest kraut in Germany. A goddamn cannibal. A twenty-pound ham in three days. Jesus Christ.

Wolf jumped off the *Strassenbahn* as it passed the mouth of the Kurfürsten Allee and walked briskly past the Metzer Strasse to further on where Mosca lived in the white stone house. Though the sun was going down the air was still hot and Wolf kept under the shade of the trees that lined the Allee. He hoped Mosca was home, but if not there was still time to pick him up at the Rathskellar or the club. No telephone on this.

Wolf opened the gate that cut the path from the sidewalk. He went up the stairs, knocked on the door, and Mosca opened it. He was dressed only in sun-tan trousers and a T shirt, his feet were bare. In his hand he held a can of PX beer.

"Come on in, Wolf," Mosca said. They went through the hall and through the door to the living room. Frau Saunders was sitting in one corner of the sofa reading a magazine. Hella was rocking the cream-colored carriage serving now as a crib. The baby was crying.

Wolf said hello to the women, and though he was impatient, looked at the baby and complimented Hella on its beauty. Then he said to Mosca, "Can I see you for a minute alone, Walter?"

"Sure," Mosca said. Still holding the can of beer he led Wolf into the bedroom.

"Listen, Walter," Wolf said excitedly, "it's finally come through, the contact on that scrip deal. I've got to meet the guy now and settle details. I want you to come with me just in case everything goes quick. O.K.?"

Mosca took a sip of beer. In the other room he could hear the murmur of voices as Frau Saunders and Hella spoke to each other and spaced in between, the tentative, discontented wailing of the baby. He was surprised and the shock was unpleasant. He had written the whole deal off and now he found he had no taste for it.

"I don't go for that any more, Wolf," Mosca said. "You'll have to get a new partner."

Wolf had already started toward the door of the bedroom. Now, stunned, he turned back again to Mosca, his white face angry and full of disbelief.

"What the hell kind of crap is that, Walter?" he said. "We knock our balls off all winter and now, everything all set, you back out? That's no good, Walter. That doesn't go."

Mosca grinned at Wolf's anger and excitement. It was an excuse not to feel ashamed of backing out. He knew he was giving Wolf a dirty deal. But he was glad the pasty-faced bastard was getting tough.

"What the hell, Wolf," he said, "we're not gangsters. It was an idea. Maybe I would have gone through with it six months ago. Now I've got a dame and kid to think about. If something screws up, what happens to them? Besides my marriage papers are coming through in a few months. I won't need all that money."

Wolf restrained his outraged anger. "Look, Walter," he said in a friendly, reasonable voice, "you're going back to the States in three or four months. Maybe you saved a thousand bucks while you've been here, maybe you made another thousand on the black market. That thousand I helped you make, Walter. In the States you have to set up a home, look for a job, a lot of other crap. You'll need dough." And then letting a hurt tone come into his voice he said earnestly. "And you're not treating me right, Walter. I lose out, too. I can't go running around for another partner. I need a guy I can trust. Come on, Walter, it'll be easy, you don't have to worry about cops, they can't turn us in. And since when have you been afraid of a couple of lousy krauts?"

"No dice," Mosca said, and took another sip from the can of beer. With his free hand he flapped out his T shirt and said, "Boy, is it hot."

"Christ." Wolf slammed the door with his hand. "Goddamn it, hangin' out with that yellow Jew and that gash hound Eddie made you lose all your guts? I thought you were a better guy than that, Walter."

Mosca put his beer can down on the dresser. "Listen, Wolf, keep my friends out. Don't talk about them any more. Now about this business. Wolf, you shrewd prick, I know you got your marriage papers; so now you can just pull off this deal and take off for the States. Meanwhile I sit here three or four months. I'm not afraid of krauts but I'm not walking around Bremen after I pull a stunt like that. If we do this it's either get out of Bremen afterwards or knock the guys off when we take the money. Right now I can't do either. And I'm not going to keep looking behind me the rest of the summer, not even for a million bucks." He paused and then said sincerely, "No shit, Wolf, I'm sorry."

Wolf stared at the floor shaking his head up and down as if pondering on something he already knew, and then, remembering the scene at the officers' club when the Adjutant had made Mosca back down, he said, "You know, Walter, I can bust this whole thing up, you and Hella. All I have to do is turn in a report at the base and at the Military Police. You're breaking a Military Government law living in a German billet. And there are a couple of other things I could really go to town on."

To his amazement and anger, Mosca burst out laughing and then said, "Wolf, for Christ's sake, have a can of beer or get the hell out. I don't mind playing gangster with you but don't for Christ's sake pull that line. I'm not one of those kraut prisoners you used to scare the shit out of."

Wolf tried to bring his head up to stare balefully at Mosca, but there was such evident power in the lightly covered body, so much force and confidence in the lean face and thin mouth, the dark serious eyes, that he could only sigh and smile weakly.

"Ah, you son of a bitch," Wolf said resignedly, "give me a beer." Adding ruefully, shaking his head. "A five-grand can of beer." But as he drank he thought of some way to pay Mosca back for the desertion. He saw there was really nothing he could do. If he turned Mosca in to the M.P.'s and then left for the States, that would not help this deal any, there would be no gain and there was always the possibility of retaliation. No, he was well off. He had a small fortune in diamonds and quite a bit of cash. Why invite any remote chance of disaster?

He sighed, sipped at his beer. It was hard to let such a fine opportunity go by. He knew he would never have the nerve to do it alone. Well, he thought, he would scrape together all the cigarettes possible, bargain around the base, buy cheaply and sell high. He might clear a thousand bucks.

Wolf held out his hand to Mosca. "No hard feelings," he said. He was a little worried now that Mosca might take his former threat seriously, and he didn't want to keep looking around his last few weeks in Germany. "I'm sorry about trying to get tough, but losing all that dough . . . Forget what I said." They shook hands.

"It's O.K.," Mosca said. He walked Wolf to the door and said to him, "Maybe you can do something on your own."

When Mosca went into the living room, both women looked up inquiringly; they had heard the anger in Wolf's loud voice. The baby was no longer crying, was sleeping in his carriage.

"Your friend left so quickly," Frau Saunders said.

"He just wanted to tell me something," Mosca said. Then to Hella who was knitting and reading at the same time. "Wolf is getting married soon, he has the papers."

Hella looked up from her book and said absently, "Yes?"

Her thin pale face went back to the book as she murmured, "I hope ours come soon."

Mosca went into the bedroom for another can of beer and a tin of peanuts. He brought them into the living room and offered the opened can to the two women. They both took a handful. "Sure you don't need a beer?" They both shook their heads and kept reading.

They all sat, eating peanuts, Mosca drinking beer, the two women reading and Hella knitting. Hella's hair was cut very short for the summer, and the fragile bones of her face were scarcely veiled by the thin curtain of flesh and skin; a tiny blue vein coursed down her cheek to her lips. The room was filled with the warm, peaceful quietness of a summer evening, a slight cooling breeze came through the open window, ruffling the flowered curtain.

Mosca studied both women. One could be his mother, the other was actually the mother of his child, and the child in the carriage was his. He sorted all this out in his mind, making it very simple because the beer had made him sleepy. But everything jumbled together.

One day, long ago, he had put on his steel helmet, taken up his rifle, and on ships, in trucks, on the back of tanks had traveled through North Africa, England, France, Belgium, the Netherlands, to search out the enemy and put him to death. And even now this did not seem wrong, or stupid, or even ironical. It just seemed queer. A hell of a thing, he thought, a hell of a thing. He was amazed now that he thought of it. He took another handful of peanuts and almost missed his mouth, some of the nuts trickling to the floor. He felt very sleepy and went to stand by the window, letting the little breeze come through the porous cotton of his T shirt and onto his warm body. He walked unsteadily over to the carriage and stared down at the baby and said solemnly and out loud, "A hell of a thing."

Both of the women smiled. "I think I'll have to put you to bed," Hella said to Mosca. Then to Frau Saunders. "This is the first time he ever really looked at the baby. Don't you believe it, Walter, that you are a father?"

"He'll be better with the second one," Frau Saunders said.

Mosca kept staring down at the child. It was not ugly now, the wrinkles of the face had been filled out to a clean, white mask. The women were reading again. Mosca went back to the window.

"Don't be so restless," Hella said, not looking up from her book.

"I'm not restless," Mosca said. And it was true. He felt more as if he were exploring the room, really looking at it for the first time. He walked over to the carriage again and watched the baby sleeping. It was getting to look almost human, he thought. Then he said to Hella, "How about us going to the country club tomorrow? We can sit on the lawn with the carriage and I'll bring you hot dogs and ice cream from the PX snack bar. We can hear the band out there, too."

Hella nodded her head, still reading. Mosca said to Frau Saunders. "How would you like to come with us?"

Frau Saunders looked up and said, "Oh, no, I have some people coming."

Hella smiled at her. "He really meant it, he wouldn't ask you otherwise. You can eat yourself sick on ice cream."

"No, really," Frau Saunders said. She went back to her reading. Mosca realized that she wouldn't go because she was too shy, that she really thought he had asked out of politeness.

"No kidding," he said.

Frau Saunders smiled. "Bring me back some ice cream," she said.

Mosca took another beer can from the bedroom; everything was O.K., he thought.

"While you're feeling so friendly," Hella said, "I have a favor to ask you. Frau Saunders has an uncle in America and she wants you to send a letter for her through your Army mail."

"Sure," Mosca said. It was standard. All the Germans were writing to their relatives in the States hinting for packages. Frau Saunders said, "Thank you." And with a wry smile, "We are all very much concerned these days for our dear uncles in America." Hella and Mosca laughed, Mosca couldn't stop and choked on a mouthful of beer he had been ready to swallow.

The women had gone back to their reading so Mosca glanced at the copy of *Stars and Stripes* that lay on the table, then said, "Maybe Leo will be back from Hamburg tomorrow and come out to the club with us."

Hella looked up. "He has been a long time this trip. I hope nothing has happened to him."

Mosca went for a fresh can of beer. "You sure you two don't want some?" They both shook their heads. He stood by the window. "I guess Leo figured he'd spend the week end there, see what's doing. Otherwise he should have been back yesterday."

Hella put her book on the table and said to Frau Saunders, "Finished. It was fine."

Frau Saunders said, "I have others in the bedroom you haven't read. Go look at them."

"Not tonight," Hella said. She went to the window and stood beside Mosca, slipping her arm around his waist, under his T shirt. They both stared out into the darkness, letting the tree-scented breeze blow against them. They could smell the vegetable gardens and the river which flowed beyond; the summer night air had only the slightest acrid taint of ruins. The full moon was screened by clouds and all around him in the quiet darkness Mosca could hear German voices and laughter from nearby houses. A radio tuned to a Bremen station was playing soft string music. He had a sudden longing to go to the Rathskellar or the club, to shoot dice or drink with Eddie and Wolf.

"Oh, you are drinking so much beer," Hella said. "I hope you can walk to bed."

Mosca stroked her hair and said, "Don't worry about me, I'm all right."

She leaned against him. "I feel good tonight," she said. "You know what I'd like?" She said this softly so that Frau Saunders could not hear.

"What?" Mosca asked, and she smiled at him and reached up to kiss his mouth.

"You're sure it's all right?" he asked, speaking as softly as she. "It's only been a month." Eddie Cassin had told him he should wait at least two months.

"I'm all right now," she said, "don't worry about me. I feel wonderful tonight, like an old family woman, as if we were together, oh, so many years."

They stood there for a few moments longer, listening to the murmurings of the city and the night and then Mosca turned and said to Frau Saunders, "Good night." He held the door of the living room open so that Hella could wheel the carriage into the bedroom. When he followed her he checked the hall door to the apartment to make sure that it was locked.

18

MOSCA SAT in the shade thrown by a great, white-painted house, the requisitioned country club. Before him stretched the archery course with its blue- and red-circled targets, beside him Hella sat in a low, comfortable chair. On the wide lawn sat G.I.'s, their wives and baby carriages.

Over everything hung the peace of late Sunday afternoon. The evening had begun to fall a little quicker than usual, Mosca thought, autumn near, coming earlier this year. Scattered through the green of the lawn were patches of brown, and there was a reddish tinge in the leaves of the great elms that screened the golf course.

He saw Eddie Cassin coming toward them, skirting the archers. Eddie sat on the grass, tapped Hella's foot and said, "Hello baby." Hella smiled down at him and kept reading *Stars and Stripes,* forming the words silently with her lips.

"I got a letter from my wife," Eddie Cassin said. "She's not coming over." He was silent for a few moments. "The final word," he said, and smiled gravely, the delicate mouth twisting. "She's going to marry her boss. I told you she was screwing for him, Walter. I didn't even know anything then. Just pure intuition. How's that for intuition, Walter?"

Mosca could see that Eddie was well on his way to a big drunk. "What the hell, Eddie, you're not a family man."

"I could be," Eddie Cassin said. "I could try." He pointed to the cream-colored carriage which sat so prettily on its green carpet of grass, the blue woolen blanket peeping out of it. "You're not a family man but you're trying."

Mosca laughed. "I'm learning," he said.

They sat in silence for a time. "How about coming to the Rathskellar tonight?" Eddie asked.

"No," Mosca said. "We got some stuff in the house. Why don't you come over?"

"I have to keep moving." Eddie got up. "I can't sit around your place all night." He wandered away, moving between the archers and their targets.

Mosca lay back against Hella's legs, raised his face to the weak rays of a dying sun. He had forgotten to ask Eddie about the marriage papers. They were due now.

He thought about going home, about coming into his mother's house with a wife and child. Gloria was married (he smiled at that) so no worry there. But it would be queer going back for good though easier now than before.

Watching the archers bend the bowstrings awkwardly and the flight of the freed arrows, he remembered an older G.I. in a farmhouse behind the lines, the farm being used to show a movie for troops in reserve. Kindling wood packed high served for seats, and this old G.I., he must have been close to forty, Mosca thought, had held one of three French kids, a six-year-old boy, between his knees and carefully combed the unruly tangled hair, parting it neatly on the side, fluffing up the front into a wave. Then he had combed the hair of the other two children, one girl and another boy, holding them in turn between his knees, combing carefully with gentle and expert strokes, turning them around to get the part right. When the old G.I. had finished he gave each of the children a bar of chocolate, picked up his rifle where it rested against the wall and held it between his knees.

Feeling it important, sitting now in green grass spotted with baby carriages, he forced his mind to go back and remember the colored G.I. who had thrown great cans of pineapple juice out of his truck as he sped by the weary troops toiling from the beach toward the sound of heavy guns, a reminder to prepare, as the sound of church bells on Sunday stirs the soul to readiness, growing louder and louder as they approached, acquiring resonance, the sound of guns becoming denser, the crack of small arms like minor chords; and before the final entry, the final act of entry when they went into a ritual of mind and body almost as if entering a church—and then his mind stopped and went back to the sweet tinny coolness of the pineapple juice, the pause in the road, the passing of the can from mouth to mouth. And from this road to a road bathed in moonlight, a French village of small stone houses, blacked out, but against which were parked clearly visible trucks, jeeps and monstrous gun carriers. At the end of the street a tank was covered with the newly washed clothing, spread to dry by moonlight.

The twang of a bowstring and its arrow's thud seemed to awaken and stir a chilly evening breeze. Hella looked up from her book and Mosca pushed himself to his feet. "Do you want something before we go?" Mosca asked.

"No," Hella said, "I'm so full. And I'm afraid my tooth is beginning to hurt again." Mosca saw a small blue lump along her jaw.

"I'll tell Eddie to get you to the dentist at the air base." They gathered their things together from the chair and grass, piled them into the carriage. The baby was still asleep. They walked off the grounds to the streetcar stop. When the car came Mosca stretched his long arms and lifted the small carriage onto the rear platform.

The baby began to cry and Hella picked him up and held him. The conductor waited for fare and Mosca said in German, "We are Americans." The conductor looked Mosca up and down but did not protest.

After a few stops two WAC's climbed aboard. One of them noticed the child in Hella's arms and said to the other, "Isn't that a cute German baby?"

The other WAC leaned over to look and said several times, loudly, "Oh, it's a lovely baby," and looking up to Hella's face to see if she understood, said, *"Schön, schön."*

Hella smiled and looked at Mosca, but he made no sign. One of the WAC's took a bar of chocolate out of her purse and as they came to a stop she quickly put it on the baby's body. Before Hella could protest they were both out of the car and walking away.

Mosca had been amused at first, but for some reason he was angry now. He took the bar of chocolate and flung it into the street.

When they had left the *Strassenbahn* and were walking home, Hella said, "Don't be so upset because they took us for Germans."

But it was more than that. He had been frightened, as if they were really Germans, and had to accept charity, humiliation as one of the conquered. "We'll be out of here soon," he said. "I'll talk to Eddie tomorrow about speeding up the papers." He felt for the first time a sense of urgency.

Eddie Cassin left the country club with no idea of where he could go. The sight of Mosca sitting on the grass, his head resting against Hella's knees, one hand on the wheel of the cream-colored carriage, the sight of this was painful to him. He caught a *Strassenbahn* and thought, "I'll go see the gorilla." This cheered him up enough to watch the girls walking their way to the center of town. At the far end of the city he walked down to the river, crossed the bridge over the Weser and caught another *Strassenbahn* that continued on through the Neustadt. He got off at the last stop before the streetcar went out to the air base.

The row of buildings here was intact. He entered one and climbed up three flights of stairs and knocked. He heard Elfreida's voice say, "One moment." Then the door opened.

Eddie Cassin was shocked each time he saw her. The soft figure, full but really fuller than it looked, the trim ankles and hips and then that monstrosity of a head with its delicate violet eyes, red rimmed like rabbit eyes.

Eddie Cassin went in and sat down on the couch against the wall. "Get me a drink, baby," he said. He kept a supply of liquor here; he felt safe doing so. He knew Elfreida never touched the stuff unless he was present. As she mixed the drink he watched with fascination the movements of her head.

It was a little too large for its body and the hair was like mounds of brassy wire spikes. The skin was old and looked like chicken skin, with the yellow, fatty sheen and huge pores. The nose was splayed as if smashed by many vicious blows and her lips, until she made them up as she always did when Eddie came, were two puffy welts the color of veal. She had a great sagging chin and jaw. But as she moved around the room and spoke to him, her voice was soft and musical and somewhere in it the trill of a long-passed adolescence. She spoke English very well, was adept at languages and made her living as a translator and interpreter. Sometimes she gave Eddie lessons in German.

Eddie felt comfortable and safe here. She always lighted

the room with candles and Eddie thought, chuckling, that probably they had other uses. On the opposite wall was a bed and near it, against the wall which faced the window was a bureau on which stood a picture of her husband, a handsome-looking fellow whose uneven teeth showed in a good-natured smile.

"I didn't expect you tonight," Elfreida said. She gave him his drink and sat away from him on the couch. She had learned that if she made any gesture of affection or desire he would leave, but that if she waited until he had drunk enough he would put out the candles and drag her violently to the bed, and she knew then she had to pretend unwillingness.

Eddie lay back on the couch drinking, staring at the picture. The dead husband had fallen before Stalingrad and Elfreida had often told him how, with her fellow countrywomen, she had donned her widow black on the special day of mourning decreed for German men who had died there, so many that now the very name Stalingrad had a terrible sound in their hearts.

"I still think he was a fairy," Eddie Cassin said. "How come he ever married you?" He watched her agitation and distress which he always caused her on his bad nights.

"Tell me, did he ever make love to you?" Eddie Cassin asked.

"Yes," Elfreida said in a low voice.

"How often?"

She didn't answer.

"Once a week?"

"More," she said.

"Well, maybe he wasn't a complete fairy," Eddie said with a judicial air. "But I'll tell you one thing, he was unfaithful to you."

"No," she said, and he noted with satisfaction that she was already crying.

Eddie stood up. "If you're going to act that way, not even talking to me, I might as well leave." He was play-acting, she knew but she knew what her response must be. She fell to her knees and clasped his legs in her arms.

"Please, Eddie, don't go. Please don't go."

"Say your husband was a fairy, tell me the truth."

"No," she said, rising to her feet and crying with anger. "Don't say that word again. He was a poet."

Eddie took another drink and said solemnly. "You see, I knew all the time. All poets are fairies. See? Besides I can tell by his teeth." He gave her a sly grin.

She was weeping hysterically now with rage and grief. "You can go," she cried out, "leave here, you beast, you dirty, filthy beast." And when he swung and hit her in the face and dragged and knocked her on the bed she knew she had fallen into a trap; that he had deliberately made her angry to excite himself. When he threw his body upon her she tried not to respond but she sank under his frenzy, and as always, succumbed to a similar frenzy of her own. But tonight was worse than it had ever been. They sank further in their bed and their passion. He made her take long drinks from the whiskey bottle and humiliated her in every way. He made her crawl on hands and knees and beg with her mouth open. He made her gallop around the room in the darkness, changing pace with his commands. Finally he took pity on her and said, "Whoa," and she stopped. Then he let her come into the bed and into his arms.

"Now say your husband was a fairy." He got ready to push her out of bed again.

With a childlike drunkenness she repeated after him,

"My husband was a fairy." She was silent after this and lay supinely on the bed. He made her sit up so that he could see the shadow of her long, cone-shaped breasts. Like footballs, almost exactly like footballs. Eddie marveled. Dressed she seemed ordinary. He had experienced a thrill of delight the first time he had discovered that treasure.

"I feel sick, Eddie," she said. "I have to go to the bathroom." He helped her there and sat her naked on the toilet bowl. Then he fixed himself a drink and lay back on the bed.

"Poor Elfreida," Eddie Cassin thought, "poor Elfreida. Do anything for a stiff dick." When he had spotted her on the *Strassenbahn* the first time, he had known everything about her from the quick look she had given him. Now, sated, void of passion and hate, he wondered at his cruelty to her, a wonder without regret, and his willful destruction of the memory of her husband. And what kind of a guy was he to marry a woman with a head like that? From what Elfreida had told him at the beginning the guy was really crazy about her, and with a body like hers you could forgive a lot of other things. But not that head, Eddie thought.

He made another drink and went back to bed. So she had the luck to find the one guy in the world who would marry her, the one person who had the eyes to see her soul beneath the mask nature had given her, and from what she said and what the picture told you, a real hell of a guy. And he was corrupting that memory.

He could hear Elfreida throwing up in the bathroom. He felt sorry for her, knowing that he had terrorized her to quell his own panic. Now, finally, irrevocably, the last roots of his life had been torn away. He couldn't blame his wife. He had never been able to hide his disgust when she was sick. And carrying the kid she had been ugly, always throwing up like Elfreida now. He had never touched her then.

Eddie took another drink. His mind became hazy but he kept thinking of his wife as if she were standing beside him, legs spread apart; and into his mind came a picture of the old ice box his mother used to have, how he went down every day to the cellar of the coal man and brought up in a heavy wooden bucket the frosty block of ice, and then emptied the great hollow basin underneath the ice box which caught the water as it melted and dripped out. And when he emptied that great basin every morning, in that murky water floated bits of decayed food, shreds of newspapers, wet clotted wads of dirt and dead cockroaches, ten, sometimes thirty, floating on their hard brown shells, their thin threadlike feelers flattened into the water like innumerable streaks of watery blood. In his mind now his wife was standing with legs thrust apart, the gray enameled basin resting on the floor between her ankles. And falling slowly down from her body were decayed bits of food, the clotted dirt and the dead, brown-shelled cockroaches, falling end over end.

He raised himself up and called out, "Elfreida." There was no answer. He went into the bathroom and found her lying on the floor, her heavy breast pressed against the tile. He lifted her and brought her back to the bed and then saw she was crying silently, weakly. Suddenly it seemed as if he were standing far away, looking down at her and Eddie Cassin. He could see his own face reflected in the candles and the summer night and a great swift spear of terror went through his body. In his mind he cried out "God. God, help me. Please help me." He kissed her face, the great mouth and nose and yellow cheeks. "Stop crying," he said, "please stop crying. Your husband was a fine man, he wasn't a fairy. I was teasing."

And into his mind from long ago, he as a boy was listening to some one read the faintly remembered fairy tales. The word so beautiful then, the fairy tales, and like everything else once innocent, corrupted now. The voice reading, "Lost lost lost in the forest. Pity the lost princess." And into his mind came now as it had come then into his boy's mind, the picture of a virginal maiden with a crown and veil of white lace, the delicate features of an angel, the slight body of an undeveloped girl with no rotundity of hip or breast, no hint of nubility to mar the purity of her form. And then (was it in school or the bedroom of his home?) looking out the window, tear-blurred eyes sweeping over a forest of stone, he had wept silently and weakly, the imploring voice behind him softly saying, "Pity the lost beauty," and going on and on and on.

That night Hella and Mosca left the baby with Frau Saunders and strolled down to Metzer Strasse where Mosca still had his official billet. Mosca carried the blue gym bag in which were towels and clean underclothing.

They were both hot and dusty and looked forward to a leisurely bath. There was no heating boiler in Frau Saunders' house.

In front of the building stood Frau Meyer. She wore white slacks and a white blouse, presents from Eddie Cassin. She was smoking an American cigarette and looking curiously smug. "Hello, you two," she said, "You haven't been to see us for a long time."

"Don't tell me you're lonely," Mosca said.

Frau Meyer laughed, the buck teeth showing from the

pulled back mouth. "No, I'm never lonely. Not with such a house full of men."

Hella asked, "Frau Meyer, do you know if Leo has returned from Hamburg?"

Frau Meyer gave them a look of surprise. "Why, he returned Friday. Hasn't he been to see you?"

"No," Mosca said, "and I haven't seen him eating at the Rathskellar or the club."

The smug look was back on Frau Meyer's face. "He's in his room now with a wonderful black eye. I teased him about it but I could see he was angry so I left him alone."

"I hope he's not sick," Hella said. They went up the stairs and knocked on the door of Leo's room. Mosca knocked louder but there was no answer. He tried the door. It was locked.

"Old Meyer missed something for once," Mosca said, "he probably went out."

They went into Mosca's room and Mosca undressed and went to the bathroom at the end of the hall. He soaked in the tub for the time to smoke one cigarette, then washed quickly. When he came back to the room Hella was resting on the bed, cradling one side of her face in her hands.

"What's the matter?" Mosca asked.

"My tooth hurts," Hella said, "all that candy and ice cream I ate today."

"I'll take you to the dentist tomorrow," Mosca said.

"No, it will go away," Hella said. "I've had it before." She undressed as Mosca was dressing, put on the damp bathrobe and went down the hall.

Mosca was tying his shoelaces when he heard someone moving around in Leo's room. For one moment he thought it might be a German domestic looting and he called out sharply, "Leo?" He waited, then he heard Leo say through the wall, "It's me."

Mosca went out of his room and Leo had unlocked the door. When he entered Leo was already walking away from him and toward the bed.

"How come you didn't drop over?" Mosca asked.

Leo got onto the bed and when he turned to lay on his back Mosca saw his face. There was a dark-blue stain under one eye and a lump on the forehead. His face looked puffy and swollen.

Mosca stared at him for a moment then walked over to the table and sat by it. He lit a cigar. He had a good idea of what had happened, the headlines he had seen in *Stars and Stripes* last night. It hadn't registered then through all the beer.

There had been a picture of a ship sailing into the harbor of Hamburg. The ship was black with people. Underneath the picture was the story of how this ship had tried to make its way to Palestine carrying former inmates of concentration camps. The British had intercepted the ship and brought it to Hamburg. The people in it had refused to disembark and had been forced to do so by armed troops.

Mosca asked quietly. "You see that business up in Hamburg, is that it?"

Leo nodded. Mosca thought for a while, smoking, putting things together, the fact that Leo hadn't come to see them, hadn't answered their knock on the door.

"You want me to beat it?" he asked Leo.

Leo shook his head. "No," he said. "Stay a bit."

"Who hit you, the Limeys?"

Leo nodded. "I tried to keep them from beating a man they had taken off the boat. I got this." He pointed to his face. Mosca noticed there was no sign of the twitch, as if the muscles had been paralyzed with shock.

"How was it?"

Leo said evasively, "Didn't you read the paper?"

Mosca made an impatient gesture. "What happened?"

Leo sat on the bed, not speaking, and suddenly the tears were rolling down his face. The tic jerked the side of his face up and down and he put his hand to hold the flesh still. He burst out, "My father was wrong. My father was wrong."

Mosca didn't say anything and after a few moments Leo dropped his hands from his face. The tic had stopped. Leo said, "I saw them beating this man they had dragged down the gangplank. I said 'Don't do that,' I was really surprised and just pushed one of them away. The other said, 'Awright you Jew bawsted, you take some of his.' " Leo imitated the cockney accent perfectly. "When I was on the ground I saw the German dockworkers laughing at me, at all of us. I thought about my father then. I didn't think he was wrong, I just thought about him, what if he should see his son like this. What would he think then?"

Mosca said slowly. "I kept telling you, this is no place. Look, I'm going back to the States when the marriage papers go through. There's a rumor the air base is closing up so I'll be out of a job anyway. Why don't you come with us?"

Leo bowed his head in his hands. The proposal aroused no emotion in him, no desire to accept, no affection for Mosca, no feeling of kinship.

"The Jews are perfectly safe in America?" Leo asked bitterly.

"I think so," Mosca said.

"You just think so?"

"Nothing's sure," Mosca said.

Leo didn't say anything. He thought about the English soldiers in their rough woolen uniforms, the same men who had wept when they had liberated him and his fellow inmates, had stripped off their own clothes, emptied their trucks of food, and he had believed his father, human beings are good, man is moved easily to pity and more to love than to hate.

"No," he said to Mosca. "I can't go with you. I've arranged to go to Palestine. I leave in a few weeks." And then feeling he owed Mosca some explanation he said. "I don't feel safe any more except with my own people." And as he said this he realized that he was reproaching Mosca, that Mosca's affection for him was personal, that Mosca in a time of danger would defend him, Leo, but would not defend a Jew he did not know or did not care for. And this affection was no longer enough, could never give him real security. He would never feel safe, even in America, no matter what kind of material success he achieved. In the back of his mind would always be the fear that all security could be destroyed in a manner he could not fight against or control, and that even friends like Mosca would not fight against that force. The face of the liberator and torturer were one face, blended, friend and enemy only the enemy. He remembered a girl he had lived with shortly after coming out of Buchenwald, a thin and merry German girl with a gleeful and almost malicious grin. He had gone into the country and come back with a goose and a brace of chickens. And when he had told her of the low amount he had given she had looked up at him and said with a disturbing intonation and smile, "So, you are a good businessman." And yet now he realized or made himself realize the attitude of mind behind what she had said, he felt only a vague bitterness against her with the others. She had been tender and loving, she had cared about him, she had treated him with every consideration and fairness except for that one time. And yet, she and the many others like her had burned the blue numerals in his arm he would carry to his grave. And where could he escape these people? Not in America, certainly not in Germany. Where could he go?

Father—Father, he cried in his mind, you never told me that every human being carries his own barbed wire, his ovens, his canes of torture, wherever they go; you never taught me to hate, to destroy, and now when I'm humiliated, jeered at, I feel only shame not even anger, as if I deserved every blow, every insult and now where can I go? In Palestine I'll find barbed wire as surely as you found it in Heaven or in Hell. And then quite simply, clearly, as if really he had known it secretly for a long time, he thought, Father too was the enemy.

There was nothing more to think about. He saw Mosca still silent, still smoking his cigar.

"I leave in two weeks, I think, for Palestine, but I leave Bremen in a few days."

Mosca said slowly, "I guess you're right, Come over to the house before you leave."

"No," Leo said, "it's nothing personal. I don't want to see anybody."

Mosca understood. He rose and held out his hand. "O.K., Leo, here's luck." They shook hands. They could hear Hella opening the door of the other room.

"I don't want to see her," Leo said.

"O.K.," Mosca said and went out.

Hella had begun to dress. "Where were you?" she asked.

"With Leo, he's back."

"Good," she said, "call him in."

Mosca thought for a moment. "He doesn't want to see anybody right now. He had a little accident and hurt his face. I guess he doesn't want you to see him."

"That's silly," Hella said. When she had finished dressing she went out of the room and knocked on Leo's door. Mosca stayed in his own room, resting on the bed. He heard Leo open the door for Hella and listened as they spoke, their voices indistinct murmurs. He didn't want to go in, there was nothing he could do.

Mosca dozed off and when he woke he felt that it was very late, it was pitch dark in the room. He could still hear Leo and Hella talking in the other room. He waited for a few minutes and then he called out, "Hey, how about getting something to eat before the Red Cross closes up?" The voices broke off and started again. Then he heard Leo's door open and a moment later Hella came into the room and snapped on the light.

"I'm ready," she said, "let's go." He saw that she was biting her lips to keep from crying.

Mosca picked up the blue gym bag into which he had stuffed the wet towels and dirty underclothing. They went down the steps and out of the building. Frau Meyer was still standing on the steps. "Did you see our friend?" she asked. There was a slightly patronizing and amused tone in her voice.

"Yes," Hella said curtly.

On the way down the Kurfürsten Allee, Mosca asked, "He tell you everything?"

"Yes," Hella said.

"What the hell did you talk about so long in there?"

She didn't say anything for a time. "About when we

were children. He grew up in the city, and I was raised on the land but a lot of the same things happened to both of us. When we were children Germany was a nice country to live in."

"Everybody is leaving," Mosca said. "First Middleton, now Leo and pretty soon Wolf. That leaves just us and Eddie. I'll have to keep an eye on you and Eddie."

Hella looked at him without smiling. Her face was tired, the eyes a very pale gray. The blue lump had spread to a long welt the length of her jaw. "I want to leave now as soon as we can," she said. "I don't like Eddie, I don't like you to be with him. I know he is a good friend, he does things for us. But I'm afraid of him. Not about me but about you."

"Don't worry," Mosca said. "Our marriage papers will get here soon. We'll leave Germany in October."

When they were nearly home, Hella said tiredly, "Walter, do you think the world will get better for helpless people?"

"I don't know," he said, "but don't worry, we're not helpless."

Then to cheer her up he said, "I wrote my mother about the whole deal. She's real happy, especially that I'm going home. She just hopes I picked a good girl." They smiled at each other.

"I think I'm good," Hella said a little sadly. "I wonder about my father and mother, what they would think of me if they were alive. They wouldn't be happy." She paused for a moment. "I'm afraid they wouldn't think me a good girl."

"We're trying, baby," Mosca said, "we're trying like hell. It's a different world."

They turned into the little path that led to their home,

following a stream of moonlight to the door. Through the walls of the stone house they could hear the baby crying, not desperately, but in perfunctory protest. Hella smiled at Mosca. "That little stinker," she said, but she ran up the steps ahead of him.

19

IT WAS the first time Hella had ever come out to the air base, and Mosca went outside the wire fence to meet her and bring her past the guards. She was very slim and chic in a suit made from officer's pink. He had bought the material with Ann Middleton's Army store card. With the suit she wore a white silk blouse and white hat and veil. The veil screened her swollen cheek. She held onto Mosca's arm as they entered the gate of the air base.

In the Civilian Personnel Office, Inge left her desk and stood up to greet Hella. They shook hands and murmured their names. Herr Topp, the chief clerk, came in from the outer office with some papers for Eddie Cassin to sign. He was all smiles and pleasantness. "We have a great dentist on the air base, American dentists are the finest," Herr Topp assured Hella.

"Did you fix it with Captain Adlock sure?" Mosca asked Eddie.

Eddie nodded, then said to Hella gently, "How do you feel?"

"It hurts a bit," Hella said. She could feel the power that Eddie and Mosca held over the people here, how respectful Herr Topp and the girl Inge were, here the role of conqueror and conquered clean-cut, not blurred by sex or personal service. It made her shy of Eddie, and Mosca too, so that she said almost defensively to Eddie, "The German dentists couldn't help."

"We have the medicines they can't get," Eddie said reassuringly. "Captain Adlock will fix you up fine." He turned to Mosca. "You can take her over there now."

Hella and Mosca left the Civilian Personnel Office. In the outer room the German clerks stopped work, as if in interested surprise, to see that the ugly American with his curt manner and cruel face had chosen a seemingly shy, sweet girl, slender and tall, directly opposite to what they had thought his choice would be.

They penetrated to the interior of the air base, crossing the many walks that radiated to the hangars, the flying fields, the Administration Building, until finally they came to the long low barrack that served as the medical dispensary and base hospital.

The dental chair of black leather was empty as was the white-walled room. Then a German doctor in white smock came in. He said, "Captain Adlock asked me to attend you. He is busy at the moment. Please." He motioned Hella toward the dental chair.

She took off her hat and veil and gave them to Mosca. She put her hand to the swollen cheek as if to hide it, then sat in the dental chair. Mosca stood near her and she reached out her hand to hold his arm. The German dentist's eyes narrowed as he saw her swollen cheek. He helped her open her mouth wide, forcing the jaws apart gently but firmly. He took one long look. Then he turned to Mosca and said. "We can do nothing until the infection is cleared up. It goes all the way down to the root, the bone. She needs penicillin and hot compresses. When the swelling goes down I can take out the root."

Mosca said, "Can you give her the shots?"

The German dentist shrugged. "I cannot do it. The penicillin is locked up and only the American doctors have the authority to use it. Shall I call Captain Adlock?" Mosca nodded. The German left the room.

Hella raised her head to smile at Mosca, as if to apologize for the trouble she was causing. Only one side of her face twisted. Mosca smiled back and said, "It's O.K." He put the hat and veil on a chair.

They waited a long time. Finally Captain Adlock came in. He was a stout, young, kind-looking man who wore his uniform with a recruit's sloppiness, the tie loosely knotted and pulled down from the unbuttoned collar, his blouse open.

"Ah, let's see now," he said cheerfully and stuck his fingers impersonally into Hella's mouth to separate her teeth. "Yes, I'm afraid my boy is right." He nodded toward the elderly German dentist who had re-entered the room. "She has to get penicillin shots and compresses. When the swelling goes down we can fix her up with no trouble at all."

Mosca knew what the answer would be but he had to ask. "Can you give her the penicillin?" He realized that his voice sounded angry, surly, that he had worded the question the wrong way. He felt Hella's hand pressing on his arm.

"I'm sorry," Captain Adlock shook his head. "You know how it is. I don't mind breaking the regulations but if I did it for you every G.I. would bring his girl here. And the penicillin has to be strictly accounted for."

"I've got my marriage papers in," Mosca said. "Does that make any difference?"

"I'm sorry," Captain Adlock said. Mosca saw the genuine regret. The Captain was thoughtful. "Look, as soon as your papers come back from Frankfort approved let me know and I'll give her full treatment. We won't have to wait for you to actually get married. I wouldn't want to wait and fool around with an infection like that."

Hella put on her hat and veil. She murmured her thanks to the Captain, who patted her shoulder and said, "Now keep putting compresses on her cheek. Possibly the swelling will go down with just that. If it gets worse take her to the German hospital." As they went out the door, Mosca saw a look of doubt on the face of the elderly German dentist, as if it were all being taken too lightly.

Back in the Personnel Office, he told Eddie what had happened. Hella sat in the chair at Mosca's desk, seemingly calm, undistressed.

Eddie clucked with sympathy. He said, "Why don't you go up to the Adjutant's office and see if he can make Frankfort rush those papers through."

Mosca said to Hella, "Can you wait here a little while, or do you want to go home now?"

"I'll wait," she said, "but don't take so long." She squeeze his hand and her palm was wet with perspiration.

"You sure you're all right," he asked.

She nodded. Mosca left.

The Adjutant was speaking over the phone, his voice polite, the bland, ingenuous face courteous with attention to the dead instrument. He raised his eyebrow to show Mosca he would be through in a moment. When he hung up he said briskly, "What can I do for you?"

Mosca stumbled over the words, feeling defensive and overawed. Then he said. "I wonder if anything came through on my marriage papers?"

"No, nothing yet," the Adjutant said politely and began

leafing through a bound volume of Army regulations.

Mosca hesitated again and then said. "Is there any way of rushing them through?"

The Adjutant didn't look up. "No," he said.

Mosca resisted the impulse to turn away and leave. "Do you think if I went down to Frankfort it would help? Maybe you could tell me who to see?"

The Adjutant closed the thick, heavily bound book and looked up at Mosca for the first time. His voice was impersonal but curt. "Look, Mosca," he said, "you lived with this girl for a year, you didn't file an application for marriage until six months after the ban was lifted. Now all of a sudden there's a big rush. I can't stop you from going to Frankfort, but I guarantee it won't help. You know how I feel about working outside the channels."

Mosca felt no anger, only embarrassment and a sense of shame. The Adjutant went on in a softer tone. "As soon as they come in I'll let you know, O.K.?" And with this dismissal, Mosca left.

Walking back to the Personnel Office he tried not to feel depressed or anxious, knowing that Hella would see it in his face. But Hella and Inge were drinking coffee together and talking. Hella had her hat and veil off and she could only take little sips of coffee but he could see from her bright eyes that she had been telling Inge all about the baby. Eddie was leaning back in his chair, listening, smiling and when he saw Mosca he asked, "How did it go?"

Mosca said, "Fine, he'll do what he can," and smiled at Hella. He would tell Eddie the truth later.

Hella put on her hat and veil and shook hands with Inge. She shook hands with Eddie and then took Mosca's arm. When they were out of the office and had gone through the gate of the air base, Mosca said, "I'm sorry, baby." She turned her veiled face to him, squeezed his arm. He turned his head away as if he could not bear her gaze without flinching.

In the early morning hours before dawn Mosca came out of sleep and heard Hella crying softly, sobbing into her pillow. He pulled her to him so she could bury her head in his naked shoulder. "Is it that bad?" he whispered. And she said, "Walter, I feel so sick, I feel so sick." Saying the words seemed to frighten her and her crying became unrestrained like the weeping of a terrified child.

In the darkness the pain swept over her, took control of her blood and the organs of her body. The memory of Mosca at the air base powerless to help her gave her a sense of terror, made her helpless to restrain her tears. She said again, "I feel so sick," and Mosca could barely make out the words, there was a curious distortion in her speech. "I'll make you some more compresses," he said and turned on the night lamp beside the bed.

He was shocked when he saw her. In the dim yellow light the side of her face was distended, the eye almost closed. There was a strange contour of her facial bones, giving her a mongoloid look. She put her hands up over her face and he went out into the kitchen to get some water for the compresses.

The ruins of the city rode on two morning sunbeams straight into the stunned eyes of Yergen's daughter. She sat on a great stone dipping her fingers into an open tin of *mirabelle* plums. The smell of rubble was just beginning to rise from the earth. The little girl serenely fished out the yellow, waxlike globes of fruit and then licked the sticky juice from her fingers. Yergen sat on a stone beside her.

He had taken her to this secluded valley of ruins so that she could eat the rare delicacy without sharing it with the German woman who cared for her during the day.

Yergen watched his daughter's face with love and sadness. The eyes showed clearly the slow fragmentation and splintering of her childish brain. The doctor had told him that there was one hope, to get her out of Germany or the continent. Yergen shook his head. All the money he made in the black market went to build a wall between his child and the suffering, the misery of the world around her. But the doctor had made him understand that this was not enough. That it all seeped through somehow.

Now at this moment he made his decision. He would buy false papers and settle in Switzerland. It would take months to prepare and a great deal of money. She would be cured, she would grow and live to happiness.

She held up a gleaming *mirabelle*, shiny pale yellow in its coat of syrup and to please her he opened his mouth to receive it. She smiled at him and the smile made him put his hand on her face, in love and protection, for in this valley of ruins his daughter seemed like a plant growing, inhuman, her eyes blank, the smile a muscular spasm.

The morning air was cold, autumn had weakened the strength of the rising sun and changed the color of the earth, turned the rubble gray and patched it with dead brown grass.

Yergen said gently, "Giselle, come now, I must take you home, I must go to work." The child let the can of *mirabelles* slip from her hand, the heavy syrup spilled out, clotted over bits of stone and brick. She began to cry.

Yergen lifted her up from the great stone she sat on and held her, pressed her head against his neck. "I'll be home early tonight, don't fret. And I'll have a present, something to wear." But he knew she would continue to cry until he carried her up the church steps to their apartment in the steeple.

Framed against the pale sky, Yergen saw a man coming over a hill of ruins and then disappear and then come over another little hill, always coming toward him, coming out of the sun's light. Yergen put the girl down and she clung to his legs. The figure came over the last little rolling hill. Yergen was surprised to see that the man was Mosca.

He was wearing his officer greens with the white civilian patch. In the morning sunlight his dark skin had a grayish tinge and lines of tiredness in his face that cut the features away from each other, making each distinct in its own right.

"I been looking all over for you," Mosca said.

Yergen stroked his daughter's head. Neither looked directly at Mosca. Yergen felt a little strange that they could be found so easily. Mosca seemed to sense this. "Your housekeeper, she told me you usually come over this way mornings."

Daylight was now at full strength, Yergen could hear the clanging of the *Strassenbahn*. He asked slowly, mistrustfully, "Why do you want to see me?"

On one of the slopes surrounding them there was a shifting and falling of rubble, a tiny landslide that sent a small cloud of dust toward the sky. Mosca shifted his feet, he could feel them sinking in the treacherous ground. He said, "I need some morphine or codeine and some penicillin for Hella. You know about that tooth. She's become really ill." He paused awkwardly. "I need it today, the morphine, she's in very bad pain. I'll pay anything you say."

Yergen picked up his daughter and began to walk over the ruins. Mosca walked beside him. "That will be very hard to do," Yergen said, but everything had already clicked together in his mind. At one stroke he would come three months closer to Switzerland. "The price will be terribly high."

Mosca stopped, and though the morning sun had no fire Yergen saw that the sweat was pouring off his face, and Yergen saw in that face an enormous relief.

"Christ," Mosca said, "I was scared you couldn't swing it. I don't care what I pay, you can steal me blind. Just get the stuff tonight."

They were standing now on the last hill and before them was that part of the city not completely destroyed, with the church Yergen lived in. "Come to me at midnight," Yergen said. "Don't come in the evening, my daughter will be alone and she is very ill, she must not be frightened." He waited for Mosca to make an expression of sympathy and felt an angry bitterness when none came. This American so concerned about his mistress, why didn't he take her to America and safety? And the fact that Mosca could do for someone he loved what he could not do for his daughter increased the bitterness in Yergen. He said almost spitefully, "If you come before midnight, I won't help you."

Mosca stood on top of the hill and watched Yergen sliding down it, the child cradled in his arms. He called after him. "Don't forget, pay anything to get the stuff." Yergen turned and nodded, the child's face in his arms staring directly upward to the autumn sky.

20

EDDIE CASSIN and Mosca left the Civilian Personnel Building, walked through the gray autumn twilight toward the hangars and the take-off strip.

"Another guy leaving the old gang," Eddie Cassin said. "First Middleton, Leo, now Wolf. I guess you'll be next, Walter."

Mosca didn't answer. They were walking against the stream of workers leaving the base, German laborers and mechanics moving toward the guarded exits. Suddenly the ground began to shake and they could hear the roar of powerful engines. Rounding a corner of the Administration Building, they came upon the great, silvery plane.

The late afternoon sun was far away across the sky. Mosca and Eddie waited, smoking cigarettes. Finally they saw the jeep come past the hangars and onto the field. They started down the ramp toward the plane and reached it the moment the jeep swung around its finned tail and came to a stop.

Wolf, Ursula and Ursula's father got out of the jeep, the father unloading the heavy Val-packs at once. Wolf gave his friends a huge, joyful grin.

"It's damn nice of you guys to see me off," he said and shook their hands, then introduced them to the father. They knew Ursula.

The propellers blasted great gusts of air that almost blew

the words away. The father went close to the airplane, ran his hands over the gray skin, then prowled around it like a hungry animal.

Eddie Cassin said jokingly to Wolf, "He going to stow away?" And Wolf laughed and said, "He couldn't stow away on the *Queen Elizabeth.*"

Ursula had not understood. She watched with quick darting eyes the luggage being carried aboard the plane, then put her hand on Wolf's arm.

Wolf extended his hand again to Mosca and Eddie and said, "Well, so long you guys. It's been a pleasure, no kidding. When you get to the States, look me up. Eddie, you got my address."

"Sure thing," Eddie said coolly.

Wolf looked into Mosca's eyes and said, "Good luck, Walter. I'm sorry that deal didn't go through, but now maybe I think you're right."

Mosca smiled and said, "Good luck, Wolf."

Wolf hesitated. Then he said. "One last piece of advice. Don't wait too long to get out of here, Walter. Get back to the States as soon as you can. That's all I can say."

Mosca smiled again and said, "Thanks, Wolf, I will."

The father came waddling around the nose of the plane. He came close to Wolf, arms extended. "Wolfgang, Wolfgang," he cried out emotionally, "you will not forget me here, Wolfgang?" He was close to tears. Wolf patted his shoulder and the fat old man embraced him. "You are like a son to me," the old man said, "I will miss you."

Mosca could see that Wolf was annoyed, bored and anxious to be off. The father took Ursula into his arms. He was sobbing now. "Ursula, my daughter, my little daughter, you're the only one I have, you won't forget your old father, you won't leave him all alone in this terrible land, eh? My little Ursula would not do such a thing?"

His daughter kissed him and murmured comfortingly, "Papa, don't take on so, you will come too as soon as I can make the papers. Please don't take on so."

Wolf had a tight little smile on his face. He touched Ursula on the shoulder and said in German, "It is time."

The fat old man let out a wail, "Ursula, Ursula." But now the girl, herself overwrought, with guilty anger at this unseemly grief for her good fortune, tore herself away and ran up the steps into the plane.

Wolf took the old man's hand. "You've upset her. Now I promise. You will leave here. You will spend the rest of your days in America with your daughter and your grandchildren. Here is my hand on it."

The old man nodded his head. "You are good, Wolfgang, you are very good."

Wolf gave Eddie and Mosca an embarrassed half-salute, then quickly went up the steps into the plane.

Through one of the windows Ursula's face appeared grimacing a farewell through dirt-streaked glass to her father. He burst into tears again and waved a great white handkerchief to her in return. The engines roared into sound again. Ground-crew men wheeled the mobile stairs away. The great silvery plane began to move slowly, pushing itself along the ground. It made a slow, seemingly wing-dragging turn and rolled away faster and faster until reluctantly, as if fighting some malignant power, it parted itself from the earth and flew toward the dark autumn sky.

Mosca watched the plane until it disappeared. Then he heard Eddie saying, "Mission accomplished, a successful man leaves Europe." There was only a faint note of bitterness in his voice.

The three of them stood silently staring at the sky, their

shadows blending into one great shadow as the sun escaped the autumn clouds before it fell below the horizon. Mosca looked at the old fat man who would never see his daughter again, who would never leave this continent. That great meat-creased face stared dumbly into the empty sky, as if searching for some hope or promise and then the small slitted eyes rested on Mosca, the voice thick with hate and despair, said, "Ach, my friends, it is gone from us."

Mosca dipped the linen rag into the hot pan of water and after wringing it out, applied the steaming cloth to Hella's face. She lay on the sofa, tears of pain in her eyes, the swollen flesh pulling the nose out of line and twisting the side of her mouth, making a grotesque distortion of the left eye. In the armchair near the foot of the sofa Frau Saunders held the baby, tilting the nippled bottle so that the infant could feed more easily.

As he kept changing compresses, Mosca spoke to Hella softly, soothingly. "We'll keep this up a couple of days and everything will be O.K., just hold still now." They had been sitting so all afternoon and the swelling had gone down a little. The baby in Frau Saunders' arms began to cry and Hella sat up on the sofa and reached for him. She pushed the compress away and said to Mosca, "I can't any more." She took the baby from Frau Saunders. She put the good side of her face against the infant's head and crooned softly, "Poor little baby, your mother can't look after you." And then with fumbling hands she began to change the wet diapers, Frau Saunders helping her.

Mosca watched. He saw that the continual pain and lack of sleep for the last week had drained her of strength. The German hospital doctors had said her case was not serious enough to warrant penicillin. His only hope was that Yergen would have the drugs for him at midnight, tonight. The last two nights Yergen had disappointed him.

Hella finished dressing the baby and Mosca took the child from her. He cradled the infant in his arms and watched Hella try to smile at him as she lay back on the sofa. As he watched he saw the tears of pain start to her eyes, and she turned her head away from him. He could hear the small, uncontrollable whimpers.

Mosca stood it as long as he could then he put the child back in the carriage. "I'm going to see if Yergen has the medicine," he said. It was a long way to midnight but the hell with it. He might catch Yergen home. It was near eight, the German supper time. He leaned over to kiss Hella and she put up her hand to touch his face. "I'll be back as soon as I can."

The Kurfürsten Allee was chilled with the first cold of winter and in the darkness he could hear the falling leaves sifting along the ground to become lost in the ruins of the city. He caught a *Strassenbahn* to the church in which Yergen lived. The side entrance was open, and he ran up the steps to the steeple. Standing a step below the door which was cut into the wall he knocked as hard as he could. He waited, there was no answer, no sound behind the door. He tried a variation of knocks, hoping that by some chance he would hit on Yergen's signal and the child would open the door and he could question her. But for some reason he did not call out. He waited again for some moments and then he heard a curious animal-like sound, monotonous, on one level shrilling tone and realized that the child behind the door was crying and would in her terror never open the door. He went down the stairs and waited outside the church for Yergen.

He waited for a long time. The wind became colder and

the night darker, the rustling of the trees and falling leaves louder and more sibilant. As he stood there waiting there grew in him a sense of certain and terrible disaster. He tried to remain still but suddenly was walking away from the church and down Kurfürsten Allee.

As soon as he had left the church and walked a few minutes the fear left him. Then the thought of watching helplessly the tears and pain he would be sure to see made him stop. All the strain and tension, the humiliations and refusals of the past week, the turning away by Dr. Adlock, the rebuke by the Adjutant, the dismissal by the German hospital doctors, and his inability to fight back in any way against them—all this overwhelmed him. He wanted a drink, three or four drinks, so bad that he was surprised. He had never needed liquor. But now, without hesitating any longer, he turned and started walking toward the avenue that led to the Officers' Club. He felt for one moment a sense of shame that he was not going home.

It was a quiet night at the club. There were some officers at the bar, but no music or dancing and only a few women. Mosca had three shots of whiskey very quick. It worked like magic. He could feel the tension flow out of his body, the fear, and he saw everything in correct proportion, that Hella had only a bad tooth and that the people who seemed such implacable enemies were only obeying laws imposed by others.

One of the officers at the bar said to him, "Your friend Eddie is upstairs shooting crap." Mosca nodded acknowledgment and another officer said with a grin, "Your other buddy is up there too, the Adjutant. He's celebrating making Major."

"I gotta have a drink on that," Mosca said and they laughed. Mosca unbuttoned his jacket and lit a cigar and had a few more drinks. He felt warm and sure that things would turn out all right. Hell, it was only a toothache, and he knew Hella was extra-sensitive to pain. It was funny how she had courage in everything except physical pain, he thought. She was a real coward about that. Not coward; he felt a sudden rush of anger at himself that he thought of such a word in connection with her. But she cried easy. And now some of the warmness left him. In the inside pocket of his open jacket he caught a flash of white and remembered that a few days ago Hella had written her first letter to his mother and he had forgotten to mail it. His mother had written asking for a letter and pictures of the baby. Mosca left the bar and dropped the letter in the mail box in the hall. He hesitated for a moment, somewhere in his mind was a faint warning not to go up, but the whiskey clouded over it. He went upstairs to the game room.

Eddie was at a corner of the table, in one hand a small sheaf of dollar scrip bills. The Adjutant was opposite him and there was something strange about the Adjutant. The ingenuous face was flushed and twisted into an expression of slyness. Mosca felt a sense of shock. Christ, the guy was loaded. For one moment he thought of turning and going out. But then curiosity made him go to the dice table. He thought, let's see if the bastard gets human on a drunk.

Eddie asked, "How's your girl?" Mosca said, "All right." A waiter came upstairs and into the room with a tray of drinks.

The game was slow—relaxation, not gambling. Mosca liked it that way tonight. He made small bets, talking casually to Eddie.

The Adjutant was the only one playing with gusto. He tried everything to goad the players into higher action. When his turn came to shoot he laid down thirty dollars.

Only ten was faded. He offered bets in various fashions, but the players, seemingly out of perversity, refused to become excited and continued to bet in one- or five-dollar amounts.

Mosca felt a little guilty. He thought, "I could leave and go home and see how Hella is and then go to Yergen." But in another hour the club would close for the night. He decided to stay.

The Adjutant, looking now for any kind of excitement and giving up hope of finding it in the game, said to Mosca. "I hear you had your *Fräulein* out to the base for some free medical treatment. You should know better than that, Walter." It was the first time he had ever used Mosca's given name.

One of the officers said, "For Christ sake, relax, don't talk shop in the club."

And in that moment Mosca knew why he had stayed, why he had come to the club. He tried to make himself leave now, tried to make his body move away from the table, tried to take his hands off the green felt. But the cruel satisfaction rose in his body and flooded over his mind and reason. All the humiliations and defeats of the past week poisoned his blood, the vessels of his brain. He thought, "All right you son of a bitch, all right, all right." But he kept his voice casual, saying, "I just thought the Doc might help." Making it sound a little nervous. He'd eaten shit all week, just this little more won't hurt.

"Things like that don't happen where I'm running things," the Adjutant said. "And when it does, and I find out, it's usually somebody's ass. And I usually find out."

"I'm not a prick," the Adjutant went on in a serious tone. "I believe in fair play. But if he treated your *Fräulein* all the G.I.'s would start bringing their clapped-up *Fräuleins* to the base for shots. Can't have that." The Adjutant's ingenuous face had a boyish, happy smile. He raised his glass and took a long drink.

Mosca stared at the dice, at the green cloth on the table. Eddie was saying something but the words were jumbled up. He made an effort and looked up. He said quietly, "I'll shoot the two bucks there."

The Adjutant put his glass on the window sill behind him, then threw a ten-dollar bill on the table. "I got you," he said.

Mosca picked up the bill and threw it back at the Adjutant. "Don't you fade me." He said it in a cold, deliberate voice. One of the other officers threw some money down and Mosca rolled the dice.

"You're pretty touchy about that *Fräulein,*" the Adjutant said. He was in a good humor, did not sense any of the tension around him. "Maybe you think those *Fräuleins* have a pure, disinterested love for your homely mugs. If it were up to me I wouldn't let any of you chumps marry here."

Mosca let the dice drop on to the table. In an almost indifferent, casual voice he asked. "That why you held up my papers, you sneaky bastard?"

The Adjutant smiled with real delight. "I'll have to deny that and ask where you got your information." He said this with his coldly formal, official manner, in it a note of menace and command.

Mosca picked up the dice. He had stopped thinking or caring. He was just waiting for the Adjutant to pass him.

"Where did you get that information?" the Adjutant asked. His bland face was serious, had its familiar look of youthful sternness. "Where did you get that information?" he repeated.

Mosca rattled the dice and threw them out carelessly. He said to the Adjutant, "You stupid prick, go scare some krauts."

Eddie Cassin broke in, "I told him and if the Colonel wants to know, I'll tell him the story. That you let the papers lay for two weeks before you sent them to Frankfort." He turned to Mosca, "Come on, Walter, let's get out of here."

The Adjutant was on that side of the table hemmed by the wall and window. Mosca wanted him to come out, to squeeze by the corner. He thought for a moment, then said, "You think this fuck gets away with it tonight?"

There was a split second before the Adjutant recognized the threat. Then, he shouted angrily, "Let's see what you'll do about it," and started to come around the table. Mosca waited until the corner would pin his arms. Then he swung as hard as he could at the profiled face. The blow glanced off the Adjutant's cheekbone and skull not hurting him, but making him fall. Mosca kicked viciously underneath the table. He felt the heel meet with a solid shock against bone. Then an officer and Eddie were pulling him away. The Adjutant, really hurt now, was put on his feet. Submissively Mosca let the officer and Eddie push him toward the door. Suddenly Mosca whirled and ran across the room. The Adjutant was standing straight up. Running he swung as hard as he could into the Adjutant's side and they both fell on the floor. The Adjutant screamed with pain. The look on Mosca's face and his attack on the defenseless man so horrified the other men that for one second they were frozen motionless. Then three of the officers swarmed over Mosca as he put his fingers inside the Adjutant's ear and tried to tear the side of his face off. One of them hit Mosca a stunning blow on the temple and then they were hustling him down the stairs and out of the club. There was no thought of retaliation in this, Eddie was helping them. The cold night air cleared Mosca's brain.

He and Eddie were alone. "That last shot queered everything," Eddie said. "Why the hell couldn't you be satisfied?"

Mosca said, "I wanted to kill the bastard, that's why." But the reaction had set in. He couldn't keep his hands from shaking when he lit his cigarette and he felt a chilly sweat over his body. Christ, he thought, over a lousy fist fight, trying to keep his hands still.

They stood together in the dark street. "I'll try to fix it," Eddie said, "but you're washed up with the Army. You know that? Don't wait, shoot down to Frankfort tomorrow and try to get those marriage papers. I'll cover you here. Don't worry about anything but the papers."

Mosca thought for a moment. "I guess that's it. Thanks Eddie." For some reason he shook hands with Cassin, awkwardly, knowing that Eddie would do everything he could to help.

"You going home now?" Eddie asked.

"No," Mosca said. "I have to see Yergen." He turned and walked away from Eddie, then called back over his shoulder, "I'll phone you from Frankfort."

A cold, autumn moon lit his way to the church. He ran up the steps and before he could knock Yergen had opened the door.

"Be very still," Yergen said, "my daughter has just fallen asleep after much trouble." They went into the room. Behind the wooden partition came the sound of the child's heavy breathing. Mosca could hear a curiously halting stitch in it. He saw that Yergen was angry and almost belligerent.

"Were you here earlier this evening?" Yergen asked.

"No," Mosca lied. But he had hesitated a fraction of a second and Yergen knew.

"I have the drugs for you," Yergen said. He was glad that Mosca had frightened his child and given him the angry courage to do what he must do. "I have the penicillin vials and the codeine tablets, but they cost a great deal." He took out of his pocket a small cardboard box, uncovered it to show Mosca the four dark-brown vials and the square box of large, red-shelled codeine tablets. Even now his instinct was to tell Mosca that the penicillin had only cost a fraction of the usual black-market price and therefore might be useless; to charge him a reasonable price for the drugs. But in that wavering moment there was a great stitching gasp in his daughter's breathing, the room was completely still. He could see Mosca looking at the wooden partition, then before either of them could move, the breathing started again, regularly, in the heavy rhythm of sleep. Yergen relaxed. "The cost will be fifty cartons of cigarettes." He saw the tiny black lights in Mosca's eyes focusing on him with a sudden cruel insight and understanding.

"All right," Mosca said. "I don't care what I pay. You sure it's good stuff?"

In time Yergen paused only for a moment but many thoughts flashed through his mind.

He needed as many cigarettes as possible, then he could swing a big deal he had planned and be out of Germany in a month. Hella probably did not really need penicillin, the Bremen doctors when they knew a girl had an American friend always asked for penicillin so that they could keep some for themselves. And he thought of his daughter again, she came before everything.

"You can be certain. I guarantee it," Yergen said. "This source has never betrayed me." He touched his breast with his hand. "I take the responsibility."

"All right," Mosca said. "Now listen. I have twenty cartons, maybe I can get some more. If I can't I'll pay you at the rate of five dollars a carton in scrip or American Express checks. Is that O.K.?" He knew that he was being fair and that Yergen was making a real steal, but the reaction of his encounter with the Adjutant still affected him. He felt an immense weariness, hopelessness and isolation. In his mind he bowed before the little German, asked for pity, for mercy. And Yergen, sensing this, became cautiously arrogant.

"I have to pay in cigarettes," Yergen said. "I think you will have to give me cigarettes."

Behind the wooden partition the little girl moaned in her sleep. Mosca remembered Hella whimpering with pain, she had expected him home long ago.

He made a last try. "I need this stuff tonight."

Yergen said, "I must have the cigarettes tonight." This time there was a malicious note of triumph in his voice, unconsciously, not knowing that he had spoken so, that he had always hated this American.

Mosca made himself not feel anything, not do anything. He was ashamed now and fearful of what would happen because of the fight in the club. He had to be careful not to make any mistakes. Gravely, without anger or menace, he picked up the cardboard box and slipped it into his jacket. He said politely, reasonably, "Come to the house with me and I'll give you the twenty cartons tonight and the money. I'll try to get you the rest of the cigarettes in the next few days and then you give the money back."

Yergen saw that nothing could keep Mosca from leaving with the drugs. He felt a moment of fear, a weakness of blood. He was no coward but was always afraid that his daughter would be left alone in the ruined land. He went behind the partition to arrange the blankets over his sleeping child and then went through the doorway of the other partition for his hat and coat. They walked to Mosca's house without exchanging a word.

Mosca let Yergen wait for his pay until he had given Hella a codeine tablet. She was still awake and he could see in the dark the white outline of the swollen jaw.

"How is it?" he asked softly, speaking almost in a whisper so as not to awaken the baby in the carriage.

She whispered to him, "It hurts very much."

"Here's something for the pain." He gave her one of the large, red-shelled codeine tablets and he could see her pushing it down her throat with her finger and then drinking the water from the glass he held to her lips. "I'll be right back," he said.

He made a package, bulky and untidy, of the cigarette cartons. He brought it to the door and gave it to Yergen, then took from his wallet the American Express checks, signed them, and put the blue thin paper in Yergen's pocket. Out of politeness and some remorse, he asked, "Will you have trouble because of curfew? Shall I take you back?"

"No, I have a curfew pass," Yergen said, and then with a soft laugh, the bulky cigarettes under his arm cheering him up, "an essential businessman."

Mosca let him out, locked the door and returned to the

bedroom. Hella was still awake. He lay down beside her, not undressing. He told her what had happened at the club and that he had to go to Frankfort the next day.

"I'll get those papers and in a month we'll be out of here, on a plane to the States," he whispered to her. He told her stories about his mother and Alf and how glad they would both be to see her. He made it all sound sure and easy, inevitable. He could feel her getting warm and sleepy and then suddenly she asked, "Can I have another tablet?" He got up to give it to her and held the water to her lips again. Then before she fell asleep he told her about the penicillin and to go to a doctor the next day to get some shots. "I'll call up every night from Frankfort," he said. "I won't be away three days even." When she fell into a sleep in which she did not even breathe he smoked a few cigarettes in a chair by the window, watching the ruins of the city fresh and clear in the autumn moonlight. Then he put on the light in the kitchen and packed his blue gym bag with the few things he would need for the trip. He made himself some eggs and tea, hoping the food would help him sleep. He lay beside Hella again and waited for dawn.

21

THROUGH THE CURTAIN of heavy, exhausted slumber and codeine Hella heard the short angry wails of hunger. Fully awake it gave her a feeling of pleasant anxiety, knowing how easily she could still the infant; she listened, then left her bed to prepare the bottle.

She felt weak though she had slept well the last two nights. The constant use of codeine had taken effect and the pain in her head and mouth was numbed. She reached up and felt surprised and shocked that her fingers and cheek met so quickly. Her face had swollen even more during the night but she had felt no pain. Waiting for the baby's milk to heat she took another codeine tablet, shoving it down her throat with her finger. It was hard now to swallow saliva. Then she brought the child his bottle and absolute quiet descended on the room.

She was very tired and she stretched out on the bed again. In the other rooms she could hear Frau Saunders moving about, cleaning her own two rooms and the living room they shared. They had been lucky with Frau Saunders, Hella thought. And Walter liked her. She hoped he would bring the marriage papers so they could leave Germany. Now she was always afraid, more about the child than anything. That if the child became ill they could not get any American medicines. They couldn't take chances on the black market where the baby was concerned.

When she felt a little stronger Hella rose from the bed and cleaned her own rooms. Then she went into the living room. Frau Saunders was already sitting by the iron stove and drinking coffee. There was a filled cup waiting for Hella.

"When is your man coming back?" Frau Saunders asked. "Wasn't he supposed to have come this morning?"

"He has to stay a few days longer," Hella said. "He will have definite news when he calls tonight on the telephone. You know what documents are."

"Have you told him about the penicillin?" Frau Saunders asked.

Hella shook her head.

"I thought this Yergen was really a friend of yours," Frau Saunders said. "How could he possibly do such a thing?"

"I don't think it was his fault," Hella said. "The doctor told me it was impossible to use because it hadn't been properly cared for. It was really penicillin. Yergen would have no way of knowing."

"He must have known," Frau Saunders said. Then dryly, "He will find his profit small when Herr Mosca goes to visit him."

In the other room the baby began to cry and Hella went to bring him out. Frau Saunders said, "Let me hold him." Hella gave her the baby and went for some clean diapers.

When she brought the fresh linen into the room Frau Saunders said, "Here, let me change him." It was a ritual they went through in the morning. Hella took the empty iron pail beside the stove and said, "I'll go down for some briquets."

"You're not strong enough yet for that," Frau Saunders said. But she was tickling the baby and spoke automatically.

The morning air was iced with autumn, dying summer sunlit trees and fallen leaves with dark-brown and reddish fire. From somewhere Hella could smell a deep, cidery tang of fallen apples; beyond the rising, gardened hills she could smell the freshness of the Weser River newly washed by autumn rains. On the other side of the Kurfürsten Allee she saw a young, pretty girl with four small children playing underneath the trees, kicking dead brown leaves piled high as snowdrifts. Then she felt very cold and went inside.

She went down the cellar stairs and unlocked the wire-mesh door which enclosed her portion of the basement. She filled the pail with oblong coal briquets. She tried to pick up the pail and to her surprise found that she could not. She made a great effort. The strength drained out of her body and she felt faint. For one moment she was frightened. She held onto the wire screen and the faintness faded away. She took three of the briquets and put them in her apron, holding the ends of it to form a basket. She snapped the lock of the wire door with her one free hand and then began to climb the stairs.

Halfway up the last flight her legs refused to move. She stood for a moment in surprise, unaware. A terrible chill struck her body. A great vessel burst and pain stabbed through her brain like an iron pike so that she did not hear the coal slip out of her apron and crash down the stairs. As in terror she began to fall, she saw Frau Saunders' veiled face leaning over the bannister, the baby in her arms, seeing them hazily but very close. She raised her arms to them and began to scream and then began to fall away from Frau Saunders' horrified face and the white swaddled baby, and still screaming, fell away from her own screams so that she never heard them.

22

EDDIE CASSIN paced up and down the Civilian Personnel Office. Inge was patiently explaining to someone at the other end that she must have the information. Then she would be switched to someone else and begin the same explanation over again.

She motioned to Eddie to come to the phone. "Yes," Eddie said into the phone.

The voice of a man, speaking almost perfect English, heavy with authority, said, "I am sorry, we cannot give information over the phone."

Eddie knew it would be hopeless to argue with that voice. He recognized the tone. The confidence of a man complying strictly with laws and regulations which governed his own little but complete world. He said, "Let me ask one thing. The woman you have in your hospital, her husband or her lover, what you will, is in Frankfort. Now. Is it serious enough that I should tell him to return immediately to see her?"

The heavy voice said, "I would advise that you do so."

Eddie Cassin said, "He is there on important business. He would not wish to return, unless it is absolutely necessary."

There was a short silence. Then the heavy voice with a surprising gentleness, said, "I think you should tell him that he must come."

Eddie hung up. He saw Inge was watching him, wide-eyed. He said, "Get me a clean glass." When she went out he picked up the phone and asked the Army operator to get him the line to Frankfort. He was still waiting when Inge came back with the glass. He let her hold the phone and made himself a strong drink from the bottle of gin and tin of grapefruit juice in his desk. Then he took back the phone.

When he got through to Frankfort, he asked for the Adjutant Section of the headquarters. He talked to three officers before he learned that Mosca had been there the day before and was now probably in the Legal Section. When he got through to the Legal Section they told him that Mosca had left an hour before. They didn't have any idea where he would be now. Eddie hung up the phone and finished his drink. He made another and picked up the phone again. He thought a moment, then when he got the Frankfort line, he asked for the message center in the I. G. Farben Building. A Sergeant answered and he explained briefly why he had to locate Mosca and asked him if he would broadcast a message over the loudspeaker for Mosca to come to the phone. The Sergeant told him to wait. Then he came back to say that the announcement would go on and that he should hold on.

Eddie waited for a long time. He had finished the second drink. Suddenly Mosca's voice came over the phone, saying, "Hello, who is this?" There was only surprise in the voice, no anxiety.

Eddie couldn't speak for a moment. Then he said, "Walter, it's Eddie. How are you making out?"

Mosca said, "I don't know yet, they just chase me from one office to another. Is anything wrong up there?"

Eddie cleared his throat. He spoke casually. "I guess

you'll have to let that deal go, Walter. Your landlady sent a messenger to Meyer that Hella was taken to the hospital. Meyer sent the messenger out to the base and I called the hospital. They wouldn't give any information over the phone but it sounds serious."

There was a pause and then Mosca's voice came over the wire, haltingly, as if he were searching for the words. "You really don't know anything else?"

"I swear to Christ," Eddie said. "But you better come back."

There was a still longer pause. Then Mosca said, "I'll catch the night train at six o'clock. Meet me at the station, Eddie. I think we get in about four in the morning."

"Sure," Eddie said. "I'm going down to the hospital as soon as I hang up. O.K.?"

"O.K. Thanks, Eddie." There was a click on the other end and Eddie Cassin hung up.

He made himself another quick drink. He said to Inge, "I won't be back today." He put the bottle and juice in his brief case and left the air base.

The city of Bremen was dark when Mosca got off the train from Frankfort. It was not quite four in the morning. In the square outside the station an olive-drab Army bus waited, barely visible. The square was illuminated only by a few weak lampposts which scattered tiny scars of light through its corners and down the streets away from the station.

Mosca looked in the waiting room, but there was no sign of Eddie Cassin. He looked up and down the street but there was no jeep waiting.

He stood uncertainly for a few moments, then followed the streetcar tracks down the Schwachhauser Heer

Strasse, swinging off into the long, curving Kurfürsten Allee, not conscious of the blue gym bag he was carrying, carefully picking his way through the ruins of the ghostly city. He never knew afterward why he did not go directly to the hospital.

As Mosca approached his home he saw in the darkness of the city one single light burning and knew it was the light in his apartment. He turned into the little gravel path. As he ran up the steps he could hear the baby crying.

He opened the door of the living room and saw Frau Saunders seated on the sofa, facing him, watching the door, pushing the baby carriage back and forth across the rug. The infant's cries were patient, hopeless, as if nothing could ease or still it. Mosca saw that Frau Saunders' face was white and strained with fatigue, the usually neat, tightly drawn-back hair now loose and straggly around her head.

He stood in the door waiting for her to speak but saw that she was frightened and would not do so.

He asked, "How is she?"

"She is in the hospital," Frau Saunders said.

"I know. How is she?"

Frau Saunders didn't answer. She stopped pushing the baby carriage and put her hands over her face. The baby's wails became louder. Frau Saunders' body began to rock back and forth. "Oh, how she screamed," she said, "oh, how she screamed." Mosca waited. "She fell down the stairs and screamed," Frau Saunders said, weeping.

She let her hands fall away from her face as if she could no longer hide her grief. She began to push the carriage back and forth again. The baby was still. Frau Saunders looked at Mosca waiting patiently in the doorway. "She is dead, she died in the evening. I waited for you." She saw Mosca still waiting there patiently, as if she had not said anything, as if he were still waiting for her to speak.

He felt only a numbness, like a tight fragile shell to keep out pain and light. He heard Frau Saunders say, "She died in the evening," again, and he believed her but could not accept it as truth. He went out of the house and through the dark streets. When he came to the hospital he followed the arc of the great iron fence until he came to the main gate.

Mosca went into the Administration Office. Behind the night-duty desk was a nun in the great white hat of her religious medical order. Then on a bench against the wall he saw Eddie Cassin.

Eddie rose and stood awkwardly. He nodded to the nun. She motioned Mosca to come with her.

Mosca followed the great white hat down the long silent corridors. He heard in the stillness, the exhausted sleeping breath of the sick. At the end of the corridor they weaved through black-clad charwomen who knelt and scrubbed the tiled floors white.

They turned into another corridor. The nun opened the door of a small room and he entered behind her. She stepped off to one side and closed the door.

Mosca took a step into the room and in the corner, framed in the white pillow, he saw Hella's face, her body covered with a white sheet to the neck. He could not see clearly and took another step into the room.

Her eyes were closed and the side of her face was no longer swollen, as if the poison and life had fled her body together. The mouth was colorless, almost white. There was no spot of red anywhere. There were no lines in her face and she looked younger than he had ever remembered; but the face was vacant, the great hollows of her closed eyes giving it the effect of blindness.

Mosca went nearer and stood beside the bed and on the sill of the draped window he could not see there stood a great vase filled with white flowers. He looked down at Hella, feeling confused, knowing now he must accept the fact of her death but not knowing what to do, not able to think or feel. Death not being strange to him in its violent form, but now seeing it as it came disguised, seeing for the first time someone he had kissed and loved physically no longer possible to contact, feeling a revulsion to the dead form here, having seen what a body became after death. He reached down to touch the blind eyes and touched her cold face and put his hand on the white sheet which covered her body. He heard a curiously crackling sound and drew down the sheet a little further.

Her body was enclosed in a shroud of heavy brown wrapping paper and he could see that underneath there were no clothes. Behind him the nun whispered, "Many wish it so, they need the clothing."

He had drawn the sheet with arrogant certainty, with faith in the armor he had grown against grief, trusting his memory of the terrible years to shield him now. But he thought, she has enough clothes to be buried in, I can do that for her. And suddenly a thousand enemies came coursing through his blood, the bile rose in his throat, a giant hand cramped the beat of his heart, drowned all light. Then without knowing how, he found himself outside the room, leaning against the wall of the corridor.

The nun waited patiently for him. Finally Mosca said to her, "I'll bring some proper clothes, will you dress her for me?" The nun made a motion of assent.

He left the hospital and began to walk. He followed the perimeter of the fence. Though it was not yet light he became conscious of the *Strassenbahn* going by and people passing him in the streets. The curfew had ended. He kept turning into deserted streets but as he entered them people seemed to spring out of the rubbled earth and buried apartments. Then there was a cold wintry sun and a pale light over the earth and he found himself on the edge of the town, walking into the countryside. The air was very cold. Mosca made himself stop.

He accepted it all now and was not surprised that everything had turned out badly. There was left only a tired hopelessness, and far down in his being a shameful guilt.

He thought of what he must do; bring a dark-colored dress to the hospital for Hella to be buried in, make arrangements for the funeral. Eddie could help him, would arrange everything. He turned back and felt something at his arm. He looked down and saw that he was still carrying the blue gym bag. He was very tired and had a long walk before him so he let it drop in the deep wet grass. He lifted his eyes to the light of the frozen morning sun and started to walk back into the city.

23

A TINY CARAVAN passed through the huge central gate of black iron, left the hospital grounds and entered the surrounding city. Gray, early morning light shrouded the ruins with ghostly sheets of vapor.

The ambulance carrying Hella's coffin led the way. The jeep, open to the wind, followed slowly behind, Eddie and Mosca hunched down to escape the cold. Frau Saunders, alone in the seat behind them, was wrapped in a brown Army blanket that hid her mourning from the world. Following the jeep came a little Opel car with its wood-burning motor and small smokestack. In it was the minister to whose church Frau Saunders belonged.

The caravan rode against the tide of the world coming to the center of the city, clanging *Strassenbahns* crammed with workers, olive-drab Army buses; people whose life-rhythm had been broken only by rest and sleep and dreams. The bitter cold of late autumn, the early cold unprepared for and unforeseen, more bitter than the cold of deepest winter, iced the metal jeep and froze the body and mind. Mosca leaned toward Eddie, "You know where the cemetery is?" Eddie nodded. Mosca said emotionlessly, "Let's get there." Eddie swung the jeep to the left and it shot forward, raced down the broad avenue winding in a slow curve through and out of the city. Then on to a little side road and through an open wooden gate and finally rolling slowly to rest on a small lawn before the long deep rows of tombstones.

They sat in the jeep, waiting. Frau Saunders put the blanket aside. She was dressed in a black coat and veiled hat and wore black stockings. Her face was gray as the winter light filtered from the descending sky. Eddie and Mosca were in dark officer greens.

The ambulance came slowly along the rutted road and entered the cemetery gate. It stopped and the driver and his helper got out. Eddie and Mosca went to help them. Mosca saw that they were the two men who had brought Hella to the hospital for childbirth. They had the two rear doors of the ambulance open and as they shoved out the black box, Mosca and Eddie gripped the handles of the end near them.

It was rough wood stained watery black, the handles dull rough iron, the color of the sky. The two ambulance men faced Mosca over the coffin but pretended not to know him. They swung the coffin around so that they would lead. It was very light. They took a path through the scarred and broken tombstones until finally they came to an open pit. Two little round-shouldered Germans in caps and dark jackets rested on their black, heart-shaped spades and watched the coffin being set down near the hole they had made. Behind them was a great pile of raw brown earth.

The little Opel car came through the gate, its smoke-stack pouring a rope of mourning to the sky. The minister came out. He was tall and thin and his craggy face was stern. He walked slowly, slightly bent, dragging his long black robe against the damp earth. He spoke a few words to Frau Saunders and then to Mosca. Mosca kept his eyes on the ground. He could not understand the heavy Bavarian accent.

The stillness of the air was broken by the even, guttural prayer of the minister. He heard the words love and pray and the German word pray was like the word beg, he heard the voice saying forgive forgive and accept accept accept and something of the wisdom and mercy and love of God. Someone gave him a handful of earth, and he threw it before him, heard it strike wood, then heard other little pats of earth. Then he heard great chunks striking like great slow steady heartbeats, growing softer and softer until there was just the inaudible sighing of earth falling on earth, and above the blood pounding in his head, Mosca could hear Frau Saunders weeping.

Finally there were no more sounds. He could hear them moving. He heard the roar of a motor, then another, then the jeep.

Mosca looked up. The mist from the city they had left behind had stolen through the graves and stones. He raised his eyes to the opaque and sunless sky as men raise their eyes to pray. In his heart he cried out, with hatred, impotent anger, "I believe, I believe." Crying out that he believed in the true God, that his vision was clear, that he saw the true tyrannical Father, merciless, pitiless, bathed in blood, drowning in terror and pain and guilt, devoured and consumed by His insane hatred for mankind. In his heart and mind great fissures opened to receive the God he saw and then a pale-gold sun appeared before the curtained sky and forced his eyes to earth.

Across the plain that lay before the city he could see the empty ambulance and the Opel car rising and falling on the bumpy road. The two black spaded men had disappeared. Frau Saunders and Eddie sat in the jeep waiting for him. Frau Saunders had the blanket wrapped around her, hiding her mourning. It was very cold. He motioned that they should leave and watched the olive-drab jeep move slowly through the gate. Frau Saunders turned for a last look, but he could not see her face. Her black veil, heavy threaded and covered with mist, shielded her eyes.

And now alone for the first time Mosca could look at Hella's grave, the mounded earth, the raw brown dirt her body had displaced. He felt no sorrow, only a bewildered sense of loss, as if there was nothing he could ever want to do and no place in all the world he could go. He looked across the open field to where the city began and under whose ruins more bones were buried than would ever fill this prepared and holy ground. The dead winter sun, shrouded in clouds, shed its pale yellow light and Mosca tried to see across the field to his own life and everything he had felt and known. He tried to reach back over a great continent of graves to the games he had played as a child, the streets he had walked in boyhood, the love his mother gave and the face of his father long dead, his first farewell. He remembered his mother always saying, "You have no father but God is your father." And saying, "You have to be extra good because you have no father and God is your father." He tried to reach back and find the love he had felt then, the streams of pity and mercy that hollowed wells for tears.

Seeking pain he thought of Hella, of her face so delicately fragile it exposed blue veins defenseless, without a veil of flesh to death and the world. He thought of her unconscious love springing like magic out of her heart and how fatal it had been, a weakness, in this world a sickness terrible and mortal as unclotting blood.

He walked down the narrow path, past the chipped, scarred tottering tombstones wounded by war. He went out the cemetery gate. Walking toward the city his mind filled with images of Hella, how she had looked when he came back and the love she gave him that he needed to stay alive, the overwhelming relief at finding her so, but now it seemed that even then he had known he would bring her to death and to this grave.

He shook his head. Bad luck, just bad luck, he thought. He remembered the many evenings he had returned for supper and found her asleep on the couch and he would put her to bed and leave and return to find her still asleep, a great deep sleep in which she was safe till morning. Bad luck, he thought again to save himself, but without hope, remembering the cruelty that had taken her away when she was completely alone, without warning, without letting her see or touch the few people she loved.

In the moment before he entered the city he tried to reach the other God, to summon him from the other world, the world his mother lived in, the upright homes, the happy, well-fed children, the virtuous women securely fastened to life with kind men and golden wedding rings. He tried to reach the world rich in drugs to soften nearly every agony, to call forth those great deep shadows of painless memories that might save him now.

And if he could have seen the city beneath him untouched, its skin of stone unlacerated, its flesh firm; and if the sun had shone and the iron sky had bled with light, and if he could have felt some love for the people groping through the shrouded winter ruins, he might have summoned that masked God who shielded his known true face with patient mercy.

Mosca descended the rolling hill to where the paved street began. Now he could not focus his mind on any real image of Hella. Just once in the misted street he thought clearly and nakedly, "It's come to an end." But that too escaped him before he could think of what it meant.

24

HE GAVE Frau Saunders money to look after the child and moved back to the billet in Metzer Strasse. In the nights that followed he went to bed early. The parties would be just starting, music and laughter in the rooms around and below him. And he would sleep through it all. But in the night, after the merriment had died and the billet was still and dark, he would come fully awake. He would look at his watch on the night table and it always read one or two o'clock. Then he would lie still, afraid to turn on the lamp because of its depressing, weak yellow light. A little before dawn he would fall asleep again and sleep through the bustle of men preparing and leaving for work. Every night it would be the same. When he woke he would lift up the watch and holding the tiny circle of yellow eyes near his face hoping it would tell him an hour near morning and light. And always he would have to smoke a cigarette and sit against the wooden headboard and prepare himself for the long dark hours he must remain awake. He would listen to the gurgling of pipes, the breathing of the couple in the next room, their drowsy moans and gurgles like death rattles and the muted cries of their somnambulist passion and then the drip of water in the bathroom. There would be little clicks and scraping of floors against walls as if they too were settling for rest. There would be a murmur of a faraway radio sometimes, and then someone alive speaking and footsteps along the hall, and in the street below his window the muted laughter of women as they left the billet. And then as dawn came Mosca would fall asleep and wake in the quiet noon of an empty house, the walls of his room painted pale lemon by winter sunlight.

On one of these afternoons, two weeks after the burial, Mosca heard the quiet broken by footsteps in the hall and then there was a knock. He got out of bed and put on his trousers. He went to the door, unlocked it and pulled it open.

Before him was the face he had seen only once but would never forget. Honny, with his skullcap of yellow hair, his fleshy nose and heavy freckles. Honny smiled and asked, "May I come in?"

Mosca stepped aside, then closed the door. Honny rested his brief case on the table and looked around the room, then said pleasantly to Mosca, "I'm sorry if I woke you."

"I was just getting up," Mosca said.

The little blond man said slowly, "I was sorry, very sorry to hear about your wife." He smiled uncertainly.

Mosca turned and walked to the bed. "We weren't married," Mosca said.

"Ah, so." Honny nervously passed his hand over the bald front of his head until he could feel the reassuring silkiness of the hair further back. "I came to tell you something very important."

Mosca cut in, "I have no cigarettes."

Honny said gravely, "I know you have no cigarettes, that you are not a PX manager, that I know since Wolfgang went back to America."

Mosca smiled at him, "So what."

"No, you misunderstand," Honny said quickly. "I came

to tell you about Yergen. That penicillin he gave you he bought through me. I was the intermediary." He stopped for a moment. "Yergen knew it was defective, he only paid a fraction of the usual price to the contact I gave him. You see?"

Mosca had to sit on the bed. He put his hand on the scar, his stomach hurt. Suddenly he had a great throbbing headache. Yergen, Yergen, he thought, Yergen who had done so much for them, made Hella happy, whose daughter Hella loved. He felt a sick humiliation that Yergen could trick him so and into such sorrow. He bowed his face into his hands.

Honny was speaking again, gently. "I learned you refused to go on with Wolf's scheme. I am not stupid. That means you spared my life. Believe me if I had known that Yergen meant his goods for you I would have stopped him. I learned too late. Yergen was willing to sacrifice me, and he was willing to sacrifice your woman." He saw that Mosca still sat on the bed with his face in his hands and so he said even more softly. "I have good news. Yergen is back in Bremen, in his old place. Your landlady, Frau Meyer sent word to him that all was in order, that he need have no fear."

Mosca stood up from the bed. He said quietly, "You're not lying?"

"No, I do not lie," Honny said. His face had gone dead white and the freckles stood out on his skin like spots of grease. "If you think back, you will know I do not lie."

Mosca went to the wardrobe and unlocked it. He felt himself moving quickly and though his head was aching he felt almost happy. From the wardrobe he took a book of blue American Express checks, signed five of them. They were each for a hundred dollars. He showed them to Honny. "Get Yergen to come here tonight and these belong to you."

Honny backed away. "No, no," he said, "I cannot do that. What made you think I can do that?"

Mosca held out the blue checks and took a step toward him. Honny backed away, murmuring, "No, no I cannot do it." Mosca saw that he would not. He took the man's brief case from the table and gave it to him. "Thanks for telling me, anyway," he said.

Alone, he stood in the center of the room. His head pounded as if a great vein was filling and emptying itself with each giant blood stroke of his heart. He felt a little faint, as if his lungs could not swallow the close air of the room. He finished dressing and left the billet.

Out in the street he was surprised by the warmth of the sun. The early winter that had invaded autumn seemed to have died away. He turned into the Kurfürsten Allee, toward what had been his home, skirting the frail shadows cast by almost bare trees. Except for the headache he felt better than he had felt in a long time. He thought, tonight I'll be able to sleep right through.

He let himself into the apartment very quietly and stood outside the door of the living room. He heard the squeak of a baby carriage, and when he went in he saw Frau Saunders pushing it back and forth. She sat on the sofa, in her left hand a book, her right on the creamy wood of the carriage. She sat straight and calm, a grave acceptance of sorrow upon her strongly lined face. The child in his carriage was asleep. Light blue veins ran through his pink forehead, and tinier veins laced one trembling eyelid into a delicate membrane leaf.

"Is he all right?" Mosca asked.

Frau Saunders nodded. "Everything is well." She freed her hands from the book and the carriage and locked her fingers together.

"Did you get the package I sent?" The week before he had sent her a great carton of food.

She nodded her head again. She looked much older. Mosca recognized something familiar in the way she sat and in the way she answered.

He didn't look at her when he asked, "Can you keep the child indefinitely? I'll pay you well, anything you say." His head felt as if it were swelling with pain, and he wondered if she would have aspirin.

Frau Saunders picked up her book again, held it unopened. The severe face had no touch of the wry humor he always remembered. "Herr Mosca," she said formally, "if you give your consent I will try to adopt your child as my son. That would solve your problem." She said this very coldly, but suddenly the tears streamed down her face. She let the book fall away to the floor and used her hands to hide and stop her tears. And Mosca recognized what he had thought familiar, she was acting like his mother when he gave her pain.

Because she was not his mother and could not really touch him, he walked over to the sofa and rested his hand on her arm for a moment. "What is it, what have I done?" His voice was calm, reasonable.

Her hands had stopped the tears and dried them. She said quietly, "You don't care for the baby, you didn't come once all this time. What if she knew you would be like this? How terrible, how terrible, she loved you both so much. She always said you were good, and when she fell down the stairs she stretched out her arms for the baby. She was in such pain and she screamed, but she thought of the baby. And now you think nothing of what she loved so much." She paused for breath, went on hysterically, "Oh, you are a terrible man, you tricked her, you are not a good man." She leaned away from him and put her two hands on the carriage.

Mosca stepped back and away from her. To help her he said, "What do you think I should do?"

"I know what she would wish. That you take the child to America, give him a safe and happy life so that he will grow old."

Mosca said simply, "We weren't married and therefore the child is German. It would take a long time."

"So," she said eagerly, "I can take care of him until then. You will do it?"

"I don't think I can," he said. And suddenly he was impatient to leave. He was conscious of his headache again.

Frau Saunders was saying in her cold voice, "Do you want me to adopt him?"

He looked at the sleeping baby. He felt nothing. He took the Express checks he had signed from his pocket and left them on the table. "I don't know what will happen," he said. He went to the door.

"When will you come to see your son again?" Frau Saunders' voice was angry. There was contempt in her face. Mosca turned back toward her.

The pain in his head was a great heavy beat, and he wanted to leave, but that look was more than he could bear. "Why don't you speak the truth, why don't you speak what is in your mind?" Not knowing his voice was rising he said, "You think it's my fault, you think she died because I didn't do enough to save her. Tell me the truth. That's why you are so angry, you look at me as if I'm an animal. You believe, 'That American, another German he killed.' Don't pretend you're angry about the child, don't pretend, don't act that lie. I know what you believe."

For the first time Frau Saunders looked at him carefully, directly into his eyes. He looked very ill, his skin was yellow and his eyes were very black, there were angry red splotches forming on his mouth. "No, no," she said. "I never thought so badly." And as she said the words she realized for the first time that he spoke some truth.

But he was under control now. He said quietly, "I'll show you it's not true." He turned and left, she could hear him running down the stairs.

Out in the street he lit a cigarette and looked up at the cloud-filled sky and then down the Kurfürsten Allee. He had nearly smoked the cigarette away before he started walking back to his billet in the Metzer Strasse. The ache in his head was hurting his eyes and the veins in his neck. He looked at his watch. It was only three o'clock. There was still a long time to wait before he could do anything about Yergen.

25

HIS ROOM was filled with afternoon shadows. He took some aspirin and lay on the bed. He was surprised at the tiredness he felt. He closed his eyes, it seemed only for a moment, and then he heard a knocking on the door, and opening his eyes he found himself in darkness. He switched on the table light and looked at his watch. It was only six o'clock. There was another knock and then the door was opened, and Eddie Cassin was in the room. He was neatly dressed, shaved and smelled of talcum.

"Christ, you should lock the door when you sleep," he said. Then casually, "How you feeling, wake you up?"

Mosca rubbed his face. "It's O.K.," he said. His headache was gone but his face felt very hot, his lips dry.

Eddie Cassin threw some letters on the table. "Picked up your mail. You got a drink?"

Mosca went to the wardrobe and took out a bottle of gin, then two glasses.

"Big party tonight," Eddie said. "Come on down."

Mosca shook his head, handed him a glass. They both drank. Then Eddie said, "Your orders come in a week. The Adjutant tried to stop it, said it was his fault. The Colonel said no good." He leaned toward Mosca. "Give the word and I'll lose some papers, give you an extra couple of weeks."

"It doesn't matter," Mosca said. He got up from the bed

and looked out the window. There was still some twilight in the streets and he could see a group of children, waiting with unlit lanterns for complete darkness. He remembered hearing their song the last few nights, its softness not shattering the light film of sleep that shielded his brain, not waking him, but seeping through somehow.

Eddie Cassin behind him said, "What about the kid?"

Mosca said, "Frau Saunders, she's keeping him."

Eddie's voice was low. "I'll go see her. Don't worry." He paused. "It's tough, Walter. Guys like you and me are jinxed. Just take it easy."

The children in the street formed two files and marched down the Metzer Strasse and out of sight, their lamps still dark. Eddie said, "Those letters are from your mother. I cabled her. I figured you not to write."

Mosca turned around to face him. "You've been a good friend," he said. "Could you do me one last favor?"

"Sure," Eddie said.

"You never told me Yergen was back in town. I want to see him. Can you get him over here?"

Eddie took another drink and watched Mosca move around the room. There was something wrong, he thought. Mosca had his voice under control, but his eyes were like black mirrors and ever so often a spasm twisted his face into what seemed a second of rage and hatred.

Eddie said slowly, "I hope you're not figuring anything stupid, Walter. The guy made a mistake. It wasn't his fault. Hell, you know Yergen went out of his way for Hella all the time."

Mosca smiled, "Hell, I just want to get back the cigarettes and money I paid for that stuff. Why should I pay?"

Eddie was so surprised and then so relieved that he let out a yelp of relief and joy. "Christ, boy, now you're back to normal. Why the hell should you pay for it?" Back in his mind flashed the thought that this was like Mosca to think of not being cheated, even in his grief. But his relief was genuine. He was glad to see that Mosca had finally come back to normal.

He was struck by an idea. He grabbed Mosca by the arm. "Look," he said, "listen to me. I'm going with Frau Meyer for a week, up to the mountains around Marburg. You come along. I'll get you a girl, a real sweet girl. We'll have lots of laughs, farmer food, liquor. C'mon, say, yes, for a buddy."

Mosca smiled at him. "Sure, O.K.," he said.

Eddie laughed out loud. "That's it, Walter. That's fine. Fine." He slapped Mosca on the shoulder. "We'll leave tomorrow night. Wait till you see those mountains. Beautiful, really beautiful." He paused for a moment and with real affection, almost fatherly, he said, "Maybe we can figure a way to get your kid back to the States with you. That's the thing you know she'd want, Walter. More than anything else." Then with an embarrassed smile, "Come on down. Just for one drink."

Mosca said, "You getting Yergen here for me?"

Eddie looked at him thoughtfully. Mosca said, "The truth is I'm broke, Eddie. I have to leave money with Frau Saunders for the kid. I need dough to go with you to Marburg." He laughed. "Unless you're treating for the whole week." He made his voice quietly sincere. "And I need the money for the trip to the States. That's all there is to it. I paid the guy a small fortune for that stuff."

Eddie was convinced. "Sure, I'll get him," he said. "I'll go right now. And then after you come down to the party. O.K.?"

"Sure," Mosca said.

When Eddie left Mosca looked round the empty room. He saw the letters on the bed, picked one up, and sat down on the bed to read it. When he finished he realized he had not understood a sentence. He went over it again. He tried to connect the words so they would mean something. They wavered through his unfocused mind, filtered through the noises of the billet.

"Please come," his mother wrote, "don't think about anything, please come home. I'll take care of the baby. You can go back to school, you're only twenty-three, I always forget how young you are and for six years you've been away. If you feel bitter now, pray to God, that is the only thing that helps. Your life is beginning . . ."

He threw the letter on the floor and stretched out on the bed. Below him he could hear the parties starting, the soft music and the laughing voices. His headache was beginning again. He switched out the light. The tiny yellow eyes of his watch told him it was six-thirty. He had plenty of time. He closed his eyes.

He thought of how it would be, the return home, seeing his mother and child every day, finding another girl and settling down. Buried inside himself he would carry this other life, his hatred for everything they believed. His life would be a stone over the grave of everything he had ever seen or done or felt. He thought with surprise of what he had shouted at Frau Saunders. It had sprung out of him. He had never even thought such a thing. But now he could see all the mistakes he had made, he forced his mind on to something else.

Drowsily the images formed into Hella carrying the child off the boat and meeting his mother. Then all of them in the living room together, and then every morning, every night, seeing each other's face. He fell asleep.

He dreamed, or thought, a fraction of his brain awake, that he was on his way home, that the sign on the door read, "Welcome Home, Walter," that he had left Hella alive in Germany and on his way home had dreamed a year away. That he had never returned to Hella, that she had not held the gray bread in her hands and let it fall to the floor, that he had opened that other door and Gloria and his mother and Alf were waiting for him, and he had come out of a nightmare to them, and they were in a great flood of light. But then his mother had a bundle of pictures in her hand, and he could see a crib in the corner and the curled back of a sleeping child and he was afraid, and then they were all sitting down and passing photos and mother said Oh what's this and he looked and saw his combat jacket and his blanket skirt and smiling over a mounded grave, That's my third victim he said and laughed and laughed, but Alf was angry and stood on one great tall leg and shouted, That's going too far, Walter, that's going too far. Everybody was standing up and his mother was wringing her hands, and he saw his face saying Good-bye Good-bye and then everything was very dark. But Wolf came with a candle and he was in the cellar with Wolf, and Wolf held his candle high in the air and said, She's not here, Walter, she's not here, and he felt the shifting rubbled floor pulling him down down below the candlelight, and he began to scream.

He was awake and knew he had made no sound. The room was completely dark, the windows painted black by night. Great shrieks of laughter filled the billet. Undulating waves of sound, music, loud male voices, many feet running up and down the stairs. In the room next to his he heard a couple making love. Then the girl saying, "Now, let's go down to the party. I want to dance." The man grumbling, angry. And the girl's voice, "Please, please I want to dance." The sighing of the bed as they rose, then the girl laughing in the hall, and he was in silence and darkness.

Eddie Cassin couldn't help dropping in on the party before he went to Yergen, but he was only a little drunk when he spotted the two young girls. They were not more than sixteen. Dressed exactly alike, in little blue hats, little blue tailored jackets, white parachute-silk blouses, they delighted his eye. Their skin and hair set off their clothes with delicate pinks, creamy whites and there were ringlets like golden coins across their foreheads. They danced with some of the men but refused all drinks and always came together when the music stopped as if they found a virtuous strength in each other.

Eddie watched them for a time, smiling, planning the attack. Then he went to the prettier one and asked her to dance. One of the men said protestingly, "Hey, Eddie, I brought her up here." Eddie said, "Don't worry, I'll fix it."

While dancing he asked her, "Is that your sister?"

The girl nodded. She had a pert little face and on it was the look of frightened haughtiness he understood so well.

"Does she always follow you around?" Eddie asked and his voice was a compliment to her, an invitation to disparage her sister in a gentle way.

The girl smiled with an innocent fatuousness he found charming. She said, "Oh, my sister is a little too shy."

The record ended and he asked, "Would you and your sister like a little supper in my room?" She was immediately frightened and shook her head. Eddie gave her his paternally sweet smile, his delicate face had an almost fatherly understanding. "Oh, I know what you think." He led her to where Frau Meyer was drinking with two men.

"Meyer," he said, "this little girl is frightened of me. She refused my invitation to supper. But if you come and chaperon, I think she will say yes."

Frau Meyer put her arm around the girl's waist, "Oh, you don't worry about him. He is the one good man in the house. I'll come with you. And he has the finest food, food you girls haven't tasted since you were in diapers." The girl blushed and went to call her sister.

Eddie went over to the man who had brought the girl. "It's all fixed," he said. "Go with Meyer to my room. Say I'll be there later." Eddie went to the door. "Save me some," he said laughing, "I'll be back in an hour."

Mosca watched the city from his window. Far away across the plateau of ruins, the heart of the city, he saw a long rope of green and yellow light, an arrow pointing as if drawn, to the blazing windows of the Metzer Strasse. He knew it was the children with their lanterns. But the shouts of laughter, the party noises of music and uneven tread of dancing feet, the small coy shrieks of drunken women, all these drowned what he listened for, the song they sang.

He left the window open and took his shaving kit and towel and went to the bathroom. He left the bathroom door open so that he would hear anyone going to his room.

He washed thoroughly, the water cool on his hot face. Then he shaved, studying the smooth and quiet features, the long thin nose, the long thin mouth with almost colorless lips, the hollow black eyes and dark bronzed skin, gray now with fatigue and splotched with fever sores.

He rinsed the soap off his face and then kept looking at it. He was surprised at how strange it seemed to him, as if he had never really seen it. He turned his head to look at each profile and how the deep eye socket cast shadows over his jaw. He saw the cruelty and evil, the black glints in the dark eyes, the firm and brutal chin. He stepped back, his hand out to cover that mirror face, but surprised, let his hand drop before it touched glass. For a moment he smiled.

In his room it was cold. There was a strange hum in the air. He went to the window and closed it. The hum ceased. The green and yellow lights crossing the ruins were much nearer. He looked at his watch. It was nearly eight o'clock. He felt suddenly weak and feverish, nausea made him sit on the bed. The ache that had been buried by aspirin broke into its steady beat, and with a terrible despair, as if he had lost final hope for salvation, he was sure that Yergen would not come. He felt very cold and went to the wardrobe and put on his old green combat jacket. From an empty cigarette carton he took the Hungarian pistol and slipped it into his pocket. He put all his cigarettes in a small suitcase, then the shaving kit and the nearly full bottle of gin. Then he sat on the bed to wait.

Eddie Cassin parked the jeep in front of the church. He went around the side entrance and up the steps to the steeple. He knocked on the door, there was no answer. He waited, then knocked again. On the other side of the door, Yergen's voice came, unexpectedly clear, "Who is there?"

Eddie said, "It is Mr. Cassin."

Yergen's voice said, "What do you want?"

Eddie Cassin said, "Frau Meyer sent me with a message."

The bolt slid back and the door opened. Yergen stood by it, waiting for him to enter.

The room was dark, except for one little table lamp in the corner, and beneath this lamp, on a small sofa, Yergen's daughter held a book of fairy tales. She rested against great cushions piled against the wall.

"Yes, what is it?" Yergen said. He looked much older, his slight figure was thinner, but his face was still sure, still proud.

Eddie put out his hand. Yergen shook it. Eddie said with a smile, "Come, we've known each other a long time, we've had many a drink together. Is this a way to act with me?"

Yergen smiled reluctantly, "Ah, Mr. Cassin, when I worked in the Metzer Strasse I was a different man. Now—"

Eddie said slowly, sincerely. "You know me, I wouldn't trick you. I've come for your benefit. My friend, Mosca, wants his money and cigarettes back. What he paid for the defective drugs."

Yergen was watching him intently, then said, "Of course, I will do that. But tell him not immediately. I cannot."

Eddie said, "He wants you to come see him tonight."

"Oh, no, oh, no," Yergen said. "I will not go to see him."

Eddie looked at Yergen's daughter lying on the sofa. She had opened her eyes into a wide, blank stare. It made him uncomfortable.

"Yergen," he said, "Mosca and I are leaving tomorrow for Marburg. When we come back he leaves for the States. Now if you don't come to see him tonight, he will come here. If he becomes angry, he will frighten the little girl when he quarrels with you."

As he had known it would, this last argument took effect. Yergen shrugged, then went to get his coat. Then he went to his daughter.

Eddie watched them. Yergen with his heavy fur-collared overcoat and neatly combed brown hair, his look of quiet dignity and seriousness, knelt humbly, sadly, to whisper into his daughter's ear. Eddie knew he was giving her the signal, so that when he returned and knocked on the door, the little girl would slide back the iron bolt. He could see the little girl's blank eyes watching him over her father's shoulder and he thought, what if she forgot the signal, what if she never answered her father's knocking on the door.

Yergen rose, took his brief case and they went out. Yergen paused, waited until he heard on the other side of the door the sound of iron sliding over wood, until he knew that his daughter was locked away from the world.

They got into Eddie's jeep. Once during the ride through the dark streets, Yergen said, "You will stay with me when we meet?" And Eddie said, "Sure, don't worry."

But now in Eddie Cassin rose a vague uneasiness. They drove into the light of the Metzer Strasse and the billet. Eddie parked the jeep and they got out. Eddie looked up. There was no light in Mosca's room. "Maybe he's at the party," Eddie said.

They went into the billet. On the first landing, Eddie said to Yergen, "Wait here." He went into the party but saw no sign of Mosca. When he went out into the hall, Yergen was waiting for him. He could see that Yergen's face was pale, and suddenly Eddie Cassin felt a terrible sense of danger. Through his mind flashed everything Mosca had said and he felt it was all false. He said to Yergen, "Come on, I'll take you home, he's not here. Come on."

Yergen said, "No, let us finish this. I am not afraid. No more—" But Eddie Cassin started to push Yergen down the steps. He was certain, almost overwhelmed with suspicious terror, and then suddenly he heard Mosca's voice above them, cold and with controlled fury say, "You fuckin' Eddie, let him go." Yergen and Eddie looked up.

He stood on the landing above them and in the weak hall light his face was sickly yellow. Two great red fever sores blistered his thin mouth. He stood very still. The green combat jacket seemed to make him bulkier than he really was. "Come on up, Yergen," he said. One hand was hidden behind his back.

"No," Yergen said in an unsteady voice. "I am leaving with Mr. Cassin."

Mosca said, "Eddie, get out of the way. Come up here."

Yergen held on to Eddie's arm. "Don't leave me," he said. "Stay here." Eddie held up his hand to Mosca and said, "Walter, for Christ sake, Walter, don't do it." Mosca took two steps down. Eddie tried to pull free from Yergen, but Yergen clutched his arm and cried out, "Don't let me stand alone—Don't, Don't—" Mosca took another step down. His eyes were black, opaque, the red fever sores on his mouth burned in the hall light. Suddenly the pistol was in his hand. Eddie flung himself away from Yergen, and Yergen alone, with a despairing cry tried to turn, tried to run down the stairs. Mosca fired. In his first step Yergen fell to his knees. He raised his head, the faded blue eyes staring upward, and Mosca fired again. Eddie Cassin ran up the steps past Mosca and kept running to the attic.

Mosca put the gun back in his pocket. The body rested flat on the landing, the head dangling over to the descending steps.

From the rooms below came a great wave of laughter, the phonograph began a loud waltz, there began a great stamping of feet and loud yodeling cries. Mosca ran up the stairs quickly to his room. Dark shadows stretched through the window. He waited and listened. He went to the window.

There was no alarm, but the ruins of the city, the great hills of rubble crawled with a mass of brilliantly hued caterpillars, bobbing lanterns that lit the coming winter night with long tracers of green fire. A great rash of sweat poured over his face and body. He began to tremble, a great circling blackness sickened him and he pushed the window open and waited.

Now, in the street below, he could hear the children singing. The lanterns he could not see swung in his mind and heart, and as the choral died away, he felt an extraordinary release from fear and tension. The cold air rushed over him and the sickness and blackness left his body.

He picked up the packed suitcase and ran down the stairs, over Yergen's body, past the party noises. Nothing had changed. Out of the billet he started walking across the black plateau of ruins, then turned for one last look.

Four great stages of light cast a burning shield against the darkness of the city and the night and from each tier came a long rolling wave of music and laughter. He stood outside that shield of light feeling no remorse, only thinking that he would never see his child or Eddie Cassin, his country or his family again. He would never see the mountains around Marburg. Finally he had become the enemy.

Far across the ruins, toiling upward toward the black and falling winter sky he could see the green and red of the children's lanterns, but he could no longer hear their song. He turned away from them and walked toward the *Strassenbahn* that would take him to the railroad station.

It was all familiar to him, the farewells to time and place and memory, and he felt no sorrow, no desolation, that finally there was no one, no human being to speed him on his way, only the wind which swept across the ruined continent he could never leave. Before him he saw the round bright glare that was the headlight of the *Strassenbahn* and heard the cold crystal clanging of its bell. Out of habit he began to run to catch it, the suitcase bumping against his leg, but after a few steps halted, knowing it made no difference whether he caught this one or the next.